ELINE VERE

LOUIS COUPERUS

ELINE VERE

Translated from the Dutch by
Ina Rilke

PUSHKIN PRESS
LONDON

First published in Dutch as *Eline Vere* 1889

English translation © Ina Rilke 2010

Afterword © Paul Binding 2010

This edition first published in 2010 by
Pushkin Press
12 Chester Terrace
London NW1 4ND

British Library Cataloguing in Publication Data:
A catalogue record for this book is available
from the British Library

ISBN 978 1 906548 26 1

Cover Illustration: *The Red Kimono* Georg-Hendrik Breitner
© Haags Gemeentemuseum The Hague
The Bridgeman Art Library

Frontispiece: Louis Couperus 1921 E O Hoppé London
© Collection Letterkundig Museum The Hague.

Set in 10 on 12 Monotype Baskerville MT
and printed on Amber Print 80 gsm
in Great Britain by TJ International

www.pushkinpress.com

ELINE VERE

I

THE DINING ROOM, doing service as a dressing room, was a hive of activity. Before a cheval glass stood Frédérique van Erlevoort, her hair loose and flowing, looking very pale under a light dusting of rice powder, her eyebrows darkened with a single brushstroke of black.

"Do hurry up, Paul! We shall never be ready in time!" she fretted, glancing at the clock.

Kneeling before her was Paul van Raat, his fingers flying as he draped a long, gauzy veil of gold and crimson about her waist, making the fabric billow over her pink underskirt; her bare shoulders and arms were snowy white with powder and all ashimmer with doubled and twisted necklaces and chains.

"Oh, there's such a draught! Do keep that door shut, Dien," grumbled Paul as the old housemaid departed with an armful of dresses. The open door offered a glimpse of the guests proceeding along the potted palms and aralias on their way from the hall to the large reception suite, the men in evening dress and the ladies in light-coloured apparel, all peering into the dining room as they passed by.

There was much merriment behind the scenes, with only Frédérique retaining some form of composure, as befitted the majesty of her role as a queen of antiquity.

"Please be quick, Paul," she pleaded. "It's gone half-past eight already!"

"Yes, yes, Freddie, don't worry, you're almost done!" he responded, deftly pinning some jewels among the gauzy folds of her drapery.

"Ready?" asked Marie and Lili Verstraeten as they emerged from the room where the stage had been set—a mysterious elevation that was barely distinguishable in the dim light.

"Ready!" answered Paul. "And now let's all calm down!" he pursued, raising his voice commandingly.

9

He had good reason to admonish them, for the youngsters acting as wardrobe assistants—three boys and five girls—were cavorting about the cluttered room, laughing, shrieking and causing the uppermost disorder, while Lili struggled in vain to wrest a golden cardboard lyre from the hands of the twelve-year-old son of the house, and the two rowdy cousins set about climbing a large white cross, which was already teetering under their onslaught.

"Come down from that cross, Jan and Karel! Give me that lyre at once, other Jan!" roared Paul. "Do take them in hand, Marie. And now—Bet and Dien, come over here, will you? Bet, you hold the lamp, and you, Dien, stand beside the sliding door. Everybody else out of the way! There won't be enough room, so some people will have to go out into the garden and watch through the window. They'll have a splendid view from there. Come along Freddie, careful now, here's your train."

"You've forgotten my crown."

"I'll put it on your head when you've taken up your pose. Come on now."

The three banished maids scurried away, the boys crouched down in a corner where they would be invisible to the audience, and Paul helped Freddie to ascend the stage.

Marie, who like Lili was not yet in costume, spoke through the closed window to the fireman outside, wrapped in his greatcoat, waiting to set off the Bengal lights in the snowy garden. A large reflector stood beside him like a pallid, lustreless sun.

"First white, then green, then red!" instructed Marie, and the fireman nodded.

The room was dark but for the lamp held aloft by Bet, while Dien stood by the door to the now deserted dressing room.

"Careful, Freddie, careful!" cautioned Paul.

Frédérique arranged herself carefully among the cushions on the couch whereupon Paul adjusted her draperies, necklaces, hair and diadem, tucking in a flower here and there.

"Is this all right?" she asked with a tremor in her voice, taking up her well-rehearsed pose.

"You look ravishing. Come along Marie and Lili, your turn now!"

Lili threw herself on the floor and Marie reclined against the couch with her head at Frédérique's feet. Paul quickly draped both girls in brightly coloured shawls and veils, and wound strings of beads around their arms and in their hair.

"Now Marie and Lili, you must look distraught! A bit more writhing with the arms, Lili! More anguish, much more anguish! Freddie, we want more despair from you—keep your eyes on the ceiling and turn down your mouth a bit more."

"Like this?"

Marie dissolved into giggles.

"Yes, that's better! Do keep still, Marie, are you ready?"

"Ready," said Marie.

Paul continued to add finishing touches, readjusting a fold here, a flower there, doubtful whether all was perfect.

"Come, let's get started," said Lili, who lay in a most awkward position.

"Bet, take the lamp away, and then you and Dien come over here and stand on either side of the sliding doors!"

Finally they all found themselves in total darkness, their hearts pounding. Paul rapped on the window, then ran to join the boys in the corner.

After a slow, sputtering start, the Bengal light flared up against the reflector; the sliding doors parted grandly, and a dazzling white blaze lit up the tableau.

A hush descended on the reception suite and conservatory as the smiling guests pressed forwards, blinded by the burst of colour and light. Gentlemen stepped aside to make room for a pair of laughing girls, and young people at the back stood up on chairs for a better view.

"*La Mort de Cléopâtre*," Betsy van Raat read out to Madame van Erlevoort, who had passed her the programme.

Cries of "Wonderful! *Magnifique!*" sounded on all sides.

In the white glow of the Bengal light, ancient Egypt came to life. Beyond the sumptuous draperies there were glimpses of an oasis, blue sky, some pyramids and a grove of palm trees, while on a couch borne by sphinxes reclined a waning Cleopatra with cascading tresses, an adder coiled round her arm and two slave girls prostrate with grief at her feet. Thus, before the gaze of a modern soirée, the poetry of antiquity was evoked by a lavish vision of oriental splendour lasting only a few seconds.

"That's Freddie! As pretty as a picture," said Betsy, pointing out the dying queen to Madame van Erlevoort, who was so nonplussed by all this opulence that it took her a moment to recognise the lovely motionless maiden as her own daughter.

"And there is Marie, and the other one, oh, that's Lili! You'd never know, would you? What splendid costumes; they went to so much trouble! You see that drapery of Lili's, the violet with silver? I lent them that."

"How do they do it?" murmured the old lady.

The light flickered and guttered down; the doors slid shut.

"Lovely, Aunt, just lovely!" Betsy exclaimed to the hostess, Madame Verstraeten, as she passed by.

Twice more the dream was reprised, first in a flood of sea-green, then in fiery red. Freddie, with her adder, lay perfectly immobile; only Lili could not help twitching in her contorted pose. Paul watched from the side, beaming—all was going well.

"How can Freddie keep so still? And it's all so lavish and yet not overdone! Just like that painting by Makart!" said Betsy, opening her feather fan.

"Your honourable daughter must be exceedingly world-weary, dear lady!" drawled young de Woude van Bergh, bending towards Madame van Erlevoort, Freddie's mama.

After the third enactment of the Egyptian dream Madame Verstraeten went to the dressing room, where she found Frédérique and Lili divesting themselves of their draperies, chattering away as they carefully picked all the pins out of the folds. Paul and Marie, perched on tall stepladders and lit by two of the maids, were busy dismantling Cleopatra's boudoir. Dien bustled about collecting discarded draperies and necklaces. The three boys were turning somersaults on a mattress.

"Did you like it, Mama?" demanded Lili.

"Did you like it, Madame Verstraeten?" Frédérique chimed in.

"It was splendid! They would all have loved to see it again."

"Not again! I'm half-dead already!" cried Lili, sweeping a pile of garments to the floor before collapsing into an armchair, her eyes heavy with fatigue. Dien was dismayed; she would never get done at this rate.

"Lili, you must rest!" cried Paul from the top of his ladder in the other room. "Your next pose will be very tiring. Aunt Verstraeten, please tell Lili she must rest!" He dragged the colourful oriental rugs off the clothesline they had been suspended from, and Dien set about folding them up.

"Dien, we need sheets and white tulle—over here!" called Marie. Dien misheard her, and brought the wrong items.

Everyone spoke at once, instructing one thing and clamouring for another in mounting disorder. Paul protested vehemently from the top of the ladder, but no one was listening.

"I'm at my wits' end!" he raged, going down on his haunches. "It's always me doing all the work!"

Paul reiterated his admonition to Lili, and Madame Verstraeten went off to remind the servants that the young artistes required refreshments. When the trays were brought in laden with glasses of wine and lemonade, cake and sandwiches, the commotion reached a frenzied pitch. The three boys insisted on being served on their mattress, upon which one of the boys called Jan spilt a stream of orangeade. Marie bore down on them, scolding at the top of her voice, and with Dien's help swiftly pulled the mattress out from under them and dragged it away.

"Frédérique, I wish you'd give me a hand with the background!" said Paul in an aggrieved tone. He had given up trying to discipline the three boys, who were now being shooed out of the room by the old biddy. Some measure of calm was restored; everyone was busy, except Lili who remained in her armchair.

"What a to-do!" she muttered under her breath as she brushed her wavy, ash-blonde hair, and then, taking a large powder puff, dusted her arms to a snowy sheen.

Dien returned, quite out of breath, shaking her head and smiling benignly.

"Quick, Dien! White sheets and tulle!" chorused Freddie, Marie and Paul. Paul had come down from his ladder to erect the unwieldy white cross on the stage, and was arranging the mattress, heaped with cushions, at the base.

"Dien, white sheets and tulle, all the tulle and gauze you can find!"

And Dien complied, along with the other maids, coming up with armfuls of more white fabrics.

Madame Verstraeten had taken a seat beside her niece, Betsy van Raat, who was married to Paul's elder brother.

"Such a shame Eline is not here; I was counting on her to entertain us during the long intervals with a little music. She has such a pretty voice."

"She is not feeling very well, Aunt. She is very sorry, you may be sure, to miss Uncle's birthday party."

"What is wrong with her?"

"Oh, I don't know … nerves, I believe."

"She shouldn't give in so easily to those moods of hers. I dare say expending a little energy would take care of her nerves."

"Ah, it is the affliction of the younger generation, Aunt, as I am sure you have heard!" said Betsy, with a smile of mock sympathy.

Madame Verstraeten sighed indulgently, shaking her head, then remarked:

"By the way, I expect the girls will be too tired to go to the opera tomorrow. So you can have our box, if you like."

Betsy reflected a moment.

"I am having a small dinner party tomorrow, Aunt, but I should love to make use of the box anyway. Only the Ferelijns and Emilie and Georges are invited, but the Ferelijns said they would be leaving early as their little Dora is poorly again, so I could easily go with Emilie and Georges and catch the second half."

"Well, that's settled then. I shall send someone round with the tickets," said Madame Verstraeten, rising.

Betsy rose too. Georges de Woude van Bergh was just about to speak to her, but she pretended not to notice. She found him exceedingly irritating tonight—both times he had spoken to her he had made exactly the same comment, some platitude about the tableaux. No, there was no conversation in him at all. And tomorrow evening she would have to put up with him yet again, so her aunt's offer of the box at the opera was a blessing. She caught sight of her husband in the conservatory with several other gentlemen—Messrs Verstraeten and Hovel, Otto van Erlevoort, and his brother Étienne. A lively discussion was going on, in which Henk had no part; he just stood there smiling sheepishly, with his bulky form pressing against the fronds of a potted palm. He irritated her, too. He bored her to tears, and he didn't cut a good figure in evening dress, either—not at all chic! He looked better in his greatcoat!

She found an opportunity to have a word with him, and said:

"I do wish you would talk to someone, Henk. You have been lurking in this corner for ages. Why don't you circulate among the guests? You look so very dull. And your necktie's askew."

He stammered a reply and raised his hand to his collar. She turned away, and soon found herself in an animated little gathering centred on the Honourable Miss Emilie de Woude. Even the sad-eyed Madame van Rijssel, Freddie's sister, was in attendance. Emilie de Woude was unmarried, and wore her thirty-eight years with enviable vitality. Her pleasant, cheerful countenance endeared her to all, and while she resembled her much younger brother Georges in appearance, she had about her a certain spiritedness that was in marked contrast to his mannered reserve.

All were irresistibly drawn to the ebullient Emilie to hear her comical anecdotes, and she was now regaling her audience with an account of a recent fall she had had on a patch of frozen snow—she had landed at the feet of a gentleman, who had stood stock still instead of helping her up.

"Can you imagine? My muff to the left, my hat to the right, me in the middle, and him standing there, staring at me open-mouthed!"

A bell tinkled, at which Emilie broke off her story to hurry to the front, where the sliding doors were opening before the assembled audience.

"I can't see a thing!" said Emilie, rising up on her toes.

"You can stand on my chair, Miss Emilie!" called a young girl in a cream-coloured frock who was taller than the rest.

"You're a darling, Cateau, that's very kind. I'm coming! May I pass, Madame van der Stoor? Your daughter has just saved my day."

Madame van der Stoor, a lady who wrote poems under a pseudonym, stepped aside with a steely smile. She was a little put out by Emilie's lack of decorum, and herself made no attempt to gain a better view.

Emilie and Cateau van der Stoor both got up on the same chair and stood with their arms around each other's waists.

"Oh, isn't it splendid!" cried Emilie, in rapt attention. From the waves of a foaming sea of gauze rose a white cross of what appeared to be rough-hewn marble, to which clung the slender, pallid form of a maiden apparently in mortal danger, her fingers gripping the Rock of Ages, her feet lapped by wavelets of tulle.

There were murmurs of: "It's Lili!"

"How graceful she is," Emilie whispered to Cateau. "But how does she do it? How can she hold that pose for so long?"

"She's bolstered up with cushions, but it's a tiring pose anyway. You can't see the cushions, of course," said Cateau.

"Of course you can't! It's very lovely; I have never seen anything more poetic. But aren't you supposed to be taking part yourself, Cateau?"

"Yes I am, but only in the final scene, together with Etienne van Erlevoort. I should be off now, to change into my costume."

She hopped down from her chair. The light flickered, the sliding doors closed. There was a clatter of applause, after which the white vision of foaming gauze reappeared; an angel now leant over the cross, extending an arm to raise the hapless maiden swooning at the base.

There was more applause, louder this time.

"Of course Marie won't be able to keep a straight face," said Emilie with a toss of her head. "She'll burst out laughing any moment now."

And sure enough, a tremor of unseemly mirth was seen to be hovering about the lips of the angel, whose soulful expression acquired a somewhat comical cast beneath a pair of nervously raised eyebrows.

Although everyone could see that the artistes were tired, since none of them were able to keep perfectly still, the final tableau was received with great jubilation. Four or five encores were demanded. It was an allegory of the five senses, enacted by the four girls, all of whom were richly draped in heavy fabrics—cloth of gold and silver, brocade and ermine—and by Etienne, the youngest of Frédérique's brothers, who was garbed as a minstrel in personification of Hearing.

Then it was all over.

Due to the long intervals between the tableaux it was now two o'clock, and the guests gravitated towards the host and hostess to take their leave.

"Will you stay to supper with Cateau?" Madame Verstraeten murmured to Madame van der Stoor. "Nothing formal, you know."

But Madame van der Stoor deemed the hour too late; she would go as soon as her daughter was ready.

The artistes, having changed as quickly as they could, repaired to the salon, where they received congratulations on their acting skills and good taste from the last departing guests. In the meantime a triumphal march could be heard being played on the piano by Emilie, who, being a close friend of the family, would stay to supper along with Henk and Betsy.

"But you'll be coming tomorrow afternoon, won't you, Cateau? The photographer will be here at two!" called Marie.

The following day was Thursday; Cateau would not be going to school in order that she might rest, and she promised to be there at two o'clock.

The fatigued artistes sat sprawled in the easy chairs of the spacious conservatory, where a light repast was laid out—turkey, salad, cake and champagne.

"Which one was the best? Which did you like most?" they clamoured.

Opinions were compared and contrasted, booed and cheered, amid the general clatter of plates, forks and spoons and the clinking of glasses filled to the brim and rapidly emptied.

II

AT HALF-PAST TWO the van Raats made their way homeward to Nassauplein. All was quiet at the house, the servants having gone to bed. As Henk slipped his key back into his pocket and drew the bolt across the front door, Betsy was reminded of her rosy little boy upstairs in his white crib, asleep with bunched fists. She took the candle from the newel post and started up the stairs, while her husband stepped into the dining room with the newspapers. The gaslight was on, tempered to a wan glow from a small, fan-shaped flame.

Betsy's dressing room was likewise illuminated. She turned the knob, causing the light to flare up brightly, and drew her fur wrap off her shoulders. In the small grate a flame leapt upwards like the fiery tongue of a heraldic lion. There was something soothing about the room, something reminiscent of a warm bath and the sweet perfume of Parma violets. For a moment she stood over the white crib in the darkened adjoining nursery, then returned and with a sigh began to undress, letting the lace gown slide down her hips like a black cloud. The door opened and Eline came in, looking rather pale in a white flannel peignoir, with her hair loose and flowing.

"Why Elly, not in bed yet?"

"No, I … I've been reading. Did you enjoy your evening?"

"Yes indeed, it was very nice. I only wish Henk weren't so insufferably dull. He never said a word, just stood there fidgeting with his watch chain and looking awkward, except when they played whist during the intervals."

Somewhat tetchily, Betsy wedged the toe of one foot against the heel of the other and kicked off a dainty shoe of gilt leather and beadwork.

Eline stretched herself languidly.

"Did you tell Madame Verstraeten I was indisposed?"

19

"Yes I did. But you know me, Sis, after a late night like this I can't wait to get to bed. We'll talk tomorrow, all right?"

Eline was used to her sister being mildly out of sorts after an evening out, regardless of whether she had enjoyed herself, desiring only to shed her clothes as soon as possible.

Nevertheless, she was tempted to make some sharp reply, but in the next instant felt too lethargic and feeble to do so. She touched her lips to Betsy's cheek and, without thinking, leant her head against her sister's shoulder in a sudden craving for tenderness.

"You're not really ill, are you?"

"No. Just feeling a bit lazy, that's all. Goodnight then."

"Sleep well."

Eline, languorous and graceful in her white peignoir, retired. Betsy picked up her lace gown from the floor and continued undressing.

In the corridor Eline felt a vague sense of banishment, which caused her momentary displeasure. She had been quite alone all evening, having given in to a whim of indolence and ennui not to go out, and any length of solitude tended to bring on melancholy, making her long for some company and light-hearted banter. She paused in the dark, undecided, then groped her way down the stairs and entered the dining room.

Henk had flung his tailcoat on the sofa, and now stood in his waistcoat and shirtsleeves preparing his nightly hot toddy. Swirls of steam rose from the glass as he replaced the kettle on the hot plate.

"Hello, my dear!" he said heartily, an affable smile spreading beneath the bushy blond moustache as he regarded her with his sleepy, blue-grey eyes. "Weren't you very bored this evening, all by yourself?"

"A little, yes. Not as bored as you, maybe," she responded with a coy smile.

"Me? Quite the contrary; the tableaux were really rather good."

He stood straddle-legged, sipping his hot drink with audible relish.

"Has the youngster been good?"

"Yes, sound asleep all evening. Are you staying up?"

"I just want to have a look at the papers. But why aren't you in bed yet?"

"Oh, no reason … "

Turning to the pier glass, she stretched her arms again lingeringly, then twisted her loose hair into a sleek, dark chignon. She felt a need to confide in him, to have a heart-to-heart talk, but in her vacant, dreamy state she was at a loss for any particular topic to engage his sympathy. She wished she could break down and weep, overcome by some not-too-lacerating grief, for the sole purpose of hearing his gentle, bass voice consoling her. But she could think of nothing to say, and continued to stretch herself with languishing gestures.

"Is anything wrong? Tell me, my dear, is anything the matter?"

Widening her eyes, she shook her head from side to side. No, nothing was wrong.

"You can tell me, you know!"

"Well, I'm just a bit upset, that's all."

"What about?"

She gave a little moan, pouting her lips.

"Oh, I don't know. It's just that I've been feeling rather nervous all day."

He laughed his gentle, sonorous laugh.

"You and your nerves! Come now, little sister, it's time you cheered up. You're such good company when you're not in one of your moods; you really shouldn't give in to them."

Feeling insufficiently eloquent to persuade her of this, he grinned and changed the subject:

"Care for a nightcap, Sis?"

"Thank you. Yes, I'll just have a sip of yours."

She turned to face him, and he, chuckling beneath his blond moustache, raised the steaming glass to her lips. Then he noted the glint of a tear in her hooded eyes, and with brusque determination set down the glass and caught her hands in his.

"There, there now, tell me what happened. Was it something between you and Betsy? Go on, you know you can tell me everything."

He cast her a look of reproof with his uncomprehending, trusting eyes like those of a good-natured Newfoundland dog.

Only then, in a voice broken with sobs, did she let loose a torrent of misery, for no apparent reason other than the prompting of his voice and his eyes. The urge to pour her heart out was too strong to resist. What was she living for? What use could she be to anyone? She wandered about the room, wringing her hands and lamenting without pause. She didn't care if she died within the hour, she didn't care about anything at all, it was just that her existence was so futile, so useless, without anything she could wholeheartedly devote herself to, and it was all becoming too much to bear.

Henk sputtered in protest, discomfited by the scene, which was no more than a repetition of so many previous ones. He began to talk about Betsy and Ben, their little boy, and about himself, and he was on the point of mentioning that she too would be mistress of her own home one day, but then thought that might be indiscreet. She for her part shook her head like a stubborn child refusing to be distracted after not getting its way, and then, in desperation, hid her face against his shoulder and sobbed there, with her arm entwined around his sturdy neck. Her nerves were frayed from the lonely hours spent in an overheated room, and she resumed her halting tirade, bemoaning the pointlessness of her existence, the wretched burden life was to her, and in her tone he detected a hint of reproach directed at him, her brother-in-law, for being the cause of all her woes. He was much confused, and also touched by the warmth of her fragrant embrace, which he could hardly return with equal tenderness. All he could do to stem the flow of disjointed sentences was murmur trite words of consolation.

Slowly, slowly, to the soft tones of his sonorous voice, she cast off her melancholy mood, as though scattering rose petals on a stream.

She fell silent at last and took a deep breath, but continued to rest her head on his shoulder. Now that she had calmed down, he thought it incumbent on him to chide her for her foolishness. What nonsense it all was, to be sure! A lot of fiddlesticks! Because, dash it all, there was no call for such a fuss, now, was there?

"But Henk, truly——" she began, raising her moist eyes to his.

"My dear girl, all this talk about there being no sense to your life—whatever gave you that idea? You know we all love you dearly."

And, recalling his earlier, unspoken consideration of her eventual marriage, he added:

"Fancy a young girl like you complaining of the futility of life! My dear sis, you must be quite mad!"

Tickled by this thought, and feeling there had been enough philosophy for now, he gave her arms a firm shake and tweaked her sad lips into a smile. She resisted, laughing, and it was as though the balance in her mind had been restored by her outburst. When a few moments later they started up the stairs together, she could barely suppress a shriek of laughter as he suddenly swept her off her feet and carried her the rest of the way while she, fearing a fall, half-ordered and half-begged him to desist.

"Now Henk, let me go! Don't be silly! Put me down at once, Henk, do you hear?"

III

E LINE VERE was the younger of the two sisters, with darker hair and eyes and a slimmer, less rounded figure. The lambent darkness of her gaze, in combination with the translucent pallor of her skin and the languishing quality of certain of her gestures, gave her something of an odalisque lost in reverie. Her beauty was of great concern to her; she made it glow and sparkle like a treasured jewel, and this sustained attention rendered her almost infatuated with what she considered her best features. She would gaze at her reflection for minutes on end, smiling as she traced the line of eyebrows and lashes with the tip of a rosy fingernail, pulling the lids sideways a fraction to make almond eyes, or rumpling her mass of brown locks into the wild exuberance of a Gypsy girl. Her wardrobe, too, was the object of long and earnest meditation, involving the effects and harmonies of the cold sheen of satin, the warmer, changeable shades of silk plush, the froth of tulle and gauze, and the sheerness of mousseline and lace. From the quivering flashes of her diamond ring to the subtle emanations of her scented sachets, the assortment of fineries gave her a pleasant sensation of luxury and delicate femininity.

Being somewhat dreamy and romantic by nature, she would sometimes while away the hours in self-indulgent remembrance of her childhood. Her memories were like beloved relics to her, to be taken out and freshened up at regular intervals, and in the course of her contemplations she would quite deliberately replace the more faded images with new, idealised ones. Calling them to mind again later, she would lose sight of what was true and what invented, and would, with complete assurance, relate all manner of trivial episodes of the old days in this polished, poetic form. Betsy, with her more practical, matter-of-fact turn of mind, never missed an opportunity to tone down anything resembling glorification of the past, and for all her nostalgic leanings, Eline, when thus corrected, would usually succeed in distinguishing the bare facts from the fantastic blooms of her imagination.

She recalled her father, a painter, a man of refined, artistic temperament but wanting in the strength to create, married at a young age to a domineering wife several years his senior. He had felt oppressed by her, and his highly strung nerves, like those of a noble musical instrument, had quivered beneath the roughness of her touch, much as Eline's now quivered beneath that of her sister. She recalled her father's features of yellowed ivory, and his pallid, transparent fingers lying idle and listless while he cogitated on some painterly masterpiece that would be abandoned after the first few brushstrokes. She had been his little confidante, as it were, and in her mind his embattled genius matched that of the great Raphael, painter of sad-eyed Madonnas with flowing tresses. Her mother had always inspired a quiet fear in her, and as her memories of the disillusionments of childhood were primarily bound up with her, she was unable to idealise her mother as she did her father.

She recalled how, after the death of her father in the disaffection of an unfulfilled life and the subsequent demise of her mother due to heart failure, she and her sister had lived under the kindly guardianship of a widowed aunt. Old-fashioned, thin and up-right, with a mournful cast to her regular features of erstwhile beauty, she loomed in Eline's memory as a figure behind a plate-glass window, her time-worn hands working four shiny knitting needles in a measured, tremulous minuet. Aunt Vere spent her days in her spacious front room amid the gently stultifying trappings of her wealth, invariably clad in sweet-smelling, velvety garments, with a thick Deventer rug underfoot, a flaming log in the grate, and by the door a Japanese screen of yellow silk embellished with scarlet peonies and storks on the wing.

The two sisters, growing up together under the same tutelage and in the same surroundings, developed along parallel mental and moral lines, but as the years went by each followed the bent of her individual temperament. Eline's languorous, lymphatic disposition entailed the need of tender reassurance and warm affection, and her nerves, delicate as the petals of a flower, often suffered, despite the plush comfort of her surroundings. She was overly sensitive to any opposition or impediment, and in self-defence took to bottling up her feelings, which led her to harbour a host of small, private grievances. Release from her long-pent-up emotion would come with the occasional outburst of temper. In Betsy's more full-blooded nature there grew an inclination to take control, which was exacerbated by Eline's want of self-reliance. At times her dominance was such that she could almost enter into the psyche of her sister, who, after the initial shock, would soon swallow her pride and even experience a measure of calm and satisfaction in being taken in hand. But neither Eline's highly strung sensitivities nor Betsy's overruling egotism had ever precipitated a tragic crisis, for within the cushioned confines of their aunt's residence the contrasting hues of their personalities blended into a uniform shade of grey.

Later—after several balls at which Eline, resplendent in floaty, pastel-coloured dresses and dainty slippers of white satin, had glided and whirled to the intoxicating three-quarter time in the arms of a succession of eager cavaliers—later, she had received two offers of marriage, both of which she had declined. They lingered in her mind as easy conquests, bringing a calm smile of satisfaction to her lips when she thought of them, although her remembrance of the first often elicited a faint sigh as well. For it was at that time that she had met Henri van Raat, and since that first encounter she often wondered how it was possible that such a big bumbling fellow, as she thought of him, a man so unlike the hero of her dreams, should appeal so strongly to her sympathies that she often found herself, quite suddenly, longing for his company. In the hero of her dreams there were touches of the idealised image of her father, and likewise of the heroes in Ouida's novels, but none at all of van Raat, with his mellow, lazy manner arising from the full-bloodedness of an overly sanguine humour, his uncomprehending, blue-grey eyes, his slow diction and unrefined laugh. And yet there was in his voice and in his glance, as in his candid bonhomie, something that attracted her, something protective, so that she sometimes felt vaguely inclined to rest her head on his shoulder. And he too sensed, with a certain pride, that he meant something to her.

That pride, however, vanished the moment Betsy drew near. He felt so intimidated by Eline's sister that he found himself on more than one occasion responding to her lively banter with even slower speech and gruffer laughter than usual. She thought it an exquisite pleasure, cruel though it was, to goad him into paying her compliments, whereupon she would mischievously twist the meaning of his words and pretend to be offended. He would apologise, stumbling in search of the right phrases, often unaware of quite what impropriety he had committed, which flustered him so greatly that he could only stammer muddled assurances of his good intentions. Then she would peal with laughter, and the sound of that full, hearty laugh, mocking him with her sense of superiority, stirred greater emotion in him than the more ethereal, needful allure of her sister. Eline's was that of a tearful, sweet-eyed siren rising from the blue of the ocean with sinuous, beckoning arms and a piteous cry, only to lapse helplessly into the deep once more, while Betsy's was more like that of a thyrsus-wielding bacchante seeking to entwine him with vine tendrils, or threatening to dash her brimming glass in his face by way of merry provocation.

And so it had come about—he could not tell precisely how—that one evening, in the green coolness of a dimly lit conservatory, he had abruptly, in a rush of words, asked Betsy to be his wife. There had been something compelling, magnetic even, about Betsy's conduct that evening that had moved him to propose. She had quite calmly accepted, without demurral, taking care to hide her delight at the prospect of being mistress of her own home beneath a veneer of serenity. She longed for a change from the dignified stuffiness of Aunt Vere's front room with its large plate-glass windows, the thick Deventer rug, the fire in the grate and the storks and peonies on the Japanese screen.

But when Eline congratulated Henk quite simply and sweetly on his betrothal, he was somewhat taken aback, and a pang of disquiet over his impetuous deed left him tongue-tied in the face of her sisterly good wishes.

Eline herself, more disturbed than she knew by this unexpected turn of events, suddenly felt on her guard with Betsy, and withdrew into melancholy aloofness. Knowing herself to be the weaker of the two, she grew haughty and irritable, and henceforth took to opposing her sister's dominating influence.

Henk and Betsy had been married a year when the girls' aunt died. Betsy had given birth to a son. Henk, at the instigation of his wife, had cast around for some employment, for he annoyed her at times with his stolid, good-tempered lassitude, which reminded her of a faithful dog forever lying at one's feet and inadvertently getting kicked as a result. He too entertained vague notions of the necessity for a young chap, regardless of the size of his personal fortune, to have some occupation. In the meantime, however, he had found nothing suitable, and had ceased his efforts. In any case, she had little to complain of. In the morning it was his habit to ride out with his two Ulmer hounds running along behind him; in the afternoon he accompanied Betsy on social calls at her behest, or, when relieved of this duty, visited his club. His evenings were frequently taken up with escorting his butterfly spouse to the theatre and soirées, where he did duty as a somewhat burdensome but indispensable accessory. He submitted to this social whirl, for he could not summon the courage to protest, and on the whole found it less daunting to get dressed and follow Betsy than to disturb the domestic peace by pitting his will against hers. But the quiet evenings spent alone together, although few, were gratifying to his innate predilection for home comforts, and his lazy contentment on those occasions did more to rouse his love than the sight of her at some social gathering, engaged in brilliant conversation. That only made him peevish, and he would retreat into sullen silence on the way home. To Betsy staying in was a dreadful bore; she would recline on the sofa with a book in the soporific glow of the gas lamp, stealing looks at her husband as he gazed upon the pages of an illustrated magazine or just sat there blowing on his tea for minutes on end, both of which habits she found exceedingly irritating. At times she became so irritated that she could not resist carping about his failure to find something to do, to which he, rudely awakened from his cosy reverie, could only give a slurred response. Nonetheless, at heart she was quite content; she loved being able to spend as much as she liked on clothes, without the need for any of the meticulous accounts her aunt had obliged her to keep, and frequently she could look back in smiling satisfaction on a week without a single evening spent at home.

Eline, meanwhile, had passed the year in glum solitude at Aunt Vere's house with its plate-glass windows and Japanese storks and peonies, only occasionally swept up in Betsy's social whirl. She had done a lot of reading, and was especially taken with Ouida's rich phantasmagoria of imagined lives in vibrant hues under the golden sunshine of Italian skies, much as in a scintillating kaleidoscope. She read her treasured Tauchnitz editions until the pages, dog-eared and crumpled, came loose and hung by a single thread. When her aunt was ill she spent long hours at her bedside, and even during these vigils, which gave her a sense of romantic fulfilment, she read and reread her novels. In the airless sickroom with its medicinal odours, Eline was enraptured by the virtues and prowess of noble heroes and the astonishing beauty of infernally wicked or divinely righteous heroines; indeed she was frequently seized with a passionate longing to reside in one of those old English castles herself, the kind of place where earls and duchesses observed such refined etiquette in their courtships, and where exquisitely romantic trysts were held in ancient parklands, with stage-like settings shimmering in the moonlight against a backdrop of blue-green boughs.

When Aunt Vere died, Henk and Betsy invited Eline to come and live with them. At first she declined, overcome by a singular dejection at the thought of the bond between her sister and brother-in-law. Eventually she succeeded in rousing herself from this dismal frame of mind, but only by an immense exertion of will-power, like a fierce beating of wings. She had always wondered at the mysterious attraction she had felt for Henk, but now that he was married to her sister the situation was different. An invisible but impenetrable barrier of restraint had risen between them, by laws of decorum and custom, so that henceforth she need surely have no qualms about showing her sympathy for him as his sister-in-law. She said to herself that it would be very childish to allow the recollection of past, undifferentiated emotions to stop her from accepting their offer. Besides, her legal guardian, Uncle Daniel Vere, who lived in Brussels, was unmarried and too young to accommodate his young niece in his home.

So Eline waived her objections and agreed to take up residence in her brother-in-law's house, jokingly insisting that she be allowed to make a modest monthly contribution towards household expenses. Henk refused outright, although Betsy shrugged her shoulders, saying that she in Eline's shoes would have wanted the same, for the sake of feeling free and independent. From the inheritance her parents left her Eline derived an annual income of two thousand guilders. With this sum fully at her disposal and by putting into practice the lessons of economy taught her by Aunt Vere, she managed to dress every bit as elegantly as Betsy did on her unlimited purse.

Three years went by, which were uneventful but for the same rounds of seasonal diversions.

IV

WHEN ELINE CAME DOWN to breakfast the morning after her tearful outburst Henk had already left, bound for the stables where his horses were kept along with the two Ulmer hounds that Betsy would not tolerate in the house. There was no one but young Ben, humming tonelessly as he poked a slice of bread and butter with his stubby little fingers. Betsy could be heard bustling about and issuing instructions to Grete, the ill-tempered kitchen maid. There would be four guests for dinner that evening—Frans and Jeanne Ferelijn and the Honourable Miss de Woude van Bergh and her brother.

Eline looked fresh and bright in a simple morning gown of dark-grey wool with a triple-flounced skirt and a close-fitting, plain bodice tied at the waist with a grey silk ribbon, and at her throat a small gold brooch in the shape of an arrow. She wore no rings or bracelets, which contributed to her air of studied simplicity and ladylike reserve. About her forehead and neck curled some delicate tendrils of hair, soft as frayed silk.

Nodding affectionately at Ben as she came in, she went to stand behind him. She placed her hands on the sides of his chubby head and, taking care to avoid his buttery fingers and lips, pressed a fond kiss on his crown.

She sat down, rather pleased with the way she looked today, and in her state of restored equanimity she felt agreeably lulled by the warmth of the stove while the snow fell outside in downy silence. Unconsciously smiling, she rubbed her slender white hands and inspected her rosy, white-tipped fingernails, and then, casting a contented glance outside, saw a fruit vendor, thin as a reed and bent double under a dingy grey shawl, pushing a barrow laden with snow-covered oranges. She took up a breakfast roll, and as she did so felt another stirring of contentment, a shade egotistically, upon overhearing the heated exchange between Betsy and the kitchen maid—shrill commands and terse, insolent ripostes ringing out above the clanging of metal pans and the porcelain rattle of a stack of plates being violently set down.

Betsy came in, eyes flashing with indignation beneath the thick brows, her small, plump lips pursed. She carried a set of cut-glass dessert plates, which she had decided to wash herself, as Grete had broken one of them. Carefully, despite her annoyance, she placed the dishes on the table, filled a basin with tepid water, and cast around for a brush.

"That dratted girl! Fancy washing my best cut glass in boiling-hot water. It's always the same; you can't trust those duffers to do anything."

Her voice sounded harsh and strident, and she pushed Ben out of her way without ceremony.

Eline, solicitous in her pleasant frame of mind, promptly offered to help, and Betsy was glad to accept. She had a great many things to do, she said, but plumped herself down on the sofa instead to watch as Eline cleaned the dishes one by one with the brush and then patted them dry in the folds of a tea towel with light, graceful movements, taking care not to get her fingers wet or spill a single drop. And Betsy sensed the contrast between her own energetic briskness, arising from her robust health, and her sister's languishing elegance, which implied a certain reluctance to exert herself or defile her hands.

"By the way, the Verstraetens said they wouldn't be going to the opera this evening, as they need some rest after yesterday's tableaux, so Aunt offered me their box. Would you care to go?"

"To the opera? What about your dinner guests?"

"Jeanne Ferelijn said she wanted to leave early as one of her children has come down with a cold again, so I thought of asking Emilie and her brother if they'd like to come along. Henk can stay at home. It's a box for four, you know."

"Good idea. Very good idea."

With a satisfied air, Eline dried the last sparkling cut-glass dish of the set, and just as she was putting away the basin another violent altercation broke out in the kitchen, accompanied by the silvery crash of cutlery. The quarrel this time was between Grete and Mina, the maid-of-all-work. Betsy ran out of the room, and there ensued another volley of irate commands and disgruntled replies.

In the meantime Ben stood where his mother had pushed him, his mouth agape in dumb consternation at the clamour in the kitchen.

"Well now, Ben, shall we go up to Auntie's room together?" asked Eline, offering him her hand with a smile. He sidled up to her, and they climbed the stairs together.

Eline occupied two rooms on the first floor: a bedroom and a spacious adjoining boudoir. With modest means yet refined taste she had succeeded in creating an impression of luxury with artistic overtones, particularly in the contrived disarray here and there, which evoked still-life compositions. Her piano stood at an angle at one end. The lush foliage of a giant aralia cast a softening shade over a low couch covered in a Persian fabric. A small writing table was littered with precious bibelots, while sculptures, paintings, feathers and palms filled every nook. A Venetian pier glass decorated with red cords and tassels hung above the pink marble mantelpiece, upon which stood the figurines of Amor and Psyche, in biscuit porcelain after Canova, with the maiden removing her veil in surrender to the lovesick, winged god.

As Eline entered with Ben, she felt the welcoming glow from the hearth on her cheeks. She gave the child some tattered picture books to keep him busy, whereupon he settled himself on the couch beneath the aralia. Eline slipped into her bedroom, where the windows displayed a few lingering frost patterns, like delicate blooms etched into crystal.

To the side stood her dressing table, abundantly flounced with tulle and lace, which she had touched up here and there with satin bows left over from ball bouquets; the top was laden with an assortment of flacons and coasters of Sèvres porcelain and cut glass. In the midst of all this pink-and-white exuberance glittered the looking glass, like a sheet of burnished metal. The bedstead was concealed behind red hangings, and in an angle of the walls stood a wide cheval glass reflecting a flood of liquid light.

Eline looked about her a moment, to see if the maid had arranged everything to her satisfaction; then, shivering from the cold in the just-aired bedroom, she returned to her sitting room and shut the door. With its muted oriental appeal it was a most pleasant retreat, while outside all was bright with frost and snow.

Eline felt her throat filled with melody. Hunting among her music books for a composition attuned to her emotion, she came upon the waltz from *Mireille*. She sang it with variations of her own devising, with sustained *points d'orgue*, finely spun like swelling threads of glass, and joyous trills as clear as a lark's. She forgot the cold and snow outside. Feeling a sting of conscience for not having practised for the past three days, she began singing scales, by turns brightening her high notes and practising difficult portamentos. Her voice rang out with plangent tones, the hint of coldness in it at once pearly and crystalline.

Although Ben was accustomed to her melodious voice echoing through the house, he stopped turning the pages of his picture book to listen open-mouthed, giving a little start now and then at a singularly piercing ti or do in the top range.

Eline was at a loss to account for her low spirits of yesterday. Where had that fit of gloom come from? She could think of no particular cause for it. How odd that it should have dissipated of itself, for she could think of no joyful occurrence to justify her change of heart. She now felt bright, gay, and in good form; she regretted not having seen the tableaux, and would have liked to have heard all about them from Betsy. She hoped the Verstraetens did not think her indisposition had been an excuse. Such a kind gentleman, Mr Verstraeten, so amusing and fun-loving, and his wife was such a dear! She was quite the nicest person she knew! And as Eline sat at her piano, now practising a roulade, then a series of shakes, her thoughts floated to all the other nice people she knew. All her acquaintances were nice in one way or another: the Ferelijns, Emilie de Woude, old Madame van Raat, Madame van Erlevoort, even Madame van der Stoor. As for young Cateau—she was adorable. And she caught herself thinking how amusing it would be to join in their theatricals herself: she heartily approved of the way

Frédérique, Marie, Lili, Paul and Etienne were always happily banding together, always planning diversions and japes. What fun it would be to wear beautiful draperies and be admired by all! And Paul had an attractive voice, too; she did so love singing duets with him, and she quite forgot that only a few days before, during a conversation with her singing master, she had remarked that Paul had no voice to speak of.

So she was in mellow mood, and sang a second waltz—that of Juliette in Gounod's opera. How she adored Gounod!

It was half-past ten when there was a knock at the door.

"Come in!" she cried, resting her slender fingers on the keys as she glanced over her shoulder.

Paul van Raat stepped into the room.

"Hello Eline. Hello there, little scamp."

"Ah, Paul!"

She rose, somewhat surprised to see him. Ben went over to his uncle and tried to climb up his legs.

"You're early! I thought you weren't coming to sing until this afternoon. But you're most welcome, naturally. Do take a seat, and tell me all about the tableaux!" Eline said warmly. Then, recalling her recent indisposition, she dropped her voice to a suitably depressed pitch:

"I was awfully sorry I couldn't go; I wasn't at all well, you know … such an appalling headache."

"I'd never have guessed from the look of you."

"But it's true, Paul! Why else do you think I'd miss the opportunity to admire your talent? Go on, do tell me all about it, I want to know every detail!" She swept the picture books off the couch and invited him to sit down.

Paul finally managed to disentangle himself from Ben, who had been clutching him tightly, teetering on his little heels.

"Now then, roly-poly, you must let me go! Well, Eline, has the headache cleared up now?"

"Oh yes, completely. I shall go and congratulate Mr Verstraeten on his birthday, and apologise for not being at the party. But in the meantime, Paul, do tell me what it was like."

"Actually, what I came to tell you is that I shan't be coming to sing this afternoon, as I have no voice left. I did so much shouting yesterday that I'm quite hoarse. But it was a great success, all things considered."

And he launched into an elaborate description of the tableaux. They had been his idea, and he had done much of the work himself, including painting the backdrops, but the girls too had been very busy for the past month, getting up the costumes and attending to a thousand details. That afternoon Losch would be coming to take photographs of the final tableau, so even if he had been in good voice he wouldn't have been able to come by to sing with her. Besides, he was as stiff as a board, for he had slaved away like a carpenter. As for the girls, they must be quite exhausted too. He had not taken part in the performance himself, as he had been far too busy making all the arrangements.

He leant back against the Persian cushions beneath the overhanging aralia, and brushed his hand over his hair. Eline was struck by how much he resembled Henk despite being his junior by ten years: of slimmer build, of course, and much more lively, with finer features and an altogether brighter look. But the occasional gesture, such as the raising of an eyebrow, brought out the resemblance to a startling degree, and while his lips were thinner beneath his light moustache than Henk's beneath his bushy whiskers, his laugh was much like his brother's: deep, and warm and hearty.

"Why don't you take proper painting lessons, Paul?" asked Eline. "Surely, if you have talent—"

"But I haven't!" he laughed. "So it wouldn't be worth it. I just dabble, you know, whether it's in painting or singing. None of it amounts to anything."

And he sighed at his own lack of energy for making the most of what little talent he might possess.

"You remind me of Papa," she said in a wistful tone, as she evoked the poeticised image of her father. "He had enormous talent, but his health was poor and in the end he was too weak to undertake anything on a big scale. He had just started work on a huge canvas, a scene from Dante's *Paradiso*, as I recall, and

36

then … then he died. Poor Papa! But you, you're young and fit; I can't imagine why you have no ambition to do something great, something out of the common."

"You know I'm to be working at Hovel's, don't you? Uncle Verstraeten saw to that for me."

Hovel was an established lawyer, and as Paul had indeed, after alternate bouts of studiousness and sloth, graduated at a relatively early age, Uncle Verstraeten thought he would be doing the young man a good turn by commending him to his friend. So it was settled that Paul would join Hovel's office until such time as he set up a practice of his own.

"At Hovel's? A very nice man! I like his wife very much, too. Oh, but that'll be splendid, Paul."

"Let's hope so."

"You know, if I were a man I'd make sure I became famous. Come along now, Ben, be a good boy, sit down on the floor and look at those pretty pictures. Wouldn't you love to be famous? You see, if I weren't Eline Vere, I'd want to be an actress!"

And she broke into a roulade, which poured from her lips like liquid diamonds.

"Famous!" he said with a dismissive shrug. "Oh no, such a childish idea, wanting to be famous! It's the last thing I'm interested in. Still, I'd like to be good at painting, or at singing, for that matter."

"So why don't you take lessons, either in painting or in music? Shall I speak to my singing teacher?"

"No thanks, not grumpy old Roberts. And besides, Eline, honestly, it wouldn't be worth it. I'd never stay the course, whatever it was. I have these sudden moods, you know, when I feel I can do anything, and off I go looking for some great subject for a painting … "

"Like Papa," she smiled sadly.

"And then I get all excited about making the best of my voice, such as it is, but before I know it all my plans and resolutions have fizzled out like so many burnt matches."

"You ought to be ashamed of yourself."

"From now on I shall be hiding the aspirations of my genius in law cases, you'll see," he said with a chuckle as he rose to his feet.

"But now I must go to Prinsessegracht—to the Verstraetens', as a matter of fact. So don't expect me this afternoon. We have a good deal to do before Losch arrives. Goodbye, Eline! Bye-bye little Ben!"

"Goodbye, then. I hope your throat will mend soon."

Paul left and Eline returned to her piano. For a while she sat thinking what a pity it was that Paul had so little energy, and from him her thoughts drifted to Henk.

But she felt altogether too cheerful to do much philosophising, so she resumed her singing with gusto, and did not pause until the tinkle of the noon bell summoned her and Ben downstairs.

Paul had said he would not be lunching at home, as he was expected at the Verstraetens'. He lived in Laan van Meerdervoort with his mother, who was Madame Verstraeten's elder sister and a respectable lady with pensive, pale-blue eyes, a slightly old-fashioned, silvery-grey coiffure, and a demeanour suffused with resignation and fatigue. As she was having increasing trouble walking, she was usually to be found sitting in her high-backed easy chair with her head bowed down and her blue-veined hands folded in her lap. She led a calm, monotonous life, the aftermath of a calm, contented and nigh cloudless existence at the side of her husband, whose portrait hung close by. She looked at it often: a handsome figure in general's uniform, strong, open features set with a pair of faithful, sensible eyes and an engaging expression about the firm, closed mouth. Life had brought her few great sorrows, and for that, in the poetic simplicity of her faith, she thanked the Lord. Of late, however, she had been feeling increasingly tired, her spirit quite broken by the loss of the man for whom she had felt affection until the end, by which time her youthful, ebullient love for him had subsided into the unruffled serenity of a becalmed lake. Since his passing she had taken to fretting over a thousand trivialities, which gave rise to daily vexations with servants and tradesmen, and these sources of annoyance had come together in her mind as an intolerable burden. She was feeling her age; life had little more to offer her, and she withdrew into a quietly egotistic state of daydreaming about the lost poetry of her past.

She had borne him three children, the youngest of whom, a girl, had died.

Of her two sons her favourite was Henk, whose sturdy posture reminded her most of her husband. But in his good-natured disposition, too, there was more of the upright robustness of their father than in Paul's high-strung wilfulness and constrained genius. Paul she had always found rather too unsettled and nervous; as a student in Leiden he had interrupted his law studies several times, and had only graduated after Uncle Verstraeten stepped in to apply some moral pressure. And she was no less concerned nowadays, what with his staying out late, his passions for painting, tableaux vivants and the singing of duets, not to mention his recurring bouts of idleness, during which he would lounge on the sofa all afternoon pretending to read a book.

In the years preceding his marriage, Henk, being more staid and homely than Paul, had fitted in better with his old mother's habits. He was not given to conversation, but she had never found fault with his taciturn habit: to her it was like being in the comforting presence of a faithful Newfoundland dog keeping a half-closed, watchful eye on its mistress. She felt so secure in dear Henk's company. She disliked being alone, for it was then that the rose-tinted remembrances of far-off times contrasted all too painfully with the uniform greyness of the present, and of Paul she saw little more than when he was bolting down his dinner in order to keep some appointment, or lazing about the house. She seldom went out, having grown unaccustomed to the noisy traffic of the streets and the hubbub of crowds.

Henk was her pet, and despite the worries clouding her mind she was ever alert where his welfare was concerned. She regretted her son's marriage to Betsy Vere. She had never considered Betsy a suitable match for her boy, nor indeed had she been able to give him her whole-hearted maternal blessing when he announced whom he intended to take for a wife. But she had made no attempt to dissuade her beloved son from his choice, for fear of causing him unhappiness. On the contrary, and somewhat to her own surprise, she had concealed her feeling of unease towards the intruder and had welcomed her as a daughter. All the same, she felt deeply concerned about Henk's future. She had been acquainted with the late Madame Vere, though not closely, and had not been taken with her: she remembered her as domineering and disagreeable, and was troubled by Betsy's resemblance to her. Although Henk was clearly possessed of much more firmness of character than Betsy's father, whom she remembered as being deathly pale and plagued by migraines while letting his wife think and act for him, although Henk had inherited his father's frank robustness and would not stand for any nonsense from a wife, she was convinced he would never be as happy with Betsy as she herself had been with her husband. Dwelling on these thoughts, she would sigh and grow moist-eyed; the maternal instinct that made her blind to Henk's failings also gave her a keen sense of an underlying truth, while her only wish was for her son to find the same happiness in marriage as she had known herself.

She was roused from her meditation by Leentje, the maid, laying the round table for one in the next room, and with weary resignation she seated herself to partake of her luncheon alone. How hateful this solitude was! Tomorrow would be the same to her as today: the summer of her life had come to an end, and though autumn and winter might be free from storms, all they brought was dreariness and cold lethargy. She might as well be dead!

The sense of loneliness and abandonment made her so dull that she did not once scold Leentje for her clumsiness, although it did not escape her that her porcelain serving dish had become severely chipped along the edges during the washing-up.

That afternoon Eline left the house earlier than usual, to call at the Verstraetens'. It was nearing the end of November, and winter had set in with a vengeance. There was a sharp frost; the snow, still bluish-white and unsullied, crackled under Eline's light, regular tread, but where possible she took to the pavements that had been swept clear of snow. With her daintily gloved hands tucked into the small muff, now and then bestowing a cordial smile and nod on some acquaintance from under her short veil of tulle, she made her way along Javastraat towards Prinsessegracht. She was still in a happy humour, content with her smart winter ensemble trimmed with brown fur, and quite unaffected by the slight argument she had just had with Betsy, who had accused her of ordering Grete to do Mina's work. This kind of disagreement was becoming increasingly frequent of late, much to Henk's dismay, for he hated nothing more than the pettiness of domestic bickering.

This time, however, Eline had paid little heed to Betsy's remark, and had responded less sharply than usual; she had no intention of letting her good humour be spoilt by such trivialities—life was too dear to her.

And, thankful for having curbed her temper, she turned the corner of Javastraat.

Arriving at the Verstraetens', she found the household still in some disarray. Dien declared that her mistress was not receiving, but Eline brushed her aside and made her way to the suite, where she came upon the lady of the house, who apologised for being in her peignoir. Losch, the photographer, had his head tucked under the green cloth of his apparatus to view the ensemble portraying the five senses. Etienne and Paul and the girls were all smiles, and Eline, after apologising to Madame Verstraeten for her absence the previous evening, said how glad she was of the opportunity to see something of the tableaux after all. But now, in the bleak daylight reflected from the snowy garden, the scene did not make the same glowing, lavish impression as the previous evening, nor were the colours as rich as they had been in the blaze of Bengal lights. The draperies hung in loose and crumpled folds, Frédérique's cloth of gold had a dingy, mottled tint, her ermine turned out to be a plain woollen blanket embroidered with black, and Etienne's blond wig was decidedly out of curl. Losch begged them to put on a more affable expression, to no avail; Lili, as the Sense of Smell, lay half-asleep on her cushions.

"I'm afraid it won't amount to much," said Marie, while Losch adjusted her robe, but young Cateau van der Stoor thought otherwise, and remained lying motionless despite the unbearable cramp in her side owing to her difficult posture.

Eline, not wishing to disturb the concentration of the posing artistes, went into the conservatory, where she seated herself beside Mr Verstraeten to offer him her birthday greetings. He laid his book aside and removed his spectacles, the better to focus his twinkling brown eyes on the smart young visitor.

"Do you know," she said, unfastening her fur-trimmed jacket, "do you know that I'm rather jealous of that happy little lot next door, always together, always jolly, brimming with ideas and fun. Why, they make me feel quite old!"

"Well I never!" said Madame Verstraeten, laughing as she stood in her peignoir behind a chair. "You're the same age as Marie, aren't you? Twenty-three, am I right?"

"Yes, dear lady, but I was never as spoilt as Marie and Lili, not that I would have minded it one bit! As you know, at our house— when I was little—Papa was often ill and naturally that made us quiet, and afterwards at Aunt Vere's ... she was extremely kind, but far older than Papa, and not very jolly either."

"You mustn't speak ill of Aunt Vere, Eline!" said Mr Verstraeten. "She was an old flame of mine, I'll have you know."

"Ah, and you mustn't poke fun at her! I loved her dearly, she was like a second mother to us, and when she died after that long illness it was a dreadful blow. I felt quite alone in the world ... So you see, I didn't have an altogether happy time growing up." She gave a wistful smile, her eyes moistening at the thought of all she had missed. "But when you look at Paul and Etienne and the girls, there's nothing but laughter and jollity. Really, it would make anyone jealous. And Cateau is a sweet girl, too."

The artistes could be heard jumping down from the stage: the photography session had come to a close. Paul and Etienne entered the conservatory with Freddie, Marie and Cateau, all in costume, while Lili went up to bed, worn out from the excitement of the last two days.

"Goodbye, Miss Vere," said Cateau, offering her small hand.

Eline felt a sudden, inexplicable affection for the young girl, so pure and unselfconsciously beguiling, and as she rose to leave she had to hide her emotion by giving Cateau a brusque, playful hug.

"Goodbye, darling!" she cooed. "Well, Madame Verstraeten, I'd better be off. I expect you have lots of things to attend to now that things are back to normal. Only, I promised Betsy I'd ask about the opera tickets. Might I take them with me, if you have them to hand, that is?"

It was still early, just gone half-past two, and it occurred to Eline that she had neglected to call on Madame van Raat for quite some time, although she knew the old lady was devoted to her and liked receiving visitors in the afternoon for a chat. Henk called on his mother faithfully every morning after his ride, invariably accompanied by the two Ulmer hounds his wife could not abide, which would gleefully bound up the stairs in his mother's house. Betsy seldom put in an appearance; she was aware of her mother-in-law's reservations towards her. Eline, however, had won Madame van Raat's heart thanks to the particularly engaging manner she had towards elderly ladies: something in her tone of voice, in her solicitous little attentions, that betokened a pleasing respectfulness.

Eline returned through Javastraat to Laan van Meerdervoort, and found Madame van Raat alone, sitting in her high-backed chair with her hands folded on her lap. The image she presented was of such utter despondency as to unsettle her young visitor; the grand but worn furnishings were redolent of nostalgia for past conviviality, and from the hallway to the front room with its sombre green-velvet curtains the sadness and yearning were almost palpable. Eline felt her heart sinking. How miserable it all was! No, life was not worth living. Why, oh why? …

Then she mastered herself. Gathering together all the thoughts that had made her so cheerful that morning, she gave a smile and adopted her habitual tone of respectful concern and affection as she enthused about Paul, about the tableaux, about that evening's dinner party and about the opera, and she promised to send Madame van Raat some books: light-hearted, entertaining literature, in which the world was viewed through rose-tinted glasses.

It pained her to keep up her lively prattle while she would have liked to have a good cry together with Henk's mother, in woeful sympathy, but she contained her emotion and even plucked up courage to broach a more serious subject. She had seen tears in the dear lady's eyes when she arrived, she said in her soothing voice, it was no use denying it; she did not wish to be inquisitive, but would love to console her if only she knew what was wrong, and besides, dear Madame had confided in her before, hadn't she?

Eline was alluding to complaints about Betsy and various other, minor preoccupations, which she thought better not to spell out.

The old lady, feeling comforted already, gave a light laugh and shook her head: truly, there was nothing wrong, it was just that she felt lonely at times, or perhaps it was merely the tedium of her years; she had so few interests nowadays, but then that was her own fault, was it not? Other old people read the newspapers and continued to keep abreast of things generally, but not she. Oh, Eline was such a dear, sweet creature; why couldn't Betsy be a bit more like her?

She perked up a little and began to talk of her girlhood, and then, gesturing towards her beloved husband's portrait, of her life with him.

It was past four o'clock when Eline took her leave and hurried away. Dusk was falling, a thaw had set in, and the darkening clouds seemed about to come down to smother her. The old lady had said that she had been happy once, very happy ... but was that really true? And then look at her, Eline: she wasn't happy, even if she was young. How would she feel if she were the same age as old Madame van Raat, and all wrinkled and ugly? She wouldn't even have the consolation of happy memories to look back on; her entire life would be a sombre shade of grey, leaden like the clouds! Dear God, she thought, why must I live if I am not to be happy?

"Why, oh why?" she whispered, quickening her step at the thought of having to dress for dinner.

It was to be a simple, informal dinner party. The Ferelijns arrived at half-past five, followed soon after by Emilie and Georges. Betsy received them in the salon and enquired after the Ferelijns' little girl.

"Much better, thank you; she no longer has a fever, but she is not yet fully recovered either," said Jeanne. "Dr Reijer was quite pleased with her progress. It was so kind of you to invite us; I haven't had the opportunity to go out lately, so this is a most welcome change from being cooped up at home. Only, I'm afraid I took you at your word about it being an informal affair, as you can see."

Her eyes darted with some anxiety between her own simple black dress and Betsy's grey satin gown.

"Oh, there won't be anyone else besides Emilie and her brother. But since you told me you'd be leaving early, I thought we'd go to the opera afterwards. Uncle Verstraeten has let us have their box. So there's nothing to upset yourself about, you were quite right to have come as you are."

Henk came in looking blithe and affable in his smoking jacket, which Jeanne found more reassuring than Betsy's casual response. Emilie, rustling with jet beads and ebullient as ever, was a close acquaintance, leaving only Georges—in a tailcoat with a gardenia in his buttonhole—to make her feel uncomfortable in her day dress.

Frans Ferelijn, a member of the East Indian colonial service, was on leave in Holland on account of his health, and his wife was an old school friend of Eline and Betsy.

Jeanne was an unassuming little woman, very subdued, and bowed by her domestic troubles. Of slight build and anaemic pallor, with soft brown eyes, she laboured under the task of raising three sickly children with restricted financial means, and moreover she was racked with homesickness for the East Indies, the land of her birth, where she had loved the simple way of life in their remote outpost. She suffered from the cold, and counted the months remaining until their departure from Holland. She told Emilie about their home at Temanggoeng in the Kadoe, where Frans was Comptroller First Class, and about their menagerie of Cochin chickens, ducks, pigeons, a Dutch cow that was milked every day, a pair of goats and a cockatoo.

"Rather like Adam and Eve in Paradise," commented Emilie.

Then Jeanne related how she used to go out each morning to tend her Persian roses and her lovely crotons, how she picked the vegetables for the day in her own back garden and how her youngsters had begun to cough and fall ill the moment they arrived in Holland. True, they had been pale in the Indies, too, but at least there she wasn't always worrying about draughts and keeping the doors properly closed. She also missed her *baboe*, whom she had been obliged to leave behind for reasons of economy. In the meantime the *baboe*, whose name was Saripa, was in service with other people at Semarang, but she had vowed to return as soon as they were back in the Indies, and Jeanne in turn had promised to bring her some lengths of pretty cotton from Holland for her to make into kebayas.

Emilie listened with friendly interest and plied her with questions, for she knew how talk of the East Indies could draw Jeanne out of her customary reticence. Betsy considered her unsuitable for larger receptions, so she usually invited her and her husband on their own or with just one or two other close acquaintances. The fact was that she found Jeanne boring and insignificant, lacking in dress sense and prone to whingeing, but that was no reason, she felt, not to invite her for the occasional informal gathering. Jeanne had been included out of pity, Emilie out of pleasure, and Georges out of duty.

While Frans Ferelijn held forth to Henk about his impending promotion to Assistant Resident, and Georges listened politely to Jeanne's account of how her husband's horse had once strayed right onto their veranda in quest of its daily treat of a banana, Betsy leant back in her chair, thinking that Eline was taking a very long time coming. She was hoping to dine early, so as to arrive at the opera in time for the second half, and she prayed that the Ferelijns would not be indiscreet and stay too long. They were seldom amusing, anyway, she thought, and she rose, masking her impatience. She touched the peacock feathers in the Makart bouquet, adjusted some bibelots on a side table and with the point of her shoe straightened a wrinkle in the tiger-skin rug before the flaming fire in the grate. She was annoyed with Eline.

At long last the door opened and Eline appeared. Jeanne was struck by how elegantly fetching she looked in her pink dress of ribbed silk, simple but beautifully made, with tiny butterfly bows dotted here and there along the low-cut bodice, in the folds of the elbow-length sleeves and at the waist. In her tawny-brown hair, dressed in the shape of a Grecian helmet, she wore an aigrette of pink plumes; her feet were daintily shod in pink, her throat was adorned with a single strand of pearls and in her hands she held her long gloves, her pink feather fan and her mother-of-pearl opera glasses.

Ferelijn and de Woude stood up to greet her, and after shaking hands with them she kissed Emilie and Jeanne lightly on the forehead. As she enquired after little Dora's health, she could not help noticing that all eyes, including those of Henk and Betsy, were fastened on her. Her toilette was clearly a success, and when Jeanne reported that Dr Reijer had pronounced the girl to be on the mend, she responded with a beaming, triumphant smile.

At table, Eline jested incessantly with her neighbour, Georges de Woude. Betsy was seated between her two male guests, Emilie between Henk and Frans, Jeanne between Eline and Henk. In the slightly sombre dining room with its antique furnishings, the snowy damask tablecloth shimmered with silverware and fine crystal, while the soft gaslight flickering on the decanters and glasses made the wines of purple-red or palest yellow appear to quiver. From a bed of flowers in a silver basket rose the prickly crown of a pineapple.

De Woude began describing the soirée at the Verstraetens' to Eline, giving her a glowing account of how truly regal the Honourable Miss van Erlevoort had looked in her poses, first as Cleopatra and then as the Sense of Sight. Emilie, Frans and Betsy were discussing the Indies, with Jeanne joining in from time to time, but she was sitting too far away and was distracted by de Woude's loquaciousness and Eline's flirtatious, high-pitched laughter. Henk ate his soup and then his fish pastry in silence, save for the occasional offer of another helping or another glass to Jeanne or Emilie. Jeanne grew increasingly withdrawn, as much from her general malaise as from having conversed at such length with Emilie after a day filled with cares. It irked her to be sitting so close to Eline, resplendent in her dinner gown, for both she and de Woude looked as if they were attending a banquet— they made her feel quite dowdy in her plain day dress. Still, she was thankful to be sitting next to Henk, and was conscious of a vague sort of sympathy with him, as he seemed to feel just as out of place as she did.

She could not help comparing herself with Eline and Betsy; there she was, struggling with her three children on a small furlough allowance, while Eline and Betsy spent their days in a whirl of sophisticated pastimes. Where was the warm friendship that had united them when they were young and carefree, walking to school together with their satchels, when Eline had filled the hood of her raincoat with cherries and Betsy had egged them on to make mischief in the classroom? She felt estranged from her young hostess, and even repelled by her condescending manner in conversation and her domineering tone towards her husband; she felt likewise estranged from Eline, whom she found vain and frivolous in the witticisms she exchanged with the dandy at her side. She could not fathom Eline; there was something strange about her, something mysterious and contradictory. Her all-too-ready laughter grated on Jeanne's nerves, and she could not imagine how someone who by all accounts sang so wonderfully could sound so disagreeable and artificial when she laughed. Oh, if only they would pipe down! She wished she was back in the narrow upstairs apartment, with her little Dora. What was she doing here, anyway? Of course, when the physician had pronounced Dora to be out of danger, Frans had been keen to accept the invitation as a much-needed diversion, but this, this was no diversion by any means, it was only making her feel nervous and shy.

And she declined Henk's offer of the sweetbreads and asparagus, which he so warmly recommended.

"I believe Mr de Woude is your brother, is he not?" Frans asked Emilie. He had not met her or Georges before, and was as much struck by the resemblance between them as by the difference.

"Indeed he is," Emilie replied in a low voice. "My very own brother, I'm proud to say. A dreadful fop, but a dear boy. He's at the Ministry of Foreign Affairs, preparing for entry into the Diplomatic Service. So don't you go getting the wrong impression!" she laughed, wagging her finger at him as if she could read Ferelijn's thoughts.

"I have scarcely exchanged half a dozen words with Mr de Woude, so I wouldn't presume to have any opinion!" he said, somewhat taken aback by Emilie's admonition.

"And quite right too; most people change their opinion of Georges once they get to know him. And as you see, I am the loyal sister leaping to her brother's defence. Would you mind pouring me some more wine?"

"You defend him even before he is attacked!" riposted Ferelijn, smiling as he complied with Emilie's request. "But I can tell he's a favourite of the ladies here, not only of his sister, but also of Madame van Raat and Miss Vere."

Betsy joined in the exchange between Eline and Georges, attracted by the latter's vivacity as he chattered on, skimming all sorts of topics: a conversation with little substance to it, not even much in the way of wit, but light and airy as soap bubbles and peppered with firecrackers. She was in her element here: serious talk, be it ever so spirited, was too heavy for her, but this kind of froth and foam was like the wine pearling in her crystal glass, and it pleased her immensely. She thought Georges far more amusing this evening than he had been at the Verstraetens', where he had twice remarked that the red illumination was more flattering than the green. Today he did not repeat himself, but, having lost his habitual reserve, discoursed volubly, now interrupting the sisters with mock impudence, then offering a droll repartee on some disputed opinion, and on the whole paying little heed to his locution.

Eline made several attempts to draw Jeanne into their lively little group, but received only a faint smile in reply or at most a monosyllable, and consequently gave up trying to amuse her. The conversation became more general; Emilie joined in with her jovial, forthright mode, and Frans, in the midst of this charmed circle, could not resist throwing in the occasional bon mot, although he frequently cast a look of concern at his quiet little wife.

To Jeanne the dinner seemed to go on for ever. Although she had no appetite, she did not wish to attract attention by declining the truffled fowl, the Henri IV gateau, the pineapple and the choice dessert, but she barely tasted her wine. Henk, beside her, ate with relish, wondering as he chewed why Jeanne took such tiny helpings. Nor did Georges de Woude eat a great deal; he was too busy holding forth. Emilie, however, ate heartily, and enjoyed her wine, too.

It was just past eight when they rose from the table and the ladies adjourned to the drawing room. Frans joined Henk and de Woude in an after-dinner cigar, as Jeanne had agreed to stay another half hour. Betsy had pressed her not to leave just yet—it would be uncivil to dispatch her guests immediately after dinner, and there was plenty of time for the opera.

"Is Dora often ill?" asked Eline. With a rustle of pink ribbed silk she sank down on a sofa beside Jeanne and took her hand. "The last time I saw her she was quite well, but even then I thought she looked rather pale and delicate."

Jeanne discreetly withdrew her hand, feeling a touch vexed by this question being put to her after the flippancy of the table talk. She came out with a perfunctory reply. But Eline, as though wishing to make up for her earlier lack of concern, put so much warmth and commiseration in her voice that Jeanne melted. She promptly voiced her fears that Dr Reijer might not have examined her little girl with sufficient thoroughness, and Eline was all ears as she spooned sugar into her cup of mocha on the silver tray held by Gerard, the manservant. Emilie and Betsy had moved to the ante-room for a look at the latest fashion plates.

"You poor thing, all those worries, and it's less than three months since you arrived in Holland. You came in September, didn't you?" asked Eline, replacing the translucent Chinese coffee cup on the side table.

Jeanne made no reply, but brusquely drew herself up and, clasping Eline's slender, cool hand in hers, broke out with:

"I say, Eline, do you remember how I always used to speak my mind? Because there is something I should like to ask you. May I?"

"Of course!" said Eline, somewhat startled.

"Well, it's just that I wonder why things aren't the same between us as they used to be, when your parents were still alive. It's four years since Frans and I got married and left for the Indies, and now that we are back, now that I have seen you again, it's just as if everything has changed. I don't know anybody in The Hague; we have practically no relations here either, and it would be so lovely to keep my old friends."

"But Jeanne—"

"Oh, I know, you probably think I'm silly to talk like this, but things are so difficult sometimes that I get very miserable. Then I wish I could let off some steam to good friend, which I can't do with my husband, obviously."

"Why not?"

"Well, he has enough troubles of his own. He's not at all well, you know, and he's losing his patience—"

"But Jeanne, I can't think what could have changed between us."

"Perhaps I'm just imagining things. But we used to spend more time together in the old days. You move in completely different circles now, you go out a good deal, while I ... Well, we seem to have become sort of estranged."

"We didn't see each other for four years, after all."

"But we wrote letters."

"Three or four letters a year isn't much, you know! It's only to be expected that one's ideas change as one grows older and one's circumstances change, surely. And I've had my share of worries, too. First there was dear Papa, and then poor Aunt Vere, whom I attended during her final illness."

"Are you happy here, do you and Betsy get on all right?"

"Oh yes, very well, otherwise I wouldn't have moved in with her, would I?"

Eline, with characteristic reserve, had no desire to go into detail.

51

"You see! You have nothing to fret about at all," Jeanne pursued. "You are free and independent, your own mistress to do as you please, whereas I—I am in a completely different situation."

"But that doesn't mean to say we've become estranged, does it? For one thing, 'estranged' has a disagreeable sound to it, and for another, it's simply not true, whichever way you put it."

"I'm afraid it is."

"No, it's not, I assure you. My dear Jeanne, if I can be of service to you in any way, just tell me. I promise I'll do what I can. I wish you'd believe me."

"I do, and thank you for your kind promise. But Eline, I wanted to take this opportunity—"

"Now?"

Jeanne was framing questions in her mind: How are you, really? Can you tell me more about yourself, so that I may get to know you the way you are now? But seeing the polite smile on Eline's pretty lips and the dreamy look in her almond eyes, Jeanne said nothing. Suddenly she regretted having spoken so candidly to the coquettish young creature opening and closing her feather fan. Oh, why had she spoken to her at all? They were worlds apart.

"Now?" repeated Eline, despite her reluctance to hear what Jeanne had to say.

"Some other time, then, when we have more privacy … " stammered Jeanne, and she rose to her feet. She was annoyed, mostly with herself, and on the brink of tears after the unpleasant dinner followed by this fruitless exchange with Eline. Just then Betsy and Emilie emerged from the boudoir.

Jeanne said it was time they went home. The three men soon appeared, and Henk helped Jeanne into her long overcoat. Forcing herself to smile amiably, she bade them goodbye, reiterating how kind Betsy had been to invite her and her husband to this intimate gathering, and again feeling a pang of annoyance when Eline kissed her on both cheeks.

"That Jeanne is such a bore!" said Betsy when the Ferelijns had gone. "She hardly said a word all evening. What on earth were you talking to her about just now, Eline?"

"Oh, about little Dora, and about her husband … nothing in particular."

"Poor Jeanne!" said Emilie with feeling. "Come, Georges, could you get me my cloak?"

But before he could do so Mina came in with the ladies' outer garments, so de Woude went off to don his ulster, leaving Henk to rub his large hands with pleasure at the prospect of staying in after his copious dinner. The carriage had been waiting for the past half-hour in the thawing snow, with Dirk the coachman and Herman the groom on the box, huddled under their capacious fur capes.

"Oh Frans, don't ever make me accept another invitation from the van Raats!" Jeanne said beseechingly, shivering on her husband's arm as they splashed along the muddy street, trying with her small, icy hand to hold the sides of her oversized coat together against the gusting wind. "Honestly, I simply don't feel at home with them any more, Betsy and Eline have changed so much."

His response was an impatient shrug of the shoulders, and they plodded onwards in their wet shoes, the monotony of their progress relieved only by the regularly spaced street lanterns shining tremulously in the puddles along the way.

The third act of *Le Tribut de Zamora* had just begun when Betsy, Emilie, Eline and Georges entered their box. Their arrival prompted a ripple in the stillness of the audience; there was a rustling of silks and satins, a turning of eyes and craning of necks and much whispering, wondering who they were.

Emilie and Eline seated themselves at the front, with Betsy and Georges behind them, and Eline glanced about a moment, smiling faintly as she laid down her fan and mother-of-pearl opera glasses. Then she slowly untied her short cloak of white plush with the pink-satin lining and let it slide off her shoulders as a pink-and-white cloud, whereupon de Woude draped the garment over the back of her chair. Affecting not to notice the looks of admiration, she savoured the triumph of her beauty.

"It's full tonight, we're in luck," whispered Emilie. "I think it's so dismal when the house is half-empty."

"Oh, I quite agree!" said Betsy. "Look, there are the Eekhofs: Ange, Léonie and their mama. They were at the Verstraetens' yesterday, too, and they're giving a *soirée dansante* next week," she concluded, returning the girls' greeting.

"Tonight we're hearing Theo Fabrice, the new baritone from Brussels," de Woude said to Eline. "Did you know two baritones have already been dismissed? This is the third one since the debuts started."

"There doesn't seem to be an end to the debuts this winter," breathed Eline, taking up her fan.

"The tenor was excellent from the start, but this Fabrice is very good too, so I have heard. Look, there he is."

The chorus of Ben-Saïd's odalisques had come to an end, and the Moorish king himself swept into his palace, leading Xaïma by the hand. Eline was not paying attention, however. She was still scanning the audience, nodding and smiling at acquaintances, and did not direct her gaze to the stage until Ben-Saïd and his slave girl were well and duly enthroned under the canopy, signalling the start of the ballet. She always enjoyed the dancing scenes, and minutely followed the ballerinas in their shiny satin bodices and full skirts of spangled tulle as they glided on tiptoe towards the Moorish arcades, beneath which they hovered in clusters, holding aloft their veils and silver-tasselled fans.

"A pretty ballet," said Emilie, yawning behind her fan as she settled back in her seat. She was feeling the effects of her lavish dinner.

Eline nodded, and while she could hear Betsy and Georges whispering behind her, she kept her eyes fixed on the prima ballerina with the glittering aigrette of diamonds in her hair, who was floating on the curved tips of her satin ballet shoes as she twirled among the other dancers and the flutter of veils and fans.

True to her dreamy and idealistic nature, Eline had a passion for the opera, not only because it gave her the opportunity to display her languorous elegance, not only because of the music and the chance to hear some celebrated chanteuse sing a particular aria, but also because of the exciting, highly romantic intrigues and melodramatic scenes of hatred and love and revenge. She did not mind the plots being predictable, nor did she aspire to find any truth in them. She had no need to forget for one moment that she was observing actors and actresses, not knights and noble ladies, or that she was in a crowded theatre gazing at a brightly lit stage with painted scenery and music from a visible orchestra, not sharing the life of the hero and heroine in some poetic medieval fantasy—she enjoyed herself anyway, as long as the singing was tolerable, the acting not too coarse and the costumes becoming.

Betsy, by contrast, went to the opera only to see and be seen, and had she known what Eline found so enjoyable, would have shrugged dismissively, saying that was childish of her. But Eline kept her enjoyment to herself, for she knew what Betsy was like and preferred to leave her sister in the belief that for her, too, the main purpose of an evening at the theatre was to see and be seen.

She now regretted having arrived so late, for she had never seen *Le Tribut de Zamora* and consequently did not know what had gone before. Emilie had fallen silent under the influence of her fish pastry and her truffled fowl, and like Eline kept her eyes fixed on the stage.

The ballet came to an end. Ben-Saïd and Xaïma descended from their thrones, and the king, having uttered the phrase *"Je m'efforce en vain de te plaire!"* in recitative, launched into the romantic air:

> *O Xaïma, daigne m'entendre!*
> *Mon âme est à toi sans retour!*

The new baritone's voice was deep and resonant, more like that of a basso cantante, and in his delivery he cast a pall of melancholy over the song.

However, his extravagant Moorish costume made him appear rather large and burly. Neither in his pose nor in his facial expression did he convey anything resembling the passionate devotion of a lover, and in the looks he directed at the *chanteuse légère*, silver-robed and with pearl-studded blonde locks, there was more fierceness than tender devotion.

Eline was not insensitive to this shortcoming of his acting, but was nonetheless charmed by the contrast between his overbearing demeanour and the humble, beseeching tone of his voice. She followed his song note by note, and when, at an abrupt, plangent fortissimo, the actress assumed an expression of great terror, she was astonished, thinking: why is she so frightened? What could have happened? He doesn't look all that wicked to me.

During the applause she cast around the audience again, and lit on a party of gentlemen who had posted themselves on the steps leading to the stalls. She saw them peering up at her box, presumably discussing its occupants, and was about to look away in a show of great unconcern when she noticed that one of the men, hat and cane in hand, was smiling at her in a courteous yet familiar way. She stared at him a moment, wide-eyed, too startled to answer the greeting, and then abruptly turned away, put her hand on Betsy's knee and whispered in her ear:

"Look, Betsy, look who's over there!"

"Where, who do you mean?"

"There in the stalls. It's Vincent; can't you see?"

"Vincent!" echoed Betsy, likewise startled. "Oh yes, so it is!"

They both nodded to Vincent in greeting. He responded by peering at them through his lorgnette, whereupon Eline hid coquettishly behind her fan.

"Who's he? Who's Vincent?" Emilie and Georges wanted to know.

"Vincent Vere, a first cousin of ours," Betsy replied. "He's a bit of a bounder, I'm afraid. No one ever knows where he is; he disappears for months and then turns up again when least expected. I had no idea he was in The Hague. Oh Eline, do stop fiddling with your fan."

"But I won't have him staring at me!" said Eline, readjusting her fan with a graceful turn of her arm, still hiding her face.

"May I venture to ask how long it is since you last saw your cousin?" enquired Georges.

"Oh, at least a year and a half. When we last spoke I believe he was about to go to London, where he'd found some position; working on a newspaper or something of that nature. Can you imagine, they say he was with the Foreign Legion in Algiers for a time, but I don't believe any of it. He's supposed to have done all sorts of things, and he never has a penny."

"Yes, I remember him now. I think we met at some time," Emilie said with a yawn. "A curious customer."

"Yes, he is, but he knows he has to behave himself after a fashion when he's in The Hague, where his relatives live, which he does, and so we put up with him."

"Ah well, there's a black sheep in most families," Emilie remarked philosophically.

Eline gave a light laugh at the popular expression, and at long last folded her pink ostrich-feather fan.

The third act passed without her comprehending much of the scene with Manoël, but she did get the gist of the great duet sung by Hermosa and Xaïma: the reunion of mother and daughter after the refrain "*Debout, enfants de l'Ibérie!*"

The curtain fell to thunderous applause, and three times the two actresses were called to the front, where they were presented with bouquets and baskets of flowers.

"Oh please, Mr de Woude, be so kind as to explain the intrigue to me. *Je n'y vois pas encore clair!*" said Eline, turning to Georges.

Before he could reply, however, Betsy proposed taking a turn in the foyer, and they all stood up and left the box. Seated on the ottoman in the foyer, Georges summarised the plot for Eline, who listened with more interest than her expression revealed. Now that she knew why Xaïma was terrified of Ben-Saïd she regretted all the more having missed the drawing of lots in the first act and Xaïma's sale into slavery in the second.

She caught sight of Vincent coming down the steps. He made his way towards them with a casual, familiar air, as if he had seen his cousins only yesterday.

"Why, Vincent! Fancy seeing you here!" exclaimed Eline.

"Hello Eline! Hello Betsy! Delighted to see you again. Ah, and the Honourable Miss van Berg en Woude, am I right?"

They shook hands.

"Nearly right! Your memory for names is admirable, unlike mine, because I had quite forgotten yours," responded Emilie.

Betsy introduced Vincent and Georges.

"And how is everybody? Well, I hope?"

"Rather astonished, really!" laughed Eline. "I suppose you have come to say that you are off again tomorrow to St Petersburg, or Constantinople, haven't you?"

He smiled, studying her through his lorgnette, his pale-blue eyes like faded porcelain behind the lenses. His features were regular and handsome, almost too handsome for a man, with a fine straight nose, a neat mouth which frequently twitched with something akin to mockery, and a thin blond moustache. But his looks were a little spoilt by his complexion, which was sallow and fatigued. Of slight build, he was dressed simply in a dark half-formal suit, beneath which his feet looked remarkably narrow. His hands, too, were finely shaped, with slender, pallid fingers like those of an artist, and they reminded Eline of her father.

He took a seat and, in reply to Eline's question, told her a touch wearily that he had only arrived in The Hague yesterday, on business. He had spent some time in Malaga recently, something to do with the wine trade, and had previously been with an insurance company in Brussels; prior to that he had invested in a carpet factory in Smyrna, which had gone bankrupt. Things had not been going his way, really, and he was beginning to tire of all the travelling; he had not sat still by any means, but fate was against him, everything seemed to go wrong. There was a chance of a position with a quinine farm on Java, but first he had to obtain the proper information. He was hoping to see van Raat on the morrow, as he had a matter he wished to discuss with him. Betsy said in that case he should come for coffee in the afternoon, because van Raat was always out in the morning. Vincent accepted the invitation with gratitude, and began to talk about the opera.

"Fabrice? Oh, he's the baritone, isn't he? Yes, a good voice, but what an unsightly, fat fellow."

"Do you think so? I don't agree, I thought he looked rather well on stage!" countered Emilie.

"Miss de Woude, you cannot be serious!"

Emilie abided by her opinion and Eline had to laugh at their difference. Then the bell sounded for the fourth act, and Vincent took his leave, declining Georges' kind offer of his seat in the box.

"Oh, thank you, much obliged, but I wouldn't wish to deprive you of your seat. Besides, I can see very well from the stalls. So we shall meet tomorrow, then? *Au revoir*, Betsy, Eline ... *au plaisir*, Miss de Woude ... a pleasure to make your acquaintance, Mr de Woude."

He bowed, pressed Georges' hand and sauntered off, swinging his slim bamboo cane.

"Isn't he odd?" said Eline, shaking her head.

"I'm always afraid he'll do something to embarrass us!" Betsy whispered in Emilie's ear. "But as I said, he's been quite well-behaved until now. I was nice to him a moment ago to be on the safe side: I wouldn't want to rub him the wrong way. You never know ... "

"I can't say he's my most favourite person!" said Emilie. They all rose to return to their box.

"Come, come, Emmy, you're only saying that because he didn't like the look of Fabrice!" teased Georges.

Emilie shrugged, and they passed into the vestibule.

"Oh, so there is not to be a fifth act! I thought there would be five!" said Eline, almost crestfallen, until de Woude quickly told her how the opera ended.

The fourth act opened with a scene in the moonlit gardens of Ben-Saïd. Eline listened intently to Manoël's cavatina, to his duet with Xaïma, and to their subsequent trio with Hermosa, but her interest mounted when the Moorish king appeared at the palace gate, where he ordered his warriors to dispatch Manoël and then himself seized the unwilling Xaïma and dragged her away with him in a sudden burst of rage. The end of the opera, where

Ben-Saïd is stabbed by the mother seeking to save her daughter, affected her more than she would have cared to admit. In his scenes with both women the new baritone acted with such fire and vehemence as to lend the melodrama a glow of romantic truth, and when, fatally wounded, he subsided onto the steps of the pavilion, Eline took up her opera glasses for a closer look at his darkened visage with the black beard and half-closed eyes.

The curtain fell, but the four actors were called back, and Eline saw him once more, taking his bows with an air of cool detachment, in great contrast to the gracious smiles of the tenor, the contralto, and the soprano.

The audience rose; the doors of the boxes swung open.

Georges assisted the ladies with their cloaks, and they proceeded along the corridor and down the steps to wait by the glass doors for their carriage. Presently the doorman cupped his hand to his mouth and announced its arrival with a long-drawn-out shout:

"Van Raa … aat!"

"Personally, I don't believe *Le Tribut de Zamora* is one of Gounod's best operas; what about you, Eline?" asked Emilie when they were seated in the carriage. "No comparison with his *Faust*, or his *Romeo et Juliette*."

"I believe you are right," murmured Eline, loath to show how moved she had been. "But it's difficult to judge a piece of music the very first time you hear it. I thought some of the melodies were rather sweet. Besides, we only saw half of it."

"I rather like seeing only a few acts; having to sit out a whole opera bores me to tears, I don't mind telling you," said Betsy, yawning.

Georges began to hum the refrain: "*Debout, enfants de l'Ibérie!*"

The de Woudes were dropped off at Noordeinde, after which Betsy and Eline rode homeward in the landau, snugly ensconced in the cushions of satin damask. They talked a little about Vincent and then both fell silent, while Eline's thoughts floated to the joyful waltz in *Mireille*, to her spat with Betsy about the maids, to the tableau of the five senses, to Madame van Raat and Emily and Georges, to her pink dress … and to Ben-Saïd.

V

ABOUT A WEEK had gone by since the *tableaux vivants*; it was afternoon, and Lili Verstraeten seated herself in the drawing-room, where they had been staged. The room had long since reverted to its normal arrangement, and a cheerful fire burnt in the grate. Outside it was cold; a strong wind was blowing, and rain seemed imminent. Marie had gone shopping with Frédérique van Erlevoort, but Lili had chosen to stay at home, and now settled back comfortably in her favourite armchair, which was old-fashioned and ample, with a tapestry cover. She had Victor Hugo's *Notre Dame de Paris* with her, but was not really in the mood for reading, so the book, bound in red calf with gilt edges, lay unopened on her lap. How pleasant it was to do nothing but muse and dream, and how silly of Marie and Freddie to go out in this horrid weather! But it was no concern of hers, she was oblivious to the wind and the rain, for indoors it was as cosy as could be, with the subdued, wintry light barely filtering through the heavy curtains. Dien had come in to tie them back, but she had sent her away. Papa was in the conservatory, reading by the window; she could just see the top of his dear grey head, and she noted how rapidly he turned the pages—he was clearly engrossed in his book, unlike her, who had brought hers along for show. She was never bored, even when she was idle. On the contrary, she would sit back and enjoy the notions drifting into her mind: rose petals wafting on a gentle breeze, soap bubbles, fragile and iridescent, which she would watch contentedly as they rose up in the air; then the petals would blow away and the bubbles would burst, but no matter, she would much rather have rose petals for thoughts than smothering tendrils of ivy, and rather a soap bubble than a balloon on the end of a string. Mama was still upstairs attending to numerous household duties. Ah well, she couldn't be of any help: Mama always insisted on doing everything herself, although Marie did her share as well. She hoped there would be no callers this afternoon; all she wanted to do was daydream, what could be more delightful than that? How fascinating it was to watch the flames curling and twisting around the glowing embers! The hearth was a vision of hell in miniature, the burning peat suggesting great boulders between which yawned chasms filled with fire and brimstone—it was like Dante's inferno, with the damned gathered together on the precipices, shuddering at the sight of the flames! Smiling at her wild imaginings, she averted her eyes, which prickled from staring into the hellish blaze. It was only last week that they had all taken their poses in this very room, before the eyes of their enthusiastic friends and relations. How different everything had looked then! Now the painted scenery, the lyres, the cross and all the other bits and pieces had been removed to the attic for storage; all the costumes had been carefully folded and put away in boxes by Dien. It had been so jolly, what with all the planning and conferring with Paul and Etienne beforehand, the choosing of the subjects for the tableaux, the costumes, and then the rehearsals, with Paul having to demonstrate each pose in turn! How many times hadn't they collapsed with hilarity, how much effort hadn't they put in for the sake of a few minutes of entertainment!

Papa read and read, and she counted how long it took him to turn the pages—first it was twenty-five seconds, then thirty. What a fast reader he was! And how the rain drummed on the windowpane, how it gurgled in the drainpipe! Freddie and Marie had gone out of their own free will, but here she was, feeling snug and safe like a purring kitten instead of bedraggled in the wet. She dug the points of her shoes into in the black fleece of the sheepskin hearth rug and nestled her blonde head against the back of the old tapestried armchair.

Freddie was going to a ball that evening. How could she bear to go out night after night! Of course she, Lili, enjoyed the occasional ball or amusing soirée, but she also liked to stay at home, reading a book, or doing embroidery, or ... doing nothing at all, without even getting bored. Her life seemed to flow onwards like a calm, rippling stream; she was so happy at home with her parents, whom she adored, and she wanted it always to stay the same, she didn't even mind if she never got married and became an old maid ... Quasimodo, Esmeralda, Phoebus de Châteaupers … oh, why hadn't she brought her copy of Longfellow instead? The Court of Miracles held no appeal for her whatsoever, what she wished for now was some verse from *Evangeline*, or from *The Golden Legend*:

My life is little,
Only a cup of water,
But pure and limpid.

Dear oh dear, she was waxing quite poetic! She smiled to herself and looked out into the garden, where the bare, dripping boughs were being whipped into a frenzy by the wind.

The doorbell rang out; she heard footsteps and laughter in the hall, and a prolonged wiping of feet on the mat. Marie had returned with Freddie; she supposed they would go upstairs, but no, they were coming this way, and entered a moment later, having divested themselves of their dripping raincoats and muddy overshoes. They were still laughing, and brought with them a rush of cold air and moisture into the warm room.

"Well I never!" exclaimed Marie. "Behold milady warming her feet by the fire! And quite right, too!"

"Would Milady like a cushion for her back?" teased Freddie.

"You can laugh as much as you like!" murmured Lili, nestling herself deeper in her chair. "Here I am, warm as toast and my feet all nice and dry, but you're very welcome to go splashing about in the mud."

Marie said she could do with some refreshment and went off to make tea, while Freddie stepped into the conservatory to greet Mr Verstraeten.

Then they all sat down together for afternoon tea, and Lili was quite happy to join in, for all that she had not been splashing about in the mud.

"How dark it is in here, Lili, how could you see to read? You know it's bad for your eyes to read in such poor light," said Marie.

"I wasn't really reading at all," responded Lili, relishing her *dolce far niente*.

"Ah, Milady has been meditating again!" said Freddie.

"Mm, divine!" said Lili, smiling with half-closed eyes. "Doing absolutely nothing ... just dreaming the time away."

They all broke into laughter at this confession of unashamed laziness. Madame Verstraeten came in, looking for the basket of keys Marie had neglected to return, and she came upon the three girls giggling over their tea while the keys lay beside the pastry dish.

Thereupon Frédérique declared that she must be going; she had been invited to the soirée dansante at the Eekhofs that evening, and still had some details to see to regarding her party dress. Madame Verstraeten pronounced it very sensible of Lili to have stayed indoors when it was raining cats and dogs, unlike Freddie and Marie.

Again there was a ring at the door. This time it was Paul, bringing with him so much cold and wet that he was sent out of the room again to wipe his shoes properly.

"Such abominable weather!" he sighed, glad to be permitted to settle into an armchair at last.

Leaving the young people to themselves, Madame Verstraeten moved to the conservatory to sit with her husband who, however, hearing of Paul's arrival, came forward to greet him.

"Hello, Uncle."

"Well hello, Paul, how are you? And how is your mama?"

"Oh I'm very well, Uncle, and Mama is well too; when I left home she was immersed in a book lent to her by Eline."

"Tell me, have you paid a visit to Hovel yet?"

"No, Uncle, not yet, I'm afraid."

"Well, don't leave it too long. Hovel is anxious to make your acquaintance."

"Paul, you said you were going to see Hovel four days ago!" cried Marie. "How can you take so long to make up your mind to do it? It's not as if it's a long journey, is it?"

"I was planning to go tomorrow."

"Well, I hope you do. I suggest you call at half-past six, he is always at home at that hour. I urgently advise you not to put it off any longer!" said Uncle Verstraeten, with a gleam of annoyance in his otherwise cheerful dark brown eyes as he returned to the conservatory with unwonted briskness.

"Paul, you naughty boy!" said Frédérique, shaking her head. "How could you be so lazy? You're worse than Lili."

"I'll do it tomorrow for sure," said Paul gruffly, lifting his cup of tea.

"You're nothing if not lazy," Marie pursued, unafraid of his temper. "And to be honest, we all disapprove."

"You're not going to give me a lecture now, are you, you old granny?"

"I don't care what you call me, I'm just giving you my opinion. You see, I think it's a shame you're like that, because there's such a lot you could achieve if only you had a bit more determination. You mark my words, if you don't pull yourself together you'll end up like Henk; he's good and kind to be sure, but not one for undertaking a great deal, is he? You know I'm not mad about Betsy, but I can quite understand her getting terribly bored at times with your brother doing nothing all day."

"Now don't you say a word against Henk! He's such a dear!" cried Frédérique.

"And besides," Marie went on, "you're much more talented than Henk, which makes your laziness and your lack of energy doubly inexcusable."

"Just leave him be, Marie," said Lili, rising from her seat, "don't get cross with poor old Paul." Then, turning to Paul, she whispered: "Now make sure you go and see Hovel tomorrow, do you hear? Then everything will be all right."

He gave her a grin and promised to better his ways if that was what they wanted.

"It looks as if I am to be placed under the guardianship of my cousins and Miss van Erlevoort," he said good-humouredly. "Well then, perhaps they will be so kind as to grant their young ward another cup of tea?"

The downpour had come to an end, but the dripping boughs were still swaying in the wind. At half-past five the doorbell sounded yet again.

"Half-past five already!" cried Frédérique. "I must dash, because I bought some ribbons this afternoon that I still I want to put on my dress. Oh, it's going to be lovely tonight—me wearing all that floaty tulle! Where did you leave my parcels, Marie?"

"Did you hear the bell?" asked Lili. "Another visitor, do you suppose?"

Frédérique waited a moment, as she had to put on her raincoat in the vestibule, and Dien came in to enquire whether they were at home to Mr de Woude van Bergh.

"I rather think not, Dien, but go and ask in the conservatory."

"Oh, not him again!" cried Lili. "He's such a prig!"

"He's not so bad," retorted Paul. "And not in the least priggish, either."

"Anyway, I have no wish to see him!" she said, and made to close the sliding door when Dien was dispatched to show the visitor in.

"Lili, don't be absurd, come along now!" said Marie.

"No thank you very much, you go yourself," she said, and slid both doors together just as de Woude stepped into the salon. He was welcomed by Marie, who led him to the conservatory.

Paul and Frédérique laughed and bade Lili goodbye, then all three passed through the dining room to the hall.

"*Au revoir*, please convey my respects to Uncle and Aunt, and tell Uncle I shall certainly go and see Hovel after supper tomorrow," said Paul.

"Please give them my regards too, and tell them I had to rush!" said Freddie.

"All right then, goodbye, have fun this evening, in your floaty tulle! Brr, how cold it is here in the hall!"

Paul and Freddie left, and Lili returned through the dining room. Georges de Woude? Oh, he was making a courtesy call after last week's soirée, that was all! No, she couldn't abide him. So affected, so stuck up! How could Paul see anything in him? Paul she thought a thousand times more agreeable and more spirited. How Marie had lectured him! Paul was all right, and if he had turned out a bit on the lazy side, what of it? He had money, after all, and could afford to enjoy himself for a time; he would get himself a position eventually, she was sure. She would tell Papa that Paul had promised to call on Hovel tomorrow, and he always kept his word.

She sat down again in the old armchair and leant forwards to poke the fire, then put on some more coal and peat, and another log. She warmed her fingers, which had grown cold, and rubbed her small hands, cool as white satin. Through the closed door she could hear the muffled exchange going on in the conservatory. Mostly she could distinguish Georges' voice—he was obviously in a very talkative frame of mind. Her curiosity being aroused, she stood up and carefully opened one of the sliding doors a crack so she could peep into the conservatory, past the broad-leafed palms. Papa and Mama were not in view, but she could just see Marie's face and Georges' back. How funny it would be if Marie saw her spying on them like this, but her sister appeared to be absorbed in what that fop Georges had to say for himself. Lili could just make out the shiny edge of his collar and the tails of his coat—very smart! There, Marie was looking up, yes she'd noticed her! She waved gaily, dropped a little curtsey, then pulled a face which made Marie frown and purse her lips so as not to burst out laughing.

It was getting dark as Frédérique hurried home to Voorhout. Willem, the manservant, let her in, and she flew down the spacious hall and up the broad staircase. She almost tripped over her niece and nephew, Madeleine and Nico van Rijssel. Their mother was her elder sister Mathilda, who, since her separation from her husband, had taken her four children to stay with Madame van Erlevoort.

"Miss Frantzen, do take care, the children will fall!" panted Frédérique when she came upon the stout nursemaid on the first-floor landing, searching high and low for the mischievous youngsters. "Madeleine and Nico are playing on the stairs."

"Have you seen Ernestine and Johan, by any chance?" asked Miss Frantzen, looking very fraught.

"No, of course not, I only just got back!" replied Frédérique indignantly, and dashed on. She burst into her room, flung aside her raincoat and, with nervous fingers, set about opening one of small parcels she had carried home in her coat pocket and muff.

"I shall never be ready in time!" she muttered nervously, sweeping aside the green damask curtain of her bedstead, where her ball gown, a diaphanous cloud of pale-blue tulle, lay spread out on the coverlet.

Frédérique's ball dress had been delivered by the dressmaker that morning, and she wanted to add a few bows but scarcely dared touch the garment for fear of tangling the filmy material.

"Oh, what shall I do?" she moaned. Then, on an impulse, she ran out of the room and called from the landing:

"Tilly, Tilly, Mathilda!"

A door opened and her sister appeared in some alarm.

"But, Freddie, whatever is the matter? Is the house on fire?"

"No, no! If it were I wouldn't be calling you specifically, now would I? The thing is, I need help, I'm at my wits' end and I'll never be ready!"

"Help? What with?"

"With my dress! I told you I wanted some little bows as a finishing touch. I thought it looked rather bare on the side, and I've bought some ribbons."

Before Mathilda could answer, the door of another room opened to reveal Madame van Erlevoort, demanding to know what the commotion was about. At the same time a shrill burst of children's laughter came from the second floor, followed by the loud patter of small feet. Frédérique's seven-year-old niece came tripping down the stairs with her six-year-old brother in hot pursuit.

"Mama! Mama!" screamed the little girl, clearing the last steps with a jump.

"Now, now, Tina and Jo! What a dreadful noise you're making! What are you doing here?" chided their mother.

"Jo keeps teasing me, he wants to tickle me and he knows I can't stand it!" explained Ernestine breathlessly, and she hid behind her grandmother's skirts while Frédérique caught hold of her brother.

"How many times have I told you not to run about indoors, and to keep your voices down!" scolded Mathilda. "You know Granny isn't getting any younger, and all this noise is too much for her."

"Never mind," soothed Madame van Erlevoort. "They were only playing."

"You'd better be careful, young man, or I shall tickle you!" cried Frédérique, and she tickled Jo under his short arms so that he fell about laughing.

"*Mais comme vous les gâtez, toutes les deux; ne les choyez donc pas, quand je suis fâchée. Je perdrai tout mon pouvoir, si vous continuez ainsi!*" fretted Mathilda. She leant over the banisters, where Madeleine and Nico were driving fat Nurse Frantzen to distraction with their disobedience.

"Madeleine and Nico! Stop that at once!" she cried.

"Oh, Mathilda, never mind the children, just come and look at my dress!" pleaded Frédérique.

"It's impossible to keep them in order!" sighed Mathilda.

"You had better hurry up, Freddie; dinner will be early today— hopefully in half an hour," said Madame van Erlevoort.

The front door opened and in came Otto and Etienne van Erlevoort, their cheerful voices mingling with the children's excited shrieks, Miss Frantzen's fruitless admonitions, and the barking of Hector, Otto's black dog.

"Mathilda, please come and look at my dress, just for a second!" Freddie wheedled in her sweetest voice.

Mathilda abandoned further attempts to discipline her brood and allowed herself to be led away by Frédérique.

"Really, I mean it; they're getting completely out of hand."

"Now, now, children, stop fighting! Be good, now!" said Madame van Erlevoort to Ernestine and Johan. "Come with me, come downstairs with Granny. It's freezing cold out here on the landing."

Madame van Erlevoort was used to the bustle and turmoil of children, which had never caused her the slightest displeasure.

As a mother of seven she had always been surrounded by laughter, squabbling and excitement, and could not imagine a large family growing up in an atmosphere any calmer than that which she had known herself. Her house had been filled with shrill jubilation, noisy disputes and the constant running to and fro of her youngsters until they grew up, all aflutter with youthful high spirits. Then, with the passing of her husband Theodore Otto, Baron van Erlevoort ter Horze, member of the Second Chamber of the States General, a period of unprecedented calm had set in, when four of her children in succession had married and left home. The first to go was Theodore, the eldest, who now managed their estates in Gelderland, and who, in possession of a young wife and numerous offspring, appeared to have transformed into a gentleman farmer as well as a youthful patriarch. Next had been Mathilda, her third daughter, whose brief marriage had been very unhappy; she was followed by the two eldest girls, Catherine and Suzanne, the former married to an English banker by the name of Percy Howard and now residing in London, and the latter to the Honourable Arnold van Stralenburg, registrar at the court of law at Zwolle.

Thus Madame van Erlevoort was left with two sons and a daughter—Otto, Assistant Commissioner at the Ministry of Home Affairs, Etienne, studying law in Leiden, and her youngest, Frédérique—and without the novel charm and refreshing emotions of being a grandmother, the comparative calm that ensued would certainly have rendered her despondent, accustomed as she was to the patter of light feet on the stairs and the song and laughter of clear voices in her spacious hall.

And now Mathilda had returned home with her children, over whom she had been granted custody after her divorce from van Rijssel. He had gone abroad, and little had been heard of him since.

Madame van Erlevoort sympathised with her daughter, who had so long and with such dignity borne her lot of wronged wife, and received her with open arms, inwardly delighting in the fresh, burgeoning life the four grandchildren brought into her house. She spoilt them all, more than she had ever spoilt her own children, and even their wildest pranks failed to rouse her anger. Mathilda, for her part, was concerned about the effect this might have on her young foursome, and begged her mother not to oppose her when she meted out some well-deserved punishment. Madame van Erlevoort conceded to this readily enough, but would forget all about it the next minute, and while Frédérique, herself a pampered child, took her sister's side, she made little attempt to instil any discipline in them either. It was only from her brother Otto that Mathilda could expect firm support, and it was indeed only to their uncle that the four rascals showed any respect. Otto had inherited his mother's kind heart and his father's common sense, and with his calm demeanour seemed older than his twenty-eight years. But his manly features were cast in such a genial, sincere mould, and there was so much sympathy and trust in those dark, shining eyes, that his general air of earnestness and sound sense was by no means unattractive. Etienne, by contrast, was all cheer and light-hearted restlessness, his mother's favourite and the very sunshine of her existence. Frédérique was devoted to both her brothers, but often called Otto 'Daddy', while she would romp with Etienne much as Madeleine did with Nico and Tina with Jo.

Madame van Erlevoort had decreed that dinner would be early—at half-past five—so that she might take a short rest before dressing for the ball at the Eekhofs, which she would attend with Freddie and her two sons. Mathilda, the quiet, sad-eyed young mother who seemed to have lost the ability to laugh, would remain at home with the children. The unruly foursome had their meals separately with Miss Frantzen, at Mathilda's urgent request, for Madame van Erlevoort would have liked nothing better than to have the whole tribe plus their stout nursemaid joining her at mealtimes, not caring a bit about gravy stains on her damask tablecloth, glasses getting broken, or small fingers being dipped in the preserves. Thus Mathilda had been unable to prevent the youngsters from stealing into the dining room one by one after their supper, to the dismay of Miss Frantzen, who would put her head round the door, round-eyed with alarm. After they had done this several times without any protest from their grandmama they had made a habit of it, in which Mathilda would acquiesce with a sigh. Etienne and Frédérique took it all as a good joke and Otto laughed too, and in the end Mathilda gave a shrug and smiled: it couldn't be helped.

"Thank you, Otto, no more for me," Frédérique said at table. "I can never eat before going to a ball, you know what I'm like."

"Still as nervous as ever?" asked Otto. "I thought it was only before a girl first comes out in society that she can't eat. You poor girl!"

"Freddie, what have you been doing to your dress? I do hope you haven't ruined it," said Madame van Erlevoort anxiously.

"No, Mama dear, I took Mathilda's advice in the end and left everything as it was. Ooh, I can't wait to show you," she went on, turning to Otto. "I'll be all ethereal in my blue tulle—you know, as if I'm floating. Ah, here come the Philistines!"

She was referring to the van Rijssel foursome, who were charging into the dining room with little Nico in front, blowing his ear-splitting toy trumpet. They had come to eat their orange with wine and sugar in the dining room; Madame van Erlevoort placed Nico beside her and prepared his dessert with care, after which the flaxen-haired rascal gobbled the sliced fruit while the juice trickled down his chin, pausing now and then to blow his trumpet.

Tina, Jo and Etienne hotly disputed the next portion, getting their forks entangled in the process, while Freddie told Otto about the people they would likely encounter at the Eekhofs.

"Well, the Hijdrechts will be there, and so will Eline Vere, as well as the van Larens, and Françoise Oudendijk. Don't you think Françoise is prettier than Marguerite van Laren? Tell me, Otto, which of them will you be courting? Oh, Nico! My poor ears! Nico!"

Tooterootoo, *tooterootoo*, sounded the trumpet.

"Nico, you're driving me demented with that din. Put that thing down this instant and eat properly. Look what you've done to your jerkin!" scolded Mathilda.

"Oh, he just likes his music—don't you, poppet?" gushed Madame van Erlevoort, and she put her arm around the child just as he aimed his trumpet at her ear and gave a loud blast in a shocking show of disrespect.

Afterwards, Freddie and Etienne played with the children while their grandmother retired to her boudoir and Otto smoked his cigar in the company of Mathilda, who had taken up her embroidery. The table was cleared by Rika, the maid, much hampered by Nico, whom she feared would upset her tray stacked with plates and glasses. The clock struck eight at last and Miss Frantzen came to fetch the children.

"*Ciel de mon âme!*" exclaimed Frédérique from the depths of the sofa, where she was half-smothered by Tina, Jo and Madeleine, and she extricated herself from their tentacular embraces. "I must get upstairs; Mathilda, will you come and help?"

"Very well," responded Mathilda, rising. "As for you, children, you must be off, it's bedtime!"

"No, I won't go to bed, first I want to see Aunt Freddie looking all pretty!" Tina bleated. "And I want to help, too."

"Aunt Freddie doesn't need your help; anyway, she always looks pretty," said Mathilda. "Be off with you now, and go with Miss Frantzen like good children."

Freddie rushed away, and as Madame van Erlevoort was resting Mathilda was able for once to impose her will. She shooed her foursome up the stairs, pausing on each tread to stop Nico from hopping down again and Madeleine from playing with Hector.

"I'll be with you in a moment, Freddie!" called Mathilda, "just as soon as the children are upstairs!"

Freddie shouted from her room that she was waiting, and began to brush her long, wavy hair, Cleopatra's cascading tresses … Mathilda was to do her hair; she was so clever at it. Then she laid out her accessories: fan, gloves, pocket handkerchief, and slipped on her dancing shoes of pale-blue satin. A nervous blush coloured her milk-white complexion as she beheld herself in the cheval glass, curving her lips into a smile to make the dimples appear in her cheeks. Not too bad, she thought, not too bad.

Half an hour later Mathilda appeared, accompanied by Martha, the upstairs maid who did duty as a chambermaid, and Frédérique sat down at her dressing table in her chemise and her blue dancing slippers.

"Just as simple and pretty as last time, please, Tilly!" said Frédérique, with Martha standing at the ready with combs, curling tongs and hairpins. "Oh, how chilly it is in here! Martha, put something on my shoulders, will you?"

Martha draped a brightly coloured shawl about her shoulders, and before long Mathilda's deft fingers had completed her hairdo.

"There!" she said, adjusting the curly fringe on her brow. "Simple, neat, and it won't sag, either. Happy now?"

Frédérique studied her reflection and touched her fingertips to the sides of her hair.

"Yes, very," she said. "And now … now for my floaty tulle."

The shawl was flung aside and rapidly retrieved by Martha, who bustled about tidying the garments that lay scattered about the room. Mathilda lifted up the cloud of delicate azure and let it sink, light as a sigh, over Freddie's head.

"It's like being a fairy, or a water nymph!" said Freddie with raised arms, while Tilly and Martha went down on their knees to fluff out the billowing skirt. La, la, la, hummed Freddie, tapping her feet.

"Do keep still, Freddie. Martha, hand me a pin; that bow has come undone."

"How do I look, Martha?"

"Ooh, lovely, Miss!"

"Isn't it a bit bare at the side now, Tilly?"

"Not at all, it's all ribbons and bows anyway. What more do you want? You're all aflutter. Oh for goodness sake, Freddie, do try and keep still."

The door began to creak, as an unseen hand gently pushed it ajar.

"What is it this time?" exclaimed Mathilda crossly when she saw Ernestine in the doorway, shivering and wraithlike in her white nightdress.

"Please, Mama," she said timidly yet with an undercurrent of mischief. "I only meant to … "

"Ernestine! You'll catch your death of cold out there in your nightdress! How disobedient you are!"

"Quick, Tina, hop into my bed, you'll be nice and warm there; mind my bodice, though!" cried Freddie, adding in a whisper: "Oh, Tilly, never mind."

Tina had already clambered into Freddie's bed and proceeded to nestle down like a dove among the blankets, happily reaching out her little fingers to touch the blue satin of Frédérique's bodice, which was still lying on the pillows.

Mathilda sighed and shrugged, resigned as ever, but moved the garment out of harm's way. With a rustle of moiré skirts, Madame van Erlevoort was the next to appear in the doorway.

"Doesn't Mama look lovely!" cried Frédérique. "You'll see, Tilly, I'll be the last to be ready! Oh, do hurry up!"

Mathilda laced up the back of the blue-satin bodice while Madame van Erlevoort looked on, smiling proudly at her diaphanous water nymph. Then came a light, scuffling sound from the landing, and looking round she spied Johan and Madeleine, both shivering in their nightwear.

"This is the limit! You're driving me to despair!" Mathilda burst out; she left Frédérique standing with her bodice half-laced and flew to the door. "How could you be so naughty? You're making Mama very sad. You'll be ill tomorrow, all of you. Go upstairs at once, this minute!"

Her voice was so sharp that the youngsters almost began to cry, but Madame van Erlevoort came to their rescue.

"Oh, Mathilda, do let them stay just a little while!"

"Get into my bed, then, quick!" said Frédérique between shrieks of laughter. "But don't you dare touch my tulle!" she added, recoiling from the outstretched paws of the two little vandals intent on clutching the filmy fabric and pulling the ribbons.

Mathilda could see that, under the circumstances, the best place for the youngsters was in Freddie's bed; for the umpteenth time she gave up with a sigh, and resumed lacing Freddie's bodice, making the satin creak as it tightened. Johan and Madeleine snuggled down under the quilted blanket beside Ernestine, and all three, starry-eyed, gazed up at the blue fairy.

"Aren't you going to put any more clothes on, Auntie?" Johan wanted to know. "Or are you staying half-naked?"

"Silly boy!" scoffed Ernestine, giving him such a hard push that he tumbled over Madeleine, who began to scream as Frédérique's bed became a heaving, tumultuous mass of woollen blankets, blond curls, pillows and rosy limbs.

Madame van Erlevoort and Frédérique laughed so much they almost cried, much to the annoyance of Mathilda, who was having great difficulty tying the laces properly, and Madame called out to Otto and Etienne, who were already in their overcoats descending the stairs, to come and witness the spectacle.

"Come into bed with us, Uncle Etienne, over here!" shouted Johan, but Etienne declined the honour, saying he was dressed to go out, not to go to bed.

"You look ravishing, Freddie!" smiled Otto.

"As if I'm floating on a puff of air, don't you think? Puff ... Tilly, haven't you finished with those laces yet?"

"How can I if you won't keep still?"

Tilly was ready at last, and everyone else was, too. Madame van Erlevoort started down the stairs to the front door, where the carriage was waiting.

"Now, children, don't all get out of bed, I will not have you running about in the cold!" cried Mathilda with authority. Meanwhile Frédérique, having charged Otto with her fan and Etienne with one of her gloves, was helped into her cloak by Martha.

"Hurry up, Freddie, Mama's waiting downstairs," said Otto, tapping the fan on the palm of his hand.

"Are you sure you've got everything?" asked Mathilda.

"I say, Freddie, where's your other glove, or will you go out wearing only one?" said Etienne, raising his voice to make himself heard over the pandemonium of the children in bed.

"Oh, how nervous you're all making me! Look, I've got the other glove half on already! Martha, my hanky! Thanks; all ready? Good! Bye-bye my little darlings!"

"Freddie, you've forgotten something!" cried Etienne.

"Oh dear, what now?"

"Your umbrella!"

"Don't be such a tease! Mama's waiting for me, and all you can do is tease and make me late! Well, goodbye everyone, bye, Tilly, bye, darlings, yes Otto, I'm coming … Goodbye, Tilly, thanks for your help. Goodbye, Martha."

"Enjoy yourself, Miss."

"Have fun, Freddie, bye-bye … "

Freddie sallied forth, followed by Otto and Etienne. The youngsters promptly leapt out of bed.

"Come here, children, at once!" cried Mathilda.

She threw some wraps about their shoulders: a shawl, a comforter and Freddie's raincoat, which trailed on the floor behind young Ernestine like a train.

"And where is Miss Frantzen? She should never have allowed you to come here!" she said testily.

"She's in the nursery with Nico, Mummy, and Nico's asleep," said Ernestine. "Please, Mummy, don't be cross!"

And she held out her little arms in the flapping raincoat sleeves, wanting to fling them about her mother.

Mathilda smiled and allowed herself to be hugged.

"Now you must all go to bed!" she said, mollified.

"Look at the state of Miss Freddie's bed," said Martha, shaking her head. "I shall have to make it up all over again, thanks to you naughty children!"

"Nice children!" countered Madeleine.

Mathilda took the child in her arms; Ernestine and Johan followed her, tripping over their improvised dressing gowns and chortling with glee that their ruse had worked.

"Shush now, children, or you'll wake Nico!"

Miss Frantzen, unaware of the youngsters' escapade, was quietly knitting with Hector at her feet while Nico lay sleeping in his crib, and was greatly distressed to see the excited cavalcade approaching. The little rogues, sneaking away like that, while she thought they were fast asleep in the next room!

The threesome were tucked into bed, shivering with cold and excitement, and Miss Frantzen had to caution them several times to stop talking and go to sleep like good children.

Mathilda gazed into the cot where her little Nico lay snugly under the covers, his eyes tightly shut, his moist lips slightly parted, his flaxen curls straggling over the pillow. How angelic he looked! And the others, too—how delightful they were! A handful of course, and quite out of control, especially with their grandmother and Freddie, and yet they were a blessing! A fourfold blessing!

She bent over and touched her lips to Nico's small mouth; she felt his light, sweet breath caressing her cheek, and her tears dropped on his forehead, so white and transparent, so soft ... her little angel!

VI

From time to time old Madame van Raat would call on her son at Nassauplein for an evening cup of tea; she would arrive in her coupé at seven, and leave again at half-past nine.

This time Betsy was still upstairs, no doubt with Ben, as Eline assured Madame van Raat, although it was actually Anna, the nursemaid, who put the little boy to bed in the evenings.

She led the old lady into the ante-room, where a small crystal chandelier spread a soft glow over the violet plush upholstery, its twinkling glass prisms reflected in the round pier glass.

"And Henk?" asked the old lady.

"Oh, still dozing, I expect!" laughed Eline. "Wait, I'll go and call him."

"No, no, leave him be," said Madame van Raat. "Let him sleep, poor dear, and stay with me a while for a chat."

She sank down on the sofa, smiling at Eline, who settled herself on a pouffe close by.

Eline took the old lady's dry, veined hand in hers.

"And how are you, dear lady? Well, I trust? You look remarkably fresh and youthful today—not a line to be seen on your brow, I do declare!"

Madame van Raat was much taken, as always, with the warmth in Eline's voice and with her beaming smile, to which she now, with or without intent, imparted a suggestion of naivety.

"You wicked girl! Making fun of me in my old age! Elly, you ought to be ashamed of yourself!" She put her arm around Eline's shoulders and kissed her on the forehead. "And how is Betsy these days, not too tiresome?" she added in a whisper.

"Ah well, you know, Betsy isn't so bad, really, just a little—a little quick-tempered in the things she says. All us Veres are quick-tempered, and I am too, although I don't remember Papa ever getting cross, but then he was a man without equal. Betsy and I get along splendidly; of course we have our little disagreements,

79

but that's only natural if you spend so much time together. I think it would even happen to you and me if I lived in your house."

"Well, I would be delighted for you to come and give it a try!"

"Oh no, I'd be far too tiresome in the long run. You think I'm nice because you don't see a great deal of me, but if you did! ... " she laughed gaily.

"What a bad girl you are, making me out to have be so short-tempered!"

"Oh no, I didn't mean it like that. But truly, Betsy has a kind heart when it comes down to it, and I assure you, she makes Henk a charming wife."

"Well, if you say so. But I'm not sure who I would have chosen for my boy if it had been up to me ... Betsy, or someone else maybe ... "

She laid her hand on the top of Eline's head and looked at her meaningfully, her eyes bleary and a sad smile about her pinched mouth.

Eline was slightly unnerved. Madame van Raat's words had called forth her own old thoughts, long passed and almost forgotten, those moments of sudden longing for Henk's company, the vague wish to lean on his shoulder and let him take charge. But it was all a long time ago, and those sentiments now seemed to her so distant, so hazy as to be merely shadows of thoughts, ghostly shadows ... They seemed rather silly now, even grotesque, and the recollection of them almost made her smile.

"Oh, madame," she murmured, giving a light, pearly laugh, "who knows how unhappy he might otherwise have been? Even if Betsy is a little domineering, he's hardly a downtrodden husband: her feet are far too tiny!"

"Hush," whispered Madame van Raat. "Someone's coming."

It was Henk. He drew aside the door curtain and declared that he had no idea it was so late. Eline laughed at him and asked if he had been having sweet dreams.

"You eat too much, that's what makes you so lazy in the evening. Oh, madame, you should see how much he eats!"

"There, Mother, now you know. This is the kind of treatment your son gets in his own home, even from his dear sister-in-law— she can be so trying!"

"Oh, stop it, Henk! It's no use pretending, because your mama won't believe any ill of me, not even from her beloved Henk! Isn't that true, madame? You can't deny it, can you?"

Eline opened her almond eyes wide and gazed up at the old lady with an air of childlike innocence. Her entire being radiated such sympathy that Madame van Raat could not resist embracing her.

"You're a darling!" she said happily, basking in the warmth of youth's bright sun shining on her old age.

When Betsy came downstairs she apologised profusely for taking so long, and suggested her mother-in-law might prefer to take tea in the salon rather than remain cooped up in the ante-room.

"Paul said he would drop by later," said Madame van Raat as Eline pulled up a marble foot-warmer for her. "Then you can sing some duets. What do you say, Elly?"

"It would be a pleasure, dear lady."

Madame van Raat brought out her spectacles and her crochet-work while Betsy seated herself by the tea tray laden with polished silver and Japanese porcelain, and prattled away about this and that, including the ball at the Eekhofs, which she had found most enjoyable.

"And you, Elly, did you enjoy yourself?" asked the old lady.

"Yes indeed, the dancing was lovely, and there was a splendid cotillion, too."

"And what about you, Henk?"

"Oh, Henk!"

They all laughed, and Eline exclaimed that he was too stout for dancing, really, although he might still cut an elegant figure doing a minuet—and minuets were coming back into fashion, as dear Madame was bound to have heard.

The old lady joined in with the merriment, and Henk had just finished his steaming cup of tea when the front doorbell rang. Paul made his entrance, announcing that he had just been to see Hovel in his office on Prinsengracht. He had meant to call at the lawyer's residence the previous evening, but having run into

Vincent Vere in Hoogstraat he had postponed his visit in order to join some friends for a glass of wine in Vincent's rooms. He had found Hovel most kind on closer acquaintance, an altogether decent fellow, very amiable, and they had come to an agreement: Paul was to start work at the office the following Monday.

Madame van Raat was unable to suppress a sigh of relief, now that the long-discussed visit had finally taken place. The last time she had seen her brother-in-law she thought there had been a hint of annoyance in his voice at the mention of Paul, and for matters concerning her youngest son she relied heavily on the aid of Verstraeten, who had been Paul's co-guardian until he came of age.

Hearing Paul's account of his visit, Betsy bit her lip; why did her Henk waste all his time on that dratted horse of his, and those dratted hounds? But what could she do? She had told him often enough, and she could hardly raise the subject yet again in the presence of her mother-in-law.

"Well, Paul?" Eline cried. "How about a song then?"

Paul said he was willing, and got to his feet; Eline sat down at the piano. They met every Thursday to practise singing together, and already boasted a modest repertoire. Paul had never had singing lessons and could barely play the piano, but took to heart all Eline's suggestions for improvement. She for her part maintained that he owed his singing ability to her alone. By now he had learnt to open his mouth wide and to keep his tongue down, but she still thought he ought to take some lessons from Roberts. No one could be expected to sing without proper study.

"What shall we have? *Une Nuit à Venise*?"

"Right you are: *Une Nuit à Venise* it shall be!"

She opened a songbook bound in red leather, with 'Eline Vere' in gilt lettering on the cover.

"Remember to sing out here, will you? But don't hold your high sol too long there," she instructed. "Better sing it in your middle register, and not from the chest; it'll sound much more melodious. And begin very softly, then you can swell there, and there. And mind you keep in good time with me towards the end, there's that flourish of notes, remember? Careful now, Paul."

She played the prelude to Lucantoni's duet, and when Paul had given a little cough to clear his voice, they broke into song together, starting softly with:

Ah, viens, la nuit est belle!
Viens, le ciel est d'azur!

His light tenor sounded a little shaky at first, but its innate charm went very well with the plangent ring of her soprano. She found great pleasure in singing together like this, provided Paul was in voice and followed her recommendations. It seemed to her that she sang with more emotion when accompanied by another voice, and particularly so in the repetition of lines such as:

Laisse-moi dans tes yeux,
Voir le reflet des cieux!

which she now infused with the languishing passion of an Italian paramour.

She fancied that in this way the duet gained in dramatic intensity, and she pictured herself with Paul as the tenor, both of them reclining in a gondola, against a painted backdrop of a Venetian canal ablaze with the magnesium glow of artificial moonlight. She saw herself richly attired as a patrician lady, him in the garb of a poor young fisherman; they loved one another, and they lay dreaming and singing in his craft as they drifted towards the lagoon before an enchanted audience.

Devant Dieu même
Dire: Je t'aime
Dans un dernier soupir …

They were nearing the final run of notes, and she began to worry that Paul would drag, so she slowed down a fraction, but no, Paul kept perfect time with her, and she exulted in the harmony of their voices as they faded away:

Dans un dernier soupir …

"Exquisite, Eline, that was exquisite!" enthused Madame van Raat, who had been listening with rapt attention.

"You're in good voice, Paul," said Betsy, for want of anything better to say.

"Well, Eline, it's time you sang us a solo now!" said Paul, pleased with his success.

In the meantime Mina had brought the newspapers, *Het Vaderland* and *Het Dagblad*, and Henk was immersed in them, taking care to make as little noise as possible turning the crisp pages.

"But Paul, what about you?" said Eline. "Don't you want to sing any more, or are you too tired?"

"I'd rather you sang on your own, Eline."

"Nonsense, if you're not too tired I would prefer another duet. Honestly, I love singing with you. How about the grand duo with Romeo? Come on then, I dare you!"

"I mean it, Eline. I don't know the part very well yet, and it's very difficult."

"Well, you knew it perfectly well the other day. If you just keep it light and sweet, and don't force your voice, you'll be fine. Look—you can sing this entire passage in the middle register. Just don't shout."

With a look of disquiet he asked her advice about a phrase here and a note there, and she was glad to oblige.

"Come now, be bold! No shouting, though, it never works. Besides, if we do get stuck, what of it?"

"Oh, all right then, if you insist."

Eline glowed with contentment, and she played the tender prelude to the grand duo in the fourth act:

Va! Je t'ai pardonné, Tybalt voulait ta mort!

she began, in splendid form, to which Paul responded with his recitative, and together they sang:

Nuit d'hyménée, ô, douce nuit d'amour!

Once more the stage version rose up before her: Juliet's chamber, with Romeo in his splendid costume reclining on the cushions at

84

her feet. And Romeo ceased to be Paul; Romeo became Fabrice, the new baritone, on whose shoulder she leant her head as she sang:

Sous tes baisers de flamme
Le ciel rayonne en moi!

Paul's voice began to waver, but Eline was hardly aware it was him singing. In her mind it was still the rich timbre of Fabrice's voice she was hearing, and hers grew in volume and resonance until she, unbeknownst to herself, entirely eclipsed her partner.

There, the lark was announcing the dawn, and she fancied herself lying in Fabrice's arms as she asked:

Qu'as tu donc … Roméo?

Paul, having recovered during the bar of rest, responded in steadier tones:

Écoute, ô Juliette!

whereupon Juliette's voice rang out in protest: no, it was no lark Romeo had heard, it was a nightingale, and the gathering light no dawn but a moonbeam, and Eline was still with Fabrice, falling into his arms as the orchestra swelled in the chords she struck on the piano. In the brief pauses between the vocal parts Eline came to earth; then the vision of the stage and Fabrice evaporated, and she saw herself in Betsy's drawing room with Paul at her side, turning the pages of the score. But the next moment she was Juliette again, Juliette admitting that it was unsafe for Romeo to stay any longer, even urging him to leave, and he answered:

Ah! reste encore, reste dans mes bras enlacés!
Un jour il sera doux, à notre amour fidèle,
De se ressouvenir de ces douleurs passées!

This was a passage in which Paul's lyrical sensibility came into its own, and Eline, waking from her reverie, smiled and thought how melancholy and dulcet his delivery was. She felt a pang of conscience, realising that it had been unfair of her to sing so loudly during the duet just now, and she vowed to be more careful in the future.

She launched into the finale, favouring a beseeching tone over impassioned despair, so that Paul's high chest notes would sound to better effect. But the vision had passed: the stage, the audience, and Fabrice—all gone.

Adieu, ma Juliette!

sang Paul, and she gave a faint cry, to which he responded with his pledge:

Toujours à toi!

"Oh, how I love singing like this!" cried Eline ecstatically, and she ran to give Madame van Raat a joyful hug. "Didn't Paul sound lovely, and isn't it a shame he won't take proper lessons? You ought to make him, you know."

Paul rejoined that Eline gave him enough lessons, and that she would be the death of him with her difficult duets. Eline, however, assured him that he had sung to perfection.

Betsy gave a quiet sigh of relief, for she thought the Veronese lovers' farewell had sounded rather too overwhelming in her salon with its delicately painted ceiling and plush hangings; it had been more of a shouting match as far as she was concerned. Why couldn't Eline sing something light-hearted and pretty, a song from some *opéra bouffe*, for instance?

Eline and Paul sat down, and the conversation drifted to other topics, day-to-day affairs and the busy stir in the streets now that the feast of St Nicholas was upon them. Then the clock struck half-past nine and Mina came to say the carriage was at the door.

"Yes, it is time I took my leave," said Madame van Raat, rising slowly to her feet, and Eline trotted off, humming to herself as she went to fetch her wraps from the ante-room: a fur-lined cloak, a woollen shawl, a hood.

The old lady placed her spectacles and crochet-work in her reticule and allowed herself to be muffled up by her dear young friend, after which she kissed everyone goodbye. Henk and Paul escorted her to the front door and helped her into her coupé.

Leaning back against the plump satin cushions as the carriage rolled off, her ears still ringing with the duets sung by Eline and Paul, she smiled wistfully as she wiped the condensation off the window to look outside, where the snow lay dirty and bespattered in the light of the street lanterns, and she thought of the good old days when she used to visit the opera with her beloved husband.

Paul remained for another hour and then departed, having celebrated the success of his duets with a good glass of wine. When he had gone Eline went upstairs—to freshen up, as she told Betsy. It was chilly in her sitting room, but the cool air felt fresh on her cheeks and hands after the overheated salon. She sank onto her couch with the Persian cushions and raised her hand to caress the leaves of the aralia, striking one of her favourite poses. And she smiled, her eyes widening dreamily as her thoughts flew back to Fabrice, with his handsome beard and splendid voice. What a shame Betsy was not more partial to the opera! They went so very rarely, while she, Eline, adored it. She would let Madame Verstraeten know in some polite, discreet fashion that she would appreciate being invited to accompany her once in a while. Mr Verstraeten never went anyway, and his wife usually asked some acquaintance to share her box. She had asked Freddie before, and Paul as well, so why not her?

She sprang to her feet, seized by an idea. Fabrice had made his third debut last night: the first had been in *Hamlet*, the second in *Le Tribut de Zamora*, in which she had seen him, and yesterday in *William Tell* …

She ran out of the room and leant over the banisters.

"Mina, Mina!" she called.

"Yes, Miss!" answered Mina, who was just crossing the hall with a tray of wine glasses.

"Bring me the newspapers, please, if they've finished with them downstairs."

"Yes, Miss, certainly."

Eline returned to her room and settled herself back on the couch. It made her laugh when she felt her heart beating with curiosity. Whatever was she thinking? In what way could it possibly be of any concern of hers?

There was Mina, climbing the stairs. She brought both papers: *Het Vaderland* and *Het Dagblad*.

"If you please, Miss."

"Thank you, Mina," said Eline, taking the newspapers with a careless gesture.

But no sooner had the maid left, shutting the door behind her, than Eline sprang into action. She quickly spread out the crackling sheets of *Het Vaderland*, scanning them excitedly for the Arts and Literature section. Ah, there it was:

The French Opera.
After successful performances in Hamlet *and* Le Tribut de Zamora, *there could have been no doubt that Mr Théo Fabrice would find favour with this season's ticket-holders for the French Opera, and so it comes as a surprise to learn of the three votes cast against this brilliant baritone. Once again, in* William Tell, *Mr Fabrice has offered proof of his fitness to fulfil the role of baritone in the Grand Opera, and we sincerely congratulate him on his appointment. This commendable artist combines a strong vocal technique with impassioned yet tasteful acting, which testifies to much dedicated study. In the duo with Arnold (Act 1), and the grand trio in the scene with Jemmy, Fabrice displayed a standard of excellence rarely encountered on our stages today.*

Eline nodded approvingly. Yes, it was all true, every word of it, and she read the article to the end, exulting in his success. Then she turned to *Het Dagblad* to see what it had to say about him.

VII

THE FERELIJNS occupied a cramped apartment over a grocer's shop in Hugo de Grootstraat, comprising on the first floor two adjoining rooms, a kitchen and a small room to the side, and on the second two bedrooms with small side rooms. Over their living quarters hung a pall of straitened means: Frans had been left only a small inheritance by his parents, and consequently had to manage with wife and children on the small salary he received while on furlough. They had decided to take up temporary residence in The Hague, the city where they had both lived from an early age, where they had first met, and where they still expected to find their friends and acquaintances, although Frans maintained that they would have done better to have gone to live in a smaller town. But also in The Hague was Jeanne's father, Mr van Tholen, a retired colonial official leading a solitary existence, rarely sought out by old friends and relations owing to his intractable temperament, and infrequently visited by his offspring once they had married or taken up appointments elsewhere, which was why Jeanne had prevailed upon her husband to stay in The Hague notwithstanding their meagre income. She promised to maintain a firm hold on the purse strings, and she kept her word, for all that she was not thrifty by nature.

So they remained in The Hague, despite numerous disappointments. Jeanne found her father much aged in the four years that they had been abroad: grimmer and more irritable than she had known him. The good old days were truly gone, she thought; her happy childhood in her sunny home with her mother and her brothers and sisters, her innocent pranks with schoolmates, her girlish dreams under the lilac and jasmine in the garden, those early days of her engagement to Frans, filled with idealistic fantasies. The memories she thought to revisit in Holland were scattered far and wide, like fallen leaves. She had yearned for the damp and mist of home when she was in the Indies, but now that she was back, with everything being so disappointing and the unrelenting struggle to make ends meet, she yearned for the uncomplicated, easygoing life she had enjoyed overseas in rural Kadoe with her cow and her chickens. But she put on a brave face and struggled valiantly to deal with the troublesome minutiae of her present existence. Dr Reijer came to visit little Dora every other day, but she thought she detected in the popular young physician a nervous haste, which made him count every second spent at the child's bedside. He would listen briefly to Dora's chest, assure Jeanne that the cough was getting better, remind her to keep the child indoors and then, after running the tip of his gold pencil down the interminable list of names in his notebook, he would jump into his coupé and vanish. It was he who had advised Frans to seek help for his migraines and fevers from a certain professor in Utrecht, with whom he had corresponded at length regarding the case. Frans duly went to Utrecht, but returned dissatisfied, for he objected to the vague, prevaricating manner in which the professor had given his opinion. So now when Dr Reijer visited Dora, Frans kept out of his way, resenting the fact that neither he nor the Utrecht professor had been able to cure him. He tried to ignore the headaches hammering at the back of his head and the fevers making him shiver as from a trickle of icy water down his spine, and took to closeting himself in the side room on the first floor, which did duty as his private little office. He remained there in sullen isolation, and although he felt a twinge of conscience when he heard Jeanne talking to the doctor upstairs and Dora loudly objecting to having her chest examined, he did not rise from his desk. All doctors were quacks as far as he was concerned, all talk, and unable to cure one when one was ill.

Jeanne accompanied the doctor down the stairs, conversing as they went, and Frans overheard Reijer enquiring after him and his wife replying, after which she called for the maid to show the doctor out. Then, as the carriage rattled off, she came into her husband's office.

"Am I disturbing you?" she said in her soft, subdued voice.

"No not at all; what is it?"

"Why didn't you come upstairs for a moment, Frans? Reijer asked after you twice."

He shrugged his shoulders.

"There wouldn't be any point," he huffed. "All he does is send one off to some celebrity in Leiden or Utrecht who charges ten guilders for a chat lasting no more than a few minutes!"

"Be reasonable, Frans. You can't expect to be cured from one day to the next of something that has been troubling you for the past two years. I think you're being quite irresponsible, doing so little about your health—and it's already three months since we arrived here. Yet that was the reason we came to Europe in the first place, wasn't it?"

"Yes, of course, but first I must find someone who inspires more confidence than Reijer. Reijer is a doctor à la mode, warmly recommended to you by the van Raats, which is all to the good, but he's too superficial to my taste, altogether too hasty. He's always gone before you know it."

"You should try being a little more forthright with him. I ask him all sorts of questions about Dora, so he's obliged to stay a while longer, and really, now that he has come to know us a little better, he seems to be taking more interest in us, too. And everybody says he's very clever; it's not just the van Raats who think the world of him."

"Well, I shall see. There's plenty of time yet. Sometimes you remind me of water dripping on a stone, drip, drip, drip—the way you go on and on about this doctor business!" he snapped. He was annoyed with himself, and with a brusque movement opened his writing case, as if to say he had matters to attend to.

She withdrew, restraining a sigh, and quietly closed the door behind her. Upstairs in the nursery she came upon their only servant, a girl of sixteen in a grimy apron with her hair cut straight across her forehead. Mietje was making the beds while Dora and the two boys, Wim and Fritsje, were in the next room playing with a handsome set of building blocks, a gift from their grandpa, Mr van Tholen.

"I'll shut the door, then you can air the bedroom, Mietje," said Jeanne, and she drew the sliding doors together. Smiling at her children, she sat down by the window at a table heaped with small garments waiting to be sorted: socks and stockings, shifts and pinnies, freshly purchased yet already in need of repair. Oh, how quickly her children wore out their clothes! She gave a sigh, stirring the heap with her small, thin hand while her eyes filled with tears. If only she had a more robust constitution, how well she would have been able to manage her little household! It was so difficult at times to raise herself above the gloom into which she felt herself sinking as into an abyss, to shake off the listlessness that held her fast with velvet arms, and yet—there was so much to be done. She must not give in to idle daydreaming, nor must she rake up her old scattered memories like so many burnt-out cinders and lose herself in nostalgia for bygone illusions: reality was staring her in the face, in the shape of Dora's badly torn new woollen skirt and the dirty laundry that needed counting before being sent off.

Even now, fingering the small socks and shirts, she felt herself being drawn deeper and deeper into the muffled depths of weariness. Unable to summon her strength and set to work, she was oblivious to Dora and Fritsje squabbling over the building blocks. How she would have loved to fill her little abode with sunshine and harmony, but she was no fairy godmother, she felt so weak and ineffectual, so daunted by the small vexations of her daily life that she did not even dare hope for a rosier future. Indeed, whenever she thought of what the future might hold, her timorous nature was overcome with a vague sense of darkness and doom, which she found impossible to put into words.

She propped up her head with her other hand, and a few teardrops fell on the laundry. Oh, if only she could have gone to sleep, gently caressed by someone who loved her and whose tenderness would make her feel calm and carefree and safe! And she thought of her Frans, and of the day he had proposed to her beneath the blossoming lilac in the garden, and of what had become of her: water dripping on a stone, drip, drip, drip …

Oh, she knew she hadn't made him happy; she was a bitter disappointment to him, but it wasn't her fault that he had refused from the start to see her for what she was: a simple, weak creature, someone in need of much, very much love, and much tenderness and intimacy, someone with a touch of sentimental poetry in her soul ...

She took a deep breath and drew herself up, telling the children not to make so much noise, for Papa was downstairs, and Papa had a headache. She looked about her for her sewing basket, but she had left it in the sitting room, so she told Dora to be a big girl and take charge of her brothers for a moment. She was in the habit of addressing the child in a tone as if she were a grown-up daughter, and Dora, flattered by her mother's trust, was glad to oblige. Casting off her lethargy, Jeanne went downstairs to her sitting-cum-dining room, and was hunting for her sewing basket when her husband came in.

Frans had heard her tread on the stairs and felt an urge to make amends for his harshness earlier. He crept up behind her in his slippers as she searched beside the chimney piece, and gently caught her by the arms.

She looked up, startled, and in his eyes she saw the old warmth she so often longed for as he murmured with a pleading, almost anxious smile:

"I say, are you angry with me?"

She shook her head, her eyes filling with tears. Then she put her arm around him and leant her head on his shoulder.

"Really not?"

She shook her head again, smiling between her tears, and closed her eyes as she felt his bristly moustache on her lips when he kissed her. How quick he was to repent when he had been harsh to her, and how good it made her feel to forgive him!

"There, there, don't cry, it's all right ... "

She heaved a sigh of relief and clung to him.

"As long as you're kind and gentle with me, oh, then I feel so ... so strong, strong enough to tackle anything!"

"My dearest little wife ... "

Again he kissed her, and in the warm tenderness of his lips she forgot the cold in the unheated room, which was making her shiver in his arms.

VIII

I T WAS 4TH DECEMBER, the Eve of St Nicholas, and since early morning the Erlevoort residence had been in a state of heightened excitement—all whispers and knowing smiles and objects being whipped out of sight the moment one entered the room.

The Verstraetens arrived a little after seven, bringing the boys, Jan and Karel, who had taken part in the tableaux. Then came the van Raats and Eline, followed by old Madame van Raat and Paul. Henk, however, did not enter the salon but slipped unseen with Jan Verstraeten into a side room, where Marie and Lili had laid out their costumes.

In the spacious salon stood Madame van Erlevoort, wreathed in smiles as she received her guests, when suddenly a deafening chorus of welcome was raised by the van Rijssel foursome and Hector, which even the combined efforts of Mathilda and fat Nurse Frantzen were barely able to quell.

"Oh, Betsy, why didn't you bring Ben?" demanded a peeved Madame van Erlevoort.

"Ben's not old enough for parties; he's only three, after all, and it would be well past his bedtime by the time we finish."

"We could have sent him home with Martha, when it's the children's bedtime. I've got him such a dear little present, too," said Madame van Erlevoort regretfully.

There was a stir in the drawing room, where the girls stood about chatting with Otto, Paul and Etienne; the van Rijssel youngsters looked up, breathless with anticipation, as Martha, the upstairs maid, came in. Grinning, she passed a whispered message to Frédérique.

"Quiet please! I have an announcement to make!" cried Frédérique, looking solemn. "St Nicholas has arrived, and he wants to know if he may make his entrance. Shall we invite him in, Mama?"

Everyone kept a straight face, stealing looks at the wide-eyed children.

St Nicholas appeared in the doorway, wearing a white tabard and a long red cloak piped with gold at the hem; he had long grey hair and a long white beard, and on his head he wore a golden mitre. He made his entrance with due ceremony, leaning on his staff, and was attended by a black page, whose fancy costume was bound to look familiar to all who had seen the tableaux. After them came Willem and the three maids, all of whom slipped into the drawing room to watch the proceedings from there.

The grown-ups, smiling self-consciously, bowed before the bishop from Spain.

St Nicholas intoned a greeting and, almost tripping over his too-long tabard, advanced across the room towards the assembled company. Occupying the sofa were old Madame van Raat and Madame Verstraeten, and around them sat Madame van Erlevoort, Mr Verstraeten, Mathilda, Betsy and Otto. No one bothered to stand up, and Madame van Erlevoort welcomed the venerable guest in a tone of cordial familiarity.

"Why did Granny stay sitting down?" whispered Ernestine, lifting her wise little face to Marie. "She always gets up when someone she doesn't know very well comes to call."

"Hark at her, how observant she is!" whispered Marie to Eline, who was standing beside her.

Eline, however, did not hear; she was laughing with Paul and Etienne at St Nicholas, whose tabard had come loose and was now trailing over his shoes, while a telltale streak of fair hair peeped out between the mitre and the sagging grey locks.

St Nicholas hitched up his tabard with a flourish. Raising his full, deep voice, he summoned the van Rijssel foursome to come forward. They were suspicious at first, but when St Nicholas took one of the sacks from his page and they both began to scatter the contents, the youngsters forgot their fear and shrieked with delight, tumbling over Hector and rolling over the floor to gather up all the goodies: russet apples, dried figs in little baskets, hazelnuts, tangerines and chocolates.

"Pick them all up, help yourselves!" urged St Nicholas. "We've got plenty more, look! And what of the big boys, wouldn't you like some too?"

The Verstraeten boys did not need to be asked twice, and happily joined the scramble.

"Will you keep this for me, Granny?" cried Nico, pouring his booty into his grandmother's lap. "Then I can go and get some more!"

"Now, now, Nico!" cautioned Mathilda.

"Never mind," soothed Madame van Erlevoort.

St Nicholas and the page shook out the last of their sacks with much ado, after which they turned them inside out to prove they were truly empty.

"Ooh, and now we'll be going to the dining room!" cried Ernestine, jumping up and clapping her hands.

"Yes, yes! To the presents!" Johan chimed in.

Everyone stood up and followed the bishop and the children into the drawing room, the girls giggling again about his wig sliding askew. But St Nicholas took no notice, and beckoned Willem and the maids.

"Now! Open the doors please, quick!" he ordered.

The sliding doors parted, and the children stormed into the brightly lit dining room, where the dining table had been replaced by four trestle tables, each with a name spelt out in chocolate letters, and each bearing a tower of toys.

The Verstraetens and the van Raats motioned for their own gifts to be brought in by the servants: a hoop, a whip, toy-gun racks, rubber balls, tin soldiers and a toy cow that gave milk.

In the meantime St Nicholas had slipped away with his page, and as it was close upon half-past eight Mathilda considered it time to return home. It took her a long while to restore order, however, even with fat Nurse Frantzen's assistance. The youngsters got muddled about what belonged to whom; hazelnuts rained from Ernestine's pockets across the floor; Johan's tin soldiers, which had been unwrapped in the blink of an eye, were impossible to get back into their corkwood box; and Madeleine ran her hoop around the room with Nico blowing his new trumpet and Hector bounding at their heels, without troubling themselves about the rest of their presents.

"Come, children!" cried Mathilda. "Hurry up now, it's time for bed."

But her four youngsters failed to hear. Mad with excitement, they ran up and down, scattering about in wildest disorder the toys painstakingly assembled by the others; then Frédérique joined the fray, giving Nico a piggyback ride while he whipped her to go faster.

The Verstraeten lads, too, joined in, chasing Ernestine and Johan down the long marble hall and making a furious stampede with their boots.

Mathilda wrung her hands in despair. No one took any notice of her, as Nurse Frantzen was helping the maids tidy up the toys and the girls were chattering to Paul and Etienne again. To her relief she caught sight of Otto talking with Betsy and Madame Verstraeten; she went up to him and clasped his hands.

"Oh, Otto, please help me! It's past the children's bedtime, and they simply won't listen to me! And you know what Mama's like, she's not any help either."

And indeed, Madame van Erlevoort was occupied in the next room filling Madeleine's toy tea set with water, milk and sugar, while old Madame van Raat and Mr Verstraeten looked on with much amusement.

"Dear me, Otto is to act the bogeyman again, is he?" he said, good-humouredly.

"No, not a bogeyman, but I'm at my wits' end! I really need your help. Have you ever seen such unruly children, Betsy? Please, Otto, will you come?"

Betsy laughed.

"I think you had better assert your authority as their uncle, Mr van Erlevoort," said Madame Verstraeten.

Otto went with Mathilda, first to Freddie.

"Now, now, Freddie, Nico must be off to bed. Down, Hector, down I say! Auntie will let you have another piggyback ride tomorrow, Nico."

"Ah, but my back has nothing to do with you!" said Freddie. "It's not your affair, do you hear? Come on, Nico, we must leave off."

Nico obeyed reluctantly, still clamouring for his trumpet as his mother took him by the hand. Then Otto went into the hall, where the two eldest were galloping up and down, and spread his arms to bring them to a halt.

"Now then, Ernestine and Jo, your mother wants you to go to bed! Do as you're told, now, or you'll make her sad."

"What a lot of presents we got this year, Uncle!" said Ernestine, quite out of breath.

Mathilda came into the hall, too, leading Nico and Madeleine by the hand.

"Would you believe it? There was Mama, calmly playing at tea parties with Ernestine!" she said, and her look of despair made Otto smile. "I honestly think it would have been midnight before she even noticed the time."

"But Mummy, mustn't we say goodnight to everyone first?" protested Johan.

"No, no! We can't have that!" wailed Mathilda, tightening her hold on all the small hands she could seize. "I'll wish everyone goodnight on your behalf, I promise! Thank you so much for your help, Otto."

She gave him a grateful nod, which he answered with his frank, genial smile.

Then Mathilda herded the children up the stairs.

"So you don't mind all this noise and commotion, I take it?" Madame van Raat asked Madame van Erlevoort with a smile, although there was a hint of disbelief in her sad, bleary eyes.

With the children finally gone, a lull ensued. The grown-ups left the dining room, which was still littered with toys, and gradually reassembled in the reception suite, to which Otto had also repaired. Madame van Erlevoort poured the tea and Willem passed the cups round.

"Do I mind the excitement, you ask? To tell you the truth, I find it invigorating; it makes me feel quite young again. I need the company of young folk, the more the merrier. I never spent a drearier time than after my son Theodore and my daughters got married, and yet I still had three children at home, including Freddie and Etienne, who are both very lively. It does me a world of good to be surrounded by a tribe of little ones, there's nothing like it for keeping one young ... Would you like some more tea?"

Madame van Raat handed over her cup, and she felt a pang of envy for her grey-haired hostess' *joie de vivre*. She drew a comparison with herself, seeing her own sense of loneliness and melancholy loom before her in cruel contrast to the cheerful bustle enjoyed by this grandmother amid her boisterous brood, with her good health and her apparent freedom from any kind of nervousness.

"And oh, you can't imagine how sorry I am to see so little of Theodore's youngsters—there are six of them now—but my son is so enamoured of life in the country that he won't hear of coming back to live in The Hague, whatever I say."

"Your daughter in England only has one child, if I'm not mistaken," remarked Madame Verstraeten. "And what about young Madame van Stralenburg?"

Madame van Erlevoort inclined her head to Madame Verstraeten and whispered something in her ear, then gave a knowing wink in response to Mr Verstraeten's raised eyebrows.

Thereupon she began to tell them all about the van Rijssel youngsters putting their shoes by the chimney the previous evening, but before she could finish the door opened and Henk, red-faced and grinning, came in, followed by Jan Verstraeten.

Mathilda, joining the company again, was met with all manner of comments on how delightful her children were. Then the front doorbell rang out, hard and long, and the cheerful conversation subsided.

All eyes were on the door, which swung open to reveal Willem and the maids heaving a large crate. They advanced towards Madame van Erlevoort.

"Ah!" cried Frédérique. "The box from London!"

Madame van Erlevoort explained to Madame van Raat that every year, on the feast of St Nicholas, her son-in-law Howard sent them a box containing something for every member of the family. Willem set to work removing screws and nails, with Etienne hovering at his elbow to offer assistance and everyone watching with bated breath. The shower of gifts and surprises could commence.

Eline beamed. She had already arranged her presents into a pretty display, exclaiming how dreadfully spoilt she had been by everyone, when Martha passed her yet another parcel. She untied the string with deliberation, inspecting the object from all angles for some sign, a seal or an initial, that might indicate who the giver was. But there were no clues, all it said on the label was her name: Mlle E Vere. The wrapping paper parted to reveal a long, slim case bound in grey leather, which she opened, thinking hard as to whom it might be from. On a grey-velvet pillow lay a fan of exquisitely carved mother-of-pearl. She lifted it out and unfolded it lingeringly, then stared at it, wide-eyed with admiration.

"Bucchi," she murmured, peering at the signature along the edge. "Bucchi … "

It was indeed a fan painted by the famous Italian artist: a fantasy of roses and fairies on ivory satin.

"Who could this be from?" she said. "It's so beautiful!"

Everyone rose from their seats to crowd round Eline, who carefully held out the precious, open fan for all to admire. She was very surprised. The bottle of scent had been a gift from Madame van Raat, of that she was certain, but surely Henk and Betsy couldn't have …

"Betsy, darling, is it you I must thank for this?" she asked, standing up.

Betsy shook her head.

"*Parole d'honneur*, Eline, it wasn't me!"

No, of course it couldn't have been Betsy, since she and Henk had already given her a bracelet … so who could possibly have sent her this fan?

"Could it be from Vincent, by any chance?" she asked.

"From Vincent? No, of course not, whatever gave you that idea? It's hardly the type of present he would give. May I have a look?"

Eline handed her the fan.

"It's magnificent," said Betsy. "Quite magnificent."

Eline shook her head slowly from side to side; she was perplexed.

The fan was passed round for inspection, and Eline scanned each face in turn, without seeing the slightest indication of complicity. There was a moment, though, when Frédérique assumed a quizzical air, which faded almost at once into apparent indifference as she drew near.

"May I see the case?" she asked.

Eline handed it over and Frédérique ran her fingertip over the grey-velvet lining.

"Are you quite sure you have no idea who it might be from?" asked Eline, throwing up her hands in a show of utter bewilderment.

Frédérique shrugged her shoulders and put the case down.

"No, I haven't the faintest idea," she said, a shade coolly, studying Eline's expression. There was something unsympathetic about that gazelle-eyed look of hers, she felt, and could not help thinking Eline's manner affected and her bewilderment about the fan's provenance insincere. From then on Frédérique ignored the much-admired fan, and was unusually quiet for the rest of the evening.

The avalanche of presents had come to an end. Madame van Erlevoort invited her guests to follow her out of the salon and drawing room, now littered with wrapping paper, straw and pieces of string, and Willem reopened the sliding doors to the dining room, where a lavishly decked table awaited them.

It was a very lively supper party. Mr Verstraeten, placed between Madame van Erlevoort and Betsy, kept the ladies amused with his witty banter, and Mathilda, who was sitting on

Betsy's other side, frequently joined in the hilarity. Henk, seated between his mother and his aunt, was quite content, while Otto and Eline conducted an animated conversation and Etienne, between Lili and Marie, talked at the top of his voice.

"Freddie, *chère amie*, you've gone very quiet," said Paul, who was alternating mouthfuls of lobster salad with attempts to draw out his otherwise so loquacious neighbour. "Are you disappointed you didn't get lots more presents?"

"Me quiet? Fiddlesticks!" retorted Freddie, and she began to prattle away with a speed and brightness much like that of her brother Etienne. However, she sounded a little overexcited, her gaiety seemed a touch forced, and she kept stealing glances at Eline, glowing with beauty as she exchanged pleasantries with Otto. Yes, there was something quite enchanting about her, something that reminded Freddie of a siren, the way her dreamy eyes narrowed when she laughed, the way the soft curve of her finely chiselled lips ended in a dimple in each cheek. And then there were her hands, dainty and pallid, fluttering so prettily about the black lace and dark red bows of her gown, and that coquettish single diamond quivering like a dewdrop amid the black tulle at her neck. Frédérique thought her enchanting indeed, but also unsympathetic, and she kept an almost fearful eye on Otto's beaming countenance as he gazed upon the siren.

Throughout this time she continued talking and laughing with Paul, with Etienne and Lili, and with Marie, eliciting from old Madame van Raat the comment from the other end of the table that Freddie was living up to her fun-loving reputation.

The champagne flowed, and Mr Verstraeten raised a toast to the ever-youthful hostess with her handsome grey locks, thanking her for the lovely party with a kiss. Eline clinked glasses with Otto at some toast which Frédérique did not catch, and which she would gladly have given her best present to hear. But she did not venture to ask …

"Etienne, you're making a terrible din!" she cried vexedly when her brother launched into a drinking song, waving his arm so as to very nearly spill his champagne over Lili's slice of cake. But presently she regretted her outburst—after all, why shouldn't the others be having fun even if she was not?

The party drew to a close, the carriages were waiting, and the guests, laden with assorted items, took their departure amid effusive thanks for the many gifts bestowed on them. Mathilda was tired and soon went upstairs, while Madame van Erlevoort and Otto drifted about, gathering up the crumpled wrapping paper lying all around.

"Look at the state of these rooms," said Frédérique, kicking a torn cardboard box out of the way. She went to the table, where the fan had lain, but Eline had taken it with her. Then she kissed her mother and Otto goodnight, rumpled Etienne's hair, and took her presents upstairs to her bedroom.

She undressed slowly, taking so long that the chilly air made her shiver. She crept into bed, and as she stretched herself under the covers Eline rose up before her again, enchanting and elegant in her black lace, smiling at Otto. It all began to whirl before her eyes, like a chaotic kaleidoscope: Henk dressed up as St Nicholas with his tabard trailing over the floor, the Verstraeten boy as his page, the box from London, the Bucchi fan …

IX

IT WAS A FEW DAYS after the feast of St Nicholas, and Eline decided to take little Ben for an afternoon stroll. The previous evening she had been to the opera with Madame Verstraeten, Marie and Lili, to see *Il Trovatore*, and that morning she had asked her old grumbler of a singing master to play the accompaniment to Leonora's aria, 'La nuit calme et sereine'.

He had shaken his head, for he did not care for the bravura songs of the Italian school, on which his opinion and that of Eline frequently clashed. She found the music of Bellini, Donizetti and Verdi elegant and melodious, as though expressly written for her crystalline soprano, whereas he was inclined to dismiss as puerile their airy little tunes, insisting on the richer depths of Wagner. But he was under her thumb, and therefore did her bidding.

"Come along now, Ben, don't dawdle, there's a good boy," Eline said to the chubby little fellow trailing a pace behind on his short legs. "Do try and keep up with Auntie. Aren't you pleased to be going to the shops with me?"

Last night at the opera, during the Comte de Luna's cavatina, Eline had conceived an idea. In a shop window she had seen several portraits of Fabrice, showing him in different costumes and poses, and a sudden craving to possess one had come over her. Now she was on her way to the shop to pick one out, secretly smiling to herself as she pictured his tall, strong build and his handsome head with the black beard. How wonderful it must be to be an actor on stage!

From Fabrice her thoughts drifted back to her new fan, which she had used last night. Betsy had told her it was idiotic to do so before she even had a clue as to who the giver was, but she had chosen to ignore her sister's advice; on the contrary, the notion of being seen with it in public gave her a thrill, and in her mind she had already conjured an episode from a romantic novel to account for the anonymous gift: Fabrice had seen her in the Verstraeten's box, he had fallen head over heels in love with her, henceforth he sang for her and her alone, and was heartbroken when he failed to spot her in the audience; it was he who had sent her the fan so discreetly addressed to Mlle E Vere, and yesterday he had seen her using it, and sooner or later he was bound to send her some signal by means of a knowing look or a particular tone to his singing …

She had to smile at her own extravagant fantasies, and in a flash remembered where she had first seen a fan decorated by Bucchi. There had been a painting show at the Academy last summer, and among the exhibits there had been several works by him: un-mounted fan paintings on silk displayed behind glass. She remembered having been full of praise for the artist at the time, saying how much she would love to possess such a fan. Somebody had obviously taken note of her wish. With whom had she gone to see the exhibition? With Emilie de Woude, or with Georges perhaps … surely Georges couldn't have … or could it possibly have been that young man she had danced with, the one who had proposed to her and whom she had turned down? Oh, it was preposterous! She gave up, she refused to think about it any more. She would find out eventually, anyway.

They walked down Parkstraat and then Oranjestraat, and were nearing the shop with the pictures at Noordeinde when she began to have qualms: wouldn't the proprietor think it strange for a young lady to come and buy a portrait of an actor? She was afraid her courage would fail her, but before she knew it there they were, standing by the plate-glass window, peering at the display. Amid the clutter of large engravings, photographs and sundry artistic items such as figurines in biscuit or terracotta, her eye was immediately drawn to a row of portraits, actors and actresses from the opera, with their names written underneath: Estelle Desvaux, Moulinat, Théo Fabrice …

"Come along, Ben!" she said, gently pushing him into the shop. Inside, there were several ladies choosing photographs, all of whom looked up as she entered. She was sure she felt her cheeks colouring slightly behind her short veil of white tulle.

"May I see some of your New Year's cards, like the ones you have in your window?" she asked the shopkeeper when he turned to serve her. "Don't touch those figurines, Ben."

A wide range of cards were brought. She inspected them with close attention, holding each one up between gloved fingertips, and laid two or three aside. Glancing about her, she lit on a stack of portraits, and reached out her hand with a gesture of languid indifference. Among them were several of Fabrice.

Which one should she choose? This soulful one, in the black-velvet costume and lace collar as Hamlet, or that one, as Tell? No, the other one, of him as Ben-Saïd, the way she had seen him the very first time. But she would also have a picture of Moulinat, the tenor, as well as one of Estelle Desvaux, the contralto; then it would be less obvious that her only interest was in Fabrice. And in that case she might just as well have the one of him as Hamlet, too.

"I'll have these cards, please; and here, these four portraits as well."

"Shall I have them delivered?"

"Oh no, there's no need. I shall pay for them now. How much do I owe you?"

She paid him the money and the shopkeeper handed her a sturdy envelope containing her purchases. Taking Ben by the hand she made her way to the door, imagining herself observed by the browsing ladies as if they could all read her innermost thoughts.

Outside, Eline's face lit up once more. Pleased with her audacity, she set off homewards in an ebullient mood, praising little Ben with the fond tones of a doting mother. When she looked across the street and caught sight of Jeanne Ferelijn in her shapeless, flapping winter coat and her plain black hat, she tightened her hold on Ben's hand and, dodging between two carriages, hurriedly led him to the other side, wreathed in smiles. She greeted Jeanne warmly, and they proceeded on their way together. Jeanne informed her that Dora was well on the way to recovery, but that she had been obliged to hire a nursemaid because Mietje was altogether too careless to look after the children properly, and consequently had an additional financial burden to contend with.

Eline had to force herself to pay attention to this latest instalment of domestic woe, but Jeanne soon cheered up and started chatting about Frans, about her father, Mr van Tholen, and about Dr Reijer, with whom her relations had much improved lately. Noting Eline's expression of sympathy as she listened, and also her mild, affectionate manner with Ben, she began to reminisce about their schooldays together, and they both laughed as they recalled Eline's hoodful of purloined cherries and all the pranks they had played. Jeanne blamed herself for her misgivings about Eline the other evening at the van Raats', for now she seemed so sincere and warm-hearted.

"But don't let me keep you any longer, Eline," she said, stopping short. "I have some tiresome errands to do. I must order some new pans, and a milk jug to replace the one broken by Mietje—such a clumsy girl."

"Oh, I'm not in a hurry; I'll come with you if you like, and if Ben isn't too tired. Ben, dear, you aren't tired, are you? He's such a fine walker, you know!"

And so Jeanne ordered her new pans and Eline helped her to pick out a pretty milk jug at a china shop. Thoughts of Fabrice crowded her mind all the while, and she could barely resist opening the envelope in her hand for a peep at the portraits. She did so love music, and Fabrice sang with such extraordinary pathos, with so much more feeling than any of the other artistes. He was quite young, she believed, and bound to become very famous—he would soon be engaged to sing in Paris, she had no doubt. Jeanne never went to the opera, so presumably she had never heard of Fabrice.

Would she, Eline, ever cross him in the street some day? What would he look like in his ordinary clothes? She decided to make some excuse to go out early one morning so she could walk past the opera house; with any luck there would have been a rehearsal and she would see the artistes leaving the building. Absorbed in her own calculations, she only heard half of what Jeanne said as they walked side by side, but glanced at her from time to time, giving the luminous smile that was her greatest attraction.

Reaching Hogewal, they bade each other goodbye and went their separate ways.

"*Au revoir* then, Jany, I shall call at your house soon, I promise. Do give my regards to Ferelijn. Don't forget, will you? Now then, Ben, shake hands with the lady."

Jeanne felt a stir of warmth and tenderness at the sound of her girlhood name, a poignant reminder of the old days, of her girlhood, when everyone called her Jany.

She hurried onward to Hugo de Grootstraat full of cheer and eager to return to her small abode, where her husband and her darling children would be waiting.

Eline smiled to herself as she struck across the park on her way home. The bare branches overhead glistened with hoarfrost, the freezing air was clear and tingling, alive with promise, and she felt an urge to burst into a brilliant roulade so that she might fill the sky with her elation.

Could it be that she was a tiny bit smitten with that … that artiste?

Oh nonsense, it was just that he sang so well!

X

THE FLAMES IN THE STOVE sent huge, elongated shadows like black ghosts flitting over the walls and ceiling in the darkened room. Wavering gleams were to be seen on an antique silver jug, on the carved edge of a sideboard looming dark and massive at the back, and on the various decorative plates and mugs displayed on the walls.

Vincent Vere reclined on his couch, watching the shadow play through half-closed eyes. The prevailing gloom shot through with that strange ruddy glow was agreeable to him, and made him forget the dinginess of his rented rooms in Spuistraat, where the shabby, bourgeois aspect was relieved only by the few personal valuables that accompanied him on his travels. He lay musing a while in the Dantesque twilight.

The last few days he had been overcome with fatigue. He was barely able to move; he felt as though there were tepid water running through his veins instead of blood, as if some sort of fog descended on his brain from time to time, robbing him of the ability to think. His veined eyelids drooped over his lacklustre, pale-blue eyes, and his lower lip was slack, thereby imparting a suggestion of suffering to his small mouth. The feeling was not new to him, but this time he blamed the atmosphere of The Hague, which he found stifling. He yearned for more space and more air, and could not imagine what had induced him to seek quarters in a city that had never held any attraction for him. Yes, he could recall, through the haze of his exhaustion, looking forward to a period of rest after his extended travels, but already he felt a nervous flickering of desire to plunge anew into the maelstrom of change. Rest and regularity had a numbing effect on him, and despite his weakness he found himself wishing for movement, for action, for ever-changing horizons. Although he lacked the energy to devote himself to any kind of employment with due determination, his capricious temperament kept driving him onwards in his fruitless search for new alliances and new circles that might be congenial to him.

The fortnight he had now spent in The Hague seemed to him like a century of tedium. The day after meeting Betsy and Eline at the opera he had called at the van Raats at coffee hour, and had asked Henk for a loan of five hundred guilders, saying he was expecting some money to arrive from Brussels any day, and would repay his debt at the very first opportunity. Henk took this promise from his wife's cousin with a pinch of salt, but did not like to refuse him, and consequently handed over the requested sum. So now Vincent was surviving on borrowed money, which he allowed to trickle through his fingers like water one day only to cling on to it with parsimonious economy the next, while the cheques from Brussels failed to materialise.

He was little concerned about the future; he had always lived from day to day, having known times of luxury in Smyrna and times of privation in Paris and London, but whatever his circumstances, he had always been spurred on by that feverish desire for change. But for the time being, faced with having to get by on five hundred guilders, he was so out of sorts that the burden of his weakness tended to be outweighed by a sheer lack of energy.

Thus his thoughts drifted on as he stared into the semi-darkness, where the ruddy glow from the stove made the furniture stand out in ghostly relief, as befitting his pessimistic frame of mind. Why bother to make plans? Once the money ran out, which would be soon, he would see his way to obtaining some more one way or another, and what was wrong with that? Notions of good and evil had no relevance in the real world, things just happened to be the way they were, as the inevitable result of a sequence of causes and effects, everything that was had a right to be; no one could alter that which was, or was to be; no one had free will; everyone had a different temperament, and it was that individual temperament, subject to environment and circumstance, that governed one's actions. That was the truth, people were always trying to fudge things up with a mixture of childish idealism and hogwash about goodness, and, as often as not, a smattering of pious poetry thrown in for good measure.

"My God, how miserable life is!" he thought, holding his head in his hands while his fingers toyed with the light-brown curls at his neck. "The life I'm leading now, anyway. If it goes on like this I'll be either insane or dead within the year. Tomorrow will the same as today: dull, dreary and boring."

He plunged into a sea of remembrance, revisiting the various countries and cities of his past, ruminating on his experiences.

"And yet, all that wasted effort!" he muttered under his breath, and his eyelids drooped as he felt the fog descending on his memory again. Beads of perspiration formed on his brow, his ears rang, and in his mind's eye he saw a fearful space, inconceivably vast, stretching away before him.

But this debility, bordering on a swoon, lasted only a second or two. A deep sigh rose from his chest, and he came to himself.

Rapid steps sounded on the stairs, and a cheery voice could be heard exchanging a word of greeting with the girl in the haberdashers' shop downstairs. He was expecting a few acquaintances to call.

The door opened …

"Good grief! It looks like a scene from hell in here, with that fire blazing in the dark. Where are you, Vere?" cried Paul van Raat from the doorway.

Vincent rose from the couch and stepped forward; he put his hands on Paul's shoulders.

"Here I am, old chap, have no fear … Wait, I'll light the lamp."

He cast around for matches, lit two old-fashioned paraffin lamps on the mantelpiece, and for an instant was blinded by the abrupt yellow glare. The Dantesque illusion was dispelled, leaving a dingy room in which the only note of cheer was the brightly burning stove; the antique sideboard bearing the silver jug and a few oriental objects looked sorely out of place beside the shabby armchairs upholstered in Utrecht velveteen, just as the antique prints on the wall struck a jarringly aristocratic note among the cheap engravings and common chromolithographs.

It was Paul's first visit to Vincent's rooms, and his attention was caught by the silver jug and the porcelain plates, which he pronounced to be admirable.

"Yes, they're quite good in their own way. Actually, the jug leaks, but the workmanship is very fine, as you can see. I went to an antique dealer today, an old Jew, to see if I could sell them. They're just dead weight, really. He said he'd come by tomorrow. Or would you be interested? They're yours for the taking."

"No, my room, or my studio if you will, is too full already."

"Come on, a few more plates won't do any harm."

"No, thanks."

"All right; I'd rather sell them to the Jew anyway. I'll get the better of him if I can, you know, and with you I'd naturally be too honest to do anything like that."

"Much obliged. And suppose he's sharper than you are?"

"Well, then he'll get the better of me, that's all. All in a day's work, eh? You have had tea, I suppose?"

"Yes. No need to put yourself out," said Paul as they both sat down. "But tell me, how long are you planning to stay in The Hague?"

Vincent raised his shoulders and his eyebrows. He really could not say; he had not yet made enquiries about the position with the quinine farm on Java, but he had heard that they would give preference to a chemist, which he was not. So he would most likely give up on that idea, and besides, he wasn't so sure the East Indian climate would agree with him. On the other hand, staying in The Hague, finding something here, was out of the question. He was already getting bored, The Hague was such a backwater, everyone knew everyone else, at least by sight, and one ran into the same people all the time—too dull for words! He had not yet made up his mind what he would do, but first he had to wait for some letters and cheques from Brussels. And he concluded by asking Paul whether he could lend him a hundred guilders for a few days. Paul thought that would be all right, but could not yet say for certain.

"You would be doing me a great service. Could you let me know by tomorrow then? Or do you think me indiscreet?"

"Not at all, not at all. Yes, all right, I'll see tomorrow."

"Well, thank you very much in advance. You know the two van Erlevoorts and de Woude are coming this evening? I invited them over for a glass of wine," Vincent said, in an altered tone.

"Yes, I know; I saw them this afternoon at the Witte club," responded Paul.

Vincent lolled against the back of the old red couch, and the lamplight gave a greyish cast to his sallow complexion, sharpening the lines of fatigue about his lips. Paul was struck by how much Vincent resembled a portrait of his uncle Vere, Eline's father, especially the way he held his hand to his head as he leant back, with a gesture such as he had frequently remarked in Eline.

It was past nine o'clock when Georges de Woude van Bergh and Etienne van Erlevoort arrived in short succession, the latter apologising for his brother's absence. Otto was not much taken with Vincent, although there had never been any disagreeableness between them; his own character was so practical and steadfast, and of such impassive reserve, that he found it impossible to feel sympathy for someone who, in his opinion, allowed himself to be governed entirely by a condition of morbid nervousness, without making the slightest mental effort to take himself in hand. Otto was one of the few people whom Vincent did not succeed in winning over. Nearly everyone he met felt on their guard with him at first, and then became intrigued, his attraction being rather like that of some sweet poison for which it is possible to acquire a taste, such as opium. Through his far-flung travels he had gained a good deal of knowledge of human nature, or rather, of how to deal tactfully with people from all walks of life, and he was able to assume any role he chose with the effortless ease of a sidewinding snake or a skilled actor. But Otto, with unselfconscious confidence in his own health and strength, looked down on Vincent for the poisonous charm he emanated to gullible associates.

Before long the room was filled with a bluish haze, Vincent having passed round a box of cigars, although he did not himself smoke. He took some bottles of Saint-Émilion from a cupboard, uncorked them, and set four wine glasses on the table. Etienne, boisterous as ever, regaled them with a stream of jokes and anecdotes told in colourful student patois, with an amount of mimicry and gesture that gave him the appearance of a gentleman-comedian in a *café chantant*. Paul and Georges laughed, but Vincent shrugged and gave a patronising little smile as he poured the wine.

"My dear Etienne, you're such a baby," he drawled.

Etienne ignored the comment and rattled on, throwing all sense of propriety to the winds, while the others listened as they savoured the bouquet of their wine. Vincent, however, continued to make fun of Etienne.

"Such a bad boy, young van Erlevoort, to say such things! Naughty, naughty," he jeered, but there was something so engaging about his smile as he said this that Etienne was undeterred.

Vincent refilled their glasses, and Georges praised the wine. He was usually rather quiet when in the company of his peers, happy to listen, for he preferred to save his efforts at sparkling conversation for the ladies. Vincent asked him about his work at the Ministry of Foreign Affairs, while Etienne and Paul exchanged meaningful looks.

"I suppose you'll be attached to some legation or other eventually?" asked Vincent.

"That's quite likely," replied Georges.

"Well, at least it's a job in which you get to see the world. How anyone can spend their entire life in an office I cannot imagine. It would be the death of me. Take van Erlevoort—no, not you, Etienne, I mean your brother."

"Well, you can leave Otto out of this," said Paul. "He'll have a brilliant career, you'll see."

"Otto's cut out to be a cabinet minister or a governor general, we all know that—at least, that's what the old woman always says. And I'm the runt of the litter!" cried Etienne.

"Yes, quite the spoilt pet, aren't you?" laughed Vincent. "How far have you got with your studies, by the way?"

"Oh, I still have some exams to sit, but I'm not attending any lectures at the moment. I'm studying here in The Hague."

"Are you so taken with life in The Hague, then?" asked Vincent, pronouncing the name in a tone of disparagement.

"It's not too bad."

"How the deuce can you say that? You fellows must be very easily satisfied, or rather, you have no idea of what the rest of the world has to offer. The Hague makes me dull and drowsy, there's something soporific in the air, it seems to me."

"You're just prejudiced, that's all!" laughed Paul.

"I dare say I am, I dare say that's why the kind of life most of you lead strikes me as quite soul-destroying. How do you people pass the time, may I ask? Going round in circles like the horses on a merry-go-round. And once you're settled in some position you find yourself doing the same old jobs day in day out, and going to the same old soirées ad infinitum. Hardly exciting, is it?"

"Well, what do you recommend we do, then?" asked Georges.

"Good heavens, you're welcome to go on vegetating like this, it's entirely up to you, but what I can't understand is that none of you seem to have any desire to go out into the world, take a look around."

"What about you, then?" exclaimed Paul, a trifle piqued by Vincent's scorn. "You've seen the world, haven't you? And where does that leave you? Jack of all trades and master of none. So you can't say you've done terribly well out of it, can you?"

A spark of annoyance lit up Vincent's pale-blue eyes while his thin lips curved into a tight smile.

"All this philosophical talk is making you forsake your duties as a host!" cried Etienne, tapping his empty glass.

"Ah well, I suppose it's a matter of temperament—mine being just a little more restive than yours, that's all," drawled Vincent. He stood up to replenish the glasses, then sank down on the couch beside Georges once more, and his eyes roamed wearily across the room.

It had grown very hot in the room, and the cigar smoke seemed to hang from the ceiling in tangible swathes. Vincent opened the door for some air. Etienne, who could not take much wine, was red-eyed and greatly excited; he had also broken his glass. Georges and Paul were highly amused by his buffoonery, but Vincent, smiling faintly, remained aloof.

He felt a sense of wonderment: how strange it was that the human character should be so fixed, that a man should always remain himself, retaining his own individual personality without ever having the possibility of changing places with someone else. Often, without the slightest cause, and even when in animated company, he would find himself wondering about this, and he chafed at the realisation of his own inescapable fate: ever to remain the same Vincent Vere, powerless to transform himself into an entirely different being, someone who would breathe and move in entirely different circumstances and societies. He would love to have experienced divergent emotions, to have lived in different ages, to have sought fulfilment in a range of metamorphoses. This desire struck him on the one hand as exceedingly puerile, being as it was a preposterous impossibility, yet on the other as quite noble, on account of the lofty aim it represented. He did not believe other people had this desire, and felt vastly superior to them for this reason. As he ruminated thus, his three visitors appeared very remote, separated from him by an impenetrable cloud of cigar smoke, and he had a sudden sensation of lightness in his brain; everything seemed to be more vividly coloured, the talk and laughter of the others sounded louder to his ears, like blows on a sheet of metal, the smell of tobacco and spilt wine became overpowering, and the veins in his temples and wrists throbbed as if they would burst.

This nervous spasm lasted several seconds, at the end of which he noticed his guests grinning at him expectantly, and although he had not taken in a word of what they had been saying, he grinned, too, pretending to share their amusement.

"I say, Vere, it's getting exceedingly stuffy in here, my eyes are stinging from all the smoke!" said Georges. "Couldn't we open a window?"

Vincent nodded and went to shut the door while Paul, who was seated by the window, raised the sash, letting a gust of cool air enter the room. Out in the street it was quiet; now and then low voices could be heard approaching and receding to the accompaniment of footfalls, or a raucous snatch from a street ditty echoing through the stillness.

The cool air brought Vincent down to earth again, and his exalted imaginings faded from his mind. Indeed, he now felt the stirrings of envy for that very state he had condemned only a moment ago as being physically and morally vegetative. He envied Paul for his health and vigour, tempered only by occasional spells of artistic languor; he envied Georges for his calm equanimity and general air of contentment, Etienne for being so young ... Why wasn't he like them, in good health, youthful and debonair, why couldn't he take life as it comes, why did he always have to go off in search of something he couldn't even define himself?

It was close upon one o'clock when the three young men rose. Paul declared that they would have to take Etienne home, as his exuberance had given way to deep dejection complete with suicidal sentiments.

"I say, Etienne, have you got your door key?" he asked.

"Key?" croaked Etienne, glassy-eyed. "Key?" he echoed dully. "Yes, in my pocket. Yes, a key, in my pocket ... here ... "

"Come on then, let's be off!" urged Georges.

Etienne went to Vincent and caught him by the arms, while the others listened with amusement.

"Vere, *au revoir*, thank you for your ho-ho-hospitality. I've always thought well of you. Vere, you're a fine fellow, do you hear? I feel a great, great deal of sympathy for you. Only this afternoon at the club I was saying ... Paul was there, he'll tell you ... I was saying that you, Vere, had a heart of gold. They're all wrong about you, Vere, but ... "

"Come on, time to go now!" cried Paul and Georges, taking Etienne by the arm. "Cut it short, will you!"

"No, no. Let me have my say. They're wrong about you, Vere, but don't you take any notice of them, old boy. It's the same with me, they're wrong about me, too. It's not fair, not fair at all, but it can't be helped. Goodbye, Vere, goodnight, sleep well."

Vincent saw them to the door with a lit candle and the threesome set off arm-in-arm with Etienne in the middle.

117

"Vere, take care now. Mind you don't catch cold standing at the door like that—and take no notice of what they say, they're all wrong, but I'll stick up for you!"

Vincent nodded amiably as they turned to go, and shut the door of the unlit shop.

"Deuced good chap, Vere!" slurred Etienne.

XI

AFTER FOUR O'CLOCK the Verstraetens were generally at home, and today was one of those days when, by sheer happenstance, there was a steady stream of visitors. When Betsy and Eline called, the Eekhofs and the Hijdrechts, Emilie de Woude and Frédérique were already there, and finally Madame van der Stoor arrived, too, accompanied by her young daughter Cateau.

Eline rested her hand on Cateau's shoulder as they admired a photograph together.

She was aware of having impressed the girl with her elegance and friendly manner, and since she, being in need of affection herself, liked to rouse sympathy in others, she lavished attention on Cateau as on a favourite house plant. But today her need was edged with triumphant pride with regard to Frédérique, whom she had suspected ever since St Nicholas' Eve of holding something against her, though she knew not why.

While Cateau was chatting to her in her pretty little voice, Eline glanced up at Frédérique to see whether she had noticed the child's adoring looks. But Frédérique was engrossed in a jocular exchange with the Eekhof girls.

"Do you often sing with Mr van Raat? Does he have a nice voice?" asked Cateau.

"Not a very strong one, but very sweet."

"Oh, I should love to hear you sing together!"

"And so you shall, one of these days."

"You have such a lovely voice, Miss Vere! Oh, I just love it when you sing, I think it's just divine!"

Eline gave a light laugh, flattered by Cateau's candid ecstasy.

"Really? But you should stop calling me Miss Vere, you know, it sounds so formal. Just call me Eline, all right?"

Blushing with pride, Cateau stroked the fur of Eline's small muff. She was utterly entranced by her heroine's melodious voice and her soft, languishing look of a gazelle.

Eline was feeling more emotional than usual, and in need of love, much love, all around her. In the secret depths of her soul her admiration for Fabrice had flared up into a passion, which dominated all her thoughts, and for which she sought an outlet without giving herself away. She felt so suffused with hidden tenderness that she seemed intent on sharing it out among deserving members of her coterie, like flowers from an exquisite bouquet. She looked about her with shining eyes, and was thrilled when she saw others regarding her with affection, but all the more upset when she detected the slightest hint of coldness towards her. She felt hurt by Frédérique's inexplicable gruffness the other evening, and although she had tried to ignore it at first out of pride, she had now made an effort to win Frédérique over, and had addressed her in her most pandering tones. But Frédérique's replies had been short and non-committal, with averted eyes; Eline was bound to notice her coolness, of course, but she was never one for hiding her emotions, she was too openhearted to have any interest in diplomatic initiatives.

The conversation turned to portraits, and Madame Verstraeten stepped past Eline and Cateau towards a side table, from which she took a photograph album that she wished to show to Madame van der Stoor and Madame Eekhof.

Distracted, and only half-listening to Cateau, Eline's thoughts flew to Fabrice as her eye fell on the album in Madame Verstraeten's hands. An idea rose up before her, like an un-pruned shoot of her rampant imagination. Yes, she would buy an album for her own private use, in which to keep portraits of Fabrice; it would be a little shrine to her love, before which she could lose herself in the contemplation of her idol, and not a soul would know about it. Her face glowed with furtive excitement at the prospect, and the notion of having something so momentous to hide from the prying eyes of those around her gave her a new sense of importance, and she felt the emptiness in her soul filling up with the treasures of her passion. She was happy, and her happiness was enhanced by a mischievous, heady elation at her possession of a secret that everyone in her set would have pronounced exceedingly foolish and improper, had they only known. A girl like her, enamoured of an actor ... what would

Madame Verstraeten and Betsy and Emilie and Cateau and Frédérique have to say about that, not to mention Henk and Paul and Vincent, if they had so much as the vaguest suspicion?

She had a sense of triumph as she surveyed her relatives and acquaintances drifting about the salon; how brave she was to be defying their conventional sense of propriety, that she should dare to have a crush on Fabrice! She laughed more merrily than called for when Emilie said something comical, indeed she was laughing at them all, exulting in her covert, forbidden passion.

"And so Mr van Raat—Mr Paul, I mean—is to be a lawyer, is he not?" asked Cateau.

Why did she keep mentioning Paul? thought Eline. It was Paul here, Paul there, his wonderful singing voice, and now his career.

"You are rather taken with Paul, I do believe!" said Eline.

"Oh yes, I like him very much!" Cateau burst out happily. "Only sometimes, you know, he can get quite cross. Fancy, the other day, during the tableaux—"

And Eline was obliged to listen to a lengthy account of how Paul had lost his temper over some detail regarding the tableaux, and also how clever he was at draping the costumes.

"She doesn't mince matters," thought Eline. "But then it doesn't necessarily mean that she's sweet on him, I suppose, even if she does talk about him all the time. Because if she were, she'd probably not breathe a word, like me."

It was half-past five; the callers began to take their leave.

"So you'll let me hear you and Paul sing?" pleaded Cateau.

"You could come on a Thursday afternoon, that's when we usually sing together."

"Oh dear, I'm at school then."

"Well, in that case you could come during the evening some time."

"Oh, I'd love that, Eline."

It was the first time Cateau had called Eline by her first name, and she beamed with gratification at her newly acquired status. Then she bade goodbye, urged to do so by her mother.

By the front door Eline, having said her farewells, found herself alone with Frédérique, quite by chance, while she waited for Betsy, who was still chatting with Mr Verstraeten. Eline was just about to say something to Freddie, but hesitated, thinking Freddie might address her first, and in the end both remained silent.

Young Cateau was ecstatic all the way home, singing the praises of Eline and Paul to her mother.

The new year arrived with freezing temperatures. Betsy had invited the Verstraetens and the van Erlevoorts as well as Madame van Raat and Paul to an oyster supper on New Year's Eve, and a very pleasant evening was passed by all in the warm luxury of her salons. The wintry days of January succeeded one another in unbroken sameness, relieved in the evenings for Betsy and Eline by a constant string of dinners and soirées. The van Raats led a busy social life, and Betsy was renowned for her elegant little dinner parties, with never fewer than ten guests and never more than a dozen, and always served with the most munificent refinement. They belonged to a coterie whose members were frequently in company with one another on terms of close familiarity, a state of affairs that caused them considerable satisfaction.

In between these light-hearted social engagements Eline fanned the flame of her secret love in mute contentment, and felt steeped in romance. One morning, as she was walking homeward along Prinsessegracht after an errand, she caught sight of Fabrice emerging from the Hague Wood. She felt her heart beating and hardly dared to look again, but after a moment allowed her eyes to chance upon him with feigned indifference. He wore a short duffel coat with a woollen muffler thrown casually around his neck, and walked at a leisurely pace with his hands in his pockets, his swarthy features and somewhat moody expression partially hidden by the wide brim of his soft felt hat. He made on her an impression of lofty reserve, which fired her imagination: he was bound to be from a good family, for there was a quality to the set of his broad shoulders that struck her as very distinguished; his parents had opposed his wish to devote himself to art, but his vocation had been impossible to resist; he had received his musical training at a conservatoire, and he had made a successful debut, but now he found himself in the throes of disillusionment and bitterness about the world of the theatre, which was too coarse and uncivilised for his artistic sensibilities; he had withdrawn into proud isolation; he thought back on his childhood, on his youth, and he could see his mother wringing her hands and imploring him to abandon his ambition and think no more of the stage …

From that day on Eline was seized with the caprice, as Betsy called it, of taking long walks in the morning. The Wood was so beautiful in winter, Eline declared; she adored the way the tall, straight trunks looked like marble pillars when it snowed; it was like being in a cathedral. Henk accompanied her a few times with Leo and Faust, the two Ulmer hounds, but he missed his habitual horse ride, and so she took to walking alone, after calling at the stable to collect the dogs, which bounded happily and protectively at her side like a pair of boisterous pageboys.

It was good for her constitution, she explained when eyebrows were raised at her new pursuit; she did not get enough exercise, and feared putting on weight like Betsy if she followed her example and never went anywhere on foot. Besides, Dr Reijer thought her morning promenades an excellent idea.

In the Wood she would see other people taking a stroll, usually the same ones, and there was an elderly grey-haired gentleman in a fur cloak, invariably coughing behind his hand, whom she crossed daily. But she seldom saw Fabrice. No doubt he was rehearsing, she told herself when the baritone failed to appear. Each time the disappointment left her feeling worn out, and she would make her way home longing for her boudoir, her warm stove and her piano. But she persisted in her walks regardless, and in due course noticed that Fabrice tended to favour Fridays. Any other day was completely unpredictable; she might see him, but then she might not. She made a point of rising early, even if she had only gone to bed at three after an exhausting soirée or a dance, and had dark rings beneath her eyes. True, she saw Fabrice quite often these days, but it was always at the opera, from a box, or the stalls, when she was accompanied by the Verstraetens or by Emilie and Georges de Woude—one evening she had even invited the Ferelijns to join her—but it was nothing like seeing him in the Wood. There she saw him differently, no longer as a vision on stage divided from her by the blaze of footlights but at close quarters, less than three paces removed from her, a man of flesh and blood.

On the days that she did catch sight of Fabrice, her heart soared, filling the high vault of snow-covered boughs with joy. She would see him coming in her direction with his manly, vigorous step, the hat at a rakish angle, the tasselled muffler fluttering from his shoulder, and when their paths crossed he would glance at her, or at the dogs sniffing his legs, with an inscrutable expression on his face. Afterwards, making her way home along the tree-lined Maliebaan, she would be overcome with a joy that made her bosom heave and the blood rush to her cool cheeks; she would not feel in the least tired, and on her return would break into jubilant song the moment she crossed the threshold. She would be in high spirits all day, her customary languid grace having ceded to quicksilver vivacity. Her eyes shone as she kept up her incessant banter; she called Henk an old lazybones and Ben a slowcoach and teased both father and son; she made the hall resound with her silver laughter and the stairs creak with her rapid footsteps.

One Friday morning, seeing Fabrice coming towards her, she made a decision. It was so childish not daring to meet his gaze, she reasoned; he was a member of the acting profession after all, and surely accustomed to being recognised in public by ladies. And so, when he was close, she tossed back her head with an air of almost haughty defiance, and looked him directly in the eye. He returned her look in his usual blank manner, and passed her without slowing his pace. Then, feeling reckless, she looked over her shoulder … Would he, too? … No, he continued walking, his hands in his pockets, and her eyes followed his retreating, broad-shouldered frame.

That morning she sped homewards, humming under her breath, with a hint of mischievous glee about her closed lips. She could think of nothing but her encounter with Fabrice. When she rang the bell at Nassauplein and Grete let her in, the dogs bounded into the hall, barking with excitement. She had to laugh: she had clean forgotten to leave Leo and Faust behind at the stable on her way home!

Betsy burst out of the dining room, fuming.

"Good heavens, Eline, are you mad? Fancy bringing those wretched dogs here! You know I can't abide them. What's come over you, going against my wishes like this? It's as if I'm not mistress in my own home! Please take them away at once."

Her voice was harsh and strident, as though she were giving orders to an inferior.

"They're thirsty, and I want to give them some water," responded Eline, affecting cool authority so that Betsy would not guess that the dogs had simply slipped her mind.

"That's as may be! I will not have them drinking water in my house, do you hear? Look at that carpet, muddy paws everywhere."

"Grete can clean it in no time."

"You don't know what you're saying! You live the life of a princess here, doing exactly as you please, taking no notice whatsoever of me! Take those filthy dogs away, I tell you!"

"They must have some water first."

"Didn't you hear me? I said I will not have them drinking water here!" cried Betsy, beside herself with vexation.

"Well, they must have their drink. I'll take them to the garden," said Eline calmly.

"Don't you dare!" shrieked her sister. "Don't you dare!"

"Come here, Leo, come here, Faust," called Eline, patting her thigh with maddening slowness.

Betsy was incensed. Her lips quivered, her hands shook, her breath came in quick, short gasps. She was speechless with rage, and wanted only to slap her sister hard, but Eline was already sauntering down the hall with the frisky hounds at her heels, into the garden, where she proceeded to fill a bucket of water at the outside tap. It gave her a subtle pleasure to anger Betsy so. The dogs drank their fill and she brought them back inside.

Betsy was still standing in the hall, glowering impotently at Eline, wishing she had run after her and wrested the bucket from her grasp.

"I warn you, Eline," she began, her voice quaking and her cheeks aflame, "I shall have to speak to Henk about this."

"Oh, see if I care!" returned Eline with a flare of temper, whereupon she flounced out of the house with the dogs, slamming the door behind her.

Fifteen minutes later she was back again, humming to herself in secret rapture about her meeting with Fabrice. Starting up the stairs, she broke into a long, pearly ripple of song, as though in deliberate provocation of Betsy, who was moping in the dining room, close to tears.

When Henk returned at midday, Betsy told him of Eline's intolerable conduct, but he had little patience with her, refusing to take sides. Betsy was outraged; she accused him of being spineless, and made a scene.

For a whole week the sisters barely spoke to one another, much to Henk's dismay, for their sulking ruined his enjoyment of the comforts of home, especially at table, where the meals were hurried through, for all that Eline chattered incessantly to him and Ben.

XII

I T HAD STRUCK FRÉDÉRIQUE during the New Year's Eve supper party at the van Raats' that Otto had talked and laughed a good deal with Eline; not remarkably so, but more than he usually did with the young ladies of their acquaintance. She had been wondering about this for several days, but the opportunity to ask her brother the question that was foremost in her mind never seemed to arise. She was brusque towards Etienne when he wanted to share a joke with her, had little patience for games with the children, and was pronounced by Lili, Marie and Paul to have grown altogether less good-humoured of late.

It was one of their evenings at home; only Etienne had gone out with some friends. The youngsters were in bed, and Madame van Erlevoort sat with Mathilda in the drawing room by the tea table, Madame with a book and Mathilda with some needlework. Frédérique came in, smiling, then went up to her mother and lovingly smoothed the grey hair at her temples.

"Freddie, would you mind ringing for Willem?" asked Mathilda. "Otto said he would like a cup of tea in his room; he's doing some work and won't be down until later."

"Why don't you just pour him a cup and I'll take it up to him," she replied.

Mathilda poured the tea, and as Frédérique climbed the stairs carrying the cup she thought this might be a good time to put her question, although she would prefer it if he started a conversation himself.

She entered Otto's room and found him wandering about with a very distracted air, his head bowed and his hands clasped behind his back, in an attitude quite contrary to his customary briskness.

"Well now, what kindness from my little sister!" he said jovially, taking the cup from her. "It will taste ten times the better for being served by such pretty hands."

"Fie, Otto!" cried Frédérique. "How could you be so banal! Don't tell me you can't come up with a more original compliment!"

She continued to smile at him, but did not catch his reply as she was too busy pondering how best to phrase her question. After all, he might take it amiss. Try as she might, she could not think of any easy, light-hearted way of introducing the subject, and to her own surprise she broke out with:

"Otto, I … I have something to say to you, something to confess."

"A sin?"

"No, not a sin, at least I don't think so; an indiscretion, maybe, which I committed against you by mistake. But first you must say you'll forgive me."

"Without knowing what for?"

"Well, it wasn't a deliberate indiscretion; besides, I wasn't as indiscreet as I would have liked to be, so you could even say I deserve a reward! But really, all I'm asking is that you forgive me."

"All right then, I shall be merciful. Tell me all about it."

"Promise you won't be angry?"

"I promise. Go on, out with it."

"It's just that, quite by accident, I happened to find out who it was … you know, on St Nicholas' Eve … "

He paled a little, observing her intently, and she was keenly aware that he hung on every word she uttered.

"So I know who sent Eline that fan … the Bucchi fan … "

She stood before him with the air of a guilt-ridden child, mortified by her confession, while he fixed her with a wide-eyed, anxious stare.

"You found out?" he stammered.

She nodded.

"Oh please, don't be angry," she begged. "I couldn't help it, honestly. I went to your room one morning because I needed to borrow your sealing wax. You never forbade me to go into your room, did you? I knocked, but you weren't there so I went in, and as I was hunting for the wax on your desk I happened to notice the leather case lying in one of the compartments, and so I recognised it straight away when I saw it again in the evening. At first I thought it might be something for me, and I was dying to take a peek inside—you know how inquisitive I am—but I didn't because I felt bad enough having discovered your gift. Oh dear, I'm afraid you are angry with me, but I couldn't help it, could I?"

"Angry? But my dear girl, there is nothing to be angry about!" he replied with forced levity. "It was a surprise gift, and surprises don't last for ever, do they? But I hope you haven't mentioned it to Eline."

"Oh no, of course not."

"Well, what of it then? There's no harm done," he said carelessly. "Or are you sorry the fan was not meant for you?"

She gave a disdainful shrug.

"I'm surprised you should think me so childish. Only—"

"Now what?"

She lifted her clear, guileless eyes to him, and he felt a slight pang of unease under her scrutiny.

"The thing is, I can't imagine any young man giving such a beautiful present to a girl unless he's extremely fond of her."

"Oh, but I am very fond of Eline, so why shouldn't I give her something for St Nicholas?"

"No, Otto, you're not being frank with me!" she said impatiently, drawing him to the sofa. "Come and sit down: I want you to listen a moment. A sensible, level-headed fellow like you doesn't give a girl a fan costing goodness knows how much unless he's in love with her, whatever you say. You never gave Eline anything before, and you didn't give Lili or Marie any presents this year either. So you see, I can tell that there's more to it!" She broke off suddenly and put her hands on his shoulders.

"Or do you think me too forward? Perhaps you'd rather not talk about it … " she faltered.

"On the contrary, my dear Freddie," he said mildly, drawing her towards him on the sofa. "I'm quite happy to talk to you about Eline. Why wouldn't I be? But suppose I did care very much for Eline, would you still think it foolish and extravagant of me? … "

"So it's true then—you love Eline?"

"You look shocked," he said, smiling.

"Oh, but Eline isn't the right kind of girl for you at all!" she cried with agitation. "No, Otto, really, Elly doesn't deserve you and she never will. I know she's beautiful and charming, but there's something about her that, well, that I find unsympathetic. Seriously, though, I think you would do better to put her out of your mind. I don't believe you and she could ever be happy together. You're so good and kind, and if you really fell deeply in love with her you'd want to surrender yourself body and soul, you'd want to do everything for her, and in return she'd give you not one tenth of what you gave her. She doesn't have a heart, all she has is egotism, stone-cold egotism."

"But Freddie, Freddie," he protested, "how you rush on! What makes you think that you have sufficient experience of human nature to know exactly what Eline is like?"

She flinched at the way he pronounced Eline's name, lingeringly, as if he were savouring it.

"Human nature? I know nothing about human nature, all I know is what my feelings tell me, which is that Eline cares about no one but herself, that she's incapable of making the slightest sacrifice for anyone. I feel—no, more than that: I am utterly convinced that marrying Eline would not make you happy in the long run. She might love you for a while, but it would still be out of egotism, sheer egotism."

"How harsh you are, Freddie!" he murmured reproachfully. "It's very kind of you to have my interests at heart like this, but you're very hard on Eline. Very hard. I don't believe you know her at all, really. Personally I'm sure she's the kind of girl who would make every conceivable sacrifice for the sake of the person she loved."

"You say that I don't really know her, but how well do you know her? You only see her when she's all smiles and sweetness."

"How can you blame her for being charming rather than impolite?"

Frédérique sighed.

"Oh, Otto, I don't know what I think, all I know is what my feelings tell me: that you'll never be happy with her," she said with full assurance.

He took her hand, smiling.

"Why, you talk as if we were to be married tomorrow."

"Oh please tell me, then—don't think I'm prying—you haven't already proposed to her, have you?"

He looked at her, still smiling, and slowly shook his head.

"In that case, I wish you'd think it over carefully. Just don't get carried away all of a sudden."

She leant her head on his shoulder, tears rising to her eyes.

"You're a dear, Freddie, but honestly—"

"You must think it ridiculous of me to try and tell you what to do!"

"Not at all. On the contrary, I appreciate your concern very, very much. Still, you shouldn't judge someone on the basis of a mere feeling, a lack of sympathy shall we say—which is quite baseless, anyway. So, little sister, be a good girl and take my advice, and I shan't think you in the least ridiculous."

She hid her face in his shoulder and he kissed her several times on the forehead.

"You will forgive me, won't you? It was tactless of me, I shouldn't have spoken to you like that."

"But I love you most of all for being honest and forthright with me, and I'm counting on you to stay that way in future."

"Then you'll only think me impolite and not at all charming, I'm sure," she said tartly.

"Now you're being a bit spiteful. You're not jealous of Eline, are you?"

"Yes I am," she replied gruffly.

"On account of the fan, I take it?" he laughed.

"Oh, you do tease me so!" she wailed. "No, not because of that—I have a dozen fans already—but because you've gone and fallen in love with her."

"Let's make a pact, then. You go and look for a nice girl who would make me a suitable consort, someone you aren't jealous of and who you like, and when you've found her, and if I like her too, I'll never think of Eline again. What do you say?"

She gave no answer and stood up, rubbing the tears from her eyes. She felt hurt by his flippant tone; clearly he hadn't taken her seriously at all. She approached the table, pointed to the cup of tea, and said:

"Your tea's getting cold, Otto; I'd drink it now if I were you."

Before he could respond she slipped away, full of contradictory feelings—on the one hand relieved to have spoken her mind and glad to have gained Otto's confidence, on the other wondering whether she would not have done better to hold her tongue.

For the past five mornings Eline had not seen Fabrice on her walk, and the disappointment soured her entire day. At first she was quiet, downcast and irritable, but soon she grew so morose that she lost all desire to sing, to the point where she cancelled her appointment with Roberts, her music teacher, as well as her Thursday-afternoon singing session with Paul van Raat. Returning from her walk one morning at about half-past ten in pensive mood, she dropped onto her couch and, leaning back, unfastened her cloak with listless fingers. Ben's company was too much for her, and she sent him off to the nursery forthwith. Her large hazel eyes, moist and glistening with unfulfilled longing, roamed idly about the room, lingering on the prints along the walls, the potted palms, the Canova figurines. She felt enveloped in a fog of despondency, and asked herself what the purpose of her life could be if all happiness were denied to her. To give her amorphous sorrow some kind of shape, she cast around for grievances and piled them up: what she needed was love, and there she was, with no one to love her. She was finding it increasingly difficult to get along with Betsy; they quarrelled frequently, and most of the time it wasn't even her fault. Then there was Frédérique, who was noticeably cool towards her, for what reason she hadn't the faintest idea, and although Madame van Raat seemed as fond of her as ever, Eline herself had not lately been minded to display the winsome, respectful openness that had endeared her to the old lady. There was no point to her life, the way she drifted aimlessly from one day to the next, and she yearned for some vague ideal, a dream without a particular contour but replete with figments of passion and love ranging from the exalted to the mundane, from the heights of idyllic romance to the simple, quiet joys of home and hearth.

She sighed, raising her hand to the overhanging aralia, and almost crushed the leaf between her nervous fingers as she tried to force her reveries to take a more determinate form. All at once, through an abrupt twist of her fancy, she saw herself with Fabrice, on stage, in a large city. They loved one another, they were famous, they were being deluged with wreaths and bouquets, and in her mind's eye rose the entire vision as it had risen that time when she and Paul were singing those love duets.

But she had not seen Fabrice for such a long time that her fantasy, being deprived of fresh impressions, foundered; the vision dissipated, leaving her in a grey, sombre frame of mind that appeared to reflect the sky outside, heavy with dark rain clouds. She felt hot tears brimming over her lashes, then a keen wish for Henk's company. At least with him she could pour out her misery; he was so devoted to her, so good at comforting her in his own kindly, gauche way—the sound of his voice alone, so deep and warm, was as balm to her soul.

She wept quietly and thought how disagreeable it was that she and Betsy were on such bad terms. The following day was her, Eline's, birthday. Would Betsy take the first step towards a reconciliation, or was she herself really to blame for their latest tiff? Had she felt sure of her sister's reaction, she would gladly have offered to make peace with her, or even apologise if necessary, but as it was she feared Betsy's coolness. So she would wait; yes, she would wait.

The afternoon seemed interminable, the hours dragged on as though weighed down by her melancholy. Then it was time to dress for dinner with the Hijdrechts, although she had not the slightest expectation of finding any amusement there. She wished she could ask Betsy to say that she was unwell and unable to join them, but no, that wouldn't do. Unlike the Verstraetens, the Hijdrechts might well be piqued by her failure to attend, and besides, Betsy might refuse point-blank to do as she asked. So she went, having worked herself up into a spirit of coquettish gaiety by which one and all were taken in, so adept was she at concealing her emotions.

The following day was 20th January and Eline's birthday. She stayed in bed longer than usual, snuggled down among the warm blankets in the soft red glow of the curtains, without the least inclination to rise, not even to go for her morning walk. She wouldn't see him anyway, even if she did go out—she could feel it in her bones. Superstitious fancies began to crowd her mind, and she wagered that if Mina came to prepare her washstand before the clock struck nine—it was now close upon the hour—she would see Fabrice in the Wood tomorrow. But Mina came after nine o'clock, and when she left again after setting out the toiletries Eline had another fancy: she would see Fabrice if she had left her bracelets on the large coaster last night, but if she had left them on one of the small coasters she would not. She sat up, swept aside the red damask bed curtain and peered at her dressing table. There lay the bracelets, on the large coaster! With a smile, she subsided onto her pillows once more.

It was time to get up, she thought, but why not stay abed in the cosy warmth, since she was so downhearted, why start a new day? In a while her friends would come to congratulate her, she would have to turn on her smiles and receive their birthday gifts with ecstatic exclamations, but her humour was by no means amenable and she had no desire to see anyone.

The clock struck half-past ten, and she thought Betsy was bound to come up before long, with a few friendly words to make up the quarrel. She listened for her sister's tread on the stairs, but heard nothing, and at last, unnerved by her own lassitude, she got out of bed and slowly proceeded to dress.

She saw her face in the glass and noticed the sad look in her eyes and the hint of bitterness about her lips, and thought herself almost ugly today. But what of it? For whose sake should she be beautiful, given that no one loved her with anything resembling the passion she knew her heart capable of?

When she was finally dressed she had qualms. If she went downstairs now, how should she approach Betsy? Should she take a passive attitude? Why didn't Betsy meet her halfway? Why did she continue to bear a grudge for so long, about such a trifling matter?

The idea of seeing Betsy in the breakfast room filled her with trepidation, and she stepped into her boudoir, where the stove was already lit and burning brightly. She slumped onto her couch, feeling bereft and abandoned. Why, oh why did she live?

She sank deeper and deeper into despondency, when relief came at last with the sound of Henk and Ben climbing the stairs. Presently they were on the landing, she could hear their voices, then there was a loud banging on her door.

"Where are you, Eline dear, still in bed?" cried Henk.

"No, I'm here, in my boudoir!" she answered, raising her voice slightly.

The door opened to reveal Henk, shaking his head from side to side, while Ben, clutching a posy in his small fist, wriggled his way in past his father's riding boots.

"Many happy returns, Auntie! Here, this is from Ben!" recited the well-rehearsed little fellow as he thrust the flowers in her lap.

"My dear girl, how could you stay cooped up in your rooms for so long? You're usually back from your walk at this hour!" exclaimed Henk.

She made no comment, merely hugged the child, fighting back her tears.

"Put them in some water, Ben, there's a good boy; tepid water is best. Thank you, thank you, poppet. Here then, take the vase, careful now."

Ben, docile as ever, went off with the vase, squeezing past his father's legs again. Eline fell back against the cushions, giving her brother-in-law a wan smile.

"I don't feel at all well this morning," she said listlessly. Henk approached her with his hands on his back.

"What, not well on your birthday?" he asked cheerily. "Come, come, it's time you went downstairs, you lazy girl, but let me give you a big kiss first! Happy birthday, dear Eline!" He pressed his lips to each cheek in turn, while she lay still, smiling weakly.

"And here's a little something for you, Elly. I hope you will like it," he continued, handing her a small box.

She gave a light laugh.

"How funny that you should come and bring me my present up here! Thank you, Henk, thank you very much."

She opened the box and saw a hairpin in the shape of a diamond spider.

"But Henk!" she cried. "How you spoil me! I can remember seeing it in the window at van Kempen's a while ago, and I know I mentioned liking it very much. I shall have to be more careful about what I say in future, I do believe," she said, with a touch of embarrassment. She was thinking of her Bucchi fan.

"Betsy made a mental note of it at the time," he responded. "We're both very happy to give you something you like."

Hearing this she almost felt annoyed at their gift, but flung her arms around his neck and kissed him anyway.

"Really, you do spoil me!" she faltered.

"Oh, fiddlesticks!" he burst out. "But now I must go for my canter. And you must come downstairs, my dear, or else I shall carry you down myself."

"No, no, that you shall not!"

"All right then, but be quick, or else——"

"Yes, yes, I'll be down in a moment. But no nonsense, Henk, do you hear?" she said firmly and with some alarm, for she could see a frolicsome intention on his part and was in no mood for banter.

He reassured her, laughing, and it was on the tip of his tongue to suggest that she make peace with his wife, but he could not think of a tactful way of raising the subject. She might fly into a rage, and besides, it would all sort itself out soon enough, he reasoned, and left the room.

Reluctantly, Eline rose from the couch, thinking that Betsy must have instructed Henk to take the present upstairs so as not to have to give it to her herself. She thought how awkward it was that it now fell to her to take the first step towards a reconciliation. It was a blow to her pride. It would look as if she was so pleased with their gift that all bad feelings were instantly forgotten. How tiresome this was, but still: she could hardly just say good morning and start eating her breakfast without referring to the gift at all. She regretted not having followed her instinct yesterday to attempt appeasement. Oh, how stupid it all was, their falling out like this, and only because of those dogs!

In an impulse of vanity she held the diamond spider this way and that to her hair, then to her neck ...

Before going downstairs Eline opened a compartment of her writing table. With a secretive smile she removed the album and opened it. It contained nothing but portraits of Fabrice in various poses and costumes, which she had been purchasing over a period of time with much discretion and nervousness, now in one shop, then in another, never returning to the same one in case the shopkeeper might guess what was on her mind. On one occasion, when she was in Amsterdam for the day to visit some friends, she had been particularly daring: she had swept into a bookshop with an air of haughty indifference and bought seven at once. No one there knew who she was, anyway, and she vowed never to set foot in that shop again for as long as she lived.

Her eyes shone with furtive delight as she surveyed her collection; on every page his swarthy features with the black beard met her gaze, and on some his expression was exactly the same as when she saw him in the Wood, wearing his soft felt hat and his muffler. Ah, there it was, that rush of emotion incomparably more intense than admiration, the sheer impropriety of which for a young lady of her station sent a little shiver down her spine. She pressed her lips to his beloved likeness; yes, she could feel it now, the passion that replenished her mind with bliss, the love for which she would make any sacrifice that might be demanded of her ... by him.

A romantic vision fired her imagination, now that her spirits had lifted somewhat thanks to Henk's cheering words, and in the heat of her fantasy she saw herself with Fabrice, waiting for their train with trepidation, fearful of being pursued.

"Auntie, Auntie! Let me in!" cried Ben from the landing.

She slipped the album out of sight and opened the door. In came Ben, hugging the water-filled vase to his chest.

"Well done, you clever boy!" said Eline. "And not a drop spilt on the stairs?"

He shook his head from side to side, proud of his achievement, for which he had Mina to thank. He began to put the flowers in the vase, and it crossed her mind that the initiative for the little boy's gift had doubtless come from Betsy, too. What a nuisance all this was.

But she braced herself and proceeded down the stairs with Ben. Betsy was in the dining room, issuing instructions to Grete.

"Good morning, Betsy," said Eline.

"Good morning, Eline, many happy returns of the day!" said Betsy, without expression.

Eline did not wish to say any more in the presence of a servant, and told Grete she could clear away.

"I shan't be having any breakfast today," she said, and to hide her unease she turned to Ben and tried to make him laugh.

Betsy remained with her back to her, poring over the bills and receipts on her writing table with the air of a dutiful housewife.

Several seconds of awkward silence ensued, broken by Betsy scolding Ben for being such a dawdler and sending him off to the nursery, after which Eline stood up. She crossed the room and put her hands on her sister's shoulders.

"Betsy—" she began.

She could not bring herself to say anything yet about the gift, the diamond spider.

"Betsy dear, wouldn't it be better if? … I can't tell you how sorry I am that we should be so … oh please don't be angry with me any more, it was wrong of me."

"Well, Eline, I am glad to hear you admit it. And I'm not angry with you."

"Are we friends again then?"

"Oh, of course. You know there's nothing I dislike more than unpleasantness. I am all for peace. So let's say no more about it, shall we?"

Her tone was icy cold to Eline, but she bent over to give Betsy a kiss.

"No truly, I am sorry; of course I had no right to go against your wishes in your own house. I do apologise."

There was something else she wanted to say, but she could not find the words, and again touched her lips to her sister's brow, at which Betsy pushed her lightly aside.

"All right then; let's drop the subject. I'm not angry any more. But please stop kissing me, you know I don't like it."

Eline spent her birthday in a sombre frame of mind. The reconciliation with Betsy had not gone as she would have wished; she had expected there to be more affection, a sisterly embrace, shared tears perhaps, after which they would have carried on in cordial companionship for a long period of time. But the reality had been, on Betsy's side, nothing but icy condescension, which had made her own contribution appear rather feeble. She knew herself to be the weaker of the two, and yet she could not resist taking a stand against Betsy from time to time, but with each act of defiance, even if it resulted in temporary victory, she felt increasingly powerless to continue her struggle. The odds were against her, and their latest disagreement was yet another proof of the fickleness of her pride, which had let her down once more, casting a pall of doom over all her thoughts.

Nonetheless, she kept up an appearance of gaiety throughout the afternoon, in the cheer of friends as they came to convey their good wishes. But Madame van Raat, in whose pensive, pale-blue eyes she would have been so glad to detect a ray of sympathy, had sent a message through Paul saying she was indisposed. This was a great disappointment to Eline, which only deepened when Madame van Erlevoort and Mathilda arrived with the news that Freddie would not be calling because she had caught a cold, and again Eline wondered why Frédérique had taken against her. Jeanne Ferelijn spoke at length of her domestic troubles, and it required all the sweet civility that Eline could muster not to betray her impatience. Not only had she been abandoned by Madame van Raat, also Cateau van der Stoor, another visitor she would have liked to receive, failed to put in an appearance. Worse, she appeared to have forgotten all about the birthday as she hadn't even sent a message. Fortunately Emilie de Woude did come, displaying her curiously irrepressible good humour. Her ebullience infused a touch of levity into the formal atmosphere of the salons, where the gas was not yet lit, and where the brightness of the gilt panelling, the sheen of the Havana-brown satin cushions, the burnished-gold plush of the curtains seemed to dissolve into the deepening shadows.

Emilie demanded to see Eline's presents, and was directed to a side table bearing diverse pretty trifles arrayed about a large basket filled with fruit and flowers.

"What a splendid basket!" cried Emilie. "Peaches, grapes, roses, how lovely! From whom, Elly?"

"From Vincent. Charming, is it not?"

"I wish I had such charming cousins!"

"Hush," whispered Eline.

Vincent had just entered, and his eyes, slightly narrowed, went in search of the hostess. Betsy, ever on her guard with their cousin, received him with her customary display of careful cordiality. Eline thanked him for his gift, catching his hands in hers.

He apologised for arriving so late; it was already a quarter past five, and the Verstraetens and the others began to take their leave in the gathering dusk, after which Gerard came in to light the gas, close the shutters and draw the curtains.

"Vincent, you will stay to dinner, won't you?" asked Betsy.

Betsy did not fancy the prospect of a dull evening at home. They had not been invited anywhere, and besides, she had not thought it right to make plans to go out on her sister's birthday while they were not on speaking terms. With Vincent being a close kinsman, she could easily extend an informal invitation at short notice. He had conversation when in good humour, and at least there would be a fresh face at the dinner table.

Vincent accepted the invitation with a laconic "Oh, with pleasure". Henk, having declared his intention to take a walk, donned only his hat and hurriedly left the house, his collar turned up and his hands in his pockets. Anna, the nursemaid, came to fetch Ben, whose chin was smeared with jelly and cream after the birthday feast. Betsy too disappeared upstairs, leaving Eline and Vincent alone in the spacious salon, now bright with gaslight.

"Let's go and sit over there," said Eline, and Vincent followed her into the violet ante-room, where the small crystal chandelier diffused a soft glow that invited intimacy and confidences. To Vincent, however, the room merely breathed an atmosphere of relaxed well-being, and with a sigh he collapsed onto the sofa. He proceeded in his usual offhand way to enquire after the guests he had seen leaving. While replying to his question, she felt a great sympathy for her cousin welling up inside her. It was that need again, springing from her passion for Fabrice, that desire to be steeped in love, to be surrounded by it on all sides, and to bestow it on others. And just as it had struck Paul by the wan glow of a paraffin lamp, so it now struck Eline under the bright gaslight flashing on the crystal pendants—Vincent bore a striking resemblance to her late beloved father, so striking as to transport her back in time to her girlhood, when her father would lean back in exactly the same way as Vincent was doing now, with the same pained expression about the mouth, the same soulful eyes contemplating some unattainable artistic vision; even the hand hanging limply over the side was exactly like her father's when he let the paintbrush slip from his fingers to the floor.

Eline felt her sympathy for Vincent reverberating with pity and poetic heartache as she listened to his murmured reminiscences of Smyrna, thinking how interesting he was, so much more so than the other young men of her acquaintance; how right he was to pronounce life in The Hague provincial and dreary, and how well she understood his desire for wider horizons, oh, if only she, too, could ...

"But I must be boring you with all this talk of my own dislikes," he continued in an altered tone, "neither is it civil on my part."

"Oh, not at all, you're not boring me in the least!" she hastened to say, a touch dismayed that he had cut the thread of her fantasy so abruptly. "Do you think I can't imagine exactly how you feel, hating the routine of sameness day in, day out, the endless going round in circles that we all do? I sometimes wish I could get away from it all myself!" she exclaimed, waving her arms as if she were a caged bird flapping its wings. "Sometimes I feel very inclined to do something outrageous!" and she gave a secret smile at the thought of Fabrice.

He returned her smile, shaking his head, and reached out to pat her lifted hand, after which it fell gracefully to her side.

"Why would you want to do anything outrageous?" he asked. "You exaggerate. Just leading your own life without depending on others, taking no notice of what society expects from you, but following your own free will as long as it makes sense, to change one's surroundings as often as one pleases—that is my ideal. There's nothing like change to keep you young."

"But being independent, doing exactly as you please … that takes more moral courage than most of us possess in this over-civilised society of ours," she replied, rather pleased with the epicurean-philosophical turn the conversation was taking.

"Moral courage? Oh no, all you need is money!" he said firmly. "If I'm rich, have good manners, do nothing outrageous, and keep up appearances before the eyes of the world, it's well in my power to achieve my ideal, without anyone accusing me of anything worse than, say, mild eccentricity."

This was rather too down-to-earth, too banal, to her way of thinking, and she countered by imposing her own, more romantic view.

"Well yes, money … of course!" she resumed, dismissing his argument with feminine facility. "But if you're not strong enough to follow your will, you'll find yourself back in the same old routine before you know it. Which is why"—he had to smile at her appealing want of logic—"which is why I would so dearly love to do something outrageous, you know, something unheard-of. Personally, I feel strong enough to go my own way whatever people might say, in fact I sometimes feel quite reckless."

He was charmed by the ardour in her shining eyes as she flaunted her defiance, and her graceful, slight frame made him think of a butterfly poised to flit away.

"But Eline!" he chuckled. "Whatever are you thinking of? What would you be reckless enough to do? Go on, confess, you naughty girl!"

She laughed.

"Oh, to elope, at the very least!"

"With me?"

"Why not? But I'm afraid you'd leave me to fend for myself before long, you'd think me rather too expensive a companion, and I'd be back where I started, with my tail between my legs. So if that was meant as an invitation, much obliged, but I'd rather wait for a rich suitor."

"No log cabin, then, in the moonlight?"

"Oh, Vincent, how dull! Never! I would die of boredom. Come to that, I'd rather be an actress ... and elope with an actor."

She sparkled with mischief and self-importance, exulting in her secret dream with Fabrice, and she looked Vincent boldly in the eye—he would never guess what she was thinking, anyway.

He laughed heartily; the vivacity that had replaced her languid elegance in the course of their conversation, combined with the radiance in her almond eyes and the way she kept patting her knee with coquettish impatience, amused him even more than what she was actually saying. And yet, her words struck a chord with him: her heartfelt longing for change was much like his own. They looked at one another a long moment, smiling, and the softness of his pale, penetrating gaze, had the mesmeric effect on her of a serpent's stare.

"How extraordinary, he looks just like dear Papa, how very extraordinary!" she thought, marvelling at the sympathy she felt for Vincent as they rose in response to the bell summoning them to the dining room.

XIII

MADAME VERSTRAETEN remained at home with Lili, who was nursing a bad cold, while Marie and Frédérique set out with Paul and Etienne, their skates slung over their shoulders, to the skating rink at Laan van Meedervoort. Mr Verstraeten was reading a book in the warm conservatory surrounded by the shiny greenery of potted palms and aralias. Lili was out of sorts, responding to her mother's occasional remarks in listless monosyllables interspersed with valiant attempts to repress her coughing. She had pronounced herself quite recovered, and being cooped up in the house like this was not doing her any good, so she was resolved to go out again in a day or two. Looking out of the window she saw the garden looking positively Siberian, with crisp white snow lacing the bushes and the trees, and the untrodden paths resembling slabs of polished marble. Madame Verstraeten concentrated on her crochet, and the rapid movements of the needle working the wool into a knotty fabric grated on Lili's nerves, as did the regular sound, a little way off, of her father turning yet another page. She herself did nothing, her hands lying idle in her lap, and while she normally enjoyed an afternoon of *dolce far niente*, she was now bored to distraction.

Secretly she envied Freddie and Marie for their good health and high spirits, while she was still convalescing and obliged to wrap up against the slightest draught. But when her sister hesitated to accompany Freddie and Etienne on their outing, Lili herself had urged her to take her skates and go; Marie could hardly be expected to stay with her all the time while she was ill, and besides, she had Mama to keep her company.

A sigh escaped her, and she took a cough lozenge from the sweet dish. Madame Verstraeten glanced at her from the corner of her eye, but made no comment, for she knew that Lili, in her irritable condition, would only huff at expressions of maternal solicitude.

The afternoon wore on slowly, without any callers to relieve either the general tedium or Lili's glum, taciturn mood, until it was past four o'clock and the doorbell sounded. A moment later Georges de Woude appeared, and again Lili was annoyed, this time because Dien had not thought to announce him first before ushering him into the salon—it wasn't as if Georges was a close friend of the family, after all. While he shook hands with her mother, she greeted him somewhat coolly with a lethargic wave of her hand, and was in no hurry to follow when her mother led him to the conservatory to meet her father. Only when they were all three seated did Lili come over, pulling up a cane chair with some deliberation, as if to say she was not particularly pleased to see him and was only joining them because it would be impolite not to do so. At the first words he addressed to her parents she looked away, pretending that the garden held more interest for her than their conversation. Madame Verstraeten asked him about Berlin, where he had been posted for three months, but he answered hurriedly, half-turning to Lili, and proceeded to enquire after her health; had she been seriously ill? Lili murmured dismissively, leaving her mama to reply in more detail, but it struck her that he had put his question with a certain anxiety, not formally at all, but in a tone of genuine concern for her welfare. What could it matter to him whether she was ill or not? But he did not appear to notice her coolness, and pursued his lively account of life in Berlin while responding in his usual agreeable manner to his hosts' interjections. He kept glancing at Lili, as though wishing to draw her into the conversation, and out of courtesy she gave a slight smile now and then, or put an idle question. What a chatterbox he was, she thought, recalling earlier occasions when she had found his talk annoying. The next instant she felt she was being unfair. He was very talkative, it was true, but his conversation was amiable and sociable, and an undeniably welcome diversion after a tedious afternoon spent watching her mother work her crochet needle. His locution was not bad, a bit rushed perhaps, but not boring, and, now that she came to think of it, not at all affected, either. His accent was perhaps a trifle too studied, but that was all; his gestures were simple, and his well-mannered voice had a pleasantly sincere ring. As for his dress, it was very neat, almost too neat, really, but at least it wasn't loud; she had to give him that.

He chatted on in response to Mr Verstraeten's queries concerning his position, and while observing him she unwittingly brightened her smile, which did not escape his notice, so that he ventured to return to his earlier question: was she feeling better, would she soon be sufficiently recovered to go out? What could it matter to him, she thought again, almost crossly; he had already asked after her health before—out of politeness, to be sure. All the same, this time she answered him herself, saying that she was no longer coughing—her words were promptly belied by a short cough—and that she was feeling very much better thanks to the good care of Mama and Marie. He was glad to hear it, he said, but he had noted the rasping in her throat and was about to advise her to stay indoors while the cold weather lasted when he thought better of it. She might think him too forward, so he asked after Marie instead.

"Oh, she is very well," replied Lili. "She has gone skating with Frédérique and Etienne and Paul. Don't you feel sorry for me, having to stay at home again, all by myself?"

"Is it such a great disappointment to you? Are you fond of skating?"

"Yes, that's to say, I do enjoy it, but I'm not very good at it, to be honest. Marie and Freddie are much better skaters, they go whirling about while I just wobble; I'm too frightened, you see."

"What about Paul and Etienne, don't they help you?"

"Oh, Paul just says it's no fun skating with someone who can't skate properly, and Etienne, well, he sometimes puts up with me for five minutes."

"But Lili, if you can't skate it's not very enjoyable for the others, is it?" objected her mother.

"I believe I was more gallant in my day," observed her father.

"Oh, I'm not accusing them of anything, just stating a fact!" said Lili, and she coughed again.

"But once you are fully recovered, when you are well enough to go out," Georges resumed, waveringly, for he knew he was taking a chance, "might I offer you some assistance on the ice one day? I am mostly in my office, but—"

"You skate, then?" cried Lili. She would never have thought it of him.

"Oh yes, I'm a keen skater!" he said. "Do you accept?"

She almost blushed as she smiled and lowered her eyes.

"Oh, with pleasure, yes indeed. But I shall be a dreadful burden to you. I'm always frightened, always hearing the ice crack beneath me. I'm afraid you don't know what you're letting yourself in for."

"Oh yes I do," he retorted. "I am sure I shall never regret having asked you."

Lili was impressed by how warm and sincere he sounded, and could think of nothing to say, so she merely smiled. There was a brief lull in the conversation, and under normal circumstances this would have prompted Georges to take his leave, but instead he stayed, broached a new topic as if he had all the time in the world, and kept up his flow of words until Lili's brother Jan came home from school with his books tucked under his arm, by which hour it was already getting dark. Georges stood up at last, with apologies for outstaying his welcome.

"Not at all, quite the contrary!" said Mr Verstraeten. "It has been a pleasure to see you again. Remember me to your father and that delightful sister of yours."

"Emilie said she couldn't manage without you!" added Madame Verstraeten. "She must be very glad to have you back again."

Lili found herself thinking that yes, she could see why Emilie would miss Georges' company, and she held out her hand with a flourish and thanked him again for his invitation.

"Good fellow, young de Woude!" said Mr Verstraeten when Georges had left. Lili returned to the drawing room just as she overheard her Mama agreeing that he was indeed a very personable young man.

"He calls quite regularly these days. But I dare say we wouldn't see so much of him if it weren't for the girls."

Lili heard no more; she smiled at her own fancy, for she could see herself with Georges, gliding on the ice, their arms crossed and hands joined.

Marie came home escorted by Freddie, Paul and Etienne, who took their leave at the door. She was tired out and cold, with red cheeks and shining eyes. It had been splendid, they had seen many friends on the ice, including the Eekhof girls and Eline, who had come with Henk.

"De Woude called earlier," remarked Madame Verstraeten. "He has been back for three days."

"Oh, really?" said Marie carelessly, and began to unfasten her short coat.

"And he invited me to go skating with him, as soon as I'm better," confided Lili, almost bashfully. She gave a slight cough.

Marie stared at her sister in astonishment.

"De Woude? With you? And what did you say?"

"That it was very kind of him, of course. What else was I supposed to say?"

Marie laughed outright.

"You going skating with de Woude? Lili, how could you? I thought you said he was a boring prig, and that you couldn't stand him."

"Well, he said he'd help me with my skating. At least he's more gallant than Paul and Etienne."

"But he can't even skate!" laughed Marie.

"He says he's very keen, though."

"Oh, don't you believe it. He's just pretending."

Lili shrugged with impatience.

"I see no reason for him to pretend about it."

"Dear me, how you leap to his defence! And you couldn't stand him before!"

"I always thought him very friendly, and polite … "

"Lili, how can you tell such barefaced fibs! You thought he was intolerable!"

"But Marie, that's no reason not to go skating with him," cried Lili, almost beseechingly. "When you go to a ball you dance with other people besides your beau, don't you?"

"Still, I hardly know what to think," Marie teased. "Off skating together, just like that! What about Mama, does she approve?"

Lili turned away with dignified contempt.

"Don't be childish," was all she said, looking down at her sister, and was dismayed to feel herself blushing yet again—for no reason, after all.

"Is Papa sleeping?" asked Georges, entering Emilie's sitting room after dinner that evening.

Emilie gave a little start. She had been slumped in her easy chair by the hearth, feeling the effects of a copious repast.

"Yes, Papa's asleep," she said, blinking.

Georges laughed.

"And you, Emilie, did you nod off as well?" he teased.

Emilie responded with like good humour. No, she had not been asleep, just resting, she assured him. Would Georges be staying for tea? She would enjoy that.

She felt a sort of motherly affection for her so much younger brother, whom she had cared for and doted on since his early childhood, and who was now back under her wing after his months abroad. He looked well, she noted with satisfaction, he had even put on a little weight, and she was glad to discern a new manliness in his fine features—or had she simply failed to notice it before he went away?

Georges sat down beside her and they chatted about this and that. She knew him well, she believed, and could sense that he had something to ask her. She was inwardly pleased at this, but saucy enough to oblige him to broach the subject without any assistance from her. He prevaricated at length, but her non-committal replies did not inspire confidence in him, and he decided to delay unburdening himself. Abruptly, and in an altered, firmer tone, he made some trivial remark, whereupon she regretted her feigned indifference and tried to think of some way of drawing him out. However, she could think of nothing tactful, so eventually asked him point-blank:

"I say, Georges, what's on your mind? What did you want to tell me?"

Now it was his turn to pretend, and with assumed amazement he echoed:

"Tell you? What do you mean?"

"Oh, I don't know, just a feeling I have. It must be the curl of your moustache!" she quipped. "Seriously, though, is there nothing the matter? Money affairs, perhaps?"

But she knew better: money posed no problem to him, it never had; so fastidious was he where finances were concerned that she, having taken charge of all their elderly father's affairs, never encountered the slightest grounds for correction. Georges smiled and shook his head, but said nothing. Could the matter at hand be so weighty as to render him speechless, she jested, a chatterbox like him?

"No, no, it's nothing," he answered. "Besides, you know what they say—silence is golden and all that."

"I beg you, Georges, don't you be coy with me! If you have something to say or to ask, please do so, and no mincing of words, please, you know that is quite unnecessary with me!" she said, almost reproachfully, but with so much warm encouragement in her tone that he took her large white hand and raised it with playful gallantry to his lips.

"Now then, out with it!" Emilie persisted, giving him a light tap under the chin with the back of the hand he had just kissed.

There was no going back now, and he plucked up the courage to speak, slowly at first, in disjointed sentences, but his query soon gathered momentum. There was his position to think about, of course, but would she think him very foolish if he considered … marriage? A tremor had come into his voice, as though his fate depended on her answer.

His words took her by surprise, for although he was all of four and twenty she still regarded him as her little boy, her pet. And here he was, thinking of marriage! But she also knew him to be grown-up and sensible under the light veneer of affection; he would not ask her opinion unless he had thought the matter out beforehand, and she did not wish to hurt his feelings by assuming an all-too-light-hearted tone. However, she felt a pang of alarm at the thought of having sooner or later to part with him.

"Marriage! Georges, are you serious?"

He gave a secretive smile, as though absorbed in some sweet vision.

"Why not?" he said, his voice sinking to a whisper.

"Are you … are you then … so much in love?" she asked in a hardly audible voice. "Is it? … " A name rose to her lips, but she left it unsaid.

He nodded happily, as if he knew she had guessed. Before his departure to Berlin she had already been teasing him about being sweet on Lili Verstraeten, of whom he talked so often. But now that he had acknowledged it, she was crestfallen. How did he know that Lili cared for him? Wasn't he building castles in the air? But she did not voice these concerns, for he seemed so happy and hopeful.

"Georges, if you are truly in earnest, well … let's see … " she resumed, moving her chair closer to his. "Suppose everything goes smoothly at first, say you propose, and she accepts, what then? You know you'll have to wait for ages before you can have a wedding."

"Why?"

"But, Georges, what are you thinking? Surely you don't mean to marry on your salary as Assistant-Consul? A mere twelve hundred guilders, am I right? Of course, there is your share of Mama's estate, but it's a bagatelle, it won't make you wealthy by any means! So I ask you, what will you live on? You can't count on the Verstraetens giving very much as a dowry; they live comfortably enough, but quite modestly. They are not rich, you know."

"My dear Emilie, if you must do my sums for me, you could at least get them right. It's true that I don't reckon on support from my … " he smiled as his voice sank to a whisper, "from my future parents-in-law, should it come to that. In fact I would not even wish to."

"I hardly think you would say no if they offered."

"I don't know, that is an aspect I haven't considered yet. It hasn't even crossed my mind, to be honest, but what I meant was that your calculations were a bit wide of the mark. Suppose I don't sit the Vice-Consular exam this year, then we're entitled to fifteen hundred guilders each, aren't we?"

"About that."

"Well then, twelve hundred plus fifteen hundred is—"

"Two thousand seven hundred guilders. And you would marry on that?"

"But Emilie, why ever not?"

She threw up her hands in exasperation.

"Forgive me for saying so, Georges, but you must be out of your mind! I wish you'd stop acting like a child and come to your senses. I suppose you've been reading that silly little book for young married couples—what is it called again? Something like *How to Live Comfortably and Respectably on Fifteen Hundred a Year*."

"No, I haven't seen it, but fifteen hundred is not the same as twenty-seven hundred, and I have reason to be confident—"

"You have reason to be confident? No, no, quite the contrary, you have no idea! What makes you think you would be able to live with a wife from January to December on a miserable two thousand and seven hundred guilders? You are confident, you say!" she burst out when he made to interrupt her. She sprang up from her easy chair. "I can just see you now, living in some poky upstairs flat with a joint of beef once a week for a treat! Not that I would know what it's like, never having been in that situation, but what I do know is that both you and Lili grew up in comfortable circumstances, so how could the pair of you possibly? … Oh come now, all this is absurd. Do be sensible. I know you too well."

"Perhaps you don't know me well enough!" he countered, his gentle tone contrasting with her stridency. "Because I'm quite sure that I shall be able to adjust my needs to my means."

"It's all very well for you to say that, but what about your wife? Do you really want to force a young girl, brought up with a certain amount of luxury, to adjust her needs to your means? Believe me, Georges dear, no one can live on air these days."

"I never thought they could."

"Let me finish. Young people like you, like Lili, need all sorts of things. For one thing they want to go out, to entertain friends, and—"

"Oh, all that going out! I did enough of that as a student to last me a lifetime."

"Egotist! Just because you went out as much as you pleased when you were young you want to stay in for economy's sake when you're married, and sit with your wife in your little upstairs apartment savouring your weekly beefsteak. A grand prospect for her, to be sure!"

"Seriously, Emilie, why all this emphasis on the need to go out every evening? I don't believe society is a good place to look for happiness, anyway."

"Until now you've been quite happy flitting from one soirée to another, in other words, you have been in a social whirl. Falling in love has given you poetic ideas, but believe me, it'll wear off, and when you have been married a while you will find yourself missing the company of friends and acquaintances."

"Granted, as far as the friends and acquaintances are concerned, but giving them up is not part of my plan, and it will not cost all that much to continue seeing them."

"It will cost a lot, Georges, believe me!" Emilie persisted. "You will receive invitations, and you won't want to appear mean so you'll be obliged to reciprocate from time to time with a dinner party, however modest, and you'll have to do so again and again, and all this on twenty-seven hundred guilders a year? I can see you at it already. Especially your poor wife, having to run a household on those paltry twenty-seven hundred guilders, or rather, on as much of it as you allow her. Well, you won't catch me coming to stay with you, I can tell you."

Her comical resentment amused him, but he was adamant.

"My dear Emilie, you can say what you like, but it's my firm belief that you can get quite far with a little money and some good sense, and be happy to boot."

"Oh, hark at Master Georges, thinks he knows better than his big sister, does he? So stubborn, it's a disgrace!" she sputtered vexedly.

"Emilie, please calm down," he soothed. "Nothing's been decided yet. I haven't actually … I'm not even sure she … "

He left his sentence unfinished, not wishing to voice a thought he could not contemplate.

"Yes, Georges, I understand," said Emilie, somewhat appeased by his tone. "Still, financial considerations need to be confronted sooner rather than later, as I'm sure you agree."

"I agree with you there, but you exaggerate the stringency of my budget. By the way," he interrupted himself with a winning smile, "talking of budgets, couldn't you do me an enormous favour and help me draw one up?"

"For an annual total of twenty-seven hundred guilders? Impossible, Georges, I couldn't do it. Why, you'd need more than that to live on if you moved into a rented apartment, even if you weren't married."

He sighed.

"So we can't reach any kind of agreement on this?"

She gave a shrug.

"How stubborn you are. You're like a child, you know nothing about life."

Georges, in spite of himself, felt his resolve weaken. His high hopes began to founder under the oppressive burden of common sense, and the future seemed to crumble before his eyes. He passed his hand across his forehead with a slow, defeated gesture and thought: Yes, perhaps it would be better to wait a while.

"Best to wait for a time, then, I suppose," he intoned in a low voice, sounding so doleful that Emilie began to have qualms about her victory.

She took his face in both her hands and peered into his sad, regretful eyes.

"You're such a dreamer!" she said, and her heart went out to him. "Well, you're still young, and perhaps one day ... you never know."

"Perhaps what?"

"Perhaps you're right and I don't know what I'm talking about!" she broke out with a pang of remorse at having pained her young brother. "Only, I beg you: be sensible and don't rush into anything, Georges!" And she pressed long kisses on his closed eyes, aware of the tears rising in them.

XIV

"GOODNIGHT, BETSY! 'Night, Henk! I'm off to bed; I'm quite worn out," Eline said in a rush of words as they entered the front hall.

"Won't you have a bite to eat first?" asked Betsy.

"Thank you all the same, but no."

Eline started up the stairs. Betsy shrugged; she could tell from the peremptory tone that her sister was in one of her nervous, irritable moods and would brook no interference.

"What's the matter with Eline?" asked Henk in the dining room, fearing another spate of strained relations.

"Oh, how should I know?" cried Betsy. "It started at the concert, and you saw how she ignored me in the carriage going home. I pretended not to notice, but I can't stand it when she goes into one of her sulks."

Eline ascended the stairs in her swansdown and plush evening cape with an air of offended majesty, and entered her sitting room. Mina had had the foresight to turn on the gaslight, and there was even a log burning in the grate. She glanced about her a moment, then tore the white-lace fichu from her head and flung away her cape, and stood there with her head bowed, staring blankly at the floor in an attitude of utter disillusionment.

Raising her eyes to the Venetian pier glass with its pretty red cords above her porcelain Amor and Psyche, whose charming idyll was in such loathsome contrast to her present emotion, she saw her reflection: shimmering in her pink rep silk and with the aigrette of pink plumes in her upswept hair, the very ensemble she had worn when she first set eyes on Fabrice, three whole months ago.

And now …

She almost laughed out loud at the sheer absurdity of it all, then cringed in self-disgust, as though she had defiled herself.

There had been a concert of the Diligentia Society at the Hall of Arts and Sciences, to which she had persuaded Henk and Betsy to accompany her. Fabrice was to perform: "*The popular baritone of the French opera has been invited to gather fresh laurels from a new audience*," the newspaper had reported. Eline had not rested until she was certain to be attending: first she had approached the Verstraetens, but Madame was not thus inclined and Lili was still ill; then she had turned to Emilie, but Emilie had a prior engagement. As a last resort she had appealed to Henk and Betsy, who, although neither enthusiastic concert-goers, had consented to go. Eline was very excited: not only would she be seeing Fabrice perform in new surroundings, but also in a new role, that of a concert-singer. Thankfully, their seats were on the balcony, close to the stage, and oh, he was bound to recognise her from the opera, he would make some sign to her, he was in love with her ... the Bucchi fan! ... She conjured illusions without end as her passion ran rampant in her soul, filling it with a second, fabulous existence, with Fabrice and her as the hero and heroine of a sublimely romantic idyll.

He was enchanted by her beauty, he worshipped her, they would run away together, they would sing on stage, suffer hardship, become rich and famous ... The dizzying prospect of seeing him again had infused the translucent pallor of her cheeks with a faint bloom like that of a velvety peach, and the ardour in her lambent gaze belied her languishing demeanour as she took her seat, radiating beauty, while every lorgnette in the audience was trained on her—a fact that had not gone unheeded by Henk, nor indeed by Betsy. The concert had commenced with a lilting symphony, which had sounded to her as a hymn of love and happiness.

Then ... then he had made his entrance, to a resounding burst of applause.

While Eline stared dazedly into the glass, reliving the moment, the image came back to her in glaring detail.

Awkward, like a burly carpenter in a dress coat that was too tight, his coarse, frizzy hair plastered down with pomade, his face flushed crimson in contrast to his snowy shirtfront, he looked common and overweight, with a disagreeable, sullen expression about the bearded mouth and in the eyes glowering from under bushy eyebrows. She had felt as if she were seeing him for the first time. Without the grand theatrical gestures and lavish stage costumes that displayed his figure to uppermost advantage, the spell he had cast on her was suddenly broken, and while his voice resounded with the same clarion flourish that had filled her with rapture at the opera, she no longer registered it, so horrified was she by the enormity of her mistake.

How could she have been so blind? How could that common carpenter have been the ideal of her wildest imaginings? She could have wept with rage and disappointment, but her face remained impassive as she sat, straight-backed, almost stiffly, merely drawing the sides of her white plush cape together with a scarcely perceptible shudder. Constricted by emotion, her breathing became fast and shallow as she continued to fix him for as long as he sang, surveying him from head to toe, as though not wishing to spare her feelings. Could this be the same figure she had seen in the Wood, with his woollen scarf and the soft felt hat that gave him the dashing look of an Italian highwayman? What had come over her?

With a tremor of panic, she cast an eye about the audience. No one was paying attention to her, no one suspected her inner turmoil, for all ears and eyes were focused on Fabrice. No one knew, thank goodness, and no one ever would.

But she found no comfort in having escaped censure in the eyes of the world. At her feet lay the shattered remains of the glass palace she had conjured up in her lovesick imaginings, the airy, frangible edifice of her fantasy that she had erected column by column, towering ever higher in sparkling crystal splendour to an apotheosis in the clouds.

And now everything was ruined, all her visions and daydreams pulverised, blown away by a single gust of wind that did not even wreak havoc, for all that was left to her was a huge, aching void—and the spectacle of that tradesman type with the red face above the white shirtfront, the too-tight frock coat and the plastered-down hair.

She could not recall ever having felt so humiliated.

For three whole months the phantom of love and romance had made her heart beat faster each time she heard mention of him or happened to see his name on a poster, and yet now it had taken just one look at that unsightly, fat fellow—Vincent's words echoed mockingly in her ears—to rip every shred of romantic feeling from her being. It was gone, all gone.

Afterwards, in the foyer, she said very little. When Betsy remarked on her pallor and asked if she was all right, Eline replied coolly that she was indeed feeling a little under the weather. The Oudendijks and the van Larens were present, too; pleasantries were exchanged and Fabrice's name was mentioned, but Eline remained seated on a banquette like a wounded dove, almost swooning with grief, yet forcing herself to smile as she mimed attentiveness to the Hijdrecht boy.

After the intermission Fabrice came on again, to the same enthusiastic applause as the first time, and Eline felt crazed in her mind, as though the audience, mad with adulation, were about to dance a satanic jig around the baritone, who stood there looking as sullen, red-faced and ungainly as before. Her forehead was beaded with perspiration, her hands were ice-cold and clammy in the tight-fitting suede gloves, and her bosom heaved from the exertion of breathing with a lump in her throat. Thank goodness, the concert was over.

Alone at last, she allowed herself to surrender to the storm of emotion raging in her heart, and with an anguished cry fell to her knees beside the Persian sofa. She pressed her throbbing forehead to the soft cushions embroidered with gold, trying to stifle her racking sobs with her hands, and in so doing her hair came loose and tumbled about her slight, shaking frame in a mass of glossy waves.

The initial pain of disillusionment had ceded to a feeling of bitterness, as if she, even if only in her own eyes, had brought ridicule upon herself and disgrace, the stain of which would cling to her for ever, haunting her like a spectre of mockery.

For a long while she remained thus, immersed in her sorrow. She heard Henk and Betsy retire to their rooms, then Gerard bolting the street door for the night, the sound of which echoed hollowly in the silent house.

After that nothing stirred, and Eline felt very alone, drowning in an ocean of wretchedness.

All at once, a thought made her start. She scrambled to her feet, tossed back her tousled locks, and with a look of wounded pride on her tear-stained features strode to her writing table, her hand shaking as she slipped the key into the lock of the once-so-beloved compartment. She took out the album, whose red-velvet cover seemed to scorch her fingers like fire. She drew up a chair by the fire, where the log was still glowing amid the ashes, and opened the book. This, then, had been the shrine of her love, the temple of her passion, the secret place where she had worshipped her idol ... And as she turned the pages the portraits filed past in procession: Ben-Saïd, Hamlet, Tell, Luna, Nélusco, Alphonse, de Nevers ... This would be the last time ... Grappling with the gilt-edged album sheets, she pulled out the photographs one by one, and without the least hesitation tore each one in half and then in half again, crumpling the stiff cardboard with vengeful fingers. She threw the pieces in the grate one by one, waiting for each successive snippet to catch fire before throwing in the next, on and on, until she finally took the poker to stir up the embers in a final act of destruction ... That was that; over and done with.

She drew herself up, in some relief.

But she was still holding the ravaged album, its velvet cover scorching her fingers, and with a stifled cry of revulsion she hurled the offending object as far away as possible, breaking a fingernail in the process. The album struck the piano, eliciting a dull groan from the vibrating cords.

She stooped to retrieve her cape and lace fichu from the floor, smoothed the rumpled silk of her dress and stepped into her bedroom, where a small night light with a milky shade diffused a pallid, cheerless glow.

She felt herself sinking once more into that ocean of misery, that abyss of disillusionment from whose depths loomed only the black spectre of her melancholy, and suddenly her latest clash with Betsy darted into her mind. It had happened a few days before, when she made a remark about Roberts, her singing master; that he was getting on in years and not very good, really, and that she was thinking of taking lessons from a proper artiste instead—Fabrice, for instance—and Betsy had said she must be mad; it was a preposterous idea, and there was no way she would put up with such silly nonsense as long as Eline was living under her roof.

Well, there would be no need for her to put up with it now.

XV

THE WINTER COLD had abated, and the onset of spring brought heavy downpours and chilly days with veils of mist hanging from the leafless trees. There was much talk of Otto van Erlevoort and the attention he had been lavishing on Eline Vere. Oh, an engagement was bound to be announced very soon, agreed the Eekhofs, the Hijdrechts, the van Larens and Madame van der Stoor. Henk was away in Gelderland, as was Etienne; they were staying at Huis ter Horze, the van Erlevoort country estate, where Theodore, the eldest son, had made a home with his wife and children. In the meantime, Otto had paid several visits to Betsy and Eline; true, these were usually in response to an invitation to join other guests at the house on Nassauplein, but still, was it not quite remarkable that he, who generally led such a quiet life and went out so little, should be such a frequent visitor at the van Raat residence? In any case, an engagement would be splendid: Otto was a likeable enough fellow with a good position, while Eline was utterly charming, elegant and believed to have a fortune of her own. They seemed made for each other, and besides, Eline was bound to jump at the chance of having a baron for a husband. Indeed, they appeared so well suited that people were at pains to find anything to criticise about the match. In the end all they could come up with was that Betsy was finding it increasingly difficult to get along with Eline, which was common knowledge, and that she would doubtless be glad of some elegant way of being relieved of her sister; it was therefore in Betsy's interest to encourage Otto, not that Eline appeared unwilling, to be sure, but had it not been for Betsy neither he nor she might ever have thought of it. Oh, of course, Betsy was charming in society, but what she was like in private, as the mistress of her own home, was a different matter altogether. She had a strong will and could be quite a vixen, witness the way she kept good old Henk under her thumb! And if Eline had been more accommodating, if she had not stood up for herself, she too would have been under Betsy's thumb! It seemed so good and generous of Betsy to take in her orphaned sister, but with the kind of money the van Raats had this was of little consequence; besides, the Vere girls had substantial private means of their own, and nobody believed it was all sweetness and light in the house by any means. Clearly Betsy thought it was time her sister found herself a husband. Eline had received several proposals of marriage already, there had been plenty of suitors, but she was a very pretty girl, hard to please, and, well—it was all up to her, wasn't it?

Eline was aware that people were talking about her and Otto, but maintained her attitude of haughty indifference. Like everyone else, she thought Otto would certainly ask her to marry him, and she thought she would accept. What she felt for van Erlevoort was not love as she understood it, but there was no reason she could think of to turn him down. It would be a very good match in every sense, although, in her heart, she would have preferred his fortune to have been a little larger than it was. But it would do. Being astute with money herself, she knew there would be enough for her to create an appropriate illusion of grandeur.

That it was all down to Betsy's encouragement of Otto was not actually the case, for although she was much in favour of the marriage, she felt no particular sympathy for Otto. His manner was too stiff and studied for her liking, and she had to make an effort to treat him with the warmth merited by a potential brother-in-law.

The van Erlevoorts, too, were subjected to indiscreet questions from time to time, but Frédérique invariably responded with a dismissive shrug of the shoulders: Eline had been engaged so many times already—according to gossip at any rate—so why not with Otto for a change, she would say, with such irony in her tone that no one would guess the truth. However, it had not escaped her notice that her mother, Mathilda and Otto had been holding mysterious discussions behind her back, some sort of family council, the outcome of which was apparently still undecided.

She felt hurt at being left out, and was too proud, since they did not seem to place any value on her opinion, to show any further interest in the affair. Only the other day, coming upon her mama, sister and brother sitting together after dinner, she had noticed how the conversation had ceased as soon as she appeared, how they had started with slight embarrassment as she stood with her hand on the doorknob, and she had turned around without a word, softly closing the door behind her, filled with bitter resentment. Nor had she sought out Otto again after the conversation they had had about the fan, for didn't he regard her as a mere child? Very well then, she would not trouble him with her childish views any further. Only with Lili and Marie did she speak of Eline, calling her a vain coquette, all smiles and poses, without a spark of real feeling. When Paul was present she kept silent; he always took Eline's side nowadays—yet another person she had twisted round her finger! It was the same with Etienne, who wouldn't hear a word spoken against her. Frédérique couldn't imagine what on earth they saw in her; as far as she was concerned Eline was all artificiality and pretence, nothing but an actress.

Notwithstanding her irritation at Etienne's loyalty to Eline, Frédérique missed her brother now that he was away, and felt quite forlorn in the big house amid the noise and bustle of the van Rijssel foursome, Hector the dog and fat Nurse Frantzen's desperate attempts to call them to order.

It was Sunday, and Paul van Raat was sitting at his easel, contemplating a half-finished still life composed of some old pieces of Delftware, an antique Bible, a glass Rhine-wine goblet and the silver jug he had bought from Vincent—all loosely disposed on an artfully rumpled Smyrna table cover. But the work proceeded very slowly, the light in the room was unsatisfactory despite repeated attempts to adjust the curtains, and he was exasperated to find how much more adapted his fingers were to arranging the various items in a pleasing composition than to portraying them with oils on canvas. It was all the weather's fault: with such rainy skies it was impossible to catch any sparkle in the goblet, while the silver jug looked positively cheap. He laid aside his brush, thrust his hands in his pockets and, whistling tonelessly, began to pace the floor. He was troubled by his lack of energy, for, much as he wished to finish the picture, he found himself unable to continue.

The artistic chaos reigning in his room was matched by the chaos of his dilettantish temperament, which was hardly conducive to the creation of serious art. Above a carved-oak cabinet hung an array of antique weapons; the walls were covered up to the ceiling with porcelain, paintings and prints, and all about the room stood female figures in marble and terracotta, a veritable harem of milk-white and amber-coloured graces. Books abounded, and then there were the portfolios spilling sketches and prints, while the floor around the easel was strewn with tubes and paintbrushes of every description. The large ashtray overflowed, and there was dust everywhere, as Leentje, the maid, was seldom permitted to enter.

As he wandered about in dismal mood, it occurred to him that he might feel better if he not only did away with all these artistic accoutrements but also banished his easel and paintbrushes to the attic. Once his room was free of artefacts, he reasoned, his desire to create art would vanish of itself, and with it his sense of disillusionment. Because, if truth be told, it was just a waste of time, he was simply lacking in talent and could find better means of distraction than this fruitless dabbling in oils. His mind turned to ways of redecorating his room: he would keep it simple and uncluttered, so that one could move about at will without bumping into statues or tripping over oriental draperies. Still, it was too bad that it had all been an illusion, and having to dispose of the last vestiges of his artistic ambition was not something he looked forward to.

His thoughts were interrupted by the sound of Eline's bright voice in the hall, and he went downstairs. He entered the drawing room just as she was greeting his mother with an embrace. She had brought Ben, and had come on Betsy's behalf to invite his mother to dinner that evening at Nassauplein. The other guests would be Madame Eekhof and her daughters Ange and Léonie, Frédérique and two of her brothers, and Vincent.

"Of course we're counting on you, too, Paul!" she said, extending her hand to him. "That goes without saying. Dear lady, I do hope you won't disappoint us; so please say yes! We won't keep you beyond your usual hour, I promise. *Ce n'est pas à refuser.*"

Madame van Raat hesitated, saying she had reservations about her place in such youthful company.

"But it'll do you good! A little diversion will take you out of yourself! Think of Madame van Erlevoort," Eline persisted, "she finds it enjoyable enough! Why don't you take her as an example?"

Madame van Raat was touched by the dear girl's persuasive tone, and consented to come. Paul too accepted the invitation. Then she turned to Eline, who was seated beside her, and fixed her with a searching look, as though pondering some question in her mind. Meanwhile Paul, finding Ben annoyingly indolent as he sat quietly on a stool at his grandmother's feet, did his best to engage the child in some play.

"Now Eline dear, there is something I want to ask you," Madame van Raat began in a conspiratorial whisper. "Tell me, is it true?"

Eline felt a faint blush rising to her cheeks, but she pretended not to understand the question.

"I don't quite know what you mean."

Madame van Raat smiled. She did not pursue the subject further, merely asked: "Did you say Frédérique would be coming, too?"

"Yes, I expect so, only … " said Eline.

"Just her?"

"No, no, she'll be coming with her brothers, Otto and Etienne … "

"Oh, indeed," said the old lady with a casual air, but she gave Eline another long, knowing look, with something like a twinkle in her otherwise bleary gaze. Eline smiled, a trifle uneasily.

"I do believe you are teasing me," she said, stroking her muff.

"Oh, you know how people talk. One hears this and that and all manner of things, and yet, once in a while one hears something that's true."

"And what have you heard?"

"Something you would have told me yourself long ago if you had placed any confidence in me. Now I had to hear it from Betsy."

Eline gave a start.

"Did Betsy say? … " she faltered.

"Yes, my dear, she did, and I would much rather have heard it from you first," said the old lady petulantly.

Eline was secretly rattled. It was true, Otto had asked her to marry him—but she had not yet made up her mind about accepting, and it was so annoying how everyone seemed to be in the know, eager to offer their opinion, how they had the audacity to address all sorts of comments to Betsy, even quite blunt ones. There had even been someone who, under the pretext of sincere friendship, had whispered in her sister's ear that she should urge Eline to declare herself. All the indiscretions were getting on her nerves, and she was on the point of giving a sharp reply, but thought better of it. Showing no emotion, she murmured in the old lady's ear:

"Well, what was there to tell, really? Yes, van Erlevoort did propose to me, but I wasn't to say anything about it until I reached a decision."

She glanced at Paul, then quickly looked away, for he had stopped playing with Ben and was watching her keenly, trying to follow what was being said. But she had no intention of satisfying either his or Madame's curiosity, so she stood up, meaning to bring the conversation to an end at the earliest opportunity. When Madame van Raat said that Otto was a very personable young man in her opinion, Eline intervened by embracing her affectionately and said she ought to be going.

The old lady kissed her in return with tremulous insistence, and this irked her, as did the gleeful look in Paul's eyes, and her annoyance was compounded by having to wait for Ben, who was taking ages to bid his grandmother goodbye.

No, Eline could not make up her mind. She was fearful of taking a step that might make her happy or unhappy for life, as though her entire future now hinged on a single word, and she could not bring herself to utter it. Fearful too of a marriage of convenience, for she knew that her heart yearned for passionate love, despite her valiant efforts to suppress all such feelings after her disillusionment. As for Otto, well … she had danced with him, she had laughed and jested with him, but not for a single moment did she find herself picturing him in her mind, indeed she seemed to forget what he looked like the moment he was out of her sight. On the other hand, he was manifestly kind and sincere, and at first the realisation that he was in love with her had certainly been gratifying, so much so that she told herself it would pain her to cause him grief, or to refuse him anything, including her hand in marriage. And while she thus wilfully blinded herself, the gentleness of his quiet adoration seemed to pour balm on her wounded heart.

In her recent state of self-delusion, the thought of becoming his wife had lulled her into a sense of calm contentment, and something akin to a rosy future had risen before her eyes. Moreover, she had considered the financial advantages.

Another cheering prospect was that of gaining her independence, being her own mistress. At last she would be able to leave her sister's house, where, notwithstanding her private income, she always felt constrained and de trop, as if she were a demanding lodger whose presence was tolerated for appearance's sake alone. But beneath all these deliberations warming her to Otto's favours there lurked, like an unseen adder, the bitter regret at the shattering of her dreams, and if she ever gave herself to him it would be for the sake of revenge, revenge upon Fabrice, upon herself.

Yet now that Otto had actually proposed, now that she was obliged to come up with an answer in the absence of a grand, all-consuming passion, she had shied away from giving it.

Otto, for his part, bided his time; at least he was discreet.

For some days past he had avoided the van Raat residence. Eline thought he deserved a reward for his tact, so she ventured to ask Betsy—she could not help blushing a little—to invite him to an informal gathering with Freddie and Etienne.

He would come, she would speak to him, and she had a sense of no longer possessing a will of her own, as though some unseen power were pushing her down a steep slope towards her inevitable fate; she felt as though blindfolded, groping for her happiness, her hands outstretched, her ears straining to catch the faintest echo of that joy, yet knowing it would elude her for ever.

Betsy poured the tea. Sharing the sofa with her were her mother-in-law and Madame Eekhof, deep in conversation with Emilie de Woude; Henk stood with his hands in his pockets listening attentively to Vincent, while Eline, Paul and the Eekhof girls discussed the music books lying on the piano. Then Otto and Etienne arrived.

"Where's Frédérique?" asked Betsy in some surprise, as she held out her hand to Otto.

"Frédérique is feeling rather tired; she asked to be excused," he answered simply.

"She's often out of sorts these days," said Etienne with finality, as though to lend weight to his brother's words.

Eline's heart began to beat faster. She felt very nervous, although she succeeded in covering her emotion with a veneer of gaiety. She felt as if everyone in the room could guess what she was thinking, and hardly dared glance about for fear of seeing all eyes fixed upon her. But when she did venture to look up, nothing had changed: the old ladies were chatting with Betsy and Emilie, Vincent was talking in an undertone to Henk, and now Etienne was shaking hands with Paul and the girls.

Otto, however, came straight towards her. She was flustered, and feared that it showed, but her secret discomfort added a trace of tentativeness to her slim figure, which was very becoming. She heard him say good evening in his simple, unassuming way, but there was something warm and generous about his voice, which sounded to her like a promise of tenderness. Suddenly she felt a new emotion, a melting softness in her heart, which she did not comprehend.

He joined the small gathering by the piano, standing close to her but chatting with Ange while Léonie giggled at Etienne's flirtatious attentions. Now and then he glanced at her, seeking to involve her in their conversation about nothing; she smiled, without hearing what passed. Her ears buzzed with the confusion of voices, and she could not keep track of her thoughts, which flittered about her brain like so many butterflies.

She knew she had to resist lapsing into one of her soothing meditations; she could hardly stand there daydreaming in the middle of a salon full of people, and after making one or two light remarks in a voice she hardly recognised as her own, so muffled did it sound, she moved away.

"You play too, don't you, Vincent?" she heard Betsy ask, while out of the corner of her eye she saw the ladies rising from the sofa and Henk moving to the salon, where he proceeded to take the mother-of-pearl counters from a Japanese box. She felt she was dreaming. She saw the cards spread out on the circular red cloth in the shape of an S; she saw the candles burning at the corners of the table, she saw Madame Eekhof's bejewelled fingers drawing a card.

Everything seemed to be happening in the remote distance. Vincent seated himself opposite Madame van Raat; Henk was to be partnered with Madame Eekhof. Betsy came up with Emilie in tow; they would take a turn later.

"Would it be all right if we made some music, or are they very serious about their game?" Léonie asked Betsy, pointing to the card table.

"Oh by all means, *amusez-vous toujours!*" responded Betsy, inviting Otto and Emilie to join her on the sofa. Her manner with those outside her family was unfailingly gracious.

"Go on, Eline, do let us hear you! We're dying to hear your lovely siren song!" Léonie continued, in irrepressible high humour. "And I shall play the accompaniment with my light-as-fairy fingers."

"Oh no, Léonie, please. I'm not in voice this evening."

"Not in voice? I don't believe you! Come! *Allons, chante ma belle!* What is it to be?"

"Yes, Eline, do sing for us!" called Madame van Raat from the adjoining salon, after which she anxiously asked her partner what was the meaning of trumps.

"No really, madame, I cannot; no, Léo, not today. I can always tell when I'm not in voice, and I hardly ever refuse, do I? But didn't you say you had brought some music with you?"

"Yes, but they aren't the right sort of songs to start the evening with; we can have them later. Let's have something serious first—please, Eline, I beg you."

"No, I can't possibly!" said Eline, shaking her head. It was out of the question: she felt herself in a fever with the blood rising to her cheeks, her eyelids drooping, her pulse throbbing, her fingers trembling. She would never be able to contain her vibrato, she had no voice today.

"Can't possibly?" she heard someone murmur behind her, and glanced round. It was Otto, gazing at her admiringly from the sofa he was sharing with Betsy and Emilie. Again she shook her head from side to side. She felt awkward as she did so, although she looked artlessly alluring to the others.

"Really, I could not ... "

She quickly averted her face, in case he might suspect the cause of her reluctance. Meeting his gaze had greatly embarrassed her, even though there was no trace of reproof in his eyes. She had a feeling there was something afoot among the friends and relations filling the adjoining rooms with their animated conversation. The atmosphere was charged, somehow, and yet, she reasoned, Betsy and Madame van Raat were the only ones there who knew that Otto had already proposed and that an answer would be expected of her this very evening. But whatever the others might suspect, they would not be so indiscreet as to press her to reveal her secret before she was ready; thankfully, they were too well bred for that.

Léonie accused Eline of being a spoilsport, whereupon Paul and Etienne clamoured for Léonie to sing instead, and offered to fetch her music book for her from the vestibule, where she had left it out of false modesty. They started for the door, but Léonie tried to stop them, causing an abrupt, frolicsome stir, at which the whist-players looked up from their cards. Etienne squeezed past her, and soon returned in triumph, waving the dog-eared score of *La Mascotte*. The Eekhof girls were duly persuaded, and launched into a laughing, halting, high-pitched rendition of the duet between Pippo and Bettina.

"*O, mon Pipo, mon Dieu, qu't'es bien!*" they sang, while Etienne played the accompaniment, frequently striking doubtful chords.

But everyone was delighted anyway, which emboldened Etienne and Paul to join in. They did so with great gusto, and the foursome warbled on in blithe disregard of both time and tune, lingering over the dreamy 'Un baiser c'est bien douce chose' and brightening over the comical air of 'Le grand singe d'Amérique'.

Eline sat on a pouffe, leaning her fevered temple against the piano, almost deafened by Etienne's vigorous striking of the keys. She was tapping her hand on her knee in time to the music so as to appear interested, but her ears ached from the thrum of the instrument, and the noise prevented her from thinking and making a decision. Her emotions kept swinging from one extreme to the other. Yes, she would accept him: his love, albeit unrequited, would make her happy, it was her fate … No, she could not go against her deepest feeling, she could not allow herself to be shackled to someone she did not love. She grew quite giddy from swinging back and forth like a pendulum, it was as if there were a clock thudding in her brain: yes, no, yes, no … What a relief it would be simply to shut her eyes and point at random to the answer. But no, she owed it to herself to think things through properly. If only that clock would stop ticking … she was in no condition to battle with her emotions, she was too frail.

She would cease all meditation, she would surrender to the invisible forces pushing her down that steep slope, she would give herself up entirely to the circumstances of the moment—let them decide. Her eyes met Otto's, and a tremor ran down her spine. She rose.

Vincent got up from the whist table; Betsy took his place.

"Well, Elly, have you thought of anything outrageous yet?" asked Vincent, imitating her tone.

The piano had fallen silent. Léonie had gone to sit with Emilie, and was giving her a vivid description of a recent dance hosted by the van Larens. Etienne spun round on the piano stool, which made Ange laugh so much that she collapsed onto the pouffe with her hands covering her face. Paul, laughing too, leafed through some sheet music.

"What? How do you mean?" faltered Eline.

"Remember you told me a while ago how you wanted to do something outrageous? Well, I'm only asking if you've thought of anything yet. I'll gladly join in."

His jocular manner irked her. In her present, unusually serious frame of mind, the mention of that frivolous outburst held an echo of her vanished hopes. No, she had no desire to indulge in anything in the least shocking or foolhardy; she wished to be sensible, as sensible as Otto was. It had been folly enough to allow herself to be disappointed in love, if she could call her craze thus, and she would never let her emotions run away with her again.

She struggled to ward off the bitter regret rearing its ugly head like an adder in her soul.

Groping for some light-hearted reply to Vincent's banter, she was seized with alarm. A new thought suddenly imposed itself. No, there was no turning back. Otto and Betsy were obviously expecting her to accept. Why would she have asked Betsy to invite him to an intimate gathering if she merely wished to see him? Surely she would have written him a note otherwise? She had made her decision, that was that, and the panic of a moment ago gave way to a sense of immense calm flooding her entire being.

"But my dear girl, I do believe your mind's rambling!" laughed Vincent. He had asked her why Georges de Woude was not in attendance, and she had murmured distractedly:

"Oh, isn't he here?"

This made Eline laugh, too, now that she was herself again. They sat down.

"Forgive me, I have a slight—" she murmured, touching her finger to a stray curl at her temple.

"Ah, a headache! I know all about them," he said, observing her quizzically. "I believe it's a family complaint, we Veres are prone to headaches."

She looked up at him, startled. Had he guessed anything?

"I had one myself just now; it was the music that brought it on—you know, all that banging on the piano. It was just as if I could see all sorts of lurid colours, green, yellow and orange. Whenever that vivacious young lady—Léonie, I believe her name is—begins to sing, I see orange."

"And what about when I sing? What do you see then?" she asked coquettishly.

"Ah that's completely different," he replied gravely. "Whenever you sing I see a harmonious plethora of pinks and purples, all soft and melting. Your low notes are pink, the high ones purple and shiny. When Paul sings everything goes grey, with a tinge of violet at times."

She began to laugh, as did Paul, who had overheard the last remark.

"But Vincent, you're hallucinating!"

"Maybe so. Still, it's an extraordinary sensation, seeing colours like that. Has it never happened to you?"

She reflected a moment, while Ange and Etienne, having caught what Vincent was saying, came closer.

"No, I don't think it has."

"Don't you ever find that certain musical notes remind you of a particular fragrance, such as opopanax or reseda? The sound of an organ is like incense. Hearing you sing Beethoven's *Ah Perfido* always brings back the scent of verbena for me, especially one of the high passages at the end. Next time you sing it I'll tell you exactly which one."

Ange giggled.

"Oh, Mr Vere, how wonderful it must be to have such a keen sense of smell!"

Everyone smiled, and Vincent too seemed in high spirits.

"But it's true, *parole d'honneur*."

"I'll tell you what: some people remind me of animals," whispered Etienne. "Henk, for instance, reminds me of a big dog, Betsy of a hen and Madame van der Stoor of a crab."

Peals of laughter ensued, at which Otto, Emilie and Léonie, rose from their seats and drew near.

"What's so funny?" asked Emilie eagerly,

"Madame van der Stoor is a crab!" hooted Ange, with tears in her eyes from laughing.

"And me, Etienne, what do I remind you of?" demanded Léonie.

"Oh, you and Ange are a pair of puppy dogs, woof, woof," cried Etienne. "As for Miss de Woude," he whispered in Ange's ear, "she reminds me of a turkey, with her double chin. Miss Frantzen's a turkey, too, of a slightly different kind. Willem the manservant is a dignified stork, and Dien, the Verstraetens' old housemaid, is a cockatoo."

"What a menagerie! A veritable Noah's ark!" tittered Léonie.

"And Eline?" asked Paul.

"Ah, Eline," echoed Etienne dreamily. "Sometimes she's a peacock, sometimes a serpent, but right now she's a little dove."

They all laughed heartily, shaking their heads at his extravagant fancies.

"Etienne is always jolly," Eline remarked to Otto when the little group had dispersed; she turned to smile and wave at Madame van Raat, who had ceded her place at the whist table to Emilie. Vincent, meanwhile, was besieged by the Eekhof girls clamouring to know whether he planned to start a perfumery store.

"Yes, indeed," said Otto. "Etienne is very jolly. He has every reason to be so, since he has everything he could wish for."

His tone was a touch wistful, as if for him that were not the case, and Eline could not think of any reply. For a while they remained standing side by side, wordlessly. She extended her hand to touch the plumes in the Makart bouquet, and the turmoil in her mind began again.

"Have you nothing to say to me?" he murmured. There was no trace of reproach in his voice.

She took a deep breath.

"Truly, I … Oh, not just yet, please forgive me. Later, I promise, in a while … "

"All right, later. I will be patient—for as long as I am able," he said, and his calm voice soothed the tangled web of her emotions. She could not refuse him now, but neither could she declare herself.

She felt a rush of admiration for his tact and gentleness as he continued to converse on various topics that held little interest for either of them. That unassuming nature was in fact his greatest asset, that was why people liked him so much; he was so sincerely himself that he seemed incapable of having any secrets he might prefer to keep hidden. While he spoke he made no pretence of discussing anything of the slightest importance, he simply wished to remain standing beside her, and for that he needed to engage her attention—it was all so evident in the warm resonance of his voice. His mind was not in the conversation, and he didn't even care if she noticed. For the first time she felt something like pity for him. She was being cruel, she was making him suffer, and again she felt that strange, melting softness in her heart.

Gerard went round bearing silver trays laden with refreshments.

"Would you like a sorbet, madame, and a pastry?" Eline asked Madame van Raat, who was sitting alone on the sofa looking rather forlorn, although she smiled now and then at the cluster of young people telling each other's fortunes with the cards.

"Look," she said to Otto. "Henk's Mama is all by herself, I had better go and keep her company."

He nodded kindly and went to listen to the horoscope Ange was drawing for Paul. Eline beckoned Gerard and took a sorbet and a pastry from the tray, which she offered to Madame van Raat. Then she seated herself beside the old lady and took her hand.

Ignoring the refreshments, Madame van Raat looked into Eline's eyes.

"Well, what is it to be?" asked Madame.

In her state of melting tenderness, Eline wasn't even annoyed by the old lady's persistence. She replied very softly, almost inaudibly:

"I … I shall say yes."

She sighed, and felt the tears welling up in her eyes as she heard herself speak. Yes, she would accept. She could find nothing more to say to the old lady, for that one statement filled her mind so completely that it absorbed every other thought. They sat together a moment in silence, with their backs half turned to the cheerful gathering across the room. Suddenly Eline became aware of Ange's shrill voice reading out the cards one by one.

"Now listen carefully, Mr van Erlevoort. I'm much cleverer at this than Madame Lenormand, you know. Here's yours: King of Hearts. You are in a vale of tears, I see, but not for long. You shall be very rich, and you shall live in a chateau in the Pyrenees. Or would you prefer a villa in Nice? Ah! There she is! The Queen of Hearts! You are rather far apart, but all the cards in between are favourable. You will have to overcome many obstacles to reach her, for she is much sought-after: look, here's the King of Clubs, and the King of Diamonds, and there's even a commoner, a social democrat if you please, the Jack of Spades!"

"Ooh, Black Jack!" cried Léonie. "Fie on him!"

Eline smiled wanly, brushing away a tear that clung to her lashes, and Madame van Raat smiled too.

"There, see how splendidly those aces are turning up!" Ange pursued excitedly. "Have no fear, Mr van Erlevoort, have no fear, it's all clearing up nicely."

"The cards seem to bode well," murmured Madame van Raat.

Eline smiled with pursed lips, but she was unnerved. Black Jack had reminded her of Fabrice.

The whist players had risen, and everyone was talking at once. The fortune-telling had given rise to merriment all round, and when Ange prophesied that Etienne would never marry, he protested vehemently, saying he had no intention of remaining a bachelor all his life.

Ange and Léonie then prevailed upon Paul to sing a piece by Massenet, to Léonie's accompaniment. While he sang, Betsy kept a watchful eye on her sister and Otto; she was sure that nothing had transpired between them as yet. Why was Eline being so coy? Betsy herself had not made such a fuss in her day, she had accepted van Raat's stammered proposal quite graciously. What was Eline dithering about? What reason could she possibly have to reject van Erlevoort? They were made for each other. She was annoyed by her sister's sentimental wavering when she had the opportunity of marrying into a good family, and a man in a fair position to boot. Her glance rested coldly on Eline's slender frame, to which that very wavering quality lent an additional allure, and Betsy noted this, as she noted the unwonted earnestness in her sister's demeanour. What a to-do about such a simple matter! But when her eye fell on her husband, who was chatting to Otto, she felt even more annoyed. What a simpleton he was! Did he really have no idea why Otto was dining at their house tonight?

Madame van Raat had already left, later than was her habit and in considerable disappointment, for she had been hoping to hear the announcement of Eline's engagement in the intimate setting of her son's home. It was now past midnight; Madame Eekhof and her daughters took their leave, as did Emilie. Vincent and Paul also prepared to go, while Henk and Etienne escorted the high-spirited girls down the hall to their carriage.

Betsy, Eline and Otto stayed behind in the ante-room. An awkward silence fell. Then Betsy went through to the salon, where she busied herself tidying the card table.

Eline felt the ground crumble beneath her feet. She could not hide her confusion from Otto, who, although he had not meant to impose on her a second time this evening, found himself unable to resist the temptation to do so, since they were alone.

"Eline," he whispered in a choked voice, "must I really leave you like this, without an answer?"

She held her breath a moment in fright; then, with a shuddering sigh, she murmured:

"Otto … truly, I … I cannot … not yet!"

"Goodnight, then, please forgive me for asking again," he said, and with that he lightly pressed her fingers and left.

She, however, suddenly felt herself melting away. Quaking all over, she almost fell to the floor, but saved herself by clutching the door curtain for support, and she cried out, in full surrender to the tide of her emotion:

"Otto! Otto!"

A low cry escaped him as he came running back to catch her in his arms, and beaming with joy he drew her into the ante-room again.

"Eline, Eline!" he cried. "Is it true?"

She did not speak, but flung herself sobbing, broken, defeated, against his chest, and felt his arms tighten about her.

"So you … you will be my wife?"

She ventured to lift her face to him, locked in his embrace, and answered him only with her tearful gaze and a fleeting smile.

"Eline, my angel," he whispered, pressing his lips to her fore-head.

From the salon came the sound of voices: Henk and Etienne had returned from the vestibule, Etienne in his greatcoat, holding his hat in his hand.

"What's keeping Otto?" Eline heard him exclaim, and she also heard Betsy whisper something in reply.

Otto looked down, smiling at Eline's emotion as she wept with her cheek to his chest.

"Shall we?" he said simply, radiating joy.

Slowly, very slowly she allowed him to lead her towards the salon, softly sobbing in his arms, her face buried in his shoulder. Betsy came towards them, smiling, and darted a glance of complicity at Otto as she shook his hand. Henk and Etienne were taken completely by surprise.

"Van Raat, may I … may I introduce you to my fiancée?" said Otto.

Henk too began to smile, while Etienne grinned from ear to ear and rolled his eyes.

"What a sly old fox you are!" he exclaimed, wagging his finger at his brother. "Keeping us in the dark like this!"

But Eline, still in tears, broke away from Otto's embrace and flung her arms around Henk's neck. He kissed her, and mumbled in his deep voice:

"Well, well, little sister, I congratulate you with all my heart! Now then, don't cry, no need for that, is there? Come on, give me a smile, there's a good girl."

She hid her face in her hands, which moved Betsy to step forward and smooth a stray curl from her sister's forehead before kissing her too.

"I'm so glad my little soirée turned out so well!" she said pointedly.

Henk wanted Otto to stay a little longer when Etienne discreetly made to slip away, but Eline murmured faintly that she was ever so tired, so Otto declined. He was too elated to wish for anything more: he would go, brimming with joy. And she thought it very sweet of him simply to shake her hand in farewell instead of kissing her in front of everyone.

As soon as the brothers had gone Eline fled to her room, where she came upon Mina lighting the lamp. The maids had already heard the news from Gerard, who had entered the salon at an inopportune moment, and Mina congratulated her, peering at her with an inquisitive smile.

"Thank you, Mina … thank you," stammered Eline.

Alone at last, she glanced in the mirror, and was shocked to see the tear-streaked pallor of her cheeks. But the next instant she felt as though her soul were sliding into a tranquil, blue lagoon, she felt the still waters close over her and found herself in what appeared to be realm of eternal peace, a nirvana of hitherto unimagined beatitude.

XVI

IT WAS A FRESH, bright day in May, after a week of nothing but rain and chilly mist. Jeanne had sent the children—Dora, Wim and Fritsje—for a walk in the Scheveningen woods with the nursemaid while she stayed behind, as there was always so much to do. She now felt lonely and forlorn in the cramped apartment over the grocer's shop, sitting there all by herself, doing the mending in the pallid ray of sunlight that she now welcomed in her abode, without a thought for her carpet and curtains. Frans was out; he had taken the train to Amsterdam to consult a specialist. It was now half-past one, she established, glancing at the mantel clock ticking loudly in the quiet room. Frans would not be back until about half-past five. The intervening hours seemed to her like an eternity, for all that she was glad of the chance to work without interruption.

When the sunbeam slanted on her face she did not mind; on the contrary, she basked in its feeble warmth. The light shimmered about her light-brown hair, giving her pale, sunken cheeks an alabaster translucence; it shimmered, too, over the slender, delicate fingers plying the needle with practised regularity. Oh, how she longed for the summer! She could not wait for May to end—all that damp, misty weather they'd been having, and so rarely a clear day! How silly of her to have expected this month of May to live up to the exalted reputation it had among all those Romantic poets!

She smiled sadly as she bent over her sewing, pressing the seam down with her nail as she stitched. How curious it was the way her illusions, even the most modest ones, kept vanishing into thin air while her life rolled on, and how the future, which held an unspeakable dread for her, kept receding to make way for the monotonous reality of her day-to-day existence. She shuddered at the presentiment lurking in her soul like a shrouded ghost, the fear that some catastrophe would strike and crush them all. Pressing her hands to her chest, she took a deep, quaking breath, and shuddered again, not for herself, not for her husband, but for her children.

She stood up. She found it impossible to continue her work, and yet she should not be idle on the rare sunny day when the children were out and there was no one to disturb her. Oh, why was she not stronger? She leant against the window, relishing the sunshine like a pale hothouse flower craving light and air, and looked down on the square patch of garden at the back of the grocery. A lilac bush was budding into leaf, but there was nothing growing in the central flower bed or along the sides, and suddenly she had a vision of Persian roses, like the ones they had grown on their estate at Temanggoeng, a riot of pink blooms diffusing the sweetest of fragrances. She could smell them now, and the remembrance of the blushing roses seemed to drive her cares away, leaving only a sense of mild nostalgia for warmth and love.

She was standing thus when the doorbell rang; a moment later Mathilda van Rijssel came in.

The two women had met a few times at the van Raats', and had found that they had a sympathy for one another.

"I have come with an ulterior motive, I must confess, because I want you to take a walk with me," said Mathilda warmly. "It's such pleasant weather, and it would do you good to take some air."

"But Tilly, the children are out, and so is Frans. So I really ought to take advantage and get some work done."

"Well, can't I tempt you anyway?" persisted Mathilda. "It's not as if you have to guard the house, is it?"

"No, but the children ... they'll be back soon, and what if they don't find me at home?"

"Oh really, Jeanne, they'll survive. You spoil them. And as for your husband being out, well, that's hardly a reason for you to stay in, is it? So please put on your hat and coat, there's a sensible girl, and come with me. You can catch up on your sewing when it rains."

Jeanne was only too relieved to be taken in hand by her new friend, in whose kind voice, even when jesting, there was an undercurrent of despondence. That was settled, then, she would go, and she ran upstairs to change, humming under her breath.

She was ready in no time, and after repeated admonitions to Mietje she accompanied Mathilda into the street. The cool breeze cleared her head and brought a little colour to her pale cheeks as her friend chatted on, explaining that she had just dropped Tina and Jo off at Nassauplein because Betsy and Eline were taking Ben on an outing and had invited the older children along.

"And the little ones?" asked Jeanne.

"Oh, Mama insisted on taking Madeleine and Nico for a walk, she dotes on her grandchildren so. Dear Mama!"

Having reached the end of Laan van Meerdervoort, they turned into the road to Scheveningen. There were few people about. Mathilda felt invigorated by the fresh air and, contrary to her habit, grew talkative.

"You have no idea how good Mama is to me," she said. "All she cares about is the family, her children and her grandchildren. She never thinks of herself, her entire life is dedicated to us. And I'm sure that if you asked her which one of us she loves the most she'd be unable to tell you. Of course she worships Etienne, he's always as happy as a sandboy, and he makes her laugh, but I have no doubt whatsoever that she's equally devoted to Frédérique and Otto, and to my little ones, too. And she's always sending letters to her far-flung offspring complaining that she doesn't see enough of them. You can imagine how affected she was when Catherine and Suzanne left home to marry. What she would really like, I do believe, is to build a sort of hotel so that she could have all of us to live with her: Theodore, Howard, Stralenburg and all the rest. Dear, kind Mama!"

Neither of them spoke for a while. The lane stretched ahead like a grey ribbon, affording a long perspective of tree trunks beneath a tracery of budding branches. The sunlight glinted on the greeny-yellow leaves unfurling against the bright blue sky, the time-worn trunks were clad in new velvety moss, and the twitter of birdsong sounded crystalline in the clear air.

"How lovely it is here!" said Mathilda. "So refreshing. But let's take one of the footpaths. Then we won't have to see those people over there, and they won't have to see us. We humans look out of place in natural surroundings. People spoil the view, I find, especially in spring, when everything is so intensely green … I'm waxing philosophical, would you believe!"

Jeanne laughed. She felt quite elated; the world was full of beauty and goodness, full of love, too, and her thoughts turned to Frans …

They sat down on a bench for a rest, and Jeanne ventured to ask:

"What about you, Mathilda? You always talk about your mama, never about yourself."

Mathilda gave a start.

"About me? I do my best not to think about myself … I … I'm nothing, nothing without my children. I'd do anything for my little ones. If it weren't for them I'd be dead."

The sadness of her words belied the resignation of her tone.

"Imagine believing you are happily married to a loving husband for whom you would sacrifice body and soul, and then waking up one day to find … But let's not talk about that now; it's all in the past."

"Is the memory of it too painful?"

"Oh no, not any more, but there was a time when the pain was so bad that I thought I was losing my mind, and I blamed God for my suffering. But since then the pain has become a blur, and I don't feel it any more. I never think of it, I only think of my four darlings. And they keep me far too busy to mope about the past. You know I have been tutoring them at home, don't you? But it's time Tina and Jo went to school, I suppose, at least that's what Otto says, but I'd miss them terribly, and of course Mama agrees with me about this. I do love them so!"

Jeanne thought she detected a hint of bitterness in Mathilda's voice, and reached out to take her friend's hand.

"You poor dear," she whispered.

"Yes, I am," replied Mathilda simply. "Poorer than you, anyway, because at least you are a wife as well as a mother!" She tried to smile, and her eyes filled with tears as she pursued: "I know you aren't having an easy time of it by any means, but you aren't as poor as I am. You can think of that as a consolation when you feel low, just think of me and how much I'd envy you if I didn't feel quite so ... so dead inside."

"Oh, Mathilda, it pains me to hear you say such a thing!"

"Well, there's no reason why it should, since I don't feel the pain any more myself. It's only a far-off memory of something that's over and done with, you know. That's all. Still, it's better not to talk about it, let bygones be bygones."

"Oh, Mathilda, how can you bear to keep it all bottled up inside you? I could never do that, I'd have to pour my heart out to someone—"

"No, Jeanne, no! I mean it! Don't ever mention the subject again, I beg you, or I ... I might come alive again."

She leant against the back of the park bench, her eyes brimming with tears. Dressed all in black, ashen-faced, she resembled an icon of infinite, lacerating woe.

She did not wish to come alive again; she wished she were dead.

Jeanne wanted to be back by the time Frans returned, so they set off homewards.

"Oh dear, I'm afraid I've made you sad, while all I wanted was to take your mind off things with a pleasant stroll," said Mathilda. "That comes of all my philosophising. I do hope you'll forgive me."

Jeanne could find nothing to say, so she merely shook her head with a smile to show that no, she was not sad. And it was true: deep in her heart she had to admit that while she had at first been distressed by Mathilda's quiet despair, she realised, now that Mathilda had resumed her air of acceptance and self-possession, that the pity she felt for her friend made her own troubles appear positively trivial by comparison. Had she herself suffered a tragedy like Mathilda's, she would never have got over it. She reproached herself for ever feeling ungrateful for all the good that had been bestowed on her, and felt remorse at having grumbled about her domestic circumstances while she had been spared so much misfortune! And dear Frans … he had his flaws, naturally, he could be short-tempered and churlish with her when he was unwell, but he always came round quite quickly once he realised he was in the wrong. And he cared for her. He loved her. Her heart lifted with pride, and she found she could no longer be sad out of pity for Mathilda. That was selfish of her, but never mind, such moments of sweet satisfaction with the circumstances of her life were so fleeting and so rare—surely a moment's egotism couldn't do any harm?

Arriving at the grocery, Mathilda said goodbye and proceeded on her way. Jeanne, left to herself in her upstairs apartment, was eager for her children to return. They soon appeared, fresh-faced from their outing, and she hugged and kissed each one in turn, wanting to know exactly where they had gone and what games they had played, and when Dora pulled a long face she did her best to make her daughter smile again with a joke and a romp. No, indeed all was quite well with the world.

XVII

LILI WAS READING A BOOK IN THE DRAWING ROOM when the doorbell rang. It was Frédérique, making her final call of the afternoon.

"Where's Marie? Is she not in?" asked Freddie.

"Yes she is," responded Lili. "We went out earlier, but she's upstairs now."

"Upstairs? How odd," said Frédérique. "She always seems to be upstairs when I call. You haven't fallen out, have you?"

"Oh no, not at all," replied Lili. "She's probably drawing, or else writing."

"Writing what? A letter?"

"Oh no, it's a novella, I think, or something like that. But don't say anything, will you? I think she means to keep it a secret."

After a pause, Frédérique asked, "Do you find Marie changed lately?"

"Changed? Marie? No, I haven't noticed anything. Why do you ask?"

"Oh, no reason, it's just that she seems forever occupied nowadays."

"But she's always been like that, she's always busy, just like Jan; I'm the only lazybones in the family, according to Papa."

Frédérique made no reply. She was surprised that Lili had not noticed how edgy and reclusive her sister had become lately, but she told herself she was probably imagining it all, or Lili would not have been so dismissive.

"You know we're going to the Oudendijks' this evening, don't you?" she said, to change the subject.

"Yes, you mentioned the invitation. Ah, so you'll be going. Just as well, too, because you've been awfully dull lately, haven't you? Becoming indisposed each time you were invited, so it seems to me," jested Lili.

"Well, I was upset," said Frédérique. "It was ... well, it was because of Otto's crush on Eline. But all that's settled now, and I've washed my hands of the whole affair. He knows best, I suppose. Anyway, it's no use fretting, because ... "

She broke off, her eyes becoming moist and her lips tightening with suppressed emotion.

"But Freddie," Lili said softly, "he's known her for such a long time, ever since she moved in with the van Raats, and if he loves her—"

"Oh, I just want everything to turn out for the good, and I hope they'll be very happy. The trouble is, I cannot abide Eline. Of course I do my best to be nice to her, but you know how hard it is for me to hide my feelings. Oh, do let's talk about something else. It can't be helped, in any case, and I'd rather not think about it either. Shall we go and look for Marie?"

Lili consented, and off they went upstairs, where they found Marie seated at the small writing table in the sitting room shared by the two sisters. Several pages of writing lay before her, but now she sat with one hand propping up her cheek and the other making squiggles on a blank sheet of paper. She gave a start when Freddie and Lili came in.

"We've come to distract you," announced Freddie, smiling broadly. "Unless you'd rather be left in peace, of course."

"Oh no, not at all. And Lili never keeps me company, anyway."

Lili made no comment. Her sister was being unfair, she thought, because it had been Marie's idea to go upstairs by herself, not hers, neither were they in the habit of spending the afternoon together in their sitting room.

"What have you been writing? Or is it a secret?" asked Freddie with a sidelong glance at the sheets of notepaper.

"No, not a secret," replied Marie with feigned indifference. "It's something I started a while ago, a sort of travel diary of the excursions we went on last year, to Thüringen and the Black Forest, and I meant to turn it into a little story. But I'm bored with it now. I don't know why I started it in the first place, really. It's not like me to want to write stories, is it now?"

"Why ever not?" said Freddie with enthusiasm. "Won't you read us something?"

"Certainly not! Bore you with my schoolgirl prose? What do you take me for? It's just something to keep me busy, that's all. I was bored, so I took up writing, just as Lili has taken up reading. Do you know what I think, Freddie?" Marie pulled a comically serious face. "I think we're getting old! Yes, downright old I say, and dreary to boot. Do you realise it's been months since we had a good laugh the way we used to?"

"Or with Paul and Etienne!" said Lili.

"With or without them. We girls used to have such fun! But nowadays ... I don't know about you, but I think we're all getting to be as dull as ditchwater! There's you, down in the dumps because you don't like Eline, and Lili going all quiet and sentimental, spending all her time daydreaming, and here I am writing about blue mountains and hazy vistas out of sheer boredom."

"Where will it all end?" laughed Freddie. "Yes, the future looks very dismal, especially in your case. I bet there's some secret lurking behind those blue mountains and distant panoramas."

"A secret?" echoed Marie. "Oh no, nothing like that. Nothing at all." She touched her hand to her temple, and Frédérique thought she was brushing away a tear. Lili concentrated on rearranging the books in one of the cabinets.

"Marie!" said Frédérique softly. "If there's anything I can do to help, I wish you'd say so. I can see perfectly well that you are upset about something. Why keep it to yourself?"

Marie stood up and averted her face.

"Why Freddie, you shouldn't jump to conclusions! You're as bad as Lili, seeing romantic reasons for everything. There's nothing the matter, except that I'm rather bored, and I'd love to have some fun for a change. Well, hello there, master Jan!"

Jan stood in the doorway with a quizzical look.

"What are you three up to? Gossiping about your beaus, I bet," he said.

"Have you ever heard such presumption!" exclaimed Marie, throwing her hands up in horror. "It's your inborn male vanity making you say that, mere stripling though you are; just you wait, I'll show you!"

She began to chase him round the table while he laughed and ducked this way and that, quickly putting chairs in her path whenever he could, much to Freddie's and Lili's amusement. Suddenly he dashed out of the room, with Marie at his heels.

"What's got into Marie?" wondered Freddie. A few moments later Marie returned, quite out of breath.

"Did you catch him?" asked Lili.

"Of course not," responded Marie. "That boy's as quick as greased lightning, and as nimble as a mountain goat too! Oh, how good it feels to run … I wish I were a boy!"

When Frédérique made to leave, Lili accompanied her downstairs; Marie said she would be down shortly.

But she lingered by the window and gazed outside, where the fading light was veiling the world with a transparent, ashen haze. She could see the canal, green and still beneath leafy overhanging boughs, and the avenue dozing beyond, melting into the dewy dusk.

She took a deep breath. She would banish that cruel sense of regret from her heart once and for all, as she had already begun doing this afternoon. She was getting old, decidedly old, she felt, she was becoming dull and weighed down with cares. But she would be brave, she would have no self-pity, she would crush the blossom within her soul, revile that vision, blot it out. It was torture, but she owed it to herself.

And as she stared vacantly into the gathering darkness, the face of her beloved rose up before her. She saw his fine head, the warm fidelity of his gaze, his kind expression, his heart-warming smile. But he was smiling at Eline, not at her.

The tramcars running between Oude Scheveningseweg and the Kurhaus were packed. At the junction of Anna Paulownastraat and Laan Copes van Cattenburch they were stormed by the waiting throng and rapidly filled to overflowing, both inside and out. There was much pushing and stepping on toes, and even ladies colourfully attired in fluttery summery dresses joined the feverish scramble for places. The bell clanged, the horses started up, and all the passengers who had managed to climb on board smiled triumphantly as the conductor shouted to the crestfallen people left behind, who promptly turned away to face the arrival of the next tram.

"Such crowds! How dreadful!" said Eline, observing the commotion with a serene smile.

She was seated next to Betsy in the open landau, facing Henk and Otto. Dirk the coachman had been obliged to halt a moment, but now the long line of vehicles began to move again. Herman, the young groom in pale-grey livery with shiny buttons, sat bolt upright with his arms folded across his chest and his lips pursed in an expression of self-importance.

"There are bound to be lots of people," said Betsy. "But as it's in the open air, there will be enough places, so we needn't fret."

Not a breath of wind stirred the dense foliage, and after a day of soaring temperatures the gathering dusk brought little relief. The air seemed torpid, leaden. Eline leant back in her seat, looking rather wan from the heat; she spoke little, merely glanced at Otto from time to time through hooded eyes, with a hint of coquettish contentment. Betsy was chatting away to van Erlevoort, as Henk found little to say. His mind was on other things, such as how much more pleasant it would have been to have stayed at home and taken tea in the garden instead of rushing off to Scheveningen immediately after dinner.

Betsy, however, felt on top of the world, relishing the sultry evening air, the soft padding of her well-appointed landau, which compared so favourably with the other private vehicles, and the sight of Herman sitting ramrod-stiff on the box with the hangings monogrammed in silver. She was pleased with herself, with the luxury that she had occasion to display, and with the company she was seen to be keeping. Eline was looking as pretty as a picture in a stylishly simple ensemble in a pale shade of pewter, her face framed by a refined little bonnet tied with a flutter of silk ribbon. And van Erlevoort was a fine-looking fellow, a man of distinction. As for Henk, he looked comfortably expansive and sleek ... No indeed, her husband was not really so bad, she could have done a lot worse for herself.

When Dirk overtook another vehicle of their acquaintance, Betsy acknowledged the occupants with her most winning smile, since she did not wish to appear to be gloating at the speed of her handsome bays.

"Oh, lovely! It's cooling down, I'm beginning to feel quite revived," murmured Eline. She took a deep breath and sat up as they came to the end of the Promenade. "Just what I needed: some fresh air after the appalling heat we had this afternoon."

"Nonsense, Elly, it was delightful!" countered Betsy. "In fact I wish we had such warm weather all the time."

"Well, it would kill me after a few weeks! Oh, Otto, you're laughing, but I'm serious, the heat makes me quite ill. Don't you believe me?"

"But Elly, of course I believe you!"

She shook her head, giving him a look of mock reproof.

"You called me Elly again," she whispered.

"So I did; how silly of me. Ah, I've just had an idea," he whispered back happily.

"What are you two conspiring about?" Henk demanded.

"Oh, nothing. Just a little secret between Otto and me … shh," she said, putting her finger to her lips, delighting in their curiosity.

For she had asked Otto not to call her by the familiar name everyone used. She wanted him to invent a special name for her, a name that only he would use, one that was not worn and stale—he did not think it childish of her, did he? He had exhausted himself trying to come up with a suitable pet name, but she was never satisfied and kept telling him to think again. And now he appeared to have found something.

"I'm dying to know," she whispered, smiling.

"Later," he mouthed, returning her smile.

"Until now I didn't find you half as tiresome as most engaged girls, and I wish you'd stop mumbling like that, it's very boring!" Betsy cried out with mild indignation.

"Well, you were no better with Henk in the old days!" riposted Eline. "Was she, Henk?"

"No, I don't believe she was!" chuckled Henk. Eline felt a pang: the thought of her sister's engagement several years since brought back long-buried moments of a certain heartache she had felt at the time. It all seemed so very long ago, yet she was perturbed.

But they had long since left Badhuisweg behind, they had passed the Gallery, they had rolled round to the rear of the Kurhaus, and now they were coming to a halt at the steps leading to the terrace overlooking the sea.

Betsy, Eline and Otto passed one by one through the turnstile, while Henk, who had the tickets, brought up the rear. They did not see the Eekhofs and the Hijdrechts, who were seated at one of the tables near the bandstand, and walked on. Otto's hand was touching Eline's arm.

"Look, there go the van Raats, and Miss Vere with van Erlevoort!" said young Hijdrecht. "They've been coming here every evening lately."

"What an absurdly plain dress Eline is wearing!" said Léonie. "I wonder who she's trying to impress … and that hat with the veil! All the girls nowadays seem to think they should have a hat with a veil as soon as they get engaged. It's preposterous!"

"Still, they make a fine couple, don't they?" opined Madame Eekhof. "And it's a splendid match."

"At least they aren't making a spectacle of themselves the way some engaged couples do," said Ange. "Not like Marguerite van Laren, for instance, for ever flicking invisible dust off her fiancé's lapels. Remember how we laughed the other day, Hijdrecht?"

Betsy, bobbing and smiling left and right as they picked their way through the multitude, said they ought to find a table soon or they would all be taken.

Fortunately it was pleasant everywhere—it was even preferable to sit at some distance from the bandstand because of the noise—so they made their way to the section adjoining the Conversation Room, which was still largely unoccupied. They chose a table at the front, where they could see and be seen by everyone strolling past.

Amid the continuous exchange of little nods and waves of the hand, Betsy and Eline exchanged whispered comments about the risible toilettes and extravagant hats passing by. Eline herself was very satisfied with the unadorned style of dress she had taken to wearing since her engagement, a sophisticated kind of simplicity, so much smarter than her former, more lavish attire, and different enough to attract notice. Simple, well-cut gowns flattered her slim figure and made her feel statuesque, and besides, they gave her an unwonted air of seriousness and modesty, which Otto, being by nature a lover of simplicity rather than ostentation, was bound to find attractive.

This was the person she now was; she knew it was difficult for her simply to be herself, it was easier to slip into a role to suit her mood, and now her role was that of the somewhat mannered but ever alluring and overjoyed fiancée of a suitable young man, someone from her own set, who was generally liked for his agreeable humour and lack of affectation. And overjoyed—that she was, for her heart's prayer for happiness was being answered—she exulted in the peace bestowed on her by his great, calm love, which she sensed rather than comprehended; she was happy in the blue stillness of that lagoon, that nirvana, into which her fantasy-ridden soul had slipped as into a bed of eiderdown; she felt so suffused with joy that her nervous tension relaxed, and quite often, to her own surprise, found herself with tears in her eyes out of sheer gratitude.

The stream of promenaders was without end, and she felt quite dazed.

"Eline, what's the matter with you? Look, there's Madame van der Stoor, and little Cateau, too!" hissed Betsy.

Eline focused her eyes and nodded her head in greeting, as disarmingly as she was able. Then she saw Vincent Vere and Paul van Raat, who were coming towards their table. They remained standing, leaning on their canes, as there were no vacant chairs in the vicinity.

"Would you two care to sit down a moment—that is, if Eline would care to take a turn with me?" asked Otto, half-rising.

Eline thought it an excellent idea, and while Vincent and Paul sat down with Henk and Betsy, she and Otto joined the meandering flow. They were approaching the bandstand, around which a semicircle of avid listeners had gathered, and they heard the crystal-clear high notes of the Lohengrin overture swelling from the violins while the conductor, standing with his back to them, controlled the rise and fall of the music with waves of his baton. When Otto guided Eline to the narrow aisle between the occupied chairs and the music lovers, she held back, whispering:

"Let's stop and listen for a while, shall we?"

He gave a nod of assent, and they halted. In her tranquil frame of mind she rejoiced in the grand swell of melody. It seemed to her that she was being engulfed, not by the music so much as by the still blue waters of her lagoon, limpid and clear as the river upon which Lohengrin's craft glided forth, and she saw majestic, beautiful swans …

At the loudest fortissimo she took a deep breath, and when the glass filaments drawn by the violins spun themselves out, thinner and thinner, the majestic swans, too, glided away.

There was a burst of applause; the semicircle of listeners dissolved.

"Lovely … that was so lovely!" murmured Eline as in a dream, feeling Otto's hand searching for her arm. Oh, life was sweet indeed …

"It's very strange, you know. I always feel so much better for listening to a beautiful piece of music; it gives me the feeling that I might not be completely unworthy of you after all," she murmured, putting her lips close to his ear so that no one would hear. "It's silly of me, I suppose, but I can't help it."

She smiled at him uncertainly, in suspense for his answer. She often felt a little uncertain, as though she might lose him by a single ill-advised word, for she had not yet fathomed how much he loved her, nor why.

"Oh, you mustn't put me on a pedestal," he said gently, lowering his voice as he spoke, so that their conversation seemed merely to hover in the air separating them. "I'm a perfectly ordinary chap, not a jot better than anyone else, and you ought not to place yourself beneath me. You, unworthy of me! The very idea! Why, I believe you don't know yourself very well at all."

Could he be right? Did she not know herself? The possibility surprised and delighted her, for she had always thought she knew herself very well. Could there really be some hidden corner of her soul that she knew nothing about, some secret wellspring of devotion to him? Would he teach her to know herself?

"Oh, Otto!" she began.

"What?" he asked softly.

"Nothing, it's just that I love you so much when you talk about us in that way," she murmured, filled with an exaltation for which she had no words. She felt the gentle touch of his hand on her arm, and a little tremor passed through her as they made their way among the jostling, laughing crowd, eagerly observed from the tables by their acquaintances and those who knew them by sight.

"There go van Erlevoort and Eline, all dreamy-eyed! They didn't even notice us, would you believe!" exclaimed Léonie to young Hijdrecht, with a touch of envy in her voice.

Hearing their names being called, Eline and Otto looked about them and caught sight of Madame Verstraeten sitting at a table with Marie, Lili and Frédérique. Georges de Woude had risen; he was beckoning amicably. They shook hands.

"Aha, Freddie!" said Otto with some surprise.

"Madame was so kind as to invite me along after dinner," she explained. "By the way, Otto, just after you left a letter came from de Horze: they are all well and send you their regards. You too, Eline."

"Thank you," said Eline warmly, sinking onto the chair Georges had vacated beside Madame Verstraeten. Marie had grown very pale, which nobody noticed as she was wearing a hat with a white veil.

"Theodore writes that Suzanne and van Stralenburg and the baby are coming to stay with them next week, and now Mama's in a great quandary."

"What, was Mama planning to go to de Horze? And Howard is coming here?"

"Yes, that's the dilemma."

"Dear Madame van Erlevoort," mused Madame Verstraeten.

"Percy let her know that he would be coming in the last week of July, while Theodore wrote a letter saying that van Stralenburg would not be staying later than the 20th. So you can imagine," continued Frédérique, forcing herself to cast a cordial look at Eline, "how complicated it is for Mama. She doesn't have much opportunity to travel to Zwolle, and leaving The Hague before the 20th while Howard and Catherine are coming, well, it wouldn't do at all."

"But Howard will be travelling on to de Horze later, won't he?" asked Otto.

"Yes, but he'll want to spend a few days in The Hague first, to take advantage of the beach at Scheveningen," replied Frédérique. "So now Mama doesn't know whether she's coming or going, and she couldn't bear it if she missed seeing her new grandchild this summer, as I'm sure you understand."

"Well, in that case I shall prevail upon Mama to let me take her to Zwolle one of these days. Simple!" said Otto. "And it would save her the journey to de Horze, which is rather more arduous."

"You might try," said Frédérique. "It would certainly solve the problem."

Lili asked to be excused as she wished to take a turn with de Woude, whereupon her mother invited Otto to sit beside her until the young people returned.

"How lovely Eline looks! Don't you agree, de Woude?" asked Lili.

Since she had been skating with him last winter she had allowed him to call her familiarly by her first name, while she had taken to addressing him simply as 'de Woude'.

"Yes, quite so," replied Georges indifferently.

"Well, I think she's really beautiful!" said Lili with conviction. "How can you not find her beautiful? Your taste is very peculiar!"

He laughed with secret pleasure.

"It's not my fault that she leaves me cold, you know. I happen to have a different idea of beauty. But if you absolutely insist that I should find her beautiful, well then, I shall take another look."

"Oh no, you needn't do that," she replied, laughing with him. "It's just that every man I know thinks she's beautiful, so I can't see why you don't. And I can't imagine why Frédérique is not fond of her. If I were a man I'd fall head over heels in love with her."

"And fight a duel with van Erlevoort, I suppose."

The first part of the programme was at an end and the listeners began to swarm away in all directions. Georges and Lili found themselves hemmed in by a mass of heads and shoulders, all pressing forward.

"This is hopeless," said Lili. "I hate being in a crowd like this. You'd think it was Sunday."

"What would you say to a stroll on the beach," he suggested softly. "The exit is just over there."

"Is it allowed?" said Lili, warming to the idea. "Do you think Mama would mind?"

"Of course not, not if you're with me," he said, sounding almost proud.

They passed through the turnstile and hurried down the steps, crossed the road, and then took the broad wooden stairs down to the sand.

The large wicker beach chairs were ranged in clusters for the night. Here and there a Scheveninger could be seen, adjusting his swagger to the slow pace of his ample-skirted wife.

The waves lapping the shore glittered in the bright lights shining from the gaslit Kurhaus.

"Phew!" said Lili. "Some space at last!"

The sea, calm and smooth, unfurled in shades of green, azure and violet, capped here and there with glistening white foam all along the beach. It was a starry night, and the Milky Way resembled a sprinkling of pearl dust in the mysterious vastness of the deep-blue sky. The air was filled with a steady murmur, as from a single, gigantic seashell.

"How wonderfully quiet it is here after all that noise! Quite divine," gushed Lili.

"Yes it is," said Georges.

She had almost tripped over something, after which he had offered her his arm, and she had taken it. There was so much he wanted to say, but he could not find the words for fear of sounding ridiculous. She too felt a sweet impulse to pour out her feelings, to tell him how awed she was by the beauty of the sea and the starry sky, but she felt a trifle embarrassed about the poetic exaltation in her heart, which was so strangely at odds with the mundanity of the circles they moved in. So they both kept silent as they strolled along the beach, with the murmur of the sea in their ears and the same tender emotion in their hearts, which each could sense in the other, and which seemed to fill the silence between them with more than words.

They had strolled wordlessly for some distance along the tranquil sea, lost in their shared solitude, when he felt he ought to say something.

"I could walk with you to the ends of the earth, or anyway all the way to Katwijk!" he said, jesting to hide his serious intent.

She laughed; it was a joke, after all.

"In that case I'd probably get very tired."

"Then I would carry you."

"You couldn't—I'm too heavy."

"If that's what you think, come here and I'll show you."

"Georges! What a shocking idea! Now I shall have to get cross—unless you beg my pardon properly, that is."

"How do you mean, properly?" he asked humbly.

"Say after me: I, Georges de Woude van Bergh, humbly apologise to Lili," she intoned, and a lot more besides. He dutifully repeated every word, and she kept adding phrases simply because she delighted in the sound of his voice.

Indeed, she was not angry at all. She wished their walk would never end, that they would stroll along the lightly foaming sea for ever, in quest of new horizons.

"I think we ought to be getting back," he said abruptly.

They turned around, and were astonished to see how far they had strayed from the Kurhaus, which was now a ruddy glow in the distance. But Lili's initial concern promptly gave way to a sense of romantic defiance—what did she care about all those people crowding the terraces? She was with him, by the sea, and that was all she cared about!

"We'd better hurry," Georges said, with a flustered laugh. "Your Mama will be wondering what's keeping us."

His urgency vexed her. Did he not feel as she did? Was he not utterly absorbed by her as she was by him, did he not feel that the only thing that mattered in the whole world was that they were together, now, by the soft whisper of the waves?

"I can't walk so fast in the sand!" she fretted, tightening her hold on his arm.

"Then you'll have to lean on me. Come on," he said resolutely. So there was severity, too, under all that sweetness and gallantry!

"But Georges, I simply can't go on, I'm exhausted!" she panted, sounding more plaintive than cross. But he only laughed and, with her arm clasped firmly in his own, swept her up the broad wooden staircase to the road, and in the end she could not help laughing too. It was rather fun, dashing about in the dark like this.

They paused to catch their breath before starting up the steps to the terrace, and while Georges felt in his pockets for the tickets, Lili shook the sand from the hem of her dress.

The interval had come to an end, and the orchestra was sounding the brass fanfares of the Queen of Sheba's march. The crowd had thinned considerably, and Lili blushed as she and Georges made their way to the table where Madame Verstraeten, Marie and Frédérique were waiting for them. Otto and Eline had left.

"Good gracious, where have you two been hiding?" cried Marie, while Georges and Lili occupied the chairs that had been kept vacant for them by draping various items over the backs. "You've been ages; I went for a stroll with Paul while you were away, and Eline and Otto couldn't hold your seats for ever."

"And it took tremendous effort on our part to keep them for you, I hope you realise," added Frédérique.

"But where on earth have you been?" demanded Madame Verstraeten. "Did you go to the Conversation Room, to watch the dancing?"

Georges proceeded to tell them of their walk along the beach, and Lili secretly admired him for his tactful replies to her mother's queries.

Henk and Vincent were the sole occupants of a table in the vicinity of the Conversation Room. Betsy, in a coquettish mood, had gone off with young Hijdrecht to take a turn about the terrace, while Eline and Otto had moved to Madame Eekhof's table in an attempt to make amends for having passed by four times without greeting her, which misdemeanour had been pointed out by Ange.

"I almost died this afternoon, the heat was so bad!" muttered Vincent.

"Eline can't stand it either," rejoined Henk, and downed his glass of Pilsner.

Vincent drank nothing; he was not feeling very well and did not enjoy the mêlée. He rarely went to Scheveningen: in the morning the heat was intolerable on the scorching beach, and in the evening he seldom had the energy. But now and then he went, just for the sake of having been there.

He was pondering how to phrase the question that was uppermost in his thoughts: a request for a loan. The last time Henk had advanced him some money he had not done so in his customary spirit of good-humoured generosity, for he was becoming annoyed at Vere's constant shortage of funds. This had not escaped Vincent, but it could not be helped, he would have to find some roundabout way of raising the subject.

"I think I shall be able to repay part of my debt later this week, van Raat, when my remittance comes. Ah well, I suppose I shall manage somehow."

Henk made no comment, only tapped his cane in time to the slow music: the orchestra was playing the overture to William Tell.

"Such a nuisance that I didn't come to an arrangement about that quinine business," continued Vincent. "But now a friend has written to me from America; he's rich and well connected, and he says he can get me an introduction to a trading company in New York. But for the moment … I say, van Raat, you'd be doing me a tremendous favour if you could lend me another fifty guilders."

Henk bridled.

"Vere, you never stop, do you? I'm getting rather tired of this business, to tell you the truth. First five hundred guilders, then it's a hundred, then fifty … What on earth are you waiting for? What do you plan to do? If you don't have financial means of your own, then why don't you find some employment? You can't expect me to keep subsidising you, can you?"

Vincent had anticipated reproof of one kind or another, and endured Henk's angry outburst without protest. Henk promptly felt embarrassed at the harshness of his tone, but pressed on nonetheless:

"All this talk about money coming from Brussels, Malaga, New York—when do you suppose it will come? It's not that it will ruin me if you don't pay me back, you understand, and I shan't trouble you for it either, but it's been nearly two thousand guilders up to now. I'm tired of it. Why don't you stop loafing around here in The Hague and do something!"

His tone was already softening, but Vincent kept silent, his eyes fixed on his shoes, which he was tapping lightly with the tip of his cane. Henk could find nothing more to say, and was relieved when Vincent finally lifted his head and spoke in a low voice: "It's unfortunate. You are quite right, of course, but it isn't my fault, really. Circumstances, you know. Ah well, I shall see what I can do. Forgive me for troubling you."

He rose purposefully to his feet, leaving Henk tongue-tied with embarrassment.

"Well, *au revoir* then," said Vincent with a faint smile and a nod at Henk. "*Au revoir*, I must be off."

Henk proffered his hand, unobserved by Vincent, who was already making his leisurely way through the crowd, languidly tipping his hat from time to time.

Henk remained alone at the table, feeling much disgruntled with himself. Soon afterwards, however, Eline and Otto returned, joking about how forlorn he looked. Betsy too made her way back to the table escorted by young Hijdrecht, whose hand she pressed warmly in farewell. It was late; many people had left before the final performance, and now that the concert was at an end the rest began to stream towards the exits. The vibrant atmosphere of music and lively chitchat had lapsed into quietude; here and there the gas lamps were already being extinguished, and only a stray group or two remained seated at the tables, enjoying the evening air, which was now tinged with briny freshness. Conversations flagged as the lingering visitors gazed out at the sea and the vast sky above, palely streaked with the Milky Way.

"What a lovely evening! Shall we stay here a little longer?" asked Betsy.

"Oh, I'd rather we went for a drive," said Eline. "Unless you think it will get too late, that is, and if the horses are up to it. What do you say, Henk?"

Betsy thought it rather eccentric of Eline to want to take a tour at this time of night, but the idea appealed to her nonetheless. So they all went down to the boulevard at the back of the Kurhaus, where their carriage was waiting in line with the others.

Eline thought the wind had risen and wished to sit forward under the half-raised hood, next to Otto. Betsy instructed Dirk to make a detour through the van Stolkpark on the way home.

The slumbering villas loomed spectrally amid dark masses of foliage stirring in the gentle breeze, and the only sounds intruding on the stillness were the thud of the horses' hooves and the light crunch of wheels on the gravelled road. No one spoke. Betsy leant back comfortably, savouring the night air. Henk fretted inwardly about his harshness towards Vincent, who was bound to feel offended, and Eline abandoned herself to the dreamy pleasure of the moment. She had removed her hat, and now inclined her head slightly to Otto, listening to his regular breathing. In the obscurity of the half-raised hood his arm had stolen around her waist, and he drew her gently towards him so that her cheek was almost touching his shoulder, while her hand brushed his knee. She felt very happy, and could imagine nothing sweeter than sitting close to him like this, feeling his breath ruffle her hair like kisses, feeling his arm encircling her waist like a girdle of love.

And, in a surge of tender emotion, she finally allowed her head to rest on his shoulder.

"What was the name you thought of for me?" she whispered in his ear.

"Nily!" he whispered back.

She felt his arm tightening about her waist, and she repeated the new name under her breath several times, exulting in his sweet term of endearment.

Mathilda van Rijssel had taken a beach tent for the summer, and had told Jeanne Ferelijn to come and join her there with her children whenever she chose. Jeanne was reluctant at first, not wishing to impose, but Mathilda had won her over, and lately she had been a frequent visitor. Sometimes they arranged to go together, leaving quite early equipped only with sandwiches, since milk for the little ones could be had from the stall. They would make themselves comfortable under the awning of the tent, in which they stored their belongings, and there they passed the time talking, reading and sewing while the youngsters set to work with their buckets and spades, digging holes in the sand nearby and building ingenious aqueducts down by the water's edge.

Jeanne fancied that her children were growing more robust and altogether more cheerful under the influence of the van Rijssel youngsters, and both she and Mathilda enjoyed watching the jolly little band of seven scampering like puppies back and forth between excavation sites and waterworks. She was very glad to keep company with Mathilda, in whom she had found a friend who understood her cares and offered sympathetic advice. They talked at length of their offspring, and also of their respective domestic arrangements, and Jeanne thought Mathilda extraordinarily frugal and practical for someone accustomed to living in comfortable circumstances.

However, the sunny days at the beach did not continue for long, as the Ferelijns had to leave. They were going to Boppard, where Frans was to take a cold-water cure. Jeanne was worried about the expense; there were the travelling costs to consider, and their accommodation, because how could the five of them afford to stay there for six weeks while the rent of the upstairs apartment in Hugo de Grootstraat needed to be paid as well?

Otto wished to introduce his fiancée to his sister's family, and Madame van Erlevoort agreed to accompany them on a visit to Zwolle for a few days. Madame was in raptures about her new grandson: the prettiest, chubbiest baby in the world, with such a fine head of dark curly hair! She was grateful to Otto for having persuaded her to come along. She visited de Horze every summer, for she was so accustomed to the journey that she saw no inconvenience in it at all, but at other times she found it nigh impossible to tear herself away from The Hague. She loved her spacious home on the Voorhout with its old-fashioned opulence, a little faded now, but still cosy and comfortable. Eline found the van Stralenburgs quite charming. Suzanne was a darling little mother, not particularly pretty and a bit careless in her dress, but so sweet-natured and so thrilled with her baby son that it was a delight to behold. As for her husband, he was an affable, humorous fellow, spoilt to the core by his wife, who fetched and carried for him with such gusto at times as to make Eline dissolve into laughter. No, she did not think she would ever manage to be like that with Otto, and trusted that he would not expect it of her! But although she warned him in jest, in the depths of her being she felt it must be heaven indeed to devote oneself heart and soul to a man the way Suzanne devoted herself to van Stralenburg, to exist for him alone, to be his loving, faithful slave, to be wholly and utterly possessed by him. Even in her current state of facility she could not resist fantasising about still greater joys to come, and conjured up elaborate visions of herself as Otto's adoring wife and of their life together in cosy, domestic bliss.

In this spirit of elation she saw happiness wherever she turned; everyone she knew seemed to her to be kind and considerate, they all seemed to be living in harmony, never flying into passions or showing the least sign of egotism. Scenes with Betsy were a thing of the past, she was sure, for she was now able to respond to her sister's disparaging remarks with mild good humour, as though there were nothing in the world that could mar her newfound joy. Her nerves were greatly soothed, and she herself was surprised to note her bright, even temper, quite undisturbed by the periodical fits of melancholy and fatigue of the past. Gone were the lowering clouds of grey-and-black gloom, for the very air that she breathed seemed changed; it was azure, flower-scented, shot through with sunbeams.

For several days after his contretemps with Vincent, Henk felt very uneasy. Being uncharitable was quite at odds with the general kindliness of his disposition, and he feared that he had hurt Vere's feelings—he might simply have been having a run of bad luck, after all. So Henk had called on Vincent to extend him the requested loan. Vincent, however, declined the offer, despite Henk's entreaties, and instead paid back a considerable portion of what he owed. Where he had procured the funds to do so was a mystery to Henk, as was everything else about Vincent.

Returning home, Henk was berated by his wife for having been tactless with her cousin. Betsy felt vaguely apprehensive about Vere, sensing in him a secret power beside which her own dominating nature paled to insignificance, and she was determined that he should not bear a grudge against her husband. Eline was going away: she had been invited to spend the month of August at de Horze by Theodore, and would travel there with the van Erlevoorts and the Howards late in July. It would be rather dismal in the big house on Nassauplein, mused Betsy. She did not wish to go on holiday with Henk just now, she preferred a trip to the south of Europe in the winter, after Eline's wedding, and so it was for reasons of both distraction and diplomacy that Betsy decided to ask Vincent to stay with them for the duration of Eline's absence. She told him how dreadfully lonely she would feel without Eline and how much she always enjoyed Vincent's company, what with all those interesting stories he had about his wanderings, so he would be doing her a great favour by coming to stay. Vincent was secretly delighted at the prospect of temporary respite from his aimless, impecunious existence. What luxury! A whole month of peace and quiet, and it would not cost him a penny. So he accepted Betsy's invitation, concealing his pleasure with a veneer of gracious condescension, as though he were deigning to allow her to make amends for her husband's heartless behaviour.

XVIII

LILI WAS VERY CROSS; her lips quivered and she was close to tears.

"I really can't see why we shouldn't ask him along," she complained to Marie. "He calls here often enough."

"Oh, Lili, have some sense! Mama already invited him to the house several times this winter, and it's not as if we know him well enough to take him on a country outing with us. Asking him along would make things stiff."

"But he's not in the least stiff!"

"No, he's not. He's much nicer than I thought at first, but still, we don't know him half as well as we know Paul and Etienne."

"Oh, them! All they do is saunter back and forth between the Witte club and the other one, dropping in at the Bordelaise or the Bodega on the way, and nowadays they're always with that wretched Vere. We haven't seen much of them at all lately. I know Paul comes by once in a while, but Etienne has become a myth as far as I'm concerned. Why don't you ask Vere as well, while you're about it?"

Marie shrugged.

"It's no use getting cross with me, Lili, just because Mama hasn't asked de Woude. It's nothing to do with me," she said gently.

"No, of course not. But it's always the same, whenever I think of something no one will hear of it. Well, I give up. I couldn't care less about the outing."

Fighting back her tears, Lili left the drawing room; Marie took up her book with a sigh.

Madame Verstraeten, seated in the conservatory with her husband, had overheard Lili's angry words, and a look of concern crossed her kind features.

"Is anything the matter?" he asked.

"Oh, it's just that de Woude," whispered Madame, so as not to be heard by Marie. "Lili wants me to invite him for the day after tomorrow."

"Why don't you, then? I have nothing against de Woude, although he is a bit of a fop. And he's rather jolly with the girls."

"But Karel, really, I don't think it would be wise. I always treat him with proper civility when I see him, but there's no need to encourage him any further, is there? What good would it do? Lili's still so young, and full of childish notions, too."

"Aren't you getting rather carried away? Why would they think of marrying? It's only a matter of an invitation, after all."

"I suppose you are right. But you never see them together the way I do. If only you'd come with us to Scheveningen some evening!"

"No, thank you very much."

"Then you'd see for yourself. He keeps hovering around our table. He's discreet enough not to accept every time I offer ice creams, but he always stays until we leave, and hardly talks to anyone else. He takes a turn with Marie now and then, to be polite, but apart from that it's Lili, Lili, all the time. I don't think it's very suitable, as you can imagine."

"And do you believe that Lili?—"

"Yes of course, it's perfectly clear! Everyone has noticed, and people are beginning to talk. I don't know quite what to do about it," said Madame Verstraeten, again looking concerned.

Mr Verstraeten sat a moment in contemplation, after which he and his wife resumed their discussion, their voices dropping to whispers.

Marie found it impossible to concentrate on her book, so she went upstairs in search of Lili. She found her lying on her bed, sobbing into the pillows.

"Lili! Whatever's the matter?" she called softly.

Lili started at the sound of Marie's voice.

"Oh, leave me alone!" she cried.

But Marie took her hands and forced her to look up.

"Lili, don't be absurd! You're so unreasonable, going off into a huff at the least provocation. Lili! Listen to me!"

"Oh, please, just leave me alone."

"Why make yourself even more miserable by coming up here to cry all alone? Why don't you just tell me what's upsetting you? It's so much better to trust each other, to be open and frank and speak your mind."

Marie herself dearly wished she could be open and frank, she would have loved to speak her mind to Lili, to Mama, to anyone, but there were some things that were best left unsaid.

Lili sat up and brushed her tousled hair from her tear-stained cheeks.

"What would you have me say, then? You know everything already. Mama's always finding fault with Georges, and I hate that."

"Come now, you exaggerate. Both Papa and Mama like him well enough."

"I know, I know! But when it comes to showing him a bit of courtesy … Anyway, you said so yourself."

"What did I say?"

"You said that taking him along would make things stiff!"

"If I'd known you cared so much, I wouldn't have said it. Only I can't bear to see you getting all upset about nothing, Lili. You carry on as if your whole life were in ruins, just because Mama thinks it better not to invite de Woude for once."

"But it's very awkward for me! I already told him about the outing, and so naturally he now thinks—"

"Well, you shouldn't have given him ideas. It's awkward for Mama, too, with people beginning to gossip about you. Only yesterday Madame Eekhof was saying—"

"I don't care a straw about what Madame Eekhof says, since we love each other! Everyone's against us, it's not fair."

"Indeed, Lili," breezed Marie, attempting to hide her own secret emotion. "It is deeply tragic. You love Georges and Georges loves you, and the whole world is against you, Mama, Madame Eekhof and everyone else, too. Very sad, my dear, very sad indeed! And of course there isn't a glimmer of hope that anything will ever change. Very sad."

"Marie, how could you? Making fun of me while you know how upset I am!"

"Yes, I'm very cruel, am I not?" Marie pursued, softening. "Come on, Lili, dry your tears and give me a kiss, all right? I didn't mean to be unkind. Shall I try and get Mama to change her mind?"

"Oh, if only you would! Mama's sure to say yes if you ask her."

"Ah yes, I'm the one no one can refuse, aren't I? And you're the one everybody's always against, aren't you? You poor thing!"

Lili had to smile through her tears. "Marie, you're so funny when you talk like that! You've made me laugh!"

"Yes, Lili dear, you can laugh. Let's all laugh while we may. Bye for now. Why don't you do up your hair, and I'll go downstairs and have a word with Mama."

Marie left the room, feeling a pang of envy for her sister's ability to unburden herself. And as she descended the stairs she smiled wistfully at the depths of Lili's despair only a moment ago, and at her infatuation with Georges. Her sister was a mere child as far as she was concerned, crying over the temporary loss of a toy, and she was confident that all would be forgotten within the half-hour. How lucky Lili was! Free to shed tears when she was sad and free to say things like: "I don't care a straw about what Madame Eekhof says, since we love each other!"

They were bound for a farmstead that was owned by an old acquaintance of the Verstraetens. The overladen charabanc rolled along Loosduinseweg under a blazing sky, with the occasional steam tram passing them as it came the other way. Madame Verstraeten and Mathilda sat in the back with Nico between them, Marie, Lili and Frédérique sat in the middle facing Paul, Etienne and Georges, and the front bench was occupied by Ernestine, Madeleine and the Verstraeten boys. Johan sat on the box, while the dickey was shared by Cateau van der Stoor and Jan. It was to be a jolly family outing, nothing formal, so everyone could relax and enjoy themselves. Marie dispensed handfuls of cherries from a large basket, and Etienne, between mouthfuls, told them that according to Marguerite van Laren going on an outing in a charabanc was a very bourgeois thing to do.

"I suppose the van Larens always go on their outings in a liveried carriage, complete with footmen in powdered wigs!" said Georges.

"Naturally! With the ladies wearing great billowing skirts like in the Watteau paintings, and leading little lambs by pink ribbons!" rejoined Lili, smiling fondly at Georges.

There was much hilarity at this; they were all in high spirits, the womenfolk in their simple cotton frocks as much as the young men in their light summer suits and straw boaters.

"Do have some cherries, Cateau," said Marie, passing her a handful. "You can share them with Jan."

"Oh yes, we'll share!" exclaimed Jan, with a roguish air. "Shall I show you a trick, Cateau?"

"What sort of trick?"

"See these twin cherries? Well, put one of them in your mouth."

"What for?" asked Cateau, doing as he suggested.

"Then I'll have the other one. Look, like this!" the rascal replied, quickly brushing her lips with his before biting into the second cherry.

"Jan! Behave yourself!" scolded Madame.

"She fell for it! Silly Cateau!" giggled Freddie.

"I had no idea what he was going to do!" protested Cateau. "Wretched boy!"

"Nonsense, you don't mean that. Of course you knew!" scoffed Paul.

The charabanc rattled on through a flat landscape of meadows with sleek, grazing cows whose black-and-white coats gleamed like satin, past endless rows of pollard willows unfurling their silvery fans.

"Willows are such melancholy trees, don't you agree, Georges?" asked Lili with feeling.

"There she goes, waxing poetical again!" Etienne cried out. "Come on then, Lili, let's hear an ode to the willow."

"I can't say anything these days without everyone poking fun at me, goodness knows why," she moaned.

Now it was Lili's turn to be teased, and they all laughed heartily as they munched their cherries.

The road began to climb towards undulating horizons. Here and there stood a country retreat, lost in the greenery, or a farmhouse surrounded by fields planted with carrot and cauliflower or beanstalks in neat rows, and gardens ablaze with sunflowers, peonies and hollyhocks. A washerwoman wringing out clothes on the bank of a stream drew herself up to smile at them as they passed, and two youngsters ran after the carriage while Jan and Cateau threw them cherries.

The road ran between fields of yellow corn and green flax dotted with blue cornflowers and red poppies, rising and falling until finally they reached the farm. The farmer's wife appeared at the gate, smiling broadly, and the young people sprang down from the charabanc while Madame Verstraeten and Mathilda took charge of unloading the cargo of boxes, cloth-covered baskets and hampers.

The coachman unhitched his steaming horses and led them to the stable.

Jan Verstraeten, Cateau and the van Rijssel foursome made a beeline for the two swings, but not before Jan had assured Madame van Rijssel that he would be very careful and Cateau had promised to pay particular attention to little Nico.

"They're just like a married couple with their offspring!" laughed Marie, following the merry band with her eyes.

"I'm going to chase them away from the swings shortly, because I want a turn myself!" declared Etienne, already a little light-headed from the sun and the fresh air. "Lili, will you join me on the other swing? If de Woude will let you, that is!" he whispered, rolling his eyes.

"De Woude has no say over what I do! But no thanks, I don't like swings. They always give me a headache."

"But I just love swings, Etienne!" cried Marie. "So I'll be counting on you as a gentleman to push me as high as I can go, really high, do you hear? Up to the clouds!"

"Let's go and find a nice spot to sit—over there, by those dunes," suggested Paul.

"He thinks it's time for a rest, how typical! But my dear Paul, it's hot in the dunes," said Freddie.

"No, there are some trees, oaks I think, over there, beyond the pavilion."

"All right, let's go. It's too hot for anything strenuous, anyway. I agree with Paul: I like a lazy outing. Just lying in the cool green shade, watching the clouds drift by overhead—lovely," said Lili.

"How poetic! Trust Lili to turn sheer idleness into a romantic occasion," laughed Marie. "For goodness' sake, de Woude, why don't you say something? Here we are, all chatting away while you're off in a trance, composing verses in your head, I shouldn't wonder."

Georges denied this with good humour, and they all set off, pushing aside the leafy twigs of overhanging bushes on their path. Lili was frightened out of her wits by a spider descending a long silvery thread, and de Woude's removal of the insect gave rise to fresh bursts of laughter and jokes about Lili being a damsel in distress and Georges a knight in shining armour coming to her rescue.

"What have we done to deserve all this attention, may I ask?" said Georges.

"Never mind, Georges, take no notice!" said Lili. "They think they're being funny. Oh, Paul, where are you taking us? It's so hot, and quite slippery underfoot, too. How much further is it to that nice spot of yours? All these tiresome branches—ouch!"

She broke off to inspect her finger, which she had scratched on a thorn.

"Why don't you let me walk in front, then," offered Georges, and he spoke so softly and slipped ahead of her so quietly that the others, still laughing heartily, did not notice. He and Lili fell behind, with him carefully holding back each intruding twig to clear the way for her.

"Let them laugh! You don't mind about them, do you?" he asked, a faraway, happy look in his eyes.

"Not in the least!" she replied calmly. She shook her head, on which she wore a wide sunhat bedecked with wild flowers, and gave an arch smile. "It's our turn to laugh at them, now. Who's that shrieking at the top of his voice?"

"Etienne, of course!" said Georges.

Paul and Etienne had found a mossy bank beneath a young chestnut tree, from which an attractive panorama was to be seen: a stretch of meadowland, grazing cows, straight lines of water-filled ditches glittering in the bright sunlight, a windmill beyond, and in the distance a line of poplars, slender and tall.

When Lili and Georges caught up with the others they found them in raptures.

"This is splendid!" said Paul. "Plenty of cool moss to lie on and a fine, sweeping view."

Everyone agreed, and they plumped themselves down on the ground, weary from their expedition. On the dark, dappled sward lay a scattering of discarded hats and lacy parasols, while stray sunbeams threw patches of shivering light on the crush of light cotton skirts.

"It's not so shady here after all. At any rate, I am in the full sun," said Lili, putting up her pink parasol. She shot an indignant glance at Paul, who had claimed a spot of deep shade, where he now lay sprawled on his back with a pocket handkerchief over his face.

"Hush, Lili, no more talking now, time for a nap!" he muttered.

"It's all very well for you to take a nap, but I'm burning to a crisp in the sun."

"Shall we go and look for a better spot, Lili?" ventured Georges.

"Yes, you do that—good idea," said Paul.

"And give us a whistle when you've found one," said Etienne.

Georges promised he would, and set off down the sandy slope with Lili clinging to his arm.

"They won't whistle, just you wait and see," said Etienne.

"Lili's so fussy!" yawned Paul.

His lethargy was too much for Etienne, who seized Paul's ankles and dragged him some way, much to the girls' amusement.

However, it was very hot, and as they were all beginning to feel lazy, they decided unanimously to wait until after lunch to take a proper walk. When peace had been restored between Paul and Etienne, Frédérique laid her head on Etienne's knees, and he tickled her ear with a blade of grass while Paul pretended to sleep. Marie sat very still, moodily gazing out at the meadows and the ditches and the cows.

The path Georges and Lili had taken was easy. Lili felt herself floating downwards as she held on to Georges' shoulders with both hands, gasping with delight as he went faster and faster. He had given her wings!

"How silly of them to stay where there isn't any proper shade; look, there's a clump of trees over there!"

"Those chestnuts?"

"They look promising. Shall we go and take a look?"

"Very well."

They made their way to the trees and found themselves in a lush, shadowy glade surrounded on all sides by blistering sunshine.

"Isn't it lovely here?" cried Lili. "Look, wild violets!"

She seated herself on the mossy bank and began to pick the wildflowers within her reach. Georges sank down at her feet, too happy to say very much, and toyed with the red tassels of her pink parasol.

"You ought to give a whistle, Georges, as a signal for the others to come," she said demurely, knowing full well that he would not.

"I can't whistle, I never could!" he responded jovially.

She laughed and began to pelt him with her violets, which he promptly gathered into a little bunch and put in his buttonhole. Then he took her hand.

"Do you love me?" he said, holding her eyes. She placed her small white hands on his shoulders and leant forward, returning his gaze.

"What?" she murmured tenderly.

"Do you love me?" he repeated, and she leant closer, so that her hair brushed against his lips, receiving kisses.

"Yes," she said, leaning her forehead against his. "Yes, I love you."

They sat thus a while, and notwithstanding the rather un-comfortable position Georges was in, he delighted in feeling the weight of her sweet head. When she finally drew herself up, he moved to sit beside her, then lifted her arm and laid it around his neck.

"By the way, my sister Emilie—" he began.

"What about her?" she said.

"Emilie has had a talk with my father. Don't you think she might talk to your parents too?"

"Oh, yes!" she replied, beaming. "But I don't know, I'm not sure whether—"

"Emilie is a very good talker."

"You love her very much, don't you?"

"Yes, and I love you, too."

With her hand on his neck she drew him a fraction closer, and kissed the side of his head—the first time she had ever kissed him. The soft, summer air beneath the leafy canopy was heavy with the scent of violets mingled with moss, and she ruffled the tawny hair above his ears with her fingers. The sensation was so delightful as to make her swoon away.

She listened blissfully to his low voice relating the conversation he had had with his sister, at a time when he didn't even know whether Lili really cared for him. He had felt very anxious at first, but now he was full of confidence, whatever challenges the future might hold.

"Emilie thought you wouldn't consider marrying a man without money," he said. "Is that true? Won't you have a penniless husband?"

"Are you penniless?"

"Well, I'm not exactly rich."

"All right then, I shall have a penniless husband. Oh, I can be very economical, you know. Sometimes I make one month's dress allowance last for three, and I think I manage to look all right, don't I?"

"You look lovely."

"But you don't strike me as being so very economical yourself. I think you probably have a great many more needs than I do."

"All I need is you. You are everything to me."

"Does Emilie like me?"

"Of course she does. She'll be like a mother to us. And you will come with me no matter where they send me? To Cairo? Constantinople? The Cape?"

"To Lapland if need be. Anywhere at all."

"My own little wife!"

He held her close to his heart, and kissed her. The air was still, the world fell away, and they were alone in paradise, united in a love of such magnitude as had never been known before.

"Mama wants to know if you're coming to lunch!" shouted young Johan van Rijssel. "How lazy you all are! You look half asleep already."

He clambered up the slope and pounced on Paul's long legs to shake them. Frédérique and Etienne sat up, saying that yes, they were quite hungry.

"Hungry from doing nothing, I suppose!" cried Jan, who came running. "We've been on the swings and the seesaw, and we had a ride in the donkey cart and climbed on top of a hay wagon, and all you've been doing is dozing!"

"Tut-tut, more respect for your elders, if you please," said Marie, with mock solemnity.

They all trooped back to the farmhouse the way they had come, picking their way through the bushes, when they heard a whistle behind them. Looking round they saw Georges and Lili exchanging complicit smiles.

"We found an excellent spot, wonderfully cool," said Georges.

"Wonderfully cool," echoed Lili.

The pair of them were assailed with questions and knowing looks, which they tried to deflect by slowing their pace, although they took care not to arrive much later than the others at table.

Madame Verstraeten and Mathilda had been very busy, notwithstanding the heat. The large table, covered with a rustic cloth of white cotton, was generously laden with bread rolls, bowls of cherries and strawberries, as well as two golden, turban-shaped sponge cakes placed on either side of a large pitcher of cream. Sixteen chairs were ranged about the feast, while the van Rijssel foursome, red-faced and bright-eyed from the heat, their hair sticking in strands to their moist brows, devoured everything with their eyes. Nico was already seated, rattling his glass and banging the table with his fork, and presently everyone was settled round the table while Madame and Mathilda pointed out the various foods.

"De Woude, dear boy, do help yourself!" said Madame, and the air was filled with cheerful voices as they all fell to. The rolls and the sponge cakes vanished at an alarming rate, while the hens clucked busily about the table, especially near Nico, who kept treating them to entire slices of bread. Jan in the meantime found a fresh reason to needle the three young men about their laziness.

Behind the farm was a wide stream, with a small rowing boat moored along the bank. Jan and Cateau had been clamouring to use the craft, but Madame Verstraeten would not give her permission unless someone older and more responsible accompanied them. So after luncheon it was agreed that Paul and Etienne would take the oars, Jan would act as the steersman and Frédérique, Marie and Cateau would be the 'freight of fair ladies', as Etienne put it.

"Georges and Lili are as thick as thieves, aren't they?" said Paul, pushing the boat away from the bank with his oar.

"Where have they got to? Oh, look, there they go, behind that hedge!" cried Frédérique. "Why, Marie, fancy you as an elder sister allowing such a thing!"

Marie smiled.

"At least they're happy," she said simply.

Etienne tried with all his might to conceal his lack of rowing skills by strenuous exertion, but Paul was not impressed.

"Oh, Etienne," he protested, "you're hopeless. Don't you know you must dip the oars cleanly, not make all those splashes!"

A shower of spray descended on them.

"You're making me all wet!" complained Frédérique.

"Come on now, are you saying I'm not a good oarsman?"

Etienne redoubled his efforts, to no avail, which Cateau and Jan found exceedingly funny. Soon they plucked up courage to ask Paul, whom they regarded as the captain, if they might have a turn at the oars. Etienne was duly displaced from his seat, as a result of which the boat almost capsized, and Cateau triumphantly sat herself down beside Paul, eager to keep perfect time with his strokes. She gripped her oar tightly with both hands, unconcerned about blisters, and was enchanted when her stroke and Paul's were as one, slicing calmly through the green water.

"Splendid, Cateau, you're doing awfully well!" said Marie. "Jan, why don't you steer us closer to those water lilies?"

Jan complied, and the boat veered slowly towards an expanse of duckweed with white and yellow water lilies surrounded by large, round lily pads. Marie leant over the side to catch hold of a lily and pulled hard on the tough, slimy stalk until it came loose and she was able to lift the flower from the water.

"There are lots more over there!" said Jan, pointing to the far bank.

They glided on, past meadows bordered by willows trailing their silvery branches in the water, and Marie, with a distracted air, continued to pull muddy flowers from the depths. She appeared not to hear the jesting and laughter, nor the heated argument going on between Cateau and Etienne as to the correct manner of wielding an oar, so engrossed was she in pulling out one lily after another and throwing the stalks at her feet like slippery eels. She tugged so hard that she tore the skin of her fingers, feeling as though she were ripping out unwanted thoughts from her mind, for whose riddance it was worth shedding blood.

The van Rijssel youngsters, whom their mama did not trust in the boat while Etienne was in it, consoled themselves with the seesaw and the swings. Tina pushed a remarkably solemn-looking Nico on one of the swings, while Johan rode the other one with Madeleine sitting between his feet. After a while Nico grew bored and surrendered his swing to Marie and Etienne, who had returned from the boat.

"Higher, Etienne, I want to go as high as the sky!" cried Marie.

They would share the swing. Etienne planted his feet firmly on the wooden seat-board and flexed his knees to set the swing in motion.

"Ah, I can see you're better on a swing than in a rowing boat!" said Marie, perched between his feet and thrusting herself forwards and backwards to help push the swing higher. Her skirts billowed and streamed, her hat flew away, and her hair fluttered about her cheeks. At the highest point, when she was suspended almost horizontally over Etienne, she gulped for breath before swinging down, then up again, and down … She had a sensation of flying over a fathomless abyss as she soared higher and higher into the blue sky, carried aloft by the wings of a great bird. Her eyes glittered with tears, her cheeks were on fire, and she imagined herself letting go of the ropes and hurtling into the gaping void.

Her eye caught the four children down below, staring up in awe at them daring to swing so very high, and she wanted to call out to them, but no sound came from her throat. Etienne seemed intoxicated by the momentum, and on they went, higher and higher.

"Enough, Etienne—that's enough," gasped Marie, shutting her eyes.

She felt quite dazed as the great bird reduced speed, gradually swinging lower and lower until it stopped altogether, and when her feet touched the ground again and she stood up she felt so giddy she almost lost her balance.

Etienne ran to retrieve her hat.

"That was good, wasn't it?" he panted.

Marie nodded and gave a faint smile as she brushed her tousled hair from her face. Etienne dashed off, calling to his cousins that they would never catch him, at which the van Rijssel foursome went in hot pursuit with little Nico bringing up the rear, running as fast as his short legs would carry him. Alone at last, Marie sank down on the grass by the swings in a flood of tears. She thought of Lili and Georges and how wrapped up in each other they had been that morning while she, Marie, had done nothing but sit and stare at the meadows and the cows until she saw stars before her eyes; and she thought of how they had stolen off together while she had sat in a boat tearing lilies out of the water until her hands ached.

XIX

"ELINE! ELINE!" a voice called from the garden.

Eline had woken with a start at half-past seven—breakfast at de Horze was served at eight—and she had to hurry with her toilette. At the sound of her name she went, half dressed, to the window, which stood open. Looking outside, she saw Theodore's two eldest girls, Marianne and Henriette, sixteen and fourteen years old.

"Good morning!" called Eline brightly.

"What, are you up already? That's quick! Will you come soon?"

"In a moment."

"Hello Eline, hello Eline!" shouted a new voice from outside. Eline looked again and saw Gustaaf, a handsome ten-year-old with bold blue eyes, ever-dirty hands and comic as a clown.

"Hello there, Gus!" she called.

"I say, Eline, remember what you promised?"

"No, what?"

"That you'd marry me instead of Uncle Otto! You promised, remember!"

"All right then, I will! But Gus dear, I must get ready now or I'll be late for breakfast!" said Eline, returning to the mirror to do her hair.

From the sunlit garden rose more voices, among which she could now distinguish Theodore's bass tones as well as the excited cries of the van Rijssel youngsters. She felt nervous, her eyes were still a little puffy with sleep and she could not get her hair to look as she wished.

"Eline! Eline!" they chanted.

"Yes, yes, I'm coming!" she called impatiently. Still tying her sash, she flew down the gloomy, oak-panelled corridor, down the grand staircase and out of the vestibule.

In the garden she saw Otto strolling with his sister, Catherine Howard. She was not beautiful, but had a pleasant, cheerful way with her, and a bright vivacity almost matching that of their younger brother Etienne.

"Oh, Otto, I can so well imagine…" sighed Catherine, clasping his arm. "I think she's very sweet. In their letters Freddie and Mathilda gave the impression that she was a society girl, so I was rather expecting her to be one of those snooty young ladies from The Hague. I have only seen her once or twice before, you know, and that was quite a while ago. Wasn't she living with that elderly widow, her aunt Vere, at the time?"

"Yes, she was," said Otto.

"Anyway, I think she's quite the sweetest thing! She talks in such a gentle, sweet way, not in the least affected, and yet she's so distinguished-looking, quite a lady. And as pretty as a picture. Beautiful, in fact."

"Do you think so?" asked Otto.

"Yes. You must be very proud of her, not every young man has your good fortune. Oh, there goes the bell! They like to make an early start at de Horze."

They made their way to the conservatory at the back of the house, where they found Madame van Erlevoort presiding over the long breakfast table. She looked up with a fond smile as they entered. Eline was talking to Theodore, noting how sturdy he was, broad-shouldered and even slightly stocky, with his thick beard trimmed short, so unlike his brothers Otto and Etienne, but in his loud, cheery voice the family resemblance was unmistakable. His wife, young Madame van Erlevoort, or Truus, as he called her, was still busy with the preparations for breakfast, assisted by Mathilda and Frédérique. Nurse Frantzen was settling the van Rijssel foursome on their chairs and tying napkins under their chins. Etienne came in from the garden with Cor, Theodore's eighteen-year-old son, a midshipman on furlough. They were followed by the girls and the boys, Willy and Gustaaf, full of fun at the expense of their Uncle Howard, whose English they did not understand and whom they were trying to teach Dutch.

"Good morning, Nily," said Otto, approaching Eline.

"Morning, Otto," answered Eline, offering her hand. She found herself enjoying the noisy bustle of a happy family. To her, who as a child had had no one but her sister to play with and had spent several years in quiet tedium with her elderly aunt, the joyous mêlée, so very far removed from the soirées and balls she was accustomed to in The Hague, was exhilarating. Everyone was so friendly, too; they all seemed to be growing quite fond of her, even Frédérique. She didn't mind when the little ones climbed onto her lap and patted her with their sticky fingers or disturbed her hair. She was seated between Otto and young Tina, on whom she doted and who kept hovering about her just as Cateau van der Stoor had done back in The Hague. That became her fixed place at table. Old Madame van Erlevoort was flanked by her two youngest grandchildren—Theodore's youngest, Edmée or Memée, and Kitty Howard, her English son-in-law's only child, and as she surveyed the long table alive with youthful gaiety she thought no one in the world could be happier than she, grey-haired but young at heart.

After breakfast Theodore proposed a visit to the Big Tree, which, he claimed, had one of the thickest trunks in Gelderland; he would go there on foot with Howard, Etienne and Cor. Eline and Otto would walk, too, they declared, and the three girls herded all the children, including Memée and Kitty, into the covered wagon.

The breakfast room was a shambles, the chairs in disarray and the table a chaos of platters and glasses while the floor was littered with napkins as well as Tina's hat, Nico's toy spade and Memée's ball.

"Are you sure you don't mind all the commotion, Mama?" asked Truus, taking Madame van Erlevoort's hand. They were still seated at the breakfast table, surveying the ruins. "Really, I'm becoming rather worried. The children are so dreadfully noisy at times that it's a relief when they're absent."

"What a thing to say!" responded Madame. "You ought to be ashamed of yourself!"

"Well, my foursome often drives me to despair, too, Truus!" Mathilda assured her.

"Now don't you worry about me, dear," said Madame. "I spent all winter looking forward to my summer visit to de Horze, and I am thrilled to be with you all. And it was sweet of you to invite Eline, too."

"I have invited them to London to join us for the season next year, once they are married," said Catherine. "I rather like her."

Truus looked away, reaching for a crumpled napkin which she proceeded to smooth and fold.

"And you, Truus?" asked Madame van Erlevoort, noting her daughter-in-law's hesitation. "You like her too, don't you?"

"Well, I don't know her very well yet. I do think it very nice of her to adapt so entirely to our ways and habits, so that we can dispense with ceremony—for which I wouldn't have time in any case; I'm far too busy. I appreciate that very much. But you know me, it takes me a while to form an opinion about people."

"That sounds remarkably diplomatic to my ears. As for me, I either like someone or I don't. It's as simple as that."

"Oh, I wasn't being diplomatic, all I meant was that I hardly know Eline since she's only been here a week. She seems very nice, but I'm not sure how I feel about her yet."

It was on the tip of Mathilda's tongue to say that she wasn't sure how she felt about Eline either, despite having known her for years, but she kept silent.

"Please don't take it amiss, Mama, but now that we're on the subject—"

"Well?"

"The thing is, there's something about Eline that makes me think she might not fit in very well with the rest of the family. She adapts herself, certainly, but I'm not sure she does so with all her heart. You don't mind my saying this, do you? There's nothing I'd like better than to find that I'm completely mistaken about her, which I probably will, once I get to know her properly."

She was loath to admit it, but she did not care for Eline. A large, sensible woman and a good mother, Truus ruled over her small empire with firmness and gentle determination, making her will pass as law, and was consequently accustomed to speaking her mind. Now, however, she had restrained herself, for she had noticed how touched her mother-in-law was by Eline's attentions and displays of affection towards her; she did not wish to disappoint the old lady, who had evidently taken Eline to her heart as her son's bride-to-be. Nonetheless, Truus couldn't help feeling that Eline looked slightly out of place in their rural family setting, there was a certain artificiality about her, something that didn't quite ring true. She was not to know that Eline was in fact feeling more herself than ever, that she felt happy in the bosom of the van Erlevoort family, and that staying at de Horze had sharpened her faculties. All Truus could see was an over-civilised, pampered society girl affecting to love the simple life in the country, and this irked her, as did the large blue bow on Eline's dress of smooth, pale-blue lawn.

Catherine Howard was all indignation. Eline would be a lovely sister-in-law, she maintained, and launched into such high praise of Eline that Madame van Erlevoort's face was soon wreathed in smiles once more.

"No, really, Truus, I don't understand your reservations. I admire Eline, especially for the way she has made herself at home with us all. I can assure you that when I first arrived in London with Howard to meet his family I felt very awkward, even though they extended me the most cordial welcome you can imagine. As for Eline—good heavens! I feel as if I have known her all my life, she is such agreeable company, so accommodating, I can't imagine anyone easier to get along with. Truly, I can't understand what makes you think she might not fit in. It's not very charitable of you to think it, either."

Truus gave a light laugh and excused herself as best she could, and as the maid had come in to clear the table, her mother-in-law, Mathilda and Catherine went out to the veranda to sit in the shade, while she herself remained invisible for the rest of the morning, absorbed in her domestic duties.

The covered wagon had long since departed. Theodore, Howard, Etienne and Cor walked in front, followed by Otto and Eline, who had opened her large lace parasol.

The men conversed in a mixture of English and Dutch; Howard claimed to understand the latter and was able to speak two or three words, while Theodore kept wavering in his English discourse on the subject of tenants and farming. Some farmhands in their Sunday suits passed by with a respectful greeting. The sun-baked road ran between russet-gold fields of rye and oats; there was not a breath of wind. Beyond, white on pink, gleamed the flowering buckwheat. On the horizon stood a farmhouse near some trees, with a faint plume of grey smoke rising up into the bright blue sky.

"I expect you feel yourself quite the king of the castle here," said Howard.

"Oh, no," replied Theodore. "I feel more like a farmer than a king, to be honest. But if you turn round a moment you'll have a fine view of my castle."

They all paused to look. Through a break in the trees de Horze could be seen in the distance, white as chalk, with its dainty shutters, its white, pointed turrets jutting into the blue and the wide verandas festooned with Virginia creeper. The pond glittered like an oval mirror in the midst of the fresh greensward, which was speckled with white doves.

"What a delightful view," enthused Eline. "Oh look, there are people waving at us!"

"Grandma and the aunts, I suppose," said Cor.

In the shade of one of the verandas they could make out the flutter of several white handkerchiefs, and they waved back, while Etienne shouted "Hurrah" at the top of his voice.

"Well, so much for the fine view," said Theodore. "Time to move on, or we'll never get to the Big Tree."

Eline spoke English quite fluently, and Howard enjoyed talking with her. He drew her into an animated conversation while she strolled arm in arm with Otto, who was holding her parasol. She was struck by how easy it was for her to engage the sympathy of men, while women only seemed to like her if she made a conscious effort to make herself agreeable to them.

While she was conversing it flashed through her mind that Madame van Erlevoort only liked her because of Otto, and Catherine only because she was friendly by nature. Their feelings did not run deep, she could tell, but on the other hand, how different it was with old Madame van Raat, with dear Cateau, and now with little Tina as well. She smiled and leant closer to Otto; what did she care about the others? She had him now, and his love was all she needed.

It was close to an hour's walk to the Big Tree. Leaving the golden cornfields behind, they took the lane along a stretch of heath flushed pink with erica, then entered the deep shade of a grove of densely columned pine trees, redolent with the pungent odour of resin.

The lane curved, and a huddle of houses came into view. It was the village likewise known as de Horze, which boasted a bakery, a vicarage, an inn with stables and a modest church in the centre. Eline looked about her with bemusement, declaring that she did not see any village.

"But that's it—right there!" said Otto.

"What? Those cottages?" gasped Eline.

They all laughed, including Howard, and Etienne asked Eline if she had been expecting to see something along the lines of Nice or Biarritz.

"Or were you were thinking of somewhere like Scheveningen, with the Kurhaus?" he quipped. "I say, Elly, can you tell the difference between rye and oats yet?"

"No, not quite. I know what buckwheat looks like, and I know flax when I see it—very pale yellow, dotted with wild flowers— and I know potatoes," said Eline, counting the crops on her graceful fingers. "But I don't know anything about rye or oats or barley. So you can stop quizzing me, Etienne! But Theodore, are you telling me you are lord and master of all this?"

She laughed beneath her wide-brimmed straw hat. There were chuckles all round at Eline's ignorance, although a look of dismay flitted across Theodore's features. Eline immediately regretted having laughed, for she did not wish to give offence, and quickly added that de Horze was a truly delightful place with the most picturesque views.

"And the Big Tree?" she asked. "Where is the Big Tree?"

They crossed the village, scattering chickens as they went. The blacksmith and some farmers doffed their caps to the landlord as they stood by the wayside, grinning and ogling the strangers in his company. Then they had to walk across a meadow and Theodore called to a young farmhand to keep the cow tethered, as Eline was clearly afraid of the massive beast with its bulging eyes and chewing, drooling maw.

When Etienne and Cor began to make mournful mooing noises at the cow, Eline became nervous and begged them to stop.

"Serves you right for making fun of de Horze, Eline!" boomed Theodore, but the veiled look she gave him so beguiled him that he hastened to add that Etienne and Cor should stop teasing. At the far end of the meadow stood the Big Tree, an oak with a colossal trunk and a mighty crown. Frédérique, Marianne, Henrietta and the children had already settled themselves between the spreading roots at the base, and raised a cheer when the walking party arrived. They clamoured for Howard and Eline to say what they thought of the Big Tree. Eline, looking very serious, complied by pronouncing it immense and prodigious, but Theodore noticed the twinkle in her eye as she said this, and wagged his finger at her accusingly until she pealed with laughter, especially when Howard solemnly concluded:

"A big tree, indeed! I never saw one quite so big. How interesting!"

"You wait! I'll catch you!" cried Theodore, and ran after Eline, who fled shrieking until she collapsed on the grass with her arms outstretched.

"Theodore, stop it! I shall call Otto!"

"I'll teach you, you wicked girl! Call Otto if you like! I'll teach you!" and he seized her wrists and shook her arms with mock force, while she pretended to be in abominable pain. Finally he helped her to her feet, and she, still giggling, promised to better her ways and show more respect for nature.

The youngsters and their English uncle were holding hands to form a ring around the tree.

"It's quite ridiculous of Theodore to make such a fuss of Eline," Frédérique muttered to herself, but Etienne overheard.

"How tiresome you've become lately!" he exclaimed. "You can't even enjoy a joke any more!"

Nearby the small church was a pine grove, where Eline reclined on a bank smooth with fallen needles, propping up her head with her hand. Otto sat beside her. They could hear the creak of the rope pulling on the headstock before each slow clang of the bell. It was time for church. Some country folk in glossy broadcloth and shiny silk aprons passed by on the road, prayer book in hand, and Eline and Otto, themselves scarcely visible among the trees, followed them with their eyes. The scattered church goers were few in number, and after a few latecomers hurried by a Sunday hush descended on the countryside. All was still save for the distant bleating of a goat.

It was true: Eline had imagined de Horze far grander and more luxurious than it had turned out to be, and the simplicity of life on the estate made her smile when she thought back on Ouida's English castles with their complement of dukes and princes, and how, during her vigils at Aunt Vere's sickbed, she had dreamt of inhabiting such a castle herself. Compared with the past splendours of that fictional aristocracy, the living conditions of these well-to-do but necessarily frugal members of an ancient house were positively austere. Yet she would not have exchanged her present circumstances for anything, and with a smile she told Otto about how enchanted she had once been by Ouida's novels and her English castles, but that she would now give preference to de Horze, just as she preferred him, her poor country squire, to some fantasy Scottish laird with an immense fortune and a name like Erceldoune or Strathmore.

Yes, Eline felt her heart swell with happiness as she sat in that quiet glade beneath the pine trees, with Otto's voice, deep and full, sounding in her ears. He told her he could scarcely believe that she was his, his alone, and that they would indeed be united for ever. He told her she had only one fault, which was that she did not know herself as he knew her. He knew her as she really was: she had untold treasures hidden within her character, and it would be his privilege to attempt to bring them to light. In the fullness of her joy she became candid, even towards herself, more than she had ever been before, and her voice was tinged with regret as she replied that he would yet, when he knew her better, discover in her much that was bad. No, no, truly, he didn't not know her as well as he thought. There was so much going on in one's heart that one got muddled at times—she did anyway—and she had to confess that her thoughts were not always of the best, neither was she always as even-tempered as she pretended to be whenever he saw her; and she could be peevish at times, without reason, or nervous, or in low spirits, but for his sake—he was such an idealist!—she would certainly endeavour to live up to the image he had formed of her. She felt pure and good making this admission, assured that she could freely reveal to him thoughts she that she scarcely dared admit to herself. Gone was the fear of losing him through some careless word; she could now see so clearly how much he loved her, and that he loved her all the more for speaking of her feelings in that frank, unguarded way. He was like the personification of her conscience, someone in whom she could confide every secret a girl might harbour. And the more she deprecated herself in such moments of sincerity and truth, the more he worshipped her, and the more he believed he could plumb the mysteries of her soul beneath that beautiful exterior.

They listened to the hymns of the peasantry drifting from the church like a soft current of simple piety, and in the tranquillity of the moment it seemed to them that the rustic voices were steeped in poetry, a poetry that mingled with the darkling boughs above, with the aroma of pine needles, with the love in their hearts. Eline was so affected with emotion that she raised herself up a little, the better to rest her head against his chest; she could not resist twining her arms about his neck, too, and all at once, feeling herself so close to him, with her bosom pressed to his heart, she was shaken by a sob.

"Goodness! Eline, whatever is the matter?" he asked gently.

"Nothing!" she replied, breathless with exaltation. "Nothing, don't mind me—it's just that I feel so—so very happy!"

And she wept in his embrace.

It was early-to-rise and early-to-bed at the country house, and the days flew by. The weather was splendid, and most of the time was spent in the fresh air, especially by the children, who only came indoors at mealtimes or to shelter from a rare shower.

With their faces and hands as brown as berries from the sun, the youngsters—the van Rijssel foursome, the two boys, Willy and Gustaaf, and Edmée and Kitty Howard—resembled a band of little Negroes cavorting on the lawns and by the pond amid the flutter of startled doves. Often they would be pursued by any one of the three nursemaids: Truus's governess, Catherine's English nanny and Nurse Frantzen, the latter being in a state of constant anxiety about the danger of Nico falling into the pond. The youngsters inspected the aviary and the stables, they befriended the head gardener and his men, as well as the coachman and his stable boy, fed the birds and the hens and the ducks, they went swimming and took turns riding Theodore's unsaddled horse under the watchful guidance of the good-natured stable boy. They also peered in the windows of the gym room to watch the men exercise, finding Theodore impressively muscular and Howard more lithe and supple, while Etienne made a show of swinging wildly on the rings and vaulting over the horse. Most of all, however, the children were in awe of Cor, who wore a rather conceited expression while effortlessly performing the most audacious turns on the rings with his strong, sinewy limbs. After coffee the boys played cricket with Howard, or they joined the girls at a game of lawn tennis in the shade of the lofty trees in the park, or lounged under a tree with a book, or simply did nothing but lie back and daydream with their hands folded beneath their heads. After supper they went for walks or took turns in the small boat to float about the pond until darkness fell, and it would be ten o'clock before they knew it.

Eline's happiness and enjoyment of country living made her feel so entirely herself that she could scarcely believe that she was the same person as she had been a few months before. She felt completely different; it was as though her soul had unwound itself from its gleaming draperies and now rose up before her like a statue of the purest white. She no longer veiled herself in affectations, no longer played a role, she was her own self, her dear Otto's little wife-to-be, and this newfound candour lent such winsomeness to her gestures, to the slightest word she uttered, that not only Truus admitted having been mistaken about Eline, much to Catherine's satisfaction, but also that Frédérique took to spending hours exchanging sisterly confidences with her, and that Madame van Erlevoort pronounced her an angel. During moments of solitary reflection on her new selfhood, tears welled up in her eyes in gratitude for all the goodness that she had received, and her only wish was that time would not fly, but stand still instead, so that the present would last for ever. Beyond that she desired nothing, and a sense of infinite rest and blissful, blue tranquillity emanated from her being.

Dusk fell slowly, and the cloudless sky turned a pearly shade of grey studded with stars. The park was a vague, shadowy mass in the background, the glass doors of the illuminated garden room stood wide open, and out on the terrace the tea table shone in the soft light coming from the house. The children were in bed, but Marianne and Henrietta were allowed to stay up a little longer. They all sat in a large circle while Truus poured the tea. Inside, Eline could be heard singing, and from time to time a star fell from heaven.

Catherine played the accompaniment while Otto sat on the sofa, listening. It sounded to Eline as if she were hearing her own voice for the first time. She was singing Mozart's *Evening Thoughts*— crystalline but with a new velvety timbre, light and almost downy, from which the previous glittery, metallic quality had vanished. She sang effortlessly, without a thought for technique or art, and not for one moment did she imagine herself on stage in front of an audience, as she used to do during her duos with Paul. She had only to part her lips and all her joy seemed to well up from her soul, charging the melancholy words of her song with a new depth of emotion. On this long, light summer evening, now that the youngsters' noisy play had ended, her music poured a melodious calmness over the happy gathering, and they loved her all the more for the poetry that she bestowed on them.

After the song there was a ripple of applause on the terrace, and Eline could be heard laughing gaily and talking to Otto and Catherine. Henrietta and Marianne ran inside to congratulate her on her performance.

"Oh, I'll never be as good as you, Eline!" cried Marianne, who, like all Theodore's offspring, addressed their future aunt familiarly by her first name. "I sing in a choir at my boarding school in Bonn, but our music master is old and boring, and I'm not learning a thing. Have you had singing lessons for long? And who is your teacher?"

Eline seated herself beside Otto on the old-fashioned, ample sofa while the two girls perched on the arms, and told them about Roberts and her duets. Catherine had gone outside.

"I say, Eline, don't you find it boring here?" asked Henrietta.

"Boring? Why should I be bored? On the contrary!"

Henrietta was surprised. She was rather heavy for her age, but still looked very boyish sitting on the arm of the sofa, wide-legged in her red stockings and riding boots with the laces undone. There was no trace as yet of coquetry; she had ginger hair in a thick plait down her back, fun-loving grey eyes, a generous mouth and beautiful teeth. In her mind she carried a confused picture of balls attended by men in gold-braided uniforms and ladies in décolleté gowns, and to her Eline was the personification of The Hague, where all that mattered was dancing and ball dresses.

"Well, I would have thought The Hague was completely different!" she exclaimed in her boyish voice. "So much more amusing, going to all those parties, I mean. I'm not sure it would suit me in the long run, but I'd love to take a look some day. I'll come and stay with you, later on, when you're married. So I thought you'd find de Horze rather boring—it's always the same. Actually, I love it here, I've got my donkey cart and my donkey, and I also have a goat, and I can't bear the idea of going away to boarding school."

"Just you wait!" interjected Marianne, who was beginning to put on ladylike airs. "Another two years, and then it'll be time for my coming out and for you to be packed off to Bonn!"

"In your donkey cart, or with your goat!" chuckled Otto.

"How horrid! To Bonn! No thank you very much! I don't care if I'm not clever. Miss Voermans is good enough for me."

"Is she your governess?" asked Eline.

"Yes. She's staying with her relatives in Limburg at the moment. She's been with us for a long time; she teaches me and the boys, but Mama says the boys are getting too old and that they must go to boarding school as well. Papa doesn't think so, he's much more sensible, he doesn't care for all that learning. Miss Voermans is all right, although she's very ugly and as thin as a rake. So you like it here, do you?"

"I certainly do. Indeed I have no intention of leaving! We've decided to stay here, haven't we, Otto?"

He smiled and took her hand.

"Come along, Henrietta, we're boring them with our talk!" cried Marianne, springing to her feet and tugging at her sister's sleeve. "Can't you see? How could you ask such a silly question, anyway?"

"What do you mean?"

"It's silly to ask Eline whether she's bored."

"Why do you think it silly?" asked Eline.

"Because people who are engaged don't get bored!"

"How would you know?" said Hetty. "It's not as if you've ever been engaged."

Otto and Eline rose, smiling at the younger sister's gruff remonstrations.

"Where are you going, Uncle?" Marianne wanted to know.

"We are going to join the others in the garden."

"That's not what you would do, is it, Marianne?" teased Hetty. "You'd steal off into a dark corner with your beloved, wouldn't you?"

Marianne looked her sister up and down for a moment and gave an aggrieved shrug, whereupon Eline cast her a smile of sympathy and took her arm.

Outside, the tea things had been cleared to make way for a large bowl of punch made with light Rhine wine flavoured with raspberries and strawberries. Animated conversation reigned over the table while Truus took a long glass ladle and filled one glass after another.

"What is keeping Theodore and Etienne?" asked the old lady, looking about her.

"They've gone for a walk in the park," responded Mathilda.

"Theodore! Etienne!" called Frédérique.

Otto offered to go and find them, and set off towards the darkness of the wood where shadows lurked between the trunks of the lofty trees. Through a break in the canopy overhead he could see a pale moon shining in the pearl-grey evening sky. He walked on, following the winding drive. Seeing no one, he shouted their names:

"Theodore! Etienne!"

A sonorous voice answered, at the sound of which he took a side path. Presently he came upon his two brothers, lost in the dark, sitting on a park bench. He could barely distinguish their faces.

"You've been sorely missed!" declared Otto. "And now punch is being served!"

He expected Etienne to leap to his feet in his usual boisterous fashion, and was most surprised to see his young brother remain huddled on the bench with his elbows on his knees and his head in his hands.

"No punch for you then?" he asked.

"Come on Etienne, let's go!" said Theodore. "Let's take our time getting back though, Otto, because there's something we ought to discuss. I have been talking to Etienne, and apparently I have not been very diplomatic. At any rate, our young brother here appears to be rather upset."

"No I'm not," growled Etienne.

"So what's wrong?" asked Otto.

"Nothing. It's just that for the past quarter of an hour Theodore has been telling me off. It turns out that I'm lazy, idle, a free-spending scamp and goodness know what else. In other words: good for nothing."

"Oh, come now," protested Theodore, "don't go off in a sulk. That won't get you anywhere. All I did was mention your future and raise the admittedly boring subject of your financial situation. No harm in that, surely. What do you say, Otto?"

"Ah, I have spoken to Etienne on those matters myself. He was quite willing to hear me out, although I don't believe he paid much attention, I have to say."

"Well, I suppose I'm not as tactful as you are. Perhaps that's all to the good, because he seems to be paying attention now, doesn't he?"

"But you make it sound as if we're as poor as church mice!" spluttered Etienne.

"And you, dear boy, sound as pathetic as a girl. I merely explained to you that we have to keep a tight rein on our expenses here at de Horze—and the same applies to Mama in The Hague—because if we don't we will be obliged to economise in the most unpleasant manner afterwards. Can you imagine what it would do to Mama if she had to leave the family home she loves so much and has lived in for so many years? It doesn't bear thinking about. And then there's Mathilda; there doesn't appear to be any money forthcoming from van Rijssel, so she has no choice but to turn to Mama for support in educating the children. We all live very frugally, as you saw for yourself when you were here last winter with van Raat, and it is no different now. The only luxury we can afford is having you all to stay with us in the summer. In the meantime you're living it up with your student friends in Leiden, all of whom are rich or pretend to be, and you get through nearly the same amount of money over there as we do here as an entire family. So you see, old chap, this cannot continue. I don't begrudge you your carefree student days, and I'm aware that it's far from easy, once one is accustomed to spending freely, to start tightening one's belt. But still, Etienne, you really must better your ways."

Etienne kept his head bowed as they went on their way, his customary high spirits dampened. He felt a sting of conscience.

"Another thing: it's time you started thinking about graduating. Because you don't seem to have been at all busy lately."

"Well, it's summer now, isn't it?" said Etienne.

"What about last winter? Did a lot of studying then, did you?"

Etienne sighed.

"No I suppose not, but I wish you'd stop nagging! You know I will graduate eventually. Wait and see. I'll work harder."

Otto smiled, feeling a twinge of pity for his young brother. Work and Etienne didn't seem to go together at all!

"All right, that's a promise!" persisted Theodore. "I can take your word for it then, can I? Come on, let's shake on it!"

Etienne put out his hand.

"Good. And no more sulking now, please, no long faces!"

"I wasn't sulking," said Etienne crossly. Theodore's admonitions had touched a raw nerve. Thinking of his exams, he realised how unprepared he was, and how hard it was going to be to keep his promise. It had never occurred to him that he had been letting them all down—Mama, Mathilda, Theodore and the children—simply by enjoying himself in Leiden and indulging in all those lavish dinners with his fraternity, and he was at a loss as to how to repair the damage. Meanwhile they had arrived at the terrace, where Truus was replenishing the glasses.

"Ah, there you are! Just in time, too, because I wouldn't have saved any punch for you if you'd made us wait much longer!" she declared with feigned vexation. "Eline was wondering what was keeping you, Otto; she was afraid you'd fallen into the pond!"

"That's not true!" huffed Eline, whereupon Catherine, Cor and the girls raised a riotous chorus of protest at her denial. There was so much jollity that Etienne quickly forgot his cares and could not resist joining the fray with whoops of laughter. Frédérique tried in vain to calm him down, while Mathilda explained to Howard what was going on.

Madame van Erlevoort shook her head in dismay.

"It is most unkind to tease her so!" she chided gently, but her defence of Eline only increased Etienne's hilarity.

The last few days had been hot and muggy. After coffee the youngsters dispersed. The doves circled round the storks' nests atop a pair of tall poles in the middle of the lawn. On the veranda with steps leading to the garden sat the old lady with her daughters, while Eline and Frédérique were inside, playing billiards with the men.

"Where are the children?" enquired Catherine, gazing out over the freshly mown lawn, deserted now but for Theodore's three dozing hounds.

"They've gone for a stroll; to the White Hollow, I believe," replied Truus.

"The White Hollow?" Mathilda cried out in dismay. "But that's an hour's walk! And I'm sure it's going to rain."

Truus stood up and peered at the sky.

"You may be right, Tilly. I shouldn't have allowed it, I suppose, but Hetty was so insistent and your little ones so eager that I gave in, without thinking of the weather. I can't think of everything, I'm afraid. All the bustle and excitement of the children makes my head spin now and then—which is not to say that I don't love having you here, mind you!"

Heavy, slate-grey clouds were massing in the sky. The light dimmed, the leaves rustled on the boughs and the surface of the pond rippled in the rising wind.

"I hope they took umbrellas!" said the old lady, standing up. Catherine and Mathilda followed suit.

"Umbrellas! I doubt it! Children don't think of such things, they won't even have taken their hats, I wager! What shall we do? There's a heavy downpour on its way."

"We can't just leave them to their fate. Are you sure they have gone to the White Hollow?" fretted Catherine.

"Sure? Well, not really, but they were talking about it. Wait, I'll go and tell Klaas to take the covered wagon to the White Hollow."

Off she went to speak to the coachman.

Scattered raindrops began to fall. The dogs on the lawn got up, stretched, and ambled into the house one after another. Madame van Erlevoort paced the floor while Catherine and Mathilda grew increasingly nervous as they waited for Klaas to hitch the horses.

The gloomy sky lit up with a sudden flash of lightning, followed by a loud rumble of thunder. Hardly had it died away than the clouds burst forth in a heavy downpour. The billiard players hurried out to the veranda, where they all stood close together in the shelter of the awning, united in their concern for the youngsters and heedless of the raindrops blowing in their direction. There were more flashes of lightning and the ensuing thunderclaps became deafening.

"I don't think we should stay here," said Catherine anxiously. "Let's go inside. Oh, my poor Kitty!"

Truus was very fraught, blaming herself for having allowed the children to go out, and in her nervous condition she snapped at Catherine and Mathilda, then at her husband, even at her mother, and finally at Etienne, who had suggested going after them with umbrellas. Umbrellas! The boy had taken leave of his senses! Why had no one thought to warn her? Why did everything go wrong the minute her back was turned? How could she possibly run this household properly under these conditions? Suddenly she rounded on Eline:

"Eline, don't just stand there by the pillars, you'll get all wet, and it's dangerous with the lightning. Oh dear, it can't be helped, so do let's go indoors! What if they've had an accident! I can't bear it! Oh, Mathilda, why didn't you warn me? I can't take responsibility for everything, you know!"

She shooed them all into the drawing room, for there was no sense in standing around getting wet, it would only make the waiting harder to bear. Nevertheless, she kept running out to the veranda to see if the youngsters were coming, while the thunderstorm continued unabated.

Inside, they seated themselves. Little was said, and the atmosphere was charged with restless expectation. They all heaved a sigh of relief when at last the old wagon returned. The hood was secured on all sides, but small hands could be seen parting the flaps and small, wide-eyed faces peering out. The ramshackle vehicle rumbled past the house on its way to the covered entrance at the back, and there was a general rush to welcome the bedraggled passengers.

One by one they emerged: first Marianne and Henrietta, then Willy and Gustaaf, after which they helped the van Rijssel foursome and Memée to alight. Catherine flew to Kitty, who was crying. They were all soaked to the skin, their shoes and hands were covered in mud and their straw hats soggy and dripping. Bedlam broke loose as the children swarmed through the vestibule into the large dining room shouting at the tops of their voices, the three barking dogs bounding alongside.

Marianne and Hetty hooted with laughter at Willy, who had left one of his shoes in the White Hollow; Tina, Johan and Madeleine shrieked in unison as they told Mathilda how Nico had very nearly been left behind because he had gone off in search of his toy spade, which he had lost in the sand. However, Truus soon showed her mettle as mistress of the house by raising her voice commandingly and rapping loudly on the table until some semblance of order was restored. The youngsters were dispatched upstairs, where Nurse Frantzen, Truus's governess and the English nursemaid ran from room to room fetching out dry socks and vests from the wardrobes while Truus distributed bath towels. The little ones were stripped of their wet clothes, and no one heeded the thunderstorm raging outside. Marianne and Henrietta went into their room and shut the door behind them for some privacy, as everyone was running in and out, including Papa and the uncles. Willy and Gustaaf were told to help themselves, and Truus threw them towels and fresh underwear, telling them to make sure they dried themselves properly, not forgetting their backs, chests, and between their toes, while she fetched them socks and shoes. Kitty was still crying; she could be heard in another room, along with Catherine and her governess, who were conversing in English.

"Oh, Tina, do take off your wet clothes," cried Mathilda, helping Johan while her mama took charge of Nico and Frédérique saw to Madeleine. Tina, however, sat on a chair and refused to budge. Just then Eline appeared, bearing a complete set of clothes for her favourite.

"Now, now, Tina dear!" said Eline indulgently, "your poor mama is quite run off her feet, so you mustn't be cross. Will you let me help you instead? What do you say?"

Tina nodded her head, pouting like a little princess. Eline crouched down on the floor, unfastened the child's mud-spattered button boots and pulled off her soaked stockings.

"My pretty poppet, you're shivering!" she cried out in dismay, and rubbed the child's clammy feet and legs with a rough towel until they were warm and rosy once more. Tina wriggled her toes in Eline's lap, happy again. She untied her belt and began to unbutton her blouse.

"Good girl! Go on, take your clothes off, and I promise I'll brush your hair afterwards. You'll like that, won't you?"

"Will you do my hair? Will you put it up like yours?"

"Gracious no, poppet, I shall make you a braid, the way you always wear it."

"Oh please, please, Eline, put it up, won't you? I want to look like a proper lady!"

"All right then, if you do as I say. Quick, Tina, let's get you undressed first."

Eline made her stand up on the chair and proceeded to undress as if she were a doll, while Tina prattled on about the White Hollow and how frightened they had been by the lightning. She rubbed the slight, shivering body until it glowed all over, after which the little girl flung her arms around Eline's neck and squeezed with all her might. Eline had to laugh.

"You have a gift for childcare, Eline! It's as though you've been doing it all your life." exclaimed Mathilda with gratitude, for she was still occupied with Johan. Madame van Erlevoort and Frédérique looked over their shoulders and smiled at Eline. Willy and Gustaaf were teasing Hetty, who had been supplied with dry stockings at last and was now pulling them on in the middle of the floor, which was littered with shoes, wet stockings, discarded underclothing and towels.

Visibly pleased with her success, Eline set about helping Tina to don her fresh set of clothing.

"How nice you look in your clean vest! Wait, I'll give you a tickle, shall I? There you go: lift this foot, now the other one, so we can get your bloomers on. Dear me, if you go on wriggling like this and waving your arms you'll muss my hair. Fasten your buttons, go on, I know you can do it! Or did you think I was going to do everything for you? Ah, where's the hairbrush? Wait, I'll go and fetch a comb!"

"And my red hair ribbon, too!" called Tina.

Eline ran off, pausing on her way to tie a large bow in Marianne's sash.

Tina grew impatient and clamoured for Eline to hurry.

"Here I am!" said Eline, returning, and began to pile Tina's hair on the top of her head in ladylike fashion, much to everyone's amusement. Tina was thrilled, but meekly submitted to having her thick brown tresses taken down again and tied into braids.

"That's better! You're as pretty as a picture!" said Eline, combing the fringe down over the little girl's forehead.

"Now children, off you go!" said Truus, regaining her confidence, and they all trooped down the stairs.

"Eline was so good with Tina," Madame van Erlevoort said to Truus in an undertone. "You should have seen them together! Such a pretty sight! Oh, I can't tell you how relieved I am that they are all back home again, safe and sound!"

Bedtime was early at de Horze; by half-past ten all was still. Eline had spent an hour chatting with Frédérique in her bedroom, very happy to perceive the growing sympathy between them. Freddie was already under the covers and Eline had perched on the side of the bed while they exchanged confidences about all kinds of subjects, stifling their occasional giggles so as not to disturb the silence prevailing in the house. At length Eline had returned to her room on tiptoe, and now she was alone at last. She lit her candle and slowly began to undress, her lips curved in an unconscious, happy smile. She paused a moment, sunk in thought, with her hair hanging loose about her bare shoulders. There was nothing else that she wanted, nothing at all: she had simply everything she could wish for.

She opened the window and looked outside. The rain had stopped and the air was fragrant with moist foliage. The sky was clear, wiped clean of leaden clouds but for some lingering streaks, from which rose a brilliant crescent moon. The far-flung fields lay muffled in silence; a lone windmill held aloft a dark, motionless sail, starkly defined against the pale sheen of the evening sky. The ditches glittered like strips of metal, and a scented freshness emanated like a gentle sigh from the slumbering landscape. Eline leant out of the window, hugging her bare arms. She felt as if that soft sigh of freshness had sweetened all her thoughts with the fragrance of wild flowers, banishing the stale, sickly smell of her former state of mind. It was like inhaling the heady perfume of musk and opopanax, and she felt very young, younger than she had ever felt before, and oh!—of this she was certain—never had she been in love as she was now, never! Her Otto! Thinking of him she felt no need whatsoever to conjure up some idealised image of him; she thought of him as he was, manly and strong in his good-natured simplicity, with one single thought governing his mind: the thought of her. His love was so rich, so full, so all-encompassing. And hers was growing by the day, she believed … no, it couldn't grow any further, that would be impossible! No further wishes, no concerns about the future; it would unfold of its own accord, a perspective tinged with a golden glow! Nothing but the stillness of that lake into which her soul had glided, nothing but the peace and love of that blue ecstasy! Nothing but that … She could not imagine what more a human being could wish for.

Only, there was one tiny blemish in all that clear expanse of blue, an inkling of fear that change might yet come! It was so very long since she had prayed, and she was unsure how to go about it, whether she should say the words aloud or just think them. Indeed, she no longer knew whether she believed in God, she no longer knew what she believed, but now, at this moment, she dearly wished to pray that it might remain as it was now, that nothing would ever change—oh, for that gentle happiness, that tranquillity of mind, that blue to remain with her for ever!

"Never again as it was, please God; make everything stay the same as it is now! I'll die if anything changes!" she whispered under her breath, and as she folded her hands in prayer, a teardrop quivered on her lashes. But it was a tear of joy, and in her joy that tiny fear drowned like a drop in the ocean.

XX

A UGUST WAS STIFLINGLY HOT IN THE HAGUE, though the evenings were refreshing on the terrace at Scheveningen or at the Tent in the Wood. It was Sunday evening, and Betsy decided to stay in for a change. It was so long since old Madame van Raat had been to see her, and so, rather than go to Scheveningen, which was less interesting on a Sunday anyway, she had instead invited her mother-in-law to visit. Tea would be taken in the green conservatory, where the glass doors already stood open. Henk took a turn about the garden with his mother, who professed admiration for his splendid long-stemmed roses. Betsy and Vincent sat alone.

"I have had a letter from Eline; she is returning with the van Erlevoorts next Wednesday. Apparently the Howards are staying on a little longer at de Horze," she said.

"Oh? And when Eline returns I am to move out, I suppose?" he responded bluntly. Betsy was taken aback, but smiled very sweetly.

"The very idea! Certainly not. You know that our home is yours until you decide where you want to go. Have you heard anything from that friend of yours in New York, what's his name again?"

"Lawrence St Clare. No, I haven't had any news for quite some time. But then it's hard to keep up with friends over such a long distance. I can't say I blame him."

He leant back in his cane armchair with a slightly aggrieved air. In reality, however, he felt very well at ease, agreeably lulled by the luxury surrounding him in the tenebrous lighting of the green conservatory. The garden beyond was well kept, rich in flowers, with an ornamental marble urn on the lawn. In that soothing environment, with the presence of Betsy in her light summer dress, elegantly poised over the softly gleaming silver and Japanese porcelain on the tea tray, he felt shielded from the discomforts of life. It was all very reposeful, monotonous even, but to him it was refreshing. He knew he had the upper hand with Betsy, but there was no need to throw his weight about just yet. Besides, he felt distinctly idle. For the present, life was easy, and he had nothing to worry about.

"What would you say if I were to look for a wife?" he asked abruptly, the sight of Betsy having put him in mind of the pleasures a wealthy marriage might offer.

"A wife? Oh, an excellent idea! Shall I try and find you one? What sort of wife did you have in mind?"

"She needn't be a beauty, just elegant. But not too naive and idealistic, please! And with money, naturally."

"Naturally. You wouldn't want to get carried away by an unsuitable passion, would you? What is your opinion of the Eekhof girls?"

"The very idea! All they do is giggle! No money there either, is there?"

"Some say there is, others say they live beyond their means. Anyway, you could find out. But are you serious, Vincent? Or were you just making conversation?"

"No indeed. I think it would be very sensible of me to get married. Don't you agree?"

Betsy looked at him intently, full of secret contempt. With his lacklustre eyes, his languid gestures, his weary drawl, he appeared to her as anything but an ideal husband for a young girl.

"Not entirely. It seems to me that you're an inveterate egotist. And I can hardly imagine a wife getting much support from you. You're weak—I mean your morale, of course."

She regretted her words on the instant, and was annoyed by her carelessness. She almost shuddered as he regarded her with that inscrutable smile of his, and those pallid, snakelike eyes.

"And a wife always needs support, eh?" he said, with slow emphasis. "As you do yourself. You find support in Henk, you can rely on him for everything, can't you? And he's strong enough—I mean his physique, of course."

Each word was uttered with what sounded to Betsy like spite, and each word pricked her like a needle, but for all her domineering nature she dared not answer back, hiding her consternation with an amiable little laugh, as if it had been mere banter on his part. He echoed her laugh with his own, equally light and amiable.

They paused a moment, both keenly aware of the resentment underlying their ostensibly jocular exchange. To end the silence Betsy launched into a plaintive account of her relations with her mother-in-law, how she was misjudged by the old lady and how she despaired of their ever getting along. But his air of utter indifference as he listened brought home to her just how much she had come to loathe him in these past weeks of proximity. If only she could send him packing there and then! But she knew that would be impossible without risking some awful scene; he would simply not go away, he would hang around for ever and ever, while she remained powerless to take matters in hand. It was all Henk's fault. If her husband had given Vincent that miserable sum of money he needed she would never have taken it into her head to invite him to stay. She despised Vincent, and she despised herself for being intimidated by him; she was rich and happy after all, so what harm could he ever do to her? But the harder she tried to shake off her fear, the more firmly lodged it became, like some debilitating idiosyncrasy of mind.

Henk and his mother returned from their leisurely stroll in the garden and seated themselves in the conservatory by one of the open glass doors. The old lady had not spoken since admiring the roses, and had grown pensive. In her son's luxuriously appointed home she now perceived a degree of coldness, an emptiness, which she found even more dispiriting than the vacancy of her own lonely abode. And suddenly it came to her: she missed Eline—Eline who radiated charm and agreeableness wherever she went. She missed the dear girl, so unlike her sister Betsy, so warm-hearted and sympathetic. And she could not help remarking dolefully:

"Your home seems so empty with Elly being away. How dreadfully we will miss her when she is married and goes away for ever. Dear, dear Elly."

She did not hear what Betsy and Vincent said in response, nor did she hear Henk's comforting words. She sat with her head bowed, staring vacantly at the veined hands she held clasped in her lap. How bleak life seemed, nothing but heartache, sad partings and tears, a grey realm peopled by tragic shadows.

A shiver passed through her, and Betsy asked if she felt cold, whereupon Henk closed the glass doors and called for the gas lamp to be lit.

Although she would never have cared to admit it, Betsy agreed with her mother-in-law that it had been lonely and dismal in the house of late, despite Vincent being there to entertain her with his supposed social graces. There was so little variation in the summer, it was always either the Tent or Scheveningen, and she was beginning to feel quite suffocated by the tedium of it all. And when Eline returned at last, radiant in her newfound happiness, it was as though a fresh country breeze blew through Betsy's plush salons. With Eline babbling on about the delights of life at de Horze, about Theodore and Truus and the children, about the Howards and the van Rijssel foursome, Betsy came to realise that her mother-in-law had been right about her home being dreary without Eline. Betsy herself began to have misgivings about her sister's departure, and her feelings towards her softened considerably. She also changed her mind about Otto, whom she had earlier found too stiff and mannered to her liking. Now that she knew him better, she found him likeable enough, and urged him to dine with them often.

Thanks to Eline's presence the talk at the dinner table became lively again, quite different from the stilted conversations she and her husband had been having with Vincent during mealtimes. Betsy was grateful for this, and cordial towards Eline as a consequence, and the sisters had endless discussions about Eline's trousseau, which she would have to hurry to assemble if they were to be married in the autumn. They spent their afternoons shopping or consulting with seamstresses; one time they accompanied Otto on a two-day trip to Brussels, where Eline wanted to order her wedding dress: extravagant yet simple, nothing but white satin, no lace trimmings or bows.

Meanwhile Eline, in all the bustle, had little time to think, only at bedtime did she find a moment's peace. The evenings were often spent at home. It was September; Scheveningen was gradually losing its appeal, and with Otto coming to dinner so often it generally grew late without their noticing it. She sat with him in the garden, or in the violet ante-room, absorbed in her tranquil felicity, as though she had never known anything else … it was all so very calm and contented that she almost wished for more diversity of emotion … but no, she loved Otto, and that single emotion was enough for her … just that sense of peace, that blue haze of serenity, lasting for ever and ever.

And yet, as she readapted herself to life in The Hague, she found her initial vivacity diminishing by degrees as she ran out of stories to relate about de Horze; the wholesome country vigour she had gained seemed to evaporate now that she no longer had occasion to romp on the floor with the children or recline in pine groves with Otto, now that she spent so much time sitting in a comfortable armchair, smiling serenely while she waited for her fiancé to reappear. The hours that she and Otto were parted were filled with the pleasant distraction of Vincent's soft voice as he held forth about his travels, the cities he had visited, the people he had met, and his own philosophy of life. Having found happiness herself, she loftily dismissed his pessimistic outlook, reasoning with a charming want of logic that made Vincent smile and shrug. That was all very well, he said, but she would discover for herself one day that making a life for oneself was not as easy as it appeared. One thing led to another; circumstances changed, influencing each other in random ways ranging from the slightest, most benign coincidences to catastrophic misfortunes, and life, well, life was the chain of fate linking all these contingencies together … and there was nothing she or anyone else could do about it.

"So you believe that everything is preordained, and that when I think I am doing something out of my own free will I am really only doing it because—how shall I put it?" she asked in some bewilderment late one afternoon during one of her tête-à-têtes with him in her room.

"You only think it's your own free will, but your will is nothing other than the outcome of hundreds of thousands of previous so-called chance occurrences. Yes indeed, that is what I believe."

"Vincent, what fatalism! In that case I might as well remain seated in this easy chair and simply wait for things to happen."

"You could do worse. But I assure you that if you did just sit there doing nothing, your passive attitude would not be the result of your own free will, but of all sorts of tiny, insignificant events which you've mostly forgotten about or didn't even notice at all."

She pondered this, giving a vague smile, then slowly nodded her head.

"It's strange, but I have a feeling you might be right. It could be true, I suppose."

She enjoyed these conversations, which generally ended with her agreeing with him. Each time she felt her old sympathy for him flare up anew, and each time she was reminded of her father, the way he spoke, his gestures, the expression on his face. She thought Vincent more interesting than he was, and one day, in a romantic mood, she suddenly felt that her love for Otto might not be enough after all. The notion flashed across her mind like a bolt of lightning, and for a split second she thought she saw a ghost. But the ghost vanished, and she laughed again. How strange to have such peculiar, nervous fancies!

"So you believe … " she resumed, still somewhat flustered.

He smiled at her.

"What?" he asked.

"You believe, for instance, that if I marry Otto all I'm doing is following a preordained path?"

He patted her hand gently.

"My dear girl, why bother your pretty little head with things like that? You love van Erlevoort, you're happy, what more could you wish for? Happiness is a butterfly: when it comes within reach it's no good trying to catch it so you can study its anatomy, it's far too delicate and ethereal a creature, and you'll only end up killing it."

She looked up in wonder. How clever he was at putting his thoughts into words, in such a plain-spoken way, without poetical affectation, as if he were saying something perfectly simple! And he was quite unselfconscious about it, too, which just showed how innately artistic he was. Then she saw, to her alarm, that he had turned deathly pale. He rose unsteadily from his seat, with wild staring eyes and a morbid, purplish look about the small, sagging mouth.

"Good heavens, Vincent, what's matter?" she cried out, springing to her feet.

"Nothing, I just need some air—could you open the window, oh please—" he gasped.

"Can I get you anything? Water?" she offered tremulously.

"No, no—air—I need air," he faltered.

She rushed over to the window, but her hands were shaking so badly that she was unable to open it, and she rang for the maid.

"My God, oh my God!" she cried.

Vincent had collapsed onto the Persian couch in a faint, and was now sliding off the cushions to the floor until only his head remained propped against the side. His forehead was bathed in perspiration and his breathing choked and rasping.

"My God!" screamed Eline in desperation.

She ran out to the landing and shouted down the stairs:

"Betsy! Mina! Henk! Help! It's Vincent—come quickly! I think he's dying!"

She ran back and tugged furiously at the bell pull.

There was a commotion in the depths of the house, and a moment later Betsy came running up the stairs followed by the three maids, Gerard the manservant, and little Ben. Henk was out.

"It's Vincent!" cried Eline. "Vincent! He's dying!"

Betsy was frightened, but remained quite calm. She promptly dispatched Anna, the nursemaid, to take Ben away, and sent Gerard to fetch the local general practitioner, as Reijer was bound to be out. With assistance from Eline and Mina she lifted Vincent onto the couch and ordered Grete to fetch some vinegar.

"Go on, hurry up!" she snapped.

Vincent lay motionless with his eyes closed, the purplish stains about the lips still showing. Betsy undid the buttons of his jacket and waistcoat, and removed his tie and collar.

"Pass me some eau de cologne, Eline. Do try and be helpful, you know I'm no good at this sort of thing!"

She began to dab Vincent's temples and wrists with hand-kerchiefs, some soaked in vinegar and some in eau de cologne. She asked Eline what had happened and Eline explained that they had been sitting down having a chat when he had suddenly stood up and then keeled over, just like that, oh, it was a terrible shock!

"Do you think he's going to die?" she asked, quaking.

"Of course not. He's fainted, that's all. It's happened before, you know. When you were at de Horze."

"It's happened before?" echoed Eline, aghast.

Betsy did not answer, and just then the door opened quietly and Otto entered.

"Grete told me Vincent has taken ill. Can I be of any help?" he asked.

"No, no, I can manage, but do take Eline away, she's so up-set."

"Oh please, do let me help you!" begged Eline.

"No, I'd rather you didn't, the doctor will be here soon, at least I hope so, and then everything will be all right. Off you go, now!"

Otto offered to check whether Reijer had returned in the meantime, but Betsy said there was no need, so he ushered Eline out of the room. He had spent the day at the office, and had arranged to go for a walk with Eline afterwards, but now he led her to the salon, where they seated themselves on the sofa. She began to cry.

"Betsy said it has happened before, but I've never seen anything like it in my whole life. I thought he was dying! Aunt Vere had the same look about her mouth when she died," she said breathlessly.

He pressed her to his chest and kissed her forehead.

"Come now my darling, you must calm down. I am sure he will be all right. Why, you're shaking!"

"Oh, I'm in such a state! My nerves … Oh, Otto!"

He patted her hand gently.

"There, there, you must try and calm down."

"I get so dreadfully upset … I can't bear this sort of thing."

She felt something like a twinge of conscience, wondering whether there could be any connection between the last words she had spoken to Vincent and his fainting fit. But she couldn't recall what their conversation had had been about, so she leant her head wearily against Otto's shoulder.

"Childish of me, isn't it?" she murmured, still trembling. "But I can't help being squeamish; I remember once seeing a dog being run over, and it still makes me shudder to think of it!"

"You're a little oversensitive," he said.

"Oh yes, I'm so … I feel so … never mind, just hold me," she murmured, leaning closer to him.

"Darling!" he whispered.

"My Otto, my very own Otto," she sighed. "Oh yes, I'm far too sensitive. How you'll put up with me I cannot imagine. I'm always so … Oh poor Vincent, I do feel sorry for him, don't you?"

"Yes I do; he doesn't seem at all well."

She continued to lean against his shoulder for some time, and gradually calmed down. Her weeping subsided, but her eyes remained moist and sad, for she was thinking of that split second when she had seen the ghost, willing herself to recall what it had looked like, the better to banish it for ever. The ghost must never, ever come back to haunt her, it was just too upsetting!

After a hurried lunch following the physician's visit, Betsy decided to send Dirk with the coupé to fetch Dr Reijer after all, and when the latter arrived she went with him to see Vincent, who had been put to bed in his room. As it was not the first time Vincent had fainted, she knew what to do: following Dr Reijer's instructions, she made sure his head was lower than the rest of his body by stuffing cushions under his back. Slowly Vincent came to himself again. He opened his eyes a moment, and trailed his hand over the coverlet. Dr Reijer turned down the light in the room and prescribed complete rest for the patient.

"It's not dangerous, is it, doctor?" asked Betsy downstairs in the salon, where Eline, Otto and Henk were waiting.

"Not immediately, dear lady," replied Reijer, hurriedly buttoning up his smart demi-season coat. "But you do realise, twice in relatively short succession … It does not bode well for Mr Vere's state of health. I have the impression he suffers from anaemia; altogether a weak constitution, very weak. What he needs is repose, as I mentioned before. Have you seen the Ferelijn family? They are all looking very well, including the children. Such a charming lady. Well now, *au revoir*. I will gladly make use of your vehicle again, thank you. *Au revoir*, Mr van Raat, I'll let myself out."

Anna the nursemaid would keep vigil at Vincent's bedside. The house was silent; Henk retired for a rest and Betsy went upstairs with Ben to put him to bed herself rather than risk a commotion by leaving this task to the erratic Mina. Otto and Eline remained in the ante-room.

"Are you feeling better?" he asked as she settled herself on a cushion at his feet.

She took a deep breath and nodded reassuringly. Indeed, she felt quite calm and safe sitting there resting her head against his knee, and had no desire to dwell on the muddled thoughts crowding her mind: Vincent's sudden illness, the conversation they had been having which she couldn't remember, the pity she felt for this cousin of hers, who reminded her so very much of her father. But no, she was determined not to think about any of these things; she was determined to be happy, here and now, close to her Otto.

"I always feel better when I'm with you. You're so good to me."

"A while ago you mentioned that you sometimes get very nervous for no reason. Melancholy, too, I believe. In this case there certainly was a reason, of course, so it is perfectly natural that you were upset. But I want you to promise me that next time you feel nervous for no reason you will come straight to me."

"Yes, of course."

"You'll come to me and tell me exactly how you feel, and you'll trust me because I love you and will always do everything in my power to make you feel better. Promise?"

"All right, I promise. I never had anyone to talk to before, except Henk, in whom I confided from time to time, but I don't believe he understood me, although he was extremely kind. At least I have you now! Oh, Otto, don't you believe that true love only happens once in a lifetime? I mean real, true love, not just having a crush on someone, which happens quite a lot, doesn't it?"

"Well, not to me; at least not any more!" he replied with a smile.

"Then you agree. You love me properly, not just because of the way I look or anything like that. At first I didn't understand why you loved me, but now I do: you love me because, because … oh dear, I don't quite know how to say it, but I can feel it deep down: I mean everything to you, don't I? But when you gave me that fan last winter, the Bucchi fan, how much did you love me then? Go on, tell me!"

He listened indulgently to her ramblings and planted a kiss on the top of her head by way of an answer. Oh yes, she knew perfectly well that she could depend on him, that she could trust him completely, and that he would make her happy again whenever she was the least bit despondent. At length, feeling increasingly fatigued after the upheaval of the past hours, she fell silent, merely humming a little from time to time with her head resting against his knee, until she dozed off in the gathering dusk. He sat very still, gazing down at her, and for the first time since falling in love he felt a pinprick of something like doubt in his mind, doubt whether everything would turn out as he had imagined. A sense of wistfulness came over him as he kept his eyes fixed on her sleeping form, pondering the notion that however great one's happiness, there was always a drop of bile in there somewhere, even if it only transpired from one's private musings and fears.

XXI

GEORGES DE WOUDE VAN BERGH was studying hard for his
Vice-Consular examination, when one day Emilie called
at the Verstraetens'. She had a long talk with Lili's parents in private, which made Lili exceedingly nervous and tearful, so much
so that Marie and Frédérique were at pains to console her. Emilie
laughingly apologised for her unceremonious visit, explaining
that her elderly father was ailing and never ventured out nowadays, which was why she had taken to managing all his affairs
and had now come on his behalf in connection with his son's
wholly honourable pretensions. She herself was not entirely in
agreement with Georges' notions of the financial necessities of
life, she had to admit, and she could very well imagine that Lili's
parents might have some reservations regarding the matter, but
on the other hand Georges' future looked decidedly promising.
Besides, the pair of them seemed so headstrong and determined
to enter a life together, in spite of everything, that it would be
quite useless to try and talk them out of it! The question was,
really, did the Verstraetens have any personal objection to him, or
would they permit the two to wait until such time as they could get
married and live together without too great a risk of starvation?
Would Lili's parents be able, when the time came, to part with
their daughter? And if they were not opposed to Lili's friendship
with Georges, what would be the best way to proceed? A proper
engagement, or just a union of hearts? It was regrettable that
Georges and Lili had made themselves somewhat conspicuous,
so that their mutual feelings were common knowledge in The
Hague, but they were young and impetuous and would doubtless
become more prudent in time. So the question was … and Emilie
reiterated her message in her genial, lively manner, but inwardly
feeling a trifle anxious as to the reply.

Madame Verstraeten sighed and shook her head with an air of
misgiving, but her husband, to Emilie's relief, did not appear to

take unkindly to her words. However, he did have objections: Lili was so young, still a child, really, and it would wiser for her to wait a while, so as to give herself a chance to make quite sure that he was Mr Right before making any definite commitment. He liked de Woude very much and believed him to be a hard-working and honourable young man, but still, he feared that Georges' views of his financial situation were unrealistic, and that his optimism was inspired by the tender feelings he had for Lili. As for young de Woude's claims to eschewing luxury, the old gentleman had some doubts. Emilie listened attentively and in some confusion, because in her heart she agreed with all Mr Verstraeten's objections and yet, now that she had been persuaded into the folly of this visit—reluctantly, but for Georges' sake—she was loath to let her beloved brother down. Now she wished to make it appear that the objections existed in Mr Verstraeten's mind alone, and found herself hotly denying them. How tiresome to be obliged to say things one didn't mean! She might even be doing Georges a disservice by pleading his cause with such fervour, but then the boy was so deeply in love, and who knows, he might be right after all! She was no oracle, and anyway there were plenty of households that managed perfectly well on a modest income, such as those of civil servants or first lieutenants. She felt flustered and foolish, but there was no going back now.

While siding with Georges, she became inwardly angry with him for putting her in this position. Why could she never refuse him anything? Why was she being forced to be an accomplice to his ruin?

But she was true to her word, and pleaded his cause so successfully that Madame Verstraeten went to fetch Lili, who burst into tears and showered Emilie with kisses. There would not be an official betrothal, it was decided, Madame not being in favour of long engagements—they sometimes went on for years, especially among those of modest means—and Emilie assured Lili that having a union of hearts with the blessing of her parents was an excellent compromise, under the circumstances. Anyway, it was better thus, was it not, because if on further acquaintance they found that they did not suit one another after all, there would be no harm done, and if on the other hand their friendship blossomed over time, well, so much the better. She ought to look on the bright side, why, she had gained quite a victory over her strict parents, so what more did she want? To marry on the instant—reception tomorrow, civil ceremony and church wedding in a day or two and then off to a tiny garret to live happily ever after? Surely not.

Lili smiled through her tears and kissed her parents. They knew best, and she would not go against their wishes.

That afternoon Georges was invited to dinner, after which a splendid September evening was spent in the garden. It was late when Georges took his leave, late, too, when Marie and Lili retired to their room and undressed. Marie listened with kind forbearance to Lili's excited chatter about her future with Georges: she would so love to travel, and Georges' position in the Diplomatic Service meant that they would do just that—later, of course, much later; her mind was quite set on it, for all that he told her not to have too many illusions. She lay back and stretched herself comfortably between the cool sheets, her arms folded behind her tousled mane of pale blonde hair, and she smiled at her rosy visions.

Marie got into bed, too, and for a moment it was quiet in the darkened room. Then there was a knock at the door, which opened almost at once. The girls were startled.

"Hush, hush, it's only me," whispered a subdued voice, and they saw a short, stooped figure in nightclothes holding a lit candle. "Hush, it's all right. I'm just popping in for a chat."

It was good old Dien, the Verstraeten family mascot, who was always so helpful when they staged plays or *tableaux vivants*. The old biddy approached, treading softly in her slippered feet, while the candlelight cast a yellow glow over the shrivelled face beneath the white nightcap.

"Dear me, Dien! You gave me quite a turn! You look like a ghost!" cried Marie.

"Shush! Everyone is in bed, but I thought you'd probably still be awake. May I come in?"

"Of course, Dien! Do come in!" said Lili cheerfully. "What have you got to tell us?"

Dien seated herself on the side of Lili's bed.

"Your old Dien may be getting on in years, but that is not to say I don't notice when something's afoot. And so I thought to myself: I had better get down to the bottom of this. You little rascal!" she said, wagging her finger at Lili.

"I don't know what you mean," said Lili.

"Come now, dearie, you can't fool your old Dien! Did you think I didn't know why you pretended to be crying this afternoon and why Miss Emilie stayed in the conservatory for such a long time? I put two and two together," she continued with a wink of her sunken eye, "and sure enough, he turned up at half-past five and stayed for dinner again!"

"Dien, you don't know what you're talking about!" protested Lili.

"You are mistaken, your old Dien knows what she knows well enough. And you too, you know what you're about."

"What, then?"

"Well, child, you're quite right. He's a steady young man if there ever was one. Such a kind face, with that neat little blond moustache. He looks just right for you, you being rather dainty yourself! They make a handsome pair, don't you think, Miss Marie?"

"They're meant for each other!" yawned Marie from under her covers.

"So you like him, do you?" asked Lili.

"He's a very fine young man!" replied Dien. "Always very civil to me and to Bet, and when I let him in he always has a kind word to say. 'How are you keeping today, Dien?' he'll ask, or some such thing. Never puts on airs, and never forgets to wipe his feet, either."

Lili broke into laughter.

"Have I said anything wrong, Miss?" asked Dien.

"Not at all! And I'm so glad you approve of him."

"You're too excited to go to sleep just yet, I'll wager. In the daytime I'm always too busy, and this is just the right time for a little heart-to-heart talk. And your old Dien may give you some advice, eh? Well, I was a wife, too, and believe you me, child, marriage is a mixed blessing. Oh yes, it all seems a rose garden at first, but then the little ones arrive, and the cares come with them. I had three myself, children I mean, and what a struggle it was to bring them up! They caused me sadness, too, because one of my boys died when he was fourteen, and the other was a bit of a firebrand until he signed up for the colonial army like so many others. But my daughter's a good girl, she's a joy to me. Did you know that she married a tailor and went to live in Rotterdam?"

"Yes, Dien, I know."

"So tell me, when do you think you'll be marrying your young man?"

"Oh, I don't know yet. Not for a long time, though, and you're not to gossip about it, do you hear?"

"No, of course not! I wouldn't dream of saying anything. But Bet has noticed, too, that something was up. Will you wait for a year, do you think?"

"Oh, at least a year, but off you go now, Dien, go to bed."

"Yes, dear, but you see, when the little ones arrive—fair-haired they'll be, what with the pair of you being fair—I shall leave your Ma's service and stay with you, all right?"

"As a nursemaid? But you're far too old!"

"Don't you believe it! Dressing them, giving them baths—you could easily leave all that to me."

"Now now, Dien, I think you're being a bit forward," said Marie.

"What's forward about it? Good gracious, it's gone midnight already! I must be off. Just one more thing, Miss Marie: it's your turn next. You won't lag behind your little sister for too long, will you?"

"I'll do my best, Dien!" said Marie.

"Well, sweet dreams then, and you too, dear Lili, sweet dreams of your young man. And tell him Dien thinks he's ever so pretty, with that little blond moustache of his. Will you tell him I said so?"

She gave Lili a playful tug on the shoulder.

"Yes, Dien, I'll tell him," giggled Lili. "But you needn't shake me so, ouch! Goodnight, Dien, sleep well."

"Night night then, my dears! Hush now, no more laughing or you'll wake up your parents … Hush, hush! I'm off."

Dien gave them another wink and tiptoed out of the room in the yellow glow of her candle.

"Funny old Dien!" said Lili with a final chuckle as she fell back on her pillow, already half asleep. Silence reigned once more, and Marie lay very still with her eyes open, staring at the ceiling in the dark.

XXII

VINCENT CONTINUED TO FEEL VERY WEAK, and Dr Reijer ordered him to stay indoors for the next few weeks, as there was a possibility he might suffer another fainting fit at the slightest provocation. He dutifully followed this advice, for which the doctor praised him, adding that had Mr Vere not become so sensible lately he would no longer be among the living. He also praised Vincent for adopting a healthier way of life by not smoking, drinking little, and taking as much rest as possible in the soothing atmosphere of his cousin's home. His only concern now was the patient's lack of appetite.

Vincent passed his days in Eline's boudoir, as Betsy could not spare him a sitting room to himself. He would make himself comfortable on the Persian couch, snugly wrapped in an ample Turkish dressing gown—a memento of his days of luxury in Smyrna. Sallow-skinned, his pale, lustreless eyes resembling dulled blue porcelain, and his light brown hair cut short, he reclined beneath Eline's aralia, his anaemic fingers holding a book in which he read not a line. He felt as though the capacity to think had vanished from his brain, that he had sunk into a mindless state of inertia akin to the fatigue caused by a stint of strenuous physical exertion. Only petty, childish thoughts floated into his mind from time to time, like so many evanescent soap bubbles, and his pleasures and disappointments were likewise petty: he felt gratified when Dr Reijer commended him for his progress, and exceedingly sorry for himself when Eline was two minutes late bringing him his breakfast. Beyond that he felt nothing, he simply lay there letting his eyes wander about Eline's room, taking in all the pictures, the potted palms, the profusion of fineries and bric-a-brac.

In the morning Eline kept him company, reading to him or singing snatches of songs to her own accompaniment on the piano, a phrase here and a roulade there, to which Vincent listened dreamily, lost in a strange vision brimming with unfamiliar fragrances and muted shades, all swirling together as in a kaleidoscope of colour and perfume. He maintained a pensive silence, and Eline too said little, suffused as she was by a romantic sense of fulfilment. During her vigils at Aunt Vere's bedside she had experienced that same gratifying emotion, which arose from selfless dedication to the care of someone in need. Her fascination for Vincent grew, her heart went out to him, and she relished the opportunity to nurse the languishing invalid in his Turkish robe and Turkish slippers.

The afternoons were usually spent at home until four, at which time Otto collected her to go for a walk. Whenever he gently rebuked her for not taking sufficient care of her own health, and for upsetting herself far too much about Vincent's illness, she would look at him tearfully in disbelief—how could he not feel the deepest, deepest sympathy for poor Vincent, who was so forsaken, so hapless and so delicate? All these cares caused her to lose interest in discussing the manifold details of her trousseau with Betsy, and one day she even remarked, with a distant look in her eyes, how awful it would be to have the wedding in November should Vincent's life still be in danger at that time. Betsy merely shrugged her shoulders and fetched out more catalogues of household linen and swatches of damask and lace, but Eline, finding it impossible to concentrate, went back to Vincent, who, so she fancied, gave her a reproachful look as she entered the room. Only recently, the conversation they had been having just before he fainted had come back to her, unleashing a flood of emotion in her soul. She remembered having asked him whether her marriage to Otto was her foreordained destiny, and could not help thinking that he might have collapsed in despair, and that the cause of his illness might be that he harboured a secret passion for her. After all, he had never spent so much time in The Hague before, almost a year it was now, whereas previously he had never stayed longer than a few weeks at a stretch. Poor Vincent! At least he had her to nurse him … Only, wasn't there a risk of her ministrations fanning the flames of his passion, a passion fated to be unrequited, since she could love only her Otto?

She wished she had someone she could take into her confidence. But it was all so complicated, and she could not think whom she could turn to. To Otto? That would not be quite seemly, she felt, and there was little point in telling Betsy, because she was bound to react as she always did—by asking where on earth Eline got her ridiculous ideas from. Madame van Raat, then?

Yes, that was a good idea, Madame van Raat would be able to advise her. She would go and visit her at home one morning alone, without Otto. Once there, however, she found it so difficult to put into words her suspicions about Vincent's feelings for her that she departed again without any mention of the subject, consoling herself with the rueful notion that Vincent might yet die before she and Otto were married, in which case her tender care would have gone some way towards sweetening his final days.

As time went by her conviction grew that Vincent was secretly in love with her, and she felt herself being engulfed by pity for her poor invalid. Her tranquil happiness, which she had believed to be unassailable, began to slip from her grasp like a wild bird bent on escape, and a nervous agitation took possession of her being, which she did not dare mention to Otto. Any thought of Vincent seemed to raise a dense fog between her and Otto, and the idea of that fog thickening any further sent shivers down her spine. After spending half the day at Vincent's side, ridden with anxiety, she would long to see her Otto again, under whose calming influence she hoped to regain her composure. He arrived at a little after four; they went for a stroll; he stayed for supper; the pair of them spent time together, and then, when he left at half-past eleven and she retired to her bedroom, she would be on the brink of tears at the realisation that his company no longer had the same soothing effect on her as before. On the contrary, his calmness even irritated her now and then; she took it as a sign of indifference, which she found increasingly objectionable, especially when she compared him to the sensitive, grief-stricken Vincent. Even Otto's plain way of speaking, in which she had only recently discovered such a wealth of love, irritated her now … Did he never have an outburst of passion about anything … anything at all? Would he always remain so calm, so stolid, so eternally even-tempered? Had he never known the torment of warring emotions? Was there nothing that could jolt him out of his calm repose, which seemed to her almost like lethargy ... Oh yes, he was good and kind all right, but his feelings did not seem to run very deep; perhaps his calmness signified nothing but egotism, perhaps he was simply insensitive to the suffering of others! And as far as she was concerned, Vincent was human suffering personified ...

Thoughts such as these made Eline feel utterly wretched. Oh God, it was those ghosts again ... here they were, evil and leering, the same as the one that had appeared to her so suddenly during her conversation with Vincent! No, she would not let them get the better of her, she would chase them away! But they kept returning, one after another, chilling her soul with doubts, and she gathered herself to do battle with them. She forced herself to think back on the sweet emotions she had known during those halcyon days at de Horze, to relive that gentle happiness, that blue haze of ecstasy ... but the happiness, the ecstasy, were gone! And then, one night as she lay in bed staring wide-eyed into the soundless dark, unable to sleep, she faced the cruel reality of her loss, and broke down into wild, racking sobs, clinging on to her pillow as though it were her very happiness, as though it were the bird struggling to escape from her grasp. She tossed her head from side to side ... No, no, she did not want this! She wanted to be happy the way she used to be, she wanted to love her Otto the way she did then, in the pine grove! Dear God, was it possible that she no longer loved him? It was unthinkable, it could not be, she would not allow it, she would summon all the fortitude of her will to go on loving him as before, she would cling on to him as she now clung to her pillow, and no leering ghost would ever pry them apart ... Listening to the silence in the house, she could make out the insistent, metallic sound of the big clock ticking in the kitchen downstairs, on and on, and she was seized with mortal fear ... fear that her happiness would not allow itself to be forced back into her soul, fear that there were invisible forces pushing her down a steep slope, while all she wanted was to rise up and up ... And then her agony turned into rage, rage because she was being assailed by thoughts she did not wish to think at all, and because she felt herself too weak to turn around and fight those invisible forces.

When Eline awoke the next morning she felt relatively calm. She was tired and had a slight headache, but the horror of the past night had faded into a bad dream, which she had no desire to recall, much less meditate on. No indeed, she would become her old self again, never again would she allow herself to think such nightmarish thoughts, which only came to her, casting her into a bottomless pit of wretchedness, because she could not sleep. That was all—she wasn't well, she had trouble sleeping, and it was always during those wakeful nights when all was quiet as the grave that those terrible notions came to torment her. She made up her mind to consult Dr Reijer about her insomnia, and oh, how much better she felt already, seeing the pale light of day coming in through a chink in the curtains. She got up early, had a little romp with Ben downstairs, took Vincent his morning roll and hot chocolate as usual—a task she never entrusted to Mina—and settled down with Betsy to go over the catalogues and swatches of materials yet again. She studied the relative merits of fine tablecloths and table napkins, and was much taken with a set of smartly monogrammed pillowcases that were very reasonably priced at the Louvre shop, and she reminded Betsy that from now on she had to be careful not to spend too much, but oh, how attractive those tea towels looked in the other catalogue!

While she kept up her bright patter there was, deep within her, a patch of gloom, like a slag of black mud on the bed of an apparently limpid blue lake. But she did her best to ignore it, and throughout their discussion Betsy noticed nothing unusual in her demeanour. Then Eline went upstairs, taking a large envelope that had been delivered for Vincent.

He was in his Turkish dressing gown as usual, lying on the couch. His condition, however, was improving: Dr Reijer had even said he might try taking a short stroll, but his repose had become dear to him, and he had replied that he did not yet feel up to it. When Eline entered he nodded affably; he relished having her waiting on him hand and foot, and his gratitude brought to his lustreless eyes an amicable glimmer, which Eline mistook for love.

She handed him the letter and asked him how he was feeling.

"Not bad; getting better, I suppose," he said tonelessly, then sat bolt upright and tore open the envelope. Eline was about to sit down at the piano.

"Ah, at last!" she heard Vincent exclaim, almost joyfully.

She gave him a questioning look. A portrait photograph slipped from the envelope onto the floor, and she bent down to retrieve it.

"It's from New York, a letter from Lawrence St Clare!" said Vincent, running his eye over the contents. "He's found something for me, apparently. There seems to be a vacancy at the trading company he's affiliated with."

Eline was startled; she studied the portrait, which had suffered some damage in the post.

"Well, what do you think?" she asked.

"About what?"

"What do you think you'll do?"

"I'll go as soon as I'm better," he said. "But that won't be for quite a while," he added mournfully.

"Go to America, you mean?"

"Yes, of course."

"Will you be glad to go, once you're better?"

"Naturally. Not much point in hanging around here, is there, now that I can get a situation."

With scarcely a thought for what he had said, he lay back on the Persian cushions, and a profusion of brightly coloured visions floated into his mind. He recalled his former life of endless variation, of ever-changing perspectives and horizons. Variety was life itself, variety would make him better, it would make him young again. He recalled his friend, a fine fellow in body and spirit, and the only man who gave him the feeling that there was more to life than world-weariness.

Eline, however, was filled with pity for Vincent.

It was only natural that he should wish to leave the country, to be well away by the time her wedding came around, so that he would be spared the agony of witnessing it. No wonder he jumped at the opportunity, really … he was obviously in love with her, and it was making him suffer!

She was still holding the portrait in her hands.

"Is this St Clare?" she asked, close to tears for the pain she thought he was going through.

"Yes," he replied, taking it from her. "It's a fine likeness! It shows him the way he is: open, upstanding, full of life and good humour."

"Is he dark or fair?"

"His hair is tawny; so is his beard. Dashing, isn't he?"

"Yes, he's handsome. But Vincent … "

"What?"

"Vincent, are you sure? Why don't you think it over? You're still very frail, you could have a relapse. You'd better ask Reijer's opinion first."

"My dear Elly, I'm the same as I ever was; my health has never been robust, and besides, who'll support me if I do stay here—not you, surely?" he asked, smiling.

To her that smile seemed wistful, and she reproached herself for trying to dissuade him. No, he was quite right to go, but on the other hand, something might happen, something that would turn everything upside down, so that there would be no need for him to leave, or at least not like this. Her head spun, she no longer knew what she wanted him to do, and she shrank from pursuing the thought that now entered her mind. It would be too awful. Too awful for Otto, and too awful for herself as well.

Vincent remained in remarkably good spirits all afternoon, and when Reijer called he advised the patient not to excite himself too much. As for America—later, perhaps, but for the time being travel was out of the question. In the interim Mr Vere would do well to take a short stroll or a brief ride in the carriage to start with, what with the weather being so mild.

Betsy promptly ordered the landau for half-past two, and off they went: Vincent, herself and Eline. In the bright light outside Eline was shocked to see how grey Vincent's complexion was above the white-silk foulard draped about his neck, how dulled and frail he looked in his smart liver-coloured demi-season costume and shiny top hat. He leant stiffly against the cushions, keeping very still,

266

his gloved hands resting on the silver knob of his cane. He felt
light in the head, even a little groggy, and had he not been seated
would have keeled over from the effect of the oxygen filling his
lungs. His eyes smarted, so he closed them a moment, while his
ears throbbed and the carriage wheels spun round in his brain.
But gradually he became accustomed to the cool, fresh air and
the wide vistas unfolding before his eyes at each bend in the
road, and his breathing became deep and regular. He felt mildly
invigorated, and his nerves regaining a little strength.

Eline did her best to converse brightly, addressing him and
Betsy by turns. Upon their return after an hour or so, she helped
Vincent alight from the carriage and took his arm to lead him
upstairs to her sitting room. She helped him out of his coat, after
which he dropped onto the couch, quite exhausted from the
outing. He asked her to leave him alone for a while, as he wished
to take a nap.

Betsy instructed the servants that she was receiving, and in due
course several callers arrived: Madame Eekhof accompanied
by Ange and Léonie, Madame Hovel and the Hijdrecht boy.
Henk had gone to his club, but Eline joined the company in
the tempered light of the salon, and presently Otto was shown
in, too. When he entered the room Eline did not feel the thrill
of warmth and contentment his appearance normally inspired
in her, but ice-cold indifference. Oh God, how could that be?
How could all that warmth have suddenly turned to ice? She
did not know, but it was so, and she was powerless to change
it. She nodded sweetly at him and extended her hand, feeling
a pang of conscience as she did so, and held on to it while she
continued telling Hijdrecht about the new *chanteuse légère* at the
opera. She could not bear to look at Otto, all she could do was
hold his hand and prattle on. What Hijdrecht said in response
she scarcely heard, for her heart brimmed with pity for Otto …
There he stood, by her side, his hand in hers, and she could feel
his soft, kindly gaze resting on her, and his breath almost ruffling
her hair as he leant over the back of her chair; there he was,
radiating love, while she … she felt as cold as ice! No, no, this
could not be, she would not allow it, she would compel herself
… she pitied him too much … he loved her too much …

"Nily, dear child, what is the matter?" he murmured while Hijdrecht and the ladies rose to their feet. He could feel the nervous pressure of her fingers on his hand.

"Me? With me? Nothing, a slight headache, that's all," she said haltingly, facing him for the first time that afternoon. He gazed into her eyes, and she felt an urge to fling herself into his arms, to hold him very tight and never let him go again …

Instead, she smiled and shook hands first with Madame Eekhof, then with Ange.

"Is there nothing to be done? Has it gone for ever?" she thought in despair.

They had a few minutes alone before dinner.

"Nily, my dearest, are you sure you are all right?" he asked anxiously. "Your hand is so cold."

"I feel a little feverish. We went for a drive this afternoon, in the open landau, with Vincent … I can't imagine why Reijer recommended it. I thought it was cold, freezing cold."

"Let's hope you haven't caught anything."

"No, it will pass, I'm sure."

She smiled at him weakly, and all at once, in a surge of hopeless anguish, she flung her arms about him.

"How sweet of you to be so concerned about me," she whispered, and her voice broke. "You are so good, and … I love you so much. I love you so very, very much … "

Vincent did not yet feel well enough to join them for lunch that day. Betsy told Otto about the letter that had arrived with news of a position for Vincent in New York.

"And when is he thinking of going?"

"As soon as he is fit again. Thank God we'll be seeing the back of him."

Eline could not contain herself.

"Reijer says he mustn't even think of travelling for the next several weeks!" she said sharply, glaring at Betsy. "But you—"

"What?"

"If it weren't for the sake of decency you'd turn him out into the street today, ill as he is!"

"If I could, yes, I certainly would. And let me tell you once and for all: I shall never have him to stay again. I haven't known anyone to outstay their welcome like this!"

"But Betsy, he's practically dying!" Eline cried out, quivering with rage.

"Don't be absurd!"

"Absurd? Can't you see how ill he looks?" she shrieked.

"Oh please, Eline, let's not quibble about Vincent. He's not worth it. You're being melodramatic; stop making such a fuss."

"Ah yes, 'Don't make a fuss'—that's what you always say when anyone shows the least bit of feeling! But you—you're just plain heartless!"

"Eline!" murmured Otto.

Gerard entered, bearing the meat dish. A painful silence prevailed.

"You forgot the gravy, Gerard," snapped Betsy, and the manservant withdrew.

"You—why, you'd trample on anyone who happened to be the least bit in your way! You won't put up with the slightest bother for the sake of anyone else! You're a downright egotist! You think of no one but yourself, and you don't even understand that not everyone is as mean as you, and—"

"Eline!" remonstrated Otto, glancing at the door as Gerard re-entered with a gravy boat.

"Oh, stop saying Eline, Eline! *Qu'est ce que me fait cet homme!*" Eline burst out, switching to French so the servant would not understand. "I don't care what he thinks! Betsy just won't see it, but I assure you, Vincent is dying. He fell asleep in my room, as white as a sheet, completely worn out by that stupid ride recommended by Dr Reijer; and I won't have you accusing him of being indiscreet or anything like that. If he hadn't been so ill I'm quite sure he would never have stayed here this long."

She spoke passionately, eyes aflame, and the words spilt from her lips with haughty, needle-sharp acuity.

Betsy too seethed with rage as she waited for Gerard to withdraw, but she said nothing. Henk gave an involuntary sigh.

"Nily my darling," said Otto, "I have nothing against Vincent, and no particular sympathy for him either, but I can't say I shall be sorry to see him go, because—"

"Not you too?" she snapped.

"May I finish?" he pursued, clasping her icy hand. "I mean that I will be glad to see him go if his presence in this house goes on upsetting you as much as it has today. You don't know what you're saying, Nily, or what you sound like."

His calm words infuriated her.

"And you—you're always calm, you never get excited about anything, do you?" she burst out, almost screaming. She sprang to her feet, throwing her napkin on the table. "It's driving me mad, all that calmness! Oh God, it's driving me mad! Betsy drives me mad with her egotism, and you with your calmness, yes, your calmness! I—I—can't stand it any more! You're suffocating me!"

"Eline!" cried Otto.

Springing up in his turn, he seized both her wrists and gazed into her eyes. She had expected some dramatic, dreadful response, that he would throw her to the floor, or smack her, but all he did was shake his head slowly from side to side, and in a tone of profound sorrow he said simply:

"Eline—for shame!"

"Oh my God! I—I'm going out of my mind!" she raged. Then, convulsed with sobs, she tore herself away from his grasp and rushed out of the room, dashing several wine glasses to the floor as she went.

Betsy made to run after Eline, but Otto restrained her.

"I beg you, just let her be!"

Henk too had jumped up, and when Gerard came in again all three of them felt acutely embarrassed about their interrupted dinner and the broken glasses.

"There's no need, no need, Gerard," said Betsy, almost apologetically. "You had better clear the table now."

They did not know where to look, as the manservant, for all his dignified stoicism, was bound to have guessed there had been a scene.

Meanwhile Eline had rushed upstairs and burst into her boudoir, startled to see Vincent, for she had forgotten he was there. She recoiled and stood in the doorway a moment, somewhat at a loss. Vincent was still dozing; his lunch tray stood untouched on the side table by the couch. The sight of him asleep gave Eline a sense of cruel, romantic satisfaction at having leapt to his defence, at having stood up for him against Betsy, and against Otto ... Not wishing to wake him just yet, she slipped into her bedroom, soundlessly closing the door behind her, and threw herself on her bed. Her sobbing had ceased quite suddenly, and, to her consternation, she found herself unable to weep. The solitude and calmness of her room cooled her agitated nerves, and although she could not remember the exact words she had spoken, she knew she had said the most appalling things, especially to Otto. Why? Why had she lashed out at him like that? Had it been because of Vincent? Because of Otto's infuriating stoicism? She no longer knew the reason; her brain was in complete turmoil, and she tossed her head from side to side on her pillow in an effort to shake off her confusion. Yes, she thought, it must have been because of Vincent, who had no one in the whole world but her and that friend of his, far away in New York. She felt sorry for him, but then, didn't she feel even more sorry for Otto? Had she actually intended to speak her mind with such vehemence? Had it been her own free will? The same will with which she had tried to force herself to continue loving Otto, because she knew she would make both him and herself miserable otherwise? Back at de Horze—how long ago that seemed!—she had never, ever, had the slightest difference of opinion with Otto, and now this! She had insulted him to his face ... Dear God, why? Whatever had made her do it? Would Vincent consider this just another inevitable outcome of a whole series of other, interconnected inevitabilities? So then what was life? What was a human being? A helpless puppet, with Fate pulling its strings? She had tried with all her might to change, of that she was certain, but she was simply too weak to go against the fate that ruled her existence, and now, now the realisation dawned on her that it was all over! She had lost, she had no choice but to admit defeat.

Slowly she began to cry, and she was relieved to feel the tears wetting her cheeks; she made herself sob properly, too, although not too loudly ... better not let Vincent notice. It grew dark; ah, she could hear him moving about in the next room, where he had evidently lit the lamp, for she could see a slit of light beneath the door. But she remained as she was, lying supine on her bed, sobbing piteously.

Otto was seated in the salon staring at the floor when Henk entered.

Noting the glint of a tear in Otto's eyes, Henk became agitated.

"Oh, van Erlevoort!" he said, laying his hand on Otto's shoulder.

Otto raised his head.

"Van Erlevoort! Come on old chap, be a man! I know it's not all plain sailing with Sis, but she's not bad at heart! You mustn't mind what she said, do you hear? She was only angry with Betsy because she's rather fond of Vincent, and you accidentally bore the brunt of her anger. You should just ignore it, that will be the best punishment for her."

Otto did not respond and remained slumped in his seat, too harrowed by doubt to be assuaged by Henk's solicitude. He thought of the time he had told Eline that she had but one fault, her lack of self-knowledge, and that she had hidden treasures slumbering within her which he would help her to rouse, but now he saw only too clearly that it would not be in his power to do so, that all he was able to rouse in her was irritation ... and that he was driving her mad ... suffocating her.

"She can be confoundedly awkward when she gets in a tantrum," Henk pursued, inwardly raging as he paced the salon trying to think of comforting things to say. "But when she's with someone she loves and respects she always sees reason in the end, and then ... I say, shall I go and have a word with her?"

"I think she should be left alone," replied Otto, with difficulty. "She's bound to come round, given time."

He tried to imagine himself in her place, to guess what she was feeling at this moment, but found himself too stunned to pursue any logical train of thought. Never had he heard her use that kind of language before, never had he known her to shout or scream, never had he seen her face contorted with such unsightly anger. Try as he might, he was unable to gather his reason owing to the pain lacerating his heart.

Henk could not bear to see him thus, bowed and despairing, and suddenly felt himself spurred into action. He had a high regard for Otto, and it was unforgivable of Eline to treat him with such contempt; no indeed, he would not allow her to get away with it, and with a new vigour he strode out of the salon. Halfway up the stairs he met Betsy, who was on her way down.

"Where is Eline?" he asked.

Betsy glanced at him, taken aback by his resolute tone.

"I don't know," she said drily.

Henk continued up the stairs and entered Eline's boudoir. Finding no one there, he assumed that Vincent was tired after his first brief spell out of doors and had already retired to bed, oblivious to the scene that had taken place downstairs. Henk knocked on the door to Eline's bedroom.

"Eline!" he called.

There was no answer, and he pushed the door open. In the half-light he saw Eline lying on the floor, her slight form shaking with stifled sobs, her face hidden in her hands. He paused for a moment on the threshold, but she did not move.

"Do get up, Eline!" he said firmly, almost commandingly.

At this she drew herself up with a violent jolt.

"What do you want?" she screamed. "What are you doing in my room? Go away!"

"Get up."

"No I won't! Just go away, will you? Go away, leave me alone!"

He bent down, flushed with emotion, and grasped her roughly by the wrists, causing her to cry out in pain.

"Damnation! Get up!" he hissed, almost beside himself with anger, and grabbed her arms to pull her up by force.

Shocked into submission by hearing him swear, by his high colour, his red face, his flashing eyes and his hoarse voice, she allowed him to raise her to her feet.

"What do you want?" she asked again, but more calmly now, and with a touch of hauteur.

"I'll tell you what I want. I want you to go down immediately—immediately, do you hear—and ask van Erlevoort to forgive you. You may not remember all the things you said when you lost your temper, but you offended him deeply, very deeply. Go downstairs at once!"

She stared, open-mouthed, shrinking from his commanding tone and his burly frame looming over her as he pointed her to the door.

"You'll find him downstairs in the salon. Go!"

"No I won't!" she cried out, shaken but still defiant.

"If you won't I shall drag you downstairs myself and make you go down on your knees to him! I mean it!" he hissed in her face, articulating each syllable with furious emphasis.

"Henk!" she cried, horrified by his vehemence.

"Well then?"

"Yes, yes, I'll go, I'll go, but—oh, Henk! Don't speak to me like that! Please don't! You're only making it worse, and heaven knows I feel bad enough already!"

"That's your own fault, all of it is your own fault, and you have no right to make cruel accusations against people, especially not against van Erlevoort."

"Yes, yes, you're right!" she said, breaking down into sobs. "I shall go, but please, Henk, please come with me!"

Leaning on him for support, she allowed him to conduct her out of the boudoir and down the stairs. Upon entering the salon she gave a start. The room was empty but for Otto, sitting huddled on the sofa with his head in his hands. She caught a glimpse of Betsy in the drawing room, and of Gerard bringing in the tea tray, so she kept silent, waiting for the manservant to leave. Then, under Henk's compelling gaze, she dared demur no longer, nor did she wish to when she saw Otto's manifest despair. Falling on her knees before him, she tried to say something, but was too convulsed with sobs to speak—genuine, heartfelt sobs this time, mingling with a flood of tears. She pressed her throbbing, flushed forehead to his knees and groped for his hands in mute desperation.

He too kept silent, gazing into her eyes.

At last she uttered the words, with great effort, while Henk stood like a judge at her side:

"Forgive me, Otto, forgive me, forgive me."

He nodded his head slowly, as yet unconsoled by her remorse, for he knew that things would never be as he had once imagined. Nonetheless he leant forwards, drew her close and kissed her brow.

"Forgive me, Otto, oh please forgive me, say you'll forgive me!"

He curved his arm gently about her shaking shoulders and pressed her to his chest, screwing up his eyes to stem the tears. Because he knew: this was the end.

He took his leave half an hour later, in low spirits, although Henk patted him on the back several times, urging him in jovial tones to stay a while now that all was well again. He bade Eline goodbye with a pained smile. Afterwards Eline also begged Betsy's pardon, likewise in Henk's presence. Betsy's only response was a brief nod of the head, but her eyes glittered with such apparent hatred that Eline recoiled and ran out of the room. Later, when Henk told Betsy how he had forced Eline to seek out van Erlevoort, the look in her eye had been one of admiration. She never thought he had it in him—fancy him standing up to Eline when she was having one of her tantrums!

Some weeks went by, during which things seemed to settle down much as they had been before. Vincent was feeling reasonably well, and went for frequent drives with the sisters. Betsy, however, ever mindful of Eline's outburst, continued to harbour a sullen resentment against her. How typical: show a little kindness and the next thing you knew you were no longer mistress of your own home. Here she was, lumbered with an ailing, loathsome cousin who caused all sorts of unpleasantness, and a sister who was becoming more insufferable by the day! The atmosphere in her lovely home was quite ruined by the pair of them—but not for much longer, she vowed. As soon as Eline was married she, Betsy, would not only go on holiday with Henk and Ben, but get rid of Vincent as well, once and for all. Never again would he set foot in her house! Not even if he lay dying on her doorstep would she let him in—yes, Eline was right there, she had to give her that!

Eline for her part felt such profound regret at having railed against Otto that she brought all her charms to bear in an effort to make amends. Since Otto was only too willing to forgive her so that he might hope once more, her efforts met with a measure of success. But the crack that had appeared in their relationship proved impossible to repair. He realised full well that everyone said things in anger which they subsequently regretted, and that Eline had simply lost her temper, only … the actual words she had spoken, now that he turned them over in his mind, were not what he would have expected of her. Had she loved him as he thought she did—granted, with a touch of egotism; not so much for his sake as for her own, and for the peace and happiness she found in him—she would never have used those words. However incensed she might have been, whether on Vincent's behalf or for any other reason, she would have expressed her feelings differently. He saw it clearly: she no longer even loved him for her own sake, because she no longer found his calm temperament soothing, on the contrary, she found it irritating; nor did she love him for himself, she never had: she forced herself to be kind to him, out of pity! All his pride bristled at the realisation, and for a moment he considered flinging her pity in her face just as she had flung his calmness in his face, but he could not. He could not do this to her, he loved her too much, nor could he do it to himself. So he suffered her contrition in a final bid to recover a fraction of the happiness she had once inspired in him, and yet he knew: it was over.

It was over; he could tell by the mildly detached air with which she greeted him when he visited, once the fervour of making amends had passed; he could tell by the way she allowed him to plant a kiss on her brow, by her alacrity to withdraw from his embrace, by her languishing silences, by everything in her manner. And for the first time he noticed how often she looked at Vincent, and how she was still at his beck and call notwithstanding his full recovery. It was something he did not wish to contemplate; the thought was too distasteful.

Eline for her part was deeply despondent; she knew she could not force herself to continue loving Otto, but suffered mortal terrors of conscience whenever he turned his mournful gaze on her. She felt a sense of total defeat. One afternoon she stayed upstairs, telling Mina to say that she was not feeling well and would not be coming down. He asked if he might see her in her room, but she sent word that she was tired and needed to rest. Slowly but surely a decision was taking shape in her mind: she had to do it, she owed it to him, and to herself. She refused to see him the following day, too, despite Henk's best efforts to persuade her, to which she responded by shaking her head with slow determination: she could not see him, she was ill. Should he call Dr Reijer? No, there was no need.

And she kept to her room, while Otto dined downstairs with Betsy, Vincent and Henk, and left early.

That evening she spent a long while lying on her couch, staring into the dark. She did not wish to see Vincent either. At last she lit the gas lamp herself, drew the curtains and sat down at her writing table. It had to be done.

Calmly she began to write, pausing frequently to read what she had written:

My dear Otto!

Forgive me, I beg you, but I have no alternative. Ask yourself whether I could ever make you happy and whether I would not be a burden to you. There was a time when I believed I could make you happy, and I shall remember it as long I live, because it was the greatest happiness I have ever known. But now—

Tears welled up in her eyes as she wrote, and suddenly, breaking into violent sobs, she tore up the sheet of paper. She was not capable of inflicting such suffering on him. Oh God, she could not do it! But then what? Let the relationship continue regardless of the pain it caused her, until such time as some other devastating variance drove them apart anyway? No, no, in that case it would be better to part in friendship now, with a last, fond letter of farewell! But she had already hurt him so deeply, without wishing to; she did not wish to hurt him further, and now—oh why did she have to struggle with her emotions like this, all alone and forsaken, with no one to turn to, and without really knowing what she wanted or even what her moral duty was? She was too weak, she simply wasn't up to it!

But she took a fresh sheet of paper and started again:

My dear Otto!

The subsequent lines, being virtually identical to the note she had torn up, followed easily enough. But how to go on from there? How to tell him? Suddenly the words came, and her pen flew over the paper, her writing becoming an almost illegible scrawl of passionate, rambling sentences.

Truly, my heart is breaking as I write to you now … now that I must ask you … whether it would not … be better for us to cease raising hopes in one another … hopes of finding happiness together. It is so cruel having to ask this, because it was such a lovely time, when we …

On and on she wrote, lost in the cruel remembrance of those days, her breast heaving with spasmodic sobs, and her head began to ache with mounting ferocity, as if there were a tight band of iron clamped around her brain and hammers pounding on her temples.

... a lovely time, when we ... were so deeply in love ... I can't tell you how I suffer in the writing of this ... more than I had thought possible for a human being to suffer, but I believe that it is my duty, and that I would cause you even greater unhappiness by not writing to you.

We must forget one another, we must never think of one another again ... That will be best, for both of us, but especially for you. Oh, if I could still hope that I might become a better person, that I might become worthy of you one day, then I would tear this paper to shreds, but all my hope is gone.

I do realise, dearest Otto, that I am causing you grief by this letter, but I beg you to forgive this final act of injury, and banish the thought of me from your mind. You are so good and kind; I am sure that one day, when you have forgotten me, you will find someone, a young girl ...

She dropped her pen, anguish-stricken, and lurched forwards, pressing her face to the tear-sodden handkerchief lying on the table. The sobs now convulsed her entire frame while the hammers pounded on her temples, between her eyes and at the base of her skull. She tossed her head from side to side, but the throbbing was aggravated by a thousand pinpricks, so she raised herself and resumed writing, intermittently striking her head with the clenched fist of her free hand. Unable to tear herself away from the missive that would set a seal on her loss of Otto, she floundered on, repeating over and over how happy she had been with him, how she suffered in losing him, and that it was her moral duty to write him this letter. The notion of duty filled her with a romantic sense of purpose, and she got quite carried away, writing the word over and over again: duty, duty, duty ... She also felt that as long as she was still putting pen to paper they would still be connected in some way; not until she had written her name at the end would it all be over, for ever after ... She could not bring herself to place her signature, and kept adding phrases to defer the moment.

Then one day you will meet someone who is worthy of you, and who will love you unconditionally. I am sure of that. Then you will be happy, and you will have forgotten me. But oh, please don't forget me completely: just forget your love for me, and think of me once in a while.

That final entreaty reverberated in the depths of her soul.

Think of me, without anger or hate, and feel a little pity for your poor Nily, who …

"I can't do it, I can't!" she moaned, grasping the tear-smudged sheet of paper with a mind to tearing it up, but instead she took a deep breath and quickly wrote a few closing words. Then she dried her eyes and set about copying out her missive, somewhat calmer now that she no longer needed to think about what to say.

A postage stamp was all she needed after this, and an envelope, upon which she wrote the address:

The Right Honourable Baron
O van Erlevoort ter Horze,
Lange Voorhout, The Hague.

She reread her letter a final time. Her anguish flared up again at the cruelty of it, and when she reached the end and had only to slide it into the envelope, she hesitated yet again. Was this really what she wanted? To break with her Otto? No, no, it was not a question of *wanting* anything, it was what she was obliged to do; it was her duty, her moral duty! So she pressed a long kiss on her letter and sealed the envelope.

Oh God, why must she live while such grief existed?

She rose, and stood for a time staring at the envelope as though willing it to vanish, but it remained there, lying squarely on the writing table with Otto's name and address on the cover.

Eline cast a rapid glance in the mirror, and she barely recognised herself in the ghostly apparition confronting her, the pallid, tear-streaked features, the dishevelled mane of hair. Then she gave two firm tugs on the bell pull, keeping her eyes fixed on the letter.

There was a knock at the door. Gerard entered.

"What time is it, Gerard?"

She was startled by how dull and hoarse her voice sounded.

"Almost midnight, Miss."

"Is the master still up?"

"The master is in his study; milady has gone to bed, and so has Mr Vincent."

"Can you take this to the post for me?"

"Yes, Miss."

"Can you do it at once?"

"Certainly, Miss."

"Here you are, then. But do it at once, will you? When is the first mail collection tomorrow morning?"

"Eight o'clock, I believe, Miss."

"Here, take it. Off you go now, all right?"

"At once, Miss."

Gerard departed with the letter, leaving Eline behind in a daze. She heard Gerard go down the stairs, she heard the thud of the front door being shut. Then all was still in the big house.

She had a sense of cold panic, like icy water trickling down her back.

At this very moment Gerard was making his way down the street, now he was turning the corner, now approaching the letter box on the Nassaulaan ... She fancied she could hear the letter drop with a dull thud, like the lid on a coffin, and was on the verge of swooning away from the monstrous visions bearing down on her like evil ghosts. And suddenly, as though jolted awake from a nightmare, she realised the finality of what she had done. She felt her entire body begin to tremble, as in a fever. By tomorrow, by tomorrow morning even, Otto would receive the letter ... her letter!

Oh God, it could not be! It must not be! It was her very happiness that she had just flung away with both hands, and only because she had found the sheer restfulness of it boring! Her life's happiness, irredeemably lost!

She felt the walls and the ceiling closing in on her, crushing her so that she could scarcely breathe. She staggered to the door, then across the landing, and burst into Betsy's bedroom.

"My God, oh my God! Betsy!" she gasped, as though a hand were clamped round her throat.

Betsy was abed in the dusky room, lit only by a weak night light; she started awake in fright, with disordered thoughts of calamities such as fire or murder.

"Who? What? What's happening? What is it, Eline?"

"I—oh my God—I—"

"What on earth is the matter, Eline?"

"I—I've written to Otto."

"What?"

"I've sent him a letter."

"A letter?"

"I—I've broken it off. I've broken off our engagement. Oh God, oh God!"

Betsy leapt out of bed and stood shivering over Eline, who had collapsed on the floor, hiding her face in her long, tousled hair.

"What did you say?" she cried in horror.

Eline only sobbed. The doors to Henk's study and Ben's nursery stood open, and Henk, who had been reading, came running.

"Is anything wrong?" he asked anxiously.

"Shut Ben's door, will you, Henk, or he'll wake up!" said Betsy, her voice shaking.

Henk shut the door.

"Eline has written to Otto, she's broken it off!" wailed Betsy.

Henk stood where he was, aghast, making no move to raise Eline to her feet. But she lifted her swollen, tear-stained face to him, and wringing her hands in a delirium of anguish, broke out with:

"Yes, that's what I've done! Oh my God! I have written him a long letter, and oh, it's awful, such an awful thing to have done! But I'm so muddled, I don't know what I'm doing any more, I don't know what I want, or what I don't want, I don't know if I love him or not, or if I love someone else. I don't know anything at all. And I can't even think with all this pounding in my head! I wrote to Otto because I considered it my duty. I would only have made him unhappy. But it's awful … maybe I was wrong to do it, maybe I could have loved him after all. I wish to God it was all over, I wish I were dead, because I can't stand it any longer, I just can't stand it … "

Her voice trailed off, then she slumped forwards and lay prostrate with her forehead against the carpet, slowly rubbing from side to side.

Betsy glanced at Henk: what would he do? The secret resentment she harboured against her sister melted away, and for a moment she was filled with pity. Henk's mute contemplation of Eline caused her a stab of annoyance—how ineffectual her husband was! She went to light the gas, threw on a peignoir, and upon her return was astonished to see the change in Eline, who was now seated on a chair, quite inert, in an attitude of numb despair, with her hands folded on her knee and red-rimmed eyes staring blankly ahead.

"Elly! Elly! How could you do such a thing!" said Henk tonelessly, thinking of Otto.

"Oh, my head is bursting!" she murmured faintly.

"Are you in pain?" asked Betsy.

"Oh—" moaned Eline.

Betsy brushed away Eline's tangled hair and dabbed her forehead and temples with a moistened handkerchief.

Henk sat down. He did not know what to do, what to say; in his mind's eye he kept seeing Otto.

"How could she? How could she?" was his only thought.

"Feeling better now?" Betsy asked gently.

Eline gave a small, scornful laugh.

"Better? Hardly. But it's refreshing, that wet hanky."

"Shall I get you something to drink?"

"No, thank you."

She was no longer sobbing, but the tears continued to flow. Then, with a faraway look in her eyes, she began slowly, almost inaudibly, to speak:

"Oh, not knowing what to do, not knowing what you want, and then doing something like this without even wanting to … poor, poor Otto! And the pain, oh my God! I'm losing my mind!"

"Henk could go to the Voorhout tomorrow morning early and get the letter back," interrupted Betsy with a brisk toss of the head. "He could ask Willem, for instance, or the maid, and then there would be no need for Otto to read it, and no one would be the wiser. What do you say, Eline?"

Eline stared dully.

"I don't know, I don't know!" she mumbled, shaking her head.

"Go on, you can still change your mind!" urged Betsy.

"No, just leave it … what's done is done. It was all ruined anyway. We could never have gone back to the way we were."

Henk sighed; both he and Betsy appeared to understand the gravity of Eline's statement, and made no further attempt to dissuade her.

"Why don't I help you get undressed so you can lie down? Would you like me to stay with you tonight?" offered Betsy.

"Yes, please—well, perhaps not; there's no need."

"Come, let me take you to your room then."

Betsy towed her sister away as if she were a child, and like a child Eline submitted to being undressed, her arms hanging limply by her sides.

"Oh my poor head!" she moaned as she fell back on her pillows. Betsy tucked in the covers, then took a damp cloth and gently moistened her sister's face once more.

"There, there. You must try to get some sleep. There's nothing we can do for the moment, but things may turn out all right again, you never can tell. Henk could still go, you know, in the morning."

Eline shook her head.

"Shall I stay with you a while?"

Eline's only answer was a blank stare. Betsy drew the red bed curtain some way across and settled herself in a chair.

Silence prevailed, but for the occasional faint whimper from Eline. The white night lamp on the table shone like a star, casting fitful gleams on the panelled wardrobe, the cheval glass, the flacons and jars ranged on the muslin-frilled dressing table, while dark shadows loomed on all sides of the room. Betsy shivered in her peignoir; she wanted to put some order in her thoughts, but could not, so consternated was she by the broken engagement. The hours crawled by, and down in the kitchen, beneath the bedroom, Betsy heard the clock strike one o'clock, then half-past. At long last the whimpering died away on the other side of the red curtain. Betsy stood up and looked in briefly at Eline, who was lying quite still with her eyes closed, apparently sleeping, and Betsy tiptoed out of the room.

She found Henk still sitting with his head in his hands. Neither of them retired to bed; they sat and talked in whispers, holding their breath now and then as they listened out for any sound coming from Eline's room. Though they both had a sense of foreboding, neither of them ventured to put their vague fears into words.

"Shh!" hissed Betsy, thinking she heard something. They strained their ears to listen. From Eline's room came the sound of piteous sobbing, the lament of a soul in agony, passionate and loud. Betsy shuddered.

"I'm so afraid," she whispered. Henk left the room as quietly as he could and stole across the unlit landing. The servants were all in bed; the house was in darkness. He went into Eline's sitting room, where the gaslight was still on, and sank onto a chair. He could hear Eline in the next room, sobbing her heart out. He had never heard her weep like this before, with hoarse, screeching howls of anguish, and with each raucous sob he felt her pain thundering in his skull.

At long last the sobbing gave way to low, intermittent moaning; then that too, ceased. All was quiet. Henk was gripped with fear in the tragic stillness enveloping him, his hair stood on end, and without knowing what he was doing he sprang to his feet. He had to make sure, he had to see her with his own eyes. Yet at the door to Eline's bedroom he hesitated, just a fraction of a second, before pushing it open and stepping inside.

On the rumpled bed, in the ruby glow of the bed curtains, lay Eline, her nightgown twisted about her limbs, her hair a tangled mass. She had thrown off the covers and appeared to be asleep, although her head and hands were twitching; she had dark circles beneath her eyes, and her breathing came with convulsive spasms, much like electric shocks coursing through her slight frame. Henk gazed upon the tormented sleeping figure, his lips quivering with dismay. Very gently he drew up the covers, and in so doing felt how cold she was. He stood there a moment, staring at her tear-stained face, then left abruptly, turning off the gaslight in Eline's boudoir as he passed through.

XXIII

O TTO HAD ALREADY GONE OUT when Willem, the man-servant, brought the letter into the dining room. Only Frédérique and her mother were present. Mathilda had gone for a walk with the children, and Etienne was still in bed.

"What's that?" asked Madame van Erlevoort.

Frédérique took the letter.

"It's for Otto, Mama. You can leave it on the sideboard, Willem—or, no, wait, let me take another look," she said, inspecting the address. "Eline's handwriting, I do believe. Such a thick envelope, too. Strange."

"Is it from Eline?" asked Madame.

"I think so."

She returned the envelope to Willem, who placed it in a Japanese charger on the sideboard, after which he left. Mother and daughter exchanged looks. Each could sense the disquiet in the other, yet each kept silent. Madame van Erlevoort returned to her housekeeping accounts and Frédérique took up the brightly coloured tapestry she was working on.

Some time went by, and the clock struck ten. Rika, the maid, came in to clear the breakfast table, leaving one setting for Etienne, when the doorbell rang. Madame van Erlevoort barely noticed, for there were tradesmen ringing at the door every morning, but to Frédérique the bell sounded ominous.

Willem came in.

"Mr van Raat has arrived, and would like to speak to you. What shall I tell him, ma'am?"

"Master Paul?" said Frédérique.

"Beg pardon, Miss, it is Mr van Raat from Nassauplein."

"Show him in!"

Madame van Erlevoort, generally so serene, was concerned. Like her daughters, she had noted how dejected and retiring

286

Otto had become lately, and how Eline seemed to avoid visiting their house.

Henk entered. His dull greeting and uncharacteristically worried expression spoke volumes. Madame waved Henk to a chair, eyeing him with anxious expectation.

"Why van Raat! What is it? What brought you here?" she asked hurriedly.

"I thought it right to call on you, dear lady. Eline has written to Otto."

"Yes, I know."

"Ah. And has he read the letter?"

"The letter? No, not yet. Willem brought it in a moment ago. Good heavens, van Raat, you don't mean to say that Eline has? … "

Henk looked away, groping for words. He had composed a whole speech in his mind on the way there, but found he could not recall a single word under the apprehensive gaze of Frédérique and her mother. When they begged him to speak he gave a helpless gesture and blurted:

"Well, yes, I'm afraid she has. She wants to break off the engagement. She has written him a long letter. I can't tell you how sorry I am."

Madame van Erlevoort sat with hunched shoulders, speechless and trembling; Frédérique had turned deathly pale.

"And Eline herself is very upset, quite heartbroken in fact. She didn't get any sleep last night, either. We heard her cry for hours."

In broken, laboured sentences, he related the events of the previous night. He had not come to try and intercept the letter before Otto had a chance to read it, since Eline had been adamant that it would not change anything, he had come because he felt impelled to do something, to express his sympathy at least, to share in their grief. That he should be the one to break the news to them compounded his misery, and he could barely put his thoughts into words.

Madame van Erlevoort was shattered. She no longer heard Henk's strained discourse, for all she could think of now was how devastated Otto would be. She tried to imagine her son's reaction, and found herself unable to picture him, as if everything might yet change, as if she had misheard. Frédérique's eyes were brimming with tears, her mind was in turmoil, and the hatred smouldering in her heart burst into flame.

Oh, she could have murdered Eline, murdered her! With a grim expression on her features she turned to her mother, who was hiding her face in her hands, sobbing quietly, while Henk stared mournfully into the distance.

Children's voices sounded in the vestibule. The door opened, and Tina, Johan, Madeleine and Nico burst in, with Mathilda at their heels. Henk stood up, flustered. Seeing her mother in tears and Frédérique glowering with impotent fury, Mathilda knew at once that something was seriously wrong.

"Not now! Take the children away!" sobbed Madame van Erlevoort, unceremoniously pushing Nico aside.

Mathilda summoned them to the door. "Off you go upstairs, now, to Nurse Frantzen, and keep your voices down!" she whispered, and they left, somewhat crestfallen, with little Nico in tears.

Mathilda closed the door and looked at Henk with fearful expectation. But it was Frédérique who, with flashing eyes and a note of pride in her voice, explained to her what had happened.

"Good heavens!" gasped Mathilda, shaking.

"How are we going to tell him? Oh, what can we say?" wept Madame. "How could Eline do this? How could she hurt him so? And all this time I thought … Oh, dear Lord!"

She drew Mathilda close and hid her weeping face in her daughter's bosom. Mathilda was used to this: everyone appealed to her for consolation of their woes, and she wrapped her arm about her mother's neck and kissed her.

"Otto's strong, Mama, he'll get over it."

"How can you say that? It's all so unexpected, oh, it will destroy him, my poor, poor boy. Oh, how could she? How could she?"

Someone came thumping down the stairs, two or three treads at a time, whistling in the shrill, jaunty tones of a street urchin. Etienne bowled into the room.

"Good morning, all! Morning, Mama! Well hello there, old chap, what brings you here? How are you?"

His customary, cheerful grin faded at the sight of the consternation written on all their faces, and he stared round-eyed at his mother when she cried out, in a choked voice:

"And you, my pet, can you understand? Can you understand why Eline has done this? How could she have stopped loving Otto?"

"What do you mean?" he asked blankly.

It took a moment for the meaning to sink in, then he ran to his dear, grey-haired mama, whose normally sunny disposition was now so rudely overturned, and flung his arms about her, showering her with childish, tender endearments. And it crossed Mathilda's mind that although her mother had turned to her for consolation, she had gained it from her darling boy, her Etienne.

While they waited for Otto to return in time for coffee, his mother and sisters agreed among themselves to greet him as calmly as possible, so as to spare his feelings. Madame van Erlevoort wondered at her son's apparent composure when Mathilda, with an air of grave intent, caught his hands and drew him to a seat. She had been expecting a different reaction from him, some outburst of horrified, violent passion, and she thanked the Lord for giving her son the strength to bear his suffering as she watched his expression change from frank and genial to an inscrutable mask, in which the only sign of emotion was a tremor of the lips.

"That letter—where is it?" he said at last.

"Otto—"

"Give me the letter, please."

Mathilda stood up and handed him the envelope. He made to leave the room, but Mathilda stepped in his path; she gave him a quick hug, whispering in his ear: "Be a man, Otto! Be a man!" Then she kissed him and let him go.

Madame van Erlevoort, who had hardly said a word to Otto, leant tearfully against Etienne's shoulder. He patted her on the back and kissed her several times, while Mathilda stared wordlessly out of the window with tears in her eyes. Frédérique sat quite still and aloof; they had no need of her, that much was clear, because what did she know about suffering? They didn't even think she knew the meaning of the word!

Tina came down, demanding attention. Mathilda wanted to send her away, but Madame van Erlevoort said, haltingly:

"Let her stay, Tilly. And call the others, too, they're bound to be hungry. But I shall not eat, I'm afraid, I have no appetite at all."

She withdrew from Etienne's embrace and was soon busying herself about the meal, slicing the top off a boiled egg for Tina and buttering the child's bread.

"Why are you crying, Grandma? Are you ill?" demanded Tina. Madame van Erlevoort shook her head, smiling dismally through her tears. Sorrow made her nervous, and her quivering hands, seeking occupation, set about helping the three other children, who had since joined them at the table. Frédérique fought back her tears as she surveyed the youngsters settling down to eat, only slightly subdued by the gloom of their elders. Such was life: no matter how much suffering there was in the world, everyone just carried on with what they were doing, eating, sleeping, laughing, all wrapped up in their egotistic materialism, and no one cared!

Otto had meant to read the letter in the privacy of his room, but passing through the salon on his way there he dropped onto a sofa and ripped the envelope open. He began to read Eline's outpouring of grief and remorse. There was no need for her to assure him that she had suffered unbearably in the writing of it, for he could read her anguish in every word even as it lacerated his soul. The letter told him, although not in so many words, that any future effort on his part to find happiness in her love—supposing he was able to rekindle it—would be in vain; it told him that the rupture was final, that they would be separated for ever, because she had lacked the strength to sustain her love. He was overcome with despair. If only she had been stronger, if only she had given herself more time, it would surely have been in his power to make her happy, for the simple reason that the constancy of his love would have offered her nerves a chance to settle down, and ultimately she would have blossomed. That was how he had seen their future unfold, but now it had all proved a grievous delusion.

He read the letter again from start to finish, as if his eyes might have deceived him, but it was true: he had lost her, she was gone for ever! Sitting in the cold gleam of the large salon with its imposing pier glasses and faded velvet hangings, he felt like a lost soul in a desolate wilderness. He looked about him, moist-eyed, and shivered. Then he slumped back against the sofa and covered his face with his hands, emitting a rasping sob. He felt as if everything inside him were breaking and snapping like a bundle of dry reeds, as if that single sob had torn through his body like a hurricane, leaving utter ruin in its wake, and in that moment he wished he were dead.

He sobbed soundlessly behind his hands, and a sombre bitterness welled up in him. What had he done to deserve this? He, who had once discovered such richness within himself; he, whose sole ambition had been to share these riches, to bestow the gift of peaceful contentment on the woman he loved? He had been spurned, his gift refused, and he found himself poorer now than the poorest man on earth, defeated and bereft of all but black despair.

The door opened softly. It was Mathilda, who, not finding him in his room, had come looking for him. She entered the salon with a look of deep compassion and seated herself on the sofa beside him. When she tried to pull his hands from his face he gave a violent start and stared at her, wild-eyed.

"Why have you come to me?" he asked disconsolately. For there was nothing left to say; he felt as if he had died.

"Why do you think? Why did you come to me that time, oh, it must be five years ago already, when I was so upset and you held me tight? And that other time, soon afterwards, that night when my husband and I … when my husband left me? Go on, tell me: why did you seek me out? Did I ask you the question you just asked me?"

Seeing his chest heave with stifled emotion, she put her arm about his neck and drew his head to her shoulder. In the depths of his own suffering he suddenly thought of his sister's grief, of which she never spoke, and he felt warmed by her wish to comfort him.

"Why bring that up?" he said, knowing her reluctance to mention her former husband.

"To show you that I understand how you feel. And to remind you that I survived, and that I must continue to do so for some time yet. But especially to remind you that you're not alone in your sorrow. Perhaps that could comfort you a little."

"Oh!" he sobbed, clinging to her; then he held out the letter, his hand shaking.

"There! Read it!" he said hoarsely.

She began to read, stroking his head all the while as though comforting one of her children, so that he could weep copious tears without shame for his unmanly conduct. And while she read, she mulled over Eline's motives.

"Does she have any idea of what she's doing?" she asked herself. "What would she do if she saw the state he is in? Is it wickedness on her part to treat him so cruelly? Is she even worthy of my beloved brother? Or is she simply an unhappy creature, like the rest of us?"

Madame van Erlevoort came in with Frédérique.

Mathilda lifted Otto's chin.

"Look, here's Mama," she said simply, as if she did not wish to detain him now that his mother was there to offer consolation. But when he saw the look of pitiful anguish on her dear face, he felt it was he who should console her.

"Mama, Mama, please don't cry! It's not the end of the world, you know!" he exclaimed.

Frédérique stood leaning against the door frame, her forearms crossed before her face. No one paid any attention to her. It was all right for Mathilda and Mama to try and comfort him, he obviously did not need her, she was only a child as far as he was concerned, and would have nothing of any consequence to say to him. She thought back on the conversation they had had about Eline all those months ago, before the engagement, but now there was nothing more to say, nothing. Her words carried no weight, she had never suffered, she had no feeling, she was made of stone.

"Stone! They think I'm made of stone!" she repeated under her breath, and continued to weep into her crossed arms, inconsolable for her inability to console Otto.

Feeling a hand on her shoulder she turned round with a look of defiance at being so sorely misjudged. But when she saw Otto's pained expression, his eyes filled with tears, his brow deeply furrowed, his lips quivering beneath the blond moustache, she flung her arms about him in a great rush of pity and smothered his face with kisses, for she had never seen him cry before.

XXIV

Betsy's compassion for Eline initially manifested itself in sisterly concern for the state of her health, but before long her old irritation returned with redoubled force. How very tiresome of Eline to go back on her word! And why, for Heaven's sake? Why had she done it? She, Betsy, could not for the life of her understand why Eline had changed her mind. Who could she possibly rather marry than Otto, even though he was perhaps not rolling in riches? Now her own plans for the future were ruined! If Eline didn't get married, she'd go on living with them for ever, and as for Vincent, he was a hanger-on if there ever was one! She was sick and tired of the pair of them, the way they were always spoiling the atmosphere with their selfish behaviour.

Another source of annoyance for Betsy was all the talk about Otto and Eline calling off their engagement. She would not have minded so much about the gossip, which she knew would die down soon enough, if Eline had given her the impression, now that she had got her way, that things would soon return to normal, that she would finally shake off this absurd act of grieving over Otto and gradually become her old self again, the younger sister whose pretty face and charming manners had been rather an asset when she entertained guests of an evening. Oh, if only Eline would be obliging and come to her senses, then Betsy's dearest wish would be for her to stay with them as long as she liked. But the fact of the matter was that Eline was permanently in a dark mood—either sullen and dazed-looking or enraged, complete with shrill vociferations. Eline never went out nowadays, and only the other evening, when Betsy had invited a few guests for dinner—just Madame Eekhof with Ange and Léonie, Marguerite van Laren and her fiancé, and young Hijdrecht—she had actually stayed up in her room under the pretext of a severe headache. Betsy's patience was running out. Why did Eline have to look so wan and weary-eyed, why didn't she bother to put her hair up properly nowadays? And those endless tête-à-têtes with Vincent! True, Vincent was their cousin and a semi-invalid at that, but there something unseemly about the way she kept sneaking off with him to the violet ante-room, or to her boudoir, or to the conservatory. She was determined to say something next time she came upon them sharing secrets; it simply wouldn't do.

In her irritable frame of mind Betsy's anger was quickly provoked, and besides delivering pinpricks of disapproval to Eline and Vincent at every opportunity, she would vent her spleen on the servants, on Ben and on her husband. Impossible to please, she bustled about the house in a pretence of housewifely fastidiousness, flying into a rage at a dust cloth left lying about or a particle of fluff on the carpet, grumbling at her young son when he was sitting quietly with his toys, or berating her husband for some misdemeanour, such as having something urgent to do elsewhere the moment she opened her mouth! Most of all she was dissatisfied with herself, for having become so ill-tempered. And yet none of it was her fault. It was all her sister's fault, and Vincent's.

One day, just before dinner, things came to a head. All that happened to ignite her rage was that she had come upon Vincent raising a glass to his lips in the dining room. The dinner bell had not yet sounded, and he had helped himself to some wine from the decanter. Forgetting all her previous caution with regard to Vincent, she lashed out at him for his abominable behaviour. Where were his manners? Didn't he know she ran a respectable house? Indeed, she had been meaning to ask him for some time whether he possessed any manners at all! Thus they stood, face to face, Vincent eyeing her with cool self-restraint while Betsy let fly, when Henk and Eline entered. Eline made no comment, not wishing to take sides, while Henk tried to pacify his wife. His efforts had the opposite effect, and she turned her fury on him, accusing him of being ineffectual and disloyal as usual. It was not the wine that she objected to—Vincent could drink as much as he liked for all she cared—what stung her was that he seemed to think he was living in a hotel, free of charge, where he could stay just as long as it suited him, helping himself to whatever took his fancy. He had no business coming down to the dining room before anyone else, before the dinner bell sounded, it was downright rude, and she wasn't having it!

Vincent kept his counsel, conceding temporary defeat, but in retreating from the room gave Betsy a look of such scorn and loathing as to strike fear into her heart. Her triumph at having put him in his place evaporated as she quickly composed herself, announcing that it was time dinner was served and motioning Henk and Eline to take their seats at the table. Henk took a deep breath and did as he was bidden; Eline too sat down, and proceeded to unfold her napkin with deliberation. Neither Betsy nor Henk said very much after that, and Eline maintained a stoic silence for the duration of the meal.

That evening Vincent packed his suitcase in preparation for his departure to London. Henk made only half-hearted attempts to dissuade him, because he knew that with Vincent out of the way there was more chance of restoring some kind of harmony in the home. He felt sorry for Vincent, to be sure, but he couldn't wait for Betsy to be relieved of this importunate cousin, whom she had first ingratiated herself with and then come to loathe from the bottom of her heart.

The next morning Vincent had a final conversation with Eline in her boudoir.

"So you really are going?" she asked.

"Of course, my dear girl. You know as well as I do that Betsy can't stand me."

"What will you do in London?"

"I have friends there, and some money matters to attend to before I go to America."

"You're going to America then?"

"You know I am: you brought me St Clare's letter yourself, remember."

"I didn't know you had decided for certain. Poor you!"

He smiled wanly, gratified to hear the concern in her voice.

"Do you feel sorry for me?"

"Yes, I do. And with you going back to your roaming existence, who knows how long it'll be before I see you again? Maybe never!"

She sighed.

"I'm always happiest when I'm roaming," he retorted.

She longed to ask him if she might accompany him on his travels, join him in his search for happiness in other lands and climates, but she could not think of how to frame her question, so she waited, hoping that he would raise the possibility himself. He was in love with her, after all; it was because of her that he had decided to go abroad in the first place, and now there was nothing to stop them being together.

"He doesn't dare ask; he doesn't dare!" she thought, unsure whether she was pleased or disappointed by his timidity.

"Happiest when you're roaming!" she echoed pensively. "It's possible, I suppose. You're a man, you're free to roam … But I am a girl, and I have lived in the same place all my life … Not that it makes me happy, though. Not by any means!"

He gave her a quizzical look. After a pause he asked:

"And why aren't you happy?"

"Why am I not happy? I don't know, really," she murmured.

She waited for him to press her for an answer, but presently told herself he might think it inappropriate to do so now, given that she had only recently broken with Otto. Yet she was sure she had heard the intonation of love in his soft voice, and she looked at him expectantly. A ray of sunshine entered the room through the parted curtains, setting aglow the slight figure on the sofa, and a pang went through her as she thought how closely he resembled her father. Her heart began to race, and she felt a great surge of love for Vincent, on account of that very likeness, on account of his suffering under the narrow-minded conventions of society, on account of her idealised, romantic perception of him.

He returned her gaze with an expression of sympathy. She had jettisoned her chance of happiness, as he himself had been known to do on several occasions in the past, although he had never been so acutely aware of it as she seemed to be now. For an instant he was of a mind to tell her as much, but then thought better of it; she would not have listened, anyway.

"Vincent!" she stammered at length, fraught with waiting for him to make some kind of declaration. "Vincent, please—we might never see each other again. Are you sure you have nothing to say to me?"

"Oh, I have lots to say to you, Elly dear. For one thing, I want to thank you for nursing me and pampering me like a true sister, here in your own room, at a time of such painful suffering for you."

"What makes you think I was suffering?"

"Because I know a thing or two about human nature."

She shook her head in denial.

"I don't think I did suffer, really. Not personally I mean, only on behalf of Otto."

She felt a twinge of guilt at that lie, but it was for Vincent's sake, Vincent who was in love with her and must not know of her heartache. He looked at her intently, wondering why she should wish to hide the truth from him. He did not understand her, but then the workings of the female mind were always hard to fathom, if not to say shrouded in mystery.

She for her part did not understand him. It was inexplicable that he had not asked her to be his, now that nothing stood in their way, now that he was on the point of going abroad. Another hour and he would be gone! Ah, but perhaps he thought it was too late. She took a deep breath, and with a new urgency in her voice she said:

"Vincent, I want you to promise me something. If there is anything I can do for you, if I can ever help you in any way, you must write to me from New York, and I shan't disappoint you. Promise me that you will write?"

"I promise. You are very kind."

"Another thing: I know you're often short of funds. If I can be of help, you must let me know. Just now, for instance, I have two hundred and fifty guilders to spare. Yours, if you need any money. Shall I get it for you?"

She rose, making to open her writing table, but he grasped her hand with a show of emotion.

"Elly, oh Elly, no—I couldn't possibly. It is extremely kind of you, and I'm deeply grateful, but I wouldn't be able to pay you back for quite some time."

"Please don't say no, I'd really like you to have it."

"I can't tell you how much I appreciate your offer, but no, truly, I cannot accept. It would not be right."

She stood quite still, her face drained of colour. Yes! Yes, of course he loved her! How could she have had the slightest doubt? Why else would he refuse the money? It was because he loved her that he wouldn't let a debt come between them! But then why didn't he say something?

At last he stood up; the cab would arrive in a few minutes.

"Can't you make it up with Betsy before you go?" she said imploringly. "It's so horrid to part under these conditions."

"I'll go to her now, and all will be put right again soon enough. But now I really must be off. Goodbye, my dear Elly. Farewell, and thank you a thousand times for everything you have done for me."

"Goodbye, Vincent, goodbye."

As he made to embrace her, she flung her arms about his neck and kissed him on both cheeks.

"Spare a thought for me now and then, will you?" he said. "I hold you very dear, and there aren't that many people I hold dear, as you well know. Farewell then, Elly, *au revoir*."

Struggling against her tears, she kissed him again, and as he moved away she subsided onto the couch, giving a final nod of farewell. He left, shutting the door behind him.

She sat staring at the door until she heard his cab rumble off. She was perplexed. How could he have kissed her so coolly in that final moment of intimacy? She dearly wished to understand his sentiments, and also to probe her own feelings so that she might know whether she really loved Vincent, but she was tired and her head felt heavy, and with a weary sigh she fell back in the cushions.

Betsy had pardoned Vincent at the last moment. In the knowledge that he was leaving at last she could afford to soften towards him, and so she made conciliatory remarks to the effect that their time together would soon have been curtailed anyway because she was planning to travel abroad in the autumn. Once he was gone she gradually became herself again, no longer venting her temper so frequently at the servants, or at Eline, Henk and Ben. She even spoke amicably to her sister from time to time: it really wasn't a good idea to shut oneself away from the world the way she was doing, it would make anyone lonely and miserable, and besides, it was bound to attract attention—people might think she was sorry to have lost van Erlevoort! No, it would be a good thing if she showed her face in public once in a while; there was no need to accept every invitation if she did not feel up to it, but sending her apologies every time was giving the wrong impression. As it happened, Madame Hovel was giving a dinner party the following week; her evenings were usually rather intimate, and this invitation was no exception. Emilie and Georges de Woude would be there, as well as Paul—in other words, should Betsy accept on Eline's behalf?

Eline herself was beginning to feel a desire for a change of scene, for she was enmeshed in her solitary thoughts, which went round and round in her head without leading anywhere. So she conceded that Betsy was quite right: she would accept Madame Hovel's invitation. It would be her first appearance in company since breaking off her engagement. The dinner party a few days hence became an anchor in her fluctuating emotions, a welcome distraction from Betsy's constant references to Vincent's tiresome sojourn in her house. What a blessing it was to be rid of that languishing, insufferable cousin of theirs! True, she had taken offence at a fairly minor breach of etiquette on his part, but it had been quite wrong of him, and she wasn't a bit sorry she had told him off, because if she hadn't done so he would still be there! Good gracious, what a bore he was! Why she had ever thought he would be good company she could not imagine. And that long face of his—rather like a reptile, quite loathsome, really. Ah well, thank goodness he was gone now, and she was glad to let bygones be bygones.

During mealtimes each day Betsy chatted on in the same mindless vein, reciting the same litany of disparagements. Henk and Eline sat in glum silence, numbed by her loquacity. Much as Eline wanted to speak out in Vincent's defence, she felt too dispirited, and simply gave a sigh of relief when Betsy finally ran out of steam. She suffered mutely for Vincent, who was in love with her and had acted so honourably.

The day of the dinner arrived. For the first time in weeks Eline took great care over her appearance. While they were waiting for the carriage to arrive, however, Betsy pronounced her to be overdressed: such a dark gown, and so formal, why, she looked as if she were going to a funeral! Eline said nothing, merely shrugged. She glanced in the hall-stand mirror and was reassured: she thought she made an impression of subdued elegance with her pale, melancholy features and her low-cut dress of black, frothy tulle.

They were the last to arrive at the Hovel residence, and when Eline made her entrance she had the feeling everyone in the room was observing her with a kind of eager curiosity. It was the first time she had ever felt ill at ease being the centre of attention, and yet she knew all the dinner guests quite intimately: Emilie and Georges de Woude, Françoise Oudendijk, Hijdrecht and Paul. On the other hand, none of them had seen her since she had called off her engagement, so there was nothing for it but to try and ignore their inquisitive glances. At the table, seated between Georges and Hijdrecht, she felt little desire to talk, and was glad of the latter's rambling conversation, to which she pretended to listen, smiling vaguely and not saying a word in response. Georges was more quiet than usual. But on the opposite side of the table a loud, jocular exchange was taking place between Emilie and Françoise, while Paul, placed between them, acted as referee.

The clamour opposite, Hijdrecht's incessant chatter at her side, and the general animation around the dinner table made Eline's head swim. The servants intoning each variety of wine as they made to replenish her glass, the copious servings, the joking and the hilarity—how very boring it all was. She was jolted out of her gloomy reverie by the mention of Vincent's name. Betsy was telling the host that her cousin had departed and might be going to America.

"To tell you the truth, I was not sorry to see him go. I don't care for him, really; in fact I think he is rather disagreeable. Of course, since he's our cousin, we can't ignore him completely, but he is very peculiar, and I couldn't help being afraid he might do something to compromise us."

Eline no longer heard what Hijdrecht was saying; she was all ears to Betsy's gossipy voice, which she could fairly easily distinguish in the hubbub. So it was not enough for Betsy to be constantly running him down in the privacy of her home, with Eline trying valiantly to keep her counsel, she was actually ventilating her hatred of Vincent in this dining room, among strangers! Eline listened with mounting rage.

"There's something creepy about him—a bit like a toad, or some reptile, don't you agree? Unnerving, too, with those pale, shifty eyes of his."

Eline could control herself no longer. The person who was dearest to her in the whole world, who reminded her so much of her father, was being vilified in society by her own sister, in the most vulgar terms imaginable! And she was making Hovel laugh! Eyes flashing, Eline burst out in tremulous indignation, raising her voice so that it would reach across the crystal centrepiece to the other side of the table:

"Betsy! Please mind what you're saying! You are not in your own home, and I advise you to find something else to amuse Mr Hovel with instead of saying such hateful things about Vincent!"

Her voice was so commanding that everyone stopped talking in mid-sentence. All eyes were fixed on Betsy and Eline as the fun succumbed to leaden embarrassment. And Eline, to whom making a scene in public would have been anathema before, sat bolt upright, glaring defiantly at Betsy and the rest of them, not caring a whit that her conduct went against the conventions of respectable society. Betsy, her face flushed with nervous agitation, was on the point of making some cutting reply, but mastered herself just in time. Turning to Hovel instead, she spoke with ostensible calm:

"I do apologise, Mr Hovel, for this interruption. My sister has been suffering from her nerves lately. Do not mind her, please."

Suppressing her anger with tact, she was soon laughing again and holding forth on another more light-hearted topic.

The hostess was rather shaken by the embarrassing episode at her dinner table, but Emilie de Woude, true to her ebullient nature, came to the rescue with more tact than Betsy could muster. She turned to Eline, who was still casting baleful looks at her sister, and addressed her directly. Her tone was placatory at first, but very soon turned humorous.

"Ah well, Eline, personally I don't find him nearly as objectionable as most people seem to. But you must understand, having someone to stay under one's roof for an extended period, as Betsy has experienced, is a different matter altogether; it's bound to lead to a certain amount of friction. It's only natural: young men always get under one's feet. I know what I'm talking about, because with Georges living at home—oh, you wouldn't believe how much bother and commotion he causes! Always getting in the way—why, it's enough to drive anyone to distraction!"

"Me?" spluttered Georges, affecting outrage. "Me?" And he defended himself with vigour.

There was a chorus of laughter at this comical tiff between siblings, who were known to be devoted to each another. It even brought a fleeting smile to Eline's face, and Madame Hovel overflowed with gratitude to Emilie.

It had rained heavily throughout the day, with strong winds lashing the trees and making the branches groan as they littered the ground with broken twigs and autumn leaves. Come the evening, when Betsy, Eline and Henk rode homewards in their carriage at half-past ten, the wind had risen to a raging storm, causing the glass shades of the street lamps to jingle in their sockets and blowing tiles off the roofs. Betsy had meant to give Eline a piece of her mind on the way, but there was so much noise that conversation was virtually impossible, and the cold coming in through a chink in the door made her shiver.

"Such stormy weather!" she fretted. "Do you think it is dangerous, Henk? Won't the horses be frightened?"

Henk shook his head. Like her, he listened to the howling wind and heard the rain drumming on the roof. Eline, too, kept silent. When they drew up at Nassauplein they were welcomed by Gerard, who flung open the front door even before Herman had time to ring the bell, and Betsy and Eline ran inside while Henk gave some last-minute instructions to Dirk concerning the horses. Eline went straight up to her room.

"What a stormy night, ma'am," said Mina as she helped Betsy out of her cape. "You'd think the end of the world was nigh! A fair number of trees will be knocked down before morning, you mark my words. Grete and I were ever so frightened. Oh, I'm so glad you're safely home again!"

Betsy did not answer, and started up the stairs with the full intention of confronting Eline. But the storm raging outside seemed to have deflected her anger, leaving her in some doubt as to what she would say. Her thoughts turned to the possibility of windows in the house having been left open and chimney stacks being blown off the roof.

"Gerard! Mina!" she called from the landing.

They both came running.

"Are you sure you have locked up properly?"

"Oh yes, ma'am!"

"Well, I want you to make quite sure all the windows are securely closed. What about the attic, for instance? Go and check, you never know."

Having dispatched the servants, Betsy regained her presence of mind. Yes, she would confront Eline in her room. Her sister was not to think she could get away with such insolence.

Betsy entered Eline's boudoir, where the gas lamp was lit. The wind rattled the window panes and made the curtains billow. Eline was taking off her cloak.

"What is it?" she asked haughtily. "I should like to be alone."

"May I remind you that you are in my house, and that I can enter any room I please? I have something to say to you."

"Well, get on with it then, because, as I said, I want to be alone."

"'I want! I want!' What gives you the right to speak to me in that tone? You are here in my house, and it is not for you to want anything!" fumed Betsy, stamping her feet. "Acting like some spoilt little princess who always gets her way! Did you think I'd let you get away with being rude to me in public? Did you? How dare you tell me what I may or may not say? I can say whatever

I like to Hovel! I don't need any prompting from you, do you hear?"

"I warn you, Betsy, that from now on, whenever I hear you speak about Vincent in that disgraceful way, even if it's in your own home, I shall put a stop to it."

"Ah, so you're warning me now are you? I have no intention of making any allowances whatsoever for your idiotic sensitivity regarding Vincent! Now he's gone, you'd think we'd have some peace again, but no! Was it he who taught you that it was perfectly all right to interrupt people in the middle of a conversation? I can't think what came over you! They must have thought you were mad. Yes, you must be mad, that's the only excuse I can think of for behaving the way you did! And you call me vulgar— what do you think that makes you? You, who dared to—"

"I know, I know—I, who dared to interrupt you at a dinner party! Yes, I dared to do so! But I promise you that I shall dare a great deal more if I hear another word spoken against Vincent. You think he's spiteful, but you're the one who's spiteful—first you invite him to stay and then you throw a tantrum over some trifle and shout at him like a fishwife so that he'll leave! You're the one who's spiteful!"

"Keep your insults to yourself, pray."

"And you keep your nasty remarks about Vincent to yourself in future!" raged Eline. "I will not hear another word spoken against him, I've put up with it long enough for the sake of peace, but now I can't stand it any longer! Do you understand?"

"You can't stand it any longer, you say? Oh, so it's because of Vincent that you can't stand Otto any more either, I suppose."

"Leave Otto out of this!" screamed Eline.

"You don't mean to say that you've taken a fancy to that reptile? Is that why you treated Otto as if he were just another beau, someone to have a little fling with? You say you won't put up with my criticism of Vincent, but I—I won't put up with any more of your compromising behaviour! Who do you think you are? First you're stupid enough to break off your engagement, out of sheer caprice, without the slightest reason, so that now we've got all the tongues wagging, then you start making a fuss of Vincent here in my house as if you're in love with him, and to cap it all you have the nerve to insult me in front of other people! I'm not having it, do you hear? If you've picked up your bad manners from all those idiotic philosophical discussions you had with Vincent, then—"

Eline was beside herself. Her nerves were strung to their highest tension, quivering under Betsy's vituperations. What Betsy had said about her and Otto, and especially about her sympathy for Vincent, which she thought she had kept hidden from everyone, filled her with helpless rage. She gripped Betsy's wrists and, hissing between her teeth, shrilled out:

"Shut up! Stop it, I tell you! Don't you dare lecture me about Otto, or Vincent for that matter, or I'll slap you. You're horrible. I've had as much as I can take of your aggravation! I warn you!"

"Eline, have you taken leave of your senses?" cried Betsy, but Eline stood where she was, shaking her fists.

"Yes, you drive me mad with all your aggravation about 'my house, my house'! I am well aware it's your house I'm living in, but I never asked to come here, and you keep harping on the fact that it's your house as if I ought to thank you for taking me in. I don't depend on you for anything, and even if I am living under your roof, that doesn't give you any say in what I do or don't do. I'm free, free to do as I please."

"No you are not. You are here, in my house, and you must conduct yourself accordingly. And if you cannot, then it is up to me to try to do something about it."

Betsy had left the door open when she came in, and their shouting reverberated through the whole house, almost drowning out the rattling of the shutters in the storm. Henk appeared in the doorway, but was unable to make himself heard over the din.

"You have nothing to say about how I should or should not behave!" shrieked Eline. "I'm free, I tell you! I don't need your house, and I swear to you that I shan't stay here for another second! I swear it! You can stuff your precious house!" She hardly knew what she was saying, having worked herself up into a paroxysm of fury, nor was she conscious of what she was doing when she snatched up her cloak off the floor and flung it about her shoulders. She made a dash for the door, but Henk stood in her path.

"Eline!" he began gravely.

"Let me go, let me go!" she raged like a wounded tigress, pushing him away with such force that he staggered back. He tried to stop her again, but she was already out of the door, flying down the stairs.

"Eline! For God's sake, Eline! You don't know what you're doing!" he called, in hot pursuit. She was deaf to his cries, for there was only one thought in her mind: to flee from this house where she was not wanted, and she was blind to Gerard and the maids staring at her in blank amazement as she rushed through the vestibule, threw open the glass-panelled inner door and swiftly drew the bolt of the street door. A blast of wind caused the inner door to slam shut, and at her back she heard the shattered glass fall to the floor.

Then the front door, too, slammed behind her, and she found herself in the street, in the driving rain with the gale blowing open her cloak and spitting at her face and neck. It was impossible for her to battle against that raging force, so she gave up and allowed herself to be propelled by the storm lashing her back like a gigantic vampire with broad, razor-sharp claws. She saw no one in the street, and as she ran ahead all alone in the doom-laden night, in the unrelenting, splashing downpour, buffeted by the gusting wind, she was seized with panic. She felt as if she had been wrenched from her familiar existence and hurled into a nightmare of disaster and despair; the rain was beating down on her bare head and she felt terror at the darkness enfolding her with calamity. The wind almost tore her cloak from her shoulders, numbing her with cold in her fluttering black tulle. Her dainty patent leather shoes went wading and splashing through puddles and mud, her dishevelled hair clung in dripping strands to her cheeks, and under her flapping cloak she felt an icy moisture gliding down her neck and shoulders. She no longer knew where she was, but hurried on regardless, shuddering with fright at each broken twig that came skittering her way, at each menacing rumble of loose roof tiles. And she saw no one, not a soul.

She was slow in coming back to reality: she had fled from her brother-in-law's house! She wanted to stand still for a moment to reflect on this, but the blustering storm drove her forward as though she were one of the autumn leaves flying past her head. And she let herself be blown along, trying to gather her thoughts as she went. Despite the direness of her self-inflicted plight, she felt no remorse, but rather, to her astonishment, a flickering of pride at her own temerity. Never had she imagined herself capable of taking flight like this, in the middle of the night, without even knowing where she was going! Heartened by this surprise, she forced herself to apply her mind to the urgent matter at hand: she could not wander about aimlessly all night, she had to think of somewhere to go.

Suddenly she noticed that she had reached Laan Copes van Cattenburgh. Driven by the wind, she rushed headlong onwards over the slippery, muddy footpath, flinching from the boughs sighing overhead. The tree trunks creaked ominously, and she was terrified that one of them would topple over and crush her to death. She battled on regardless, summoning all her will-power to put some order in her thoughts. Where for the love of God should she go? She felt great staring eyes fixed on her in the darkness. Whom could she turn to? Old Madame van Raat? Oh, she might have been fond of Eline once, but now she was bound to take sides with her son and daughter-in-law! To the Verstraetens, then, who were her brother-in-law's relatives? She felt herself sinking into a muddy abyss of despair. Otto loomed up in her mind, and she thought how willingly she would have traded the rest of her life just to have him appear at her side at this moment, to be drawn into his embrace, to be borne away to a safe place full of warmth, light and love. His name rose to her lips like a supplication, but her voice was drowned out by the storm. She was barely able to take another step, she was ready to let herself fall into the mud at her feet and lie there, lashed by the wind, until she died! But that would be a cowardly thing to do, while she had found the courage to follow her impulse to leave, and so she forced herself to focus on the question as to whom she could possibly turn in her distress. Not to Madame van Raat—not to the Verstraetens, either—oh God, where should she go? Suddenly, like a bolt of lightning in that night of torment and dread, it came to her. Jeanne! In her mind's eye she saw her old school friend's sitting room in the cramped abode over the greengrocer's shop. Yes, that's where she would go! It was a last resort, but she could not think of anything better, and besides, her strength was failing her. So she turned to face the driving wind and, with faltering steps, fought to cross the square at Alexanderveld in the direction of Hugo de Grootstraat, clutching the collar of her cloak tightly about her neck, drenched to the skin and shivering with cold. On the far side of the green she could just see the backs of the houses on Nassauplein. There were still lights in a few windows, but she was too far away to distinguish which ones were Betsy's—hers no longer—and a pang of longing and regret went through her at the realisation of what she had left behind. With a sinking feeling she calculated how much longer it would take her to reach the Ferelijns' apartment. She was exhausted, exhausted from the quarrel with Betsy, from the unrelenting, icy rain striking her in the face, from the wind buffeting her from side to side, from her sodden patent leather shoes, heavy with mud and threatening to slip off at each step. She felt she was about to die of misery, desolation, hardship.

But she pushed her way doggedly onwards against the gale until she reached Javastraat, where she turned right towards Laan van Meerdervoort. A gust of wind almost made her lose her footing, and a broken branch came flying through the air, striking her on the shoulder and grazing her cheek, at which she let out a scream. Fear, pain and utter despair took possession of her as she laboured to make her legs go faster … To the Ferelijns'! To the Ferelijns'! But the raging wind was against her, compelling her to fight every step of the way.

"Oh God! What have I done?" she moaned in helpless agony. The streets so familiar by day had been transformed into a diabolical maze of darkness and clamour, in which she felt like a lost soul, ghostlike and God-forsaken, and when she found herself going past old Madame van Raat's house she had to summon all her fortitude not to ring the bell, by which she would have gained immediate admittance to warmth and light. But no, it was too late in the night, Madame would be asleep by now, and besides, she would not take kindly to Eline's flight from Nassauplein. And she trudged past the door without stopping, driven onwards by the wind as much as by her newfound passion to reach the Ferelijns, frantically putting one foot in front of the other in her mud-clotted evening shoes. She turned into van de Spiegelstraat—how much longer would she have to endure this torment? There, at long last, Hugo de Grootstraat!

With the rain stinging her face and the wind tearing harder than ever at her cloak, she found herself—thank Heavens!—standing on their doorstep. The house was in total darkness, but she did not hesitate. This was her only salvation. She seized the bell pull and rang for all her worth, wildly, passionately, and rang again, and again.

How long it was taking! It seemed like an eternity, but at last she heard someone thumping down the stairs, then the squeak of the bolt being drawn across the door. It opened a crack, and a face appeared.

"For the love of God!" she cried, thrusting the door open and rushing inside. "It's me, Eline!"

The door fell to behind her. She stood in the unlit stairwell, face to face with Frans Ferelijn, who cried out her name in disbelief. Jeanne appeared at the top of the stairs, holding a lamp. All Eline could think of at that moment was the promise of light, warmth and comfort, and, mustering the very last of her energy, she ran up the stairs.

"Jeanne! Jeanne! I beg you, help me! It's me, Eline! Oh, please help me!"

"Good heavens, Eline!" gasped Jeanne.

"Help me, I beg you! I—I have run away! Oh please, help me, or I'll die!"

She sank down in a wet, crumpled heap at Jeanne's feet.

"Eline! Eline!" cried Jeanne in dismay.

Breaking into violent sobs, Eline remained hunched on the floor, where puddles were forming about the hem of her cloak. Jeanne struggled to lift her to her feet.

"Oh Eline! What have you done? What's happened? You're wet through! And quite frozen! Heavens above!"

She led Eline, who could barely stand, into Frans's little study, and set down the lamp. Eline collapsed onto a chair, muddy water oozing from her clothes.

"I've run away! I've run away from Nassauplein!" she wailed. "I couldn't bear it any longer—and I came here because … well, because I had nowhere else to go. Oh, Jeanne, please, you will help me, won't you?"

Jeanne was overwhelmed with pity.

"You can tell me about it later, Eline. Come, let's get you out of those wet clothes, or you'll catch your death of cold."

"Oh yes, please, help me take them off. Here's my cloak. Oh, and my shoes! What a disgusting state I'm in, all covered in mud! Lord in heaven, I wish I were dead!"

She slumped against the back of her chair, weeping.

"Frans, just look at her!" said Jeanne tremulously. "I do hope she won't fall ill—she didn't even have a hat, and look what she's wearing, just a flimsy evening dress!"

"I'll go down and light the stove, then, while you get her some dry clothes," said Frans, in a subdued voice. He too was profoundly moved by the sight of Eline slumped in their armchair, her dripping hair in streaks across her marble-white throat and jaw, her black silk dress clinging wetly to her limp form. He went off, glad for something to do.

Outside, the storm raged unabated.

In the Ferelijns' sitting room, lying on the couch, which Frans had moved up close to the glowing stove, Eline shivered feverishly under a blanket. Nonetheless, in that room suffused with light and warmth she experienced a grateful sense of well-being, and her relief at having escaped from the diabolical powers of darkness knew no bounds. With a start, she drew herself up.

"Forgive me!" she cried hoarsely to Jeanne, who was preparing a hot toddy. "Please, please, forgive me for disturbing you in the middle of the night like this! I am so sorry! But where else could I go? There I was, out in the dark street, in the wind and the rain! I can't bear to think of it! It was terrible, the most terrible night in my life! But you must understand, I simply had to leave … I couldn't stay there another minute! Oh, Betsy's so mean! How I hate her!"

"There, there, Eline, you must try to get some rest now."

"Why did she have to bring Otto into it? She had no right to do that! I hate her! I hate her!"

"Eline! Eline!" said Jeanne, clasping her hands beseechingly.

She fell to her knees before the couch. "I beg you, Eline, for Heaven's sake calm yourself! Lie down, now. You really must rest."

Eline stared a moment, wild-eyed, then wrapped her arm around Jeanne's neck.

"You must try and relax, Eline. Lie down and repose yourself, if you can't sleep."

A hollow sob rasped in Eline's throat.

"You're an angel!" she whispered hoarsely. "I shall never forget what you've done for me, not as long as I live. You saved my life! Oh, all that horrible mud! You do love me, Jany, don't you?"

"Yes, Eline, I love you, but you must take some rest now."

"Ah … rest!"

The word pierced Jeanne's soul. Eline had uttered it in a voice full of despair, as if to say that there would be no rest for her ever again, but she lay back in the cushions obediently, and drank the hot toddy proffered by Jeanne.

"Thank you … thank you," she faltered.

Jeanne tucked her up in the blanket and sat down beside her. The window panes rattled in their frames, whipped by the branches outside. The mantel clock struck three.

It had also struck three in the van Raat residence when Frans Ferelijn pulled up at their front door. The storm was still raging like a wounded monster in the sky over the darkened city. Frans sprang down from the cab and rang the bell. He could see that the light was on in the vestibule.

"I have no money on me, I'm afraid, so please come to my house in the morning to collect what I owe you!" he called to the driver.

The door was opened almost immediately by Henk, who appeared to be expecting someone. But on seeing Frans rush inside, he stepped back in wonder.

"Why, is that you, Ferelijn?" he exclaimed.

"Yes, it's me, don't be alarmed," said Frans. "It's all right, Eline is at our house."

He stepped forward, crushing the broken glass that lay scattered on the floor.

"At your house? Oh, thank God for that!" cried Henk. "I was worried sick, I didn't know what to do. What a relief!"

"Do come through, Ferelijn," Betsy called from the dining-room door. The maids and Gerard, who had crept into the hallway to hear what was going on, were likewise relieved, and withdrew to the kitchen whispering among themselves. Henk ushered Frans into the dining room.

"There is no cause for alarm, Madame van Raat. Truly, this is the best solution for the moment. Eline was soaked to the skin, but Jeanne has taken good care of her. You can't imagine what a fright it gave us to hear the doorbell at such a late hour, and then to find her on the doorstep, dripping wet," said Frans, his voice trailing off as he stared at Henk.

"What on earth has happened to you? Your cheek—it's bleeding!"

"Oh, nothing serious. When Eline ran out of the house I wanted to go after her, but the wind slammed the vestibule door shut, shattering the glass. Some fragments sprang into my face and eyes, so I couldn't go in pursuit of her at once, but as soon as I was able, Gerard and I ran out, meaning to drag her home again if necessary. But it was so confoundedly dark—the gas lamps had all gone out in the storm—and she was nowhere to be seen. I didn't know what to do. In the end we went to the police station on Schelpkade, and they sent out a party of nightwatchmen to search for her. She was in a terrible state when she left—I thought she might do herself an injury, and in this infernal weather anything could have happened. My eye is still hurting. I think I'd better see an oculist tomorrow."

Betsy sighed and fell into a chair. "Dreadful! How very upsetting all this is," she said. "Eline must have taken leave of her senses."

"And you're the one who drove her to it!" fumed Henk, with his hand to his painful eye.

"Oh, so now it's my fault, is it?"

"Van Raat, there are a few things we ought to discuss," interposed Frans. "I came here without a moment's delay, of course, because I thought you would be frantic with worry."

"My dear chap, I can't thank you enough."

"Never mind about that. The thing is, Eline has positively declared that she has no intention of going back. Needless to say, an affair such as this is bound to be talked about. People will gossip, which is most disagreeable! Gossip only makes things worse. The servants know what has transpired, I presume?"

Betsy cast Frans an approving look for raising that point.

"Well, it can't be helped!" said Henk impatiently. "People always gossip."

"That's true. Still, I think it would be a good idea for you to come round to our house in the morning. See if you can persuade Eline to return home—at least if she's well enough, because she seemed rather feverish to me when I left. I suggest you let her get some rest now, but come over as soon as you can in the morning."

"Very well," said Henk, looking dazed.

"I believe she may have been delirious when I left the house in search of a cab, but she seemed very determined. She gave me her house keys, and kept saying that she would never go back. She also asked me to settle her affairs here," he said, looking askance at Betsy, "and to arrange for her clothes to be sent on, but I think she said all this in the heat of passion. In any case, I hope we will have come to some amicable arrangement by this time tomorrow."

"Look here, Ferelijn," said Betsy uneasily, "I hope you realise how upsetting this is for me. Goodness knows this is not the first

314

time Eline and I have fallen out, but who could have imagined that she would go and do something so silly? And as you say: it will be the talk of The Hague! So if you can manage to persuade her to change her mind, I'd be eternally grateful. Our house is always open to her. As for her keys, you can leave them here. Yes, I expect it will turn out all right in the end. I'm so glad it was you she went to! But can you imagine—in the middle of the night, in that storm? How could she do it? How on earth could she do it?"

Frans and Henk resumed their conversation, and Henk suggested he stay the night, as Frans had sent away the cab and the storm had not abated. Gerard showed Frans to Henk's dressing room for a dry set of clothes.

"Henk, you might ask Ferelijn discreetly how much he paid for that cab," Betsy suggested when she was alone with her husband once more. "It must have cost him a pretty penny, and it was very kind of him to come at once."

"Discreetly, you say—you don't know the meaning of the word!" spluttered Henk, and he left the room, shuddering to think of what people were going to say.

Early the next morning Henk drove with Frans Ferelijn to an oculist. There was slight damage to the veins in one eye, and after the removal of a small splinter of glass he felt greatly relieved. His cheek, however, displayed a nasty gash.

"I look as if I've been to war!" he jested grimly when they were back in the cab on their way to Hugo de Grootstraat. "And indeed, my dear Frans, at the moment my house does seem like a battlefield! I, for one, have had quite enough of it."

Ferelijn's heart went out to Henk, whose kindly, honest face now wore an expression of utter despondency.

Henk was clearly dreading his interview with Eline. In the event, however, he was spared the ordeal. Eline refused categorically to see him, and from the adjoining room he listened anxiously as she remonstrated with Frans. Why had Frans brought Henk to see her, and why had he taken her keys? Was there no one she could trust? Not even Frans?

Eline sounded hoarse and strident, and it seemed to Henk that she must still be delirious. He could hear Jeanne trying to pacify her, although he could not distinguish the words, then Eline sobbing with self-recrimination and remorse.

Presently Frans returned, raising his shoulders apologetically.

"She won't see you. You'd better resign yourself to it for the moment, as she seems to be running a high fever. Do you think Reijer might still be at home at this hour? Perhaps you could drive there and ask him to come over."

"Very well," said Henk forlornly. "I'll do that."

Eline moaned softly as she lay on the couch, her limbs twitching restlessly under the woollen comforter. Jeanne had told the children to keep out of the way.

"You're so good to me, Jany! But, you see, I can't possibly stay here and put you to so much trouble!" she said. "You haven't much room to spare; I'd only get in your way. I shall go to a hotel this afternoon."

Jeanne sat down on the edge of the couch and took Eline's hands in hers.

"Eline, please be sensible. Don't you worry your head about anything like that. You're ill, you know. You can stay here, honestly. I'm not saying you must go back to Betsy's house, but I certainly don't want you going to a hotel."

"Yes, but what if I'm ill—not that I think I am, but you seem to think so. If I'm ill I shan't be able to leave again for some time. And—and—oh, I know it's just not possible. Dear, dear Jany, please forgive me for saying this, but it would be beyond your means, and—"

Jeanne's eyes filled with tears.

"If that's what's troubling you, Eline, you can stay with us and pay for your keep. Just don't mention the word hotel any more, I beg you. I shan't be embarrassed; indeed you're welcome to share in the expenses if that makes you feel better. But do please stay."

Eline gave a start and shook her tousled locks, which Jeanne tried in vain to brush away from her face. Then she flung her arms around Jeanne and clung to her, the better to savour the flood of sympathy.

"Oh, you're such an angel!" she cried. "Forgive me, I didn't mean to hurt your feelings in any way, but yes, I should love to stay. May I? You are so kind, so very kind!"

That afternoon Madame van Raat and Madame Verstraeten called at the Ferelijns', their minds set on persuading Eline to return to Nassauplein. Betsy came too, having been prevailed upon by Jeanne to apologise to her sister. Eline, however, refused flatly to receive them. In the adjoining room the visitors held their breath as they listened to Eline protesting to Jeanne in no uncertain terms that she would not see anyone, whoever they were. Jeanne—yes, she would see Jeanne, but nobody else!

The news soon spread among their friends and acquaintances that Eline had fallen out with the van Raats, and that she had sought refuge, as it were, with the Ferelijns. The fact that she had dined with the Hovels the previous evening roused considerable curiosity, and young Hijdrecht, who had been present at the dinner, was reported as saying that there had been some disagreement between the sisters. He had been seated beside Eline, and had never been so bored by her company as that evening: she had hardly said a word. The details of the dispute were unclear, only—and of this everyone was certain—Eline had been seen in a cab on that stormy night in the company of a nightwatchman, or of a young man; strange goings-on, to say the least.

Eline had displayed a penchant for eccentricity before, what with her habit of taking solitary walks in the Wood last winter— hardly the thing for a respectable young lady—and then there was that unfortunate business with van Erlevoort, and now this nocturnal escapade with a young man and a nightwatchman! Such a shame it was, too, for she was such a sweet girl, really, so pretty and so elegant! But then the Veres had always been a trifle eccentric, had they not?

Betsy agonised over all the gossip, which she could sense was spreading apace, and as she scarcely dared show her face in public, she had recourse only to the Verstraetens and Emilie de Woude for company.

XXV

A MONTH HAD PASSED since Eline's arrival at the Ferelijns', as Jeanne had refused to let her go until she was fully recovered. Reijer's diagnosis was that Eline had caught a severe cold which, if neglected, might prove fatal, and Jeanne nursed her with fond indulgence. She had turned Frans's small study into a bedroom for Eline, despite the latter's protestations that she could easily go to a hotel. Frans too had assured her that he did not need the room, as his specialist in Amsterdam had advised him to work less hard, and so she hugged Jeanne with passionate gratitude and stayed on, her violent fits of coughing echoing grievously throughout the small upstairs apartment.

Her cough was now subsiding, and the pain in her chest had eased. However, she had grown very thin and hollow-eyed, with a sallow hue to her features. She settled herself in the ample chair close to the small stove and looked out of the window, listlessly following the progress of the butcher, greengrocer and milkman from door to door and watching the housemaids take charge of the deliveries: a plump red-haired one on this doorstep, a scrawny one on the other, and on the third the mistress of the house in person, wearing a black apron and a dingy lace cap.

At length she stood up, coughing, and glanced in the small looking glass, which had a plain black frame, as plain as everything else in the Ferelijns' abode. She was expecting a visitor, someone she had not seen for some time, and she studied her reflection with misgiving, wondering what sort of impression she would make. Betsy had written a long letter to their uncle, Daniel Vere, who had acted as Eline's guardian while she was still under age. As he had still been single when old Aunt Vere died, the possibility of Eline going to live with him in his Brussels residence had not arisen at the time, but he had recently married. He seldom came to The Hague, and when he received Betsy's letter informing him that Eline had left the house at Nassauplein, his first reaction had been dismissive: why should this be of any concern to him? On second thoughts, however, he replied to the letter and also wrote to Eline, saying he should like to see her. His letter came as a very welcome surprise, for she was becoming increasingly fretful about what she should do once she was well again, and thought he might be able to advise her. So she responded in the most amicable terms, saying she would be glad to receive him at his convenience, so long as he did not expect her to make her peace with Betsy and return to the van Raats—under no circumstances would she do that, for she had learnt to her cost that Betsy and she simply did not get along, never mind who was to blame.

Vere promptly telegraphed the date and hour of his intended visit. And now Eline was waiting for him to arrive, anxiously surveying her gaunt features in the glass, fearing that her power to win every man's heart with her beguiling charm had deserted her. She drew the curtain a little, to temper the light falling on her face. Come afternoon, Jeanne showed the visitor to Eline's room. He was tall and spare, with the somewhat languorous gestures that were so typical of the Veres, with the exception of Betsy, who was more like her mother. Eline thought he looked agreeably distinguished and worldly in his fur coat, and felt a trifle embarrassed about receiving her uncle in these humble surroundings. She rose and stepped forward with queenly demeanour, while Jeanne withdrew, closing the door behind her.

"Hello, Uncle!" said Eline softly, unsure of what lay ahead. "I am very glad to see you, very glad indeed."

She extended her hand and motioned him to a chair. He sat down, looked at her intently, smiled a little and finally shook his head from side to side.

"For shame, Eline!" he began. "How sad you have made me. What a disagreeable state of affairs this is, my dear cousin."

"I presume Betsy had plenty to say about me in her letter?" she asked, hiding her curiosity with an air of indifference.

"Betsy's news came like a bolt from the blue. I had no idea you were so out of sympathy with your sister. I thought you were happy at the van Raats'. Last spring I received a happy letter from you saying you were to marry van Erlevoort, and now I'm told that you broke off your engagement some months ago. But why that should lead to your taking flight in this unfortunate manner is beyond me. My dear Eline, how could you allow yourself to be so carried away by your emotions?"

He spoke with some caution, gauging her mood, for he did not wish to antagonise her. The news of her dramatic flight had given him the idea that she must be exceedingly impetuous and hot-tempered, and he did not quite trust her subdued manner, thinking she might suddenly leap up and do something desperate. But she maintained her even composure and responded in cordial tones.

"Uncle, the fact that I ran away from Betsy and Henk does not mean that everything I do is unconsidered and foolish. It's true that I was very angry with Betsy, and with hindsight I am sorry that I lost my temper, I am sorry that I didn't simply turn my back on her and arrange to move out of her house on the morrow, when things had calmed down. But I think you will agree that there are moments in life when one—well, when one forgets oneself!"

"So have you considered going back?"

"I thought I made my decision perfectly clear to you in my letter," she replied, with an edge of disdain.

"So you did, but I was hoping—I thought you might re-consider."

"Never!" she said resolutely.

"Very well then, we need not pursue the subject any further. I am sorry I mentioned it. But you sound very determined; I hope you have given ample consideration to the consequences of your decision."

"Certainly!" she said, and broke into coughing.

"In that case some alternative will have to be found. First you must get rid of that nasty cough, of course, but do you have any plans after that?"

Eline's pride dissolved into anxiety.

"Well, I have been doing a lot of thinking. I haven't made up my mind yet, but I might find somewhere to live by myself. I can afford it, and anyway I'm not a spendthrift. I could hire a live-in maid."

In her fancy she saw herself living in a cramped upstairs apartment like this one, and tears came to her eyes.

"That sounds reasonable. Here in The Hague?"

"I suppose so. I'm not sure yet. Or some smaller town, perhaps."

"Ah well, we can leave that till later. Because, you see, I have a proposition to make."

He took her hand and looked at her through narrowed eyes. She thought he might invite her to join him in Brussels, and wondered whether she should accept.

"Your Aunt Eliza and I are planning to go abroad for a few months. It makes me laugh to call her 'your aunt', because as you know Eliza is only five years older than you. So when you have been introduced you will be calling each other by your first names. We are first going to Paris, and then on to Spain, probably. What I was wishing to propose, my dear, is that you accompany us. A change of scene would do you good after all you've been through. We might stay away all winter, possibly longer. If you get bored you could always return to Holland and find yourself an apartment, as you suggested earlier. You have not met my wife yet, but I dare say you will find her sympathetic: she is lively and gay, a real *française*. How does my proposal appeal to you?"

Eline's eyes widened. To be sure, she could do with a change of scene! Fancy travelling abroad all though the winter! She had a sense of glorious sunshine flooding into the sombre darkness of her soul. Oh, variety at last! And variety was life itself, as Vincent was wont to say.

"Oh, Uncle, I don't know what to think!" she began, with feeling. "I am not very cheerful these days, and I hardly think I'd make a good travelling companion."

"My dear girl, you never can tell. Finding oneself in different surroundings and meeting new people often has the effect of lifting the spirits. Variety is the first necessity of life."

She gave a start, then smiled warmly at him. He sounded just like Vincent! She felt a surge of gratitude, how very kind of him to make her this offer! And how pleasant his manner was! Yes, she would accept—gladly!

"You can come and stay with us in Brussels first, before we leave. We do quite a lot of travelling, and we do it economically, without denying ourselves any pleasures—we're rather good at getting by—and as for you, you're comfortably off, aren't you? An excellent catch, as they say!" he concluded, laughing.

"An excellent catch? Me? I'm not all that rich, you know, and not all that eligible any more either," she said with a wry smile. "I'm getting old—an old maid."

He spoke with blithe assurance: their trip would cure her of all those gloomy notions. After Jeanne had been told of the plan he took his leave, saying he still had to call on van Raat at Nassauplein.

Eline remained alone while Jeanne saw him out. A multitude of thoughts danced about her mind like so many rose petals, sunbeams, iridescent soap bubbles. She looked out of the window, but all she could see were clouds of dust whirling up from the road. The grey autumn sky made her shiver, and she turned away. As her gaze slid around the room she was struck by the sight of Frans Ferelijn's tear-off calendar up on the wall. The date was printed in bold type: 1st November.

That was the very date she and Otto had picked for their wedding! She stared at the calendar, transfixed. Then a wave of wild, hopeless anguish swept over her, and she flung herself into her armchair, sobbing piteously.

The Eekhofs, the Hijdrechts and the van Larens were all agog at the news: Eline Vere was going abroad with her uncle, Daniel Vere, who lived in Brussels and had only been married a year. Henk and Betsy, with their young son, would also be leaving The Hague for some time: they were thought to be travelling to Algiers.

XXVI

Eighteen months had passed. The Verstraetens' residence on Prinsessegracht was splendidly decorated from top to bottom, with the vestibule, dining room, salons and conservatory made to resemble lush winter gardens by means of artfully disposed palm trees in the angles of the walls, which formed pyramids of verdure flanked by red and white clusters of azaleas. For there was a bride in the house, and it was time for celebration.

The reception was in full swing, with a jostling multitude of friends and relations come to bestow their good wishes. In the main salon the easy chairs had been arranged in a semicircle on either side of the sofa, with their backs to the greenery obscuring the garden window. Georges de Woude van Bergh and Lili Verstraeten stood in attendance by the sofa, like a princely pair holding court. The twenty-year-old bride, wearing white silk with orange blossom in her hair, was radiant with joy, and did not tire of breathing sweet words of thanks to all who came to congratulate her.

"Thank you! Thank you! And thank you so much for your lovely present!"

The groom, sporting a white rose in the lapel of his tailcoat, likewise offered thanks, inwardly longing for the parade to end but nonetheless wreathed in smiles. Madame Verstraeten stood beside her daughter while Emilie de Woude hovered restlessly near her brother, disappearing frequently for brief forays among the buzzing crowd of well-wishers. The bridesmaids were Marie and Frédérique, in pink, and the best men were Paul and Etienne, in tails with flowers in their buttonholes. The latter took turns escorting guests to the conservatory, where the wedding presents were displayed on a long table. Old Mr de Woude's gift of a silver tea service occupied the centre, surrounded by further offerings of silverware, cut glass and fine porcelain from friends and relations. From the van Raat cousins, Henk and Paul, they had received a pretty suite of drawing room furniture upholstered in glossy blue satin, the various components of which stood about, cluttering up most of the space. The gift from the bride's parents was not on view as there was simply not enough room: it was an entire bedroom suite, of fine quality but not overly luxurious, which, as Emilie explained to Madame van der Stoor and Cateau, was as it should be for a young couple who had yet to make their fortune.

"They will be going to live in Atjehstraat, will they not?" asked Madame van der Stoor, her eyes riveted on an agate-handled serving spoon and fork.

"Yes, a small apartment in Atjehstraat, quite suitable for two young things like them. Just imagine, mere children! And getting married, too! Ah well, they know best, I suppose," responded Emilie with a rueful smile, and Madame van der Stoor smiled in return. Cateau was full of admiration for the satin suite.

"This was given by your brother and sister-in-law, wasn't it, Master Paul?" she said.

"And by yours truly!" responded Paul, pointing to himself. "But how ladylike you've grown, Cateau!" he continued, surveying her approvingly. "With your hair piled up like that—most impressive!"

"Well, why shouldn't I be a lady and wear my hair up?" Cateau said loftily. She was piqued by his familiarity; she was almost seventeen now, and there was no reason why he should always address her by her first name while she never knew what to call him—Mr van Raat, Master Paul, or simply van Raat? Indeed, she found him decidedly disagreeable lately, and then there was his bad behaviour, for ever gadding about and squandering money!

"But you are a lady!" said Paul with a sarcastic smile. "You're every inch a lady; did you think I hadn't noticed? I say, Cateau, do you remember me draping those robes around you for the tableau of the five senses? How long ago was that?"

Cateau blushed.

"Oh, that was ages ago. Let me think—it must have been at least two and a half years since we did the tableaux. I was only a child then. I wouldn't let you dress me up now, I can assure you!"

How dare he bring up that subject! With a toss of the head she turned away, while he smiled at her indignation. Then, catching sight of Frédérique, he made his way to the main salon, where his mother was taking leave of her.

"Is Mama going already?" he wanted to know.

"Yes, she's a little tired!" she replied tartly, without meeting his eye.

He noted her coolness towards him, and felt hurt. They all seemed to be against him these days, first Cateau, and now Freddie, too.

"Ah, Freddie!" he said with forced gaiety. "You aren't in a very festive mood, are you?"

"Why do you say that?" she asked blankly.

"You haven't said anything in the least nice to me all day. You're not angry with me are you?"

"Me? Oh no, not at all. Why should I be?"

"Can't I make it up to you? If only I knew what I've done wrong."

Etienne came towards them.

"I say, you two: please remember your duties! Two old ladies have just arrived, whom I've never seen before; they can't take their eyes off the wedding presents, and I'm afraid they might be light-fingered or something, you never know. Come on, Marie has also been looking for you everywhere!"

They followed him to the conservatory, which was thronged with guests. Paul was annoyed that Etienne had interrupted his moment with Freddie; for days he had been meaning to have a word with her, because all she did was pout, and it was getting on his nerves.

Henk and Betsy entered the dining room, where they encountered the groom's father deep in conversation with Otto van Erlevoort. Old Mr de Woude had dull, kindly features and thinning grey hair; he sat with his cane propped between his knees and, being hard of hearing, with his head cocked to his interlocutor, whom he kept asking to repeat himself. Otto and the van Raats no longer called on each other these days, but they did meet from time to time at the Verstraetens' or at the homes of other mutual friends, and had remained on amicable terms.

They found little to say to one another, for there was a mist of unhappiness between them. Betsy and Henk moved on, having extended their good wishes to Mr Verstraeten, who was chatting with Mathilda van Rijssel in the drawing room.

"Well then, goodbye Betsy, goodbye Henk. Thank you so much! By the way, did you hear what Madame van Rijssel just told me?"

"No, what did she say, Uncle?" asked Betsy.

"That your old friend Jeanne, Ferelijn's wife, is gravely ill."

"Jeanne? Is she ill?"

"A letter arrived yesterday, from Ferelijn in Bangil," Mathilda said softly.

"Where's Bangil?" asked Betsy.

"In Pasoeroean. Jeanne had just given birth to another baby when he wrote the letter, and her life was apparently in danger."

"Really? Oh dear, poor girl! We have not been in touch lately, but I have always been very fond of her, and … "

It was on the tip of Betsy's tongue to add: "and we owe her a great deal," for she was thinking of Eline. But all she said was:

"Please, Mathilda, if you hear any more news, you will let me know, won't you? I'd be most grateful."

"Yes I will," said Mathilda, and Betsy moved away with Henk in search of the bride and groom. Mathilda's thoughts turned to Jeanne, her hapless friend who had followed her husband to the Indies six months ago, and whom she might never see again.

Henk and Betsy approached Georges and Lili.

"Ah, Betsy and Henk!" exclaimed Lili. "How you have spoilt us! It was such a splendid surprise, too! A truly beautiful gift!"

She gave them both a hug of thanks for the blue-satin suite.

"Let's hope it won't look too grand!" said Georges, after expressing his thanks.

"Nonsense!" cried Lili. "Men are such ungrateful creatures, aren't they, Betsy? But I'm awfully grateful; I'm thrilled with it, truly thrilled!"

"She's as happy as a little girl with a new doll's house!" Emilie chuckled, glancing at Betsy.

Meanwhile, in the conservatory, Marie and Etienne were testing the blue satin suite for comfort and plumpness. Marie had been in remarkably good cheer lately, quite elated even. They bounced up and down, giggling merrily, with no regard at all for the creaking springs.

Well, there was every reason to be light-hearted, even if it was her sister's wedding and not her own. Once Lili had gone there would be time enough to be glum, for it would be lonely without her, but Marie had no intention of letting that prospect spoil her enjoyment of this happy day.

Mathilda and Otto wandered into the conservatory to view the wedding gifts, and Marie promptly pointed out each item in turn, announcing who the giver was.

"Why don't you come to the dance tomorrow?" she asked Otto. "It would be so nice if you were there."

He smiled and shook his head.

"It's no use insisting. Forgive me for refusing the invitation, but my decision is final. My dancing days are over."

"You're becoming a veritable recluse!"

"I am getting old."

"Fiddlesticks! Doesn't it amuse you any more to see people amusing themselves?"

"Yes it does, now and then, but on the whole I prefer to stay at home."

His tone was wistful, and she desisted from further effort to persuade him. To change the subject, she indicated a large basket of flowers with a wave of her hand.

"Just look at those lovely roses! And so early in the season, too. I do so love it when all the flowers come out. It looks as if we'll be having a wonderful summer."

"Yes, and we are having a wonderful spring, too," he said dully.

She was somewhat piqued by his tone, despite the pity she felt for his quiet sorrow, and kept silent. He must have been thinking of a previous spring, a previous summer …

The 'union of hearts' between Georges and Lili, for which Emilie had sought permission from the Verstraetens on her brother's behalf some eighteen months before, had quite quickly developed into a stronger alliance, for although Georges kept his promise to observe due discretion in the affair, it had become common knowledge in The Hague. Lili's parents had been in something of a quandary, what with their daughter chafing at the restrictions they imposed on her dealings with her beau, and Emilie beginning to exert pressure on them as well. Madame Verstraeten had approached her sister Dora, Madame van Raat, in the hope of some moral support, but had not received it. Why not have a formal engagement, Madame van Raat had suggested in her soft, sad voice, then everything would surely sort itself out. Lili had been overjoyed when she heard of her elderly aunt's advice, pronouncing her to be the dearest, sweetest aunt in the whole world.

And so it happened that, as soon as Georges had passed his Vice-Consular examination, the engagement was officially announced. Georges had gone off to Paris and Hamburg on tours of duty, and upon his return Emilie and Lili joined forces in persuading her parents that it was time to contemplate the next step. After much deliberation it had been decided that, provided Georges, now at the Ministry of Foreign Affairs, was as careful with money as he claimed to be, and provided Lili became a little more sensible—for she was by no means sensible enough according to her mother—they might entertain the idea of marriage with a small financial contribution from the Verstraetens. The big day was planned for the 20th of May. Madame Verstraeten, Emilie, Marie and Lili devoted themselves to assembling the trousseau, and no one was happier in The Hague than Georges and Lili, whom Emilie insisted on calling 'the babes in the wood', much to Marie's amusement.

Marie had grown so vivacious lately that Frédérique quite forgot how nervous and moody her sister had been only a short while ago, shutting herself up in her room for hours, purportedly to work on her travelogue. Nowadays she ran up and down the house bubbling with laughter, playing jokes on Lili and Jan and taking Dien by the shoulders to whirl her around. Her rather plain features seemed to glow with a new freshness, her hazel eyes sparkled, and everyone in her set noted the change—Marie looked positively pretty these days!

The radiance of her expression reflected the new hope that was dawning in her heart. Nowadays, when she stood by her window looking out over the avenue glistening with morning dew in the mild May sunshine, and at the Wood beyond, swathed in myriad shades of vibrant green, her heart no longer ached—it sang.

She was now free to think about Otto, there was nothing to stop her admitting to herself that she loved him. And it seemed to her that the pity she felt for him made her love him even more passionately than before, when she had been racked with secret jealousy of the fiancée who had so cruelly tossed him aside as if he were some worthless object.

He still seemed to be mourning his loss, but that did not mean there was no hope, and the hope in her heart rose up to infuse her face, lending beauty to her smile.

That evening, when the reception was over, the Verstraetens were worn out. They exchanged their formal wear for more comfortable clothing, and Mr Verstraeten retired to his study while his wife went upstairs to take some much-needed repose. Lili, overtired from hours on her feet giving effusive thanks to everyone for their gifts and good wishes, flung herself in her favourite armchair with the old tapestry cover, and leant back, half-closing her eyes.

"Lili, why don't you go upstairs and lie down for a while?" said Marie.

"Oh no thanks, I can't be bothered. I'm so tired, as tired as can be."

Georges looked concerned. He sat down beside his bride, took her hand in his, and whispered to her in the dimmed light. Frédérique, Paul and Etienne had stayed to supper, as had Georges, but now Etienne came to take his leave as he had a prior engagement to meet some friends.

"Are you coming, Paul?" he asked.

Paul lifted his head, turning the question over in his mind, then stretched his limbs.

"No thanks, I don't feel up to it."

"But they're expecting you!"

"Well, I'm not in the mood. You'll have to excuse me."

Etienne left, somewhat disgruntled. Marie hummed to herself as she sauntered about the salons with Frédérique, tidying up the various bouquets and flower baskets and dipping her fingers into a bowl of water to flick the drops onto the blooms. Marie was the only one still wearing her party clothes, but now she too went off to exchange her pink frock for something simpler, as the atmosphere was becoming so dull anyway, with Lili's head lolling on Georges' shoulder and Paul sprawled in an armchair with his legs flung wide.

"Freddie, be a dear and put that big basket on the side table in the conservatory, will you? It will only get in the way of the dancers tomorrow. I'm off upstairs now," said Marie.

"All right," said Frédérique.

Marie left the room and Frédérique made to lift the flower basket, whereupon Paul drew himself up.

"Need some help?" he offered.

"Yes, you could put this on the side table over there. Thank you."

She took the bowl of water and followed Paul into the conservatory, from which all the wedding gifts had been removed save for the blue-satin suite. Now that the lights were out the place resembled a dark, leafy arbour. Paul stood with his hands in his pockets watching Frédérique as she besprinkled the flowers with water.

"Freddie," he began, "there is something I want to ask you."

"Oh? What?"

"You seem to have taken against me lately. Can you tell me why?"

"Taken against you? Not at all. It's just that I don't feel particularly fond of you at the moment."

"And why not, may I ask?"

"You'd know if you bothered to think about it," she replied. She moved away with her bowl of water, but he clasped both her wrists.

"Don't go off in a huff; put that bowl down and answer me properly."

With gentle force he sat her down on a chair, and as he took the bowl from her she snatched her hands from his grasp. But she felt a moment's triumph at the imploring look on his face, and made no effort to stand up again.

"Now will you tell me what you have against me?"

The urgency in his tone flustered her.

"You know what my main weakness is, Paul!" she began. "You know I'm no good at pretending. It's true that I am a bit annoyed with you, and apparently I can't help showing it. I am sorry about that, but I assure you that I don't do it on purpose at all. I shall try harder to hide my feelings then, shall I?"

"There's no need to be so bitter, Freddie. Why don't you just tell me what's bothering you?"

"My dear Paul, what is there to say? I might start reproaching you, and I have no right to reproach you for anything at all."

"What if I gave you the right? I would rather hear your reproaches than all those snubs and cutting remarks I've been getting lately."

"Are you sure you want a lecture from me?" she asked, softening towards him.

"Oh yes, please, I would love that."

"You see? You're joking already. I am perfectly happy to joke, but then let's talk about something else and go back inside."

"No, no, not yet, this is the perfect place for a private conversation, and I am absolutely serious, honestly."

She peered into his eyes, but it was too dark in the sombre shadow of the palm fronds for her to make out their expression. Lately she had noticed an edge of sarcasm creeping into his voice, which made her uneasy, and she could hear it even now, as he pleaded with her to speak her mind.

"Well, you're rather self-satisfied aren't you? You talk about everything in such a flippant, patronising way these days."

"Ah, now we're getting somewhere. Flippant, patronising—no, I was not aware that I spoke in that way. But why should I not be satisfied?"

"Why not indeed? You lead such a useful life, don't you?"

"Oh, I can see what you're getting at. You mean that I'm not working at Hovel's any more. Actually, I'm planning to establish myself as a lawyer."

"Yes I know, at least, so I've heard."

"Well then, doesn't that put your mind at rest?"

"Put my mind at rest? Nonsense, Paul, there's no need for that. Oh please let's talk about something else. Far be it from me to urge you to make something of yourself. Honestly, I don't care what you do, or if you do nothing at all. Shall we adjourn to the salon?"

"Oh please, Freddie, don't be so short with me. Georges and Lili are in the salon, spooning, as it happens, and we'd only disturb them if we went in there. I wish the two of us could be friends again, though."

"I didn't know we were enemies."

"We're not, but I can't say a thing without you taking it amiss. And the fact that I'm not working at the moment can't be the only reason why you're so cool towards me. Go on, out with it, what else is there?"

She felt somewhat embarrassed, but tried not to show it.

"As I told you before," she said, "what bothers me sometimes is your flippancy, and your patronising tone. You can sound awfully arrogant, you know. Like the other day, when you were talking about Georges and Lili."

"You mean because I thought it absurd—and I still do—that they should want to live together while they're as poor as church mice? It's entirely up to them what they do, of course, but why should it be arrogant to say what I think?"

"Because not everyone is a millionaire, Paul."

He looked at her intently.

"I don't know what you mean."

"It's hardly difficult to understand, surely!" she retorted with a short laugh.

"You're not saying I'm arrogant about not being penniless myself, are you?"

"Well, yes I am, in a way."

"Oh come now, don't be silly!"

"Well, you do seem to be throwing your money around. You have a circle of friends, I gather, who take advantage of your purse, and you hold orgies with them at home, too, making it impossible for your poor mama to get any sleep."

"Who told you that?"

"You seem to forget that I have a brother who's in the same set as you. And that your mama sometimes needs to let off steam."

"Oh, I'm planning to move out in any case. I'll find a place of my own. It's hard being young and having to adjust to a so-called orderly household. Actually, I've seen an apartment that looks suitable, so Mama needn't be kept awake by my orgies any longer."

"An apartment? Well, if I were you I'd take an entire hotel, with plenty of rooms for all your penniless friends."

"I wish you'd stop harping on my penniless friends! Who do you mean, anyway? Hijdrecht isn't penniless, nor is Oudendijk!"

"Those two are the only decent chaps in your set."

"You haven't met the others, Frédérique."

"No, thank goodness I haven't!"

"So what do you know of them? How can you judge them if you don't even know them?"

"What I do know is that they are parasites, only after your money."

"Oh, is that what you think? I expect Etienne happened to mention that there's someone I used to help out now and then. Etienne ought to know better than to tell tales about his friends. It's perfectly normal for young men to lend each other small sums of money when they need it. He doesn't know what he's talking about."

"If you say so. Let's drop the subject then, shall we?"

There were sounds in the salon, and the gaslight was turned up. Frédérique rose.

"So we have not made peace, then?" asked Paul, likewise rising.

"We were not at war, Paul," responded Frédérique. "You said you wanted to talk with me, and you have. If I have offended you in any way, please just forget we ever had this conversation. As I said, I have no right to reproach you, and I wouldn't have said anything if you hadn't asked. You're old enough to make your own decisions. What would I know about anything, anyway? You don't need any advice from a young girl, I'm sure."

She went into the salon, where Georges and Lili had been joined by Madame Verstraeten and Marie. Just then Dien came in with the tea tray, and Lili asked Frédérique what had kept her.

"Paul and I were in the conservatory, waiting for teatime. I'm dying for a cup," replied Freddie.

Paul, however, took his leave. He would seek out Etienne and his friends after all, he said with a defiant edge to his voice.

"Until tomorrow, then. Goodbye, everyone! Goodbye, Freddie!"

"Goodbye, Paul, I hope you enjoy yourself. Till tomorrow," Freddie replied coolly, her fingers barely touching his outstretched hand.

Feeling not a bit pleased with himself, Paul made his way along Prinsessegracht. He tried hard to shake off his unease, initially without success, for it had cast a grey shroud over his usually carefree attitude, and the more he struggled to free himself from its hampering folds the more constricted he became. There was no reason he should be so bothered by Frédérique's disapproval: after all, she was just a girl who happened to have heard some gossip about what he got up to with his friends and who had got quite carried away, imagining him to be leading a life of romantic dissolution, complete with rivers of champagne, showers of gold coins and ladies with beckoning arms. What had Frédérique's criticism amounted to, really? That he was not at present gainfully employed? What was wrong with enjoying life if he could afford it? And what was the use of looking for a position which he did not need, and which, if taken by him, meant denying some poor chap the opportunity of earning his living? That would be rather unfair, wouldn't it? He for his part would be glad to work in congenial surroundings, but interesting positions were few and far between, and so Frédérique should by rights be commending him for his unselfishness instead of lecturing him about his bad behaviour. As for his so-called penniless friends, Frédérique had quite rightly observed that not everybody was a millionaire, so she could hardly expect him to consort exclusively with nabobs! What was wrong with helping one's friends when they were in need, if all it took was a visit to his banker? But what a blabbermouth Etienne was when it came to matters which one did not discuss with ladies or relatives!

He badly needed telling off for his indiscretion, the young blackguard! Little did Frédérique know that Etienne himself was no better: forever asking him for small sums of money, and sometimes quite large ones, too.

Squaring his shoulders and lifting his chin, he went on his way in the gathering dusk. A devil-may-care glint came into his eyes. What a burden it was to be rich, he thought to himself, chuckling under his breath. It was too bad the way one was under pressure from some to spend freely and from others to keep a tight rein on one's purse. Still, it made for a certain popularity, especially among ladies with daughters of marriageable age, such as Madame Eekhof, who seemed determined to pair him off with Ange or Léonie, and Madame Oudendijk, who invited him at least once a week and then left him alone with Françoise for hours on end, and now that Cateau was coming of age Madame van der Stoor had likewise taken to fawning on him. So many mamas with so many daughters to be married off—he saw them file past in his mind's eye, a procession of matrons all wreathed in smiles, presenting to him their appropriately blushing daughters as though he were a Pasha with a mind to forming a harem. He had only to put out his hand and he would have ten comely fortune-hunters clinging to each finger. Oh, the burden of being rich!

He turned into the Korte Voorhout, feeling much better for the entertaining vision of eager matrons vying with each other to extol their wares. He would have none of it, of course; he had no intention of giving up his freedom for a long time yet. Supposing he were poor, though, how many of those pretty young things would still want him? Françoise would, he thought, because she was always making eyes at him as if she were truly smitten. Then there were Ange and Léonie with their trim little figures, who kept hovering around him wanting to play catch-me-if-you-can: had he gone after them they would certainly have swooned away in his arms. And then there was Cateau, the youngest of them all and the only one to put on airs with him.

While he was thus reviewing all their charms with affectionate derision, his thoughts drifted to Frédérique, who appeared to him as a lone princess towering above the ranks of mere odalisques.

For her he felt no derision, nor was she attended by a matron offering her for sale. She stood alone, regarding him with calm self-assurance; she would not have fallen into his arms or knelt at his feet like the others. For her he felt respect.

"At least I didn't leave her cold, or she would not have been annoyed with me," he mused as he went past the theatre and turned into Houtstraat. "It's all very well her saying that she doesn't care what I do or don't do, whether I live in this way or that, but if it really made no difference to her then why was she so cool towards me? Why did she bother to tell me what she thought? Ah well, we have known each other for such a long time, so I suppose it's hardly surprising that she should take an interest. And she obviously hears an awful lot of bad things about me from Mama and Aunt and the cousins. She's a sweet, sensible girl, and I like her very much indeed."

He almost felt flattered that such a sweet and sensible girl should have taken it upon herself to voice her criticism of him, and he looked forward to a reprise of their tête-à-tête beneath the overhanging palm fronds in the conservatory.

"Of course, she's quite young, and so she knows nothing about the world apart from what she reads in novels, probably bad ones at that, but what she said about those parasites being after my money was rather clever. She's bound to have read that somewhere! She sounded just like a professor! Little Miss Know-it-all … I think I'll call her 'professor' from now on."

He began to laugh inwardly once more, but for all that he was tickled by what he saw as Frédérique's pompousness, in his fancy she remained on her pedestal, aloof from the other girls who were being pressed into his arms by their eager mamas.

As he approached the Witte club where he would join his friends, he could not help thinking again, with secret relish, oh, what a burden it was to be rich!

The dance party at the Verstraetens' the following evening was very animated. As only friends and relations had been invited, the atmosphere had the relaxed familiarity of a family gathering, notwithstanding the lavish decorations and the formality of the young people's dress: floaty evening gowns for the ladies and white tie and tails for the men. Most of the guests knew each other quite intimately, and so it was that both young and old indulged in light-hearted chitchat and sparkling repartee.

Paul's late arrival meant that he was too late for the polonaise and the polka, and when he greeted the bride with a stiff little bow, she responded by berating him.

"Naughty man, keeping away from my party for so long! I hope you'll be punished for your sins, you horrid boy!"

He apologised with his laughing eyes and mocking mouth, sniffed her splendid white bouquet in its lace foil, tucked his opera hat under his arm and pulled at the fingers of his pearl-grey gloves. He thought she looked almost ethereal in the white froth of her tulle and orange blossom, with her pale, delicate features and the pouting lips of a spoilt child.

"I hope every single girl is taken for the next dance, so that you'll be left all by yourself!" she said, rising to her feet.

"Ah, what a severe bride you are! Will you wager with me that I shall not be left by myself, and that I shall be dancing all evening?" he murmured in her ear, imitating her high voice.

"No, not a wager! I know you—getting up to mischief as usual! You'd better behave yourself this evening, I warn you!" she said, wagging her finger at him.

Just then Paul spotted Cateau van der Stoor standing with her back to some azaleas, in conversation with a tall, spindly young man whom he did not know. From across the room he gave her a cheery, indulgent nod, as if she were a small child, to which her only response was a stony look. The little minx! He resolved not to ask her to dance all evening; he might even ignore her entirely, just to teach her a lesson.

He was in the mood for larking about, and his eyes lit on Frédérique and Marie, both in pink tulle.

"Well I never! A fine best man you make!" exclaimed Marie. "I'm surprised that you even dare to show your face at this late hour. Are you blushing?"

Ignoring Marie's reprimand, he turned to Freddie. She had promised him several dances, so he reminded her, and he was wondering about the next waltz.

"Of course!" said Freddie. "I thought you'd forgotten all about me."

From the conservatory came the opening strains of *Invitation à la valse*.

"And we'll carry on with last night's philosophical discussion while we dance, shall we, Freddie?" he asked.

"Oh no, no more philosophy please! I just want to dance and enjoy myself."

She sounded happy, elated even, and smiled at him so winsomely that his heart began to beat apace. No cold shoulders now, thank goodness. How lovely she looked this evening, her face aglow with the rosy reflection of her pink toilette, her eyes sparkling with fun! Oh, she was prettier than all the others, to be sure, prettier even than the pale young bride across the room. He felt an urge to enfold her in his arms, but gazed into her eyes instead.

"You've kept the polka before the intermission for me, haven't you? And the waltz after supper? And the cotillion, too, I hope?"

"Yes, I've kept them all for you," she replied, colouring. "Not that you deserve it by any means. But I always keep my word. As you can see, all my other dances are already taken."

She showed him her dance card. Grinning broadly, he scrawled a large capital P in each of the remaining blanks.

The waltz had already started, and just as he curved his arm around Frédérique's waist he caught sight of Cateau dancing with the spindly young man. He gave her another patronising nod, noting to his considerable satisfaction that her cheeks were on fire as she glared at him over her lanky cavalier's shoulder. After that he no longer thought of her, but only of Freddie.

He could not recall ever having enjoyed a waltz as much as now, with Freddie floating in his arms as they glided among the other dancing couples. He could not resist drawing her close, pressing her lightly to his chest, and his laughing eyes slid down her throat to her lovely, firm shoulders. The whirling pink froth of her skirts made him feel quite giddy, and with his head almost leaning on her shoulder, he fastened his gaze on the silken tendrils of hair curled against the nape of her neck. Miss Know-it-all had vanished without trace, so had the little professor; it was only Freddie now, dancing like a dream. This is the life, he thought to himself, a long, sweet waltz going round and round in a soft, mesmerising rhythm, on and on, the pretty little head at his shoulder, the graceful creature in his arms, the pink whirlwind of rustling pleats like a flurry of rose petals, the silky tendrils of hair, the gentle curve of her lily-white shoulder, on and on …

"Paul, you needn't hold me so tight, I am not about to run away, you know!" she whispered, smiling. He gazed into her shining eyes but did not relax his hold, and she resigned herself to his embrace with good grace. They fell silent.

When the music stopped he felt as if he were waking from a wonderful dream.

"Oh, Freddie, can't we go on waltzing together for ever and ever, until our dying day?"

She smiled and murmured a reply, which he did not hear, for in his fancy they were off again, dancing the waltz.

For the lancers Paul was on the same side as the bride, Frédérique, Marie, Cateau, Georges, Etienne and young Jan, and each time his hand touched Cateau's he gave her fingers a little squeeze. He had been teasing her all evening with his mocking glances, and Cateau now looked daggers at him. He could not think why he was feeling so waggish this evening, but he simply could not resist pulling everyone's leg. He was now playing the dandy, surrounded by a bevy of girls, treating each of them in turn to an impertinent remark which only made them giggle. He pretended to ignore Françoise Oudendijk when she posed some comical questions, then suddenly spun round to gaze into her eyes, his face a grimace of incredulity.

"I say, Paul, how you've changed! You're so mad nowadays! What's come over you?" she said, reaching out to touch the gardenia in his buttonhole.

"Can't you guess?" he retorted in an undertone, batting his eyelashes flirtatiously. "Can't you guess?"

"Me? No, how could I?"

"May I tell you the reason later? May I?" he begged.

"Oh yes, please!"

"Well then, join me for half a dance-conversation during the Scottish reel," he said quickly.

"What do you mean by half a dance-conversation?"

"I hereby promote the first Scottish to a dance-conversation with two ladies, but I shan't be talking first with the one and then with the other, but with both at the same time. My first partner is Léonie Eekhof, so if you will be my second, I promise I'll tell you the reason for my madness. What do you say?"

She stared at him a moment, unsure whether she should take offence or not.

"If that's all you have to offer, then no thank you!" she rejoined, affecting indignation.

"As you wish!" he concluded, giving her such a mocking look that she turned her back on him.

The other girls were still chattering nineteen to the dozen.

"My dear children, I fear you are making me quite deaf!" he said pompously, pushing them out of his way as he made for the drawing room. It was time for a lark with the mamas sitting in a row at the back admiring their daughters, but he was checked by Betsy, who was having a conversation with Emilie.

"Hello, gadfly!" said Betsy, touching his sleeve. "Where are you gadding off to now?"

"To the old wallflowers," he whispered in reply. "And what about you—not dancing? This is not an invitation, mind; I am only showing an interest."

She promptly took up the gauntlet, assailing him with reproach for his impertinence, whereupon they launched into a hilarious exchange that brought tears of laughter to Emilie's eyes. Betsy beamed; she too was impressed by the startling transformation he had undergone: he had become so dashing, no wonder he was doted on by all the women! It had taken him rather a long time to shake off his old lethargy, and he had roused himself at an age when his peers were already settling down, but there was something about him, a touch of the Don Juan with his tawny hair and brazen grey-blue eyes, something that would play on the heartstrings of every girl. She watched as Paul made his way towards the matrons in the drawing room. He bowed to Madame Eekhof and Madame van der Stoor, seated side by side on the sofa.

After a brief exchange of civilities, Madame Eekhof enquired:

"Aren't you dancing tonight, van Raat? I can hear the music starting up again."

Replying that he did not care for the mazurka, Paul requested the ladies to make room for him on the sofa, and he nestled himself between them with remarkably little ceremony. He listened with an air of rapt attention to their questions and responded willingly, toying with his opera hat all the while. No, he had abandoned painting entirely—the smell of oils was so disagreeable—and he had even banished his easel to the attic. He had given up music, too, since Eline Vere was no longer there to sing duets with. He smiled graciously, twisting the ends of his thick blond moustache when Madame Eekhof protested that it was a shame to let his talents go to waste, and did he not recall how Cateau used to fall into a swoon whenever she heard him sing?

"Talking of Eline," Madame van der Stoor interposed, "do you happen to know when she will return? Is she still travelling?"

"You know she went to Spain with her uncle and aunt, don't you? She stayed with them for quite a while in Brussels after that, and then all three of them went to Nice. She also spent some time with relatives of her aunt's, in a chateau somewhere near Bordeaux, and goodness knows where else she has been."

Paul was beginning to find the conversation tedious, for he was singularly uninterested in Eline at the moment. Having no wish to hear Madame Eekhof raking up the sorry affair, he rose abruptly and took his leave. He turned to the row of matrons, each of whom he greeted with due charm and ceremony, taking great relish in their eagerness to speak to him. Ah, there was Madame Oudendijk, who seemed to think he was minded to propose to Françoise this very evening, for there was a touch of the mother-in-law in the way she rested her hand on his arm, to which he responded by showering her with refined little compliments about her daughter, and oh, how she lapped them up! He said Françoise had mentioned to him that she would love to ride; perhaps her mother could buy her a horse? What a pretty picture she would make riding side saddle! Waiting for her answer, he imagined he could read her thoughts: let him give Françoise a horse if that's what she wants, and himself into the bargain! But he had no intention of doing anything of the kind.

He moved away, and in passing overheard Uncle Verstraeten and Henk discussing the likelihood of Eline returning to The Hague in the summer. He recalled having heard something about Eline having plans to stay with his mother. Well, that would be very nice, having such a pretty girl in the house ... How old was she now? Twenty-five, at a guess—young enough at any rate to be good company, and he resolved to see if he could make her fall in love with him, just for fun.

Returning to the salon, he found the bride and groom and their entourage besieged by the crowd. His appearance caused a stir, and when several girls ran towards him to berate him for shirking his duties as best man, he put up a comical defence.

"Paul's such a card nowadays!" giggled Léonie.

He gave a condescending smile and looked past her at Frédérique, who was talking to Georges as they waited for the music to begin.

"Come on, I've got so much to tell you!" he said to Léonie, feeling a twinge of regret at the distance between him and Frédérique. "But remember, we're supposed to be talking, not dancing."

"Oh, please, Paul, just a little whirl?"

But after that first whirl he resolutely steered his young partner through the crowd to a settee at the back shaded by overhanging palms.

"Léonie, now be a good girl and say something nice!"

"But I thought you had so much to tell me!" she countered coquettishly.

He was about to reply when he caught sight of Françoise coming towards them, fluttering her hands as she threaded her way through the surge of dancers.

"Is there any room for me on the sofa?" she asked. "You invited me to be your conversation partner, remember?"

"Ah! So you've decided to accept after all, simply because you haven't found a dancing partner I suppose. Well, now it's my turn to decline—be off! Away with you!"

"Oh, Paul, have mercy on me! Let me sit here with you, it was hard enough getting here in the crush, please don't send me away!"

He was merciful and shifted to the middle of the sofa so that Françoise could sit on his other side, which left him half submerged in their bouffant tarlatan skirts.

"And now for some fun with the grand parade!" he said, in a lordly manner.

The threesome settled back to observe the black tails and billowing skirts reeling past. Paul borrowed Françoise's fan to beat time with, and leant back like a sultan to enjoy the running commentary of his mirthful companions.

"Ah, there's Freddie! An excellent dancer!" exclaimed Françoise as Georges and Freddie hove into view, and the threesome clapped their hands so vigorously that they caused the settee to jolt on its legs.

"Sheer, sheer madness!" cried Paul, bouncing up and down, crumpling their frocks.

"Ah, talk about being mad!" said Françoise. "So tell me, Paul, why you're so mad these days? You were going to tell me, remember?"

"Because I'm mad about you!" he gushed. "Yes, mad about you, Françoise! I'm dying of love for you! Let me kiss you!"

Françoise recoiled in mock horror, upon which Léonie exploded with laughter.

The music stopped for the intermission; it was time to bring in the trestle tables, which had been laid up beforehand to enable the swift conversion of the reception suite into an elegant restaurant.

The guests dispersed themselves about the hall and the conservatory, whence the pianist had departed, forming small clusters amid much banter and fluttering of fans, and a magical golden dust seemed to descend on the entire gathering, setting each glance, each smile, each peal of laughter aglow with contagious euphoria.

Madame Verstraeten approached the young bride and whispered in her ear: was she not tired? Lili assured her she was not. She lay back in her cane chair and sniffed the wilting jasmine in her bouquet, rejoicing in the sight of so much celebration and laughter—and all of it in her honour, simply because she was marrying her Georges! She felt quite the little queen appearing before a cheering multitude, especially now that Paul's loud voice had drawn everyone to the conservatory. Everyone crowded round to hear what he was saying to the bride and groom, and when he was finished he jokingly invited Léonie and Françoise to come and sit on his lap, one on each knee.

Marie's accusations that his manners were worsening by the day fell on deaf ears: he had already sprung to his feet, having caught sight of young Cateau van der Stoor peering round the door of the conservatory. Ah, he would now show compunction for a change.

"Are you very cross with me, Cateau, for pulling your leg?"

"Oh, I didn't even notice," she said, but her quivering lip betrayed her.

He offered her his sincere apologies, rolling his eyes and begging her to reserve a dance for him.

"I have no dances left!" Cateau retorted triumphantly, showing her dance card.

"But I must dance with you! I insist! Let me see: Hijdrecht, Hijdrecht—two dances with Hijdrecht! But that's not fair! Why don't you go and tell him you want to dance with me?"

"But I daren't!"

"He won't bite, you know! Please, Cateau, come with me, I want that dance!"

He pulled her along in search of Hijdrecht and made her retract her promise for the next Scottish reel.

Cateau was somewhat annoyed with herself for letting him have his way, but it was impossible to refuse Paul anything.

"Right then, see you later, and you're not angry with me any more, are you, dearest Cateau?" he murmured beseechingly.

"I'm not your dearest Cateau by any means!" she scoffed, inwardly gratified by his effort to make amends.

The long table in the centre was occupied by the bride and groom and their entourage, while the smaller tables were occupied by groups of four. Paul was in excellent humour, for he had not only danced the polka with Frédérique but also found himself placed beside her at the table, and he submitted with remarkably good grace to Marie's admonitions about his forwardness with all the girls. Etienne was flushed from drinking champagne, and grew maudlin, lamenting the pointlessness of dancing and disporting oneself when life was so short and sad!

After supper Paul waltzed again with Freddie, and it seemed to him that this second waltz was even sweeter than the first, the effect of several toasts of sparkling champagne being compounded by the intoxicating whirl of pink tulle, and all was froth and ebullience between them. Yet he had a feeling that he could not be truly in love with her, because although she was certainly the prettiest of them all, the other girls struck him as rather attractive, too, and afterwards, when he and Etienne led the cotillion, he outdid himself in inventing brand-new figures for them all to follow.

With the party drawing to a close he was mobbed by the girls, who pranced about challenging him to run and catch them, and in the middle of the last dance he played an impromptu game of tag, which ended with Ange and Françoise crashing into a potted azalea and Emilie de Woude pronouncing the ball to have degenerated into a veritable bacchanal.

"Oh, it's all Paul's fault, it's Paul's fault!" they all cried out.

The wraps were brought into the dining room and the guests began to leave. It was three o'clock in the morning.

"You were so much nicer this evening than yesterday, Freddie," said Paul, helping her with her cloak.

She smiled dreamily, wondering whether she had said anything she shouldn't have, but she could not recall anything untoward.

Paul set off homeward with several other young men. He turned up his collar, thrust his hands in his pockets, and thought back on how he had fared this evening. Well, there was no doubt in his mind—they were all mad about him, every single one of them!

The church wedding took place the following Thursday morning. All agreed that Lili made a lovely young bride as she entered the church on the arm of her young husband-to-be, delicately pale and blonde in the white mist of her veil, with her long train of heavy white moiré and her pageboys Ben van Raat and Nico van Rijssel. Behind them followed Mr de Woude and Madame Verstraeten, then Mr Verstraeten and Emilie, with the ushers and bridesmaids, the witnesses and other members of the family bringing up the rear. At one o'clock the carriages departed to Prinsessegracht for the wedding breakfast, the final event in the celebrations, during which well-wishing toasts were brought out and tears were shed, notably by Madame Verstraeten, and also by Lili and Marie. By seven o'clock there was only a small gathering of intimates left in the drawing room. The newly-weds, bound for a fortnight in Paris, had slipped away earlier, but not before Marie had whispered tearful assurances to Lili that their love nest in Atjehstraat would be in perfect order for them when they returned.

Old Madame van Raat and Emilie, Henk and Betsy, Frédérique, Otto and Paul stayed a while to keep the Verstraetens company. Attempts were made to keep up a lively conversation, but a pall of melancholy seemed to have settled on the drawing room, mingling with the dying perfumes of the bouquets and flower baskets. Mr Verstraeten dithered about, irked by all the flowers and greenery and inwardly more moved than he cared to admit, now and then tapping his wife on the shoulder in passing to press a rapid kiss on her brow. Emilie said it was time she was going, and gave him a farewell embrace, whispering that she hoped he was not vexed with her for her persistence on behalf of her young brother's love for his daughter … When Otto, too, took his leave, Marie was so moved by the sadness in his voice that she had to fight back her tears, and she fled upstairs to the rooms she had shared with Lili for as long as she could remember, which would henceforth be hers alone.

The first sight to meet her eyes was Lili's wedding dress lying across the deserted bed, with its long white train hanging over the side and trailing on the carpet; her veil and orange blossom lay in a crumpled heap on a chair, the dainty white satin shoes discarded at some distance from each other. She sat on the side of Lili's bed in tears, and took up a rustling handful of the moiré train. It reminded her of a shroud. She had a sense of utter desolation—Lili was gone, and it almost felt as if she was dead and buried. Then the door opened and Dien came in.

"There, there, dearie, don't upset yourself! You know she'll be back soon, and they won't be living far away. You can see her every day if you want. My oh my! How pretty she looked in her white wedding dress! Such a fine-looking pair, too," said Dien, with a catch in her voice. She crossed to the window and drew the net curtain away to let the afternoon sun stream into the room.

"Ah yes, so it goes, so it goes. You raise your children for all those years and then they go off to the Indies, or they get married, and leave you all lonely and forlorn. Fancy you, crying! Did you really believe you would stay in this house for the rest of your life? You'll see, you'll find a husband, too; when the time is right you will marry, that's how it always goes, you mark my words!"

Marie smiled through her tears. "Oh, what would you know about it, Dien! I might become an old maid for all you know!"

"My dear child, you must be joking! No, that would never suit you. It will be your turn next, you mark my words!"

Marie had to laugh. The sun slanting in was like a ray of hope and expectation, and it set the creased moiré of the wedding dress ashimmer with dazzling light. That was no shroud, it was a festive dress, white as snowdrops, worn to mark the most wonderful of occasions! She felt a rush of optimism, and sat back, giving herself up to the sweet promise of spring sunshine until all budded and blossomed in her soul.

XXVII

IT WAS TWO O'CLOCK in the afternoon when Paul awoke. He had been out with friends the previous evening, and had not returned home until daybreak. He took a cold bath and dressed at leisure, so that it was past three by the time he went down to the dining room, where his breakfast awaited him. He felt hungry, and noted with relish the jellied chicken and bottle of Hochheimer wine. But first he took a couple of raw eggs from the dresser and, whistling a tune, stirred them into a glass of cognac. He did not like the taste, but downed the drink anyway for its restorative properties, after which he took his seat at the table and helped himself to a slice of the tender cold chicken in pale golden aspic. He was in no hurry at all, and wished to enjoy every mouthful.

It was a cloudy day in early June, and still quite chilly. The bleak light coming in through the window showed up the decaying opulence of the room. Paul was a little discomfited by the faded, old-fashioned drapes, the threadbare chair covers and ancient Deventer rugs, and had on several occasions tried to persuade his mother to redecorate her home, but without success. So he had resigned himself to the situation, for he realised that Madame van Raat, at her age, would not feel at ease with a more modern style, and also that each timeworn object in her home was aglow with memories and associations that she held dear and wished to surround herself with for the rest of her days.

As he savoured his chicken and Hochheimer his thoughts took a philosophical turn. Life was not so bad at all, he mused, and he could not imagine why he had ever felt differently. His student days floated into in his mind, chiefly as a time of youthful waywardness, but there was also Uncle Verstraeten hovering in the background, urging him to sit one exam after another. All those exams—there had seemed to be no end to them! On the other hand, it was just as well his uncle had kept such a stern eye on him. Because what would he have achieved otherwise? Had he been left to his own devices, free to do as he pleased as he was nowadays, he would probably still be a student! After graduating he had gone through that period of artistic ambition, and what a disillusion it had been to discover that he had insufficient talent for either painting or music! Well, he had got over all that; he no longer painted, no longer sang, and, thank God, no longer suffered despair at his piteous lack of creative genius. Now his sole aim was to enjoy life for its own sake, to lead a comfortable, heedless existence, indulging his spendthrift inclination—which he did with gusto—and sure enough, he found himself more energetic and in better spirits than he had ever been before, either as a student or an aspiring artist. Pursuing his materialistic and epicurean tastes gave him a sense of hearty well-being, indeed, he sometimes felt rather like a young bull frisking in a sun-drenched meadow at the height of summer! Thus he mulled over his transformation from what Betsy had been known to call a 'feckless fatty', into the devil-may-care, fun-loving young blade he was today. His meditations did not run deep, however; he was merely letting his thoughts roam for want of a conversation partner at his breakfast table.

Having eaten his fill, he lit a cigar and looked idly about him. Through the window he caught a glimpse of Aunt Verstraeten and Marie passing by; a moment later the doorbell rang. Knowing how slow Leentje was getting in her old age, he answered the door himself.

"Ah, good day, Aunt, good day, Marie."

"Good morning to you, Paul. Is your mama in?" enquired Madame Verstraeten.

"I expect she is, Aunt, but to be honest I haven't seen her. I got up rather late, you see."

They went upstairs together and found Madame van Raat in her dimly lit room at the back; she was sitting by the window with her hands folded on her lap, gazing into the garden. A book by Gustave Droz, *Tristesses et sourires*, lay open on the table beside her. She rose to welcome her visitors; kisses were exchanged, after which Paul, too, planted a kiss on his mother's cheek. When they were all seated Madame van Raat asked after Lili and Georges.

"They are very well. Apparently, they ran into Eline at the home of some French relatives of Vere's wife," reported Madame Verstraeten. "They seem to be enjoying Paris very much, although in her letter Lili did mention that she couldn't wait to move into their new home!"

Curling his lip sarcastically beneath his moustache, Paul gave an almost imperceptible shrug.

"Such dear young things!" smiled Madame van Raat. "Their little abode is nearly ready, then, I take it?"

"Nearly, Aunt," replied Marie. "I pop in there every day, and I keep finding things that still need seeing to. Actually, I ran into Emilie there a few times, too—she has a spare key, you know."

"How touching!" said Paul. "The doting sisters!"

"There's nothing touching or doting about it," retorted Marie loftily. "We happen to think it good fun to put our doll's house in order, as we call it. But you wouldn't understand such simple pleasures, would you? By the way, you said you had got up late—and at what time would that have been, then?"

"Ah, checking up on me now, are you?"

"Go on then, what time was it? Or is it too embarrassing to tell me?"

He responded facetiously, and again caught Eline's name being mentioned by the ladies.

"Oh, they find Eline very gay and winsome—well, quite the way we always thought of her, too, didn't we?" said Madame Verstraeten. "They dined with those French people, apparently. And Eline has turned into a proper Parisienne, Lili said, didn't she Marie?"

Marie gave a faint smile. She pictured Eline, and in her mind's eye Otto appeared beside her.

"Yes, Eline mentioned Georges and Lili in her letter to me too," observed Madame van Raat.

"What's that? Did you get a letter from Eline, Mama?" exclaimed Paul. "And you never said a word about it to me!"

"My dear boy, I have not seen you since dinner yesterday evening. And yes, this morning I received a very sweet letter. She is very pleased that I asked her to come and live with me. Poor child, she tells me she feels very lonely amongst all those strangers, however kind they are to her. She says she's relieved to be able to settle down at last."

"So she's coming to live here, with us?" said Paul. "Such a shame I'm just moving out!"

"You were always very fond of Eline, weren't you, Aunt?" said Marie. "What an excellent idea to invite her to stay with you."

"Yes, dear, I agree. I think it will be for the best," sighed Madame van Raat. "Besides, the idea of engaging some lady's companion does not appeal to me at all, and having a sweet, considerate girl like Eline, who is part of the family after all, to keep me company is a different proposition entirely. I am so glad you approve, because I confess I did have some concerns at first."

"Betsy seems to take a positive view of it too, at least so I have heard," said Madame Verstraeten.

"That does not surprise me. Eline wouldn't dream of going back to live in their house, and with her coming to live here Betsy needn't worry about any talk of a rift between her and her sister."

"A solution satisfactory to all parties," said Paul, rubbing his hands. "All is well with the world, then, which is just how I like it."

Madame van Raat, shocked by her son's playful tone, looked at him sharply. Just then there was a knock at the door and old Leentje came in to announce that the carriage was waiting.

Paul rose.

"Much obliged, beauteous Helen! My dear Aunt, would you care to join me for a drive? It's such a fine day."

His aunt declined his offer, as she had some calls to make.

"You could drop me off at Atjehstraat, if you wouldn't mind," suggested Marie. "There's something I need to do there anyway."

He declared himself willing to conduct his beloved cousin to the North Pole if need be, and they departed together.

Madame van Raat shook her head.

"That Paul! I don't know what's got into him lately!" she said, sighing.

But Madame Verstraeten came to his defence.

"Never mind, Dora, he's not a bad boy at heart. He's simply a young man with money to spend … what can you expect?"

"Henk was never like that. It's a shocking way to live one's life! To start with, he never gets up before eleven, and then he goes for a ride on horseback or in his buggy, after which he's off to his club. He usually dines at home, thank Heavens! As for the evenings—well, goodness knows what he gets up to."

"He looks well enough, though."

"His constitution is robust, fortunately, and until now his health does not seem to have suffered from the ridiculous hours he keeps. But as I said before, it's a shocking way to live. He was less wayward as a student than he is nowadays. No indeed, Henk wasn't in the least like that when he was Paul's age!"

She continued in the same vein for some time, drawing comparisons between her eldest son, her favourite whom she thought sensible and solid, and Paul, whom she accused of being irresponsible and egotistical. For that was what he was, egotistical, there was no other word for it, taking no heed whatsoever of his mother's wishes, offering her no companionship to speak of, and treating her house much like a hotel! He had no thought for his old mother, he lived only for himself, for his own enjoyment.

Madame Verstraeten could think of nothing to say except that Paul was a good boy at heart and that this was just a stage he was going through. Although unable to express her feelings in words, she had a sharp sense of regret at the cruelty of Nature's laws, by which the generations inevitably became estranged once the children grew up and embarked on their own lives, entering new realms of mental and material consciousness from which their elders were excluded. The gulf of incomprehension dividing parents from their adult offspring did not signify a lack of love on either part, it was simply the outcome of that single, fateful law dictating ultimate alienation. It was not so much that all the ties of kindred love were suddenly severed, they were successively unwound, unravelled, frayed, until such time as they were slack and inconsequential. She had become painfully aware of this when Lili took against her on account of her love for Georges, and she was reminded of it again now, for it had not escaped her that Marie's behaviour had changed of late, which was bound to portend yet another estrangement, another parting. And then there was Jan, whose turn would come a few years from now. No one was to blame, either; not the parents, who were merely victims of their own parental love, nor the children, who, once they were parents themselves, would have to bear the same martyrdom in their turn.

The weather was cool and Marie felt the wind on her face as she perched on the high box beside Paul, who was holding the reins.

"What do you keep going to that house for?" asked Paul. "You just can't get enough of it, can you?"

She had to laugh, because he had guessed the truth. The cosy little nest was all ready and waiting to receive the two lovebirds, and yet she couldn't wait to spend time there, as if it were a brand new toy.

They rolled along Bankaplein towards Atjehstraat, with Marie giving directions to Paul.

"Do you always carry their house key in your pocket? Whatever will you do when you've given it back?" he teased, drawing the buggy to a halt. The groom jumped down from the back to help Marie alight.

"I shall ring the bell and hope to be let in!" she replied, laughing. "But why don't you come in for a moment, Paul? Then you can see your wedding present in its proper surroundings."

"No thanks, I can quite imagine what it looks like!" he responded. "Have fun!"

"Thank you for the ride … "

She slipped her key in the lock, pausing to watch as Paul's elegant, frail-looking vehicle rolled away with the smart little groom at the back.

Stepping inside, she heard someone singing upstairs. "Dear Emilie," she thought, smiling to herself. But she did not climb the stairs at once; instead, she slipped into the salon for a quick glance at the pretty suite of furniture, blue and shiny with newness in the soft light entering through the cream-coloured lace curtains. The silver tea service glowed under its tulle dust cover on a side table. The mantelpiece, too, was prettily adorned with vases on either side of an artistic jester's head in terracotta, which was reflected in the glass. Only the walls were still a little bare, as were the walls of the dining room, which was very simply furnished with a round dining table and chairs, a modest nut-wood dresser and a brown-leather settee.

"It all looks so new," thought Marie. "Not very cosy yet—but that will come, all in good time."

Everything was indeed very shiny. The kitchen was the shiniest area of all, from brand-new pots and pans to a gleaming range that had yet to be lit for the first time. True, there was no life in the place yet, but all in all the ground floor was very fetching. Marie went upstairs. Emilie was still singing, and not at all surprised to see Marie, who was busy in Georges' study arranging countless souvenirs from his boyhood room in his parental home.

"Oh, how cosy it's beginning to look here!" said Marie. "Those knick-knacks make all the difference. It's still a bit bare downstairs, I think."

She opened the door to a side room which had been made into a small, frilly boudoir for Lili.

"Now isn't this just too lovely?" gushed Marie.

"Yes, isn't it?" rejoined Emilie. "Just think: young Georges at his desk over there while milady sits in her boudoir, daydreaming."

"Daydreaming? Milady will be far too busy running her household!" said Marie. "Oh, I can just see Lili getting all flustered giving instructions to her new housemaid! How will she ever manage?"

They both pealed with laughter, and in high good humour set about removing Georges' books from their boxes and ranging them on the shelves of the tall, antique bookcase, another relic of his study at Noordeinde. Marie was in such high spirits that she kept dissolving into helpless hilarity, which severely impeded their progress.

"There, there, Marie," chuckled Emilie. "Pull yourself together! We'll never get anything done at this rate. You can't stop laughing, can you? You seem very happy—any particular reason?"

Marie gave a start and blushed.

"Happy? How do you mean? No, no particular reason. But every time I come here I have a fit of the giggles, I can't imagine why," she said, and a fresh peal of laughter ensued. "Just look at us, feathering the lovebirds' nest for them! Would they do the same for us, do you think?"

Still laughing, the pair of them made a quick survey of the bedroom, which they still found to be lacking in cosiness. There was the same untouched, formal sheen of newness whichever way they looked, and when they opened one of the closets the sight of immaculate shelves bearing stiff little piles of starched household linen tied with pink and blue ribbons caused yet more merriment. Marie plumped herself down on the unmade bed.

"Oh please, Marie, do tell me why you're in such a jolly mood! Are you keeping something from me?" said Emilie.

"What makes you think I have a secret? But seriously, Emilie, I wish you would tell me why you never married. I mean, you must have been courted at some time?"

"Yes, I was, by a cavalry officer. He was big and strong, and he had soulful eyes, and then, one day—oh, you naughty girl, stop laughing at me, do you hear?" she protested, whereupon Marie sprang up, pulled Emilie to her feet and waltzed her around the highly polished floor.

XXVIII

ELINE SAT ALONE in the ladies' compartment, her head tilted back against the red-velvet padding. She listened attentively to the wheels pounding the rails, thinking she could distinguish a nervous three-quarter time in the harsh, metallic monotone. Now and then she rubbed the steamed-up window with her pocket handkerchief to look outside, where the grey shadows of twilight were deepening. She saw swirls of mist rising over the meadows and the faint yellow glow of scattered farms in the distance as the train chugged onwards to The Hague. The Hague! She had been away for so long that the city seemed dear to her now, a place where she might yet find something of a home.

For the past eighteen months she had been abroad, either travelling and living in hotels surrounded by strangers or staying at her uncle's house in Brussels, never having a place she could call her own. Her varied existence had made the time pass very quickly, her mind having been constantly occupied by touring new cities and meeting new people, but lately she had begun to tire of that endless diversity. She now yearned for peace and tranquillity, for a long, dull period of complete repose, untroubled by dreams or sadness of any kind.

Something of a home! Would she find such a home with dear old Madame van Raat, that mournful, grey-haired lady who loved her but who did not know her as she was now: a sad, subdued creature, weary of her young life. Because from now on that was what she would be, sad, subdued, and weary; no longer would she work herself up to be vivacious and gay at all times, the way she had been obliged to do among strangers, the way Georges and Lili had seen her only a few days ago. A proper Parisienne, Lili had called her—fancy Lili being taken in by her veneer of sophistication! Ah well, she felt too weak for any kind of performance now. Something had broken in her spirit, and now everything else was slowly but surely breaking down all around her. What a mess it all was …

The train whistled shrilly and the lights glimmering through the mist multiplied. In a few minutes she would be in The Hague. Slowly she drew herself up in her seat, adjusted her hat and veil, placed her book and scent bottle in her leather travelling bag and waited, tense and ramrod-straight. She appeared rather slight and wan in her grey travelling coat, gazing ahead with hollow eyes as the train rolled into the station and ground noisily to a halt.

Her heart beat faster and she could feel the tears welling up in her eyes. The train conductor shouted "Hague! Hague!", and through the steamed-up glass she saw the jostling crowd on the platform, bathed in the dismal glow of gas lanterns.

The carriage door was wrenched open from the outside; she stood up, gripping her bag in one hand and several parasols rolled up in her travelling rug in the other. She scanned the stream of disembarking passengers for any sign of Paul, whom she had been told to expect, and was astonished to see another familiar figure coming in her direction.

"Why, Henk!" she cried.

As he helped her down to the platform she almost tumbled into his arms, while Paul, who arrived a moment later, relieved her of her hand luggage.

"Elly, dear child! My dearest Elly!" Henk said with a catch in his voice, and he kissed her softly as she leant against him, weeping. She barely heard Paul's greeting, merely handed him her luggage ticket so that he would see to her trunks. A sob escaped her, but Henk chatted on regardless, taking her arm and steering her to the station exit where his carriage was waiting. She responded meekly, her mind awhirl with undefined thoughts and nostalgic sentiments, and she was glad of his strong hand helping her up to her seat. She recognised the landau in which she had ridden so often, but she noted that the groom was different; in the old days it would have been Herman.

"Paul will be here soon, and then we'll be off," said Henk, seating himself beside her.

She did not answer, but leant back, covering her face with her hands to hide her emotion.

"I had not expected to see you, Henk! How very kind of you!" she said after a pause. "So very kind!"

He pressed her hand and put his head round the open door to look for Paul, who was just arriving with the luggage.

"All set!" cried Paul, jumping in. "Well, Elly, what a pleasure to see you again! A great pleasure, I must say."

The groom shut the door and the carriage rumbled off. Paul said no more; neither did Eline and Henk. With each gas lantern they passed Paul caught another glimpse of Eline leaning back in her seat with her hands to her face, motionless but for her heaving breast.

It was past ten when they drew up at the house on Laan van Meerdervoort. The groom rang the bell; the door was opened; they alighted. In the vestibule stood Madame van Raat, trembling with emotion as Eline rushed forward and flung her arms about her.

"My dear, dear lady! How glad I am to see you!" she sobbed. "So you will have me? You wish me to stay with you?"

Madame van Raat, weeping like a child, drew Eline to the brightly lit dining room, where the table was spread for supper.

"Oh, I can't tell you how grateful I am! You're such an angel!" Eline cried out. "I'm so delighted to be here with you."

They clung together tearfully as they moved to the sofa, where they sat down side by side. The old lady put her arm fondly about Eline's waist. How long it had been since they had seen one another! How sorely she had missed her! And how had Eline fared in the meantime? Was she well?

"Oh yes, certainly! I am very well!" cried Eline, kissing her again and again.

Madame van Raat undid Eline's veil, helped her to remove her hat and her coat, and was dismayed to see the frail shoulders, the gaunt cheeks, the forlorn expression in the eyes.

"My dear child!" she gasped, unable to contain herself. "My dear child! How you have changed! Look at you!"

Eline embraced her passionately, hiding her flushed face in the old lady's bosom.

"Oh, I'm perfectly all right, only a little pale, probably, and tired after my journey. Just being with you will make me look as a fresh as a daisy again in no time, you'll see!"

She smiled through her tears and kissed her repeatedly, now on the cheek, now on the backs of her wrinkled hands. They were soon joined by Henk and Paul, who were likewise shocked to see how thin Eline had grown, without however making any comment on her appearance.

After a while the old lady, who could not take her eyes off Eline, suggested that she might like to freshen up in her room.

"No, not yet!" objected Eline. "I hardly feel dusty at all, so never mind that. But ah, there he is—Henk! Good, kind Henk!"

She beckoned him to the sofa where she was sitting with his mother, drew him close and cupped his face in her small hands.

"You're not cross with me, are you, Henk?" she murmured in his ear.

He bit his lip.

"I was never cross with you," he stammered.

She kissed him, let him go, took a deep breath and cast a leisurely glance about the room. She had found something of a home.

They all seated themselves at the table. Eline was not hungry: she barely looked at her soup, avoided the meat dish and ate only some slivers of duck accompanied by a few lettuce leaves. She was thirsty, however, and eager to have her glass replenished by Paul. The wine and the excitement had brought a red flush to her sallow cheeks, and when the old lady wondered aloud why her uncle Daniel had not seen fit to escort her to The Hague, she responded with loud, nervous laughter. Oh, there had been no need, it was no hardship for her to make the journey from Brussels to The Hague alone; besides, her uncle had offered to accompany her but she had not wished it—she was so accustomed to travelling that she felt perfectly at ease! Travelling, there was nothing to it: you packed your valise, found out about itineraries and such, and off you went to catch your train. Ah, if dear Madame would ever feel inclined to undertake a journey with her, Eline would show her what an expert traveller she had become!

She prattled on, holding her wine glass all the while and pausing only to raise it to her lips for another sip. She spoke of Eliza, her young aunt, who was adorable, so lively and gay, always on the go, always thinking up amusing things for them to do. She and Uncle Daniel seemed to disagree about practically everything—oh, how they squabbled!—but they did so in such a funny way that it was quite hilarious, really. Eliza's relatives in Paris were very nice, too, but she also had an uncle and aunt in Bordeaux, who were quite, quite delightful. Their name was des Luynes and they owned a chateau, where she, Eline, had been invited to attend the grape festival; such a pretty pastoral scene it had been, which reminded her of something she had read in a novel, a novel by Georges Sand, she believed; wasn't it Georges Sand who wrote *La Petite Fadette*? Well, then! And Spain, oh, she was mad about Spain, especially the south with all those Moorish influences, like the Alhambra in Granada—it was magnificent! But she had refused to go to a bullfight, which Eliza had thought ridiculous of her, but she couldn't stand the idea of those poor bulls lying in pools of blood, it was simply too horrid.

Paul laughed, saying he agreed about the pitiful bulls, and she laughed too as she embarked on yet another topic. Again Madame van Raat begged her to eat some more, since she had hardly touched her food.

"No, really, dear lady; thank you but no. I am rather thirsty, though; may I have another glass?"

"My dear, are you sure you aren't drinking a little too much?"

"Oh no, it helps me sleep, you know—otherwise I lie awake all night long, which is such a bore. Cordoba is a lovely town, too, the mosque there is quite superb," and she was off again, on yet another nervous stream of delightful reminiscences of her wanderings. She could not imagine why Paul did not travel more; had she been a man, especially a young man of means like him, she would still be roaming even now; she would have travelled far and wide, on the Great Pacific, for instance, from New York all the way to San Francisco, and then across the Pacific Ocean to Japan—halfway across the world by ship! How divine that would be! But travelling in a railway carriage was divine, too: she wouldn't mind living in one!

The old lady shook her head, smiling indulgently at Eline's excitement.

"But coming to live here with you is the best thing of all! Oh, you're such a darling, such an angel!" Eline cried out ecstatically.

After supper Madame van Raat urged Eline to rest a while in her room. Eline said she would, but held back, pleading with her to keep her company. Paul said that he had an appointment and Henk, too, stood up to take his leave.

"May Betsy come and see you tomorrow?" he whispered anxiously. She gave a faint smile and pressed his hand.

"By all means!" she said. "Give her a kiss from me, will you? And how is little Ben? Has he grown much?"

"Yes indeed, he's a big boy now. You will see him tomorrow, no doubt. Goodbye for now, then, Elly. Sleep well."

"Goodnight, Henk. Till tomorrow."

When Henk had gone his mother offered to show Eline her room.

"I am afraid that I cannot give you a sitting room of your own for the moment, Elly dear," she said as they climbed the stairs. "Not until Paul leaves, that is."

"Where is he planning to go?"

"He wants to live independently, which is better for a young man, I suppose. But your bedroom is quite large; you probably remember it—the room next to mine."

"Yes I do remember. What a lovely room!"

The lamps had been lit by Leentje and the doors to the balcony were open to admit the cool summer air. Eline began to cough as she entered.

"It's getting a little chilly," said Madame, and moved to shut the doors.

Eline glanced about her in deep astonishment, and her eyes grew moist. "Good gracious! Whatever have you done?" she cried.

Wherever she looked there were mementoes of her rooms at Nassauplein. Her very own dressing table with the mirror, her writing table, her couch, her Venetian pier glass, and over there, in tasteful profusion, stood her figurines and other trinkets. The only item that was new was the ample bedstead, over which dark-blue curtains were suspended like a canopy jutting from the wall.

"Do you approve?" asked Madame van Raat. "I thought you would like your own things best. But my dear child, why are you crying?"

Eline clung to her, weeping on her shoulder and kissing her again and again. Madame van Raat made her sit on the couch beside her, and Eline nestled up against her like a child seeking comfort from its mother.

"Oh, at last, I shall be able to get some rest!" she said wearily. "Because I am so tired, so very tired."

"Shall I leave you alone then, so you can take a nap?"

"No, no, please don't leave me. I'm not tired from spending five hours on a train, I'm just tired … tired of everything, and going to sleep now won't help. But I feel so much better already, just sitting here close to you, because I know you care for me. You see, this is what I missed so dreadfully while I was away, with all those strangers for company and no one to lean on and comfort me with a kind word. People were friendly and considerate, but cool at the same time. Uncle Daniel is like that too: amiable and considerate to the point of gallantry, but rather cold. I got on quite well with Eliza, who is very gay, so we laughed and joked a great deal, but she is a cold sort of person, too, cynical even. And there I was, on my best behaviour and permanently wreathed in smiles, because no one likes a guest with a long face, do they? Besides, where else could I go?"

"You could have come to me, my child; I would have written to you earlier had I known of your feelings. I thought you were happy over there."

"Happy!" Eline gave a hollow laugh. "As happy as a horse on its last legs, having to be whipped to make it go! Giddy-up, giddy-up!"

Her laughter speared the old lady's heart. Too moved to speak, her bleary eyes aglitter with fresh tears, and she could only press Eline closer to her breast.

"Yes, hold me fast," murmured Eline. "Now I can relax … Oh, you're such a comfort to me, like a darling mama of my very own."

They remained thus for a long moment, saying very little, until Madame van Raat said Eline should try to get some to sleep.

"If you want anything, just call me; I shall be in the next room. I want you to be entirely at home here, so please don't be too discreet. That would pain me. So if there is anything you need, you will say so, won't you?"

Eline promised she would, and Madame van Raat left the room. But Eline still felt too restless to go to bed. She let her eyes drift about the room, and wherever she looked she recognised her own vases, pictures, and photographs.

"How very kind of her," she murmured under her breath, smiling wistfully. The nervous agitation in her soul seemed to ebb away into a comforting sense of relief and well-being, for she felt safe among the relics of her former life. She rose from the couch to wander about, pausing to trace her finger along her treasured terracotta and biscuit figurines, touching a photograph here and a trinket there. Each beloved object awakened a host of memories and associations in her mind, some like scented flowers, others like painful, scorching sparks, and suddenly it came to her that the time she had spent abroad had not passed quickly at all, that it had been a full year and a half, and that the last time she had set eyes on any of these things had been on that terrible night when she had run away and sought refuge at Jeanne Ferelijn's house.

But she continued to take stock of her new room, and her glance fell upon the Japanese box which Madame van Raat had placed on her writing table. She automatically tried to raise the lid, but found it locked. Beside it lay her old bunch of keys, the same collection of small keys on a silver ring that she had entrusted to Frans Ferelijn such a long time ago, and she took it up, picked out the key belonging to the Japanese box and opened it. The box was filled with letters, discoloured with age. Among them were letters from Aunt Vere, sent to her when she was at boarding school, and from old schoolmates. She resolved to tear up the latter as she no longer cared for the sentimental outpourings of schoolgirls whose existence she had forgotten, much as they had no doubt forgotten hers. She also found a batch of letters written by her beloved father, who had been such a wonderful man; those she kissed reverently, as though they were sacred. As she rifled through the sheets, a small oval-shaped piece of cardboard slipped out and fell to the floor. She bent down to retrieve it, and turned deathly pale.

It was a medallion portrait of Otto.

What was it doing there among her letters? Then she remembered: it was a rejected proof of a portrait he had once ordered as a gift to her. The portrait itself, which she had kept with her at all times during her engagement, she had sent back to Otto along with the other presents he had given her—including the Bucchi fan—in a final, heartless gesture of rebuffal.

Moaning quietly as she wept, she pressed the portrait to her lips. The rejected proof, which she had never given another thought after it got lost among her old correspondence, was now dearer to her than anything else in the world, and she vowed that she would never part with it, not until the day she died! It was all that was left of her great happiness, the happiness that had slipped through her fingers like a captive bird bent on escape, leaving her with nothing but a stray feather!

"Otto! Oh, Otto!" she faltered, covering the oval card with tears and kisses.

Madame van Raat sat for a while in the next room, her own bedchamber, tearfully shaking her head from side to side as she ruminated upon Eline's plight.

How was it possible that she had known such lasting happiness with her husband, while poor dear Elly was so bereft? Being of devout mind, with the childlike piety of a simple heart, she was thankful for such goodness as she had received, and folded her wrinkled hands to say a prayer for her beloved, unhappy Eline.

The next morning, when Eline had finished dressing, she opened the glass doors to the balcony and saw Madame van Raat among the rose bushes, wielding a pair of pruning scissors. Eline hurried downstairs to join her in the garden.

"I am not too late, am I? I hope I haven't kept you from your breakfast," she said sweetly. The old lady kissed her, telling her she could get up at whatever time she liked, and that she had waited with breakfast.

"I can tell you have every intention of spoiling me! Oh dear, and then I shall become a burden to you eventually, I'm afraid. My, how pretty the garden looks! May I pick some flowers?"

Smiling her approval, Madame van Raat handed over the scissors and trailed after Eline as she sauntered along the beds, going up on tiptoe by the tall bushes to draw the blossoms towards her, snipping off sprays of the deep purple and creamy white lilac, the bright yellow laburnum, the snowy elder, while the glistening dewdrops rolled like bright diamonds over her fingers. It was a pity the jasmine was not yet in flower, she mused.

"Do you have a vase? Then I shall make you a nice big bouquet, but I need more lilac blossom, lilacs above all … "

The scissors flew through a large bush, the choicest of them all, and the purple-headed stems tumbled down on the dewy grass. She gathered them up and went into the house, where her hostess was already preparing their hot chocolate. Eline set about arranging the flowers in a large vase on the dresser.

"Flowers work wonders to brighten up a room, don't you agree?" she exclaimed, taking a few steps back to consider the effect of her mixed bouquet.

Madame van Raat chided her gently for letting her chocolate go cold, and Eline sat down with a sigh. The previous evening the old lady had been struck by how restless Eline seemed, picking up objects and putting them down again, adjusting their position ever so slightly, darting furtive looks at the window, the door or the ceiling in what seemed like alarm, twitching her head, drumming her fingers on the table; all of this alternating with sudden fits of apathy, when she dropped into a chair and leant back with an air of utter exhaustion.

This morning, too, Eline was showing signs of nervousness, but at least she was drinking her cup of fragrant hot chocolate.

"What will you have for breakfast, my child? A soft-boiled egg and a slice of bread?"

Eline smiled anxiously.

"Oh, must I, dear lady? I'd rather not, to be honest. The chocolate is delicious, though."

"Elly, my pet, you must have some breakfast. You hardly ate a thing last night! Have a boiled egg then; just for my sake."

Eline consented and Madame sliced the top off her egg for her as though indulging a child.

"You really ought to eat more, Elly dear," she pursued. "You're far too thin. Why, you almost look starved! We must get some weight on you. Plenty of milk, eggs and meat, that will do you good."

Eline merely smiled and regarded her egg with slight revulsion, which she was unable to conceal. After a few tastes of the egg she pushed it away.

"Please don't be cross, but honestly, I can't have any more. It doesn't agree with me."

She looked so miserable that the old lady abandoned further attempts to make her eat. In the end she consumed one rusk, just to appease her hostess: that would be quite enough, she insisted, and anyway she was not accustomed to having such an early breakfast.

"What about Paul? Is he still asleep?"

"Yes he is."

Madame van Raat went on to say that Paul always breakfasted alone, or rather, that he skipped breakfast altogether most days, contenting himself with a cup of coffee; in fact, he gave her very little trouble, but then he did not give her much pleasure either.

"Girls are so much easier to get on with than boys, aren't they? Well, you could pretend that you have a daughter staying in your house!" Eline said fondly. "Oh, do you remember suggesting—it was many moons ago—that I could come and live with you, and I said that you only loved me because you saw so little of me, but that you would find my presence irksome if you saw me every day. Do you remember?"

The old lady smiled vaguely, casting back her mind, but the memory escaped her.

"Oh, I know exactly when it was! It was at Nassauplein, in the violet ante-room. Who would have thought I'd ever seek shelter with you? But I promise I shall try my best not to be a nuisance."

She toyed nervously with an ornament dangling from her watch chain: a locket of black enamel studded with seed pearls which she had not worn for years. It had been a gift from her father for her tenth birthday, and when he died she had vowed never to wear it again, but this morning she had changed her mind. The locket now held the slip of cardboard she had found among her letters.

"Dear lady," she began in a tremulous voice, taking Madame van Raat's hand. "There is something I should like to ask you, if I may. It's about Otto van Erlevoort—have you seen him at all lately, or have you heard from him?"

Madame van Raat looked intently at Eline, trying to read her mind, but could infer nothing from her feverish glances and fluttering hands.

"Why do you ask, Elly?"

It was the first time that Otto's name passed between them since Eline had broken off her engagement.

"Oh, I'd just like to know whether he was much affected, and whether he is happy now. Do you never see him?"

"I saw him a few times at my brother-in-law's house."

"How does he look?"

"Much the same, outwardly; a little older maybe, but not that you would notice. He is certainly rather quiet, but then he was never very exuberant, was he?"

"No, he wasn't," murmured Eline, brimming over with memories.

"He's not in The Hague at the moment. I believe he's gone to de Horze."

Could he be avoiding me? thought Eline. Then, not wishing to give the impression that her interest in Otto's welfare was in any way personal, she said softly:

"Then I suppose he has got over it. All I want is for him to be happy; he deserves it—such a good man."

The old lady said nothing and Eline struggled not to cry. Here she was, working herself up again to hide her true feelings, even in front of dear, dear Madame van Raat! Life was so full of sham and make-believe! She had always been someone who pretended, to herself as well as to everybody else, and she was still doing it—she could not do otherwise, so ingrained a habit had it become.

"And now I would like to show you something that I hope will please you," said Madame van Raat, sensing Eline's emotion. "Come with me."

She led her to the salon, where Eline had not yet been, and opened the door.

"You remember I had that old, rather battered piano? The one Paul used to tinkle on for his singing practice? Well, look what I have now!"

They went in, and Eline saw a brand-new Bechstein. Her music books, bound in red leather with gilt lettering, lay on top.

"It will suit your voice very well, the sound is so lovely and clear."

Eline's lips began to tremble.

"But Madame!" she stammered. "Oh, you shouldn't have! You shouldn't have! Because I—I don't sing any more, you see."

"What? Why ever not?" cried Madame.

Eline sighed deeply and sank down on a chair.

"I am not allowed to!" she almost wailed, for the new instrument was a cruel reminder of the lovely voice she had once had. "The doctors I consulted in Paris forbade it. The thing is, during the winter my cough is rather bad; it only goes away in the summer. The past two winters I was coughing all the time, and I always had a pain, here in my chest. But I'm perfectly all right in the summer!"

"My dear child!" said Madame anxiously. "I hope you took good care of yourself while you were abroad."

"Oh yes, the Des Luynes referred me to some lung specialists in Paris, and they tapped me and osculated me so thoroughly that I simply couldn't stand it any more! Besides that I underwent regular treatment by two doctors, but after a while I'd had enough of them: they were not making me better, anyway, they just kept saying I ought to live in a warmer climate, but I could hardly go and live all by myself in Algiers or goodness knows where; in any case, Uncle Daniel had to return to Brussels. So you see," she concluded with a nervous titter, "I'm a complete wreck, both on the outside and on the inside!"

The old lady's eyes filled with tears, and she pressed Eline to her bosom.

"Shame about the lovely instrument, though!" said Eline, extricating herself. She seated herself at the piano. What a wonderful sound it had, so rich and full!

Her fingers glided deftly over the keys, playing a succession of scales that seemed to lament the loss of her singing voice. Madame van Raat watched her sadly; she had cherished the illusion that Eline would sing with her Paul, and that Paul might succumb to the melodious, convivial atmosphere and take to staying in of an evening, but all she heard was loud, sobbing arpeggios, the weeping dewdrops of a chromatic tremolo, and the big, splashing tears of painful staccatos.

"I shall have to practise my piano-playing. I never was a great pianist, but I shall do my best! Because you shall have music, dear lady, I promise you! What a lovely instrument this is!"

And the lovely notes gushed forth in an outpouring of sorrow.

In Eline's honour, Paul made sure he was at home for coffee at half-past midday. In the afternoon Marie and her parents called, followed by Emilie de Woude. Eline received them cordially, and showed herself pleased to see them again. She told them about her meeting with Georges and Lili and what a delightful impression the young couple had made on everyone, including the Des Luynes and the Moulangers and Aunt Eliza's other relatives. And it had been sweet of Georges and Lili to call on her so soon after their arrival; she had greatly appreciated it.

It gave Marie a strange feeling to see Eline again, almost as if she feared that Eline would find her changed, too. But Eline did not appear to notice anything, and chatted on about her travels, the cities she had visited, the people she had met, on and on in a rush of nervous expatiation. It was the same nervousness that came over her nowadays whenever she was in the company of others, no matter how small and intimate the gathering, and it kept her fingers in constant motion, now crumpling her handkerchief into a tight ball, then fidgeting with the fringe of a tablecloth or plucking the tassels on her chair to make them swing to and fro. Her elegant languor of old, her graceful poise, had vanished.

It was close to four o'clock when the door of the salon opened and Betsy appeared, leading Ben by the hand. Eline sprang up and ran towards her in order to hide her own misgivings with a show of excitement. She embraced her sister with effusive tenderness, and fortunately Betsy was able to respond with like enthusiasm. Then Eline bent down to smother Ben with kisses. He was large for a five-year-old, and thick-set, and in his eyes there was the blank, drowsy look of a backward child. Yet he seemed to remember something pleasant, for his lips parted in a happy smile and he threw his chubby arms around Eline's neck to kiss her in return.

Neither sister seemed to have any inclination to exchange confidences, because Betsy left at the same time as the Verstraetens and Emilie, and Eline did not press her to stay. Each of them was conscious of the distance that had grown between them, and that their sisterhood was something they would henceforth honour for the sake of appearances rather than out of love. They had been parted for a year and a half, and now that they were reunited she felt as if they had become strangers to one another, exchanging polite words of interest while their hearts were cool and indifferent.

Eline felt rather tired when the visitors had gone, and the two women settled themselves in the armchairs by the glass doors to the veranda. Between them stood a low velvet-covered tabouret bearing a basket of crochet-work and some books and illustrated magazines. She smiled wanly at the old lady, then leant back and closed her eyes, pleasantly lulled by the restful, cosy atmosphere.

Madame van Raat took up her crochet and began to work her needle with unwonted verve, for she felt a new vigour stirring in her old, stiff limbs, and suddenly it came to her that she might yet have a goal in life. That goal would be to inspire the poor lamb with some vitality and hope, so that she might yet find the kind of happiness that she herself had known in her youth. Her heart swelled with munificent sympathy, and a gleam came into her old eyes as she regarded Eline, wasted and pale, slumped in the armchair beside her.

"Eline," she began softly. "I must speak with you, seriously."

Eline opened her eyes with a questioning look.

"This morning you mentioned that you underwent treatment in Paris. Would you mind if I sent Reijer a note asking him to call one of these days? Not that he is my doctor, but I know you used to see him occasionally."

Eline gave a start.

"Oh no, no doctors for me!" she cried with passion, almost commandingly. "They are such a bore, and none of them can cure me anyway. I suppose it's my cough you are thinking of?"

"Not just your cough. In my opinion you don't look at all well, in fact I think you must be suffering from some illness, although I wouldn't be able to say which one."

Eline laughed out loud.

"My dear little Mama, how you exaggerate! Now that I'm not coughing so much any more I feel perfectly all right, honestly! It is very sweet of you to worry about me so, but truly—"

"So I may not write to Reijer?" said the old lady in a wheedling tone.

Eline, fearing that she had gone too far by laughing so disparagingly, gave one of her most winsome smiles.

"You may do whatever you wish!" she murmured ingratiatingly. "And if it pleases you, I shall swallow whatever they give me and they can tap me and hammer me as much as they like. I don't believe it will do any good, but if that is your wish, it will be my command. So send a note to Reijer, then; far be it from me to stop you from doing anything, anything at all."

Madame van Raat was grateful, and, for the moment, somewhat reassured.

XXIX

FINE, THE SOUR-FACED maid-of-all-work Madame Verstraeten had engaged for Lili, was busy in the dining room at Atjehstraat, spreading a brand-new cloth on the round dining table, Emilie was pattering about the salon lighting the lamps, and Marie hummed as she arranged flowers in various vases. The French doors stood open in the pearl-grey dusk.

"Let there be light!" Emilie exclaimed happily, turning up all three gas jets of the chandelier to full blaze. "They can start counting pennies tomorrow," she muttered softly so that Fine would not hear.

"The china cupboard is locked, ma'am!" Fine burst out accusingly.

"So it is, Fine. Here, take the key. What do you need from the cupboard?"

"The tableware, ma'am; the settings. I need plates and dishes and the soup tureen. And I don't see any cutlery, either. But I must go and see to my chops, or they'll burn to a crisp."

"Very well, Fine. Off you go then, you can leave the table to us."

Fine returned to the kitchen and Emilie opened the china cupboard.

"Marie, do stop fussing with those flowers and lend me a hand with this instead! We'll never finish on time otherwise."

The two women bustled about in playful humour, laying the table for two. Emilie tucked the napkins into the wine glasses as a finishing touch.

"Good heavens no! That won't do at all! That's what they do in restaurants!" remonstrated Marie as she made to remove the napkins.

"Don't you dare!" cried Emilie, clasping her wrists. "Don't you dare touch my creation!"

Several mock skirmishes later, when Emilie had uncorked the wine, Marie declared that it would be a shame not to use the new cut-glass decanters.

"Excellent idea!" responded Emilie. "They're upstairs, in Georges' room. Quick, go and fetch them."

Marie returned bearing a pair of elegant crystal carafes with silver-chained labels, into which the wine was decanted.

"See how stylish they look!" said Marie admiringly. "And now for the flowers—let's have two vases on the table, one for the master and one for the mistress."

"A single vase of flowers is quite enough."

"No, no! Two looks much nicer!"

When after much good-natured argument they were finally satisfied with their elaborate table setting, Emilie announced that she was going upstairs. Marie would join her later; first she wanted to put the finishing touches to her flower arrangements elsewhere in the house.

Upstairs Emilie found all the doors wide open and the gas lamps blazing in every room. The bedroom, with the neatly made-up bed and assortment of toiletries ranged on the washstand and dressing table, was coming alive already, and tomorrow, tomorrow the whole place would be alive with young love! She dithered about the rooms for a final inspection, adjusting the position of a chair here, straightening a lace mat there. Everything was in perfect order, from the bedroom to the small study, where the antique bookcase was now neatly filled with leather-bound tomes, and the boudoir, where the chairs stood around the low table as if they had been vacated just two minutes previously. Marie came running up the stairs and burst into the room, crying: "Emilie, it's nearly ten! We must be off!"

"Our cab hasn't arrived yet."

"For what time did you order it?"

"For ten o'clock. Don't fret, they won't be here until ten-past— I know, because I checked the railway timetable. Oh, how I wish I could be a fly on the wall when they arrive!"

"Shall we go and hide?"

"No, of course not!"

"Are you afraid you'll see something you shouldn't?"

Their eyes met and they exchanged complicit smiles at the thought of Georges and Lili going into raptures upon entering their fairy-tale abode.

"Wait! I have an idea!" Emilie cried out. "Are there any flowers left?"

"Yes, a few with short stems, which I couldn't fit into my vases. Why do you ask?"

"We could use them to make a sort of ring around the night light. Oh, that would look so sweet! Quick, run and get them, will you?" By the time Marie returned with the leftover flowers Emilie had lit the night light, and they set about arranging and rearranging the blooms with mounting agitation, finding it difficult to coax them into a shape to both their satisfaction.

"We must hurry," admonished Emilie. "It's nearly ten o'clock."

A cab drew up outside and a moment later the bell rang.

"That must be our cab! Come along now, Marie, hurry up! Let's turn off the main light, then the night light will look all the more enchanting! Leave the flowers as they are! Do hurry!"

Emilie turned off the gaslight and forcibly drew Marie to the landing. Then, to their alarm, they heard the rattle of wheels on the cobbles outside as a second vehicle drew up, followed by a shouted exchange by the drivers.

"Oh dear! Just as I feared—we're too late!" wailed Emilie.

The doorbell rang, and they stared at each other in horror.

"They'll have seen our cab!" cried Marie. "What are we to do?"

"Tell Fine to wait before answering the door! No, it's too late for that!"

"Then we'll have to hide," said Marie.

"No, no, Marie, that's absurd."

"Well, then I shall go and hide even if you won't!" cried Marie, running into Lili's boudoir. Emilie couldn't think what to do, so she ran after her. They closed the door behind them, turned off the gas and hid behind the curtains. There they cowered, stifling their giggles, like a pair of mischievous schoolgirls, while Emilie did her best not to cause a bulge in the curtain. They heard Fine open the front door. They heard the coachman bringing in the suitcases. And they heard Georges and Lili's voices.

"Hello, Fine! There's a cab waiting outside—do you know who it is for?"

They could not make out Fine's reply, for she spoke in a low, genteel tone.

"Emilie! Marie!" called Georges and Lili from downstairs.

"Shh! Not a word!" hissed Emilie.

"How like Fine to have given us away," Marie whispered plaintively. Their names were called again, and then, straining their ears, they heard Lili's happy voice as she drifted from the salon to the dining room.

"Oh! Georges, come over here! Look what a pretty table setting! And all those lovely flowers!"

After a moment's pause, during which Georges and Lili were presumably in raptures, they heard their names being called yet again.

Emilie and Marie held their breath.

"Wait! I know, let's go and look for them!" they heard Georges cry, followed by the sound of him and his young bride running up the stairs.

"Oh, Marie! They're coming!" whispered Emilie.

Georges and Lili burst into the bedroom, and after that nothing was heard but muffled whisperings, a soft laugh, the sound of a kiss. Marie could contain herself no longer and let out a giggle.

"I heard someone laugh!" exclaimed Lili. "They must be hiding somewhere. Where are you, Marie and Emilie, you can come out now!"

But Emilie and Marie kept as quiet as mice, listening to Georges and Lili's footsteps as they searched the study and the small dressing room before entering the boudoir. Georges lit the gas, and promptly saw the bulge behind the curtains.

"Look! Lili, look over there!"

"We've found them!" rejoiced Lili. "Oh, what madcaps they are!"

The curtains were thrust aside to reveal Emilie and Marie, red-faced and brimming with laughter. Boisterous greetings were exchanged, and everyone spoke at once.

XXX

MADAME VAN RAAT had written to Dr Reijer, and he had responded by paying Eline a visit. They had greeted each other warmly, and had made light conversation on various topics. Reijer had left it at that during that first visit, as it was clear to him from the outset that Eline was reluctant to engage with him in his capacity as physician. Madame van Raat, present at that encounter, was not favourably impressed by the smart young doctor who spoke with such facility about Spain and Paris instead of touching on the delicate matter at hand. When Reijer called again two days later, she gave him a somewhat chilly welcome. However, she soon noticed the penetrating looks he directed at Eline when he was not glancing distractedly about the room, and her opinion of him improved: he evidently wished to spare Eline's feelings. Appreciating his tact and delicacy, she left them alone for a while. When Reijer had gone Eline reported that he had examined her thoroughly, and although the old lady was surprised to hear of the young doctor's powers of persuasion, she was only too happy to place her trust in his expertise. On his third visit he had a word with her in private after seeing Eline. She found him plain-spoken and firm in his opinion; he said outright that he had no wish to mislead her, that he held it incumbent on him to tell her the truth. He had discovered the germs of pulmonary consumption in Eline, the consequence of neglecting a severe cold from which she had mistakenly thought she had recovered. He for his part would naturally exert all his efforts to combat those germs. Beyond that, however, he perceived in Eline's frame of mind the signs of what he termed 'the fate of the Veres'. Her late father had been highly strung, too, and so was her cousin Vincent. In Eline's case it was a soul-disturbing agitation of her nerves, which were tangled like the strings of a broken musical instrument. He would not presume to exaggerate the extent of his knowledge, and believed it would not be in his power to restore full harmony to her mind, no more than he was able to reverse the damage caused by rough handling of a delicate flower. Madame van Raat herself was far better equipped to lavish care on a flower, she was in a position to administer the very remedy Eline was most in need of in her present condition: a restful environment with plenty of warmth and tender care. Come winter, though, a milder climate than that of Holland might be desirable.

He did not mention the quinine drops he had prescribed for Eline.

Madame van Raat's eyes filled with tears as she listened to the doctor's verdict, and she pressed his hand with warm sympathy when he took his leave. But the task he had entrusted to her weighed heavily on her frail shoulders, for all that she dearly wished to devote herself entirely to Eline. She feared that Reijer overestimated the healing power of her love for the poor girl, and suspected that for her to recover her health completely another kind of love would need to enter her life.

Eline, however, seemed assuaged, and began to look forward to Reijer's visits.

The days passed in soothing repose. Eline was reluctant to venture out of the house, despite Reijer's recommendation that she go for a stroll, preferably late in the day in order to improve her chances of sleeping well at night. But she was more partial to sitting out on the veranda with Madame van Raat of an evening, comfortably installed in a wide wicker chair with a cup of tea, looking up at the darkening sky with the stars coming out one by one like daisies in a meadow. She spoke little, because the old lady always chided her ever so gently when she got carried away and couldn't stop talking; she was grateful for such gentle correction, and kept silent for long moments, gazing at the stars. Now and then Paul joined them on the veranda for tea. He would perch on the balustrade and indicate a few constellations with a casual wave of the hand—Ursa Major, Cassiopeia, the Lyre—promising to point them out to her on his celestial globe some time. Then, when he was gone, she would tilt back her head and seek out the star patterns all over again, for it seemed to her that they shone softly into her soul.

It was July; the heat of day had succumbed to the long hours of twilight, and she remembered a similar evening at de Horze, a few years ago. They sat on the veranda for a long while, until Madame van Raat announced that she was tired and wanted to go to bed. Eline too retired to her room. She closed the windows, undressed and lay down. The night light spread a soft glow amid the looming shadows, and the curtains over the French windows shimmered in the light of the rising moon. Eline closed her eyes and tried to sleep.

Instead of sinking into slumber, however, she felt tense and wide awake. Her mind was filled with a jumble of illogical thoughts and associations—one moment she was in Spain, the next in Brussels jesting with Eliza, or she was embracing Betsy, who had come towards her leading Ben by the hand, her ears ringing with a tune she had heard someone sing in Madrid; she was in a garden with a Moorish ruin and citrus groves; she was dining at the Moulangers, riding in a carriage at dusk in the environs of the Des Luynes' chateau, consulting with her doctors in Paris, recoiling from the leering beggar who had given her such a fright in Nice—one scene after another with constantly changing characters and settings.

Her face and neck were beaded with perspiration and she threw off the bed sheet. The slightest sound set her nerves jangling, and suddenly she was struck by the sound of her watch ticking away, which seemed deafeningly loud although she had been wholly unaware of it a moment ago. She heard the wardrobe begin to creak, then what sounded like a fingernail scratching the wallpaper, and suddenly, from outside, came a horrible cry of someone being throttled, and she held her breath in terror—but no, it was merely a cock crowing in the distance.

She turned over with a sigh, opened her eyes and brushed her damp hair from her forehead. Looking up she saw the ghostly reflection of the illuminated curtain in the pier glass. Then her slippers, on the floor at the foot of her bed, caught her attention, and she imagined how horrified she would be if a hand appeared suddenly from under the bedstead to snatch them away. In the looming shadows, which the night light did not dispel, black beasts began to prowl, so she closed her eyes again.

But still sleep escaped her; notwithstanding her shuttered vision, she felt more awake than ever. The creaking of the wardrobe grew louder, as did the scratching on the wallpaper, and any moment now she expected to hear her slippers being snatched away by the hand. She broke out in a sweat when she opened her eyes again and saw her white petticoat draped over a chair—it was a shroud!

Making no movement, not even daring to look away, she stared in wide-eyed horror at the corpse, certain that she had seen it move.

Then, in the deep silence that filled the house, she heard the scrape of a key as it found the lock in the front door, and a wave of relief washed over her. It was Paul, returning home to bed, and she followed his every movement as he crept up the stairs, tiptoed across the landing and let himself into his room. A few moments later she heard him setting down his boots in the corridor and shutting his door. After that, all was still.

The knowledge that Paul was close by brought Eline back to earth, and she saw that the corpse was nothing but her petticoat. She got up, took the night light and crouched down to look under her bed—there was no hand to be seen. But then, as she was setting the lamp on the table, the shadows began to heave again with wild animals on the prowl, and she ran back to bed, shivering with fear as she drew up the clammy, rumpled sheet. Her next thought was of the hand under the bed.

However hard she tried to halt the workings of her brain so that she might sleep, she stayed awake, filled with a dark sense of foreboding. Madame van Raat might die all of a sudden, and then what? She conjured up all manner of confused, illogical scenes illustrating the circumstances of her passing: a protracted illness, like the one Aunt Vere had suffered, complete with bouts of ill temper which Eline would bear with infinite forbearance, or a sudden heart attack, or else a fatal accident, such as a railway disaster. Or something even more dramatic: there was a man, for instance, a man with a grudge bent on revenge, he was dragging the old lady over the floor by her grey hair, stabbing her with a kitchen knife so that she lay dying in a pool of blood, until Eline broke down and sobbed at her fantasised horror.

How grief-stricken she would be, how she would cling to the lifeless body, how she would scream when forcibly dragged away! In a flash, the tragedy was transformed into a gentle scene, filled with love and happiness: a reconciliation between her and Otto, who came towards her, pressed her to his chest and kissed her. With their arms about each other, they wandered off into a Spanish landscape, only for her to push him away abruptly and for him to fall at her feet in a flood of tears. She raised him up again, and they were standing on top of a bridge, swaying sky-high over a thunderous waterfall, deafened by the noise; then he enfolded her in his arms, and together, exhausted from their grief and the roaring in their ears, they jumped into the deep.

Outside, the cock crowed again, and Eline sat up with a jolt. Had she been asleep, had she been dreaming? How could that be? She could have sworn that she had not slept a wink. Panting and clammy with perspiration, she got out of bed. Her throat was parched, and after moistening her face with a wet towel she gulped down a glass of water, then another and another in rapid succession. She shivered, despite the warm stuffiness of the room, and donned a grey woollen peignoir. Then she lifted the edge of the window curtain and looked outside, where the night was beginning to pale. It was half-past three; the cock crowed yet again, and this time its cry was answered by several others.

Her fevered imagination came to rest in the bleak onset of dawn, and she turned away from the window. The sight of her rumpled bed, on which she had spent so many hours tossing and turning, filled her with distaste, so she lay down on the Persian couch instead. From there she could just see the leafy crowns of the chestnut trees outside, and she focused her attention on the ruffled foliage.

Inside, the night light sputtered, flickered, then went out, leaving the wick smoking.

Eline dropped off to asleep, exhausted in mind and body, as the gathering light of day played on her sallow, waxen features.

Reijer was not due to call on her that morning, but Eline sent him an urgent summons and he came forthwith. She almost begged him to give her something to make her sleep, saying that she would surely go mad if the horrendous experience of the past sleepless nights repeated itself. Reijer replied that he could of course prescribe a sleep-inducing medicine, but she would be far better off trying to regain a normal sleep pattern without artificial means. She should take exercise, go for walks. Eline sighed and shrugged her shoulders impatiently. She had barely had the strength to get out of bed this morning, and even now she could only drag herself with difficulty from one chair to the next! Take exercise—in this warm weather? She was simply not up to it, so she stayed at home, only feeling slightly revived in the fresh air of evening, in her large wicker chair on the veranda. Madame van Raat eyed her with concern.

Come the evening, Paul joined them again for tea, as was becoming his habit. Regarding Eline from his perch on the balustrade he was reminded of the dance party for Lili's wedding, when he had conceived the idea of setting his cap at Eline, just for the sport of it. Although she was not as fresh-faced as she used to be, and much thinner, she made on him an impression of ethereal elegance; indeed, he found her rather beautiful with her dark, sunken eyes and her sad little mouth. However, he dismissed all thought of engaging her attention with honeyed tones and blandishments, for he could see that her spirit was broken. He recalled how dazzling she used to be, how coquettish and vivacious, with laughter pearling from her lips, and the memory filled him with a deep sense of pity for her. She had said her life was in ruins, and he thought that might well be the case.

"How are you feeling, Eline? Better than this afternoon?" he asked, and in his voice there was something, a certain warmth, that reminded her of Henk.

She nodded faintly, and he pointed to the stars that were beginning to twinkle in the dusk, asking whether she would like to see his celestial globe; this was as good an occasion as any, especially since he had brought it down from the attic that very morning. She was in no mind for astronomy, but did not wish to disappoint him, so off he went to fetch the globe. He placed himself beside her, and she sat up straight in readiness for instruction. Madame van Raat looked on as Paul, having availed himself of her crochet needle, used it to point out the constellations, after which Eline obligingly tried to identify the corresponding figures in the sky, smiling as she raised her finger to trace imaginary lines from one star to the next.

Paul's mother noted the sweetness of Eline's smile, and was likewise impressed by her son's affable tone, in which there was not a trace of the cynicism and breezy condescension he so often affected. A vague sense of optimism came over her: to be sure, time was when she would have liked to see Eline wedded to her son Henk, but she could not help thinking that a measure of tenderness had crept into Eline's exchanges with Paul of late. Even now she was responding with some animation while Paul pursued his elementary lesson in astronomy, circumstantially explaining that since she was looking down at the stars on the astronomy globe whereas she looked up at them in the sky, she should try and imagine herself at the centre of the globe.

That evening Paul stayed at home until the ladies made to retire at eleven. When he took his leave, his mother clasped his hand and kissed him on the forehead, instead of nodding a perfunctory goodbye as she usually did.

XXXI

FRÉDÉRIQUE felt very annoyed with herself. She had discovered that Paul had been lending Etienne money again, and when she found herself alone with him she had given him a piece of her mind. Oh, why couldn't she resist meddling in their affairs? What they did was none of her business, really. With Etienne it was different: he was still a boy, and as his older sister she had every right to tell him off when he behaved badly. Paul, on the other hand, must be getting sick and tired of her, what with her lecturing him and going off into a huff whenever she took exception to his behaviour. Because that was what she had done, yet again. Why had she not simply asked him not to lend Etienne any money in future, why complicate matters by giving him the cold shoulder first? There was no need for any of that!

She sat with her mother and Mathilda in the conservatory after lunch, watching Ernestine and Jo busy themselves in the garden with the long rubber watering hose. They took aim with the brass nozzle, making a jetting fan of water descend on the roses and resedas, the verbenas and heliotropes, geraniums and begonias, making the flower heads bounce in the spray and the lawn glisten with droplets.

Madeleine and Nico pranced about with Hector on the gravel path beyond, shrieking and dashing away whenever the hose wavered in their direction.

"Careful now, Tina! Don't let the children get wet! And don't be too rough watering the flowers! Gently does it!" cautioned Mathilda.

Yes, Paul must find her intolerable, mused Frédérique, putting her book down to watch the youngsters' antics. It was ridiculous of her to lecture him at all, but that time when she had criticised him for being lazy and arrogant and having the wrong kind of friends had been even more ridiculous. What made it worse was that there had been a ball the very next day, during which she

384

had been completely won over by his irrepressible sense of fun. She did so enjoy some gaiety, she loved dancing, and she was glad that he had asked her to dance, but afterwards, when it was all over, she had felt very dissatisfied with herself. Not that she could think of anything she had done wrong, but still.

"Madeleine, do stop teasing Hector! You'll get bitten if you're not careful," Mathilda cried out.

Frédérique found it hard to concentrate her thoughts with the spray pattering on the broad rhubarb leaves, the children whooping with excitement and Hector's constant yapping, but she kept wondering what she had done to make herself feel so dissatisfied.

She did have a vague idea, but shied away from thinking it through. Paul's flirtatious behaviour with all those girls had stung her; he danced attendance on every one of them, and he didn't mean a word of what he said. Were they taken in by his blandishments? Was it just innocent fun, or was there a touch of malice there? But he was not a bounder, nor did she even think him frivolous, really; he was just getting a bit too big for his boots because he was handsome and had money. His heart was in the right place, though; he wouldn't hurt a fly. Besides, what concern was it of hers? What did she care if he flirted with Ange and Léonie, not to mention that goose of a Françoise! Why did she mind any more about that than about the behaviour of any other young man in her social circle? Because he was a friend of the family? Because he was Marie and Lili's cousin? Surely not.

It irritated her that she did not dare confront the stirrings of her soul with the same honesty as when she looked in the mirror.

Still, she couldn't help noticing that he was different with her than with the other girls, in both manner and tone, and she was flattered by this. Clearly he had more respect for her. Or was it just that he knew she wouldn't be impressed by his cajolery? Could he be a little in awe of her, just because she gave him a piece of her mind from time to time? Oh, she would hate him to be in awe of her! If that were true she would never dare to have another tête-à-tête with him; she would, if the worst came to the worst, have to be like all the other girls and play the coquette.

But no, she could never do that! Besides, what difference did it make if Paul was in awe of her?

All those questions went round and round in her head, as though trapped in a labyrinth without issue. Deep down, however, she did have an inkling of where the exit might be, but was not ready to admit it to herself.

"Freddie, would you be so kind as to help me pack?" asked Mathilda. "Then I'll start by putting the children to bed."

Freddie promised to give assistance. The youngsters rolled up the garden hose with much ado, after which Mathilda joined forces with Miss Frantzen to shoo the boisterous foursome upstairs. In the morning the whole party would be leaving for de Horze. That they should spend the summer months in the country had been Theodore van Erlevoort's idea; life was less expensive on the estate, and it was becoming increasingly difficult for his mother to keep up the standards expected of her in the big house on the Voorhout. She had even considered moving permanently to de Horze, but had come to the conclusion that leaving her beloved home in The Hague would be too great a sacrifice. As it was, she would try to extend her stay at de Horze, possibly until November, and she looked forward to a happy sojourn in the countryside in the bosom of Theodore's dear little family.

Mathilda, too, was glad to go to de Horze, and had agreed to take Tina and Jo out of school a few months before the summer holidays: she would see to their lessons herself, as she had done in the old days, and was secretly delighted at the prospect. Freddie felt less enthusiastic about leaving The Hague, and her own puzzlement at this increased her dissatisfaction. On the surface, however, she was the same as ever, cheerful and on friendly terms with everyone in the house, except with Etienne, whom she had treated rather coldly earlier that day, not only because of that business about borrowing money from Paul but also because he kept grumbling about them all going away. He said he was thinking of taking a room somewhere in the interim, in Leiden or The Hague; he had not yet decided which.

Otto had been a regular visitor at de Horze of late. He had spoken at length with Theodore, as he was thinking of taking a position in the provinces and leaving The Hague for good.

In fact he already had something in his sights: thanks to an old friend of his father's, he had a good chance of being appointed steward of the royal estates in Gelderland.

Although Madame van Erlevoort warned him repeatedly about the dangers of becoming a recluse, he had grown too disaffected with The Hague to find any distraction there. He was so despondent nowadays, desiring nothing but to be left alone in his private quarters, where he would not bother anyone with his gloomy presence. To her he seemed cowed and broken, languishing under his irredeemable loss. Not that he ever complained, nor did he stoop to the indignities of impatience or churlishness; in that respect he resembled Mathilda.

Madame van Erlevoort had dozed off in the stillness that prevailed now that the children were in bed. Frédérique, too, left the room, just as Etienne came running down the stairs.

"Where are you off to?" he asked.

"I said I would help Mathilda with her packing," she replied.

"Oh, but it's me you should be helping!" he exclaimed. "Mathilda already has the nursemaid to help her, and I can't find the patience to fold up all my clothes properly."

"Have you rented a room then? Here or in Leiden?"

"To tell you the truth, I haven't rented a room. I am going to de Horze with the rest of you. I shall be able to study for my finals there, in peace and quiet. It's no use being in Leiden during the holidays anyway, and if I stay here I shan't get anything done. And I must, you see," he said, his voice dropping to a whisper. "I can't very well hang around here, can I? What with Mama saying we can't make ends meet and Theodore telling us we ought to economise."

She looked at him fixedly as he stood before her in doubtful expectation.

"All right then," she said. "I'll give you a hand."

"Come and take a look in my room then, will you?" he asked brightly, relieved at her amenable tone.

They went upstairs to his room. His suitcase was wide open, as was the wardrobe.

"I'll throw all the stuff I want to take on my bed, shall I, then you can put it in the suitcase."

"Very well."

"And you're not angry with me any more, on account of that loan?" he said in the wheedling voice of a spoilt child.

"No, but you must pay Paul back when you see him tonight. I can help you out if you like, because I've got some extra money."

"You don't have anything against Paul, do you?"

"Oh no, not at all!" she said. "Still, it's better not to be in debt."

"But Freddie! He's my best friend! I'm not afraid of owing him a little money."

"Indeed. He's very kind, but the sensible thing to do is to pay him back, don't you agree?"

He agreed. Yet again she felt annoyed with herself. There she was, meddling in other people's affairs again! They would both start hating her if she wasn't careful. But Etienne did not hate her at all, on the contrary, he adored her for doing his packing for him.

"There: shirts, collars, socks. Well, you can find the rest for yourself. I'll go and look for Paul—at least, if you will advance me the money."

She was prepared for this, and reached into her pocket to hand him the required sum.

"Thank you. We are leaving early in the morning, I gather. Oh yes, would you tell Willem to wake me up in good time? Bye for now."

He made to leave, but she took his head in her hands and kissed him.

"I'm really glad you're coming to de Horze with us. Mama will be thrilled. And so will Theodore, especially when he hears of your studious intentions," she concluded sweetly.

He was delighted that they had made up, and a moment later she heard him whistling as he ran down the stairs.

The following evening Theodore van Erlevoort and Klaas the coachman drove to the railway station at Elzen to collect the party of visitors, and at about nine o'clock the old covered wagon rumbled up the oak-lined drive to de Horze. Marianne, who had returned from her final term at boarding school, came running to meet them, with Edmée and the two van Stralenburg toddlers close at her heels. The little ones frolicked like young puppies, trying to keep up with the wagon amid shrieks of "Hello, Gran! Hello, Aunt Tilly! Hello, Aunt Freddie! Hello, Uncle Etienne!" in complete disregard of Marianne's frantic efforts to restrain them.

Between the pillars of the veranda stood Truus beside Suzanne and her husband, Arnold van Stralenburg. After a grand, rattling sweep around the pond, the wagon drew up by the entrance to disgorge its passengers on all sides. For a few moments pandemonium reigned in the mêlée of happy reunion, with the children hugging and kissing everyone in sight and Theodore's large hunting hounds barking and bumping the littlest ones off their feet.

Madame van Erlevoort was the last to alight, and was promptly stormed by her high-spirited grandchildren, who squeezed past the long legs of their uncle from Zwolle to fling their short arms about her.

Truus, Mathilda and Suzanne allowed the children to play for a while, but before long Miss Frantzen and the two other nursemaids came to fetch them. They were served sandwiches and then unceremoniously bundled off to bed. Mathilda went after them to make sure they were all well settled.

They had not seen each other all winter, and the air was filled with questions to catch up on everybody's news. Madame van Erlevoort glanced around, as though missing someone.

"Where is Hetty? And where are the boys?" she asked eagerly.

"Still at school, Mama dear; the holidays haven't started yet," replied Truus, smiling at her mother-in-law's disappointment. "Hetty is doing very well in Bonn; she writes long letters home. Cor was in Buenos Aires recently, with his ship."

"And Miss Voermans has left, hasn't she?"

"Yes she has; the dear old soul took her leave with tears in her eyes. But she was no longer needed, and we couldn't afford to keep her on for old time's sake, more's the pity. Theodore is having trouble enough with his tenants as it is."

Overhearing this, Theodore assured them that he had no reason to complain, especially now that his dear kinfolk had arrived. "Why, Freddie! You look remarkably well! Prettier by the year! Look, Truus, what a fine-looking young lady she is! Wouldn't you love to have a sister like that?"

He placed his hands on her waist, displaying her to his wife, who responded with a warm smile.

"And how is your heart faring? All well I hope?" he whispered in her ear. "Anyone making it beat faster yet—pitter-patter, pitter-patter?"

Freddie's laugh was as clear as a bell.

"Oh no, no one yet! Don't fret, it won't happen for a while."

"So you send all your suitors packing, do you?"

"Oh yes, I keep them at a distance. A long distance!" she chuckled. "I haven't found anyone I care for, no one at all."

"Ooh, little Miss Sharp!" he retorted. "You'll frighten them all away if you're not careful."

She laughed more merrily than ever. How lovely she was when she laughed! She reminded him of the goddess Diana, a young, mocking Diana, lithe and strong with her proud head thrown back defiantly as she fixed him with her shining, challenging eyes. Despite her playful manner there was in her beauty a sense of truth and sincerity, a certain dignity telling him that she was not being coquettish, but that she possessed a sense of pride.

"Ah, so that's how you feel!" he continued. "Well, I can't say I'm sorry. It just goes to show that you have a sense of breeding."

And he looked at her once more, gratified to see in her a true van Erlevoort.

"And what do you think of Etienne?" gushed Madame. "He has come to study for his exams!"

"It is indeed a most pleasant surprise!" said Theodore, bowing deeply.

Frédérique began to laugh again.

"Oh, he's such a card!" she said to van Stralenburg. "Just imagine, Arnold, he very nearly forgot to take his study material! He turned up with a great stack of books at the very last minute, so there was some legal treatise or history book tucked away in almost every one of our suitcases!"

"You can't expect me to think of everything!" said Etienne defensively.

"No, of course not! You have so much on your mind already, don't you?" quipped Arnold, narrowing his eyes. "All that correspondence to see to, all those conferences and consultations!"

He was in the habit of teasing his young brother-in-law at every opportunity, and Etienne was quick to rise to the bait, which often resulted in volleys of comic repartee followed by mock sparring matches.

"Now, Arnold, don't you start squabbling with Etienne!" cried Suzanne. "Tell them to stop it, Mama, or they'll be at each other's throats again!"

"Uncle Arnold and Etienne are always at each other's throats!" tittered Marianne.

Arnold, however, declared that the sheer joy of this family reunion had completely undermined his combative spirit, and with a theatrical flourish he spread his long arms to welcome Etienne. Locked in their embrace, they swayed from side to side a long moment until, without warning and utterly straight-faced, Etienne forcibly pushed Arnold's head down and vaulted over his stooping frame. As though by design, without a word or the slightest hesitation, Arnold proceeded to vault over Etienne and vice versa, in a succession of leapfrogs provoking hilarity all around.

"When they're not at each other's throats they're just like clowns!" shrieked Marianne. "Just like clowns!"

Frédérique and Marianne, who called each other by their first names despite being aunt and niece, shared a vast, high-ceilinged room, in which stood a monumental, old-fashioned oak bedstead with a dark-brown canopy. The doors were likewise made of oak, as was the wainscoting; the ceiling was decorated with a large medallion within which disporting nymphs and cupids could still be faintly discerned.

"I am so glad we're sharing a room," said Marianne as they were getting ready for bed. "Oh, I couldn't bear to sleep here alone! I'd be terrified, wouldn't you?"

"I don't expect so; I'm not that easily frightened," replied Freddie.

"I think this room is awfully romantic, everything looks so ancient," said Marianne. "It's easy to imagine yourself living in the Middle Ages, with all this dark panelling on the walls and the coats of arms over the doors."

Frédérique donned her nightgown and crawled into the four-poster bed.

"It's big enough to drown in!" she laughed. "I've never slept here before."

Marianne, still dithering about in her bare feet, lifted the window curtain a moment, letting a shaft of moonlight into the room.

"Look, Freddie, how eerie! Don't I look like a ghost in this light?"

"Oh, Marianne, stop fussing, will you? Why don't you come to bed, then we can have a nice gossip."

Marianne dropped the curtain, undressed hurriedly and nestled herself beside Freddie.

"Good gracious! This bed is gigantic! Oh, I'd die if I had to sleep in it by myself. Don't you think it's scary? Not even a little?"

"Of course not. It's your imagination, that's all."

"Yes, I'm always imagining things, such as seeing ghosts, or being in a haunted house, or other things like meeting a knight in shining armour. But you're different, all cool and collected, so I don't suppose you dream up all sorts of stories for yourself the way I do."

"Stories? No, no. What sort of stories?"

"Oh, entire novels sometimes. Then I imagine that I am a noble damsel, and that the boys are my grooms and the little ones my pages. And then I fall in love with a knight, who wants me to elope with him because my father's so cruel and bloodthirsty, and won't have him for a son-in-law."

"What a flattering portrait of your papa!" giggled Frédérique. "And what about your knight—is he dark or fair?"

"That depends on my mood. I say, Freddie, have you ever been in love?"

"Of course not."

"Truly not? I've fallen in love a dozen times already, but it never lasts very long with me, just three or four weeks at the most. In Bonn, for instance, I had a drawing master whom I adored. And then there was a young man—fair hair and blue eyes, he had—who used to bring me bon-bons on the sly."

An elaborate enumeration of Marianne's beaus followed.

"But tell me, Marianne, how old are you now? Seventeen? Eighteen?"

"I'm already eighteen!"

"Goodness me!" laughed Frédérique. "And your head is still full of ghosts and drawing masters! You're as bad as Etienne, he never seems to grow up either."

Marianne took offence at this and began to shake Freddie, whose laughter only increased.

"And what about you? You've never even been in love! How grown-up is that?"

"It's time we went to sleep, Marianne. I wish you sweet dreams of a certain blue-eyed someone, then!" laughed Freddie.

Marianne soon drifted into sleep, with her head touching Freddie's shoulder.

Freddie lay awake for a long time; she had to smile at how childish Marianne seemed, despite being all of eighteen years old! She herself was twenty-three—quite a difference with Marianne there—and all that romantic fantasising about knights in armour and noble damsels was a thing of the past as far as she was concerned. But what kind of thoughts did she have nowadays? She often thought badly of herself, it was true—but who else did she think about? There was one person she thought about rather often, someone she wished were different in some ways, although in which ways she was not sure. So why did she think about him at all, if he was not as she would have liked him to be?

"It's so peculiar, so very peculiar," she murmured to herself. "Why I keep thinking of him is beyond me. It isn't as if I want to think of him, I just can't get him out of my mind."

She was tempted to drift off into some pleasant daydream, but checked herself, sensing the stirrings of pride in her heart. She had self-worth, Theodore had said; she had breeding! The person she kept thinking of did not deserve her wholehearted attention. He was—she could see it quite clearly now—unserious, and besides, he was egotistic, the sort of person who made himself popular with everyone.

Theodore's words had struck a chord, for there in her character a trait that she had barely been conscious of before: a sense of pride, not merely pride in her high birth and her surname, but an innate pride inherited from noble forebears, which resonated in every nerve of her being. Yes indeed, she was proud, but that did not mean to say that she felt satisfied with herself. On the contrary! Oh, on the contrary!

She lay awake for hours, staring at the faded nymphs and cupids on the ceiling with Marianne beside her, fast asleep, breathing softly and regularly like a child. Countless times she asked herself the unanswerable question: why did she keep thinking of Paul?

The following morning saw the arrival of Otto, who was to spend a week at de Horze before taking up his new position of steward to the royal estates. His appointment was in the environs of Elzen, and he would therefore be living fairly close by, a consoling thought to Madame van Erlevoort, who felt that the proximity of the happy household of de Horze might assist him in casting off his sorrows.

Theodore was out for the day, taking Arnold van Stralenburg on a tour of the grounds, and Truus was busy in the house while the children played in the park and the gym room under the supervision of the nursemaids. Otto joined the ladies—Madame van Erlevoort, Mathilda, Suzanne, Frédérique and Marianne—on one of the spacious, creepered verandas.

"How is Etienne getting on?" he asked.

Madame van Erlevoort beamed.

"He got up early," said Freddie. "He made a tremendous to-do rearranging the furniture in his room when he arrived, to make himself a proper study, and he's putting it to good use, as you see."

Marianne stood up.

"Where are you off to, Marianne?" Suzanne wanted to know.

"I am going to my favourite little spot at the back of the park!" she said. "Oh, Freddie, it's so lovely there, full of lilies of the valley. Why don't you come with me? Then I can tell you all about the book I'm reading: *Ein Gebet*, by Carmen Sylva—oh, it's just wonderful!"

Marianne left with Frédérique in tow, after which Otto and Suzanne set out for a stroll together. They had not seen each other for a long time, as Otto had gone to stay with his relatives in London the previous summer instead of coming to de Horze. Suzanne found him altered: he look older, and his face resembled a mask of quiet mourning, in which she detected a trace of bitterness.

She took his arm, and wordlessly they wandered down the broad oak-lined avenue, shaded from the baking July sunshine by the lush foliage. Giant ferns spread their fans along the ditches all ashimmer with metallic hues, delicate spider webs festooned the bushes like filaments of silvery glass, and now and then, through a break in the trees, they glimpsed a weather-beaten statue on a pedestal, a Flora or Pomona velvety with moss. The sweet-smelling wild honeysuckle ran riot along the verges, flinging its tangled shoots in every direction, while the blossoming cow parsley raised its flat heads of white froth. Otto and Suzanne proceeded at a leisurely pace. Ahead of them, in the distance, they saw two small figures in light-coloured clothes plunging into the greenery: Frédérique and Marianne, bound for the lilies of the valley. At their back they heard peals of laughter from the children frolicking on a heap of sand in the shade of the big house.

"How beautiful it is here!" Suzanne said at length. "I am so glad Theodore is letting nature have its way in the park, even if it's only for the sake of economy. It looks like a jungle! I can remember when I was little Papa had a whole regiment of groundsmen, and the park always looked as tidy as a garden, with gazebos and vases and statues. And now it's all tumbling down—some of the statues are broken, too. Oh, do you remember that time when you climbed on top of that nymph over there? You broke her arm, remember?"

"So I did," said Otto.

"Papa was furious! You were sent to your room and put on bread and water for three whole days, remember?"

"Yes I do," said Otto, smiling.

"And you refused to beg Papa's pardon for answering back when he told you off, and then Mama insisted you should anyway. Remember?"

He squeezed her arm gently in response, moved almost to tears. The remembrance of that summer in his boyhood evoked a whole train of associations with another summer, during which he had strolled in this very park not with Suzanne, but with …

"I say, Otto!" Suzanne said abruptly. "Won't you be homesick for The Hague, living all by yourself in Elzen?"

"Oh no!" he exclaimed with feeling. "Not at all! I have no desire to be in The Hague."

She glanced at him, startled by his emotion.

"Life in the country appeals to me, and I look forward to my new office," he added.

"Is there any particular reason you want to leave The Hague?" she asked softly.

"A particular reason? No, none at all."

He seated himself on a park bench, but she remained standing, absently plucking sprays of blossom from the overhanging honeysuckle while she tried to find the words to continue.

"Oh, Otto, it's not on account of—on account of?—" she faltered.

He looked straight ahead a moment, then replied in a slow, dull voice.

"My dear Suzanne, what are you thinking? That I want to leave The Hague because of Eline?"

"Yes," she said timidly. She sat down beside him and began to arrange the flowers into a posy.

"My dear Sis," he resumed, sounding as if he were reciting a rehearsed response, "whatever gave you that idea? Did you really think a fellow would spend the rest of his life mourning a girl who goes back on her word? Of course I was sorry at first, and I was sad, too. But it's all over now, I assure you. Over and done with … One stops seeing the other person, gradually one stops thinking about them, and in due course one forgets. A broken heart never killed anyone in real life, and besides, a man's heart does not break as easily as you might think: men have work to do, business to attend to, and life simply goes on, leaving them little time to ponder their losses, even if they wished to. It is different with women, I believe; they give in to their feelings more readily, don't they?"

He stood up, as in a dream, and she followed him.

"Yes, I suppose they do," she said, with little conviction.

"One forgets," he continued in the same dull tone, "and so it can easily happen, after a time, that one meets someone else, someone one can love and who will make one happy. It happens all the time. That's life."

"Yes, I suppose it is," she said, and he was reminded of something Eline had said in her letter: "then you will find a girl who is worthy of you, and who will make you happy."

"So don't you go thinking I am pining with romantic love!" he concluded, with a strained smile. "I'm not that far gone, you know."

She fell silent, saddened by his response. He was like Mathilda, too proud to share his grief with anyone, preferring to maintain a certain stoic, outward composure. She did not let him notice that she was undeceived by his pose, and they walked on for a while, saying little. All at once they caught the sound of animated chatter some way off. It was Marianne, ensconced among the lilies of the valley, relating the story of *Ein Gebet* to Frédérique.

"It's a bit melodramatic, but so lovely, so moving! You see, Raoul is doing penance for his mother, who was a tremendous sinner, apparently, although I cannot imagine she could have done anything really wicked. He enters the priesthood and chastises himself. I didn't sleep a wink after I'd read the bit about him blessing the marriage of Rassillo and Editha. Editha is ever so soft-hearted and sweet, and Raoul has always loved her.

397

Berthalda, though, is incredibly passionate, oh, exaggeratedly so! Anyway, as I was telling you, Berthalda put poison on the wafer, and so, when Raoul gives Editha the wafer she collapses, and instead of repeating the marriage vows, she cries out 'Raoul!' and dies. Sad, isn't it? I couldn't stop crying! Berthalda does penance too; she enters a convent, a subterranean one where the sun never shines, and Raoul's hair turns white overnight."

Otto and Suzanne, who had been hiding behind some trees to eavesdrop, went on their way again.

"Look at my hair, Suzanne!" said Otto with the same strained smile: "It didn't turn white overnight! I am not a bit like Raoul, you see!"

She said nothing, trying to smile as she clung to his arm, swinging her honeysuckle posy with her free hand, and to end the silence she hummed a tune.

At de Horze life continued at a steady, unhurried pace. Otto had left for Elzen, and Etienne was extraordinarily diligent, taking off straight after breakfast to study in his room upstairs and disappearing again after lunch for more work. In the evening he joined the rest of the company for a little entertainment, such as leapfrogging over van Stralenburg and throwing mock punches at him, but when everybody retired he went back to his desk to put in a few more hours of study. He had a veritable craze for his books, in Madame van Erlevoort's opinion, and seemed not to be deterred by any anxious looks or complaints about his pallor from her or anyone else.

One day Etienne received a letter from Paul, telling him of his plan to visit de Horze in the near future, after which he would travel on to Germany or Italy for an extended tour. Theodore responded somewhat scoffingly to this news, fearing that Paul would lure Etienne away from his books and even try to persuade him to accompany him on his travels. Madame van Erlevoort, however, was very pleased, for she thought Paul's presence would do Etienne a world of good—the boy was working far too hard, all that zealous studying was bound to make him ill.

Frédérique had given a radiant smile when she heard of Paul's intended visit, but had said nothing. She wore the same radiant smile when she studied her rosy reflection in the glass on the morning of his arrival. With her brown eyes sparkling like dark gems, her thick, chestnut hair curling silkily about her milk-white neck, she could not help thinking how pretty she looked in her simple dress of pink cotton, lithe and strong, smiling in that regal, munificent, way. Yes indeed, she was quite exhilarated!

Was it because of the sun lighting up her eyes and the peachy glow on her cheeks? Or was it because the person she could not get out of her mind was about to arrive? As she surveyed her appearance, lost in conjecture, she forgot her sense of pride, she forgot all about wanting Paul to be different in certain ways; she found herself being swept away on a wave of emotion that she was powerless to resist, and she was thrilled by her own weakness before the sublime effervescence invading her soul.

He arrived, and when she shook his hand she had the sensation that she had never seen him before. How tall he was, and how handsome, with his cheerful blue-grey eyes, his bushy moustache and his white teeth! How infectious his laughter, hearty and full, and so disarming! She returned his laugh with her own, uttered some pleasantries, and was struck by his manner towards her: it was not a bit like the way he laughed and joked with Françoise, Ange, or Léonie, or with any of the other girls for that matter. There was a gentle intimacy in his gaze, as there was in his tone of voice, from which every trace of cynicism or forwardness had vanished.

Was it the country air that made him look so attractive, so fresh-faced and sincere? Theodore at any rate was pleased to see Paul in such good form, and promptly pressed him to stay with them for a few days, on condition that he should not distract Etienne too much from his books. Paul gave his solemn promise and accepted the invitation with gratitude. When they were all gathered together on the veranda to enjoy a light May wine, Frédérique could not help noticing how he held everyone's attention. No, he wasn't half as vain and frivolous as she had thought, and she—well, she found him very engaging, to say the least.

It was a clear, starry evening, and the boat on the lake beckoned. Paul and Arnold van Stralenburg took the oars, Marianne and Etienne teased one another, and Freddie, holding the tiller, hummed a song which carried softly over the water in the violet dusk. Suddenly Paul broke in with a snatch of the duet he used to sing with Eline.

Ah! Viens, la nuit est belle!
Viens, le ciel est d'azur!

Freddie was delighted to hear him sing. The scene was so simple and so delightfully familiar: Paul's song, the lake they were drifting on, the illuminated veranda with Mama, Mathilda, Suzanne and Theodore sitting together, the looming dark-green mass of the trees and the twinkling stars above. How extraordinary that she had never realised how poetic it all was! Paul concluded his barcarole with a soft, drawn-out high C in falsetto, and she fancied she heard nightingales in the jasmine-scented air, like a silvery vibration in her heart.

How would he comport himself with Marianne, she wondered. Marianne had a pretty face with soulful eyes, and a pert, slightly coquettish demeanour. But he showed no inclination to flirt with her, by which Frédérique was both surprised and gratified.

Since that first day, however, she had recovered herself. She had been too forgiving, she believed; she had seen him the way she wished to see him—which might even have been the way he temporarily happened to be by some extraordinary coincidence. But had she then forgotten what he had been like in The Hague, dancing attendance on all those girls, inconsiderate to his mother, hanging around with those so-called friends of his who were nothing but spongers? By what stroke of magic could he have ceased to be frivolous and vain, egotistic and weak?

Whatever the case, now that he was away from all the girls, away from his mother and from his friends, he made a decidedly better impression. She vowed not to voice any criticism she might have, in case he took a permanent dislike to her. Nor would it be hard to keep her vow, for Paul was making things remarkably easy: for the moment he gave no cause for criticism of any kind.

It had rained for several days, and the morning was clear, with a well-rinsed brightness to the sky. Klaas had saddled the two riding horses, one of which was a sorrel; the other, fitted with a side saddle, had a blaze down its forehead. Paul was checking the horses' tackles when Freddie emerged from the veranda with the train of her riding costume over her arm and a small top hat with a white veil on her head. She buttoned her gloves and smiled.

"All set!" said Paul, turning to face her.

He gave Freddie a leg up to her blazed horse; once seated, she leant forward to pat its gleaming neck. Paul mounted the sorrel and together they ambled off under the watchful eye of Klaas, who thought them a fine-looking pair, both of them healthy and strong, bright-eyed and rosy-cheeked. He noted that Freddie sat ramrod-straight on her side saddle, and deemed her companion to be a full-bodied young fellow. He approved of full-bodied men.

Paul and Freddie rode to the front of the big house, chatting happily.

"Hullo there! Where are you off to?" a voice called from above.

Looking up, they saw Etienne leaning out of his upstairs window, looking rather unkempt in his shirtsleeves and with tousled hair, which made Freddie laugh.

"Well, you two! Where are you off to?" demanded Etienne, with a hint of envy in his tone.

"We haven't decided yet!"

"Why isn't Marianne with you?"

"Marianne said she was quite happy reading Carmen Sylva's *Ein Gebet* all over again! Don't you trust us?"

"Well, yes, but did you have to pass under my window? Couldn't you have taken another route?"

"You're the last person we were thinking of!" Paul cried mercilessly.

"I'm not surprised!" spluttered Etienne. "You think of no one but yourselves, going off for a nice ride while I'm stuck indoors with my books. Well, bad luck to both of you, you heartless creatures!"

"*Merci bien*, my charitable brother!" exclaimed Freddie, waving her whip in his direction. "Here's hoping you'll be more favourably disposed when we return. *Au revoir*!"

"Enjoy your books! *Au revoir*!" rejoined Paul, and with that they rode off at a leisurely pace, down the long oak-lined avenue. Reaching the country lane, where the blazing sunshine swathed the oats and barley on either side with gold, they urged their horses to a canter.

"Why don't we go to the White Hollow? We could take the long way round and ride through the pine wood," suggested Freddie.

"Yes, let's do that," said Paul.

They reined in their horses as they approached the farmstead, which stood in the shade of some chestnut trees. The farmer's dogs, recognising them, sprang up and ran to the ends of their chains, barking enthusiastically, at which the farmer's wife appeared at the door to wave. Then they entered the wood beyond, relieved to exchange the scorching sun for cooling, deep-green shade, where the horses' hooves sounded muffled on the carpet of pine needles.

It was the first time since Paul's arrival at de Horze that Freddie found herself alone with him, and she felt strangely nervous, as if this was the first time ever, yet she had often gone riding with him in previous summers, and there had also been plenty of occasions in the past when they had been alone together, talking quite confidentially. So why did she barely dare to look at him, if she were afraid of what his appearance might reveal?

She mustered her courage and looked him in the eye as he chatted on. She would not allow herself to be swayed by sentimental emotions; she would show him that she was the same girl she had always been, someone who had no qualms about speaking her mind. She would not say anything against him if she could help it, but neither would she flinch from his blue-grey gaze—that would be too much!

A challenging glint came into her eyes at that thought, but what was there to challenge? He was being neither sarcastic nor flippant, nor was he being pompous, indeed he was conversing with marked indulgence about all sorts of people she had known him to disparage on previous occasions.

"Take Georges and Lili," he said, and she was astonished by the genial tone of his voice as he uttered those two names. "It's so amusing to see them together! They're so wrapped up in each other that they're quite blind to what goes on in the world. They think everything revolves around them! And it's not that they are arrogant, they are just naive! Try telling them they aren't the only two people in the world to be madly in love with each other and they'll shake their heads in disbelief. They're Adam and Eve all over again—everything starts from them."

Frédérique smiled, curiously moved by his words.

"I think they are quite delightful together," continued Paul, "but you must admit that they're rather superficial souls, when it comes down to it. Neither of them has much depth, really. Yes, Georges is a good, sensible young man, but apart from that—"

"Good and sensible; well, that's a start anyway!" she said musingly.

"Yes it is, but I don't believe Georges has ever found himself confronted by any kind of mental struggle. Until now his life has been a smooth path, which is how it will always be for him."

"Well, what about you? Have you experienced mental struggles?" she asked lightly.

"More than Georges!" he responded. "I thought I was an artist, but then I found out that I wasn't. And it takes quite a struggle to admit to yourself that you've made that kind of mistake, don't you see?"

"Yes I do. It must have taken a lot of energy, too, I imagine."

Her remark sounded a trifle snide, and she instantly regretted it. Why hint at his failure to pursue his artistic ambition if he was lacking in genius anyway? But he did not seem to have heard.

"Do you know what I find so strange?" he pursued. "That Georges and Lili knew that they were made for each other almost from the moment they first met. And then there are all those other people who have known each other for ages and

403

think nothing of it, until one day they wake up, and then—they see the light—"

She could feel her heart beating and the blood rising to her cheeks. Keeping her head down to hide her colour, she affected deep concentration as she smoothed the folds of her riding costume with her whip.

"Don't you agree?" he asked.

"I—I don't know," she stammered. "I have never thought about it, really."

Neither spoke for a moment.

"How oppressive it is here, under the trees!" she murmured at length, blinking her eyes. "I can barely breathe! Let's take this turning, shall we? It will take us back to the road, and then we can have a fine gallop to the White Hollow."

She felt very strange—she, who never suffered from the heat, was overcome with a sense of dizziness; she felt suffocated by the tight bodice of her riding habit, and her hands holding the reins began to shake. With faint vision, she veered into the narrow overgrown path and spurred on her horse. She heard a warning shout from Paul, and before she knew it her hat had been knocked off her head and her hair was violently pulled, causing a searing pain on her scalp.

"Ouch," she cried out, drawing up her horse, which halted, quivering.

She had not noticed the limb of a pine tree reaching out across the path; it had grazed her forehead and now her hair was caught in the branch. She leant back to avoid pulling it further.

"Oh! Oh!" she whimpered.

Paul rode up beside her, took her reins and patted both horses on the withers.

"I tried to warn you about that tree!" he lamented. "Here, lean on my shoulder, and I'll untangle your hair."

He flung down his whip, pulled off his gloves and carefully set about freeing her snarled, dark-brown locks, scattering hairpins in the process.

"Does it hurt?" he asked.

"Yes," she moaned. "Ouch, ouch!"

"Is this better?"

"Yes—oh, yes—that's better."

He tried to be as deft as possible, and the tenderness of his movements made her forget the pain. When he was done at last she remained leaning against his shoulder, their two horses quivering side by side. She was spellbound by his smile, which reminded her of some extraordinarily beautiful young god. She closed her eyes, and everything sank away …

Suddenly she became conscious of his breath near her face, then she felt the hot pressure of his lips on hers. As if she had received an electric shock, she sat bolt upright and stared at him with flashing eyes.

"Paul!" she cried.

She was at a loss for what to say or what to do. He continued to hold her eyes, half bashfully, half beseechingly, still wearing that winsome smile. Then, without warning, she slid down from her mount, retrieved her hat, clapped it on her dishevelled hair, picked up her whip and swung herself up to the saddle, at which her horse reared and sped off along the narrow path, beneath the overhanging pine branches.

She charged ahead without once looking back, filled with impotent fury, as though his kiss had stung her like a bee. Turning onto the country road, she urged her horse to go faster, and on she galloped between the fields of burnished gold, her hair and white veil streaming behind her, her skirt flapping wildly, causing the farmhands to pause in their labours and stare. Gradually she took possession of herself; her hands became steady again and she slowed the horse to a trot as she traversed the oak wood. At the sandy hollow she dismounted, tethered the horse to a beech sapling and, lifting the train of her habit with one hand, picked her way down the slope. The sand shifted beneath her tread, setting off small avalanches that left tree roots exposed on a layer of reddish earth. At the deepest point she halted and stood quite still a moment, with her eyes closed. Then she sighed, threw off her top hat and subsided onto the cool, shady ground. Burying her face in her arms, she began softly to cry.

Paul's kiss had shocked her, and she was annoyed with herself for having fled instead of telling him off for his effrontery. Of course, it was not the first time he had chased her in fun and stolen a kiss, but they had only been children then—well, she had been a child, anyway. This time had been different; there had been a warm urgency in his kiss, a sensation that was new to her, and frightening, too. Why, oh why had he done it? That kiss had turned everything upside down, throwing into utter confusion what she had thought of as a gentle, budding friendship.

In her tearful distress she did not hear the soft thud of hooves reverberating in the sand as Paul rode up to the rim of the White Hollow, where he dismounted. After tethering his horse with hers, he clambered down to where she lay and softly called her name.

She raised herself up and stared at him through her tears. He was kneeling before her with such an engaging, fond expression in his eyes that she felt her anger ebb away.

"Why did you rush away like that?" he asked gently. "Did I make you angry? Was it so wrong of me?"

"Yes it certainly was!" she exclaimed, her resolute tone belying the frisson of pleasure at her recollection of Paul's offending lips. "I never gave you permission to kiss me! Not ever!"

She waited for his response. He would no doubt remind her of those playful kisses of past summers, for which no permission had been given either. But he said nothing. Could that mean that the kiss had been different for him, too? She hid her face in her arms again.

"What if I asked your permission, Freddie? What if I asked your permission now, as I have wanted to for such a long time? Tell me, would that be so wrong of me?"

"I don't know what you mean," she murmured almost inaudibly.

"Don't you understand what I am saying? I love you, and I'm asking you if you love me enough to be my wife!"

Blushing scarlet, with trembling lips, she felt her heart melting in secret rapture at the idea of falling into his arms with unconditional abandon. But in the next instant her indomitable pride reared its lofty head, tearing the blindfold from her eyes, and in a flash she saw him as she had seen him in The Hague: egotistic, frivolous, vain.

"You don't mean that, Paul!" she replied with icy self-control, and calmly set about winding her flowing tresses into a chignon.

"I don't mean it?" he echoed, casting her a pained, searching look.

"You may think you mean what you say," she said, and then, with more conviction: "But you are mistaken. You are just imagining that you have feelings for me—it's got nothing to do with love. You'll feel the exactly the same about someone else tomorrow, about Léonie Eekhof, for instance, or Françoise Oudendijk and goodness knows who else the day after. If I weren't wearing my riding costume—which I dare say is quite becoming—it wouldn't even have entered your head to ask anything so silly."

He had never heard her speak in such a sharp, sarcastic tone. For a moment he was unsure what to answer, then his indignation got the better of him: "Does it ever occur to you, Freddie, that the things you say might be hurtful?"

"I would be sorry if that were the case, Paul," she responded, struggling to keep her tender feelings at bay. "But I have no doubt you can understand why I was offended by that kiss you gave me."

"I meant to ask you to marry me before I kissed you, Freddie! So is this the only answer I get?"

She paused, fighting back her tears.

"That is all I have to say, Paul. Believe me, I probably know you better than you know yourself. You don't love me in the way I wish to be loved by the man I marry. You are fond of me, I know. You may even think you have fallen in love with me. But you love yourself too dearly to care very much for anyone else."

"How well you know me!" he said bitterly, pursing his lips beneath the blond moustache.

"But do let's remain friends!" she said, extending her hand unsteadily. "We would never be happy together, and one day you will thank me for not taking you up on your—on your proposal of marriage."

But he did not take the proffered hand, and she withdrew it.

"Ah yes, how well you know me!" he repeated cynically. "I was not aware that my character was an object of study to you, indeed, I was not aware that I could be deemed worthy of such studious interest."

"It doesn't take much study to fathom you, you know!" she said in a high, almost scathing tone of voice. "Whatever the case, for someone like me, who has seen the way you behave with the girls in our set, it is impossible to take any declarations of love on your part at all seriously."

"Do you really believe I was courting all those girls? I would have thought you could tell the difference between innocent fun and serious intent. Anyway, I didn't know it was a sin to be jolly."

"That kind of fun and jollity ought to be beneath you, Paul. And I might remind you that some people are more susceptible than others when it comes to your ill-advised pleasantries."

There she was, preaching again; she hated herself for it, but a twinge of jealousy had impelled her to speak her mind.

"Are you accusing me of being a heartbreaker?" he said with a forced laugh. "Believe me, Freddie, you are mistaken. Those girls are not naive, you know; they are perfectly capable of telling when I am being serious or just having a lark. It seems that you are not. And I can assure you that if my intentions towards any of them had been in the least serious, my behaviour would have been totally different."

There was a hostile edge to his voice, which almost made her fearful, and she kept silent.

"But you said just now," he continued in a gentler tone, "that you couldn't take me seriously when I said I loved you. So tell me honestly, Freddie, what would I have to do to make you believe me?"

She was greatly confused, which did not escape his notice.

"Go on, Freddie, please tell me!" he urged.

"If I believed you, Paul," she said, recovering herself, "I would feel very sorry for you. As it is, I believe you will get over your disappointment in no time, and so I would really like us to remain friends. There's no need for either of us to have any hard feelings simply because you took it into your head to propose and I didn't take you seriously. And I am not naive, either, I'll have you know."

He said nothing, crushed by her contempt, inwardly incensed at her dismissive attitude. Slowly he rose to his feet.

"Very well, then," he said evenly. "So be it."

He took his whip and tapped the sand off the legs of his velvet riding breeches, then consulted his watch.

"Ah, almost midday. We should be getting back, don't you think?" he asked, as if nothing had happened.

"Yes, we should," she replied.

She too stood up, donned her hat and adjusted the veil, then shook out her train and arranged it over her arm before starting up the sandy incline.

"Will you take my arm?" he offered coldly.

"No thank you, I am all right," she said.

At the top he untied the horses and silently helped her to mount.

"Merci," she said.

They rode off side by side, but very soon he urged his horse to go faster, so that he was ahead of her. At the end of the wood they took the country lane, where he quickened his pace further. She followed at some distance in the scorching midday sun, her eyes fixed on his back, her mind filled with consternation. A bleak sense of dissatisfaction came over her, and she feared that she might have been wrong to respond as she did, that the victory of her family pride and self-esteem might have been gained at too great a cost.

When Paul reached the iron gateway of de Horze he halted his horse and waited for her to catch up, after which they rode side by side up the drive to the big house. At the stables beyond they found Klaas and the stable boy cleaning the wheels of the old covered wagon.

Paul and Freddie dismounted. Coffee would be served presently, and Freddie hurried indoors to change out of her riding habit. In the vestibule she brushed past Etienne, who was looking more civilised now, in a jacket and with combed hair.

"Ah, there you are!" he snapped. "Back at last! You ought to be ashamed of yourself—going off for a ride like that without me."

She turned on him irritably.

"And I hope you won't wish me bad luck ever again, even as a joke!" she burst out. "I very nearly cut my face on an overhanging branch—I missed it by a hair's breadth! Look at this scratch on my forehead! Don't you ever say something like that again, do you hear? I'm more superstitious than you think!"

Paul announced that he would be leaving the following morning to join his friend Oudendijk, Françoise's brother, in Cologne, whence the young men would travel together across Switzerland to Italy. During dinner he was the same as usual, conversing on various topics in sarcastic tones with a supercilious expression hovering beneath the blond moustache. Frédérique was very subdued; it was generally assumed that she was suffering from the after-effects of the accident with the branch when out riding.

But it would not have been so easy for them to dissemble what had transpired between them had not that very afternoon seen the riotous homecoming of young Willy and Gustaaf. The two boys, fourteen and fifteen years old, were thrilled to be home from boarding school for the summer holidays, and in the midst of their boisterous capers with the children no one noticed that Paul and Frédérique were avoiding each other.

That evening, in the big bed, Frédérique was thankful for Marianne's chatter about the novels she had been reading, as her rambling discourse on the psychological and philosophical ramifications of *Adam Bede* and *Romola* safeguarded Frédérique from thinking her own thoughts. The following morning, when Paul took his leave, she offered him her hand, which he pressed briefly. Not a word passed between them. When he had gone she felt sad and distraught, and longed to unburden herself. But to whom could she turn? Not to Marianne, for she was only a child, and not to Mama either, because it always upset her to see any of her offspring suffer. To her older sister, then?

She went looking for Mathilda and found her in the sitting room with her foursome, about to begin their daily lessons. Schoolbooks and copybooks lay scattered on the table. Nico was scribbling noisily on his slate.

"Oh, I have disturbed you! I am so sorry!" said Freddie. "I had forgotten all about your lesson. I just wanted a chat, that's all."

410

She made to withdraw, but looked so crestfallen that Mathilda checked her.

"What about?" she asked.

Frédérique hesitated, glancing at the children.

"I'll come back later, shall I?" she said.

But Mathilda told the children they could have an hour's break-time, and they rushed happily out of the room and down the stairs. Frédérique began to cry and Mathilda drew her to the sofa.

"I simply had to come and tell you!" said Freddie between sobs. "Yesterday morning Paul proposed to me, and I turned him down!"

Mathilda was taken aback. Paul and Freddie had known each other for a long time; they were friends, of course, but she had never imagined the amity between them blossoming into love on either part, let alone his.

"I'm afraid I was too harsh with him," continued Freddie. "I hurt his feelings without meaning to. It's strange how one can be driven to say things one has no intention of saying at all! I mean, there was no need to be cruel. Why couldn't I simply have told him I didn't love him enough to marry him, instead of telling him it was impossible for me to believe him when he said he loved me."

"Did you wish you could believe him, then?" asked Mathilda, curving her arm about Freddie's waist.

Mathilda was asking her almost the same question as Paul! But Freddie could not bring herself to disclose her true feelings, even to her sister, and she demurred.

"Well, no!" she said, blushing. "No, I didn't; it was just that afterwards I regretted having been so inconsiderate. I didn't regret it at the time, though, so why should I regret it now? How awkward it is when there's something you know you have to do, but you don't know how to do it. I don't think I have ever felt quite so unsure of myself."

"I know what you mean," murmured Mathilda encouragingly, for she could tell that Frédérique was not telling her the whole truth. "Decisions can be so heart-rending. Sometimes you make a decision without thinking, in a blur of happiness, and you regret it afterwards, and sometimes you consider all the aspects carefully beforehand, only to discover after a time that your feelings have changed, which doesn't get you anywhere either. And sometimes you simply aren't brave enough to commit yourself one way or the other—"

Mathilda's voice trailed off as her thoughts drifted to Eline, then to Freddie, who, she could guess, had not dared to make the decision of her choice, and whose refusal to commit herself seemed to her to stem from indecision rather than indifference.

"Yes, that's exactly right!" Freddie cried. "I wasn't brave enough, I didn't have the courage! Why? Because I was stupid enough to put myself up on a pedestal, because of my wretched self-worth, as Theodore calls it. Oh yes, I know: Paul has his faults, quite big ones actually, but I love him with all his faults, maybe I love him because of his egotism, because he's no paragon of genius and virtue, but a man of flesh and blood, with all the good and the bad! Who do I think I am, placing myself above him, thinking he might not be worthy of me? As if I can claim to be a paragon of genius and virtue! Me, with my preposterous pride! My breeding! Oh yes, I have breeding all right!"

She burst into tears and threw her arms about her sister. Mathilda was overcome with sympathy for Freddie—Freddie, who was humbling herself for the sake of the man she loved! But her humility came too late. She should have humbled herself before, if it was happiness she was after.

The following week Hetty returned from her boarding school in Bonn to spend the holidays with her family at de Horze. The van Stralenburgs left for Zwolle, and in their place the Howards arrived from London. Notwithstanding the bustle of arrivals and departures, and notwithstanding Mathilda's sympathy, Frédérique felt lonely. She suggested inviting Marie Verstraeten to stay, and Theodore and his wife were happy to oblige, as there was plenty of room in the big house.

Frédérique went to fetch her friend from the station in the old-fashioned buggy, taking the reins herself, and during the ride homeward the girls chatted nineteen to the dozen. Although they were alone—Freddie having left the stable boy at home—she did not feel ready to bare her soul.

"What about Paul? Has he been amusing?" asked Marie.

"Oh, that can wait; I'll tell you about him later," said Freddie.

There was a strange note of anxiety in her voice; Marie looked at her a moment in wonder, then quickly changed the subject to the practicalities of her luggage, which she had left at the station to be collected by wheelbarrow later. When they pulled up at the entrance to the house all the children came running to give Marie a joyous welcome. That night Marianne kindly gave up her place in the large bedroom for Marie, and it was then that Freddie finally confided her secret in her friend.

Wearing their white nightgowns, they settled themselves on the wide window seat overlooking the cavernous room, which was lit by a single night light. Frédérique began to cry, covering her face with her hands, which Marie tried gently to prise apart.

"But Freddie, if you love him surely things can be put right. All he wants is for you to love him. I shall write him a letter."

Frédérique straightened up.

"No, Marie," she said firmly, between her tears. "I would never allow you to do that. I turned him down, and I can't go back on my word and make demands on him now. I'm not crying because I've lost him, I'm just upset because I was unnecessarily harsh with him, because I got on my high horse and didn't take him seriously. So if he feels hurt, it's my fault. And I respect him for the way he kept his dignity with me afterwards, which just goes to show that his sense of self-worth is just as strong as my ridiculous pride. He has 'breeding' too, as much as I do."

"That leaves you butting your heads together like a pair of stubborn goats, just because you both have breeding," Marie exclaimed. "Very sensible, I must say! No, Freddie, be honest, why don't you admit that you misjudged his character, then you can set things right. What do you have against him, anyway? His egotism? All men are egotistic, so how can you expect him to be any different! Try and be sensible, take things as they are.

I am not referring to your brothers, mind: Otto is in a class of his own, and besides," she continued, lowering her voice almost to a whisper, "besides, Otto has been through so much. As for Etienne, he's still a boy, he's good and kind, but only a boy nonetheless. So it's no use comparing Paul with them; just think of Paul as someone who happens to have money and who simply wants to enjoy life. I'm not saying that Paul has a strong character, that he's his own man, quite the opposite, in fact. I'm saying he's a bit weak."

"I could never love a man who is weak," responded Freddie gruffly.

Marie put her arm around Freddie's shoulder.

"My dear Freddie," she said, "after everything you've told me, you can't expect me to believe that you're not in love with him. He may be weak, he may be an egotist, he may be anything under the sun—but it's quite obvious that you love him."

"Yes," said Freddie, with a rueful smile. "I suppose I do. You are right. I've already confessed to Mathilda that I love him, faults and all. I didn't tell you before because you rose to his defence, and it was such a relief to hear you do so."

"Well, let me write him a letter, then."

"No!" said Freddie. "You must promise me you won't write to him. Not ever. I don't want you abusing my confidence. I have been very foolish, I have thrown away my chance of happiness, and I will suffer for it. That is as it should be."

The summer drew to a close without Paul and Freddie meeting again. The Howards went back to London, Hetty and the boys returned to their respective boarding schools, and Marie, too, took her leave. Freddie soon received a letter from Marie in The Hague, with news of Paul: he had fallen in with a group of artists in Rome and had rented a studio there in which to paint.

However, when the van Erlevoorts returned to The Hague in October, Frédérique heard that Paul was no longer painting in Italy. He was reported to have taken up residence in the town of Bodegraven, where he had found a position in local government, and that he was planning to become a mayor.

XXXII

D R REIJER had urged Eline yet again to find an occupation of some kind to distract her from the melancholy she languished in from morning till night. Eline had blamed her lethargy on the hot summer weather, which she found oppressive. Now that the leaves had begun to fall and the cool breezes of autumn refreshed her face, it seemed to her that she could breathe more freely, and she declared her resolve to find something to do with her time. Madame van Raat continued to regard Eline with anxiety, for her rasping, hacking cough had returned along with the improvement in her humour. In the meantime she had begun to lavish far more care on her appearance again, and took to practising diligently on the new Bechstein piano. But music alone did not satisfy her, and she looked further afield for something to do.

Although she had neglected her acquaintances of late, she still saw them from time to time at Betsy's salons. On one of these occasions she agreed, out of sheer ennui, to accompany the Honourable Miss Eekhof, an elderly maiden aunt of Ange and Léonie, to a service in the French chapel the following Sunday. She had not been there for years, and on the Saturday felt so disinclined to go that she was on the point of sending the honourable lady a note to excuse herself. Madame van Raat, however, would not hear of it, so Eline obliged. There was a new preacher, with large, dark, soulful eyes and pale, aristocratic hands. Eline returned home all excited, full of news about the wonderful sermon and how she had hung on to the preacher's every word. Her only regret was that the interior of Protestant churches was so bare, and the singing so poor, oh, if only she were Roman Catholic, then her soul would have been borne aloft on the wings of a soaring Ave Maria or Gloria in Excelsis, she would have been able to lose herself in the mystical splendour of the altar and the holy sacrament, she would have swooned away in the theatrical piety diffused by clouds of incense.

But she was not Roman Catholic, so she had to make do with her French chapel, going there several times in the company of the Eekhof girls' maiden aunt. Before long she was in attendance every Sunday, nodding gravely at her acquaintances with a soft, melting look in her eyes and a sorrowful cast to her closed lips, and word of Eline Vere's astonishing, newfound piety spread quickly in The Hague.

Miss Eekhof was on the committee of numerous ladies' associations devoted to good works, and it took little persuasion on her part to induce Eline to join two of these charities. She was even, at Miss Eekhof's instigation, appointed to the board overseeing the crèches for the children of paupers, which kept her occupied on fixed days. She spent a whole week working hard for a fancy fair, without however going so far as to participate in the sale of items on the day itself. And the honourable lady frequently persuaded Eline to accompany her on her visits to the poor.

At first she found a certain fulfilment in her virtuous, philanthropic pastimes, but before the month was out she found herself getting bored by the preacher's repetitive style of officiation; she could predict the exact moment at which he would raise his eyes to heaven during a hymn, the exact gesture his pale hand would make for the benediction. The singing set her nerves on edge, for the voices were hoarse and untrained, and she was increasingly irked by the plainness of the white-walled interior with its lectern and wooden pews. She began to have misgivings about the congregation, suspecting them of hypocrisy. The preacher was probably a hypocrite, too, and so were the high-and-mighty deacons; the same could be said of Miss Eekhof, sitting beside her—and Eline herself, with her melting eyes and grave expression, was no better.

From Miss Eekhof she had heard about all sorts of petty disagreements and rivalries existing between the ladies governing the various institutions, which made her wonder about the good they professed to be doing. The entire notion of good works became odious to her; she found herself unable to believe in the sincerity of any of the ladies of her recent acquaintance, not even the ones who had become friends; they were all insincere and self-serving, every one of them; they all had their secret motives, thinking only of themselves under the guise of helping others. Quite what those motives were she could not tell, but they all had them, of that she was certain.

The visits to the poor in the company of the elderly maiden aunt now filled her with revulsion. Their crowded, airless dwellings, the misery and privation, constricted her throat, and she felt she would suffocate to death if obliged to spend a single day in such filthy, cramped conditions. Having lost her trust in the bountiful ladies, she now distrusted the poor themselves. She had read somewhere that there were people in London who posed as beggars while secretly possessing vast amounts of money, which they spent on lavish feasts with streams of champagne and beautiful women. All the paupers to whom she and Miss Eekhof dispensed alms actually had hoards of jewels and gold sewn into their repulsive mattresses, and whether their response was grovelling gratitude or dumb brutishness made no difference; it was sham, like everything else about them.

While remaining a member of various charities and continuing to give Miss Eekhof money intended for this ailing widow or that blind organ-grinder, she stopped going to church; she also stopped visiting the repugnant poor and resigned from her position on the governing board of the crèches.

Winter arrived, and Eline's cough kept her indoors. She dragged herself from one uneventful day to the next in monotonous indolence with only Madame van Raat for company, and for the umpteenth time Eline asked herself what purpose there could possibly be to her life if she was not to be happy.

After the disillusionments of philanthropy and religion, she no longer trusted anyone. Looking about her, she could not believe that Georges and Lili were truly in love now that they were married; of course they were disappointed in each other, and only pretending to be happy. She did not believe that Betsy was happy, either, even though she was rich, because how could she love Henk? How could she not long for more passion? Nor did Eline believe that Otto had ever truly loved her; how could he, while his character was so very different from hers? Her feelings of distrust reached such a pitch that she even doubted whether

Madame van Raat's love for her was sincere. Madame had been hoping to find in her an agreeable lady's companion, that was all, and it was obvious that Eline did not live up to her expectations. Henk's mother was a hypocrite, like everybody else.

At one time such bitter sentiments would have thrown Eline into black despair, but as it was her soul had become so numbed that she was unaffected by them. She did not care; what difference did it make to her that life was one great lie? It was so, and could not be helped, least of all by her, so she might as well lie like everybody else.

Rather, she would lie as a last resort, when forced by circumstance to show some emotion, some sign of 'life'. For the rest she would submerge herself in the torpor of detachment.

Such were her thoughts, and she forced her youth to bend under the yoke of apathy and listlessness. Her drift into self-willed indifference even caused her charming manner of old to desert her, and the sympathy she evoked among her associates dwindled as she grew increasingly sullen and unapproachable.

She would stay in bed for the greater part of the morning, and although Madame van Raat disapproved, she permitted Eline's breakfast to be served in her room, as that was the only way she could be brought to eat anything at all.

Even so, Eline often left it untouched. When she finally rose she did not get dressed at once; instead, she slipped on a peignoir and lounged on her couch or in a chair, staring vacantly out the window. She did not go downstairs until around noon, bowed by the lassitude that seemed to run in her veins like some debilitating, tepid fluid. Reijer called regularly, and insisted that she go out and brave rain, wind or snow, but although secretly she longed for some fresh air, she either remained closeted indoors, or returned home after five minutes. Her only movement would be to hobble from her seat by the window to a chair by the stove, coughing and shivering, with ice-cold fingers, glazed eyes, and her lips tightly pursed.

Madame van Raat lost all hope of her ability to restore some measure of vitality in Eline. It was as she had feared: the task Reijer had assigned to her, and which she so dearly wished to fulfil, was proving beyond her powers. Her hopes faded, and she subsided into the grey mists of her own private melancholy. Hours went by during which the old lady and the young girl sat together in the same room without exchanging a single word, each of them lost in hopeless reverie.

Eline was aware that this desultory cohabitation could not last. There was something about Madame van Raat and about her home, something she could not define, that irritated her. She found herself unable to contain her exasperation at times, and would burst out with some harsh, unkind remark, often for no reason whatsoever. The old lady's only answer would be a momentary, wounded stare, which would instantly fill Eline with remorse. Sometimes she could not bring herself to apologise, and would scarcely open her mouth for the rest of the day. At other times she was so consumed by guilt that she went down on her knees and hid her face in the old lady's lap, weeping and begging to be forgiven, lamenting that when she was in one of her black moods … she knew not where they came from or how to control them … oh, it was like being possessed by demons, as if she had no will of her own!

Madame van Raat dissolved in tears, too, and kissed her, but the next day the same demons bore down on Eline to crush her will.

Something had to be done, thought Eline. She wrote a long letter to her uncle Daniel and Eliza, in which she bared her soul more than she had ever dared before. She informed them that she felt utterly miserable in The Hague, that she would die of dreariness if she stayed much longer with Madame van Raat, notwithstanding the latter's great kindness to her, and that she longed desperately for a change of environment. Uncle Daniel came to The Hague and declared to Eline, in the old lady's presence although without mentioning the letter, that he and his wife missed her and wondered whether she would pay them another visit.

Eline was undecided, but Madame van Raat urged her in mournful tones to accept her uncle's kind invitation, and it was arranged there and then that she should accompany him to Brussels two days later.

When Daniel Vere was gone, Madame van Raat sat slumped in her chair, her grey head sunk down upon her breast, shattered by the immensity of her disappointment. Another two days and Eline would leave! That would be the end of it! Weak as she was, she had hoped to make herself useful, she had hoped to infuse just a little fresh vigour into the dear young creature's listless existence, but she could not help seeing that she was defeated: Eline was languishing in her home, Eline yearned for variety! How could she, an old woman, have had such presumption!

Seeing the old lady's mute sorrow, Eline was overcome with despair, despair over her own egotism. She had not given the slightest thought to Madame van Raat when she wrote that letter to her uncle Daniel; she had thought only of herself, and now she was causing the old lady great distress, even though she herself was convinced that exchanging The Hague for Brussels would not change anything, really, least of all rid her of the fatigue that had plagued her body and soul for the past two years.

"My dear little Mama!" she cried tearfully. "Are you very sad to see me go? I can hardly think you would have wished to keep me with you, me, ungrateful, cross creature that I am!"

She sank down on a low stool at the old lady's feet and kissed her hand.

"Sad? Yes, it makes me sad, Elly!" faltered Madame van Raat, gently stroking Eline's forehead. "But it will be for the best. Far be it from me to wish you to leave, even if you are not always as sweet-tempered with me as you used to be. Oh, if only I could be confident that you would find happiness here eventually, then I would not tell you to go. But as it is, I say to you: go, my poor child, with my blessing, and come back whenever you wish."

Eline began to sob.

"It's all my fault, I know it is! You are such a dear, you have been so very kind to me, and I have yet to hear you utter a single word against me. You spoil me as if I were your own flesh and blood, and in return I fly into rages and say abominable things! Oh, what a wretched creature I am! How I wish I could be different! Time was when I would have loved nothing more than to be spoilt by you, but now … now it makes no difference! It's not that I don't love you, because I do, I love you more than anyone else in the world, but, you see, nothing matters to me any more, nothing, nothing!"

"Fie, Eline, fie! You shouldn't say such things."

"Oh, I know I'm horrid! But am I to blame? Don't you think I would much rather be good and kind and happy? But I cannot change the way I am, it's impossible! You told me that I ought to pray, you said it would make me feel better. Well, I went to church, and it didn't help … and I can't pray properly the way you do, either! I did pray for something once, a long time ago, but my prayer went unanswered."

She thought of that night at de Horze, when she had prayed to God that her happiness, the gentle felicity she had found with Otto, might remain with her for ever.

"I'll tell you what I prayed for!" she pursued hoarsely, coughing as she rose to her feet and began to walk aimlessly about the room, wringing her thin hands as if they were ice-cold. "I was so happy then, happier than I thought I could ever be. It was a lovely time, so peaceful and so tranquil; everyone was good and kind to me. I couldn't imagine what I had done to deserve such great happiness, and then … then all of a sudden I began to be afraid that things might change. That was when I prayed to God to make that wondrous happiness last for ever. And from that moment on—when I was afraid and prayed to God—from that moment on things did begin to change, very slowly, but surely. I can see it so clearly now! I shouldn't have given in to doubt, I shouldn't have been afraid, I shouldn't have prayed! Don't you see? That is why I cannot and will not pray any more."

She flung herself on the sofa in a nervous flood of tears, but jumped up again immediately with a wild, hunted look. Her eyes darted this way and that and her fingers were in constant motion, touching a vase here or a flower basket there, toying with the fringe of the window curtain, tracing arabesques on the steamed-up panes. Abruptly recovering herself, she found that she could not recall what she had just said.

"I don't suppose you understand, do you?" she said doubtfully to Madame van Raat, whose mournful gaze had followed her every movement.

"Yes, my dear, I believe I do," she stammered, overcome with grief over Eline's lost chance of happiness.

Eline stared. For a moment she deeply regretted her half-remembered confession, but the sympathy beaming from Madame's eyes reassured her.

"So you understand what I mean? You understand why I can never be happy again?" she asked, sinking down on the footstool once more.

Madame van Raat did not answer; with tears in her eyes she put her arm around Eline's neck and kissed her. They remained thus a moment, in silence.

"And will you forgive me, just a little, for leaving you?"

"Oh, why won't you stay with me?"

"I'm a burden to you; my company is anything but agreeable. There is nothing I can do for you, just as there is nothing you can do for me!"

It was the truth. Madame could do nothing for her. No one could.

They found no more to say to one another. Each was painfully aware of her inability to lighten the load of the other's existence by means of mutual consolation. But Madame, pressing Eline to her bosom, was not convinced that there would be any consolation to be found in the company of Uncle Daniel and Eliza either.

Dusk fell, and as the fire was almost out it grew chilly in the room, with dark, vague shadows looming in the angles of the walls and among the furniture. Madame van Raat was shivering, but she did not rise to attend to the fire or ring for the maid, because Eline's head was resting on her lap. She had fallen asleep, and with her eyes closed it seemed to the old lady that, had it not been for the laboured breathing, she would have thought the girl had died, so waxen and livid was the shade of her emaciated features.

Eline slept on, and the temperature in the room dropped further. Madame van Raat peered at the grate: not a trace of fire to be seen. With slow deliberation she took off the woollen shawl she invariably wore around her shoulders, and carefully spread it out over Eline.

XXXIII

Daniel Vere and his young wife, Eliza Moulanger, occupied a spacious apartment on Avenue Louise. The reception room was vast, with five windows overlooking the street; half salon, half drawing room, the space was decorated in no particular style, but rather with artistic flamboyance. Although the furniture and ornaments looked as if they had been picked up here and there at various auctions, together they constituted an attractive ensemble of muted shades and pleasing contours. The walls were lined with softly gilt leather, and from the ceiling, patterned in the Moorish manner with soft blues, pale reds and dull gold, hung a many-branched chandelier of coloured Venetian glass. A generous fire burnt in the grand, old-fashioned hearth with a richly carved oak surround, and whichever way one turned there were potted palms, curios from Turkey and China, and artefacts of antique porcelain, all in artistic profusion.

The central bay window, wider than the others, formed a kind of interior balcony, where Eliza and Eline often sat together. A week had gone by since her arrival, and Eline found herself warming to the company of her uncle and her youthful aunt. The sheer lavishness of the reception room, almost like a museum, gratified her aesthetic sensibilities while exuding an atmosphere of warmth and conviviality. The modern luxury of Betsy's salon, full of gilt, plush and satin, seemed ordinary and tasteless to her now, compared to the somewhat haphazard, slightly dusty, yet cosy abundance of her present surroundings.

It was morning, and in the bay window sat Aunt Eliza, attired in a Chinese robe of grey silk with red tassels, painting at a table strewn with paints and brushes. Eline was seated by the large fire with a book on her lap, an unconscious smile playing on her pale lips as her gaze slid searchingly about the room.

"I love the way you have decorated your apartment!" she said in French to Eliza, who was humming softly as she rinsed out her brush. "You can sit here quietly by the fire and conjure up the most delightful fancies, because every single thing here sparks some idea that you can embroider. If you look around the room, you feel as if you're travelling."

Eliza licked the tip of her brush and laughed.

"You have such curious ideas, Eline!" she said, rising abruptly. She untied her mass of tightly curled hair, which was ever dishevelled, shook it, and twisted it into a loose knot. "I've spent practically all my time in this room for the past three years, never have any of my things given me the feeling I was travelling! But all of you have such curious ideas! You and Daniel and Vincent, too. It's very amusing; I keep being taken by surprise! So curious, and so original, you know. Is your sister Betsy like that, too?"

Eline smiled at her in wonder.

"Betsy?" she echoed pensively. "No, I don't believe so. Betsy has a very practical nature, very resolute. Betsy takes after our Mama, not after the Veres at all."

Eliza smiled gaily.

"Shall I tell you what I think? You're all a bit peculiar, I do declare, a bit peculiar, every one of you! Believe me, it's true!" She said this in such a joking, friendly fashion that Eline could not take offence. "But you know, I rather like a whiff of peculiarity. I can't abide ordinariness. Ordinary people—ugh! So you see, that's why I adore you: you aren't a bit ordinary, you're interesting and original!"

"Really?" said Eline forcing a laugh. "Well, I can assure you that I would give half my life for the privilege of not being original or interesting, but ordinary instead, as ordinary as it is possible to be."

"My dear girl! What an absurd privilege to aspire to! The way I see it, one shouldn't aspire to anything, one ought to want to take life as it comes, and be satisfied with one's lot. *Voilà le secret du bonheur!* You are original, Eline, so you might as well be satisfied with your interesting personality. But there you go, wanting to be different—wanting to be ordinary, no less! Shame on you!"

She seated herself beside Eline and stretched out her hands to the fire.

"I'll tell you something else, Eline, something that has always puzzled me about you. You are a very pretty girl, you have enough money to do exactly as you please, and yet you don't enjoy life. You're always dreaming, dear girl, but dreaming is not the same as living, is it? Had I been in your shoes before I got married, I'd have made sure I enjoyed life to the full. But I didn't have a penny to my name, and I was a plain-looking girl—as I still am. Daniel fell for me anyway, and I accepted him. Of course I did! If I'd been pretty like you and if I'd had a little money of my own I would have made sure I amused myself—but it would have been without Daniel, you see. With who else? Well, I couldn't say at this stage, but I know I would have had lots of fun! As for you—*mais c'est une pitié!*—you're simply bored, bored to death if you ask me. It's a crying shame! In a word, you're a mystery to me. And that's exactly what I like about you."

Eline gave a rueful smile, remaining silent.

"Ah well, I don't know your personal history, all I know is that you left your sister's home in the middle of the night, during a storm. Not everyone would do that, you see, and that's what appeals to me. It's intriguing, to say the least. I dare say you have some dramatic story to tell, but then who hasn't? A romantic story, perhaps? If so, I pity you, because you obviously made some foolish mistake."

She paused in anticipation of some response from Eline, but none was forthcoming.

"Don't misunderstand me," she prattled on, relishing the occasion to air her views. "I think love is a fine thing. It is most enjoyable. But I also think it ought to remain enjoyable. Once romantic love becomes a source of heartache it's not worth pursuing, in my opinion. I don't believe there is such a thing as all-consuming love, like a big flame that won't tolerate any flamelets in its vicinity. It's an impossibility, when you think about it. Take me. I have always lived here in Brussels. Daniel happened to be living here, too, and so we met. We fell in love, as they say, and we got married. All well and good, but what if I had been living in Lapland, and Daniel on the South Pole? Just think about it. We would never have set eyes on each other, and each of us would have met someone else—me an Eskimo, and

Daniel someone from the South Pole. Stands to reason, no? Love simply happens, and people can fall in love hundreds of times. Why, Eline, you've gone all quiet. I'm not boring you am I?"

"On the contrary!" laughed Eline. "I love it when you're in one of your talkative moods!"

Eliza blinked happily.

"Well, I am rather a chatterbox, aren't I? But I meant what I said about you not enjoying life enough. You might bear that in mind, my dear; you're still young enough to change your attitude."

Eline was certain that there was nothing she could do to change her attitude. She was simply not up to it—she had allowed herself to be driven down a steep slope, further and further until she could see the abyss gaping beneath her, and even then she had not mustered the strength to climb back up.

"Do you know what I think your weakness is, Eline? You're too sensitive. Altogether too emotional. What you need in life's struggle is a good dose of indifference. You see, we have little choice: we happen to be among the living, and we must live our lives as best we can. So we might as well make things as agreeable as possible for ourselves. As for you, you have the means to do just that. You have no responsibilities, no dependents to provide for, you can do exactly as you please. The trouble is that you think too much, and thinking too much is depressing. Me? I don't think. I only have impulses, little ideas that occur to me; but I never think. And thank goodness for that. I may be philosophising now, but I am not thinking."

This light-hearted chat amused Eline; she even caught herself thinking Eliza might be quite right to take such a heedless attitude. But Eline herself was different: there was no way she could cast off the melancholy that seemed to have infiltrated into the very marrow of her being, and she was sure that she would end her days without having enjoyed life—or at least not in the way Eliza meant. Nor did she desire such enjoyment, for she had experienced happiness of a higher order—the happiness of being with him, with Otto.

Eliza thought her indolent, but she herself took pleasure in doing nothing. She gave herself up wholeheartedly to her languorous inertia. Most days she stayed at home, pleading her cough, though in reality all she wanted to do was to nestle herself among the Turkish cushions in the big armchair by the fire and while away the hours daydreaming. She made an effort to be like Eliza and not think, and to a certain extent she succeeded in this endeavour. Only, she began to have a sense of waiting for something, waiting and waiting.

Although she seldom went out, she saw plenty of people. Uncle Daniel was always bringing home friends, sometimes accompanied by their wives, and they often stayed for dinner. The social circle Eline found herself in was not entirely new to her, for she had met various of its members when she first stayed in Brussels. But she did not feel wholly at ease with them; they were unconventional in ways that both fascinated and shocked her. In The Hague she had always moved in circles limited to her own class, where everyone, despite variations in personal fortunes, held the same views when it came to morals and manners, and where everyone observed the same rules of etiquette and exchanged the same pleasantries when they visited each other's homes. No such rules seemed to apply in Brussels. People vented the most outlandish opinions, on topics unheard of in Betsy's salon or at the Eekhofs'. She found her new, free-spirited acquaintances somewhat unnerving, but at the same time interestingly exotic.

It was indeed a motley assortment of friends that Uncle Daniel had gathered around him. One evening he had invited some count or other to dinner, who, much to Eline's surprise, entered wearing evening dress with a diamond-studded dress shirt that looked decidedly the worse for wear, as well as rather oversized cameo rings on his fingers; he was handsome in a faded sort of way, with a lock of black hair tumbling over his brow, and wrote poetry; he offered Eline a volume of his poems and a booklet containing reprints of flattering reviews of his works. He was said to be rich, and Eliza thought him witty. Eline, however, felt a twinge of dislike on shaking his hand. Another evening it would be an actor, which made Eline worry about the possibility of

Fabrice turning up one day. Or it would be a well-known jeweller accompanied by an enormously stout, blonde lady wearing a lot of rouge and a red-velvet gown. But from time to time the Moulangers and the Des Luynes came over from Bordeaux, and Eline would be greatly relieved to recognise in them a modicum of respectability and distinction.

With the exception of these two families, though, visitors at avenue Louise behaved with a remarkable degree of informality. They either came to dinner unannounced or arrived at eleven o'clock at night, when Eline was feeling ready for bed, and stayed until the small hours drinking champagne and smoking. Eline would smoke along with them, and laugh very loudly. Uncle Daniel would lounge in a chair, smiling somewhat wearily, and Eline often had the impression that all these strange people were in some way useful to him. She had never quite understood how he obtained his money, since he did not seem to have had any employment. But she dismissed the thought, for she was determined not to think at all, like Eliza, and as time went on she found a certain measure of satisfaction in this society, so very different from what she had been used to in the salons of The Hague.

Above all, Eline liked conversing with Uncle Daniel's physician, a man of indeterminate age who was remarkably polite in both manner and speech, and who always seemed to be watching her closely. His interest in her had initially put her on her guard, as if he might discover something within her that she herself was unaware of, some secret that would put her to shame. Yet she was drawn to his amicable, steady gaze as to a magnet, and before long she took to asking him, when she had one of her headaches, to hold his cool outstretched hand close to her forehead for a moment. The first time he had done so had been on his own initiative, and Eline had immediately felt as though a refreshing, invigorating current were passing through her brain. Since then she had become addicted, in a manner of speaking, to the emanations of that hand, which, without even touching, seemed capable of making a cool breeze blow through her over-heated skull.

Eline had told him of the difficulties she had sleeping at night, and he had said he would like to try and induce her to sleep by the sheer force of his will, but she had begged him not to: she had so little will-power of her own, and feared losing it altogether if he were capable of exerting such a strong influence on her from afar. Thereupon he had supplied her with a sleeping draught of morphine, which was extremely expensive and which he had mixed himself; he counted out the drops for her in a glass of water. That night she laid herself down to sleep in a haze of blissful contentment; she felt her body becoming weightless, rising up from her bed, her pillows and sheets, and for a moment she found herself floating on currents of softly swirling blue air.

Then she sank into a profound slumber, from which she did not wake until late in the morning. And she was full of praise for Uncle Daniel's physician for having succeeded where Reijer had always failed—at least he knew how to send her to sleep.

Life went on in much the same manner, with Eline accommodating herself to the humour of the moment. She still had a bad cough, but felt comparatively content nonetheless. Eliza, though a compulsive talker, seemed to like her well enough, and Uncle Daniel, ever gallant if a touch remote, was no less well-disposed towards her. Sometimes, however, she had the feeling that they were putting on an act, in the same way that everyone had put on an act in The Hague. But she had no desire to analyse this doubt, preferring to let her brain slumber in untrammelled lethargy.

One day an envelope arrived from Vincent Vere in New York; it was addressed to Uncle Daniel, to whom it came as rather a surprise, as they were not in the habit of writing to one another. But Eline, who had not heard from her cousin for some time, was all aflutter at the unexpected mention of his name, and couldn't wait to hear what her uncle would say about the letter. She would not be surprised if Vincent were asking for money.

But in this Eline was mistaken. He had not asked for money, nor did he need a letter of introduction or some other favour. Vincent simply wanted to let them know that he and his friend Lawrence St Clare were planning a trip to Europe, and that they would be stopping in Brussels. They would be sailing to Liverpool, from where they would travel to London and Paris before arriving in Brussels. By the time Uncle Daniel received this news they were already halfway across the Atlantic.

Vincent's letter revived Eline to some degree from her psychic lethargy. She remembered how Vincent, pale and sickly, had lain on her couch in his Turkish chamber cloak, and how she had nursed him back to health. Her next thought was of Otto, and she fumbled agitatedly for the black enamelled locket on her watch chain. Had she not fancied that Vincent was in love with her, and she with him? Were there any such feelings still lingering in her heart? No, those feelings were far, far away, like birds that had vanished out of sight.

Uncle and Eliza discussed Vincent's impending visit briefly, then said no more on the subject. But Eline, though she kept silent, thought a great deal about him and his American friend. She recalled having seen the photograph of St Clare when it fell out of his letter to Vincent; it was on the same day that she had lost her temper with Otto during dinner. She recalled having asked Vincent whether his friend's hair was fair or dark, but not what he had replied. Nor could she recall what St Clare looked like. She was very curious to see them both.

After some weeks a second letter from Vincent arrived; this time posted from Paris. A few days later the two friends arrived; it was late afternoon, and they stayed to dinner. Uncle and Eliza offered to put them up, out of courtesy, but St Clare declined politely: they had already taken rooms at the Hotel des Flandres.

Vincent had not changed a whit, either in appearance or demeanour. When he and Eline were standing side by side, talking, she caught their reflection in the pier glass, and suddenly noticed that she had aged. He was the same elegantly dressed young man as two years before, and beside her sallow skin and sunken cheeks he looked healthier than she had ever seen him. She, in black lace—she wore nothing else these days—stood there with her thin shoulders and lacklustre eyes gazing at the ruins of her former youthful radiance ... ruined inside and out.

Lawrence St Clare directly made a very favourable impression upon both ladies. Eline had rather imagined him, as an American, to be a little coarse and uncivilised—possibly even spitting, swearing, or demanding whiskey—and she was pleasantly surprised by his engaging, easy manner. He was tall and rugged, with a full, dark-blond beard, and in his clear eyes there gleamed a certain pride, but it was a pride that, without a trace of arrogance, betokened character and strength of will. His masterful bearing and air of independence inspired confidence in Eline. Although Vincent had not told her very much about St Clare, she felt almost at once that she had known him for a long time. His frank smile and mild yet penetrating gaze pleased her, and when she glanced about the dinner table she was struck by the calm, wholesome uprightness he exuded, compared to which her uncle's civility and Eliza's frothy chitchat, as well as the vague melancholy shared by herself and Vincent, seemed to her false and jaded.

After dinner they took coffee in the reception room. Eline felt at ease in St Clare's company, and hoped there would be no further callers to disturb them. She had little opportunity to converse with him, though, as Eliza bombarded him with questions about New York, Philadelphia and St Louis. He replied in French, speaking slowly, with a strange accent that Eline found rather charming.

Vincent clasped her hands and stared at her intently; he was grateful for what she had done for him in The Hague, and now felt a pang of compassion for her.

"I have missed you, Elly!" he said as they settled themselves in the balcony. "But you really ought to put on some weight, you know!"

She gave a light laugh and nervously poked the tip of her shoe into the fleecy white rug.

"I am quite all right!" she said. "Indeed, I have been feeling rather well lately. Better than before, anyway. And I am very glad to see you again, very glad. You know I have always been fond of you."

She put out her hand with a generous gesture; he pressed it and moved his chair a little closer.

"And what do you think of Lawrence?" he asked. "Do you like him?"

"Yes, he seems very nice."

"He is the only man I have ever known who is as good as his word. I don't trust anyone, not a soul, you see; not even you, not even myself, but I do trust him … Don't you find his French accent rather amusing?"

"He speaks French very well!" responded Eline.

"Oh, you can't imagine how loyal he is to his friends!" Vincent continued familiarly. "If I were to tell you all the things he has done for me, you wouldn't believe me. To be honest, his generosity towards me has been enormous, almost embarrassingly so, as it happens. You see, I was taken very ill in New York, very ill indeed—my life was in danger. At that time I was employed by the same company St Clare has invested his money in. He took me into his home and looked after me with almost as much tender care as you showed me in The Hague. I don't know what I have done to deserve his friendship, nor can I ever repay him. But I don't think there is anything I would not do for him. If there is a grain of goodness in me at all, it is thanks to his influence. During my illness he arranged for a temporary replacement for my position—I was second in command in the accounts department—so that I would not be without an income once I had recovered. But then a while ago he conceived the idea of going on a tour; he knew little about Europe, and was concerned about my working too hard. In short, he invited me to accompany him on his travels. I declined at first, because I was already so beholden to him, but he insisted, and in the end I agreed. He wants to go as far as Petersburg and Moscow this winter, and to spend next summer touring southern Europe. Well, as you know, I have done a fair bit of travelling myself, and so I am glad to offer my services as a guide. But I have never travelled in such style before! We stay at the best hotels, no expense is spared. Nothing but the best, don't you know!"

He paused, tiring of his prolonged whispering.

"Has he so much sympathy for you?" murmured Eline. "How remarkable! Of course, I hardly know him, but it seems to me that his temperament is not a bit like yours, Vincent."

"No, it is not; you are quite right. Maybe that is why he likes me. At any rate, he's always saying I'm a better person than everyone seems to think, myself included. Which is quite a consolation, wouldn't you say?"

"Perhaps he finds you as interesting as Eliza finds me!" said Eline, laughing disparagingly in spite of herself. Seeing St Clare coming towards them, she felt a pang of conscience—how could she have compared the proud sincerity emanating from his person with the trivial coolness of Eliza!

Meanwhile Eliza busied herself with the liqueurs, asking Vincent whether he preferred kirsch or curaçao, or would he rather have a glass of cognac? Vincent went to sit with her and Uncle Daniel by the fire, while St Clare seated himself in the balcony beside Eline.

"Ah, so you are the dear cousin Vincent told me so much about! The cousin who took such good care of him," he said, smiling as he put his hands in his pockets and fixed Eline with his frank stare.

Eline was about to say that he too had proved his merit in that department, but checked the impulse, thinking it might be inappropriate to let on how much Vincent had already told her about their friendship.

"Yes, I am the cousin who cared for him!" she replied, in French. Her English was good, but she found his French so charming that she had not offered to speak with him in his native language.

"That was in The Hague, wasn't it?"

"Yes it was; he was staying at my brother-in-law's house."

"And you were living there too at the time, weren't you?"

This seemed a touch inquisitive on his part, but he spoke in a tone of such candid interest that she didn't feel offended.

"Yes," she answered. "Did Vincent tell you that?"

"He did. Vincent often spoke of you."

He sounded as if he knew quite a lot about her. She had written to Vincent after her flight from Betsy and Henk's house, so he probably knew about that, too.

"And you have done a good deal of travelling?" he pursued.

"Oh yes, with my uncle and aunt. A great deal. You intend to travel extensively yourself, I gather?"

"As far as Russia this coming winter."

Neither of them spoke for a moment. It seemed to Eline that they both had much to say to one another, but did not know where to begin. She already felt she had known him for a long while, and now it turned out that she was no stranger to him either.

"Do you care very much for Vincent?" she asked.

"Very much. I feel very sorry for him. Had his health been more robust, he would certainly have made his mark on the world. He possesses energy and a hard-working spirit, as well as a broad view of life. But his physical weakness prevents him from giving his mind to one thing and bringing it to fruition. Most people have the wrong idea about Vincent. They think him lazy, capricious, egotistic, and refuse to see that he is simply ill. I can't think of anybody else who would be capable, despite suffering from such ill health, of sharing so much of his talent and intelligence with the rest of mankind."

She had always had great sympathy for Vincent, but had never seen him in this light.

"Yes, I believe you are right!" she said after a short pause. "But don't you think the trip you have in mind will be too tiring for Vincent? All the way to Russia, in winter?"

"Oh no. The cold climate will have an invigorating effect on him. And he won't have to exert himself. I don't even want him to accompany me on every expedition I have in mind. But travelling by train poses no problem—all it requires is for him to put on his fur coat and sit in a railway car."

His words made her suspect, as she had suspected from her conversation with Vincent, that St Clare set inordinate store by his friend's comfort and well-being.

"I do believe you are very kind-hearted!" she could not help exclaiming.

He gave her a puzzled look.

"What makes you say that?" he asked, laughing.

"I don't know!" she said, smiling and colouring slightly. "It's just an impression I have. But I may be mistaken, of course."

He gestured vaguely with his hand. A hint of coquetry had crept into her voice at the last, which she regretted.

"Just now you spoke of energy and a hard-working spirit," she resumed. "And you said that if someone is ill, that person deserves to be forgiven for not being energetic and hard-working."

"Naturally. What do you mean?"

There was an unhesitating singleness of purpose about his manner, which flustered her. During her tête-à-têtes with Vincent in the old days, their rambling, philosophical speculations had wavered this way and that without aim, rather like coils of smoke dissipating in the air, and the sheer directness of St Clare's question caught her unprepared.

"I mean," she replied hesitantly, "wouldn't you be even more inclined to excuse the lack of energy and activity in someone who had suffered a great sadness, than in someone like Vincent, whose only trouble is poor health?"

He held her gaze.

"Yes I would—provided he had tried to be energetic, and had succumbed in the attempt. Not otherwise, not if he had given himself up to the force of sheer circumstance without a struggle, as if it were his foreordained destiny. A fatalistic attitude; Vincent is no stranger to it either. And there is nothing more undermining than that kind of fatalism. Life would turn into moral death if we all just sat down with our hands in our laps and thought: What will be, will be."

Eline was nonplussed.

Had she possessed energy? Had she given herself up to the force of circumstance? She had no answer. She felt small in his forceful presence, and could not concentrate her thoughts.

"But what if that person's suffering were caused by remorse over something he had done in the past?" she whispered almost pleadingly, with moist eyes, nervously fingering the black locket and digging the point of her shoe into the sheepskin rug. His expression softened into pity.

"In that case—oh yes, he would deserve to be forgiven!" he whispered with indulgent reassurance.

But the indulgence of his tone discomfited her; suddenly she felt that she had given herself away, that she had been open-hearted in a way that was not fitting, that she ought to have had the strength to maintain her reserve.

St Clare was uncertain how long he would stay in Brussels, as he wished to take short trips from there to Mechelen, Antwerp, Bruges and Ghent. Aunt Eliza found him very likeable indeed, but frowned on his intention to tour the northern countries during winter. She was in favour of travelling, but not of suffering from freezing temperatures. St Clare laughed, saying that neither he nor Vincent minded about the cold.

Vincent accompanied him on some of his excursions away from the city, though not all, and during their absences there was much talk of them among the eccentric friends visiting Avenue Louise at eleven o'clock of an evening. The Count remarked that he had met St Clare some years since; he appeared to be some sort of *chevalier d'industrie*, and the Veres would do well to tread with caution. At this Uncle Daniel shrugged his shoulders, but Eline fixed the Count with a stare of withering contempt. Soon afterwards she retired to her bedroom, where she could still hear the high-pitched vociferations of the blonde lady in red velvet and Eliza's shrieks of laughter.

The carousal in the reception room prevented her from sleeping, notwithstanding the drops she had taken. But despite her wakefulness and the aggravation of the noise, she felt surprisingly calm. The thought of St Clare was reassuring to her, more soothing even than the cool liquid prescribed by the physician. Maybe there was more to life than hypocrisy after all, maybe there was such a thing as true friendship and devotion, in a word: truth.

St Clare and Vincent stayed away for a week, during which they were sorely missed by Eline. They arrived on the day before New Year's Eve, and Eliza invited them to the soirée she was holding the following evening, which promised to be very grand.

At about half-past nine the following evening the motley collection of guests began to arrive, and Uncle Daniel and Eliza welcomed them warmly. The Count, the actor, the jeweller and his blowsy consort were the first to make their appearance, after which Eline saw a strange review of guests parade past the host and hostess, the men with an air of the nouveau riche, or with bohemian flamboyance, the ladies with oversized diamonds and limp trains to their gowns.

She did not feel at home in this setting, and yet she was amused by all those remarkable people drifting about the reception room so extravagantly furnished with bibelots. The candlelight diffused by the Venetian chandelier glinted strangely over the arrays of antique bronze, antique porcelain and antique fabrics. The guests were all unusual in one way or another, in keeping with Eliza's avowed dislike of the mundane.

Eline remained somewhat aloof, hovering at the elbows of her uncle and aunt, and was glad to catch sight of St Clare and Vincent as they entered the room. Both were in evening dress, and she found them a markedly distinguished-looking pair.

Once they had presented themselves to their hosts, however, they did not seem to notice Eline in the crush, and she felt rather lost. She was at the mercy of a diminutive, elderly lady with little red plumes in her hair and a face as brown and wrinkled as a walnut, who was talking incessantly of all the deserving painters and sculptors of her acquaintance, and of how she, as a patron of the arts, championed their cause.

"It is to be an artistic soirée tonight, is it not?" she asked, narrowing her eyes.

"Yes I believe it is," replied Eline, with mounting discomfiture.

"You sing, do you not?"

"Oh no, not any more; my doctor has forbidden it."

"I suppose you would have gone on the stage otherwise?"

"Oh no, I don't think so … "

Several gentlemen came forward and bowed to the elderly lady, after which she introduced them all to Eline: composers, musicians, actors, painters, gifted yet misunderstood artists to a man, whose names would doubtless be on everyone's lips before long.

Being thus encircled by misunderstood geniuses made Eline feel quite dizzy, and she was greatly relieved when she saw St Clare making his way towards her.

"What a siege!" he laughed softly. "I could hardly get through the crowd."

Eline pouted.

"Let's move to the side a little, there is more room there!" she lisped, deftly making her escape from the geniuses. With a sigh she subsided on to a pouffe, nervously patting the burnished gold beadwork along her low-cut bodice of black satin.

"Oh dear, I was already getting quite bored," she said with light distaste. "But do tell me, how did you fare in Ghent and Bruges?"

He remained standing beside her and told her a little of his excursion, while the throng eddied all around them and footmen went round offering wine, sorbets and cakes.

"By the way," said St Clare, breaking off his account, "do you know what the entertainments are to be this evening?" All eyes were turned on Eliza, who was bobbing and weaving before the Count in apparent supplication.

The Count responded with a show of modest reluctance.

"Oh, but you can't let me down! I beseech you!" wheedled Eliza.

"I expect she asked him to declaim some poetry, and he's too shy!" laughed Eline.

She was right. Eliza darted a look of triumph at the ladies in her vicinity when the Count finally relented. He struck a declamatory pose and cleared his throat. He would recite an epic poem that told of Pizarro's conquest of Mexico, of Montezuma and the Aztecs.

Voices sank to low whispers, and in the ensuing hush the Count launched into wave upon wave of thunderous alexandrine verse, with plenty of burring *r*s. From the far side of the room Vincent sent Eline a mischievous nod. The Count's voice rose to a shout.

"Sublime, don't you agree?" ventured the elderly lady with the red plumes, who had reappeared at Eline's side.

Eline gave a confirming nod.

The audience, however, was not unanimous in its appreciation; here and there despairing looks and sighs were exchanged, and the whispering grew louder.

"Patience and resignation!" murmured Eline, smiling at St Clare.

He returned her smile. With him standing so close to her, she thought, the long poem didn't seem half as boring.

When the Count's final stanza died away at last, the audience was galvanised into motion. There was laughing and jostling once more, and several ladies made a beeline for the Count to congratulate him on his performance.

"Couldn't we seek refuge before the next entertainment begins?" asked St Clare with a light laugh.

"We will be more at liberty in the conservatory," said Eline.

With some difficulty they threaded their way through the crowd to the small winter garden. It was empty save for a pair of elderly gentlemen seated at a table bearing an assortment of empty wine glasses, and a young man in active conversation with a young lady who kept tapping her knee with her fan. A sultry perfume like a breath of the tropics floated beneath the potted palms, vanilla bushes and orchids. Through the windows they saw a snowstorm of white down whirling in the night.

No sooner had they seated themselves than they heard chords being struck on the piano in the reception room. The actor, a frequent visitor, was in possession of a bass voice, and was to sing some duets with the jeweller's blonde lady friend, who had garbed herself in blue plush for the occasion. St Clare and Eline could see them reflected in one of the mirrors adorning the winter garden; they were taking up their positions by the piano while their accompanist—one of the misunderstood composers—seated himself to play.

"I had no idea that she sang!" Eline burst out. "*La bonne surprise!* But do go on with what you were saying."

A blush began to tingle on her cheeks, and she regained a shade of her former beauty and charm. She listened to him with keen interest, raising her glass of champagne to her lips from time to time to take a sip. From the reception room proceeded the high shrieks of the soprano vying with the low growl of the bass in a cacophony of song.

Gradually, the winter garden filled up with the bustle of guests, laughing and chatting with relief at escaping from the duets. Vincent, too, sauntered in, and catching sight of St Clare and Eline made his way towards them.

"Do you mind if I join you?" he asked in French.

"By all means!" said Eline.

They felt rather removed from the rest of the crowd, as though they were attending some kind of public fête; they knew hardly anyone, and watched the scene unfolding around them with quiet derision. The two elderly gentlemen's collection of empty wine glasses had expanded considerably, and beneath an overhanging banana frond the young man could be seen slipping his arm about his companion's waist. From another corner came the sound of broken glass, whereupon a rowdy guest, identified by Vincent as a self-proclaimed Russian prince, began to disport himself with two female circus riders. Vincent could not imagine how they had managed to be introduced to Uncle Daniel.

"Oh, they must have slipped in through the back door! I'm sure Eliza doesn't know they are here!" laughed Eline.

The entertainments took their course in the reception suite with more songs, serious poetry and comic monologues. The audience's attention to the performers, however, flagged as the evening wore on, and the hubbub grew louder. The Russian prince began to chase the circus riders round the winter garden, trying to kiss them, and the two elderly gentlemen, rather the worse for drink, broke into a violent argument.

The young paramours had slipped away.

"I believe I should advise you to remain a little closer to your uncle and aunt; the company here seems to be getting rather mixed," St Clare said to Eline. Vincent had left them. Eline stood up in some alarm; St Clare followed suit. But in the salon they found Eliza at the centre of a very noisy gathering; champagne was being spilt, and several ladies were smoking cigarettes.

St Clare led Eline to the balcony. A stern look came into his proud eyes and his lips quivered an instant as he observed Eliza and her friends.

"How do you come to be here?" he asked abruptly, in a tone of ill-concealed censure. "How is it possible that I should have met you here?"

She looked at him in surprise.

"I don't know what you mean," she replied coldly.

"I'm asking you what brought you here in the first place. I wouldn't have thought this sort of company to be congenial to you. Is it?"

She began to see his meaning, and was shocked by his forwardness.

"Not congenial to me? This sort of company?" she echoed slowly. "May I remind you that I am in the house of my uncle and aunt?"

"I know that, but the company your uncle and aunt keep is hardly up to your standards, it seems to me. You are here with the consent of your other relatives, I take it?"

She began to tremble all over, and fixed him with the haughtiest stare she could muster.

"Mr St Clare! I cannot think why you feel entitled to subject me to a cross-examination. I thought I was free to do as I please, and old enough to choose my friends without prior consent from anyone at all, not from my 'other relatives' and not from you either."

Her tone was needle-sharp. She made to turn away. He caught her hand. She snatched it away.

"Do stay a moment, I beg you. Forgive me if I have hurt your feelings: that was not my intention. But I can't help taking an interest in you. I have heard so much about you from Vincent. I knew you before I had ever set eyes on you. I thought of you as, how shall I put it, as an unknown sister, just as I thought of Vincent as my brother. And here you are, mixing with people who—"

"Thank you most kindly for your good intentions," she broke in icily. "But be so good as to find more appropriate means of expressing your fraternal interest in future. You knew me before you met me, you say. *C'est possible.* I have known you for a week. Hardly long enough for you to dare to speak to me as if I required guidance. I am much obliged for your solicitude, but I have no need for it."

He gestured impatiently and restrained her once more. She was still quivering with rage, but stood her ground.

"Oh, please, don't be angry with me!" he said warmly. "Perhaps I was too outspoken. But what about you—would you yourself qualify the present company as suitable?"

"I see no reason why the acquaintances of my uncle and aunt should not be mine, too. Whatever the case, it is no concern of yours."

"Why won't you allow me take an interest in you?"

"Because it's presumptuous of you."

"Is there no pardon for such presumption, if it arises from a sense of true friendship?" he asked, extending his hand.

"Oh, certainly!" she said coldly, ignoring his hand. "But please spare me your presumption as well as your all-too-friendly feelings in future. Too much interest can be tiresome."

She turned on her heel and swept out of the balcony. St Clare, now alone, watched her as she mingled with the throng, rubbing shoulders with the circus riders and the Russian prince, with the blonde lady, the two inebriated old gentlemen, and the Count-cum-poet.

The party was over at last, and in the solitude of her room Eline reflected on her bruised feelings. It was five o'clock in the morning, and she felt almost too exhausted to shed her clothes.

It was not so much his presumption that riled her, but it had been such a long time since she had been able to forget her sorrows, even temporarily. That evening she had actually begun to enjoy herself a little, like in the old days, and he had gone and spoilt her innocent pleasure with his remarks about the company being unsuitable. As if she didn't know that! And it was precisely because she did know, and because deep down she could not but agree with him, that she felt hurt. Why couldn't he have granted her that brief evening of amusement? Why did he have to mention her 'other relatives'? What would Betsy and Henk care if she took up with some unconventional acquaintance of her uncle's? But she hadn't taken up with anyone; the only people she had exchanged more than a few words with were Vincent and him. She had enjoyed herself in spite of the company, couldn't he see that?

Still wearing her black-satin gown, she threw herself down on a couch to think. The more she pondered the affront she had suffered the more tenuous it became, but before it eluded her completely she checked herself. Yes, she did feel hurt, she thought with grim resolve. Very hurt indeed.

On the other hand, was it really so serious? He had raised objections, on her behalf, to the unconventional coterie she found herself in, taking them for a disreputable lot. He had expressed his disapproval with brutal frankness, and she could still hear him say: "How do you come to be here? Are you here with the consent of your other relatives?"

In other words, he was interested in her welfare: genuinely, frankly interested. And she was seized with longing to beg his forgiveness and ask him what action he would advise her to take. What bliss it would be simply to follow his lead, to give herself up in complete surrender … how restful … how sweet.

At noon, after a brief slumber, she entered the reception room, looking very pale, with dark circles under her eyes. Eliza was bustling about with the maid and manservant, tidying up the remains of the previous evening's orgy. She declared herself very pleased with her soirée.

"Happy New Year, Eline!" she said. "You can't imagine how many glasses got broken last night! Thank goodness they were only hired. If you want some breakfast, you'll find it in the *salle à manger*. Off you go now, you'll only get in the way here, if you don't mind my saying so. But it was fun last night, wasn't it?"

Eline repaired to the dining room. She nibbled a piece of toast and lingered a while, hoping that St Clare would call. But neither he nor Vincent put in an appearance that day. Not the next day either, or the one after that. If Eline had dared, she would have sent him a note.

Before the week was out she received a letter from Madame van Raat, with news about Paul, whom she saw from time to time even though he had gone to live in Bodegraven; he seemed unhappy about something, but his mother knew not what. She was sorry to say that she and her son seemed to have become somewhat estranged, and expressed doubt as to whether she had been a sufficiently loving mother to him as a child.

"She, not loving enough?" Eline thought to herself. "I have never known anyone so loving ... to me, at any rate."

She read on, and learnt that Lili was expecting a baby, due in March. But at the end of the letter she received a shock. Jeanne Ferelijn had died in Bangil. Eline's eyes filled with tears.

"Oh my God! Oh my God!" she repeated slowly, and a nervous sob shook her frame. Her poor friend was dead! Oh, how tenderly Jeanne had nursed her when she was ill with bronchitis in that cramped little upstairs apartment! How kind and comforting she had always been, and how devoted to her husband and children! And now she had died ... What had life given her? Nothing, oh, nothing! Madame van Raat had her own sorrows; so did Paul. And Lili would receive her share of sadness and disappointment too, now that she was to be a mother. What was life but one great misery ...

"Jeanne is dead! Jeanne is dead!" hissed a voice in her ears and in her brain. She had so much to thank Jeanne for, and she would never see her again, for Jeanne was dead! Oh God, she was dead!

She threw herself back in her chair and hid her face in her hands. Hearing footsteps in the ante-room she looked up, and before she had time to compose herself, a figure appeared in the doorway. It was St Clare. She stared at him blankly through her tears.

"I hope you will forgive me for disturbing you," he said softly, seeing that she was crying. "The maid said you were at home and receiving. Would you rather I came back tomorrow?"

She drew herself up, wiped her eyes and gave a sad smile.

"Do you wish to go already?" she said. "You are not disturbing me; on the contrary, I am glad to see you. Do take a seat. Is Vincent well?"

"Thank you, he is very well!" he said, and in his tone Eline could hear the affection he bore Vincent. "We have been to Liège and Verviers to visit some factories."

"Is that the only reason I have not seen you since the soirée?"

He looked at her a moment.

"Yes," he said. "That is the only reason."

"So you were not angry with me?"

"Not in the least. I was the one who was wrong. I ought not to have spoken to you like that. You were right."

"I don't believe I was," she said. "I was rude to you, and I am sorry. Will you forgive me? Or will you refuse me your hand, just as I refused you mine?"

She held out her hand. He held it fast.

"I forgive you, gladly!" he responded. "And I do appreciate your willingness to admit to being a little mistaken."

"So will you continue to take an interest in me? Will you believe me when I say that your friendship and concern are not in the least tiresome to me, unlike what I said before? May I depend on that?"

"Certainly you may."

"Thank you. Thank you so much. I was not mistaken when I said you were kind-hearted. You are more than kind, you are noble."

He gave a short laugh.

"How formal you sound!" he said. "Very dignified!"

"No!" she protested. "I am not dignified, and I wasn't being formal either. Please don't say that. I meant what I said. I can't tell you how pleased I am that you have come to see me, and that you aren't angry with me. Especially now. I was so downhearted."

"You were crying, weren't you?"

Teardrops trembled on her lashes.

"I just received some very sad news: a dear friend of mine has died. She was so frail, and yet so needed; what will become of her poor husband and children I cannot imagine. But what can you do? People who lead useful lives die. And people like me, who are a burden to everyone, including themselves, live on."

"Why do you say that? Are you sure there is no one who needs you and loves you? And is there no one you love?"

She gave a wry smile.

"Because there must be people who care about you," he persisted.

"What can I say? Both my parents have died, and my sister— well, I expect Vincent told you about her. Did you know I ran away from my brother-in-law's house?"

"Yes."

"Since then I have been drifting from one place to the next. Always among strangers. And now my uncle and aunt have taken me in, but in a way they are strangers, too. Back in The Hague I lived with my brother-in-law's elderly mother for a time; she was extremely kind to me, and I was devoted to her. But I wasn't at all kind to her, I'm ashamed to say."

"I feel for you very much!" he said. "I wish there was something I could do to help. Have you considered finding something to occupy yourself with? Aren't you rather bored? Couldn't that be the cause of your unhappiness?"

"I did look for things to do in The Hague. And I did a fair amount of travelling, but I still felt unhappy. It's all my own fault, you see. I threw away my chance of happiness."

She began to cry, holding her head in her hands.

"Tell me, is there anything I can do?" he pleaded.

"Nothing, thank you. I am beyond help … from anyone."

"But submerging oneself in unhappy thoughts to the exclusion of all else is never a good thing. I strongly advise against it. You need to be brave, so as to raise yourself from your suffering. Everybody suffers at one time or another. Come, promise me that from now on you will try to be brave."

"But I'm not brave, I'm weak!" she sobbed. "I am broken, ruined."

She sounded so powerless and distraught that he did not know what to say. His heart overflowed with pity, a pity mingled with despair at finding the means to help her. And yet his only wish was to try and console her, come what may.

"No!" he exclaimed firmly. "You are not broken. That is just a phrase people use. You are young, you have your whole life ahead of you. Break with your past, put it out of your mind."

"But how?" she wept. "How could I possibly do that?"

He was aware that he, too, had used just such a phrase. He was also aware that the human psyche could become permanently warped by anguish suffered in the past.

"My heart goes out to you!" he said. "I feel such pity for you, more than I have ever felt for anyone before."

"That is the only thing you can do for me!" she cried out with passion. "Give me your pity! It will do me good! Didn't you say that you knew me before you met me, that I was like an unknown sister to you?"

He stood up, placed his hands on her frail shoulders and held her gaze.

"Certainly!" he said warmly, and she could have died, so profoundly grateful did she feel. "And now that I have met you properly, I shall do everything in my power to help you. You must tell me all about yourself. I will make you brave, you'll see."

He gave her a pat on the shoulder, in comradely fashion. Her heart was frantic with regret: why, oh why had she not met him sooner? How wonderful it had felt to humble herself before him and beg forgiveness!

A week elapsed, during which the Veres saw neither Vincent nor St Clare, as they were away in Holland. There was talk of a masked ball, hosted by the Count. Uncle Daniel would not attend in fancy dress, but Eliza would be going as an oriental dancer, and Eline, whose imagination had deserted her, was thinking of doing the same.

When the invitation arrived Eline thought of St Clare. What would he say if she accepted? But she had no desire to spend the evening at home alone, so she banished the thought from her mind and concentrated on her costume.

The two friends returned on the day before the ball. Eline thought she saw a flicker of concern in St Clare's eyes when he heard of the event, but he made no comment. The following evening at around half-past eight he and Vincent called at Avenue Louise. Both of them had been invited to be of the party; Vincent had accepted, St Clare had not. He wished to see Eline, but was told that she had just started her toilette. When St Clare reiterated his request with some urgency, Eline sent word that she would see him shortly and asked him to wait.

The reception room was deserted, as Uncle Daniel and Eliza were also preparing themselves. Vincent, in evening dress, settled himself on a couch and took up *L'Indépendance* to skim the news. St Clare posted himself in the balcony with his hands thrust in his pockets, staring out of the window at the snow gleaming dingily beneath the street lamps. The servant entered with tea for the gentlemen.

"I must say I admire your pluck, Lawrence!" Vincent remarked in English as he slowly stirred his tea. "Are you sure she will take it all in good part?"

"I have no choice. It is the only way," St Clare replied resolutely, and declined the offer of tea.

When the servant was gone they kept silent for a time, until Eline entered. A rosy blush of face powder hid the sallowness of her skin; her hair was already dressed for the ball with chains of glittering coins, which fell in three tiers across her forehead. Further than that she had not proceeded with her costume, and had wrapped a white-flannel peignoir about her in some haste. Vincent stood up, and she apologised for the state she was in. Nonetheless, she looked alluring.

"You wanted to speak to me urgently, I believe?" she said softly to St Clare, extending her hand. "So please excuse my undress. Do take a seat."

They sat down, while Vincent repaired to the winter garden with his newspaper. St Clare looked intently at Eline.

"What do you wish to say to me?" she asked.

"First of all, I must apologise for disturbing you so rudely during your preparations for the ball."

"Oh that's all right; I have plenty of time."

"I am very grateful that you came at once. I hope you understand that I would not have intruded had it not been for a good reason. I have a request to make you."

"An urgent request?"

"Indeed, an urgent request. And I run the risk that you will be very angry with me when I tell you what it is; that you will feel hurt, and that you will tell me to mind my own business."

It began to dawn on her, vaguely, what his request would be.

"Come on then, out with it!" she said simply.

"You said I might take the same interest in you as a brother would take in a sister. Is that right, or am I mistaken?"

"No, that is quite right."

"Well, if you were my sister, I would ask you to do me a great favour by not going to that ball tonight."

She did not answer.

"If you were my sister, I would tell you that Vincent and I made some enquiries as to the guest list for the ball, and that I am certain that a large proportion of the guests are even less reputable than some of the people your uncle and aunt count among their friends. If you were my sister I could hardly express myself more plainly. But I hope you will understand my concern, now that you have some idea of the type of people that have been invited."

She lowered her eyes.

"And therefore, at the risk of interfering in a matter that does not concern me, at the risk of your uncle and aunt taking offence at my meddling in your affairs, at the risk of you yourself, having forgiven me one indiscretion already, becoming very angry with me, I ask you again: please don't go to the ball. You do not belong there."

Still she remained silent, twisting the sash of her peignoir around her finger.

"Are you very angry?" he asked.

"No," she replied very softly after a pause. "No, I am not angry. And I shall do as you ask. I shan't go."

"Do you mean that?" he exclaimed joyfully.

"I mean it," she said. "I shan't go. I am very grateful to you for making enquiries about the kind of people who will be there. To tell you the truth, I had a feeling that you might not approve, but I dreaded having to stay at home all by myself. I find it so depressing."

"You had a feeling I might not approve?" he echoed, smiling.

"Yes!" she replied. "You are such a good friend to me; I would hate to do anything against your wishes. As for tonight—your wish is my command."

"Thank you!" he murmured, pressing her hand. "I appreciate that very much."

"Oh, as well you might!" she said brightly, although she was somewhat startled by her own submissiveness. "Do you realise that it took me almost an hour to arrange all those coins in my hair? And all for nothing!"

"I am serious—I appreciate it very much, really!" he said earnestly.

Uncle Daniel came in.

"*Bonsoir*, St Clare. You are not coming with us, are you? But Eline! Shouldn't you be getting dressed?"

Eline's stammered reply was lost in the vociferations of Eliza, who was berating the manservant in the adjoining room, and a moment later Eliza swept in, resplendent in Algerian draperies and a headdress of coins, with dainty Moorish mules on her feet.

"*Bonsoir*, St Clare! What a shame you won't be joining us! Good gracious, Eline, look at you!"

Vincent emerged from the winter garden.

"It's almost half-past nine and you've only done your hair!" pursued Eliza. "What's the matter with you?"

"I don't believe your niece will be accompanying you, dear lady," said St Clare, as Eline was too flustered to speak. "We heard, Vincent and I, that the society would be rather mixed this evening—and consequently I have advised Miss Vere to stay at home rather than expose herself to undesirable encounters. I hope you don't mind. Of course I knew she would be in safe hands with her uncle and you to chaperone her, but I couldn't help feeling that keeping such company would be rather less suitable for a young girl than for a married lady—even such a charming one as yourself! Was I very wrong?"

Eliza wondered whether or not she should take offence, since his tone, though determined, was friendly enough. Daniel Vere shrugged his shoulders.

"Wrong?" echoed Eliza. "Well, I wouldn't know. Of course Eline can do as she likes. If she would rather not go, *eh bien, soit*, then we shall have to pretend she has a headache. Easy as kiss-your-thumb. But you will be abysmally bored, Eline."

"No, really, I would rather stay at home," said Eline. "That is, if you don't mind."

"Not at all, my dear. *Liberté chérie*, as they say."

The servant came in with the fur coats, and announced that the carriage was waiting. He held up Eline's cloak.

"If your uncle and aunt have no objection, I should like to keep you company for a little while," said St Clare.

They had no objection, and Eline felt mildly confused.

"Goodbye, have fun!" she said with a timid smile when Uncle Daniel, Eliza and Vincent took their departure.

"Ridiculous," grumbled Uncle Daniel when they were seated in the carriage. "Ridiculous! He won't have her going to the ball, but thinks it perfectly all right for him to stay with her and keep her company. I suppose it must be American! I mean, which is more compromising—going to a ball with us or spending an evening alone with a young man? Ridiculous!"

Vincent, thinking it beneath his dignity to defend his friend, made no comment. With much ado Eliza prevailed upon her husband to keep silent, saying that it would not do to speak ill of a niece who was living under his roof, nor of a friend whom they saw so frequently.

"Speak ill of him? Not at all!" huffed Uncle Daniel. "He's American! And he has American ways, I suppose."

Eline was still flustered.

"I don't think my uncle was very pleased that I took your advice," she said when they were alone. "Nor did he seem to approve of—of you staying behind."

St Clare looked at her in calm surprise.

"Then why didn't he say so? I asked him if he had any objection. And you? Would you rather I left?"

"Oh no, I'd be very grateful if you stayed a while."

"With pleasure. Because I have another favour to ask of you, albeit a less important one."

"What is it?"

"Could I have one of those coins you have taken so much trouble to arrange in your hair?"

Eline smiled; carefully she unwound the string of coins from her head and pulled one off, which she presented to him.

"Thank you!" he said, and attached it to his watch chain.

Eline was bemused. She felt very pleased, happy even, and yet somewhat abashed. And she wondered which Betsy would have thought the greater evil: going to the ball chaperoned by her uncle and aunt, or spending the evening unchaperoned with St Clare—in her peignoir, of all things. The latter to be sure, she thought. But he seemed to consider it all so simple and natural that she didn't even dare to excuse herself to go and change her dress.

"And now let's have a nice chat!" he said, settling himself in a Turkish armchair while she remained seated on the couch, shyly fingering the string of coins. "Why don't you tell me some more about yourself, about your childhood, or your travels, perhaps?"

She said she did not know what to tell him, so he asked her questions, which she answered with pleasure and growing confidence. She told him about Aunt Vere, about how much she had enjoyed reading Ouida's novels, and above all about her father and the large canvases that he never completed. She told him about her singing, and about Betsy and Henk, adding that she used to think quite differently then, and that she used to look quite different, too.

"What do you mean by 'then'?"

"I mean before my illness and before I went travelling with my uncle and aunt. Before … before my engagement."

"And how did you look then?"

"Much healthier, and … fresher."

"You mean: more beautiful?"

That he could read her thoughts made her laugh, and also that he did not make the slightest effort to be gallant. She suggested that he might be interested in seeing some of her photographs from those days, and as she reached for one of the albums lying on a console, it occurred to her that she might as well give him leave to call her by her first name, but in the next instant forgot her intention.

He leafed through the album, which contained many fine portraits of her: with a ribbon in her hair, wearing a pearl necklace, and several in a low-necked gown.

"Well? What do you think?" she asked, in response to his silence.

"Very pretty," he said indifferently. "But that smile ... so co-quettish, so sweet ... a pretentious kind of sweetness. A bit off-putting. Did you always look like that, or were you doing it for the photograph?"

She was piqued.

"Goodness me, I didn't know you could be so harsh!" she said accusingly.

"Was I harsh? If so, I beg your pardon. They are portraits of you, after all. I was confused. It's hard for me to recognise you in them. But to be quite honest, I would have been put off if I had seen you looking like that. Beautiful, but off-putting. You look thinner now, and rather frail, but there is something very appealing about your expression, whereas the portraits are just coquettish poses. I prefer you as you are now."

He closed the album and laid it aside.

"And you?" he resumed. "Would you rather be the way you were then? Do you miss your old life?"

"Oh no," she sighed. "I wasn't happy then, either."

"But from now on you will do your best to be happy, won't you?"

She laughed softly and shrugged her shoulders.

"Happiness can't be forced," she murmured dreamily, in English.

"I didn't know you spoke English!" he exclaimed.

"Me?" she responded in French, waking from her dream.

"Yes, you!"

"Me? Speaking English?"

"Not now; a moment ago."

"Was I speaking English? I didn't realise—"

"Why did you never speak English to me before?"

"I don't know."

"Yes you do."

"No, truly, I don't."

"Of course you know. Come now, tell me why."

She gave a light, gay laugh.

"Because of the way you speak French! Your accent is so charming."

"So you have been laughing at me behind my back all this time?"

"No, truly I have not!"

"Then which language shall we speak from now on? English or French?"

"French, or you'll only think I was laughing anyway."

"There's no logic at all in what you're saying."

"I dare say, but I want to go on speaking French."

"See? You aren't as weak as you thought. You're getting braver already."

"Am I?"

"This is the first time I've heard you say 'I want'. It's a good start. Mark my words: first you exercise your will over some small matter, and soon it will become firmer. Once it's firm and strong, you'll become brave. Promise me you'll try to cultivate that small will of yours, think of it as a hothouse seedling that needs a lot of care."

She continued to smile sweetly.

"I could become very wilful under your influence."

"Well, I hope not. But I'd be delighted if you became a little braver under my influence."

"I shall do my best."

"And I shall keep you to your word. Now I must be off. It is nearly eleven."

She wanted to exclaim 'What, already?", but checked the impulse.

"Now tell me honestly, don't you think you are far better off going to bed early and getting a good night's sleep instead of staying up until six in the morning and dancing with strange men and associating with an even stranger assortment of ladies?"

"You are absolutely right. I am very grateful to you."

"And so am I to you, for the coin you have given me."

She sensed that his gratitude extended further than the coin.

"And now I must take my leave. Goodnight, Eline."

She was moved to hear him call her by her first name; it struck a new note of familiarity and warmth.

"Goodnight, Lawrence," she whispered.

She extended her slender hand. He held it a moment, gazing into her eyes, then let go.

"Adieu!" he said with a final cordial nod, and left.

She remained standing a while, sunk in thought, then ordered the servant to turn off the light in the reception room, and retired to her bedroom. She took the string of coins from her hair and laid it on her dressing table. The shimmering draperies of her oriental costume were spread out on a chair, with her Moorish mules on the floor beside it.

While she was getting dressed for bed she could hear his voice speaking in that light accent of his. She tidied away her jewellery with deliberation. Her eye fell on her watch, and from there on the black locket attached to the chain. She opened the locket and gazed at it for a long moment, moist-eyed.

Then she pressed a soft kiss on the likeness it contained, as though she were kissing someone who had just died. She had a momentary impulse to detach the locket from the chain and put it away in one of the little drawers of her jewellery box, where she kept various trinkets that she no longer wore. But she did not act on it.

She climbed into bed. She did not sleep. Nor did she take any drops. At half-past five she heard Uncle Daniel and Eliza return home, sighing with exhaustion. But her wakeful hours had been undisturbed by grim thoughts of any kind; indeed, she felt bathed in a calm, rosy glow of repose.

Towards morning she dozed off, and when she awoke she felt less lethargic than usual.

Eline did not see Eliza again until lunch the following day. Uncle Daniel had already left on one of his numerous missions, the nature of which was never fully disclosed, so that his occupation remained a mystery to Eline. She asked Eliza whether she had amused herself at the ball.

"Oh, yes, well enough," Eliza responded genially. "Rather a brouhaha. Perhaps it was just as well that you didn't go. You would have been a nervous wreck. *Le cher poète était désolé.* Did St Clare stay long?"

"Until eleven."

"Ah well, personally I didn't mind about him advising you to stay in. But Daniel thought it a bit strange that you were so easily persuaded. He's got over it now, though! You are as free as you like as far as we're concerned, you know that."

Eline said nothing.

"But you have to admit," Eliza continued with a chuckle, "that it was a bit odd. Makes you think, doesn't it?"

"Well, what does it make you think?" asked Eline warily.

"My dear girl, that is private. I am not going to tell you. You know I don't go in for much thinking, but right now I do have some ideas. Don't be alarmed: I am all in favour of it, if what I suspect is true."

Eline sensed that this was an allusion to something she was barely conscious of herself.

She kept silent, whereupon Eliza, still fatigued from the ball, settled herself on a couch with a book and soon dozed off. Eline went to the balcony and sat down to think. She had thought little during the last few days, which had passed in a haze of contented submission, but now Eliza's words had impinged on her consciousness. A bit odd … it made you think … True, that St Clare should have been so bold as to ask her not to go to the ball was slightly odd, to say the least, and it was no less odd of her to have consented! What this made her think of she dared not formulate in her mind, although the temptation to do so was almost irresistible. But she knew that nothing could come of it, that it could never be … Oh, why had she not met him sooner? How cruel fate was!

She began to have qualms about her behaviour towards him. Perhaps she ought to have rebuffed him, told him not to meddle in her affairs. Nor had there been any need for her to apologise to him the other day for her coldness, really. But, on the other hand, how wonderful it had felt simply to bend to his will! He was so strong and protective, so deeply reassuring to her. It had never entered her mind that he might fall in love with her, ailing, broken creature that she was. It would be a foolish thing for him to do … but it was probably too late now to try and stop him.

When he called again a few days later, he found her alone in the reception room. The weather was cold, and Eline hardly ever went out with her uncle and aunt due to her cough. She was seated in the Turkish chair by the fire, while outside a driving wind sent the snowflakes whirling against the window panes.

"I was sure I would find you at home; that's why I came!" he said, taking a seat. "Have your uncle and aunt gone out?"

"Yes they have; I don't know where to—some auction I believe, to buy antiques."

She meant to maintain some reserve in her answers, but his company was so welcome to her that she found it impossible to do so, and in spite of herself she said:

"It's lovely to see you again."

He smiled briefly and made some comments on the purchase of antiques with particular reference to the porcelain items dotted about the room. Then he said:

"I shall soon be leaving you for an extended period. We are travelling via Cologne to Berlin, and then onward from there."

She felt her throat tighten.

"When will you be leaving?" she asked mechanically.

"In a few days."

"And you will be going all the way to Petersburg, to Moscow?"

"Yes."

"Does Russia attract you?"

He responded somewhat absently, in short, halting sentences. Listening to him, she had to fight back her tears, and his words came to her in a blur when she heard him say, as though interrupting himself:

457

"But there is something I wanted to ask you. I wanted to ask you to think of me once in a while, during my absence."

"Of course I'll think of you!" she said tremulously. "You have been so good to me, so kind—and I shall always remember you with pleasure."

"Thank you," he said softly. "It is sad, I find, having to say goodbye so soon to a new acquaintance with whom one has a sympathetic rapport."

"Yes, but then life is filled with disappointments, is it not?"

"I know what you are going to say," he went on, following his own train of thought. "You are going to say that I can stay in Brussels as long as I please, because I'm travelling for pleasure and can alter my plans at will. Actually, I might even prefer so stay in Brussels."

She began to tremble all over, but recovered herself in time to murmur:

"Why should you alter your plans? Why not see what you can of the world?"

"Because I love you," he said calmly, fixing her with his penetrating gaze. "And because I dread having to part from you. I would like to remain with you for ever, to care for you and protect you. I shudder to think of leaving you behind, as if something might happen to you while I'm away."

"But that's impossible!"

"Why impossible?" he retorted. "Why is it impossible for me to be with you for ever, or rather, for you to be with me for ever? Tell me, Eline, why?"

"Because it cannot be so," she replied, weeping.

"Yes it can! It can, if you love me. You could come with me and I could take care of you; you would be my wife."

"And I would make you unhappy!" she wept.

"No, no. On the contrary, I would do everything in my power to make you happy, and I am certain I would succeed. Listen to me. I cared about you even before we met, because of what Vincent had told me about you. The first time I saw you I felt sorry for you, because it was so clear to me that you had suffered some terrible grief. I tried to think of some way of making you happy again, but found nothing. Only, during our conversations together I thought you were beginning to look and sound slightly more cheerful. It might have been my imagination, but that was my impression. I also imagined, perhaps out of vanity, that I might have had a hand in lifting your spirits a little. I watched you talking with other people, but with them you appeared to be cool and reserved, whereas with me you seemed quite happy to talk; you even grew confidential. That is when I felt a great longing to dedicate myself entirely to you, because I thought, if I can do that, she might be able shake off her gloomy view of life and be happy again. My darling Elly, you're still so young, and you think it's too late for things to change. Don't think like that any more; put your trust in me, then we can set out together to discover whether life really is as dismal as you believe. Tell me, Elly, will you? Will you let me show you that you have a whole new life waiting for you?"

She sobbed quietly and raised her tear-filled eyes to his, clasping her hands almost beseechingly.

"Oh, why must you ask me that?" she cried. "Why must you ask me? Why must I hurt you? Not you, too! But it's impossible; it could never be, not ever."

"Why not?"

"Why not?" she echoed. "Because, even though I'm young, I'm quite broken. Why won't you believe me? Because everything in me is shattered, because my soul is in ruins."

"Eline, there's no need for such big words. Calm down."

"I am not using big words, I am quite calm. I speak with reason, oh, with hopeless reason!" she cried, standing up to face him. He caught her hands in his. "I know what I am saying, and I can't bear it! Listen to me, Lawrence. You know that I was engaged to be married, don't you?"

"Yes. You broke it off."

"Yes I did. I broke it off, and yet I loved him. Even when I was writing that final letter telling him it was over, I loved him. Do you realise how awful that is?"

His only answer was a look of bewilderment.

"You don't understand, do you?" she burst out, her hands shaking in his grasp. "You have no idea what it feels like to be a woman whose heart is lacerated by the most horrible doubts!

I don't even know what I feel sometimes, or what I want, or even what I'm thinking! You see, there's a part of me that is undeveloped, incomplete. I'm always racked with doubt, never sure about anything. I loved him—oh, please forgive me saying this to you now, but I loved him so very much, he was so good and he would have given his life for me! And then one day I began to wonder whether I really loved him. I even thought I loved someone else for a time, while I loved no one but him. I know that now, but I discovered it too late, and I may have ruined his life!"

"Why do you think that, Eline?"

"I just know it. When I was in The Hague people gave me to understand that he had got over the disappointment. But I never believed them! Now that it's too late, it has all become clear to me, only now do I realise how much he loved me. And he hasn't forgotten me; if I had heard that he had married someone else in the meantime, I still wouldn't believe he had forgotten all about me. I know he still thinks of me, just as often as I still think of him."

"Do you still love him?" he asked dully.

"Not the way I loved him before. Not any more, Lawrence. I think what I feel for him now is pity more than anything else. But I think of him often. I have his portrait here."

She opened the locket and held it out for him to see Otto's likeness. He stared at it.

"Do you keep it with you at all times?" he asked softly.

"Yes, I do," she said in a barely audible whisper. "Always. It is sacred to me. And that is why, Lawrence—oh, that is why it can never be! The thought of him would always come between us. I could have been happy with you, if it weren't for that thought haunting me. But I could never be happy while I knew him to be sad, oh, no, I could never do that!"

When he failed to respond she sank to the floor, convulsed with sobs, and pressed her forehead to his knees.

"Oh forgive me, Lawrence, forgive me! I never thought you could love me! I felt so ill, always coughing, too weak to do anything! I thought I'd grown ugly, and that no man would ever want me! Otherwise I wouldn't have shown you that I cared for you! You spoke of us as brother and sister! Why do you speak differently now? And now I have caused you pain, but I had no choice. It would be wicked of me to become your wife while I have this weighing on my conscience."

He pulled her gently to her feet and drew her towards him.

"Eline!" he said. "You once told me that you had thrown away your happiness. I did not ask what you meant by that. But I am asking you now. Did you mean the letter you wrote to Otto?"

"Yes!" she sobbed.

"You threw away your happiness by writing that letter, is that it? Are you quite sure that you won't be throwing it away again if you stand by the answer you gave me? Or could I never make you happy? Only Otto?"

"Oh, Lawrence!" she murmured passionately, stepping closer. "If only I had met you when I was younger, before all those things happened, I could never have loved anyone but you. But it was not to be. It was my fate."

"Oh, don't talk about fate. Fate is just a word. Everyone shapes their own fate. You are too weak to take yourself in hand. Let me be your fate."

"It's impossible!" she wept, tossing her head from side to side against his chest. "I can't help it, but it's impossible!"

"No, Eline, it is not impossible!" he replied. "You say you could have loved no one but me if you had met me before. But if we had met before, you might not have had the same effect on me; in any case, all that is mere speculation, and beside the point. The point is that I love you; I love you the way you are now. You say that you are ill, but I know that you will recover. I can feel it."

"You can't be sure!" she wept.

"That is true, but neither can you be sure that you ruined Otto's happiness. You can see that, can't you? You don't know for certain."

"Oh, but I am! I can feel it!"

"But you don't know for certain," he persisted. "And you tell me, when I ask you to be my wife, that it's impossible, out of the question. Aren't you being rather cruel?"

"Oh, please don't say that!" she sobbed.

"You said yourself a moment ago that you are always doubting, never certain about anything. So what makes you so certain that you can't marry me? How do you know you won't regret your decision when I'm gone, when it's too late?"

"Oh," she moaned. "How can you make me suffer like this? You're tormenting me—"

He lifted her face to his.

"I shall stop tormenting you, Eline. There is just one more thing. Please don't give me a flat refusal. You might yet have a change of heart. At least allow me to hope. Vincent and I are leaving the day after tomorrow. Five months from now you will see me again. I shall ask Vincent to write to you from time to time, so that you always know where to reach me. One word from you and I shall come straight back. You needn't promise me anything, just don't refuse me just yet. Allow me to hope, and try to be hopeful yourself. Will you do that for me? Is that asking too much?"

"No," she whispered. "Oh no, it's not too much. I will give you my answer five months from now."

"Good," he said. "That's all I ask. And now I will wait here for your uncle and aunt to return, so that I can take my leave of them. Vincent will look in tomorrow. And, since we're alone now, may I take this opportunity to say goodbye to you?"

She did not answer, but held his gaze until he took her in his arms and kissed her.

"Five months from now?" he whispered, smiling.

Drawing back a moment, she looked at him intently, then flung her arms about his neck and pressed a long, tender kiss on his forehead.

"Five months from now," she echoed.

XXXIV

A T THE ONSET OF WINTER it seemed to Frédérique that her soul, which had previously felt as light and free as a bird, was labouring under a burden of lead. It seemed to her that she had committed some secret crime, that she had murdered Paul, as it were, and that Mathilda and Marie were the only people in the world who knew about it. She had grown taciturn and withdrawn, and her remorse tempered the dark shimmer of her eyes to a soft, soulful glow.

She had not seen Paul since he had moved to Bodegraven, and he very rarely visited The Hague nowadays. Had he left on her account? Or was his ambition to become a mayor just another fad, much like his earlier efforts at making a career out of singing, or painting, or his short spell at Hovel's law office? Did he ever think of her? Or had he forgotten all about that sunny morning at de Horze when he kissed her and asked her to be his wife? And supposing he still thought of her, was it with regret or with indifference?

She could not answer these questions, which plagued her the moment she found herself alone.

At length she had resigned herself to the idea that she would not be seeing Paul any more, so it came as rather a shock when she spotted him in the street one day, coming in her direction. Her heart pounded, the blood left her cheeks, and had she been obliged to speak she would have found it impossible to utter a syllable. When he drew near he tipped his hat, to which she responded with a brief nod of the head, and they passed one another wordlessly. She proceeded on her way with quaking knees, wondering whether he had noted her consternation.

That afternoon, when she rang the bell at Prinsessegracht and the door was answered by Bet, she began by asking:

"Are there any other callers?"

"Yes, Miss, that is to say, young Madame van Raat with her young lad, and also the Eekhof ladies."

"No one else?"

"No, no one else, Miss."

Frédérique hesitated a moment. Paul might yet arrive. But it was also possible that he had already called earlier. Whatever the case, she could say she was pressed for time and leave quickly; it was just that she dearly wished to see Marie for a moment.

Frédérique went in. The elders were in the conservatory with Betsy; Marie was in the drawing room with Ange and Léonie; Ben sat quietly on Ange's lap while tea was being served. After greeting Marie's parents, Frédérique went to sit with the girls. Suddenly she overheard Betsy in the adjoining conservatory:

"Paul is in town, you know. He had coffee with us today."

Ben twisted round on his aunt's lap, slowly repeating in his slurred voice:

"Uncle Paul—Uncle Paul had coffee with us."

"Did he now? And did you like that, my podgy little poppet?" cooed Ange, slightly disconcerted by the child's docility.

The conversation turned to Paul; the Eekhof girls asked how he was getting on in Bodegraven and would it be long before he was appointed mayor. They thought it very odd of Paul to want to be a mayor—surely he was not stiff enough.

"Has he been here?" Frédérique asked with apparent indifference, but Marie understood how much she cared.

"No," she answered. "He might drop by later, though."

Frédérique's mind was a blur: did she want him to see him arrive unexpectedly, or did she not really want to see him at all? She had come because she wanted to see Marie, and here she was, with Marie, but she could hardly pour her heart out in the presence of the Eekhof girls. Ah well, perhaps that was a good thing.

What was there to say, anyway? Words were no help.

She accepted Betsy's offer to drop her off on her way home, and in the carriage she almost wept at the thought of that first, fleeting encounter with Paul after so many months of silence.

A few days later, when Frédérique thought Paul had already returned to Bodegraven, she ran into him again. She had decided on a whim to call at the Verstraetens', and, setting eyes on him in the salon, she felt the blood drain from her cheeks just like the first time, but it was late afternoon and the light was dim, so no one noticed. Georges and Lili were there too, and after greeting everyone Frédérique extended her hand to Paul, who had risen when she made her entrance. She wavered between calling him Paul or Mr van Raat, but only for a moment, realising that the latter form of address would attract undue attention. He answered quite simply:

"Hello, Freddie."

Lili was complaining to Madame Verstraeten about her butcher and her milkman, until Marie broke in, saying she was becoming a dreadful bore with her constant fretting about her housekeeping. Lili countered that she was not fretting at all, it was just that she would not tolerate being treated lightly by tradesmen. Paul had been conversing with Uncle Verstraeten, but he now turned to Frédérique, addressing her in such a relaxed, natural tone of voice that she was quite taken aback.

"It has been such a long time since we met, Freddie! How are you? And your family?"

"Oh, very well thank you."

"Next time I come I shall pay a visit to your mama. Do give her my warm regards, will you? And Mathilda, too, of course. Is Etienne still hard at work?"

"Yes, he's extraordinarily diligent these days."

Paul laughed.

"Poor boy. I am glad to hear he is coping so well. Have you been going out much this winter? How is the season?"

"It has only just started, really. The Eekhofs will be giving their annual ball in February—in the Hotel des Indes this time."

"Yes, I know. Ange asked me to come over for it."

She was mortified by the triviality of his remarks, to which she felt she had to respond in kind while her heart was convulsed with emotion. Had he really forgotten?

It seemed that he had, for he continued in the same vein, asking after the opera, the Diligentia concerts, Marguerite van

Laren's wedding and so forth, and although Marie frequently put in a word or two, all those inconsequential questions struck Frédérique like arrows aimed exclusively at her. Mustering all her strength, however, she recovered her old sense of dignity, and succeeded in conversing with appropriate lightness. She recalled what she had said to him that morning at de Horze: that there was no reason for any hard feelings just because he had proposed to her and she hadn't taken him seriously, and that she wasn't naive like the other girls.

Oh, she knew she had dealt a blow to his pride by her haughty rebuffal of his advances, and however amiable and relaxed he sounded now, in reality he was seething with resentment against her.

That evening, after dinner, Paul flung himself in an easy chair.

"When will you return to Bodegraven?" his mother asked softly.

"Tomorrow morning."

"Will you stay the night?"

"Yes, I suppose so."

"Do feel free to light a cigar, my dear, I don't mind if you smoke. Would you like some coffee?"

"If it's not too much trouble."

Leentje was summoned to provide coffee, and Madame seated herself in her favourite armchair for her moment of postprandial repose. She closed her eyes, sunk in thought. How pleasant it was to have Paul sitting across the room with his glass of cognac and cigar; such a shame, though, that he and she seemed to have drifted apart lately. They seemed to have become quite estranged. She searched her conscience for clues to explain the distance that had come between them, but found nothing, although it was true that she had doted on Henk when he was a boy, and also that Paul had caused her concern at times with his capricious, indolent nature. She felt a great, instinctive surge of pity for her younger son, in whom she surmised some kind of grief that was beyond her comprehension, yet the more she pitied him, the more remote he seemed to her.

Through half-closed eyes she stole a glance at Paul, who was staring at the ceiling and blowing rings of cigar smoke in apparent rumination. He gave a start when she addressed him softly:

"Tell me, Paul, are you are sure you are all right? You are not ill, are you?"

He sat up and smiled.

"Whatever makes you say that?" he asked. "I don't look ill, do I? In fact everybody tells me I have grown stouter."

He gave her a searching look: what was she thinking? He was touched by her concern, for it was soothing to him, albeit futile.

"That is as may be," responded Madame van Raat hopefully. "Still, you must admit that you have changed. Am I right in thinking that there might be something troubling you?"

"Something troubling me? Of course not!"

"Is your work disappointing? Don't you find it rather dull, living in a village?"

"Well, it's not the height of entertainment, of course. But I don't mind. The Hague gets boring too, after a while."

"So you are sure you are all right, then?"

"Oh, mother, please stop fussing! There's nothing wrong with me. I'm as fit as a fiddle."

"I am glad to hear it, my dear boy."

She suppressed a sigh, leant back in her chair and closed her eyes. The gulf between them was as wide as ever. Time passed, and Paul thought she was asleep. At the sound of a stifled sob he looked up to see her weeping quietly, her face hidden in her hands.

"Mama dear, what's the matter?" he cried.

"Nothing, it's nothing," she murmured.

He rose from his armchair and went to sit beside his mother.

"Tell me, why are you crying? It's my fault, isn't it?"

The unwonted gentleness in his tone made her melt away in sorrow.

"No, my child, it is none of your fault, but it is so sad, so very sad—"

"What is?"

467

"The way young people always lock themselves up so you can't reach them any more. Eline was just the same, and it distressed me greatly. And now it's your turn—my own child! Because I can sense that you are keeping something from me, something that is causing you sadness."

"I assure you—"

"Don't assure me that is not the case, there's no need to spare my feelings. I know, my child, believe me, I know. I have known for months. And I dearly wanted to ask you to confide in me, but I was afraid you would tell me that it was no concern of mine. And I am not asking you to confide in me now, either, I'm only crying because it all makes me so sad. Nor do I blame you for being the way you are; all you young people are the same, refusing to put your faith in your elders. And yet, you know, it can do a world of good to share your troubles with someone who loves you. And who could love you more than your own mother? But no, you just keep a still tongue in your head. People only think of themselves nowadays, of their own joys and their own sorrows. Ah well, I suppose it can't be helped. But it makes me sad, so very sad."

She wept noiselessly, bowed by that cruel ruling of fate by which parents become estranged from their offspring. Her son, with quivering lips and tears in his eyes, remained silent.

"You see your child labouring under some dreadful burden as the months go by, and yet his heart is closed to you; there is nothing you can do because you have nothing to offer. The less said the better, everyone seems to think."

A sob of compassion for his mother escaped him, and he buried his face in his hands. She laid her arm gently about his neck, and it broke her heart to feel her tall, strong son weeping in her embrace. She pressed her lips to his head of thick, tawny hair.

"I am not reproaching you for anything, my darling boy, there, there, don't cry."

"Can't you understand that some things are too painful to talk about? That it's less painful to keep them to oneself?" he murmured, clinging to her.

"For a time, yes, but don't you think you would feel a great deal better for having shared your sorrow with someone?"

"I don't know, I really don't know!" he faltered.

She said nothing, but he remained in her arms, savouring the sweet consolation of maternal love. He waited, hoping that she would urge him again to confide in her. But she did not, and to end the silence he began to speak of his own accord.

"I can't imagine how you knew. I thought I was putting on a pretty good face, that I was the same as ever. I didn't even want to think about it either, because I couldn't stand how much it affected me. As if I couldn't live without that creature!"

He related to his mother how he had proposed to Frédérique and how she had rejected him in such a disdainful, insulting manner. He admitted that for some time he had felt very low as a result, but he would soon get over it: it was too absurd.

"Don't you love her any more?" asked Madame van Raat.

Hearing him say 'that creature', her first thought had been of Eline, and when she discovered that he meant Freddie, she could not help feeling a flicker of relief.

"No, no I don't love her!" he replied, shaking his head vigorously. "Oh no! Not any more."

She lifted his chin with her hand and gazed into his eyes a long moment.

"Why are you so different from the way you used to be?" she asked reproachfully, doubting his denial. "Why have you become so quiet lately, and so unforthcoming? But I won't quiz you any further, my child; you need not tell me more than you wish. Only, please do not deceive me, Paul, I should prefer you to say nothing rather than that."

"Oh, you are such a dear!" he faltered. "And it has done me a power of good to have told you, even though it's rather embarrassing."

"If you no longer love her," she pursued, tousling his hair with her fingers, "then it is only your vanity that has been hurt, Paul, and that is something you can easily put behind you. Still, I find it hard to believe that you should have stopped caring for Freddie. But as I said, my dear boy, I do not wish to pry, nor do I wish to cause you pain. I just want to thank you for trusting me enough to share your troubles with me at last. Now tell me, you do believe that your old mother loves you, don't you?"

He nodded, tightening his embrace. All at once she noticed how much he resembled his father in the life-sized portrait on the wall—more so than Henk—and she had a sense of wonder at the overwhelming rush of love she felt for her young son in his time of heartache.

Marie's bouts of gaiety were over. She no longer collapsed into fits of helpless, happy laughter as she had done so often when she and Emilie de Woude had such fun putting the finishing touches to Georges and Lili's new abode. She became resigned to the disillusionment she had suffered, and she saw her life stretching ahead of her like a dismal fog of monotonous grey, especially now that her brother Jan had left for the military academy in Breda and the house had grown distressingly dull. She longed for some animation, and envied Frédérique the lively company of the van Rijssel children, who filled Madame van Erlevoort's spacious home with such cheer.

Otto never visited The Hague. She had not seen him since August, when she had been staying at de Horze, and she cherished the memory of the few occasions she had found herself alone with him, when they had talked and strolled together in the park. Not that their conversations had been in any way intimate or important, but to her they were like small, sweet oases in the desert of her disappointment.

Only once, during those early months of winter, had her subdued mood of acceptance been disrupted by a crisis of emotion. It was brought on by a remark made by Frédérique, who, talking of how lonely it must be for Otto in the village of Elzen, suddenly exclaimed:

"Oh, Marie, you would have made Otto such a good wife! At least you would have appreciated him."

"Me?" she had responded timidly, attempting to smile. After Frédérique had gone she had lapsed into a flood of bitter tears. But after an hour everything was the same as before: blanketed by a grey fog of disillusionment, to which she, as usual, accommodated herself.

One day, Marie was surprised to receive a visit from Madame van Raat. Marie said she was sorry that Aunt Dora had not chosen a more propitious moment to call, as her father had gone to visit Lili and her mother was out shopping, but her aunt maintained that she would be delighted to have a chat with Marie instead, and plumped herself down in an armchair. She was not usually talkative, but this time she launched into all manner of topics, even enquiring after the ball given by the Eekhof girls. She mentioned a letter from Eline, and what a good thing it was that Paul was doing so well in Bodegraven and that he seemed very steady in his resolve to pursue his chosen career. Marie was glad to hear her speak so approvingly of her son, as until then she had only known her to frown on Paul's behaviour. She also thought it very amiable of Aunt Dora to say, in parting:

"By the way, how is Freddie? I have not seen her for such a long time. You can tell her from me that I am beginning to think she has forgotten all about me—she has not called on me for months! Tell her she is a naughty girl, will you?"

"Yes, Aunt, so I shall!" responded Marie with a light smile. Madame van Raat departed, leaving Marie wondering whether Aunt Dora had any notion of what had transpired between Paul and Freddie.

When Frédérique heard from Marie that Madame van Raat was expecting her to call, her feelings were mixed. She had been avoiding the house at Laan van Meerdervoort out of a sense of discretion mingled with regret and embarrassment. But now that she had been summoned, she thought it likely that Paul's mother had no knowledge of her son's proposal. Besides, Paul had made it quite clear that he wanted to let bygones be bygones, and so, thinking it would be impolite of her to neglect the dear old lady any longer, she decided to pay her a visit.

But her heart beat fearfully as she rang the bell. Here she was, calling on Madame van Raat as a mere acquaintance, whereas if only things had been different, she might have come as her daughter-in-law.

Madame van Raat gave Frédérique a warm welcome. She was eager to know how her young visitor was keeping, and eyed her intently as she responded to various innocuous questions. Her thoughts flew back to the time when, observing Paul with Eline, she had entertained something akin to a hopeful expectation, and now she could not resist drawing a comparison between Eline's faded elegance and Frédérique's rosy freshness, tinged only by the faintest suggestion of melancholy. But notwithstanding the girl's beauty, Paul's mother felt a pang of aggrievement, on behalf of her son. Frédérique was so lovely, so healthy, and she was making her poor son suffer in silence. She did not think herself possessed of a talent for diplomacy, nor did she have a clear notion of her own eventual motives, all she knew was that she dearly wished to deepen her acquaintance with Frédérique. With any luck she would gain some insight into what the girl was feeling as she chatted to the mother of the suitor she had rejected. But the time was not ripe for plumbing the depths of Frédérique's character, and the rules of polite society were not to be transgressed. On the other hand, she could not help thinking how agreeable the girl was, how open-hearted and amiable, and how winsome, with none of Eline's self-conscious airs and graces! No, it was inconceivable that Freddie should have wilfully toyed with Paul's emotions ... she simply did not love him enough, or ... there might be other reasons, which she preferred not to dwell on for the time being.

"Well my dear, at least you have made amends now!" said Madame van Raat when Freddie took her leave. "But you won't make me send out a summons again, will you? I am all alone here, and I do so like to see a young face from time to time."

Frédérique kissed her goodbye, promising to call again soon.

In the days that followed Madame van Raat went about her business with a faintly knowing smile on her lips and a calculating look in her eye. Through the mist of her habitually passive disposition she had caught a glimpse of a new goal to her existence. That goal was not going to be easy to attain, nor was it by any means near. She knew she had been too optimistic in trusting Dr Reijer's judgement when he maintained that she had the ability to contribute to Eline's recovery, and was afraid she might risk an even greater disillusionment now that the happiness of her own child was at stake. But being a pious soul, she prayed to God for guidance.

The next time Paul spent a few days in The Hague his mother did not breathe a word to him about Frédérique, nor about the conversation she had had with her. When she received a second visit from Frédérique she mentioned how much she enjoyed having someone read to her. Eline used to read to her sometimes in the past, but had grown tired very quickly. Lately Marie had been so kind as to do her this favour on several occasions. Why did not Frédérique join them one evening? Frédérique promised to do so, with some misgivings, because the more amicable Madame became, the more awkward she felt, for the old lady never gave any intimation that Paul had told her of his proposal, and if she had known, she would surely not have been quite so effusive in her manner towards her. But Frédérique allowed herself to be persuaded, and became a regular visitor at Laan van Meerdervoort. She never met Paul there, as she did not visit when she knew him to be in town; nor did Madame, who kept her deepening friendship with Frédérique secret from her son, ask to see her at those times.

One blustery evening, when Madame van Raat was expecting Marie and Frédérique, the latter came alone, as Marie was feeling indisposed. Frédérique offered to take Marie's place as reader, and the women settled themselves in the spacious salon, where the red-shaded gas lamps spread a rosy glow and the kettle sang for tea. On a low table lay Volume II of Tolstoy's *War and Peace*.

This time, however, the book was to remain unopened, as Madame was more in the mood for conversation. She talked of nothing but Paul: how serious he had become, and how he had always been a good boy at heart. He had sown his wild oats, but had now developed into a fine, sensible young man. It could have been so different—after all, for a young man to have a fortune was not always a good thing. Oh, she was very pleased with how he had turned out; and Freddie had always liked him too, had she not?

"Well, you always liked him, didn't you?" Madame van Raat repeated with feeling, after Freddie had stammered an unintelligible reply.

"Oh yes, indeed!" Freddie managed to say.

"Talking of Paul," Madame pursued in a confidential tone, "there is something that I have been wanting to ask you, Freddie. You don't mind, do you?"

She had laid her hand on the girl's arm, and could feel it trembling. Frédérique had a sense of being trapped: the old lady had spun a web of sympathy and familiarity around her, from which she could not disentangle herself.

"Of course not! Ask what you wish," she stammered, dreading the question.

"I wanted to ask you whether, by any chance, there has been any unpleasantness between you and Paul. What made me wonder was that he seems to act rather strangely every time someone happens to mention your name. There's something troubling him, I can tell. And because I know he can be quite rude at times, I thought he might have offended you in some way. I do hope that is not the case. Is it?"

"Oh no, not at all, I assure you."

"Go on, dear, you can confide in me, you know. Paul is not always on his best behaviour, in fact I'm afraid he is a bit of a prankster, and when I see the way he teases Françoise van Oudendijk and the Eekhof girls I can't help being amazed that they don't seem to mind at all. Or rather, I used to see him acting flirtatiously, but he has become much more sensible lately. So you see, I can well imagine that you were annoyed with him for some reason or another, and he with you in return. Now if you would only tell me what that reason was … "

"But dear lady, I assure you, nothing happened!" she cried, struggling against her tears. "There was nothing, nothing at all!"

Paul's mother gave her an incredulous stare.

"My dear, what a fibber you are! Fie on you! Can't you see that if you do not tell me the truth I shall only be worried, allowing all manner of things to enter my head—disagreeable ones, too! But my dear, you are not crying, are you?"

The evening had been torture for Frédérique from the moment she arrived, owing to Madame van Raat's constant allusions to the strained relation between Paul and herself, and she could contain herself no longer.

"Why won't you believe me?" she broke out, with an accusatory sob.

"Because if nothing happened," said Madame van Raat, putting her arms about Frédérique, "there is no reason for you to be so upset, is there? Forgive me if I have caused you pain, but what did you expect me to think, Freddie? What am I to think of your being so upset?"

"Nothing! Don't think anything! There is nothing the matter!" Freddie wailed.

Madame van Raat drew her closer. "Now listen, Freddie, listen to me! Do you love Paul?" she murmured.

Racked with sobs, Freddie tried to extricate herself, but the old lady only tightened her embrace.

"Don't go, Freddie, just stay close to me a moment and answer my question: do you love Paul? Do you love him very, very much?"

"Why are you asking me that? Why do you want me to tell you?"

"Because I believe that he loves you."

"No, no, he doesn't care about me, he doesn't love me, not any more."

"But he did once, and he may do so again! Oh, do tell me the truth, my dear—tell me what happened between you. Well, if you won't tell me, shall I guess? Paul made advances to you, he trifled with your affection, and then neglected you. Is that what happened?"

"No, no! Nothing like that, honestly! It was all my fault!" Frédérique cried out. "How could you think such as thing of your son!"

"Was it really your fault? Well then, did he ask you to marry him? And did you say no? I am only guessing, because of course I don't know anything. But you shouldn't tell fibs, my dear, just tell me the truth."

Frédérique felt too worn out by this persistence to offer any more opposition, and she admitted defeat with a despairing nod, after which she hid her blazing face in Madame van Raat's shoulder.

"Why did you reject him?"

"I think it was my pride … it got the better of me."

"Did you not think my boy good enough?"

"No, no, it wasn't pride, really; it was more like jealousy, I think. He was so charming to all the other girls … Oh, I'm not even sure why I turned him down."

"And do you regret it, my child?"

Frédérique recoiled in dismay.

"But you mustn't mention a word of this to him!" she cried. "Not a word! Oh, please, promise me that you won't say anything! You say you think he might yet love me, but I know for certain that it cannot be the case. And I would die of shame if he had any idea that I … Oh, will you promise me that you won't say anything?"

"Of course I promise, my child. But there is no need for all this distress, now is there? I'm afraid I have made you unhappy, for which I am truly sorry. But really, don't you think you have behaved rather foolishly? Now listen to me. Try looking on the bright side. Personally, I would not be at all surprised if Paul still loves you; in other words, anything might still happen."

"But I was horrible to him! He hates me!"

"Nonsense, dear! There, there, you must stop crying, Freddie. But now it is my turn to ask a promise of you now: will you try to believe that Paul still loves you? Will you try for my sake?"

Freddie gazed at through her tears.

"I wish I could, but … it wouldn't be right!" she said tonelessly.

Madame's knowing smile never left her face; she kissed Frédérique and gently brushed the teardrops from her cheeks.

When Frédérique had gone, Madame van Raat did not betake herself to bed at once as she usually did, but stayed up for a long while afterwards, musing contentedly on her efforts to inveigle Frédérique into an admission. Never had she imagined herself capable of such a feat of diplomacy!

So now she knew: Freddie loved her boy. Why she had rebuffed him was still unclear, but her motives for doing so no longer seemed to be clear to Freddie herself either. He had proposed, so much was evident. The next day Madame van Raat sent a note to her son asking him to come and visit her without delay, as she wished to hear his opinion on certain money matters. Paul complied with promptness and astonishment. Money matters? It was always Henk whom she consulted regarding the family finances, and besides, what did he know about money? That was exactly why she had summoned him, she declared: it was high time that he learnt to manage his own financial affairs. He shrugged, saying that he was sure that his brother was much better at such things than he was, whereupon she launched into a long and convoluted exposé to persuade him of the necessity of taking himself in hand, at the end of which she remarked, as though at random:

"Freddie came to see me yesterday evening. Such a sweet girl. Such a shame … "

"Freddie? I didn't know you and she saw each other."

"Oh yes, quite often."

"Often? I thought … "

"What, dear boy? Freddie often comes by of an evening, with Marie; they read to me, you see. Didn't you know?"

"No, I didn't."

"How odd; I thought you knew. We talk about you sometimes."

"About me? Does she talk about me?"

"Well, not all the time, but whenever I mention you she responds very sweetly. Of course she doesn't know you've told me everything, dear boy. So she is not aware that I know what passed between you."

"It's a bit surprising that she should call on you, though."

"Not at all. No one knows about that, anyway."

"It still seems rather strange to me. I mean, that she can bring herself to come here. And also that you can sit and talk with her, exchanging pleasantries as if nothing had happened."

"Indeed, my dear Paul. It is true that I was vexed with her at first, but I have grown very fond of her since. Actually, I firmly believe that she loves you. Paul. And it is because that is what I believe, or rather, because I know it for certain, that I no longer have any ill feeling towards her."

"Oh, Mama!" he faltered. "How can you be so sure?"

"I can't explain, but everything tells me that it is so. Little things she says … a word here, a word there … "

He was too dazed by the rosy prospects unfolding in his mind's eye to respond, and his mother pursued with her counsel:

"It is perfectly clear that she loves you. The pair of you could still find happiness together. Next time you see her, try not to behave as if you don't care, as if you have put it all behind you. You ought to get to know her a little better."

"Don't you think I know her well enough?"

"No, Paul, you do not. I assure you, God help me, that she loves you!"

"But she can't!" he stammered. "It's impossible! Oh, Mama, it's impossible."

"That is what she said, too!" thought the old lady, rising. She enfolded him in her arms once more.

"But she does! She does love you, my dear, dear boy!" she whispered. A radiant smile crossed her features, making her seem ten years younger than her age.

She thought it best to leave them be for a while, now that she had instilled in both their minds the notion of a misapprehension that might yet be rectified, and she bided her time.

Paul kept delaying his return to Bodegraven. The day after his conversation with his mother he called at the Verstraetens'. He arrived at four, an hour at which the family was usually gathered together and there was most chance of Freddie dropping by. So disappointed was he when she did not appear that he could not help asking Marie in an urgent undertone:

"Won't Freddie be coming this afternoon?"

She was startled by the question. "I don't know, Paul. Why do you ask?"

"It's been so long since I've seen her," he almost whispered.

Marie blushed; she wished she could tell him how sorry Freddie had been about how things had turned out last summer, but she did not dare, for fear of inadvertently snarling the delicate fabric of emotion between them. It was up to them to find a resolution, but when would they do so? Perhaps never, thought Marie.

Paul did not see Freddie that afternoon. During dinner he asked his mother:

"What would you say if I paid the van Erlevoorts a visit this evening?"

"I'm sure they would like that," she replied.

"How can you be so sure?"

"Oh, just a word here and a word there. Enough for me to look on the bright side, at any rate. You'll see, Paul."

Her response did not clarify matters, but was reassuring to him nonetheless. After dinner he grew agitated and began to pace the room sunk in thought.

"Do sit down, Paul, and don't let your coffee go cold."

"At what time do you think I should call on Madame van Erlevoort?"

"Not before eight, my dear. Between eight and half-past."

"I used to call at any time, quite casually!"

"And that is precisely why you ought to avoid any suggestion of a casual call."

He sighed. In that case he would have a glass of cognac first, he decided, wondering what Freddie could possibly have said to his mother. He took a book and pretended to read. Madame pretended to doze, but in reality she was no less nervous than Paul.

The clock struck half-past seven, and he flung his book aside.

"It's stuffy in here; I need some air. I think I'll take a stroll first," he said. "I'm off."

She smiled. "Good luck, my dear," she said softly.

That evening the Verstraetens, accompanied by Georges and Lili, made their way to the Voorhout; a cable had been sent to Etienne in Leiden summoning him home, and Madame van Erlevoort had asked Henk and Betsy to come, too.

For the latter it was the first time since the rupture between Eline and Otto that they had visited the van Erlevoort residence.

However, all feelings of antagonism had vanished. The festive spirit ran high, for the news of Paul and Freddie's betrothal had come as a complete and very welcome surprise.

When Madame van Raat returned home that evening, worn out from the emotion, she felt too tired to undress for bed, and sank into her easy chair to sit for a while, her veined hands folded on her lap, her chin sunk onto her breast, filled with wonder at the successful outcome of her instinctive machinations. That she, for all her despondence and lassitude, had had a hand in it! But then it was her son's happiness that was at stake, and her piety had given her strength.

XXXV

U NCLE DANIEL AND AUNT ELIZA showed no surprise whatever when, a few days after St Clare and Vincent had taken their departure, Eline announced her intention to return to The Hague. They knew her to be capricious by nature, wanting first this and then that, never satisfied. But this was no caprice. The idea had been growing in her mind ever since that evening when St Clare had asked her so bluntly "How do you come to be here?", and she had felt as though a curtain had been swept aside, revealing to her with devastating clarity that she did not indeed belong in her uncle's Brussels apartment, and even less so among the coterie he and his wife associated themselves with. And it was out of her feelings for St Clare—respect, friendship and possibly even love—that she had resolved to leave Brussels.

She wrote to Henk, asking him to rent two rooms for her in a ladies' boarding house, or else in one of the new chic hotels. She received a prompt reply from him, as well as notes from Betsy and old Madame van Raat, all protesting that she should not take rooms but make her home with them instead. Betsy wrote saying that it was time to forgive and forget what had passed between them, and imploring Eline not to be so eccentric as to go and live on her own when there was plenty of room for her at Nassauplein. Old Madame van Raat extended a similarly urgent and affectionate invitation. But Eline declined their offers with effusive thanks, and was not to be dissuaded from her pursuit.

So Henk gave up with a forlorn shrug and went with Betsy to pick out a handsome two-room apartment in a spacious boarding house on Bezuidenhout. Thereupon Eline returned to The Hague.

She recalled how tired she had been from all her travels when she arrived in The Hague the previous summer to make her stay with old Madame van Raat. She compared the fatigue she had felt then with her present state of exhaustion, which seemed to

481

have robbed her even of the capacity to shed tears. For St Clare's sake she had mustered the last remnants of her strength to show herself the way she had once been: attractive and engaging, if not radiant. And now that St Clare had gone, she realised that although she had tried to be candid and guileless with him, she had found herself putting on an act yet again, to avoid letting him see her as utterly broken-spirited—at death's door even. Now that it was no longer necessary to work herself up to a pitch she was falling apart, and besides, the emotional upheaval of that final confession had left her feeling so drained that she felt sure she would never get well again, mentally or physically.

Her cough was very bad, and she sought treatment from Dr Reijer once more. But she did not mention the morphine drops prescribed by her physician in Brussels, mindful as she was of Reijer's earlier refusal to supply her with a sleeping draught. It was February, bitterly cold, and she kept to her rooms.

Rising from her bed in the morning she was overcome by the same sense of purposelessness as when she was staying with Madame van Raat, and rather than get dressed she would slip on her peignoir and recline on a couch, savouring the restful feeling that nothing was demanded of her, that there was no earthly reason for her to get dressed, and there was nothing to stop her remaining as she was, in her slippers, with her hair undone, for as long as she chose. She had been found thus, undressed, dishevelled and vacantly staring out of the window by various callers, including Madame van Raat, Betsy, Madame Verstraeten, and Marie and Lili. She did not read, she did nothing at all, and hours went by during which even her thoughts came to a standstill. At times she would abruptly throw herself on the floor and lie there pressing her face to the carpet with her eyes tightly closed, until a knock at the door—the maid bringing her lunch tray—made her scramble to her feet in sudden fright. She barely touched her food, and a grim little smile, half satiric and half crazed, etched itself on her features.

The evenings inflicted hours of agony on Eline. Her mind would be in a frenzy of agitation, as though electrified by the dread of a sleepless night. A vertiginous glare flooded her brain, her ears were filled with an incessant hum. A maelstrom of remembrances whirled by, and visions rose up before her. She started in fear at a shadow looming on the wall or the glint of a pin on the floor. But she took her drops, and was muffled at last by a leaden mantle of sleep.

For long moments she stood staring in the glass at her faded beauty. Tears would rise to her eyes, whose brightness seemed to have been snuffed out for ever, and her mind drifted to her past. She was filled with yearning for those former days, having lost sight of what they had entailed, for she was finding it increasingly difficult to think clearly. It was as if there were certain limits to what she might think about, which she might not venture beyond. However, the sluggishness of her powers of reason lessened her melancholy, which, had she been of clear mind, would have mounted to a dangerous crisis. Instead, she now spent hour upon hour racked with doubt as to what she could possibly do with her useless body and her useless existence, dragging herself from one spasm of coughing to the next in the prison of her rooms. She shed bitter tears over her unfulfilled desires and lay writhing on the floor, her arms outstretched towards a phantom lover, for both in her dreams and in the daytime ramblings of her mind she had begun to confound Otto with St Clare, unconsciously attributing the utterances and ideas of the one to the other, so that she no longer knew which of the two she had ever truly loved, or still loved. When, during such fits of equivocation, she tried to battle through to a resolution, she came up against those thought-confining limits again, and became so enraged by her powerlessness that she thumped her head with her fists, as though trying to discipline her wayward brain by force.

"What is the matter with me?" she asked herself in despair. "Why can I remember nothing of hundreds of things that have happened, except that I know that they happened? Oh, the dullness in my head! I'd rather be in terrible pain than suffer this dullness! I must be going mad ... "

A shudder ran down her spine like a cold snake. Suppose she did go mad, what would they do with her? It did not bear thinking about, and yet, even as she struggled to banish the spectre of encroaching insanity, she had a sense of crossing a forbidden limit. Because if that was what she was doing then she must be … losing her mind!

At such moments she would cover her eyes and her ears with her hands to block out all sight and sound, as though the first impression she might now receive would push her over the brink into madness. So terrified was she of this happening that she did not breathe a word to Reijer about the befuddlement in her brain.

During her prolonged spells of inactivity she became enslaved by strange fantasies and delusions, often rising to a bizarre strain of ecstasy, from which she would suddenly start awake in shock. Reclining on her couch, nervously toying with the tassels on the cushions or twisting a strand of her long, tousled hair, she mused on the theatrical illusions she had cherished in the old days of her duets with Paul, when she thought she loved Fabrice. Then she became an actress, she was on stage, she could see the audience, she smiled and bowed, it rained flowers …

She rose to her feet in a daze, and began to hum some recitative, or a few phrases from an Italian aria as she drifted about the room, throwing up her hands in despair, reaching out beseechingly to a fleeing lover, falling down on her knees and begging for mercy even as she was being forcibly dragged away … Diverse roles floated into her mind: Marguerite, Juliette, Lucie, Isabelle, Mireille, and in her transport of excitement she became all these heroines, acting out their most tragic moments in swift succession, only to wake abruptly from her delirium to find herself all alone in her room, making strange gesticulations.

Coming to herself again, she thought:

"Oh God! Is it true? Am I going mad?"

She sank onto the couch again and kept very still, wide-eyed with fear, as though some horrible catastrophe were about to strike, as though the faces in the paintings and prints on the walls had suddenly come alive, jeering at her and grimacing like demons.

After such a day she would resolve, in quiet dread, to take possession of herself. The following morning, upon waking from her leaden, artificial slumber, she rose promptly from her bed and dressed with care, after which she went out to make some purchase, take coffee with Henk and Betsy, or call on either the Verstraetens or Madame van Raat. She said she was lonely, and people invited her to dinner now and then out of pity. On such occasions the evening passed quite cheerfully, and she returned to her rooms afterwards glad to have reached the end of another day, but almost fainting with exhaustion from her unwonted animation, her forced brightness, her unnatural, shrill laugh, not to mention her endless coughing. And she would pay heavily at night: the drops had no effect; she remained wide, wide awake, prey to the wildest phantasms conjured by her sick mind as she relived the day's strenuous activities.

She was the subject of much talk, and Betsy frequently remarked with a worried frown that she feared Eline was ill; she was acting so strangely these days, and Reijer was not at all satisfied either. And everyone felt sorry for her: poor, poor Eline, who used to be so elegant and alluring, so gay! Now she was like a shadow of her former self on the rare occasions that she was seen venturing out in the street with nervous, unsteady gait, her muff pressed to her lips, and there was something almost timid in the way she tilted her head in greeting the van Larens, the Hijdrechts, the Oudendijks. No indeed, she was not at all well; it was evident for all to see.

It was raining: a cold, driving March rain, and Betsy was at home, sitting in the violet ante-room by the conservatory with her armchair pushed into the light so that she could read her book, *Pêcheur d'Islande* by Pierre Loti. But the story bored her: she could not imagine fishermen being quite so sentimental. Beyond the potted palms in the conservatory she could see into the garden, where the bare trees glistened starkly in the downpour. Ben sat on the floor by his mother, his head lolling against her skirts, his eyes fixed on the leafless branch of an elm tree tossing madly in the wind and rain. He heaved a sigh.

"What's the matter Ben, is anything wrong?" asked Betsy.

"No, Ma," he said in his slurred voice, looking up at her in wonder.

"Then why did you sigh, darling?"

"Don't know, Ma."

She looked at him intently a moment, then laid aside her book.

"Come here, Ben."

"Where, Mama?"

"Here, on my knee."

Smiling, he clambered onto her lap. Her tone, formerly sharp when addressing her only child, had softened of late.

"Do you love your mama?" she asked fondly.

"Yes."

"Give me a hug, then."

He threw his short arms about her neck.

"And now give me a kiss."

Beaming doltishly, he kissed her.

"Mama is never bad, is she?" asked Betsy.

"No."

"Do you like sitting on Mama's lap?"

"Yes."

The overgrown seven-year-old snuggled up against her bosom.

"Tell me, Ben, is there anything you'd like to have? Shall Mama give you something nice?"

"No, thank you."

"Not even a cart, for instance, with a pony, a proper pony? Then Herman could teach you to drive."

"No, thank you," he said blankly.

She grew impatient, and was on the point of scolding him for being so witless, but stopped herself just in time. She held him close and kissed him.

"Well, if there's anything else you want to have, you must tell me, do you hear?" she resumed, almost in tears. "You'll tell me, won't you, Ben? What do you say, little man? Promise you'll tell Mama?"

"Yes," he replied in a tone of blissful contentment.

And she shut her eyes, shuddering at the thought that she had an idiot son. What had she ever done to deserve such a punishment?

She sat there holding her child on her lap for some time, when she heard someone approaching through the salon. It was Eline.

"Well hello, Elly."

"Hello, Betsy. Hello, Ben."

"So you went out in spite of the rain?"

"I took a cab; I couldn't stay indoors a moment longer. This weather makes me so dreary, and I thought ... I thought I was going mad with boredom. Oh, God!"

With a strangled cry she dropped into a chair and tore off her short veil, as if she needed air.

"Just imagine: the same four walls of your room day in day out, all by yourself, with nothing to distract you—surely that would drive anyone mad? Anyway, I can't stand it any more; if it goes on much longer I'll go insane ... "

"Eline, *prends garde: l'enfant t'écoute.*"

"Oh, him ... he doesn't understand, and I don't think he ever will!" she ranted hoarsely. "Come over here, Ben, and listen to me. Shall I tell you what to do when you grow up? Never think about anything, poppet! Don't think at all! Just eat, drink and have fun for as long as you can, and then ... then you must marry! But don't start thinking, whatever you do!"

"Eline, *vraiment tu es folle*! Mind what you're saying!" Betsy burst out, more concerned for her child than for her sister.

Eline laughed out loud; the shrill, crazed edge to her voice frightened Ben, who gazed up at her round-eyed, his mouth gaping. But she went on laughing.

"Oh, he has no idea, does he, the little mite! No, you don't know what Auntie's raving about, do you? But it feels so good to rant and rave for once! I wish I could do something outrageous, something quite mad, but there's nothing I can think of. I'm so dull nowadays that I can't even think at all. If only Eliza were here, she'd know what to do. Do you know what Eliza and I did once, that first time I was staying in Brussels? I never dared to tell anyone before, but now I don't care, I can say whatever I like. Just imagine, one evening we went out, just the two us, for a walk; we were feeling adventurous, you know. Mind you, don't breathe a word of this to anyone. Then we met two gentlemen, two very nice gentlemen, whom we'd never met before. And we went for a drive with them … in an open landau, and then we … we went to a café."

Her whole speech had been punctuated by nervous, shrill giggles, and by the end of it she was laughing hysterically, with frenzied tears running down her contorted features. Not a word of it was true, but to her it was all real.

"Just fancy! We were in café! A café! And then—"

"Eline, please! Stop being so silly," Betsy said quietly.

"Oh, you think it's terribly shocking, don't you? Well, you can put your mind at rest; it wasn't that bad."

She gave another wild, forced laugh and then broke down into sobs.

"Oh, that wretched Reijer! I have this constant pain here, in my head, and he doesn't even care, all he goes on about is my cough. I know I cough, I don't need him to tell me. Oh, God! And that boarding house is so awful."

"Then why don't you come back to live with us?"

"We'd only be at each other's throats again after the first three days!" Eline laughed hollowly. "Now that we don't see very much of each other we seem to get on rather better than before, I find."

"Honestly, I'd do my best to make you feel at home!" pleaded Betsy, feeling increasingly concerned about the state of Eline's nerves. "We could take care of you properly! I'd accommodate myself to your wishes."

"But I wouldn't accommodate myself to yours! No, thank you very much! Freedom above all. You talk such nonsense. We'd start bickering in no time—I mean, just look at us, we're bickering already."

"Why do you say that? I am not bickering, not by any means. All I want is for you to come back to us as soon as possible— tonight, preferably."

"Betsy, if you don't shut up about that I shall leave now and never come back. I have no desire to live in your house, do you hear? I will not live with you, and that's final."

She hummed a little.

"Will you stay for supper, at least?" asked Betsy.

488

"Yes please! But I'm exhausted, so I won't have much con-versation. What are your plans for later this evening?"

"We're going to the Oudendijks'. Haven't you been invited?"

"No, I've stopped going out."

"Why?"

"Drat the Oudendijks! Oh, my poor head! I'm half dead … do you mind if I go and lie down for a while?"

"Please do."

"Then I'll go to Henk's room; there's a comfy couch there."

"The fire isn't lit, though."

"Oh, I don't mind."

She went upstairs to Henk's sitting room. Henk was out. She removed her coat and hat. Then she took a cigar from a cigar box, bit the tip off and lit it, but the bitter taste disgusted her and she stubbed it out. She lay down on the couch. Her wandering eyes lit on a weapon rack, a trophy of swords, daggers and pistols. What if she wanted to kill herself, how would she do it? A dagger through her heart? A bullet in her mouth? Oh no, no, she would never have the courage, and anyway she wouldn't know how to handle a dagger or a pistol. She might just wound herself, mutilate herself, and … go on living. Besides, death was even worse than life. Death was something she never dared to think about, something infinitely, unspeakably vast and empty. Would there be life after death, would there be a God? She remembered having sweet visions of azure landscapes bathed in a luminous glow, with singing angels flitting about on silvery wings, and far away in the hazy distance a throne of clouds occupied by an ethereal being of majestic allure. The vision came back to her now, and she felt herself being borne aloft on the soft strains of heavenly song. But then she had a sense of falling down to earth at dizzying speed with the room wheeling all around her, until her eyes came to rest on the weapon rack again. No, no, not a pistol, not a dagger! Not poison, either, because she would turn blue and green and they'd find her with her face twisted and swollen and everybody would be appalled by her ugliness. What if she drowned? Then, too, she would be ugly, with her body all bloated by the time they fished her out of the lake. But drowning was supposed to be a gentle death; you saw the water closing over your head in a gorgeous swirl of lovely colours and then you gradually dropped off to sleep, sinking deeper and deeper into a billowing, downy softness, and in death you were like Ophelia, adorned with water lilies and reeds. But she couldn't think of any lake with lilies and reeds in The Hague, there were only canals with foul-smelling, green water ... oh no, not that! The lake in the woods, then? Or the sea at Scheveningen? No, no, she would be too terrified, and anyway she was too weak; she wouldn't even have the strength now to run away in the middle of the night during a storm as she had done so long ago, all alone, battling against the wind and the driving rain. And she came to the conclusion that she would never find the courage to hang herself, or to suffocate herself; the fact was that she was too cowardly to kill herself at all. She began to quake as in a fever, so horrified was she by her thoughts.

Why did she have to be like this? Why couldn't she have been happy with Otto? Why hadn't she met St Clare when she was eighteen? What had she done to deserve such wretchedness? Who had she ever harmed? Hadn't she taken good care of Aunt Vere in her final illness, hadn't she sacrificed her own good fortune for Vincent? Oh, if only she had been capable of happiness, then she would have shared it with everyone around her. St Clare—or was it Otto?—had once told her there were treasures slumbering in her soul. Well, she would have shared out those treasures, she would have bestowed the jewels of her joy wherever she went. But it had not come to pass, she had been crushed by the sheer weight of her existence, and now she was so tired from the struggle that her only wish was that it should end. Oh, if only she were dead ...

The rain had stopped; it grew dark. Exhausted from her sombre ruminations, she lay back, numb, her mind a blank, and at length dozed off. She was roused by a heavy footfall in the hallway, and before she was fully awake, Henk entered.

"My dear Sis! What are you doing here in the dark? My, how cold it is in here!"

"Cold?" she echoed with the dazed look of a sleepwalker. "Yes, so it is, I can feel it now—I'm shivering. I must have been asleep."

"Why don't you come downstairs with me? Dinner will soon be served. Betsy said you were staying, is that right?"

"Yes. Oh, Henk, how awful that I fell asleep."

"Awful? Why?"

"Now I won't sleep a wink tonight!" she sobbed, burying her head in his shoulder.

"Why won't you come back to live with us, Elly?" he asked softly. "It would be so much better all round."

"No, no, I don't want that."

"Why not?"

"It wouldn't do, Henk. I am certain of that. It's very sweet of you to ask, but it simply wouldn't do. I have these sudden moods when I feel like smacking Betsy, for instance, especially when she's being nice to me. I very nearly hit her this afternoon."

He sighed with a hopeless expression. She was ever a mystery to him.

"Let's go down," he said, and as they descended the stairs together she leant heavily on his arm, shivering from the cold that had now truly overtaken her.

Winter came to an end and Eline's condition remained unchanged. It was May, and although the weather had been wintry only the previous week, the summer season had burst forth with soaring temperatures. Eline lay on her couch, felled by the heat.

"Don't you think it would do you good to spend some time in the country this summer?" suggested Reijer. "I don't mean travelling from one place to another, that would be too tiring. I am thinking along the lines of a holiday in some cool, shady retreat, a place where you would find a caring environment."

She thought of de Horze. Oh, if only she had married Otto! Then she would have had all the cool shade and loving care she needed!

"I wouldn't know where to go," she answered dully.

"I might be able to help you there. I know some people in Gelderland, a most agreeable couple who run a small country estate with a fine wood of pine trees nearby."

"Not pine trees, for Heaven's sake!" cried Eline with passion.

"The country air would agree with you."

"Nothing will agree with me. I do wish you'd stop nagging, Dr Reijer."

"Have you been sleeping well lately?"

"Oh yes, very well."

It was not true; she did not sleep at all at night, only dozed off from time to time during the day. The drops no longer sent her to sleep; instead, they left her in a permanent state of hazy exaltation, a crazed semi-consciousness veering between extreme lassitude and mortal fear, during which she had spells of becoming an actress moaning and writhing in agony on the floor.

Reijer regarded her intently.

"Miss Vere, pray tell me the truth. Have you been taking any other medicines besides the ones I have prescribed ?"

"Why do you ask?"

"I should like an honest answer, Miss Vere."

"Of course I haven't! How could you think I would do such a thing! I wouldn't dare! No, no, you may rest quite assured about that."

Reijer left, and in his carriage he forgot about his notebook for a moment while reflecting on the plight of Miss Vere. Then he heaved a sigh of defeat.

No sooner had he gone than Eline stood up; her room was unbearably hot and stuffy, even though the door to the balcony was open. She wore only a thin grey peignoir carelessly draped over her emaciated frame. Standing before the mirror, she plunged her hands into her loose hair. It had grown very thin, and she laughed as she twisted a strand between her fingers. Then she flung herself on the floor.

I refuse to see him again! she thought to herself. *That Reijer! He only makes me feel worse. I can't stand him. I shall write and tell him he's discharged.*

But she knew she would not have the spirit to do this, and remained crouched down, tracing the floral patterns on the carpet with her finger. She began to hum to herself.

The sun shining in through the open balcony door cast a rectangle of gold on the floor, with myriad dust particles dancing above it. The glare disturbed Eline, and she drew back.

"The sun!" she whispered inaudibly, with strangely staring, glazed eyes. "How I hate the sun! I want the rain and the wind, cold rain and cold wind, I want to feel the rain trickling down the décolletage of my black tulle dress."

Suddenly she scrambled to her feet and wrung her hands on her chest as though holding the sides of a cloak to prevent the wind from tearing it from her shoulders.

"Jeanne, Jeanne," she moaned in her delirium. "Please let me in, I beg you. I have run away from home, because Betsy's so horrid to me, you see, and during dinner at Hovel's this evening she said all sorts of hateful things about Vincent. And you know how much I love Vincent. It was because of him that I broke off my engagement, my engagement to St Clare. Oh, he bored me to tears with his calmness. So calm he was, forever calm. It drove me mad! But truly, Henk, I shall go to Lawrence and ask his pardon, only don't hit me, Henk. Oh, Lawrence, I beg you, I love you so much, don't be angry with me, Lawrence—Lawrence! See if I don't love you! Look, I have your portrait right here! I keep it with me all the time."

She fell to her knees by the sofa and lifted her face, as if she had seen someone, then gave a violent start and rose unsteadily to her feet.

"Oh God, there it is again!" she thought, recovering herself.

She felt as if there was a war going on inside her brain, with her powers of reason fighting a losing battle against the madness assailing her. She groped for a book that was lying on the table, and opened it, to force herself to be sensible and to read. It was the score of *Le Tribut de Zamora*, which she had bought long ago, during her passion for Fabrice.

She dared not look up, fearing that her madness would take some hideous form before her eyes. She dared not move, out of terror for herself, and in her wandering mind salvation would come if only she could pass out of her body, as it were, and into the sunlight, which was now flooding her entire room, rippling over the satin curtains and bathing the delicate Japanese porcelain and polished brass ornaments in a golden glow.

Softly she began to sing, without thinking what, in a voice hoarse and raw with endless coughing. But there was a knock at the door.

"Who's there?" she asked anxiously

"It's me, Miss," a voice cried. "Bringing you your lunch."

"Thank you, Sophie, but I have no appetite. Dr Reijer said I wasn't to eat too much."

"Shall I take it away then, Miss?"

"Yes, take it away."

"You will ring if you want anything, won't you?"

"Yes, yes."

She heard the rattle of plates and glasses on the tray as the maid descended the stairs, and tried to focus her mind on Xaïma's score. She drew herself up, held her head high and made a regal gesture with her hand as she broke into song, only to crumple up in a fit of coughing.

There was another knock at the door.

"Oh, what is it now?" cried Eline, greatly perturbed.

"May I come in a moment, Miss Vere?" It was a different voice, affable and genteel.

Eline thought hard a moment, then closed the songbook and sank down on the couch. She lay back against the cushions and half-closed her eyes.

"Yes you may," she answered graciously.

The door opened and the proprietress, a buxom lady dressed entirely in black, stepped into the room.

"I just popped in to see how you are," she said with warm civility. "Are you not well?"

"No, I am not!" groaned Eline, closing her eyes. "I feel very weak."

In reality she was feeling full of nervous, manic energy which she was minded to express by means of song, but it had become a habit to say that she felt weak when people asked after her health.

"Won't you have a bite to eat?"

"Dr Reijer said—" Eline began.

The proprietress shook her head.

"My dear Miss Vere, shame on you for trying to mislead me. I just heard from Dr Reijer that you would benefit from a cup of hot broth."

"I am afraid hot broth would make me nauseous."

"But you must eat something, Miss Vere."

"I assure you, I feel too ill to eat now."

"Well, later then. May I prepare a wholesome meal for you? What would you fancy?"

"Do whatever you like. My appetite may come back to me, I suppose. But in the meantime would you be so kind as to tell any callers, including my sister, that I cannot receive them? I feel very low this afternoon. I can't tell you how low."

"Is there anything you need? Anything I can do for you?"

"You are very kind, but really, I have no need of anything. Except perhaps some ice, come to think of it. I am rather thirsty."

"A chilled carafe?"

"I would rather have a slab of ice."

"Are you running a fever?"

"No, but I like the feel of a lump of ice melting in my mouth. And please remember what I said—I am not at home to callers this afternoon."

"Certainly. I shall send for some ice at once. But you won't mind if I let down the blinds, will you? Spare a thought for my poor furniture, Miss Vere!"

The proprietress lowered the blinds and left. Eline sat up, smiling and clicking her tongue in anticipation of the cooling ice, took up the songbook again and pictured herself as Xaïma.

She was standing tall, like a queen on a precipice, pointing to the dreamt ravine at her feet. Fancying that she heard a response from Ben-Saïd, she remained a moment thus transfixed, then resumed her portrayal of Xaïma, humming now rather than singing. But her voice cracked so that she had to clear her throat, which made her cough several times, and soon she was coughing so violently that she laid aside the score and sat down with her hands pressed to her constricted throat.

"What's the matter with me?" she thought. "I'm not making any sense! I want to make sense!"

But the turmoil in her mind persisted as wave upon wave of confused memories washed over her, drowning her reason. Her eyes darted feverishly about her.

"I want to make sense!" she kept telling herself, and this aim became a wheel spinning in her brain. "I want to make sense!"

Her head felt leaden, and her theatrical excitement subsided into the mental torpor that she so feared. At such moments of desolation her only desire was to see St Clare. If only he had been there with her! He would have known what to do, he would have comforted her and made her see sense again. Their parting words in Brussels flashed into her mind. Five months from now, they had said. That had been in January, now it was March. He had said it would take only one word from her and he would rush back to her side. The idea was so tempting that she resolved to write him a note—she knew where to send it thanks to her correspondence with Vincent—oh, just a few words, just enough to make him come back! A soothing perspective opened before her eyes, and for a moment she felt very calm, and even happy. But that very calmness enabled her to take possession of herself, and her illusion evaporated. She shook her head from side to side: St Clare loved her out of pity, out of a desire to heal a fellow creature's suffering, and even if he were indeed able to give her some measure of happiness, she had no right to chain her wilted life to his. And her next thought was of Otto. So she knew that it could never be. Never.

Notwithstanding the lowered blinds, the heat in the room was rising. Sophie, the maid, knocked at the door.

"I've brought you some ice, Miss!"

She came in bearing a tray of ice. As soon as she was gone Eline put a shard in her mouth, then took several others and rubbed them over her forehead until the large, icy drops trickled down between her fingers.

Sophie brought her repast at half-past five, and laid the small round table with much care. But Eline merely picked at the various dishes, and was glad when Sophie came to clear them away. The weather was too hot; the smell of food turned her stomach.

She glanced at the calling cards Sophie had brought in with her tray: one from Madame Verstraeten and another from Lili.

"Old Madame van Raat also came by this afternoon, Miss!" said Sophie, and left.

Eline was alone; the evening crept forward. The sun sank leisurely behind the horizon, and it did not grow dark for a long time, so she raised the blinds again. Then she took from her cabinet a small phial and carefully counted out her drops in a glass of water. She drank slowly. Ah, if only they would bring some relief this time! They didn't seem half as effective as they used to be.

Worn out from her long day of inertia, prey to the ramblings of her troubled mind, she decided to have an early night. She would not light the gas lamp; she would sit in the dusk a little longer and then try to get some sleep.

But her head began to seethe and simmer with unrelenting insistence. The cool evening air wafted into the room, yet she felt suffocated. She let the grey peignoir slide off her shoulders. Her arms were thin, her chest almost hollow, and with a sad smile she surveyed her wasted frame. She ran her fingers through her long, thin hair. And because the light was fading, because she dreaded not sleeping despite the drops, because of the livid pallor of her skin beside the lace-edged nightdress, because she grew fearful of the deepening shadows, the madness rose up in her once more.

Ah, perfido! Spergiuro!

She began to hum, and she raised her arm in a wild gesture of accusation. This was the Beethoven aria that used to remind Vincent of the fragrance of verbena … Then, her features twisting with grief and vengeance, she broke into song, raging at the faithless lover, commanding him out of her sight, invoking the wrath of the gods to punish him to the end of his days. With a sudden movement she pulled the sheet off her bed and draped the long white fabric about her, so that it resembled a robe of marble in the grey dusk.

Ah no! Fermate, vindici Dei!

She sang hoarsely, pausing repeatedly to cough. Her expression had altered, for she was now imploring the gods to have mercy on him—however cruel his betrayal, the constancy of her devotion was unchanged, and she would not seek revenge; for him she had lived and for him she wished to die. Slowly she intoned the adagio, very slowly, while the white folds of her drapery billowed and swayed to the supplicating gestures of her arms. She sang on and on, until a heart-rending cry forced itself from her throat, and in that final plaint she suddenly became an actress, a prima donna in the noble art of the opera. Her lover had fled, and she saw herself turning to chorus surrounding her with pity:

Se in tanto affa … a … a … anno

She sang, almost weeping, with grief-stricken cadenzas, and in her agonised lamentation her voice rose to a shriek:

Non son degna di pietà

She gave a violent start, appalled by the shrill, screeching sound of her ruined voice, then flung off the white sheet and sank down on a chair, trembling. Had anyone heard her? She darted a quick glance through the open door of her balcony at the street below. No, there were only a few strollers in the gathering dusk, and no one was looking up. What about inside? Had they heard?

Ah well, if so, it couldn't be helped. But from now on, she vowed, she would be more sensible.

She was sobbing, and yet she laughed, too—at herself, for being so silly as to get all carried away like that! No wonder she wasn't feeling in the least drowsy! She laid herself down on the rumpled bed and kept her eyes firmly closed. But sleep did not come.

"Dear God," she moaned. "Dear God, let me sleep, I beg you, let me sleep!"

She wept bitterly, unceasingly. Then a thought flashed into her brain. What if she took a few more drops than the dose prescribed by that physician in Brussels? There would be no harm in that, would there? It was hardly likely, given that her normal dose didn't seem to do anything for her these days. How many more drops would it be safe for her to take?

The same amount again? No, that would be too much, obviously. Goodness knows what might happen. Half the amount, then? Another three drops? No, no, she did not dare: the doctor had given her dire warnings about the dangers. Still, it was tempting … and she got out of bed.

She took up her phial to count out the drops.

One … two … three, four-five. The last two spilt out just as she righted the phial. Five … would that be too much? She hesitated a moment. Those five drops would be enough to send her to sleep, of that she was certain.

She hesitated yet again. Abruptly, she made up her mind: yes, she would sleep. And she drank her potion.

She lay down on the floor, close to the open door to the balcony.

Perspiring with fear, she felt herself sliding into numbness; but what a strange sensation it was this time … how different from the numbness she had grown accustomed to.

"Oh my God!" she thought. "My God! My God! Could it have been … too much?"

No, no, that would be too awful! Death was so black, so empty, so unspeakable! And yet, what if she had taken too much? All at once her fear melted away, and a sense of infinite peace came over her. If that was what she had done, so be it.

And she began to laugh, with stifled, nervous titters, while the numbness pressed down on her, as though with giant, leaden fists. She tried to ward off the fists with her flailing hands, and her fingers became entangled in the chain she wore about her neck. Oh, his portrait, Otto's portrait!

Had she really taken too much? Would she? ... She shivered. Would they come knocking at her door in the morning, and find no answer? Would they return later and knock again, and come upon her lying on the floor like this?

A terrible thought! Her fingers, moist with perspiration, groped for the locket. They must not find that portrait on her breast!

She raised herself to a sitting position and prised the small oval card from its casing. She could not see it, because it had grown dark in her room and her vision was already clouding over; only the yellow glow of the street lamp by the entrance dispelled the gloom. But she imagined it vividly, and she fondled the slip of cardboard, pressing it to her lips again and again.

"Oh, Otto!" she faltered, her speech slurring. "It was only you, my Otto, not Vincent, not St Clare, only you ... you ... Otto ... oh my God!"

She was torn between fear of death and acquiescence. Then, in the passion of her kisses, she took the card in her mouth. Yes, she would swallow it, since she no longer had the strength to tear it up or destroy it in any other way! A shuddering sigh convulsed her frame, and she began to chew the rejected proof of Otto's portrait.

Her tears were still flowing, but she no longer sobbed. The bitterness had ebbed away, and she wept like a child, with soft, childish whimpers and plaintive little moans. Now and then she gave a short, crazed laugh, and at length grew quiet, seated on the floor by the open door to the balcony with her forearms crossed before her face.

She made no movement, petrified by the state she was in, by what lay in store. She had a sense of a sea tossing within her, a dark sea flooding her thoughts, drowning her; she wanted to push the sea away, but its force was too great, and she lurched over and fell, deafened by the dull roar in her ears and in her brain.

"God! God! Oh God!" she moaned in a choked, fading voice of powerless despair.

Then her consciousness seeped away, drop by drop, and the sleep of death came over her.

The street lamp was extinguished, and the spacious room was transformed into a dark crypt, a mausoleum of blackness in which a lifeless body lay, ghostly white.

The night air grew chill, and slowly the pearl-grey pallor of dawn arose.

Henk van Raat sent a letter at once to Daniel Vere in Brussels, notifying him of Eline's decease. Uncle Daniel and Eliza both wrote back, full of sympathy for poor Eline. Daniel also informed him that Vincent had returned from Russia a few days previously, accompanied by the American friend whom Eline had met in Brussels, and that they would be travelling to The Hague to attend the funeral.

XXXVI

MORE THAN A YEAR had passed since Eline's death. For the van Erlevoorts momentous changes had taken place. Madame van Erlevoort had been persuaded by her son Theodore to sell the house on the Voorhout, the beloved family home where all her children had been born, and she had moved to de Horze along with Mathilda and the four grandchildren. Paul and Frédérique were married and living in the small town of Heibeek, where Paul had been appointed mayor. Etienne had obtained his degree, and there had been talk of him making a career in the Indies, but his mother could not bear the thought of parting from her youngest boy, and in the end he had established himself as a lawyer in The Hague. Although Madame van Erlevoort was sad at first to lose her home in The Hague, she soon accommodated herself to the warmth and cosiness of her eldest son's family circle, to which Henrietta, like Marianne before her, had returned from her last term at boarding school, while the boys put in an appearance from time to time. The van Rijssel foursome—Tina was now eleven years old—were thriving alongside Memée in the wholesome country air.

Paul had begged his mother to follow Madame van Erlevoort's example by selling her house and coming to live with him and Frédérique at Heibeek, but to no avail. Madame van Raat promised that she would visit them often, but she did not wish to take up residence in their home, fearing that her world-weariness, which had deepened since the death of her beloved Eline, would cast a pall on their sunny, fresh happiness. The excitement of Paul's engagement and his subsequent marriage had taken her out of herself for a while, but now that her son had what he wanted and most needed, she gradually became submerged once more in the half-life of her listless despondence.

The Verstraeten household was hushed, and Marie often shed bitter tears. She had so much love locked away inside her, and all

502

of it would go to waste; she felt as if she would shrivel up, like an overlooked flower. Lili was far too busy with her household and the care for her two fair-haired little ones to pay much attention to her, but she did not blame her sister for not realising how she unhappy she was. Besides, what difference would it have made, even if Lili had known; how could that have comforted her?

Paul and Freddie invited Marie to spend the summer months with them, and she felt better there than at home, for all that she doted on her papa and mama. At least with Paul and Freddie she could laugh and joke now and then, especially when they reminisced about all the fun they had had putting on those *tableaux vivants* in the old days. Fancy her having lectured Paul about being lazy! And did he and Freddie remember that Lili couldn't abide de Woude back then? Well, Lili said it wasn't true; she claimed that she had always adored him, and got very cross whenever anyone so much as hinted that this might not have been the case!

The villa in which Paul and Freddie had taken up residence was quite splendid. Built by the previous mayor of Heibeek, it had a colonial aspect to it, with a white-columned porch at the front and an enclosed veranda rather like a large conservatory at the back. Paul had furnished his new home with considerable luxury, which Frédérique thought somewhat exaggerated, given that it was a backwater they were living in where they received no one but the local church minister. But she did not go against her young husband's extravagant tastes, in which she saw the reflection of unfulfilled artistic ambition; she was happy to see him the way he was now, with a warm heart for the community and contented in his position.

Otto came over from Elzen now and then to spend a few days with his sister and brother-in-law, and on a few occasions his visit coincided with that of Marie. Frédérique had the feeling that Marie was a shade subdued in Otto's presence, and she was reminded with some unease of a remark she had made to her some years since.

"Oh, Marie, you would have made Otto such a good wife!" she had said, and she could still hear Marie's stammered reply:

"Who, me?"

Now she wondered whether she had caused Marie pain with those words. But she consoled herself with the thought that her impression might be quite wrong, that she had merely imagined Marie to be affected in her demeanour.

For Otto the year had passed in sombre, oppressive dejection. After Eline died there had been unpleasant rumours; she was known to have been ill, of course, but the suddenness of her death had given rise to much whispered speculation as to its cause. This had not escaped Otto, who plunged into renewed grief over his loss of Eline. He looked stricken and almost old, and when Frédérique tried to cheer him up, telling him it wouldn't do to submerge himself entirely in his gloom, he protested gently with the same words he had once used to reassure Suzanne at de Horze: a man's heart does not break as easily as you think; men have work to do, business to attend to, they do not ponder a lost love for the rest of their days.

Back then, at de Horze, he had not meant what he said. But lately it had seemed to him that there might be a measure of truth in those words after all. The heaviness in his heart seemed less leaden than it used to be; it was more like a lingering soreness from past hurt and sorrow. He had pangs of conscience whenever he felt his spirits lifting, and would vow to dedicate himself entirely to his grief and to the memory of Eline. But he did not reckon with the fact that time, at once cruel and kind, healed wounds, and that the wound he had come to prize would at length be no more than a scar.

And now, in midsummer, strolling in Paul and Freddie's garden with Marie at his side, he felt happy in spite of himself. He had asked her to marry him, which had initially thrown her into confusion and subsequently made her weep, whereupon he had begged her not to turn him away simply because he had previously given his heart to another. He had grown to love her deeply, he loved her for her candid simplicity and her sweet, affectionate nature, in which he found solace—oh, he would not deny it, his love for her was utterly egotistic, but she was not to scorn him for that, since he had suffered so much for that other love. As for Marie, she had no desire to refuse him. Her heart brimmed over with infinite compassion; her tears were not for herself, they were tears of joy that he had come to her at last, not tears of frustration at his mention of the past, they were for him alone, for the suffering he had gone through.

So she accepted, moist-eyed, and pressed a light kiss on his brow. He was unaware that she had always loved him, unaware of how much she, too, had suffered during his courtship of Eline. He had yet to perceive the depth of her love for him, he saw only the depth of her pity, but that alone was like a soothing balm to his soul.

Through the dense, spreading bushes glimmered the villa, and seated between the columns on the porch, in the light shining from inside, was an animated gathering, for Paul and Freddie had invited more friends to their abode: Georges and Lili with their two small children, and Etienne, boisterous and youthful as ever.

Otto and Marie made their way back slowly, lingering along the flower beds. All around were rose bushes in full bloom, suffusing the freshness of evening with their sultry fragrance. Beyond, on the porch, Etienne appeared to be teasing poor Lili, for they could hear her cries of indignation followed by peals of laughter from the others.

Marie hung back, as though embarrassed by the joy welling up inside her; then she stooped to shake the stems of a few overblown roses and watch their petals flutter down to the ground.

"Come," he murmured. "Let's go and surprise them with our good news."

And as he led her by the hand he felt he could breathe again; he had a new sense of energy, even of rebirth, for the consoling passage of time had not only effaced his sorrow, it seemed to have rekindled his lust for life.

AFTERWORD

Almost halfway through *Eline Vere* we find its eponymous heroine in a state of conscious happiness. Eline, whose life has hitherto centred round the entertainments of high society in The Hague, is staying at de Horze in Gelderland, the country property of the family into which she has agreed to marry. The more she sees of her betrothed, Otto van Erlevoort, the more she appreciates his kindly, virtuous character. Herself highly strung and only too frequently dissatisfied, she has found deep contentment in surrendering to the slow rhythms of the rural summer. These have enabled her to get on with members of the large van Erlevoort family so well that they are now obviously fond of her—even Otto's sister Frédérique, who has never much cared for her. Eline is quite aware that she has significantly changed:

> *During moments of solitary reflection on her new selfhood, tears welled up in her eyes in gratitude for all the goodness that she had received, and her only wish was that time would not fly, but stand still instead, so that the present would last for ever. Beyond that she desired nothing, and a sense of infinite rest and blissful, blue tranquility emanated from her being.*

Yet the God to whom she prays for this stasis does not answer her prayer, for time by its very nature cannot stand still. And moving and even sympathetic though we may find Eline's thoughts here, we can also detect in them signs of the pernicious weakness that will destroy her. Her hopes are unrealistic, and fear plays too great a part in them; indeed, they amount to a desperate desire to have subtracted from existence anything demanding or painful. They are also self-centred; in this respect Eline's "new selfhood" differs little, if at all, from her former one. Does her fiancé have his rightful part in these wishes of hers for the future to be cancelled?

When Eline returns from de Horze to her sister and brother-in-law's house in The Hague, she finds that her older cousin, Vincent, is in temporary residence. Vincent has led a rackety life, which has taken its toll on him both physically and financially (he endlessly cadges money). Eline's sister Betsy— practical, conventional, insensitive—loathes him, but on Eline he exerts a curious fascination, particularly as the Gelderland days recede, and the all-too-familiar tedium of her life in The Hague engulfs her anew. Vincent reminds Eline of the father she so loved and revered, a failed artist who could never find the energy to complete one of his ambitious canvases. Indeed, for all his dabbling in doubtful commercial enterprises, Vincent, with his collection of bric-a-brac, could himself be called a failed artist, and this is how he sees himself. A man more unlike Otto van Erlevoort than this seedy, yet somehow magnetic, individual could scarcely be imagined, and in fact we readers know that Otto, unlike the other more impressionable young men in his social circle, actually despises him: "But Otto, with unselfconscious confidence in his own health and strength, looked down on Vincent for the poisonous charm he emanated to gullible associates." But Eline, much to her sister's irritation, takes to having long, lazy, philosophical conversations with him:

> *"So you believe that everything is preordained, and that when I think I am doing something out of my own free will I am really only doing it because? … "*
>
> *"You only think it's your own free will, but your will is nothing other than the outcome of hundreds and thousands of previous so-called chance occurrences. Yes indeed, that is what I believe."*
>
> *[…]*
>
> *"You believe, for instance, that if I marry Otto all I'm doing is following a preordained path?"*

But only seconds after she asks him this, Vincent, in poor condition anyway, faints. The effect on Eline of both his remarks and his swoon is astonishing, and yet, on reflection—for this is a novel of great subtlety in its psychological and social observation—

perhaps we should not be so very astonished. Eline now begins to wonder that "her love for Otto might not be enough after all"; for an instant she has seen behind her imaginings of her married life-to-come an alarming "ghost". Vincent's faint draws her, emotionally, romantically, towards him—though there is no evidence of any deeper feeling for her on his part than cousinly affection and gratitude. (Indeed, perhaps if there had been, she would not be so drawn.) Couperus, born in 1863, was twelve years the senior of Carl Gustav Jung (1875–1961) yet *Eline Vere* (1889) strikingly anticipates key Jungian ideas, present also in his subsequent fiction. Vincent, sick, seedy, idle, is the *shadow* to Otto in Eline's psyche, and indeed embodies important features of her own self. Hence her fleeting but frightening vision of the "ghost", which is this shadow's projection. Eline's consequent casting-off of the Otto she still loves—causing her genuine anguish in which, for all her egotism, concern for the rejected young man is a strong component—is, in truth, an unconsciously motivated attempt to assert her personality in all its complexity on behalf of its unending quest, its driving need for wholeness. It may also be seen, of course, as a revolt against that very preordination—societal and circumstantial—that her cousin was proclaiming before he passed out.

But there is more still to be discovered in Eline's action. Her moods, her nervousness, her preposterous fantasies which spiral away from those who have inspired them, her bouts of illness (or indefinable unwellness), may exasperate us readers almost as much as they do her elder sister, Betsy. But when we stand back and view them collectively, do they not reveal her unwitting, instinctive recognition of what is dead or dull in her society, of what may be pleasing, even admirable on the agreeable, convention-hallowed surface but which never addresses what runs deeper? In hoping for a suspension of time's movement, Eline at twenty-three may have been entertaining the dreams of a silly adolescent, but is she not, in the very fervour of her wishes, also fighting herself and her own frightening powers of understanding? Hasn't she all along had an appreciation of life's darker side—whereas the less complicated Otto, at any rate up to this point, has not? Eline's problems derive from her not knowing how to cope with her troubling appreciation, receiving no guidance here from the largely stultifying codes by which her more adjusted friends and relations live.

Eline's rejection of Otto constitutes the heart, both structural and moral, of the novel. As the above adumbrates, her action is a far from simple matter. Lionel Trilling wrote about Jane Austen's novel *Emma* (in *Beyond Culture*, 1965): "We never know where to have it. If we finish it at night and think we know what it is up to, we wake the next morning to believe it is up to something quite else; it has become a different book." This holds true for *Eline Vere* too. And in both cases the book's ability to change itself in our minds is inextricable from the delineation of the woman who gives it its title.

Louis Couperus was only twenty-six when *Eline Vere* came out, and had previously published only unsatisfactory and derivative poems (in 1883 and 1884). Though it is a literary artefact of precocious sophistication and accomplishment, the novel is also palpably the creation of a young man whose years were a great advantage to him in its composition. For Couperus is still very much *of* the milieu he is recreating, aware though he is of its limitations and faults, and he clearly was intimately familiar, as a member himself of youthful Hague society, of the very pleasures, expectations and hopes he ascribes to his large cast of characters, almost all of them his contemporaries. Their gossip and banter, their flirtations, their little tiffs and misunderstandings and reconciliations, their plans for and doubts about the nature of their future adult lives convince us (and never more so than in Ina Rilke's spirited and linguistically sensitive English) because they are done essentially from the inside. A young man like Etienne van Erlevoort, lazy and industrious, facetious and affectionate by turns, springs to life off the pages—on which he performs no absolutely essential dramatic act—as though a relation of the author's own, slyly observed over many years, were being presented to us.

Youth surely accounts also for the infectious physicality of the work. We disport ourselves with its characters at the beaches and by the dunes of Scheveningen, and deep in the woods of Gelderland too; we are present at amiable wrestling matches, ending with one boy leap-frogging over his partner, and are right there on the little boat as it is steered down a country stream past thick pads of waterlilies. These are all triumphs of the writer's kinaesthetic powers, and stand in contrast to, and perhaps at variance with, his other less healthy and wholesome aesthetic abilities, when he draws us near that sombre and threatening shadowland which those such as Vincent Vere know only too well.

Couperus was helped in his chosen task of bringing his own society to life by two important features of the contemporary literary scene. He called *Eline Vere* 'A Novel of The Hague', partly because there actually flourished at the time a popular genre known simply as 'The Hague novel'. This dealt with the city's social life, in something of the manner of those English 'silver-fork' novels of the period 1825–50, or of such now-forgotten but once widely read English novelists of the 1880s as Rhoda Broughton and W E Norris. Its principal readers were female, drawn largely from a lower social class than its books' protagonists; it therefore appealed to their eagerness to hear what was going on in such elegant streets of the Dutch administrative capital as the Nassauplein where Eline lives with Henk and Betsy van Raat, in a house which Couperus himself had inhabited. We can see how *Eline Vere*, which was hugely successful from the very first, partakes of this category and could meet the wishes of its enthusiasts. From its opening description of the gleeful preparations for a society *tableau vivant* to its closing evocation of the "quite splendid" villa furnished "with considerable luxury" in which the recently wed Paul and Frédérique are now living (admittedly not in The Hague but in Heibeek), the novel leaves us in no doubt whatever that we are moving among the well-off and well-connected, whom the author knows at first hand. And a good measure of both the charm and the interest of these people with whom we are concerned does indeed derive from their favoured station: their easy manners and articulate conversation, the pleasantness of the innumerable dinner parties and expeditions which amply set off their developing personalities, their ability, if they so wish, to yield to impulse and pursue some hobby or passing enthusiasm (Paul van Raat's excursions into singing and painting conspicuously come to mind), or even to take their time over their studies and thus over deciding what they should be doing in life (Etienne is a good, and a happy, example). And some of them, of course, never do make any satisfactory decision, and yet do not seem to us much the worse for it; in truth the very leisureliness of their lives gives them enviable scope for exercising fundamentally amiable qualities. The superbly realised Henk van Raat, with his two devoted Ulmer hounds, himself several times likened to a Newfoundland dog, is perhaps the best instance of this. Yet the important plot lines of Paul's relationship with Frédérique van Erlevoort, Georges de Woude van Bergh's with Lili Verstraeten, Marie's with Otto would not at all be out of place in a run-of-the-mill 'Hague novel', and, like that genre's intended readers, we are ceaselessly stirred to read on by asking ourselves (even on rereadings, such are Couperus' narrative gifts): "Will they ... or won't they? Will she ... or won't she?", such questions and their answers providing the story's dynamics.

What stands apart from the usual interests of such a novel is, obviously, the portrait of Eline herself—disturbing, multifaceted, unforgettable—which transcends, or, if you like, subverts, the genre in which it commandingly stands, lifting the individual work into another species of literary endeavour entirely.

But a second feature of the literary climate is even more important in considering the production of this twenty-six-year-old author: the enormous reputation then, throughout the reading world, of Leo Tolstoy (1828–1910). In one of the later chapters we find elderly Madame van Raat reading French and Russian novels, and *War and Peace* (published 1865–9) is specifically cited.

Tolstoy builds up his great novel from innumerable small episodes of ordinary life, familial, domestic, social and sometimes seemingly trivial (and, we should add here, it is our ease of reception of these and our belief in their complete authenticity that enable us to identify with those they feature when 'history' overtakes them in the form of Napoleon and his invasion of Russia). Just as Jane Austen said that "three or four families in a country village is the very thing to work on", Tolstoy spoke of his fiction as deriving from the affairs of the *deux cents familles* to which he himself belonged. Couperus, in his first novel, was similarly drawn to writing about people of his own class (the only ones probably with whom he feels thoroughly at home), and profited by Tolstoy's example. Indeed, as we follow the doings of the van Erlevoorts, Verstraetens, van Raats, and de Woude van Berghs, we can easily envisage them as friends of Tolstoy's Rostovs. They would all have been perfectly at home at Natasha's first ball. (And yet, for all their breeding, with the van Erlevoorts prominent here, and their money, with the van Raats the richest, Couperus' people are far nearer in their values and mores to ourselves than are Tolstoy's; both their pastimes and their more serious aspirations belong to a modern capitalist society based on commerce rather than to the semi-feudal one we encounter in the great Russian.)

But I suspect that the young Couperus was even more influenced by the Tolstoy of *Anna Karenina* (published 1875–7). Whereas the cumulative episodes of *War and Peace* unite into an epic of a people during a significant segment of historical time, those out of which *Anna Karenina* is constructed are shot through with our intensifying awareness of its central figure, and the predicament she apparently wills onto herself and, involuntarily, onto those close to her. This, unlike its predecessor, is above all a novel of moral and psychological investigation and dissection. "*Vengeance is mine, saith the Lord, and I shall repay*" is the motto Tolstoy chose for it, and in retrospect we can see how it informs every scene, no matter what sense of the humdrum, of the randomness of existence, it may also offer. *Eline Vere* works on us in this manner too. We can see this in the very way Couperus has decided to introduce us to Eline.

From the merry preparations of the young people in the very first chapter she is conspicuously absent. "Such a shame Eline is not here," her aunt-through-marriage exclaims. "She is not feeling very well," Madame Verstraeten is told; it is a question of "nerves" apparently, "the affliction of the younger generation".

So we do not meet Eline until the *second* chapter, and when we do, we encounter her at night-time, at half-past two in the morning. (To the British and American readers of today these members of Hague society keep astoundingly late hours, just as they all have a surprising amount to drink.) And we first see her "looking rather pale in a white flannel peignoir, with her hair loose and flowing", the last a favourite symbol in nineteenth-century paintings, from the Pre-Raphaelites through to Edvard Munch, of a girl's rejection of the restraints of conventional respectability. "Languorous and graceful", Eline has absented herself from the jollifications of her peers through a "whim of indolence and ennui", and has been regretting it ever since, unable to relieve her melancholy even by reading. When her brother-in-law, Henk, chides her for yielding to yet another black mood—Henk, the first man she was ever seriously attracted to, and who, probably more than any other, still holds her heart— she breaks down in tears:

> *The urge to pour her heart out was too strong to resist. What was she living for? What use could she be to anyone? She wandered about the room, wringing her hands and lamenting without pause. She didn't care if she died within the hour, she didn't care about anything at all, it was just that her existence was so futile, so useless, without anything she could wholeheartedly devote herself to, and it was all becoming too much to bear.*

What is Eline's malady, and what is its meaning when viewed in the context of her social world? Which is also to ask, what is its meaning for the novel as a whole? In Anna Karenina's case the cause of her undoing is her trust in the truth of passion over other truths, other considerations. On account of this trust she undervalues the importance of society itself, which exacts retribution on her of both an outward and an inward kind. This is not to say that Tolstoy accepts society on its own (so often hypocritical or cynical) evaluation—far from it. But he does believe that it is only through principled unselfishness that a satisfactory life can be led, and that this entails taking society into account. We see in *Anna Karenina* how the erratic Levin, who, like *War and Peace*'s Pierre before him, has a normal man's dissolute

514

past, realises that a reciprocally giving married life with Kitty will benefit not just himself but the larger world as well.

Such thinking is present also in *Eline Vere*. Paul van Raat is as silly and selfish as young men often are, indeed maybe more so than many because of the wealth and lofty social position into which he was born, the very thought of which makes him proud and a touch reckless. But he is also warm-hearted and observant of others, and through the love he feels for Frédérique and the marriage with her that he will sustain, he can not only repay his debts to society but make it a better place (this being fittingly emblemised in his becoming mayor of a comparatively small provincial community). But Eline will make no contribution of this kind whatsoever. In common with Tolstoy's Anna, what she will bequeath to the society that has produced and nurtured her is a death that at once distresses and disconcerts it. Why? What went wrong?

Eline's flaw is *not*, like the Russian tragic heroine's, related to intensity of sexual reaction. If anything Eline strikes us as deficient in normal erotic feelings. The baritone Fabrice, Otto for the greater part (she has to be cajoled into accepting him as fiancé), Vincent, the mysterious figure of Lawrence St Clare—there is no evidence that she is sexually aroused by any of them. Nor is there much evidence that men generally, while admiring her beauty and her social grace, respond to her physically, as—to take examples from literature—men, including her own husband, do to Flaubert's Emma Bovary, or those in Christiania's elite do to Hedda Gabler in Ibsen's virtually contemporaneous play (1890). What attractions Eline feels for the men in her life, what emotions they have brought out in her very quickly dissolve into daydream. Fabrice—whose picture she will buy for her albums, like any starstruck shop girl—scarcely has any reality for her off the boards of the stage on which he sings Gounod. Vincent's secretive disposition, compounded by his insecurities of money and health, she soon distorts into a novelette invalid's yearning for love, which she might somehow satisfy. Even Otto, for whom she does know something not unlike love, becomes for her chiefly an embodiment of masculine good sense on which she will be able eternally to depend.

Unlike Emma Bovary or Hedda Gabler, however, Eline is not unintelligent or even notably unintellectual, nor is she—as Ibsen, in his preparatory notes on his play, says of Hedda—conventional. Couperus is insistent that Eline's English is positively good, and her French is clearly proficient also: she reads as well as speaks both languages. She is interested in the arts, even if she does have an inordinate admiration for the outrageous Ouida, is cognisant of cultures outside the Netherlands, and, if anything, is rather too much at ease among the bohemian, heterodox folk whom her uncle Daniel and his younger wife, Eliza, take up with. Her discussions with Vincent might not impress a professional philosopher any more than they please her irascible sister, Betsy, but they show her to have, for all her languor, a certain liveliness of mind, a wish to explore further than the bounds of the immediately perceptible. It is hard to imagine the other young members of her circle engaging in them. Furthermore she has the ability—often, admittedly, coming to the fore too late or with insufficient force—to stand back from her fantasies and even her behaviour. (Think of her sad, bemused awareness of how badly she can behave to kind old Madame van Raat.) Likewise, she has the ability to discern the sham even when it is she herself who, through her heightened theatrical tendencies, is doing the shamming. When, in her despair, she turns to churchgoing, she can see through her own religiosity—so akin to the swooning over opera which led her to idolise the sorry, shabby Fabrice—and also through the hypocrisies of her fellow worshippers.

No, Eline's tragedy—for it is nothing less—is not the consequence of her having too much erotic passion in her or too little sharpened an intellect. It is that she has too abundant and fertile an imagination in a society which gravely undervalues this quality, indeed scarcely even pays lip-service to it. Imagination is not an attribute one could ascribe to any other character in the book—with the possible exception of Eline's shadow self, Vincent, and perhaps Frédérique, in her own frustrated way. Her milieu is one of fundamentally practical, pragmatic persons, sensible once they have put youthful idleness behind them, incurious, rarely looking beyond their own set, dabbling in the arts (as Paul van Raat does) while unaware that these have profounder purposes than amusement, worried about money in a household-expenditure kind of way, but never seriously discomposed by current affairs—and accordingly disinclined ever to challenge the status quo.

Eline surely emanates from that part of Couperus' own experience which made him, in a vital respect, an outsider in the social world in which he was so accepted. The Couperus family had a long connection with the Dutch East Indies. Louis Couperus' own father, John Ricus Couperus, was born there in 1816. In 1872, when Louis was only nine years old, Couperus senior took his family away from The Hague back to the Indies, where they had property, and they did not return to Holland until 1878, when the boy was fifteen. Couperus was therefore something of a stranger in those circles which were so open to him, and in which he was expected to have a role. And his kinship here with spoilt, orphaned Eline becomes the clearer when we realise what a pampered, luxurious life he knew as a child in Batavia (Java's capital) as a child of its ruling class. What he also was aware of in the Javanese life all round him was its rich vein of inherited lore, its reliance on instinct rather than rational precepts, its attention to natural phenomena which the folk mind read as emanations of mysterious powers, often dark, hostile and running contrary to humankind's conscious intentions or will. Such knowledge he could not have gained remaining in The Hague.

In one of his greatest subsequent novels, *De Stille Kracht* (*The Hidden Force*, 1900), Couperus depicts van Oudijck, a Dutchman who holds the eminent position of Resident of a Javanese province: kindly, conscientious, ready to be a paterfamilias with all the responsibilities and demonstrations of affection that entails, even prepared to face up to his own sensuality. But he is lacking in imagination, and vigorously suppresses any signs of that quality which tentatively surface. His failure here— demonstrated in his dealings with the mother of the Javanese Regent, or chief nobleman—has dire consequences for many, but before these have become fully apparent, he and those close to him experience hideous, terrifying manifestations of hostile occult spirits, whom the superstitious local folk can name but whom the educated Dutch refuse even to acknowledge until far too late. These are emanations from the shadowland, the vast region of the collective unconscious which the colonialists have chosen first to despise and then to deliberately ignore.

Eline Vere is thus of the East Indies without being aware of this. The "ghost" she sees behind her picture of life with Otto, the fantasies she embroiders round the decadent figure of Vincent, the terrifying cavalcade of images that haunt her on her last day of life—these relate intimately to what torments van Oudijck and his wife in *The Hidden Force*.

The importance of the East Indies to Louis Couperus is evidenced in his marrying his cousin Elisabeth Baud, whose family had distinguished itself in Indies service, and in the couple's living there from March 1899 to February 1900, returning again for four months during their long travels of October 1921–October 1922. Of the generous cast in *Eline Vere* the irrepressible Etienne van Erlevoort is tempted to join the colonial administration but in the end prefers to stay at home. But there is one very important character in the novel connected with Java—the ill and indigent Jeanne Ferelijn, whose husband is on poorly paid furlough and who pines in what she sees as the drabness of Holland for the richness of her Indies, whither she returns and where she dies. Significantly when Eline, in her hysterical passion, flees the van Raats' house at night, it is to Jeanne she goes, Jeanne with whom she was warmly friendly when they were both schoolgirls, and who now in her illness will console and sustain her. And when later Eline learns of Jeanne's death, she is dreadfully upset; indeed we can see her reception of this news as the most authentic moment of her life. This then is Eline's tragedy: to have been born with too large a supply of imagination in a society too focused on the cash nexus and on living comfortably. Her neighbours and kinsfolk in The Hague represent only too well the dominant culture of their times, extending from Gilt Age America to Queen Victoria's Diamond Jubilee in Britain and France on the eve of the Dreyfus affair.

Tolstoy was not the only influence on the keen, probing mind of the young Couperus. And of Tolstoyanism itself, with its emphasis on the word of the Gospels and on the quietist faith of ordinary folk, I can see only mild manifestations. Mesdames van Erlevoort and van Raat are undogmatically pious, the lives of both women being dominated by a warm, compassionate, maternal feeling commendably inclusive of others outside their immediate family, and therefore exemplary. (See the treatment of Eline by both women.) Couperus tenderly evokes simple country churchgoing for us, indeed his whole portrayal of Gelderland life as more conducive to ethical health and spiritual contentment than the sophisticated urban round of The Hague could loosely be described as Tolstoyan. Similarly his preference for the good-hearted in all circumstances—whether represented by indolent Henk or hard-working Jeanne Ferelijn—relates to Tolstoy's admiration for certain of *his* characters, Count Nicholas Rostov and Princess Mary in *War and Peace* for example. But all these can, and probably should, be seen mainly as expressions of temperamental priorities and preoccupations, as well as of the contemporary fear that the age, in its obsession with productivity and wealth, had brought about rather too radical a severance from the natural life. As discernible as that to Tolstoy is Couperus' debt—one is tempted to call it ideological—to Émile Zola (1840–1902). By the time of *Eline Vere*'s appearance fifteen novels in Zola's great twenty-volume Rougon-Macquart sequence had appeared, its ambition to show, through two interconnected families, both the laws of human heredity and the development (illustrating these laws) of France up to the fall of the Second Empire. Among these books were such influential and powerful works as *L'Assommoir* (1877), *Germinal* (1885) and *La Terre* (1887)—while a sixteenth came out the same year as Couperus' first novel, *Le Rêve* (1888).

Heredity is most evidently a preoccupation of *Eline Vere*. Great emphasis is placed on the two sisters' inheritance from their parents. Madame Vere was, we are told, an intimidating, unlovable woman, and from her come Betsy's blunted sensibility and her bossiness. Eline, as she herself believes, inherits from her father, a refined, dreamy, weak-willed, indecisive person. So far so convincing, but, graduate of the school of Zola as he felt himself, Couperus wishes us to go further. Both Eline and nephew Vincent exhibit the late Mr Vere's fatal lack of robustness, which appears also, modified, in his younger brother, Daniel, with his fondness for luxurious surroundings and for the company of bohemian riff-raff, *flâneurs* and useless expatriates. Eline's readiness to fall in with her uncle and aunt's way of living is a manifestation of her own share of this regrettable, determining trait, clearly associated in Couperus' mind—as in Zola's and, later, Thomas Mann's—with the make-up of the artist. Only a family, and by extension a society, in decline devotes itself to art, would seem the implication.

Take by way of contrast the case of Paul van Raat, a virile and lively young man, despite those bouts of laziness and dissipation ascribable to the phase of life through which he is passing. Paul, at two important points in the novel, is much taken with being an artist. It isn't, we realise, so much the case of his not having enough talent to become one (though that statement is true enough), as his having rather too healthy a physical inheritance. The van Erlevoort clan into which he befittingly marries is clearly an excellent genetic pool; descriptions of the youngest generation abound in tributes to their vitality and physical attractiveness. This can be darkly counterpointed by the case of Paul's own nephew. His brother Henk has a child, Ben, by a Vere, and neither Henk's rude health nor Betsy's maternally received energy can prevent the likeable, indeed the imaginative little boy from being a backward child—a predicament poignantly rendered. Is this then another reason why Eline feels she cannot, must not marry Otto? She could not give that splendid specimen of normality a satisfactory child who would one day himself continue a strong line.

For me this aspect of *Eline Vere* is its least convincing, perhaps because it is not sufficiently thought out. Moreover—very unlike any production of Zola's—the novel does not allocate to the figures in the foreground any convincing background connecting them to society in the wider sense of the term. The occupations of Paul and Otto, who do indeed become responsible public servants, are perfunctorily rendered; they interest us because they fit into the overall formal pattern, rather than because they have much validity in their own right. With regard to the specific instances in the novel of biological inheritance, Couperus has nothing like Zola's command of detail, his intensity of interest in, and insight into, specific cases. Ben van Raat's backwardness, like Eline's concluding helpless capitulation to psychic and physical illness, smacks of literature—if aided by sincere human sympathy—rather than life studied scientifically by the author himself. But there is surely another factor at work here.

Though Couperus found in his wife Elisabeth a veritable model of companionship and unsparing support, their union is generally assumed to have been a *mariage blanc*. The very idea of procreation horrified Couperus whose erotic inclinations—and practice—were, by general agreement now among experts on the writer, homosexual. Thus Eline's increasing non-progenitive detachment from her society can be seen as a correlative for Couperus' homosexual position. And homosexuality must stand behind the novel's most baffling couple, Vincent Vere and Lawrence St Clare.

For whatever else can it be that holds these two men together, so that they are in constant communication when apart, and are prepared to travel together for many months without significant interruptions? The one is an American *"chevalier d'industrie"*—which may be a polite way of saying he is a successful businessmen not above a sharp piratical manoeuvre or two—the other a drifter with ideas of himself way above his actual accomplishments. St Clare thinks of Vincent as a brother, he says, yet his Vincent is not the man we ourselves have come to know. He tells Eline:

> *"Most people have the wrong idea about Vincent. They think him lazy, capricious, egotistic, and refuse to see that he is simply ill. I can't think of anybody else who would be capable, despite suffering from such ill health, of sharing so much of his talent and intelligence with the rest of mankind."*
>
> *She had always had great sympathy for Vincent, but had never seen him in this light.*
>
> *"Yes, I believe you are right!" she said ...*

What a contrast to how Otto van Erlevoort sees Vincent!

Vincent Vere has told St Clare so much already about his cousin (combining the complimentary with the compassionate) that already, before their actual meeting-up in Brussels, the latter has thought of her as an 'unknown sister'. Hence his intense solicitude on her behalf, his unique ability to elicit from her truths about her deepest feelings (including her great grief for her friend Jeanne Ferelijn), his insistence, which she accepts, that she keep apart from the dubious crew with whom her uncle and aunt socialise, and his proposal of marriage, which, though moved, she refuses. What kind of marriage can St Clare be offering Eline? Primarily, we feel, one of concerned companionship such as Louis Couperus and Elisabeth Baud enjoyed, though the sincerity of not just his feelings but of his regard for her is not in doubt. Watching Eline improve in Brussels, largely because of his own caring converse with her, he has begun to feel:

> *a great longing to dedicate myself entirely to you, because I thought, if I can do that, she might be able to shake off her gloomy view of life and be happy again. My darling Elly, you're still so young, and you think it's too late for things to change. Don't think like that any more; put your trust in me, then we can set out together to discover whether life really is as dismal as you believe.*

Perhaps there is too much of the crusader, of the benevolent pedagogue and too little of the lover in this declaration, though we cannot but respect the man for making it—just as Eline does, though it also makes her weep. But she has to decline, continually tormented as she is by her memories of her failed engagement to Otto (broken off by herself, after all, for intimate, never wholly articulated reasons). Perhaps in her refusal Eline is acknowledging that, outside Ouidaesque fantasies, the whole domain of the carnal is not congenial to her, just as it apparently was not to her creator. In Couperus' mind sexuality results in misery as much as it does in children, and even the latter (from whom he so recoiled) rarely quite vanquish the former. It is an essential but terrible part of humankind's lot that it has not yet arrived at an ability to cope adequately and painlessly with its sexual instinct, evolution being as yet incomplete in this respect. And evolution is the key word here.

For Couperus was of the post-Darwin generation, quite unable to accept the explanations and consolations of orthodox religion, and obsessed, as though by a fresh discovery, by the distress, the mutual destructiveness inherent in existence itself, an awareness memorably expressed in the anguished personal writings of Darwin himself occasioned by his observation of the cruelty rampant throughout the animal world. It is the duty of the honest writer, according to this view, to face up to the bleakness, the terror, to the fact that what laws one can detect operating in life take no consideration of the feelings of those they control. Everywhere there is appalling waste, and waste is represented here by the sterile careers of Vincent and St Clare, by such an un-partnered woman as Emilie de Woude van Bergh, who deals with her plight by adopting a hearty, jolly persona, and, supremely, by Eline herself. That fine novelist of the American South, ten years Couperus' junior, Ellen Glasgow (1873–1945), had a similar *Weltanschauung* both compounded and aided by a not dissimilar refined sensibility. In her novel *Virginia* (1913) Glasgow writes of a young man destined never to become the writer he dreams of being:

> *But at the age of twenty-two … he was pathetically ignorant of his own place in the extravagance of Nature. With the rest of us, he would have been astounded at the suggestion that he might have been born to be wasted. Other things were wasted, he knew, since those who called Nature an economist had grossly flattered her. Types and races and revolutions were squandered with royal prodigality—but that he himself should be so was clearly unthinkable.*

Against this waste humankind has created art, and Couperus belonged to the generation who, even while seeing them as a sport of Nature, peculiarly valued artists, as able to provide invaluable bulwarks against the ultimate emptiness of existence. Much taken with, and in his turn admired by, members of the Aesthetic Movement, including Oscar Wilde himself, Couperus made his own great contribution to the art of literature, not so much through his own aestheticism—shown in his dandyism, his epicurean pleasures, his tendency to lushness of prose—as in those deeply serious novels, of which *Eline Vere* is the first, in which, with scrupulous honesty, artistry of design and intense care for minutiae he faces up to life's complexity.

His masterpiece, *Van oude mensen de dingen die voorbijgaan* (*Old People and the Things That Pass*, 1906), deals with two old people who, when younger and living in the East Indies as members of its colonial service, committed a horrendous crime—just how horrendous comes as a shock even to readers long anticipating its revelation, so savage, treacherous and pitiless was it. Undiscovered and therefore unpunished for decades, the murder has nonetheless worked a long-enduring, baleful power on the intertwined ramified families of the culprits in The Hague (of the same milieu as the protagonists of *Eline Vere*). A novel of deceptions, ignorance, half-understandings, reluctant or nervous uncoverings, it imports into a restricted Dutch circle that disruptive 'hidden force' so ineluctably bound up with passion and with a culture not founded on reason, showing how it lurks behind even the most conventional or formal interchanges. Intricate in form though it is, with its all-important glimpses of the lurid pasts of an extremely aged man and woman, it describes a trajectory as relentless and seemingly swift of movement as some well-aimed deadly arrow. The Tolstoyan openness of *Eline Vere*, with its many scenes of the hustle and bustle of the unremarkable social life of mostly unremarkable individuals, must not detract from our realising that it is also closely worked and forms a devastating trajectory. Again, the book is less close to *War and Peace* than to *Anna Karenina*, from the structure of which it surely learnt valuable lessons. The novel opens with an exchange between Paul and Frédérique, who, like Beatrice and Benedick, are to continue to spar throughout the novel, the girl perpetually showing up the shortcomings of the young man while revealing her deep affection for, even her belief in, him, and showing up too—with continual shrewdness, if with limited charity—the faults in Eline that will lead to her decline and demise. Paul and Frédérique's is to be the union of those approved of by Nature and so, fittingly, it is with a window into their young married life, and with Otto and Marie determined to emulate it, that the novel concludes.

Between the opening and the final episode of Paul and Frédérique's love lie, as if between bookmarks, the stories of other couples, and, too, of those Nature has marginalised. Of these Eline herself is not merely a representative but at times a passionate spokesperson, too often foolish and futile, but in her sensibility rightly judged worthy of having named after her one of the richest, most satisfying novels of the late nineteenth century.

Couperus wrote as a summary of himself:

ZOO IK IETS BEN, BEN IK EEN HAGENAAR
Whatever else I am, I am a man of The Hague.

His love of his native city pervades his first novel, so that to visit The Hague, and nearby Scheveningen, is to live again the experiences it recounts. But *Eline Vere* reveals also that, through being so faithfully and feelingly a man of The Hague, Couperus could speak to, and for, the whole of humanity.

PAUL BINDING